CEMETERY ROAD

CEMETERY ROAD

A Novel

GREG ILES

wm

WILLIAM MORROW
An Imprint of HarperCollins*Publishers*

CEMETERY ROAD. Copyright © 2019 by Greg Iles. All rights reserved. Printed in the United States of America. No part of this book may be used or reproduced in any manner whatsoever without written permission except in the case of brief quotations embodied in critical articles and reviews. For information, address HarperCollins Publishers, 195 Broadway, New York, NY 10007.

HarperCollins books may be purchased for educational, business, or sales promotional use. For information, please email the Special Markets Department at SPsales@harpercollins.com.

FIRST EDITION

Library of Congress Cataloging-in-Publication Data

Names: Iles, Greg.
Title: Cemetery Road : a novel / Greg Iles.
Description: New York, NY : William Morrow, 2019. |
Identifiers: LCCN 2018057445 (print) | LCCN 2018059594 (ebook)
  | ISBN 9780062824639 (ebook) | ISBN 0062824635 (ebook) | ISBN 9780062824615 (hardback)
  | ISBN 0062824619 (hardcover) | ISBN 9780062824622 (international paperback)
Subjects: | BISAC: FICTION / Suspense. | GSAFD: Suspense fiction.
Classification: LCC PS3559.L47 (ebook) | LCC PS3559.L47 C46 2019 (print) | DDC 813/.54--dc23
LC record available at https://lccn.loc.gov/2018057445

ISBN 978-0-06-282461-5 (hardcover)
ISBN 978-0-06-282462-2 (international edition)

19 20 21 22 23 LSC 10 9 8 7 6 5 4 3 2 1

To all those adults who return home
to repay the debt of childhood,
and find they never really left.
Listen while you still can.

A secret is not something untold.
It's something which can't be told.

—Terence McKenna

CEMETERY ROAD

CHAPTER 1

I NEVER MEANT to kill my brother. I never set out to hate my father. I never dreamed I would bury my own son. Nor could I have imagined that I would betray the childhood friend who saved my life, or win a Pulitzer Prize for telling a lie.

All these things I have done, yet most people I know would call me an honorable man. I wouldn't go that far. But I try to be a good man, and most of the time, I believe I succeed. How is this possible? These are complicated times.

And it's not easy to be good.

CHAPTER 2

HUNCHED ON HIS knees, Buck Ferris pulled a ball of fired clay from the sandy soil beside the Mississippi River, then got to his feet with a groan and climbed out of the hole beside the foundation pier. It was difficult to be certain about the era by moonlight, and he couldn't risk a light—not here. And yet . . . he *was* certain. The sphere sitting in his palm had been fired a few centuries before Moses started wandering through the desert with the children of Israel. Ferris had been an archaeologist for forty-six years, but he'd never discovered anything like this. He felt as though the little ball were vibrating in his hand. The last human to touch this clay had lived nearly four thousand years ago—two millennia before Jesus of Nazareth walked the sands of Palestine. Buck had waited all his life to find this artifact; it dwarfed everything he'd ever done. If he was right, then the ground upon which he stood was the most important undiscovered archaeological site in North America.

"What you got there, Buck?" asked a male voice.

Blue-white light stabbed Ferris's eyes. He nearly pissed himself, he was so stunned. He'd thought he was alone on the vast, low-lying ground of the industrial park. A quarter mile to the west, the eternal river flowed past, oblivious.

"Who are you?" Ferris asked, throwing up his left hand to shield his eyes. "Who is that?"

"You were warned not to disturb this ground," said the man behind the light. "It's private property."

The speaker had a refined Southern accent that tickled Buck's memory. He couldn't quite place it, though. Nor could Buck say much in his own defense. He'd applied for permission to dig in this earth seven times over the past forty years, and he'd been turned down every time. But five days ago, the county had cleared the debris of the electroplating factory that had stood here since World War II. And two days from now, a Chinese company would begin building a new paper mill in its place. If anyone was going to find out what lay beneath this ground, it was now—the consequences be damned.

"Where did you come from?" Buck asked. "I didn't see anybody when I came down here."

"Oh, Buck . . . You always were a good ol' boy. Why couldn't you have left well enough alone?"

"Do I know you?" Ferris asked, certain that he'd heard that voice before.

"You don't seem to."

"I don't think you understand the *value* of what I have here," Ferris said, his voice edged with excitement.

"You don't have anything there," said the voice. "You're not here."

Buck got the gist of it then, and something started thrumming in his belly, like stretched-taut wire plucked hard. "Wait, listen," he tried, "this ground you're standing on . . . it's an Indian settlement that's four thousand years old. Maybe five or six thousand, depending on what I find if we dig deeper."

"You hoping for a PBS series?"

"God, no. Don't you understand what I'm telling you?"

"Sure. You found some Injun bones. Thing is, that's bad news for everybody."

"No, *listen*. There's a site just like this only fifty miles from here, in Louisiana. It's called Poverty Point. It's a UNESCO World Heritage site. Thousands of tourists visit it every year."

"I've been there. A couple of mounds of dirt, and the grass needs cutting."

Buck realized then that this was like trying to tell a hillbilly about Bach. "That's ridiculous. You—"

"A billion dollars," the man cut in.

"Beg your pardon?"

"A *billion dollars*. That's what you could cost this town."

Buck tried to focus on the conversation, but the ball in his hand still felt like it was vibrating. Known as a "Poverty Point object," it had been used by Indians to cook meat under dirt. God only knew what else lay in the loess soil beneath their feet. Pottery, spear points, jewelry, religious artifacts, *bones*. How could someone not understand what it meant to stand on this ground and know what he knew? How could someone *not care*?

"This doesn't have to ruin your deal," he said. "Situations like this get handled all the time, to the satisfaction of all parties. The Department of Archives and History comes in, assesses the site, and then they move things, if that's even necessary. To protect them. That's all."

"Would they have moved all of Poverty Point to build a paper mill, Buck?"

No, he thought. *They wouldn't.*

"A billion dollars," the man said again. "In Mississippi. That's like ten billion in the real world. And that doesn't begin to address what it could cost me personally to lose the mill."

"Could you take that light out of my eyes?" Buck asked. "Can't we talk like civilized men?"

"Do it," said the voice.

"What?" Buck said. "Do what?"

"I always liked your guitar pickin'," said the man. "You should've stuck to that."

Buck heard something shift on the ground behind him, but he couldn't turn fast enough to see who was there, or to protect himself. A white afterimage on his retinas filled his eyes, and out of that whiteness came a dense black rectangle.

Brick.

He threw up his hands, but too late. The brick crashed into his skull, scrambling his perception. He felt only pain and the lurching nausea of falling into darkness. His wife's face flickered in his mind, pale with worry when he'd left her earlier tonight. As he collided with the earth, he thought of Hernando de Soto, who died near the Mississippi in 1542, not far from here. He wondered if these men would bury him beside the river he'd loved so long.

"Hit him again," said the voice. "Beat his brains out."

Buck tried to cover his head, but his arms wouldn't move.

CHAPTER 3

MY NAME IS Marshall McEwan.

I ran away from home when I was eighteen. It wasn't Mississippi I was running from—it was my father. I swore I would never go back, and for twenty-six years I kept my promise, excepting a few brief visits to see my mother. The road was not an easy one, but I eventually became one of the most successful journalists in Washington, D.C. People say it must be the ink in my blood; my father was a legendary newspaper editor and publisher in the 1960s—the "Conscience of Mississippi," the *New York Times* called him—but I didn't learn my trade from Duncan McEwan. My dad was a legend who became a drunk and, like most drunks, remained one. Still, he haunted me, like a second shadow at my side. So I suppose it was inevitable that his death would be the thing that brought me home.

Oh, he's not dead yet. His death has been approaching like a lone black ship that makes itself felt by the waves pushed ahead of it, dark waves that disturb a once-keen mind and roll over the protective boundaries of a family. What drives that black ship is what the doctors call co-morbid conditions: Parkinson's disease, heart failure, hypertension, an alcoholic's liver. I ignored the situation for as long as I could. I've watched brilliant colleagues—most ten or fifteen years my senior—struggle to care for ailing parents back in the small towns of the republic, and in every case their careers suffered. By chance or by karma, my career entered a meteoric phase after Trump's election in 2016. I had no desire to leap from my meteor, land back in Mississippi, and start babysitting the eighty-four-year-old man who had pretended I didn't exist since I was fourteen years old.

I finally surrendered because my father was so ill that I could no longer help my mother manage him from a thousand miles away. Dad has spent the past three decades sliding ever deeper into anger and depression, making those around him miserable and ruining his health in the process. But since I'm a good Southern boy at heart, the fact that an unbridgeable gulf had existed between him and me for more than thirty years was irrelevant. It's an unwritten law down here: when your father is dying, you go home and sit the deathwatch with your mother. Besides, our family business—the Bienville *Watchman* (founded 1865)— was disintegrating under his increasingly erratic stewardship, and since he'd stubbornly refused to sell our dinosaur of a newspaper for the past two decades, I had to keep it a going concern until what remained could be sold for salvage upon his death.

That's what I told myself, anyway.

In truth my motive was more complicated. We rarely act from logic when facing the critical choices of our lives. I couldn't recognize my self-deception then. I was still in a state of prolonged shock from a marriage that had endured a tragedy—or more accurately, failed to endure one—then spiraled into divorce as my professional life entered the stratosphere, but I see it now.

I came home because of a woman.

She was only a girl when I left home, and I, a confused boy. But no matter how relentlessly life tried to beat the softness out of me, to encase me in the hard, brittle carapace of cynicism, one pure thing remained alive and true: the half-Jordanian, half-Mississippian girl who unfolded the secret joys of life for me was so deeply imprinted upon my soul that no other woman ever measured up to her. Twenty-eight years of separation had proved insufficient to kill my yearning to be near her again. Sometimes I worry that my mother has known my hidden motive from the start (or maybe only sensed it and prayed that she was wrong). But whether she knows or whether she remains as ignorant as I was on the day I finally gave in, I took a leave of absence from my print and TV gigs, packed up my essentials, and made a white-knuckled drive south to test Thomas Wolfe's most famous dictum.

Of course you can go home again, answered my pride. *At least for a little while. You can do your filial duty. For what man who thinks of himself as a gentleman would not? And once that duty is discharged, and Himself is*

dead, perhaps you can persuade your mother to return with you to Wash-
ington. Truth be told, I probably knew this was a forlorn hope, but it
gave me something to tell myself, rather than think too deeply about
the unsolvable problem. No, not my father's situation. The girl. She's
a woman now, of course, a woman with a husband, who is probably
my best friend from childhood. She also has a son, who is twelve years
old. And while this knot may not seem particularly Gordian in our
age of universal divorce, other factors ensure that it is. My father's
plight, on the other hand . . . will inevitably resolve itself.

I sound cold, I suppose.

I don't say that Dad bears all the blame for his situation. He endured
his share of suffering, God knows—enough to cure him of religion for
life. Two years before he married my mother, he lost his first wife and
baby daughter in a car crash. As if that weren't enough, when I was in
the ninth grade my eighteen-year-old brother also died in an accident,
a tragedy that struck our town like a bomb dropped from an invisible
height. Perhaps losing two children in succession broke my father. I
could understand that. When my brother, Adam, died, it was as though
God reached out and switched off the lights of the world, leaving me to
stumble through the next two years like a blind man unable to adapt to
his new affliction.

But "God" wasn't done with me yet. Twenty years after Adam's
death, I lost my two-year-old son—my only child—in the most domestic
of accidents. I know what it means to be broken by fate.

I do, however, still function.

I work sources, write stories, go on CNN and MSNBC to comment
on the issues of the day. I even make speeches for $35,000 a pop (or I
used to, before I moved back to my third-world state and sent my market quote into irreversible decline). The point is I suffered, but I got on
with it. That's what I was taught to do—by my mother, of course, not
my father. Also by Buck Ferris, the archaeologist and scoutmaster who
stepped in after my father opted out of his paternal duty and did what
he could to make a man of me. After all my success, Buck figured he'd
accomplished that. I've never been sure. If I do prove it to myself one
day, he'll never know. Because sometime last night, Buck Ferris was
murdered.

Buck's passing seems a natural place to begin this story, because that's the way these things generally start. A death provides a convenient line of demarcation, kicking off the familiar tableau of investigation, the assigning of guilt, the determining of punishment. But beginnings are complex things. It can take decades to determine the exact chain of cause and effect that led to any single outcome. My degree in history taught me that, if little else. But I can't wait twenty years to address these events. For while I'm healthy at this moment—and I've done what I can to protect myself—there are people who would prefer me otherwise. Best to get it on paper now.

But as we dance these familiar steps together, please remember that nothing is what it seems. While Buck's murder provides a natural jumping-off point, this story really began when I was fourteen years old. The people whose lives would intertwine with fatal consequences were alive then, and some were already lovers. To understand this story, you must swim between two times like a person moving from wakefulness to sleep and then back again. Given the nature of the mind, we'll consider the dreams of sleep to be the past, never quite accurate in recollection, always made to serve our desires (except when haunting us for our sins). And the wakeful present . . . well, it, too, holds its dangers.

When I was thirteen, I came upon a bobwhite quail perched upon a log in the woods. Another quail lay at its feet. It appeared to be dead, but I knelt very near and watched them both for half a minute, one motionless, the other making inquisitive movements, as though waiting impatiently for its partner to rise. Only after my eyes lost focus, perhaps from strain, did I notice the rattlesnake coiled two feet away, tensing to strike. The heavy eastern diamondback was four feet long, and focused on me, not the bird.

I lived that day, and I learned: Close enough to see is close enough to kill.

CHAPTER 4

BY THE TIME I got word that there was a body in the Mississippi River, the sheriff had already deployed the county rescue boat to recover the corpse. Normally, I would dispatch a staff reporter to document this, but because my source sounded pretty sure the dead man was Buck Ferris, I know I have to go myself. Which presents difficulties. For me, water and death are inextricably entwined. I never go down to the river—or even drive across it on the high bridge—unless I have no other choice. That can make living in a river town pretty inconvenient.

Today I have no choice.

Before I leave the *Watchman* offices, I call Quinn Ferris, Buck's wife. Quinn treated me like a son when I was at her house, which was often and for long periods. Despite my having been absent from Bienville for twenty-eight years (excepting the last five months), we're close enough that I know she would rather get tragic news from me than from the police or the coroner. As I feared, word has already reached her—the curse of a small town. She's running around her house, trying to find her keys so that she can get down to the river. Because she lives fifteen miles out in the county, Quinn desperately wants to start toward town, but I somehow persuade her to wait at home until I call with confirmation of what is still only a rumor.

My SUV is parked in the employee lot behind the newspaper building. We're only four blocks from the bluff, where Front Street slices down the two-hundred-foot drop to the river at a forty-degree angle. Pulling out onto Buchanan Street, I go over what my source told me on the phone. About 8:40 A.M. a retired kayaker discovered a man he believed to be Buck Ferris wedged in the fork of a cottonwood snag in the Mississippi River, four hundred yards south of the Bienville landing. The kayaker didn't know Buck well, but he'd attended a couple of his archaeological presentations at the Indian Village. Anyone who knows the Mississippi River recognizes this story as a miracle. If Buck hadn't floated by chance into the fork of that tree, he might have drifted all the way to Baton Rouge or New Orleans before being discovered, if he was found at all. A lot of people drown in the Mississippi, and while most are eventually recovered, there are times when the river god refuses to give up his dead.

Dread settles in my stomach as I drive down the steep incline of Front Street to what locals call Lower'ville—short for Lower Bienville—but which the Chamber of Commerce calls the Riverfront. The Mississippi is already high, even for spring, and a brisk breeze is kicking up whitecaps on its broad, muddy surface. Pulling my eyes from the water, I focus on the cars parked along the timber guardrail blocking the precipitous drop to the river, but this does little to calm my anxiety. I've tried for more than thirty years to rid myself of what is surely a phobia about this river, but I've failed.

I'm going to have to gut it out.

TWO NARROW STREETS ARE all that remain of Lower'ville, the den of the demimonde who lived in the shadow of the Bienville bluff in the nineteenth century. Two hundred years ago, this infamous river landing offered flatboatmen and steamboat crews everything from gambling and fancy women to prime whiskey and rentable dueling pistols. Through Lower'ville moved a brisk trade in everything from long-staple cotton to African slaves, enriching the nabobs who lived in the glittering palaces atop the bluff and whose money flowed back into the district as payment for exclusive vices.

Today all that has changed. The relentless river has reduced Lower'ville to two parallel streets and the five short alleys that link them, most of which are lined with tourist bars and restaurants. The Sun King Gaming Company maintains a small office and transit bus stop here to serve its garish Louis Quatorze–themed casino, which stands a mile upriver. A local tour operator runs open-air buses from down here, and a whiskey distiller practices his craft in an old warehouse butted against the foot of the bluff. Everything else is overpriced shops. There are no whores, steamboat captains, knife-wielding flatboatmen, or pistol duels. The duels happen in Bucktown these days, the weapons of choice being the Glock and the AR-15. For gambling you have to shuttle upriver to the Sun King. I almost never visit this part of town, and on the rare occasion that I'm forced to meet someone in one of the river-facing restaurants, I sit with my back to the picture windows, so I don't have to look at the big water.

Today I won't have the luxury of avoiding my stressor. Parking my Ford Flex a few feet from the river's edge, I spy the county rescue boat anchored in the current a quarter mile south of the landing, a hundred yards out in the river. A broken line of people stands watching the desultory action on the water. Three-quarters of a mile beyond the bobbing boat, the low shore of Louisiana hovers above the river. The sight from this angle brings on a wave of nausea, partly because of the river, but also because I'm starting to internalize the reality that Buck Ferris could have left the planet last night while I slept in my bed. I knew he might be in danger, yet wherever he went last night, he went alone.

Forcing myself to look away from the opposite shore, I walk downstream from the gawkers to get a clear line of sight to the boat. Without binoculars I can't see much, but the two deputies on board appear to be trying to wrestle something out of the water on the far side of the boat.

There are three kinds of snags in the river, all of which could, and did, wreck many a steamboat back in the age of Mark Twain. The worst is the "planter," which occurs when an entire tree uprooted by the river wedges itself into the bottom and becomes braced by accumulating silt. Often showing only a foot or two of wood above the water, these massive trees lever gently up and down in the current, waiting to rip deadly gashes in the hulls of boats steered by careless pilots. Given the deputies' obvious difficulties, I figure they're struggling to free the corpse from a half-submerged fork in a planter. Even after accomplishing this, they'll have to deadlift his body over the gunwale of the rescue boat, which is no easy task. As I ponder their predicament, the obvious question runs through my mind: What are the odds that a man who fell into a mile-wide river would float into one of the few obstacles that could have stopped him from being washed toward the Gulf of Mexico?

While I watch the sweat-stained backs of the deputies, a whirring like a swarm of hornets passes over my head, pulling my attention from the boat. Looking up, I see a small quad-rotor drone—a DJI, I think—zoom out over the water at about a hundred feet of altitude, making for the sheriff's department boat. The drone ascends rapidly as it approaches the craft; whoever is piloting it obviously hopes to avoid pissing off the deputies. Knowing the Tenisaw County Sheriff's Department as I do, I doubt that pilot will have much luck.

One deputy has already noticed the drone. He waves angrily at the sky, then lifts binoculars to his face and starts panning the riverbank in search of the pilot. I follow his gaze, but all I see is a couple of city cops doing the same thing I am, scanning the line of rubberneckers for someone holding a joystick unit in their hands.

After thirty fruitless seconds of this, I decide the pilot must be guiding the drone from atop the bluff behind us. If the drone pilot *is* working from the bluff, which rises two hundred feet above the river, flying a low approach to the county boat was smart. That gave the deputies the feeling that he or she must be working from the low bank. Without tilting my head back, I scan the iron fence atop the bluff. It doesn't take long to notice a slight figure 150 yards south of the landing, standing attentively at the fence with something in its hands.

While I can't make out features or even gender at this distance, the sight gives me a ping of recognition. I know a kid with a knack for capturing newsworthy events on his aerial camera: the son of a girl I went to high school with. Though only fourteen, Denny Allman is a genius with drones, and I've posted some of his footage on the paper's website. Most kids wouldn't have a way to get to the bluff on a Tuesday morning while school is in session, but Denny is homeschooled, which means he can get away from the house if, say, he hears about a dead body on the police scanner he begged his mother to buy him last Christmas.

As I watch the figure on the bluff, the coroner's wagon rumbles down Front Street. It's a 1960s vintage Chevy panel truck. Rather than stop in the turnaround, as I did, the driver pulls onto the hard dirt and drives downstream along the riverbank, finally stopping about thirty yards from where I stand. Byron Ellis, the county coroner, climbs out and walks toward me, avoiding the gawkers who pepper him with questions.

You don't have to be an M.D. to get elected coroner in Bienville, Mississippi. Byron Ellis is a former ambulance driver and paramedic who, as he approached his sixtieth birthday, decided to become the first African American to secure the position. Byron and I have gotten to know each other well over the last five months, for a tragic reason. Bienville is in the grip of a violent crime wave that's 100 percent confined to the black community. About six months before I arrived, black teenagers began killing each other in ambushes and shoot-outs that have terrified the citizenry, both black and white. Despite the best efforts of law enforcement and dedicated intervention by church, school, and neighborhood leaders, the cycle of retribution has only escalated. Byron and I have stood alone over too many bullet-riddled children, facing the inarguable fact that our society has gone mad.

"Who's out there, Marshall?" Byron asks as he nears me.

"I've heard it's Buck Ferris. Don't know for sure yet. I hope to hell it's not."

"You and me both." Byron slaps my offered hand. "That man never hurt a fly."

I look back at the deputies struggling in the boat. "I figured you'd beat me down here."

"Got another kid in my wagon. Been sweating my ass off already."

I turn to him in surprise. "I didn't hear about any shooting last night."

He shrugs. "Nobody reported this kid missing till his mama went in to give him his Cap'n Crunch this morning and saw he wasn't in his bed. Convict road crew found him lying in a ditch out where Cemetery Road crosses Highway 61. He took eighteen rounds, best I could count. I pulled what looks like a .223 slug out of what was almost an exit wound in his back."

"Goddamn, Byron. This is getting out of hand."

"Oh, we're way past that, brother. We in a war zone now. Drowned archaeologist seems kinda tame after that, don't it?"

It takes all my willpower to hold a straight face. Byron has no idea that Buck Ferris was like a father to me, and there's no point making him feel bad by telling him now. "Maybe," I murmur. "I'll be surprised if this was an accidental death, though. I've got a feeling there's something serious behind this. Some powerful people."

"Yeah? Well, that sounds like your department." Byron chuckles, the low laughter rumbling in his generous belly. "Look at them keystone cops out there. Deputy Dawg, man. That drone 'bout to run 'em crazy!"

"I'll call you later," I tell him. "I've got work to do."

"Sure, man. Just leave me out in this sun. Don't worry 'bout me."

Byron winks as I give him a mock salute.

Getting back into the Flex, I push the engine button and head up Foundry Road, which ascends the bluff on an opposite angle to Front Street. As my motor strains on the incline, a pistol shot cracks over the river, echoes off the bluff face. I jump in my seat, stunned by the reckless idiocy of a deputy firing into the air in a populated area to try to hit a drone. Another shot pops off below me. I hope they don't have a shotgun on board the boat. If they do, they can probably bring down the little aircraft, which by law must carry a registration number. And since Bienville has an asshole for a sheriff, the pilot will wind up in a lot of trouble. If the pilot is who I think it is, that's a story I don't want to have to cover.

I don't pray, but all the way up the hill I beg the universe to grant me one dispensation in the midst of its daily creation and destruction: *Let that body belong to someone else. Don't let it be the man who stopped me from killing myself at fifteen.*

Don't let it be Buck.

CHAPTER 5

ON THE BIENVILLE bluff, you can't park closer than thirty yards from the edge. Within the city limits, there's a buffer of green space between Battery Row and the iron fence that keeps kids and drunks from killing themselves on a daily basis. As I'd hoped, the slight figure standing at the fence turns out to be my friend's son, fourteen-year-old Denny Allman. Denny surely recognized my Flex as I parked it—if he hadn't, he would have bolted.

I lift my hand in greeting as I approach him. Denny tosses his head in acknowledgment, then turns back to the river, his hands never leaving the drone controller. Even with his back to me, I can see his mother in his stance. Dixie Allman was athletic and attractive in high school. A C student, mostly because of laziness, she had a quick mind. Her problem was that from age ten she'd focused it solely on getting male attention. She married at eighteen—pregnant—and divorced by twenty-five. Denny's father was her third husband, and he abandoned them when Denny was five or six. Dixie has done her best to raise the boy right, and that's one reason I've encouraged him by posting his stuff on our website.

"Did they shoot at your drone?" I call to him.

"Shit, yeah! Morons."

I force a laugh and walk up to the fence. Denny has a salty vocabulary for an eighth grader, but so did my friends and I at that age. "They probably called a backup car to hunt for you."

"They did, but it went down to the river. I grabbed some altitude and landed behind some trees farther south. They're trying to work their way down there now. They'll never make it through the kudzu."

The drone controller in his hands mates an iPad Mini to a joystick unit. Denny has strapped a sun hood onto his iPad, so I can't see the screen with a casual glance. Looking over the fence, I see the county boat down on the river. It's headed toward the dock now. The deputies must have finally taken their cargo on board.

"Did you get a good look at the body?" I ask.

"Not live," Denny replies, focusing on his screen. "I had to keep my eyes on the deputies while I was shooting."

"Can we look now?"

He shrugs. "Sure. What's the rush?"

"Did you ever meet Dr. Ferris, out at the Indian mounds?"

"Yeah. He came to my school a couple of times. I—" Denny goes pale. "That's him in the water? Old Dr. Buck?"

"It might be."

"Oh, man. What happened to him?"

"I don't know. Maybe he was looking for arrowheads or something and walked too far out on a sandbar. They collapse under people sometimes."

The boy shakes his head forcefully. "Dr. Buck wouldn't do that. He walked rivers and creeks all the time hunting for stuff, usually after storms. He found tons of Indian swag, even mastodon bones. You should see the stuff he's found for the museum in Jackson."

"I have."

"Then you know there's no way he fell into the Mississippi. Not unless he had a heart attack or something."

"Maybe that's what happened," I say, though I don't believe it. "Or a stroke. Buck was over seventy. With some luck, we'll find out where he went in. That might tell us what he was doing."

I can see Denny making mental calculations. "I need to leave the DJI down there till the cops leave," he says, "but I can access the file from here. It just eats up a lot of my monthly data allowance."

"I'll reimburse you."

His face lights up. "Awesome!"

He stabs the iPad screen, waves me closer. Thanks to the sun hood, I now have a glare-free view of what Denny shot only a few minutes ago. On the screen, two deputies with no experience at hauling corpses out of water are attempting to do just that. All I can see of the dead man is one side of a gray-fleshed face and a thin arm trailing in the muddy current. Then the head lolls over on the current, and a wave of nausea rolls through me. My mouth goes dry.

It's Buck.

I can't see his whole head, but the far side of his skull appears to have been broken open by some sort of fracture. As I strain to see more, his head sinks back into the water. "Fast-forward," I urge.

Denny's already doing it. At triple speed, the deputies dart around the deck of the rescue boat like cartoon characters, occasionally leaning over the gunwale to try to yank Buck's body free of the tree fork holding him in the water. Suddenly one looks skyward and begins waving his arms. Then he starts yelling, draws his pistol, and fires at the camera suspended beneath the drone.

"What a freakin' idiot," Denny mutters, as the deputy fires again.

"Does he not realize those bullets have to come down somewhere?" I ask.

"He flunked physics."

"Don't they teach gravity in grade school?"

After holstering his gun, the deputy stomps back to a hatch in the stern and removes what looks like a ski rope. Then he makes a loop in the rope, leans over the gunwale, and starts trying to float the lasso he made down over Buck's body.

"No, damn it!" I bellow. "Have some goddamn respect!"

Denny snorts at this notion.

"He needs to tie the rope around his waist," I mutter, "then get in the water himself and free the body."

"You're dreaming," Denny says in the lilt of a choirboy whose voice has not yet broken. "He's gonna lasso the body, gun the motor, and leave a rooster tail all the way back to the dock."

"And rip Buck's body in half in the process."

"Was it Buck for sure?" he asks. "I couldn't tell."

"Yeah. It's him."

Denny lowers his head over the screen.

It takes some time, but the deputy eventually gets the rope around Buck, and he does in fact use the motor to tear him free of the snag's grasp. Thankfully, the corpse appears to stay in one piece, and after the boat stops, the deputies slowly drag it up over the transom.

"Oh, man," Denny mutters.

"What?"

"Look at his *head*. The side of it. It's all messed up."

It doesn't take a CIA analyst to see that something caved in the left side of Buck Ferris's skull. The vault of his cranium has a hole the size of a Sunkist orange in it. Now that he's out of the water, his face looks oddly deflated. "I saw."

"What did that?" Denny asks. "A baseball bat?"

"Maybe. Could have been a gunshot. Gunshot wounds don't look like they do on TV, or even in the movies. But it might be blunt force trauma. A big rock could have done that. Maybe he took a fall before he went into the river."

"Where?" Denny asks, incredulous. "There's hardly any rocks around here. Even if you fell off the bluff, you wouldn't hit one. Not igneous rocks. You'd have to hit concrete or something to do that."

"He could have fallen onto some riprap," I suggest, meaning the large gray rocks the Corps of Engineers carpets the riverbanks with to slow erosion.

"I guess. But those are right down by the water, not under the bluff."

"And he would have had to fall from a height to smash his skull like that." Despite my emotional state, I'm suddenly wondering about the legal implications of Denny's drone excursion. "You know, you really need to turn this footage over to the sheriff."

"It's not *footage,* man. It's a *file.* And it's mine."

"The district attorney would probably dispute that. Are you licensed to fly that drone?"

"I don't need a license."

"You do for commercial work. And if I put it up on our website, or pay your data bill, you're doing this for hire."

Denny scowls in my direction. "So don't pay me."

"You're missing the point, Denny."

"No, I'm not. I don't like the sheriff. And the chief of police I like even less. They hassle me all the time. Until they need me, of course. That time they had a car wreck down in a gully by Highway 61, they called me to fly down in there and check to see if anybody was alive. They were glad to see me then. And at the prison riot, too. Although they stole my micro SD cards and copied them. But any other time, they're major A-holes."

"I heard they have their own drone now."

Once again, Denny snorts in contempt.

"You know what I'm thinking?" I say.

"Nope."

"The next thing we need to know is where Buck's truck is. He drives an old GMC pickup. It's bound to be upstream from where he was found—unless something isn't what it appears to be."

Denny is nodding. "You want me to fly the banks and look for his truck?"

"Seems like the thing to do, doesn't it? You got enough battery left?"

"Two is one, one is none."

"What?"

"Navy SEAL motto. Meaning I brought some extras." Denny leans over the fence and looks down the sharp incline of Front Street. "Looks like they're loading him into the coroner's wagon. Let the deputies get clear, and I'll fly the drone back up here, change out my battery, and start checking the banks."

"Sounds good. Let's try the Mississippi shore first."

"Yep."

We stand at the fence together, looking down into Lower'ville, which on most mornings would be virtually empty (except in March, which is peak tourist season for our city). But on this May morning, death has drawn a crowd. Though they're almost stick figures from our perspective, I recognize Byron Ellis helping the deputies slide the sheet-covered body from his gurney into the old Chevy. Watching them wrestle that mortal weight, I hear a snatch of music: Robert Johnson playing "Preachin' Blues." Turning back to the road, I look for a passing car but see none. Then I realize the music was in my head. "Preachin' Blues" was one of the first songs Buck taught me on guitar. The harmless man lying beneath the coroner's sheet with his skull cracked open salvaged my young life. The realization that he has been murdered—possibly on the river—is so surreal that I have to force it into some inaccessible place in my mind.

"Hey, are you okay?" Denny asks in a hesitant voice.

I wipe my eyes and turn back to him. "Yeah. Buck and I were close back when I lived here. When I was a kid."

"Oh. Can I ask you something?"

He's going to ask me about my brother dying, I think, searching for a way to avoid the subject. Seeing Buck pulled from the river has already knocked me off-balance. I don't want to dwell on the nightmare that poisoned the river for me.

"Sure," I reply, sounding anything but.

"I knew you won a Pulitzer Prize and all, when you were in Washington. But I didn't realize what it was for. I was online last week and saw it was for something you wrote about being embedded in Iraq. Were you with the SEALs or somebody like that? Delta Force?"

A fourteen-year-old boy's question. "Sometimes," I tell him, relief coursing through me. "I was embedded in Afghanistan before Iraq, with the Marines. But in Iraq I was with private security contractors. Do you know what those are?"

"Like Blackwater and stuff?"

"Exactly. Most guys who do that work in Afghanistan are former soldiers: Rangers, Delta, SEALs. But a lot of them in Iraq were just regular cops back in the world, believe it or not. And lots of those were from the South. They go over there for the money. It's the only way they can make that kind of paycheck. They earn four times what the regular soldiers do. More than generals."

"That doesn't seem fair."

"It's not."

Denny thinks about this. "So what's it like? For real. Is it like *Call of Duty* come to life?"

"Not even close. But until you've been there, you can't really understand it. And I hope you never do. Only a few things in life are like that."

"Such as?"

"That's a different conversation. One for you and your mom."

"Come on. Tell me something cool about it."

I try to think like a fourteen-year-old for a minute. "You can tell what units the contractors came from by the sunglasses they wear. Wraparound Oakleys for Delta Force. SEALs wear Maui Jims. Special Forces, Wiley X."

"No way. What about Ray-Bans?"

"Over there? Only for punks and phonies. Over here, that's what I wear." I glance at my wristwatch. "I need to call Buck's wife, Denny."

"Sure, okay. But like, how did you get that kind of job? I mean, that kind of access?"

"A guy I went to high school with helped me out. He was an Army Ranger a long time ago, during the Persian Gulf War. He got me that gig with the private contractors. He also saved my life over there. That's what won me the Pulitzer, that assignment. What I saw over there."

Denny nods like he understands all this, but I have a feeling he'll be buying my book online this afternoon.

"Save your money," I tell him. "I'll give you a copy."

"Cool. Who was the guy? Your friend?"

"Paul Matheson."

His eyes widen. "Kevin Matheson's dad?"

"That's right."

"That dude's like, rich. *Really* rich."

"I guess he is, yeah. Paul didn't go over there for the money, though. It started as a sort of Hemingway trip for him. Do you know what I mean by that?"

"Not really."

"A macho thing. He had problems with his father. He felt like he had a lot to prove."

"That I understand."

I'll bet you do.

"Hey," Denny says, his voice suddenly bright. "We should go up to the cemetery to run this search. That ground's like forty feet higher than here, counting the hills. Better line of sight up there, which gives me better control."

The thought of the Bienville Cemetery resurrects the dread I felt earlier. "Let's just do it from here, okay? I'm on a tight schedule this morning."

The boy gives me a strange look. "What you gotta do?"

"They're breaking ground on the new paper mill at eleven A.M. I need to be there for that."

He laughs. "The Mississippi Miracle? I'll believe it when they build it."

Denny sounds like he's quoting someone else. "Where'd you hear that line?"

He looks sheepish. "My uncle Buddy."

Denny's uncle is a mostly out-of-work contractor who spends his days getting high in front of the TV. "That paper mill's the real deal. The Chinese have the money. And a billion-dollar investment could put this town in the black for the next fifty years."

Denny looks a little less skeptical. "My mom's been kind of hoping to get work out there."

"I'll bet. The average salary's going to be sixty thousand dollars. And *that*," I think aloud, "is why I'm afraid that the new paper mill might have played some part in Buck's death."

Denny's head whips toward me. Even a fourteen-year-old boy can put this together. "I read your article about the artifact Buck found. Would that mess up the paper mill somehow?"

"It could. It scared the shit out of most people in this town. The whole county, really."

"You think somebody would *kill* Buck over that?"

"I can think of about thirty-six thousand suspects at this point."

"For real?"

"Kids are killing kids over cell phones in this town, Denny. What do you think people will do for a *billion* dollars?"

"A billion dollars?"

"That's what the Chinese are investing here, not counting all the millions that will come with the new bridge and interstate."

"Wow. I see what you mean. Well . . ." He looks over the fence again. "The coroner's splitting. I'll get the drone back up here and start checking the riverbanks."

I give him a thumbs-up. "I'm going to walk down the fence and make a few calls. Holler if you see anything."

"I will."

For a second I wonder if I could be putting him in danger by having him search for Buck's pickup, but I can't see how. Turning, I walk north along the fence, looking down at the roof of the coroner's wagon as it hauls Buck's remains up from the river for the final time. I really have only one call to make, because the call I *want* to make, I can't. Not for several hours yet. The call I *must* make I'd give anything to avoid.

Taking out my iPhone, I dial Buck's house. Not even one full ring passes before his wife pounces on the phone.

"Marshall?" Quinn Ferris says breathlessly.

"It was him," I tell her, knowing the slightest delay would only make it worse. "Buck's dead."

There's a deep-space silence for two full seconds, and then Quinn says in a tiny voice, "You're sure?"

"I saw his face, Quinn."

"Oh, God. Marshall . . . what do I do? Is he all right? Is he comfortable? I mean—"

"I know what you mean. They're treating him with respect. Byron Ellis picked him up. I imagine they'll take Buck to the hospital for a brief period. There's going to have to be an autopsy in Jackson."

"Oh . . . no. They're going to cut him open?"

"There's no way around it, I'm afraid."

"Was it not an accident?"

Here a little soft-pedaling won't hurt anyone. Not in the short run. "They don't know yet. But anyone who dies while not under a physician's care has to have a postmortem."

"Dear Lord. I'm trying to get my mind around it."

"I think you should stay at home for a while, Quinn."

"I can't. I have to see him. Marshall, does he look all right?"

"He was in the river. That doesn't do anybody any favors. I think you should stay out at your place for a bit. I'll drive out to see you in a couple of hours."

"No. No, I'm coming in. I can take it. He was my husband."

"Quinn, listen. This is me, not the police, asking. Do you know where Buck was last night?"

"Of course. He was going back to the industrial park to try to find some bones."

I fight the urge to groan. The industrial park is the site of the new paper mill, where the groundbreaking will happen in two hours. Buck was jailed for five hours for digging at that site the first time, and charged with felony trespass. He knew he would only get in more trouble if he went back there. But more important, that site lies *downstream* from where Buck was found.

"Did they kill him?" Quinn asks. "Did some of those greedy bastards murder my husband because of their stupid mill?"

"I don't know yet, Quinn. But I'm going to find out."

"If you don't, we'll never know. I don't trust one of those sons of bitches in the sheriff's department. They're all owned by the local big shots. You know who I'm talking about."

I grunt but say nothing.

"The goddamn Bienville Poker Club," she says.

"You could be right. But we don't know that."

"*I* know. They don't care about anything but money. Money and their mansions and their spoiled rotten kids and—oh, I don't know what I'm saying. It's just not right. Buck was so . . . *good*."

"He was," I agree.

"And nobody gives a damn," she says in a desolate voice. "All the good he did, all those years, and in the end nobody cares about anything but money."

"They think the mill means survival for the town. Boom times again."

"*Damn* this town," she says savagely. "If they had to kill my husband to get their mill, Bienville doesn't deserve to survive."

There it is.

"You need to call Jet Matheson," she says. "She's the only one with the guts to take on the Poker Club. Not that you haven't done some things. I mean, you've printed stories and all. But Jet's own father-in-law is a member, and she's still gone after a couple of them like a pit bull. She took Dr. Warren Lacey to court and damn near stripped him of his license."

Quinn got to know Jet during our senior year in high school, and better during the years I was away. "Jet's out of town this morning," I tell her, "taking a deposition in a lawsuit. I'll speak to her when she gets back."

"Good."

Quinn goes silent, but I can almost hear her mind spinning, frantically searching for anything to distract her from the immediate, awful reality. I wait, but the new widow says nothing more, probably realizing that no matter what I do, or what Jet Matheson or anyone else does, her husband will still be dead.

"Quinn, I need to get back to work. I'll check in with you soon, I promise. You call me if you have any trouble with anyone or anything today."

"I can handle it, Marshall. I'm a tough old girl. Come out later if you get a chance. This house is going to seem pretty empty. You'll remind me of better times. All my old Eagle Scouts around the dinner table. Well, Buck's, really."

Quinn and Buck married in their early forties, and she was never able to have children of her own. Buck's Boy Scouts always got an extra dose of maternal affection from her, one much needed by some.

"Yours too, Quinn."

"They were. And all the music. Lord, you and Buck played through till dawn so many nights. I'd get so mad knowing we had to be up the next day, but I never said anything. It was so pure. I knew how lucky we were, even then."

And with that, my first tears come. "I remember you complaining a time or two," I tell her.

"Well, somebody had to be responsible." She laughs softly, then her voice drops to a confiding whisper. "I know you know what I'm going through, Marshall. Because of Adam."

I close my eyes, and tears roll down my cheeks. "I've gotta go, Quinn."

"I didn't mean to— Oh, hell. Death *sucks*."

"I'll call you this afternoon."

I hang up and strike off down the bluff, away from Denny Allman, who doesn't need to see me crying right now. Denny's father abandoned him a long time ago, and while it might be good for him to see how grown men react to death, I don't want to explain that the loss robbing me of my composure now didn't happen last night, but thirty-one years ago.

A fourteen-year-old boy doesn't need to know grief can last that long.

CHAPTER 6

WHILE DENNY ALLMAN flies his drone up the bluff face to change batteries and begin searching for Buck Ferris's truck, I walk north along the fence and try to get myself under control. It's tough with the Mississippi River dominating my field of view. Seeing Buck pulled dead from that water kicked open a door between the man I am now and the boy I was at fourteen, the year fate ripped my life inside out. That door has been wedged shut for more years than I want to think about. Now, rather than face the dark opening, my mind casts about for something to distract itself from peering into the past.

My finger itches to make that call I cannot make, but the person I want to talk to can't take a call from me right now. I've slept with married women twice in my life. The first time was in my twenties, and she was French—my professor at Georgetown. I didn't even know she was married when I started sleeping with her; her husband lived most of the year in France. The risks during that affair never rose above the possibility of an awkward meeting at a restaurant, which might have resulted in a sharp word later, for her not me. The woman I'm sleeping with now has a husband quite capable of killing me, were he to learn of our affair. If I called her now, she could try to play it off as business, but even people of marginal intelligence can detect intimacy in the human voice. I don't intend to have my life upended—or even ended—because of an unguarded syllable decoded by a nosy paralegal. I could send a text, of course, but SMS messages leave a digital trail.

For now I must suffer in silence.

A group of women power walking along the bluff approaches from a distance. An asphalt trail follows the bluff for two miles—the Mark Twain Riverwalk—and in the early mornings and evenings it's quite busy. Thankfully, by nine thirty most of the serious walkers have retreated to coffee shops or to their SUVs for morning errands. For the first hundred yards, I keep my eyes rightward, on the buildings that line Battery Row. I pass the old clock tower, the Planters' Hotel, two antebellum mansions. Behind them stands the tallest building in the city, the Aurora Hotel. Next comes the memorial fountain enshrining 173 Confederate dead. It's a stone's throw from the emplacements where thirty-two-pounder Seacoast guns covered the Mississippi River during the Civil War. Across from the fountain stand a couple of bars and restaurants, another antebellum home, and then the new amphitheater, paid for by casino money.

The old railroad depot functions as the hub of the bluff, with its small café, convenience shop, tourist information office, and herd of blue bicycles for rent. Past the depot stands the only modern building on the bluff, the Holland Development Company, headquarters of our local real estate king. Just down the street from that crouches the Twelve Bar, a ratty blues club owned by a native son who's turned down stunning sums to hold on to his pride and joy. Across from the Twelve Bar is a graded site awaiting the granite slab of a promised civil rights memorial, but somehow the final money never seems to get appropriated. I've walked this route too many times over the past months to be distracted for long. Eventually the gravity of the river draws my gaze to the west.

From the midpoint of the Bienville bluff, you can see seventeen miles of river. Thanks to the misguided Corps of Engineers, the Mississippi upstream from Bienville looks like a canal. It's a nine-mile run to the first meander, and two meanders above that stands the siege city of Vicksburg. Besieged by Yankees during the Civil War and by economic woes today, the city fights hard to survive. It's a grim reality, but the river towns are dying in Mississippi, by a slow exsanguination of people and talent that functions like a wasting disease. Most have changed so little over time that if you resurrected a citizen who lived in the 1890s, they would still recognize the streets they once walked. In Natchez and Bienville, you could do that with someone from the 1850s.

Of all the famous Mississippi cotton towns—from Clarksdale in the

Delta to Natchez on its bluff—only Bienville is holding its own against the tides of time, race, and terminal nostalgia. The reason is complex, largely illegal, and has occupied much of my thoughts and work since I moved back here five months ago. My gut tells me that Buck Ferris's death will ultimately be added to the list of smaller crimes committed in the quest for Bienville's economic survival, but right now my mind refuses to track on that.

Right now I'm thinking how this day feels a lot like the day my feelings about the Mississippi River changed forever. It was May then, too. A glorious May. I loved the river then. As a boy, I'd fished in it, hunted along it, canoed across it, camped above it as a Boy Scout, even skied over its backwaters during flood years. The Mississippi was as much a part of me then as it ever was of Huck Finn or Sam Clemens. The year I left Bienville to attend college at the University of Virginia, I came across a letter by T. S. Eliot, who I had always vaguely assumed was English. To my surprise, I discovered that Eliot had grown up along the same river I had, in St. Louis, and to a friend he wrote this about the Mississippi: *I feel that there is something in having passed one's childhood beside the big river, which is incommunicable to those who have not. I consider myself fortunate to have been born here, rather than in Boston, or New York, or London.* I knew exactly what Eliot meant.

All my life, I've felt a constant, subterranean pull from the great river that divides America into east and west, this slow juggernaut of water that was the border of my home, a force that tugged at me like spiritual gravity. But after one day in 1987, what it pulled *on* in me changed. Today smells a lot like that day: Confederate jasmine and honeysuckle, late-blooming azaleas. The sun is hot, but the air is cool. And the river's running high, just as it was thirty-one years ago.

But unlike today, which began with death, that day began in glory. Glory for my family and my friends. The idea that the angel of death was circling over us would have seemed preposterous.

My brother and I had spent the afternoon in Jackson, the state capital, running in the state track meet for St. Mark's Episcopal Day School. When I write "Episcopal Day School," don't picture an ivy-walled temple of learning. Picture three gray corrugated aluminum buildings without air-conditioning and a bumpy football field in a former cow pasture. Correction: The teacher's lounge and the library had window

AC units. The school board couldn't have hired anyone to teach us without them. Academic rigor was stressed at St. Mark's, but—as in the rest of the former Confederacy—football was a religion. Basketball and baseball also rated as manly sports, though second tier, while running track was viewed merely as training duty. Golf, tennis, and swimming were hobbies pursued by dandies. Swimming was the one activity at which I truly excelled, but St. Mark's didn't have a team. I had to swim for the City of Bienville.

Thanks to my brother Adam and his senior classmates, St. Mark's had thus far won both the Class A state championship in football and the Overall State championship in basketball, defeating the preeminent Quad A school in the state, Capital Prep in Jackson. This miracle had been accomplished only twice in the state's history. It was *Hoosiers,* rewritten for the Deep South. We'd only managed to win South State in baseball, but at the track meet on that day we racked up our third state title.

Though I was still three weeks shy of turning fifteen, I ran in both the mile and two-mile relays (we won firsts), and I took third place in the high jump. But my older brother was the star of the team. Adam had filled that role in every sport for St. Mark's since his sophomore year, when he began playing quarterback for the varsity football team. That year Adam McEwan led the Crusaders to a South State title, beginning his meteoric rise to statewide legend status. There's nothing unusual in that, of course. Every couple of years, a kid from some little Mississippi town gets canonized as the Next Big Thing, the next Hot College Prospect who's "maybe good enough to go pro." My brother happened to be that kid. The thing was, most people who canonized him had no idea how unique he really was.

Adam wasn't like the other small-town demigods—phenomenal at one sport, or two, or even three. He was gifted at everything he put his hand to. I once saw him (having touched a bow and arrow only once, as a boy at day camp) try a compound bow at a demonstration being given by a hunting expert at a local gun show. After an hour of informal advice, Adam outshot every hunter present and even matched the instructor on distance shots.

But Adam's embarrassment of riches did not end with sports. As a junior, with no background in music, Adam walked onto the stage during the St. Mark's production of *My Fair Lady* and sang "On the Street Where You Live" in a tenor voice so tender yet powerful that it literally stopped the show. To add insult to injury, Adam was as beloved by his English teachers as by those who taught calculus and physics. His SAT scores came in fifty points higher than anyone else's in the senior class, cementing a National Merit Scholarship, and by the afternoon of that track meet in 1987, he'd been accepted to five Ivy League universities. Our father wanted him to attend Sewanee, his own alma mater, but in a rare rebellion, Adam told me he planned to insist on Brown University.

I loved him for that, for breaking free from our father's life template. Mississippians with Adam's gifts rarely leave Mississippi, much less the South. When you're from Mississippi, Vanderbilt is considered a northern school. My brother not only decided to attend an Ivy League school in the *far* north, but the least structured institution of them all. Oh, I loved him for that.

Yet even so, it was tough to have a brother like Adam.

The three years between us might have provided a protective cushion with a normally gifted older brother, but there was simply no escaping Adam's shadow. The glare of the spotlight he walked in whited out everything around him. And while I stood six feet tall as a ninth grader, and was no slouch in the classroom, I couldn't possibly stand tall enough to escape the penumbra around my brother. Yet as I watched him stride like Apollo through our earthly realm, what amazed me most was his humility. Despite being subjected to near continuous adulation, Adam did not "get the big head." He kept himself apart from all cliques, treated everyone as an equal, and he almost never got angry. Adam seemed, by any measure of human frailty, too good to be true. And while someone so universally admired almost inevitably generates resentment or outright enmity in some people, Adam seemed the exception. Even teams he embarrassed on the hotly contested fields of Mississippi embraced him as a kind of hero, someone they would later boast they had played against.

By the end of his senior year—at least the athletic year, of which that track meet marked the coda—Adam wasn't the only high school boy feeling immortal. As soon as the coaches handed out our trophies, we broke out in spectacular fashion. After holding ourselves in check for most of the year—limiting ourselves to a few beers on weekends—we switched to Jack Daniel's or vodka for the ride home, and some guys even broke out the weed. By ten P.M. in Bienville, every member of every St. Mark's boys' athletic team was wasted.

We started in one big group, a convoy of cars and trucks that hit all the high school hangout spots like a motorized Roman triumph. McDonald's, the mall parking lot, the recently closed electroplating factory, and finally the sandbar by the river. But as the hours wore on, the liquor and grass began culling the weaker members of the tribe. Some left to find girlfriends for late-night rendezvous, while others simply passed out in cars at various places around the city. By midnight, we were down to a core squad of six guys in two vehicles.

Adam and I were riding in Joey Burrell's beat-up Nissan 280ZX 2+2. In the other car were Paul Matheson and his two cousins from Jackson— prize assholes and stars at Capital Prep. Like Paul, they were blond and annoyingly handsome (our cheerleaders loved them, the bastards). Having won the Quad A division of the state track meet, the Matheson cousins had driven their sparkling new IROC-Z Camaro the forty miles from Jackson to Bienville to "teach Cousin Paul how to celebrate."

Paul Matheson didn't need any lessons in that department. It was Paul who'd supplied the weed after we got back from Jackson, and I was pretty sure he'd been smoking it all year long, between seventh period and afternoon practices. Though only a year older than I, Paul was talented enough to outplay most of us stoned. His father, Max, had been a football legend at Bienville's public high school in 1969, before he went to Vietnam, and the son had inherited enough of those genes to return punts and kickoffs for the varsity and to take people's heads off as a strong safety on the starting defense. Paul had also been sixth man on the championship basketball team that defeated Capital Prep—something that drove his cousins crazy.

Despite the age difference between us, Paul and I had been friends on and off since we were young boys. Back then, his house wasn't far from mine; we swam at the same pool, and by the time I was seven we were playing on the same sports teams. After going through Cub Scouts and Boy Scouts together, we found ourselves playing for St. Mark's junior high. In that sense, we were comrades in arms and close to brothers. The main thing that separated us was money.

Paul's father was rich. His uncle in Jackson was richer still. Paul's family owned the lumber mill in town and also a wood treatment plant by the river. The uncle was a big contractor who did a lot of state jobs. My father earned a decent living publishing the Bienville *Watchman,* but our family cars were ten years old, and we lived in a tract house built in 1958. We had no second home on Lake Comeaux, no killer stereo or projection TV, and no kids' phone line or swimming pool in the backyard as we hit our teenage years.

As a boy, I never noticed this wealth gap. Paul shared what he had, and money didn't seem important. Besides, his dad had won some big medals for bravery in Vietnam, and not many people begrudge a veteran success when he survives combat. But having Max Matheson for an old man was a heavy cross to bear for Paul. The war hero was a hardass, despite being known to party on occasion, and he pressured his son to win every contest in which he participated.

From the way Paul's cousins acted the night of the track meet, I figured the uncle must be an even bigger bastard than Max. They'd come to Bienville still angry about losing Overall State to us back in February. By the time they found us, they were toasted on some combination of grass and speed. Not that we were sober. Even Adam—who always imbibed in moderation—had skipped the Miller ponies in favor of Jack Daniel's. The hours before midnight passed amicably enough, but after twelve, things started to get contentious. The Matheson cousins had been digging at us all night, and we had been paying them back with interest. But around two A.M., things drifted out of control.

We were parked at the foot of the big electrical tower near the port, close enough to the river to get hit by barge searchlights as they passed. The Matheson boys weren't rocket scientists, but they had the animal cleverness of natural predators. Dooley was seventeen, his brother Trey a year older. Dooley had the mean streak. All night they'd been calling us faggots, losers, and cheaters—because if we hadn't cheated, how else could Capital Prep have been beaten by a pissant Single A team? The fact that we'd won by only one point was to them clear evidence that we'd bribed a referee, at the least.

I didn't give a damn what they said, but for some reason Adam couldn't endure their incessant ragging. This got my attention, because my brother was the most unflappable guy I knew. And somehow, before

I understood what was happening, Adam had accepted a challenge for a hundred-yard sprint along the road beneath the tower. One minute we were a group of griping drunks, the next we were lined up along the asphalt in the beam of the IROC-Z's headlights, smashing bottles and waiting for the starting gun.

Joey Burrell kept a pistol in his car, a little .25. He fired it into the sky, sending us all blazing down the road with adrenaline, alcohol, and cannabis roaring in our veins. I ran so hard I thought my heart might burst, but I only came in fourth place. Adam won the race, beating Paul by half a step. Trey Matheson was third, then me, and finally Dooley Matheson, the complainingest son of a bitch I'd ever met. All the way back to the cars, Dooley bitched about Adam and Paul getting a head start.

We should have stopped then, but when we reached the foot of the tower, Dooley demanded a chance to get his own back. He didn't want to do it on foot, though. He wanted a drag race along the levee road. This was preposterous. Their IROC-Z boasted a hundred more horsepower than Joey's 280ZX, but nevertheless I soon found myself sitting shotgun in the Nissan while Dooley and his brother revved the big engine of the IROC-Z. Adam sat in the backseat behind me, his seat belt cinched tight, while Paul angrily took the backseat of his cousins' car to keep the weight distribution even. The finish line was a grain elevator at the end of Port Road, roughly two miles away. After Joey and Dooley shouted a mutual countdown from five, we were off, blasting along the levee, watching the taillights of the IROC-Z as it vanished like an F-16 ahead of us. That Camaro beat us so badly that by the time we reached the grain elevator, the Mathesons were lounging against their car drinking beer.

At that point, we should have quit while we were behind, but the drag race only sparked further madness. We were boys, after all, and the testosterone was flowing. After handing out the embarrassing loss, the Mathesons insisted on giving us a chance to "win our pride back." I didn't know what they were talking about until Dooley pointed up at the electrical tower standing two miles back at the starting line. At six hundred feet tall, that tower—and its twin on the Louisiana shore a mile away—supported the high-voltage transmission lines that carried electrical power across the Mississippi River. I knew a few guys who'd claimed to have climbed that tower, but I'd never believed them. Nor could I see how climbing a six-hundred-foot-tall erector set represented any kind of winnable contest. But as the drunken discussion progressed, it became apparent that this was more of a test of manhood than a contest.

Once again, I was shocked to see my older brother buy into this idea. On any other night, Adam would have laughed at the absurdity of the dare. But *that* night, he let himself be baited. As subtly as I could, I tried to stop him. I wasn't scared of much back then, but heights I did not handle well. That tower was as tall as a fifty-five-story building. Even standing with both feet planted squarely on the ground, I felt the soles of my feet tingle as I looked up at the metal beams and struts silhouetted against a moonlit cloud.

By the time we'd driven over to the tower's massive base, the Mathesons had imposed a penalty for chickening out. Anyone who didn't make it to the top would have to streak stark naked down six blocks of Main Street at dawn. *Great,* I thought, picturing myself sprinting down Main with one hand over my cock and balls. Just getting up to the main ladder proved difficult. First we had to park a car beneath a tree that grew near one of the tower's four legs. Climbing onto the roof, we managed to grab the lowest limb on the tree, and that ultimately took us to a point where we could stretch precariously over a twenty-foot drop and grab the metal pegs that served as the ladder for the first hundred feet of the climb. (The power company had undoubtedly designed this obstacle to prevent drunken fools such as ourselves from attempting the suicidal climb. Clearly, they underestimated our stupidity.)

While still in the tree, Joey Burrell decided he was too drunk to try crossing to the metal pegs, so he turned back, becoming the first to earn the penalty. But soon the rest of us were clinging to the tower leg, like newborn raccoons afraid to follow their mother up a tree. Trey Matheson was highest, followed by his brother Dooley. Then Paul, Adam, and, last of all, me. I went last because something told me I might have to make a strategic retreat. I didn't want to, but I wasn't so deluded as to think I might not get into trouble.

For most of the climb, I stared only at the ladder rungs, focusing on the few square inches where I would place my free hand, then release the other and reach up again, finding the next rung—again and again and again. I heard birds and bats flying around me, but I didn't turn to see them. Mosquitoes bit me, sucking my blood without interruption as the wind whipped my shirt, tearing at my body. I sweated continuously, soaking my clothes. The boys above me chattered and laughed, and the Mathesons whooped like madmen every minute or two. All this I ignored to keep my Zen-like focus.

Two-thirds of the way up—at about four hundred feet—I made the mistake of looking out over the river. A paralyzing wave of vertigo hit me, and it was all I could do not to vomit. My vision blurred. I became vaguely aware of the lights of faraway towns and farms, and the great glittering serpent of the river running beneath us. From six hundred feet in the air you can see thirty miles. At only four hundred feet, I was incapacitated.

Adam soon realized I was in trouble. He stopped climbing and offered to come back and follow me down, discarding any thought of the climb as a test of manhood. But since we were already two-thirds of the way up, I decided to go on. I didn't want to suffer the penalty and risk arrest for indecent exposure; nor did I want to suffer Paul and his preppy cousins ragging me for all eternity.

I made it fifty more feet. Then my nerve broke.

It was the signal failure of my life. While the Mathesons hooted with derision from above, yelling *"Pussy!"* at the top of their lungs, I clung to that ladder like an arthritic old lady asked to scale the Matterhorn. This time Adam insisted on escorting me down. Shivering in terror, I told him I would descend only if he pushed on to the top. Besides, I whimpered, we were on a ladder. How the hell could he help me get to the ground? Adam said he would tie one end of his belt to his ankle and the other to my left arm, so that if I slipped, I'd have an instant to catch myself before the belt broke and I went into free fall.

I wasn't going to put my brother in that kind of danger. When Adam saw that I wouldn't change my mind, he finally started up again. My subsequent descent was a triumph of courage over abject terror. I was still two hundred feet off the ground when I saw the others "summit" the tower. And once they were on the platform, six hundred feet in the sky, I learned just how crazy the Matheson cousins were. Dooley, the seventeen-year-old, climbed onto the top strut where the aircraft

warning lights were mounted. There he stood up like a gymnast on a
balance beam. There was nothing to hold him, not a safety rail, not a
belt . . . *nothing*. A single gust of wind could have plucked him off that
tower like a dandelion seed. Watching him dance along that strut like
a drunken court jester nauseated me. Dooley Matheson was willing to
throw away his life to try to get back at my brother for a basketball loss
that could never be erased. *That,* I thought, *is what makes McEwans superior to Mathesons on the evolutionary scale.*

Then, to my horror, I saw my celebrated brother prove he was
just as crazy as Dooley Matheson. As Dooley climbed down into his
brother's arms, Adam mounted the strut and not only walked along
it, but extended his arms like wings while his shirt parachuted around
him in the wind. When I saw the wind whipping his shirt like a sail in
a storm, I finally puked. After I recovered myself and looked back up,
I saw Adam bend his knees, take Paul's hand, and drop back onto the
platform. Relief surged through me like an anesthetic.

Then, as Adam started down the ladder, I saw Trey Matheson leap
from the platform and catch hold of a high-voltage line where it passed
over a horizontal strut that protruded from the tower. My heart started
slapping my chest wall. The madman was hanging from a wire carrying 50,000 volts of electricity across the Mississippi River! God only
knew what he must have been feeling: every hair on his body had to be
standing on end. What I couldn't see was how he would get back onto
the tower without killing himself. If he grounded his body to the metal,
the electrical current would blow off his legs as it shorted out his brain
and heart. I watched Trey the way I'd watched the trapeze artist from
the Ringling Bros. Circus as a little boy, until the elder Matheson finally
swung himself repeatedly to gain velocity, then let go of the wire and
flew back to the tower ladder like Spider-Man.

The shame and abuse they heaped on me when they finally reached
the foot of that tower was almost unbearable. I heard the word *pussy*
a hundred times in five minutes. Dooley crowed about how I had
"pussied out, like all faggots do when the going gets tough." Trey stared
at us with a trancelike glaze in his eyes, claiming he'd gotten a massive
hard-on as soon as he grabbed the high-voltage line. Pretty soon they
were bragging that there was nothing that required balls they couldn't
beat us at. The basketball championship had obviously been a fluke.

Then Dooley started singing "The Ballad of Casey Jones," substituting profanity at every available opportunity. *"Marshall McEwan was a pussy from hell, born sucking dicks in Bee-en-VILLE, tried to climb a tower with some ree-ul men, then he pussied out all over again!"*

I laughed, even as some part of me wondered why Dooley seemed so obsessed with homosexuality. Did he really hate queers that much? Or was he secretly gay himself? As he started another verse, I wondered whether Dooley's IQ might be marginally higher than I'd initially guessed—but Adam wasn't having any. He told Paul to shut his cousin up, or he'd shut his mouth for him. I hadn't seen Adam make such a threat since he'd defended me from a bully when I was ten years old. Dooley started squaring up to fight Adam, and Adam's eyes went strangely flat. Paul Matheson looked worried. Paul knew all too well what Adam could do to someone on the football field when he felt no particular animus toward them. *What would happen if Adam McEwan decided to really mess somebody up?* I could see Paul wondering. There was more tension in the air than there had been atop that electrical tower, but Paul's cousins didn't seem to realize the danger.

Then I heard myself say, "There's something I can beat you assholes at. And I'll bet any amount of money you want on it."

This took their attention off Adam, and quick. *What was I talking about?* they demanded. Some kind of fag parlor game, like bridge?

"I can beat you across the river," I said.

"What do you mean?" Trey demanded. "Like racing over the bridge? We already won the drag race."

"Not in the cars," I said, feeling eerily calm. "Swimming."

That stopped them. I knew then that, whatever they might say, they couldn't refuse my challenge. Refusal didn't fit into their fantasy of themselves. I had them cornered.

"Bull-fuckin'-shit," Dooley said finally. "You won't swim that river. It's a mile wide."

"More like half a mile. Three-quarters maybe, with the high water. And I'll beat you by a hundred yards, you stupid cow-fucker."

They looked at me like I was delusional.

"You ever swum it before?" Trey asked cannily.

"No."

"He lying?" Dooley asked Paul, over his shoulder.

"No. But he's a hell of a swimmer."

"Well, shit. I'm a hell of a swimmer, too!" Dooley crowed. "I'm a *great* swimmer! I won the hundred-meter freestyle when I was thirteen."

"Blue ribbon," I said with mock awe. "So you're all ready."

"Fuck you," Dooley growled. "I was born ready."

"Nobody's getting into that river," Adam said with sobering authority. He sounded exactly like our father. "We're all wasted, and a sober man would be crazy to try to swim that river, especially at night. Not to mention at high water, which only a lunatic would try at noon. Plus, that water is runoff from the north. It's iceberg cold. So forget it."

"I can do it," I said quietly.

"I said forget it," Adam snapped. "We're going home."

"You go if you want. I'm swimming it."

"Then put your money where your mouth is," said Trey Matheson. "I don't get wet for free."

In the end, we bet four hundred dollars on the race. Four hundred dollars then was like forty thousand to me now. More. It was all I had in the world, every dollar saved from working minimum-wage jobs. But I risked it, because I believed in myself. But what happened afterward—

"Hey, Marshall!" calls a high-pitched voice. *Not Adam's . . .*

I blink myself from my trance and see the river two hundred feet below the bluff, stretching north through clear sunlight, not cloaked in fog like that terrible night—

"Marshall!" Denny Allman calls, running along the fence on the bluff's edge. "Come see! I found the truck! I found Dr. Buck's truck!"

By the time Denny reaches me, panting like mad, I've come back to myself. He jams the shaded screen of his iPad Mini up to my face. A green sea of treetops glides past below the flying camera, as though shot by Stanley Kubrick.

"Is that a live shot?" I ask.

"No, the drone's flying back on autopilot. My battery was low. This is recorded. There's the truck! See it?"

Denny apparently put his drone into a hover over a local make-out and picnic spot north of town called Lafitte's Den. The den is a geologic anomaly, a sandstone cave set low in the loess bluff, long said to have been the hideout of pirate Jean Lafitte while he evaded U.S. Navy ships pursuing him from New Orleans. No one has ever satisfactorily explained where Lafitte could have concealed his ships while he hid in the cave, and historians consider the story more legend than fact. As Denny's drone descends toward the treetops on the screen, I see the rusted orange roof of Buck Ferris's GMC pickup.

"That's it," I marvel. "You did it!"

Denny is beaming with pride. "Yep. I thought about flying down and looking into the windows, but the trees are pretty tight, and we're at the limit of my range."

"No, this is great. Don't risk your drone."

Staring at the abandoned truck parked in the dirt turnaround by Lafitte's Den, I'm sure of only one thing: Buck wouldn't have wasted five minutes digging at that natural homeless shelter. Thanks to the Lafitte legend, over the decades the earth in and around that sandstone cave has been ratholed like a block of cheese by an army of gomers with metal detectors, ten-year-olds with toy shovels, and housewives with garden spades. The most anyone has ever found there are arrow points and pottery shards, which can be picked up anywhere in or around Bienville after a heavy rain. No one in the past two hundred years has ever found a single gold piece of eight.

"Buck wouldn't dig there," Denny says, reading my mind. "There's nothing at that cave except empty beer cans and used rubbers."

This kid. "You're right. Something's wrong here."

"But there is sandstone in the ground around the cave. Could falling on that have crushed Buck's head like we saw?"

"I don't think so. First, most of the ground is covered with dirt. Second, even the sandstone is so soft you can dig a hole in it with a car key. Third, the cave is deep but not high, so he couldn't have fallen that far."

"Unless he fell from the top of the bluff," Denny points out.

"If that's what happened, he'll have multiple broken bones. Also, there should be traces of sandstone in Buck's wound."

"What are you gonna do?"

I look down into the boy's expectant face. I always see his mother when I do that. Like a lot of guys, I slept with her a few times in high school. Dixie was a good person, but I knew even then that she would never get out of this town or even to college. "Do you want credit for finding Buck's truck?"

Denny thinks about it for a few seconds. "That won't make up for the sheriff finding out for sure it was me filming his morons on the river earlier."

"Probably not. Somebody will find that truck in the next few hours, but the sooner the better, as far as making a murder case. How about an anonymous call?"

Denny nods.

"Okay, then. I'll handle it."

"How? There's no pay phones anymore."

With my burner phone, of course, I think. "Don't worry about it."

"Okay," he says skeptically. "So what's next?"

I start to ask him what he means, but I know. And I'm glad. Because though Denny's only fourteen, he has a resource I can't easily replace.

"I've got a feeling I know where Buck was really digging last night. And it wasn't that cave."

Denny's eyes light up. "Where?"

"The new paper mill site, in the industrial park. I think we could use a little aerial surveillance out there. Check for signs of recent digging."

"But you said they have the groundbreaking ceremony there today."

I glance at my watch. "In an hour and a half. The time for an over-flight is this afternoon. Can you meet me out there later if I call your mother and make sure it's okay?"

"You bet your ass! I mean—no problem."

"Thanks, Denny. You need a ride home?"

"Nah. I'm good. Going over to the depot for some food."

"Okay." I pat him on the shoulder and start back in the direction of the Flex, but he stops me by calling my name.

"What is it?" I ask, turning back.

"Are you okay?" he asks, looking genuinely worried.

"Yeah, yeah. I was just thinking about something that happened a long time ago."

Denny Allman doesn't look puzzled or even curious. He works his mouth around for a few seconds, then says, "Your brother?"

So he does know. "Yeah. Who told you about that?"

"My mom."

Of course. "I figured."

"She said it was the worst thing that ever happened in this town."

That doesn't surprise me. "That's what it felt like, at the time. Actually, some pretty bad things have happened in this town since it was founded."

Denny bites his bottom lip and looks at the ground. "Maybe one happened last night, huh?"

"That's what I'm thinking. You get home and do your schoolwork. I'll call your mom later on."

Before I turn to go, the hornet humming of the drone sounds above us, and Denny's DJI quad-rotor descends rapidly on autopilot, hovers for a few seconds, then slowly lands thirty yards away from us.

He grins proudly. "Pretty cool, huh?"

"Pretty cool."

CHAPTER 7

AFTER LEAVING DENNY Allman near the old railroad depot, I walk back to the Flex and start the engine but leave it in Park. My anonymous call made, the rush of discovering Buck's pickup has already faded. Seeing my surrogate father dragged from the river has left a deep shadow over me, one I sense will not pass for a long time.

I have an hour and fifteen minutes to wait before the groundbreaking ceremony for the new paper mill, but I have no desire to go back to the office. I'm craving coffee, but I'm in no condition to go to Nadine's, which is where I usually spend my morning coffee break. Nadine Sullivan is about ten times more perceptive than Denny Allman, and I don't want her picking at my soul until I get my defenses back up. The thing about kicking open a door to the past is that sometimes what's behind it comes out under its own power. You can try to run, but no matter how fast you do, you're dragging your demons behind you. At a certain point, you might as well stop, turn, and let them roll over you, enfold you. If you're lucky, maybe they'll die in the light of day.

Quinn Ferris's accusations about the Bienville Poker Club still ring in my ears, but I don't care to think about that right now. I'll see those guys at the groundbreaking, where there'll be plenty of time to study them in their native environment. Putting the Flex in gear, I drive slowly north along the bluff, skirting the edge of town, moving toward the Garden District, where six blocks of lovingly preserved Victorians stand between the commercial district and the high ground of the city cemetery. As I drive, I realize that despite being back in Bienville for five months, I've yet to go out to the cemetery once.

Soon after losing sight of the bluff, I turn left onto Hallam Avenue, which will carry me through the Garden District to Cemetery Road, which runs west-to-east from the graveyard to the eastern forests of Tenisaw County. Two- and three-story gingerbread houses drift past on both sides of my SUV, set back behind wrought-iron fences, but I don't really see them. In my mind I'm standing on the bank of the river with my brother, peering through the fog at the Louisiana shore, which has never seemed so far away.

On that night, we drove down the levee in the Camaro and the Nissan until we came to a place where the river lay only twenty yards away. As soon as we arrived, Adam—speaking in my father's voice again—declared that no one was getting into the water before the sun came up. That meant an hour's wait at least. Hoping to talk me out of the swim, Adam asked me to sit in the car with him for a minute. Instead, I walked up and down the levee fifty yards at a time, breathing deeply, limbering my muscles, and trying to burn off as much alcohol as possible. After my failure to climb the electrical tower, I felt exultant at the prospect of redeeming myself and teaching Paul's cousins a much-needed lesson.

Trey and Dooley Matheson sat in their IROC-Z, steadily taking hits from a Cheech-and-Chong-size joint. While the moon set and the sky grew blacker, two strings of barges moved downriver, and one moved up. As the last barge passed, its big diesels vibrating the ground beneath our feet, I noticed fog building over the surface of the river. That wouldn't interfere with our swim, but it made me wonder about the temperature of the water.

When the eastern horizon began to lighten, four of us walked down the levee to the water's edge: Trey, Dooley, Adam, and me. A thousand yards of river lay in front of us, a sheet of fog six feet thick hovering over the surface. It looked like the edge of the Atlantic Ocean. Joey Burrell stood on the levee behind us, telling us we were crazy to even consider trying to swim it. Paul stood silent beside him, watching intently. Joey was simply afraid, which showed he had good sense. But I'd never seen Paul display fear, and he knew his cousins would give him hell for skipping this. His refusal told me that either Paul knew I was the best swimmer and didn't need his help to beat his cousins, or he'd assessed the situation and, despite his considerable athletic ability, decided the risk of death was too great to chance the river.

That should have given me pause.

It didn't. I wanted to show those rich bastards that they weren't invincible, or blessed, or any more than just plain average. I wasn't sure Adam was going to come with me, but when the Mathesons and I pulled off our Levi's, Adam followed suit. At that point I told him he didn't need to go, but he quietly replied that he couldn't let me try the swim alone. If I drowned, Adam said, he'd never be able to face our parents and tell them what had happened. For a moment I thought of arguing with him, but in truth I was glad he would be with me out there.

The coldness of the river shocked me when we waded in, and the Mathesons howled. Adam and I made no sound, other than a quick sucking in of breath, then grunts of acceptance as we pushed off the flooded levee grass with our toes and joined the main current of the river.

"Nothing to it," I told him. "Just do what I do."

"Lead on," he said. "I'm right behind you."

It was strange, being the leader for once. But Adam didn't hesitate to yield authority to me in the water. The fog was thicker than it looked from the levee, but I knew we could make the swim. In a pool I could cover the distance in twenty minutes. In a flooded river moving at eight or ten miles per hour—and with the added responsibility of shepherding Adam across—I'd need to drift as much as swim. If I guessed right, and we made steady progress, we would end up maybe four miles downstream on the Louisiana shore. The whole thing ought to take half an hour. Forty minutes, tops.

I looked back and relayed all this to Adam in a loud whisper. He nodded and said we should stay as far as we could from Trey and Dooley. I agreed, but before we were thirty yards into the current, Dooley swam over and tried to push me under the water. I easily avoided him, but he threw an arm backward and got hold of Adam before Adam saw the danger. They struggled for half a minute, Dooley managing to duck him until I went deep, grabbed Dooley's leg, and dragged his head under. He fought hard, but I held him down until I heard him screaming. When I surfaced, I saw that Adam had bloodied Trey's nose in a skirmish I'd missed. As soon as Adam saw that I was okay, we started kicking toward

Louisiana, half swimming, half floating, staying high in the water like cottonmouth moccasins.

That worked well for fifteen minutes. Then we got separated. I'm still not sure how it happened. Maybe one of us got into an eddy, a boil, a whirlpool, something—but we lost sight of each other, and in the fog voices proved hard to track. The treachery of the Mississippi lies in its currents, which flow at different speeds and depths. This process creates dangerous surface effects. I'd thought I could handle them, but I was growing less sure as time passed. For the first ten minutes of the swim, I'd heard the Mathesons yelling and cursing, hooting insults. But for the last five minutes I'd heard nothing. Even stoned, they must have figured out that wasting energy in the river would kill them.

Tiring more quickly than I'd expected to, I started to worry about Adam. Certain he was behind me, I swam back and started a zigzag search, calling his name every ten seconds. The effort cost me two minutes, but I felt better after I collided with him in the fog. Then I saw that he looked pale, and he was panting in a way I'd never heard before. When I asked if he was okay, Adam told me somebody had been pulling at his legs, dragging him under. I was pretty sure the Mathesons were ahead of us, not behind, so I had no idea what might have been bothering him. An alligator gar? A big catfish? Both were unlikely.

I managed to stay close to him for another five minutes, but then we got separated again. Adam called out that he was okay and I should keep going. I did, but much more slowly than I could have, and I did a voice check every twenty seconds or so. I risked going a little ahead because I wanted to sight the opposite shore as soon as possible, to correct our course if we weren't moving aggressively enough across the current. The sun had cleared the horizon by then, but with the fog it didn't help much. As I swam, I realized my teeth were chattering. I wondered how long I had been shivering. I also sensed a vibration in the water, a subsonic rumble that felt more like my body was generating it than some external source. When Adam cried out for help, I turned back instantly, but again it took some time to find him in the fog.

As soon as I did, I saw he was in trouble. He was doubled over in the water, struggling even to stay afloat.

"My legs cramped up," he choked out. His face was gray, his eyes glassy, and his teeth were chattering. "My *calves*. I can't get them loose!"

I knew what had happened. The past thirty-six hours—which included the state track meet, serious alcohol intake, the foot race on the levee, and the long tower climb—had depleted Adam's potassium to the point that his skeletal muscles wouldn't function properly. I tried diving to massage the cramps out, but it did little good. I needed to get him to shore.

"Trey!" I shouted. "Dooley! Adam's in trouble! We need help!"

"They won't help," Adam said. "They'll be lucky to make it themselves."

"Listen, I need you to go limp. Try to relax. I'm going to put you in a buddy tow and swim you to shore."

"You can't tow me that far. Not in this river."

"Bullshit. You know I can. Do what I say."

"I can make it," Adam insisted, trying to pull himself through the water.

"Not cramped like that, you can't. Lie back! I'm going to tow you to Louisiana."

"Just gotta wait for my legs to . . ."

He fell silent. Adam had heard what I had. The rumble I'd barely perceived before seemed suddenly upon us, around us, beneath us. Somewhere in that fog, not far away, a string of barges was being pushed by a tugboat. Pushed toward us. Panic bloomed in my chest, and Adam saw it in my eyes.

"We've gotta move!" I cried. "Lie back!"

I'd never seen my brother's eyes fill with fear, nor his face look so exhausted that I doubted his ability to continue. I had never seen him *helpless*. I couldn't have imagined it. No one in Bienville could. But in that river, on that morning, our golden Apollo was as helpless as a newborn baby. Worse off, actually, since I could have easily hauled a baby to shore, whereas dragging 190 pounds of muscle would be like trying to swim an anchor through the water. Nevertheless, I dove and swam behind Adam, then surfaced and got my arm around his neck, up under his chin, and my left hip beneath his lower back. Then I started the "combat stroke" I'd been taught by my swimming coach, a former navy rescue swimmer. I had long since abandoned any thought of the Mathesons. From that point on, our lives depended on me.

The tugboat was closer, I could feel it. That meant the barges, which might extend a quarter mile in front of the tug, could run us over any second. Abandoning the alternating scissor-kick-and-pull stroke, I kicked constantly, with all the power in my legs. But as I did, I realized something that took my fear to a higher pitch: I was shivering; Adam wasn't. His core temperature had dropped. The combination of cold water, exhaustion, dehydration, and alcohol was killing him. If I let go, he could sink without even struggling.

Summoning every atom of energy in my body, I kicked with focused violence and pulled water with my right hand, vowing I could do the work of two. But after the long day's exertion, this was akin to hauling my brother up a mountain on my back. Worse, the diesel rumble had steadily grown louder, yet the fog still prevented me from determining the exact direction of the threat. I only knew it was upstream from us.

"You're fading!" Adam gasped in my ear. "You can't do it, Marsh."

"Bullshit," I panted, worried I was hyperventilating.

"You're gonna kill us both. That barge is coming downstream, hauling ass."

"Shut up, why don't you?" I snapped, kicking like a madman.

"Can you see the shore?"

"Not yet . . . can't be far, though."

Before Adam spoke again, a gray wall as tall as a house appeared out of the fog to my right. It was the flat bow of the lead barge, maybe thirty-five yards away, growing larger by the second. I couldn't scream or speak.

"Let me go," Adam coughed.

I suddenly realized that I'd stopped swimming. I started kicking again, searching the fog for the edge of that wall.

"Let go!" Adam screamed. "You can still make it!"

Tears streaming from my eyes, I kicked with everything I had left, but it wasn't enough. I felt five years old. The next time I looked up, the barge was twenty yards away. In that moment Adam bit into my neck. As searing pain arced through me, my brother punched me in the face, then kicked free of me. Separated by three feet of water, we looked into each other's eyes with desperate intensity. Then a mass of water lifted us both, shoving us several feet downstream.

"Go," Adam said with a calmness that haunts me to this day. Then he smiled sadly and slid beneath the surface.

For some fraction of time that will always be eternal, I stared at the empty space where my brother had been. Then my brainstem took control of my body. Freed from Adam's weight, I cut across the water in a freestyle that felt like flying. The barge's bow crashed past my feet so closely that the wake lifted me like a surfer catching a wave. A vicious undertow grasped at my lower body, pulling me back toward the steel hulk, but terror must have granted me superhuman strength. I fought my way clear.

After twenty more strokes, I spied the low shore of Louisiana 150 yards away. White sand, gray riprap, waist-high weeds. When I reached the rocks, I didn't have the strength to climb out of the water, only to get my head clear and rest my weight on the submerged stones.

Some of what followed I can't bear to think about even now. What I do remember is the search for Adam's body. It will be remembered as long as men live and work along the Lower Mississippi. Everyone took part: the Coast Guard, twelve sheriff's departments, four tugboat companies, a hundred private boaters, professional salvage divers, and even the Boy Scouts in a dozen counties and parishes lining the Mississippi River.

Nobody found him.

My father borrowed a Boston Whaler from a friend and went up and down the river for months, searching the banks and islands for his lost son. I would have gone with him, but Dad didn't want me in that boat. Though my eyes were far sharper than his, he couldn't bear my presence during his search.

That's how it began. Not so much his withdrawal into himself, which my mother also went through, but his erasure of me, the guilty survivor. That was not Duncan McEwan's first voyage into grief, of course. He had lost a child once before. I knew about that, but I'd never really thought deeply about it. That before he married my mother, he'd had another family. Sure, my father had always been older than my friends' dads, but it never seemed like an issue. Yet in the wake of my brother's loss—while I sat alone at home and my father plied the river in the vain hope of a miracle—his first wife and daughter seemed suddenly relevant.

Eloise and Emily. Emmie was the daughter. Two years old. My mother told me that they'd died in a one-car accident on Cemetery Road in 1966, taking a shortcut home after visiting Dad at the newspaper. I'd ridden over that exact spot a thousand times. It's a dogleg turn where three sets of railroad tracks cross through the asphalt. Deep gullies gape on both sides of the road. At night, in a blinding rain, their car—Dad's car, actually, an Oldsmobile Delta 88—spun off the road and tumbled into one of the ravines, coming to rest upside down in three feet of runoff water. Mother and child drowned in less than a minute. I can't imagine what that must have been like for my father, to have endured that and then have built another life—to have been gifted a son like Adam—and then be told that he'd been taken by the river during a stupid teenage dare. It was more than my father could bear. And without a corpse to mourn, he simply refused to believe that Adam *was* dead. Who could blame him? When you're blessed with a god for a son, it's tough to accept mortality.

Thinking of my father like that, boarding that Boston Whaler down below Front Street every day, on a hopeless quest for his dead son, I suddenly realize that I've come to the low stone wall that borders the Bienville Cemetery. Hallam Avenue has intersected Cemetery Road. The bluff and the river aren't quite visible from here, but I see Laurel Hill, the westernmost hill in the Bienville necropolis, where the monument to Adam stands. The statue—of an athletic young man who appears to mournfully stand watch over the river—was sculpted in Italy, by an artist my father met while working in Rome as an army reporter for *Stars and Stripes*. Another story for another day. The statue is famous among barge crews, who call it "the Watchman." Poised 240 feet above the river, it's the first thing the crews look for as they pass north of Bienville. Despite the tragedy behind the statue's existence, it reassures them somehow, like a life-size St. Christopher medal.

Its effect on the town was impossible to foresee. Within hours after being erected on the hill, Adam's statue became a shrine for local teenagers. By that time I was in a pit of despair, suffering from what doctors would later diagnose as PTSD. But I still went to school, and I heard the stories. On any given weekend, you could find kids leaning against its pedestal, watching the sunset. At dawn you'd find different kids watching the sunrise from the same spot. Since coming back home, I've been told this still happens, thirty-one years later, even though the present generation knows nothing about Adam beyond what their parents have told them. Pilgrims have prayed to Adam's statue, conceived children under it, left rafts of flowers and poems at its feet. But I haven't stood before it in twenty-eight years. I can't bear to. The last time I did, the experience hurled me back to that terrible morning in the river—just as seeing Buck's body did today. But the worst hour of that morning, worse even than abandoning my brother to his death under that barge, was the soul-scalding act of walking into my family's home with the sheriff and telling my parents that their oldest son wouldn't be coming home ever again.

And then explaining why.

Parked beside the cemetery wall, only two hundred yards from Adam's statue, I decide I'm still not ready to confront his marble doppelgänger from any closer proximity. Not yet, at least. Better to drive back to town and have a cup of coffee at Nadine's, settle my nerves, then ride out to the groundbreaking and try to figure out which of my fine fellow citizens acted on the nearly universal desire to silence Buck Ferris.

CHAPTER 8

MY DAILY SANCTUARY is a bookstore/coffee shop called Constant Reader, which is nestled between two large buildings on Second Street near the bluff. Bienville has had five bookstores during the modern era, none of which survived more than fifteen years. A big chain store in the mall hung on until a couple of years ago but finally gave up the ghost. After this grim record, Nadine Sullivan wisely opened Constant Reader only two blocks from Battery Row and one block from the Aurora Hotel, the art deco grande dame of Bienville, which serves as the primary downtown landmark of the postbellum era. While the Aurora is currently shut down for renovations, nearly every tourist coming up from the riverboats or walking the bluff still passes Nadine's door, and most step inside for coffee and a muffin, if not to buy books, those musty relics of the twentieth century.

Nadine is eight years younger than I, but like me, she attended St. Mark's Episcopal. She was far enough behind me that I barely knew she existed, but she graduated knowing a fair bit about me. Neither of us could have known that decades after high school, a common experience would make us close friends. The daughter of a traveling pharmaceutical rep who left town permanently when she was nine, Nadine became a highly successful personal injury lawyer in Raleigh, North Carolina. Married at twenty-seven, she divorced at thirty-one, with no children to fight over. After winning a huge settlement against a drug company, she was planning to open an indie bookstore in Charleston, South Carolina, when her mother was diagnosed with terminal cancer. Nadine moved home for what she thought would be a brief nursing period, but her mother rallied under her care and lived two more years. (Though my father has not rallied, this similar experience made Nadine and me natural confidants.) During the period that Mrs. Sullivan was ill, Nadine ran a weekly book club for her and a few close friends. So no one was surprised when, after her mother died, Nadine purchased a nineteenth-century pharmacy building downtown, restored it, and opened Constant Reader. Only tourists and newcomers refer to the store by its official name. Natives call it "Nadine's place" or simply "Nadine's."

In the five months since I've been back, Nadine has hosted book signings by some of the finest writers in the South. She was one of the first to recognize the genius of Jesmyn Ward and Angie Thomas, and she's also hosted small concerts by famous musicians she came to know while living in the Carolinas. Nadine is the kind of person who effortlessly pulls people into her orbit. Her gift for dealing with people can't be attributed to any identifiable personal style, but rather to the vibe she radiates. Nadine Sullivan simply settles your soul, the way being around a baby does. Not that she has any childish quality; I know for a fact that she was a shark in the courtroom. But that's difficult to imagine now. There is a purity about Nadine, a clarity in her eyes that—combined with a lack of any detectable tendency to judge people—invites the world in on its own terms. That said, her store is not merely a shelter for those in need of sympathy or conversation. Her author parties and musical events are webcast live to tens of thousands of followers, and she does good business mailing autographed books and CDs all over the world.

Most mornings, I drop by the store about 10:15, after the old men have finished bitching about "libtards" and the walking ladies have scarfed down their power waters and muffins. Nadine usually brings my coffee over herself, then lingers to chat for a couple of minutes, depending on how busy she is. Most days she remains on her feet, catching me up on any local gossip worth hearing. But some days she sits and sounds me out on events she's thinking of scheduling, or just talks about the world in general. We've told each other about our respective divorces, and our shared commiseration imparted an intimacy that has made some of her customers wonder if we're sleeping together. We're not. But were I not committed elsewhere, I would certainly have tested her feelings on the matter.

Nadine says people gossip about us because until I showed up, the word around town was that she's gay. That rumor started after she rejected just about every single man in Bienville, plus a lot of the married strays. Her target status is no mystery. Bienville is brimming with fake blondes with fake tits. Nadine, on the other hand, is a natural blonde with a sharp wit and a mischievous twinkle in her eye. Two years shy of forty, her body remains well distributed and finely calibrated when it moves, which alone would draw men to her. She's assured me that her constant rejections have less to do with her sexual orientation than her strict standards when it comes to men. When she wants sex, she goes out of town. I don't know where, and I don't ask. Nor has Nadine volunteered the information. I must admit that, despite our familiarity, I find myself intrigued by the air of mystery that surrounds that part of her life.

A brass bell clangs as I step into the shop, and the scent of hot coffee pulls me through the bookselling area like a rope around my neck. The café tables in back are empty but for a young couple who have the look of French tourists. Nadine stands behind the counter, cleaning her espresso machine. She smiles over her shoulder, then says sotto voce, "Is it true about Buck?"

I move up to the counter before answering. "What did you hear?"

"They found him in the river. Dead."

I nod, then shiver as the air-conditioning chills my sweaty shirt. "I just watched them pull him out."

She shakes her head, then drops her rag and turns away from the gleaming machine. "Accident?"

"Between you and me? No way."

She sucks in her lips and looks down at her counter, absorbing the news. "Was it the Indian artifacts? The threat to the paper mill?"

"I think so. Which, if you include residents of the county, gives us about thirty-six thousand suspects."

"That sounds about right. You want coffee? I figured you'd be out at the groundbreaking."

"I'm going, but I needed my caffeine."

Her eyes probe mine with almost physical thoroughness. "You need something stronger than that. Are you okay? Seriously."

I look down at the oversized muffins under the glass. "That scene at the river . . . no good for me."

She reaches over the counter and squeezes my hand, then turns to prepare my coffee. "You going to sit? Or you in too much of a hurry?"

"Do you have time to sit?"

She looks around the store and smiles again. "Be there in a sec. How's your dad doing?"

"'Bout the same," I lie, from habit.

As I survey the eight café tables, I hear the couple speaking French while consulting a guidebook. On the round table before them lie copies of Richard Grant's *Dispatches from Pluto* and Richard Wright's *Native Son*. Anticipating the conversation Nadine and I will have, I detour into the book-signing nook, a C-shaped banquette set on a large dais raised two feet above the rest of the café.

The walls above the banquette are covered with signed author photos, most black-and-white. Facing me as I take a seat are Rick Bragg, Chris Offutt, Kathryn Stockett, John Grisham, and Pat Conroy (that one signed shortly before his death). Above these, a dozen more photos climb toward the ceiling. Behind me hangs a collection of signed photos given to Nadine by loyal customers. These include Eudora Welty, James Dickey, and Donna Tartt, as well as Mississippi blues singers Sam Chatmon and Son Thomas. Placed side by side to my left are signed publicity shots of the young Elvis and Jerry Lee Lewis, wearing their 1950s duds. Jerry Lee is considered practically a native son, since he hails from Ferriday, Louisiana, just forty miles down the river. Rarest of all is a signed photo of Bobbie Gentry, the reclusive singer of "Ode to Billie Joe."

Waiting for Nadine, I recall a weekend when Buck recruited a group of musician friends from around the South to play this store. Despite the superior musicianship, Buck included me both nights. We had two guitars, a mandolin, a fiddle, a bass, a harmonica, and a trap kit. After one set, the crowd got so big that people spilled out into the street, and rather than interfere, the cops closed Second Street to auto traffic and gave us a block party. Sometimes living in a small town is cool.

Nadine walks lightly up the steps to the nook and sets a heavy china mug in front of me. She joins me at the table with a cup of green tea and gives me a smile designed to buck up my spirits.

"No avoidance today," she says. "The river, I mean. It was bad, huh?"

"Bad enough. To tell you the truth, I feel like I killed Buck."

Her eyes darken. "Oh, come on. That's bullshit."

"Is it? I knew when I published that story it would make people furious. I tried to argue him out of it, but Buck wanted it in the paper. It was so unlike him to stir up controversy. All the years he lived here, he never did anything like that. He went out of his way not to. But this was like a mission for him. A life quest."

"Why was it so important to him? I'm guessing you know a lot more than you put in the paper."

"Some. But I hadn't talked to him in a couple of days. I was really sort of waiting for the next shoe to drop."

"I guess it has." Nadine blows air across her tea. "Just not the way you were hoping."

"I was hoping the Department of Archives and History would come in here and take over the site. They've got a lot of power in these situations. They appoint their own board, and in theory are immune to political pressure. They can place a preservation easement on public land—which the mill site is—and that would give them control of the site. At least while they survey and assess it."

"That's exactly what people are afraid of, right? It would have delayed construction?"

"No doubt."

"Possibly even ended it?"

"If the site is what Buck believed it was."

"Which is what? A site like Poverty Point? A potential UNESCO World Heritage site?"

"Yep. And I think it is. Poverty Point is only forty miles from here, as the crow flies. And there are remnants of that same culture down at Anna's Bottom, north of Natchez. Buck believed that a deeper strata might hold evidence of an even older culture, like the one at Watson Brake, Louisiana. That's only seventy miles from here, and it predates both the Giza pyramids and Stonehenge."

Nadine is smiling with what looks like wistfulness. "My dad took me to Poverty Point when I was a little girl. I never told you that. It's one of my few good memories of him. We had a picnic there. When you think about people living along the river before the pyramids, that's pretty mind-blowing."

"If only Buck had made his finds in the middle of nowhere, rather than an industrial park."

Nadine pulls a wry face. "One that was nearly awarded Superfund status for its toxic sludge. What did you leave out of your article?"

"Mostly Buck's persistence. About thirty years back, some small clues got him thinking there might have been an ancient civilization near here, one that vastly predated the known tribes. The Indians we're famous for—the Natchez, mainly—were relative latecomers. They're fascinating because they were sun-worshipping, corn-growing mound-builders, like the Maya. Buck first made his reputation by documenting their involvement with the French and English in slave trading."

"The Indians were involved in the slave trade?"

"Big time. Anyway, the electroplating factory that used to sit on the paper mill site was built during World War Two. Buck had heard rumors that the construction workers turned over artifacts every day with their bulldozers. He tracked down a few old-timers, checked out the relics they'd given to their kids. But it was all later-era stuff—1500 to 1730. A lot of guys would have quit there, but Buck had seen descriptions of the site that predated even its agricultural use. Before that land was plowed up during the early 1800s by tobacco and cotton farmers, there were supposedly semicircular rings on the ground— raised concentric ridges facing the river, possibly built up on an older bend where the river used to flow. That's exactly how Poverty Point is oriented."

"I remember." Nadine is nodding and smiling as though reliving her childhood picnic. "Buck couldn't prove that?"

"No. Most of the acreage around the factory had been graded flat and paved over. The company refused to let him dig out there—even on the fringes—and Buck was so busy with other projects that he just let it go."

Nadine sips her tea. "So what made him suddenly dig at the mill site this month? Finding that mysterious map?"

"Yeah. I was vague in the article, because the guy who found it didn't want to be named."

Nadine gives me a look that says she fully expects me to take her into my confidence. When I hesitate, she says, "It's in the vault."

"Okay. Six weeks ago—just as the county started tearing down the old factory in anticipation of the Chinese deal going through—old Bob

Mortimer, the antique dealer, came into possession of some books from the attic of a local antebellum home. Folded into one he found some papers. Three sheets were early nineteenth-century maps that turned out to be hand-drawn by a guy named Benjamin L. C. Wailes."

"The famous historian mentioned in your story."

"Right. The first geologist in this part of Mississippi. Wailes's maps are like the Bible of archaeology in this region."

"And this new map showed what, exactly? Indian mounds?"

"Yes, but also the concentric semicircular ridges Buck had heard about. Plus some depressions that might be holes for wooden posts, like Mayan stelae. Posts oriented into a Woodhenge, a huge circle for astronomical observations."

"Like Stonehenge?"

"Exactly like that. Or Cahokia, a similar site up in Illinois. Anyway, as soon as Buck saw the map, he intuited the whole history of the place. He figured a succession of tribes had built over the original earthwork of that first Neolithic culture, because the site was so good. And once Buck saw that Wailes map, nothing was going to stop him from digging."

"And a week ago, the county conveniently finished tearing down the old factory. Even the parking lot, right?"

"Yep. Of course, no one was going to give him legal permission to dig there. The Chinese won't either, once all the papers go through."

"And soon there'll be a billion-dollar paper mill sitting on top of it. So he did it guerrilla style." Nadine smiles with fond admiration. "Who bailed him out of jail? I'm guessing you."

"I should have left him there. Maybe he'd still be alive."

She sips her tea and checks on the French tourists. "So why hasn't the state come in and roped off the site?"

"Normally they would. But that mill—plus the interstate and the new bridge to service it—is going to transform all of southwest Mississippi. It's like the Nissan plant going to Canton. The goddamn governor is going to be out there in an hour blessing the ground. Trump's commerce secretary is flying in for a photo op, for God's sake. In a perfect world, MDAH would have shut it down yesterday, if not over the weekend. Buck's case was very strong. As I wrote in the article, a lot of archaeologists believe Poverty Point was a pre-pottery culture.

That its builders only used carved stone bowls obtained from other tribes. But the potsherds Buck found help support the theory that Poverty Point was the original pottery-making center of the Lower Mississippi Valley. There's no tempering material mixed into the clay of the fragments he found. He also found drilled beads that match Poverty Point artifacts, as well as what are called Pontchartrain projectiles. He had no doubt about what he'd discovered. But a boatload of academics could be hired to refute his assertions. So. While the Department of Archives and History may have the legal power to act in this situation, we live in the real world."

Nadine laughs. "You call Mississippi the real world?"

"Sadly, yes. The only thing that could change the equation is bones. And that's what Buck went back last night to find."

She looks confused. "I thought Buck died in the river."

I shake my head. "Quinn told me he went back to the mill site last night."

"You think he was killed there, then dumped upstream?"

"We found his truck at Lafitte's Den, half an hour ago."

"We?"

"Denny Allman. My drone pilot."

Nadine shakes her head. "I know that kid. Reads way over his age level." The bell on the front door rings, but Nadine only glances in that direction. "So who would have caught Buck at the mill site? There aren't lights out there anymore, right? It's Bumfuck, Egypt."

"The night after I ran my story about Buck, somebody posted guards out there. They patrol all night."

"Who?"

"Maybe the Chinese? Maybe the county. I don't know yet."

"You think security guards killed him?"

I shrug. "Seems unlikely, and risky, but who knows? That could explain the body being moved. Guards at the mill site would have to explain how he died."

Nadine purses her lips, pondering all I've told her. "Tell me why finding bones would make such a difference."

I'm about to answer when a short man wearing a coat and tie steps up into the banquette. He's about sixty, and he's holding a James Patterson novel, but he's staring intently at me. He looks oddly familiar (as have hundreds of people I've seen since getting back to town), but I can't place him. Then Nadine says, "Hello, Dr. Bortles."

He gives her a tight smile but keeps his eyes on me. "Do you remember me, Mr. McEwan?"

"Sure," I tell him, racking my memory for anything to add. "You're the . . . dentist, right?"

"Orthodontist. I came over because I was very disheartened to read your story on Buck Ferris's recent digging by the river."

Oh boy. Here it comes. "The *Watchman* prints the news, Dr. Bortles."

He smirks at this. "Bad news, in that instance."

"I could debate that. But even if you're right, what's your thesis? I'm not supposed to print bad news?"

He makes a sour face, as though he's being forced to converse with an idiot. "You know, it's easy for you to stir this up. You don't live here anymore, not really. After your father passes, you'll go back to Washington and spend your nights on TV, telling people how smart you are. What do you care if this town dries up and blows away?"

"I happen to care a lot about that."

"Then stop printing stories about crazy Buck Ferris and his Indians. Keep it up, and you can rename *this* town Poverty Point. Nobody will have a job that pays more than minimum wage."

Anger flares in my gut, but I force myself to stay in my seat. I look closer at him, at the meticulous comb-over, the plastic surgery around his eyes, the Apple watch with the $5,000 band. "Buck Ferris wasn't crazy," I tell him. "But you don't have to worry about Buck anymore. Somebody killed him."

Shock blanks the orthodontist's face. "What?"

"The next thing I'll be printing about Buck is his obituary."

Dr. Bortles stands blinking like a rodent after someone hit the lights in a dirty kitchen, disoriented but not entirely unhappy. "Do you mean that he died? Or that someone killed him?"

"Read tomorrow's paper and find out."

Bortles shakes his head. "Well. You can't say he didn't ask for it."

My right fist tightens, and I'm halfway out of my chair when Nadine touches my arm and gives me a sharp look.

"Why don't you let us finish our conversation, Doctor?" she says in a syrupy Southern voice that bears little resemblance to her own.

The round-faced Bortles looks surprised, then indignant. He's clearly unaccustomed to being dismissed by anyone. "You've certainly gotten rude all of a sudden, Ms. Sullivan."

Nadine gives him the too-broad smile of a woman whose mouth wouldn't melt butter. "I never knew you were an asshole before, Doctor. Now I do."

Bortles draws himself up to his full five feet six inches and in a pompous voice announces, "I will never buy another book in this shop. You have lost my patronage, Ms. Sullivan. Forever."

The French tourists are watching from their table.

"Then why are you still standing here?" Nadine asks. She waves in Bortles's face with mock solicitude. "Toodle-loo. You have a *blessed* day."

Bortles huffs a couple of times but doesn't manage any coherent response. Then he marches out, dropping his book loudly on a display table before slamming the door and filling the shop with the high clanging of the bell.

"Well," I say. "You are something, Ms. Sullivan."

She waves her hand in disgust. "The only reason I can do that is because I have some money. If I relied on this store to put food on my table, I'd have had to sit here and listen to that shit."

I nod, dispirited. "That prick is probably an accurate reflection of how most people in town will feel about Buck's death."

"Were you telling the truth? Is Buck's obit the next thing you'll write about him? Or are you going to blow this story wide open tomorrow?"

"I don't know. I need more facts before I can do anything."

She nods thoughtfully. "You never answered my question. Why were bones the Holy Grail of Buck's little Indiana Jones excursion?"

I smile. Like any good lawyer, she doesn't lose the thread of the narrative, no matter the distractions. "You're the lawyer."

"*Oh.* Does Mississippi have some kind of grave-desecration statute? I know they differ from state to state."

"Mississippi *does,* thank God. Anybody who comes across human remains in this state must report them. And a discovery like that stops whatever's going on around it. Even major construction. Doesn't matter whether the land is public or private."

"Oh, man. The local politicians would crap their drawers." Nadine is working it all out in her mind. "But for how long? It's one thing if a team comes in, catalogs things, then moves them to a museum. But you can't move a Poverty Point. That's like discovering the pyramids."

"You're right. That level of find would kill the paper mill. The Chinese would move on to one of their alternate sites. Arkansas or Alabama."

"Is the paperwork not fully completed? They're breaking ground in less than an hour, for God's sake."

"That's all for show. Gold shovels and glad-handing. The Chinese company has an office here and reps, but nothing's final-final. The associated state projects are finishing the planning stage. The I-14 route is on the verge of final approval, but technically the mill is at binding letters of intent. There's still due diligence to be done. If the Chinese *really* wanted to, they could fold up their tents and leave next week."

Nadine sits back in her chair. "I'd say that's a motive for murder."

"I'm not sure how many people truly understand that risk at this point."

"Does it matter? Anybody who fears the worst could have killed Buck. Even some hotheaded version of Dr. Bortles."

"I guess so. Well, the powers that be will want this to go down as an accidental death. But it'll be tough to hide. Buck has a massive skull wound, maybe from a rifle bullet, maybe a rock."

Nadine is studying me as though trying to see behind my eyes. "What are you thinking, Marshall? I know you. You're going to go out there and try to dig up some bones yourself, aren't you?"

I take another long sip of coffee. "I'm not anxious to get my skull caved in. But Buck was right. Old B. L. C. Wailes wouldn't have wasted time drawing maps of nothing. I think there are bones out there, thousands of them. The bones of people who were living in this county four millennia ago, and maybe five or six. Right where you and I grew up."

Nadine steeples her fingers and smiles the way my favorite English teacher used to, as if she's about to test me in some private way. "In a vacuum," she intones, "I'd say that's one of the coolest things I've ever heard. But the way things are now . . ." She sighs.

"Go on."

"Bortles is an asshole, but he raised a real dilemma. What if you go out tonight and dig up some bones? You trace out the Woodhenge and uncover a major archaeological site. A new Poverty Point. Would you kill the paper mill deal to do that? Would you kill the future of this town to do it?"

There's surprising passion in her voice. "Killing that mill deal wouldn't kill the town."

"Don't be so sure." She raises her right forefinger, and again I flash back to school. "The new white-flight neighborhoods in the eastern part of the county have brought in some money from Jackson, and there's some smaller commercial activity going on—indie retail, like my store—and some light industry. But to *really* survive, Bienville has to have something like that paper mill. Hundreds of jobs that pay sixty or seventy grand, with good benefits. God knows how many ancillary jobs will be created. The construction alone will be a bonanza for this town. Then—"

I lift my right hand to stop her. "You're right, no question. The bridge and the interstate alone mean hundreds of millions. Even the ancillary stuff . . ." I look up into her bright eyes. "They killed Buck, Nadine. You know? They *murdered* him."

"Who's 'they,' Marshall?"

I sigh heavily. "Quinn Ferris thinks the Poker Club did it."

"The venerable Bienville Poker Club," Nadine whispers. She raises her hands and makes a mock show of reverence. "The descendants of the hallowed founders. I'd say Quinn's instincts are dead-on, as usual."

"I'm about to see most of them at the groundbreaking ceremony. I may try to talk to a few."

The front bell rings again. Nadine looks over to see a familiar customer, an older lady, who walks to the mystery section. Turning back to me, she whispers, "What does Jet say about all this?"

"I haven't spoken to Jet."

She looks surprised. "Why not?"

"She's out of town today, taking a deposition in that suit over rigged construction bids. She probably hasn't even heard Buck's dead."

Nadine slowly shakes her head. "That's going to hit her hard. But she's going to have some ideas about who did it. She knows more about the Poker Club than we ever will."

"Because she married into it," I say in a sour voice. I look at my watch, then gulp the rest of my coffee. "I need to get moving if I'm going to make it."

"You want a go cup?"

"No, thanks." I start to stand, but Nadine reaches out and catches my right forearm, holding me in my seat.

"One second."

"What's the matter?"

"I see something in your eyes. Something I haven't seen before. Not even when you talked about your divorce. Or . . . your son."

A cold blade slices through my heart. "I'm okay."

"Come on. This is me. When you came in, you said the river got to you this morning. Did it make you think about Adam? The day he drowned?"

God, this woman knows me. After a few seconds, I nod. "It's like Buck's death pulled a cork on something, and the past came rushing out. It feels like water rising over my head."

She nods slowly. "Should you talk to somebody?"

"I'm talking to you."

"A professional."

"Come on. I haven't talked to a shrink since I was fifteen."

"Maybe you didn't need to. Do you want to come back here after lunch?"

"No, I'm fine." I move to get up again, but something holds me in my place. "I think how I feel has as much to do with my dad as Adam."

"That was the start of your problems, right? Him blaming you for Adam's death."

"Yeah. And it *was* my fault, as much as something can be your fault when you're fourteen. The thing is, after Dad stopped hunting for Adam's body, he finally apologized. This was like four months after the memorial service. I'm pretty sure my mother made him do it."

"Why do you say that?"

"Because he didn't mean it. Dad *wasn't* sorry he'd blamed me. He's blamed me every day since. That was the central fact of my life for three years. He never said it out loud again. But he never truly made eye contact with me after that day. Not unless I caught him staring at me when he thought I was preoccupied. And when I did catch him, I could read his mind like a neon sign blinking on his forehead."

"Don't say it, Marshall."

"*Why are you here?* That's what the sign said. *Why are you here when he's gone? Where's the justice in that?*"

"That's your guilt talking," Nadine insists. "You're flagellating yourself. Your father's a good man. He just couldn't—"

"Sure, sure," I say angrily. "A hero to millions. The Conscience of Mississippi, right? But to me? He was a living rebuke. Never mind that the tower climb could have killed Adam just as easily."

Nadine takes my hands in hers. "Don't you get it? This is why you're back here. You didn't come only because your mother needed you, or even because he's sick. You came because you have to settle this between you. You have to forgive each other before he goes."

I appreciate Nadine's efforts, but very gently I remove my hands from hers. "That's not going to happen. I've been alone with him several times now, hard as that is, and he hasn't said one word about it. He just sits there and yells at the television. The news, of course."

"He'll get there," she says with absolute assurance. "He probably carries unimaginable guilt for doing that to you. He had to blame somebody. He could have blamed God, but he didn't believe in God. You were handier."

For five seconds I allow myself to recall the black hole of my life from the end of ninth through tenth grade. The black hole that Buck Ferris pulled me out of. I sigh heavily, then stand. "Thanks for the coffee. Also the floor show with Dr. Bortles. I'll update you tomorrow morning."

She walks me to the door. "Hey, have you heard the rumor about the party tonight? On the roof of the Aurora?"

"The celebration of the mill deal? What about it?"

"They say Jerry Lee Lewis is going to be there. He's supposed to play a set, like he used to in the old days."

"No way. Isn't he like eighty-five or something?"

"Eighty-two." Nadine has gotten that glint in her eye. "But the Killer still brings it."

"They said Trump was coming to the groundbreaking ceremony, too, but all we get is the secretary of commerce."

"I've got faith in Jerry Lee."

"That'd be something to see, all right. But I'm not invited."

Nadine looks genuinely surprised. "But the Mathesons are co-hosting. Surely Jet or Paul—"

"I'm persona non grata since writing that piece about Buck's discovery."

Nadine stops at the door and turns to me with her mischievous smile. "Well, *I'm* invited. Why don't you be my plus-one?"

I start to decline, but this is Nadine. And the party would be a damn good opportunity to study a lot of people who are profiting off the paper mill deal. "Can I get back to you in a bit?"

She shrugs. "Open invitation."

"I'm a little confused," I say, unable to resist needling her. "I heard you were gay."

She laughs out loud. "Come to the party with me, and we'll kill that rumor for good. People will have us engaged by morning."

As I open the door, her smile fades, and she follows me outside.

"Take a hard look at the Poker Club at the groundbreaking," she says. "They're bastards to a man. They've ruled this town for a hundred and fifty-three years, and not one of them would lose a minute's sleep over killing Buck."

"I actually hope that's not true."

She points at a display of mysteries and thrillers in her front window. "Despite my trade, the truth is there's not much mystery to real-life murders. Cui bono, honey. That's the only question that matters. I'd bet my store that one of those Poker Club assholes killed Buck. But don't kid yourself about what it would mean to take them on. They'd kill you, too. Wouldn't hesitate. Keep that in mind during your editorial meetings."

With that, Nadine goes inside and closes her door, leaving me to walk away with the muted ring of her bell in my ears.

CHAPTER 9

THE RIDE FROM Nadine's to the paper mill site takes ten to fifteen minutes. The land called the "industrial park" sits below the bluff south of
town, where four or five large factories and a few smaller ones operated
from the 1940s through the 1980s and '90s, before going through down
cycles, changes of ownership by second- and third-tier companies, and
finally the sheriff chaining the gates shut. It's the same story all over the
South—all over America, really.

I drive along the bluff most of the way, thinking about Buck and
who might have killed him. Both his widow and Nadine believe the
Bienville Poker Club must be behind the crime. I don't disagree in principle, but I've yet to see any evidence. Before I forget, I text Ben Tate, my
editor at the *Watchman,* and ask him to find out who employed the security guards who started covering the industrial park after we published
our story on Buck and whether any were on duty last night.

Again the river dominates my view for most of the route, this time
on my right, as I drive south along the bluff, which is mostly covered
with kudzu here. Searching the Sirius channels for some of the music
Buck and I used to play together, I realize I'm thinking about my son,
whom Nadine mentioned back in her bookshop. He was in my mind
earlier, at the cemetery wall, just below the dark drama of Adam and
my father. My talk with Nadine dispelled the clouds of sediment that
memory raised, and during the drive along the bluff my little boy rises
from the deep darkness.

I got married fourteen years ago, to a colleague in Washington. Her
name is Molly McGeary, and quite a few TV viewers still remember

her. After starting as a reporter at the *Washington Times,* Molly became one of the first print journalists to make the jump to television. First she moved to *USA Today* as a political reporter. Then a producer at NBC happened to catch her on a panel at a conference in New York, and she was off. In no time she was making appearances on the *Today* show, covering Washington stories and the business side of the entertainment sector.

At the time I married Molly, I believed I loved her. But looking back later, I realized I was in that situation where everyone you know— lifelong friends, colleagues, old classmates—has already been married for years and is having children, some their second or third child. Faced with this, you start wondering if you were put on earth merely to work and have a succession of sexual relationships that ultimately go nowhere. That kind of anxiety skews your objectivity, makes you persuade yourself that you're feeling things you're really not. You believe you *ought* to be feeling those things, so eventually—with the help of your parents, your cajoling friends, and a romantic co-conspirator—you do. That was my state of mind *before* I went to Iraq. By the time I got back, I knew that life could be snatched away at any moment, and the only sensible thing to do was get married and start procreating.

Molly and I were still in the glow of infatuation when we walked down the aisle. The first year was a good one. But after she got pregnant—a planned decision—the reality of having a child started to come home to us, and particularly to her. To my consternation, as the fetus grew inside her, and she ballooned up in the later months, she began to feel that our baby was a parasitical being, sapping the life from her, changing her irrevocably. At first I thought Molly was only half-serious. And surely, I reasoned, such feelings must be common among professional women? They would inevitably pass. But within two weeks of delivering Adam (yes, I named my son after my dead brother), I witnessed something I had never quite understood before: postpartum depression.

With the clarity of hindsight, I now believe Molly never recovered from that condition—not while we were together. We consulted a parade of medical experts, tried several promising therapies, and went to great lengths to get first-class child care so that Molly could return to her career. Nothing worked. Two years passed like that—a mostly wonderful time for Adam and me, but for Molly a sort of shadow play that never quite became real. She stayed emotionally muted, exhausted, and irritable when she did feel alert. She resented the demands of motherhood, but also the demands of her job. And then—just as I was considering a radical job change to try to improve the situation—I discovered that death had been hovering over us once more, just as it had when I was fourteen.

In late August, I was working in the main offices of the *Post,* on Fifteenth and L, where Woodward and Bernstein did the work that made me want to follow in their footsteps. I was supposed to be home by six thirty, to take over caring for Adam so that Molly could attend a network event. Then I got a call from CNN. Could I run over to their studio and appear on *Lou Dobbs Tonight* to discuss President Bush signing the bailout bill, and the suspension of trading on both Russian stock exchanges? This was before the era of ubiquitous pundits on television every night, so it was something I felt I should do. Molly agreed, though she let me know she wasn't happy about giving up her evening to babysit our two-year-old.

I was in the midst of the interview when my cell phone vibrated an emergency code in my pocket. By the time I got off camera and checked it, the emergency was over. Molly had taken Adam to a friend's condo about fifty yards up the street from ours. She and Taryn Waller had started drinking wine and commiserating over their husbands' unreasonable work hours, while Adam—comatose after an ice cream cone—slept in the TV room down the hall. Taryn was pouring their fourth glass of wine when Molly realized she hadn't checked on Adam in a while. When she went to the TV room, she didn't see him.

They found him behind the condo, at the bottom of the Wallers' swimming pool. While Molly and Taryn were talking, our son had awakened and somehow crawled through a homemade pet entrance set in the Wallers' back door. He wandered onto the patio, where there was no pool fence or motion alarm. The police report said it appeared that Adam had simply walked off the edge of the swimming pool into six feet of water. He never made a sound. None that Molly heard, anyway.

Our marriage did not survive his loss.

You hear all the time how the death of a child always leads to divorce. In truth, most times it doesn't. Sometimes that kind of tragedy strengthens a marriage. I can see how it would happen, if you were married to the right person. I wasn't. For four years I had tried to convince myself that I was, but the fissure that opened in our relationship after Adam died proved me wrong. I tried not to blame Molly. Whether I was successful in that effort or not, she believed that I blamed her, and that—combined with her own sense of guilt—had a corrosive effect on both our marriage and her mental state.

For me, the irony was nearly fatal. Twenty-one years after my brother drowned in the Mississippi River, I had to endure my son drowning in six feet of water. Worse, I—who had been blamed by my father for my brother's death—was now in the position of persecutor. *How could she have left him unattended for more than an hour?* I wondered. *A two-year-old! How could she not have heard him when he woke up? Surely Adam had made some sound, called out for me or his mother, as was his habit. Especially after waking in an unfamiliar room. Or finding himself alone on a dark patio.* I asked myself these questions thousands of times. And then, when I could stand it no more, I asked her. Molly hit back with the obvious: if I hadn't forced her to cancel her plans so that I could race over and appear on CNN, Adam would still be alive.

This was unquestionably true. But accepting it did nothing to alleviate our suffering. I'll omit the awful, protracted descent into hell that followed this exchange. Suffice to say that by the time we divorced eleven months later, we were both emotionally scarred, and Molly had lost her job. I was nearly fired myself, and were it not for the benevolence of a sympathetic friend in management, I would have been out. Instead, they kept me on, and I slowly worked my way back to some semblance of normalcy, often taking risky assignments as a way of penetrating the emotional damper that grief wraps around us.

But it was the advent of the Trump circus in 2015 that not only resurrected my career, but lifted it to new heights. I became a regular on MSNBC and an occasional guest on CNN. This spurred me into a kind of mental overdrive. Using my most closely held sources in Washington and New York, I began researching Donald Trump's financial ties to Russian oligarchs. At the same time, I started writing a book about how the Trump phenomenon had exposed the grim truth that the sins for which the South had always been excoriated—racism, tribalism, and xenophobia—were deeply embedded in the white body politic across the United States. I was halfway through my first draft when

I discovered how ill my father truly was and decided to come home. The Trump-Russia story I had to leave to others. And I was less than fours hours south of Washington when I realized that all that work I had been doing—maintaining a pace that had shocked even my most intense colleagues—had but one purpose: to shield me from the pain of losing my little boy.

Nadine knows about Adam's death. The facts, anyway, and what it did to my marriage. She understands that I've never fully dealt with his loss, any more than I've dealt with my brother's. As regards healthy grieving, I've been stuck in a state of arrested anger for decades. The death of my son piled onto the death of my brother gave me a psychological burden—or perhaps a soul burden—that requires much of my fortitude to carry through each day. "My two Adams," I sometimes call them. I've had countless nightmares about both tragedies, my brother's more than my son's, which may seem odd. But recently, it's my little boy I see in the long watches of my restless nights.

I see him awakening confused, even scared, calling out for me or his mother, then getting to his feet and searching the darkened condo for us, his arms stretched out before him. Drawn by the light of the little plastic trapdoor, he somehow uses his ingenuity to get it open and then crawl through, after which he scrambles to his feet and wanders out to the undulating bright blue surface of the swimming pool. Perhaps Adam sees himself reflected in the water. Perhaps he leans over to see better, looks into his own eyes . . . and then tips over.

That dream is worse than the one in which I'm pursued by savage soldiers with guns and knives who want to hurt me so badly that I consider suicide rather than capture. I have lived through that situation in the real world. It pales next to the image of my son sinking through cerulean water with no comprehension of what's happening to him. *Did he surface?* I've wondered a million times. *Did he flail his little arms? Did he scream for help, sucking in chlorine? Or did he die in silence at the cold, airless bottom?*

I've never asked an expert that question. I didn't even google it. In the last analysis, I probably don't really want to know. But maybe I'll meet an expert someday. Maybe I'll find the courage to ask. Because however hesitant I might be to face reality, I'm a human being, and that's something we have to know sooner or later. Did our loved one suffer? And if so . . . how badly?

It took a long time for me to start seeing women after that. Eventually I did. The first couple of tries didn't go very well. I found it difficult to be at ease with a woman once other people were removed from the equation. Then I met Eleanor Attie, a producer at one of the cable networks. Eleanor sensed that I carried some deep pain, but she never pushed me about it, and that made intimacy possible. We'd been dating for about four months when I realized I needed to return to Bienville. We kept in close touch at first, but after three weeks or so, our calls started getting further apart and our emails less frequent—weekly, almost perfunctory things. When you leave the small, hyperconnected family that is the Washington media circus, it's like falling off the earth—at least to the people still working under the big top.

After all, it wasn't like I was sending in weekly reports from Zabul Province in Afghanistan. I was in Mississippi, which from Washington looks like a fourth-world country. The newspaper I'd taken over focused mostly on local matters, except for the occasional blistering screed against the depredations of Trump and his cronies, authored by my father. But it's been two months since Dad printed one of those. Mortality is having its way with him. His diminished editorial output has cut into the profits of our local glazier, who was making good money replacing the plate-glass windows on the ground floor of our downtown office. Before Dad slowed his pace, not even security cameras stopped the angry Trump supporter who simply wore a mask as he marched up to the windows with brick in hand to make his feelings known.

As I reach the head of Port Road, which leads down the bluff to the industrial park, the sun flashes off a large gathering of cars about a mile away. This confuses me for a few seconds, because it looks more than anything like cars gathered for a sporting event. Then I realize this crowd must have assembled for the groundbreaking. As the Flex coasts down the steep bluff road, I start to make out tents set up on the actual paper mill site, where Buck found his artifacts. Several large groups of people are moving around the tents, and as I reach the level ground of the industrial park, logos on those tents become legible.

One belongs to the casino and reads SUN KING RESORT in gold letters. A larger tent reads AZURE DRAGON PAPER, which is the parent company of the mill that will be built here. The mill will operate under the name PulpCore, Inc., but Azure Dragon will own it. Off to the right, Claude Buckman's Bienville Southern Bank has two tents set up side by side, but the grandest tent of all reads PRIME SHOT PREMIUM HUNTING GEAR. These logos tell me that the men who truly run this city are out in force today. And why not? All their years of machinations have brought them to this moment. The town took a serious hit in the '90s, and another after 2008, but unlike the other river towns, Bienville has come through the recession strong enough to not only maintain its population, but also to expand its tax base. The twelve members of the Bienville Poker Club stand on the threshold of a billion-dollar payoff. Bigger, really, when you add in the ancillary elements of the deal. A new interstate highway that will run from El Paso, Texas, to Augusta, Georgia, passing over the new Bienville bridge as it carries Azure Dragon paper pulp to market. Weighed against all this, one archaeologist's life wouldn't have counted for much.

"Marshall McEwan!" cries a male voice as I get out of the Flex.

I turn to find New Jersey émigré Tommy Russo hurrying along the road in a close-fitting tailored suit. The owner of the Sun King Casino is walking in the direction of the tents. I figured Russo would have been here an hour ago, working the governor and the secretary of commerce. The only non-native-born member of the Poker Club, Tommy Russo plans to bring in a second casino as soon as I-14 becomes a reality. Bienville has a long gambling history, dating back to the Lower'ville saloons and a nineteenth-century horse track on the river. But Tommy has updated the old riverboat gambler stereotype and brought *The Sopranos* to Bienville. He's quick to smile, but you sense menace just behind his eyes. He's like a friendly snake with his fangs folded out of sight.

"I guess the Chinks are really going to make us rich after all," he says, as I fall into step beside him. "Off the record, of course."

"I take it a day at a time, Tommy."

"Come on, brah. None of that pessimism. A billion dollars is like the second coming. That's real money, even to me. Hey, did you hear about Buck Ferris?"

I show no reaction. "What about him?"

"They found him in the river this morning. I figured you'd be all over that."

"I'll wait and see what the police tell me."

Russo's predatory eyes read every line and shadow on my face. "Yeah? Good. That's good. Last thing we need around here is more bullshit stories to upset the Chinamen. This town's on the right track, while everybody else is starving."

"Looks that way. I'll catch you later, Tommy."

Just as I start to break away, another member of the Poker Club emerges from the parked cars and calls, "Tommy Flash! What you doin' fraternizing with the enemy?"

Beau Holland is a real estate developer, and he likes to tell people that his family can trace itself back eight generations in Bienville. If you let him talk, Beau will swear he's descended from French royalty. A few years shy of fifty, Holland is the second-youngest member of the Poker Club. He owns property all over south Mississippi, and he developed both white-flight subdivisions on the eastern edge of the county that have attracted affluent young professionals from Jackson. Word is he's speculated heavily in all sorts of ventures since finding out that Azure Dragon would be building its newest mill at Bienville.

"Marshall's not the enemy," Russo says as Holland catches up to us, wearing a suit that probably cost more than my entire wardrobe. "He's just doin' his job."

"Could've fooled me with that story on Buck Ferris."

Beau Holland always sounds like an irritated spinster to me. He reminds me of some Mississippi Delta boys I met when I went to Boys' State as a junior in high school. They weren't gay, but they spoke with a soft lisp and a passive-aggressive sarcasm that fit the old stereotype. What they were was mama's boys.

"At least we won't have to worry about Buck anymore," Beau adds, finding it impossible to suppress his bile.

"I wouldn't be too sure of that," I mutter.

"What?" he asks sharply, reaching out to stop me.

I keep walking, and Tommy stays apace.

"I'm talking to you, McEwan!" Holland snaps.

"Keep talking," I call over my shoulder. "Maybe somebody will come by who gives a shit."

Tommy Russo snickers under his breath.

As we come to the tents, I say, "Catch you later, Tommy," then break away and push into the edge of the crowd, trying to avoid eye contact where possible. I don't want to suffer through fishing expeditions by people wanting information about Buck's death.

Moving into the crowd's center, I see Max Matheson holding court beneath the Prime Shot tent. Max radiates the same vitality he always did as a younger man, his lean build, deep tan, and hard blue eyes making it easy to visualize him in a sergeant's uniform in a Vietnam rice paddy. As I focus on his gray-blond head, I see his son standing to his left and, beside Paul, several attractive young women wearing Prime Shot polo shirts. Something tells me they're here to keep the Chinese officials entertained. As I hover between two tents, a dark-skinned, black-haired beauty behind the Prime Shot girls draws my gaze. She's wearing an indigo sundress that exposes perfect shoulders. She's older than the Prime Shot girls, but even behind large sunglasses, she's clearly out of their league. As I shield my eyes against the glare of the sun, I curse out loud.

The unknown beauty is Jet Matheson. And she's looking right at me. Glancing at her husband's back, Jet points to her right, where a refreshments bar has been set up. Without nodding, I head in that direction, my heart rate increasing with each step. *What is Jet doing here?* She's supposed to be taking a deposition in Jackson. I get into the queue at the refreshments bar and force myself to focus on a stack of soft drinks and bottled water.

I can't believe I was looking right at Jet without recognizing her. Especially since she's one of the most unusual-looking women I've ever seen. Buck Ferris once described her as an Arabic Emmylou Harris. Jet's father was Jordanian, her mother American. That's one reason she always stands out in Mississippi crowds. I suppose the Jackie O sunglasses and the crowd of Prime Shot hostesses obscured enough of her to confuse me, and my belief that she was sixty miles away did the rest.

"I heard about Buck's death before I went into the deposition," Jet whispers from behind me in the line. "I canceled it and headed straight back. I had Josh with me, so I didn't text you."

Josh Germany is her paralegal.

"Are you all right?" she goes on. "I know what he meant to you."

I nod but say nothing.

"Do you know who killed him?"

Almost imperceptibly, I shake my head.

"Betsy Peters!" Jet says effusively. "My God, it's been an age. What a pretty day, isn't it? What a crowd."

"It's awesome," says a woman with a heavy Southern accent. "Good times are finally coming. I'm *so* ready for that party tonight."

"Me, too," Jet gushes, as though she has all day to shoot the breeze. "I was actually thinking of quitting early today. By three, probably."

My heart thumps. Jet's last statement was code, telling me that she wants to meet me in private. Today—at three P.M. Our default meeting place is my home.

"Did you hear about old Buck Ferris?" Betsy Peters asks in a softer voice. "They found him dead in the river."

"I did," Jet replies.

"I hate to say it," Betsy goes on at 50 percent volume, "but it's a damn lucky thing for Bienville. We don't need that old crank screwing up this China deal. I don't care if the damned Indians raised the dead on this ground we're standing on. Their time's done. This is *survival*."

"It is," Jet says, but her tone sounds contemplative rather than indicative of assent.

After Betsy passes on, I turn as though looking casually around. "Jet Matheson!" I cry, feigning surprise. "What are you doing here? Spying on the enemy?"

Through her sunglass lenses, I see Jet's eyes cut over to the Prime Shot tent. "You could say that," she answers in a theatrical voice. "But God knows I want success for this town. I just want it to be on the up-and-up."

She's wearing sapphire stud earrings and a silver pendant necklace that hangs just above the neckline of her sundress. Beads of sweat glisten around the pendant, which appears to be an Arabic symbol. Smiling at her, I glance quickly around, taking in everyone standing within thirty feet of us. A couple of faces look familiar, but none do I know well. Of course, that doesn't mean they don't know me.

"I'm jealous," I tell her. "I'm way too busy to take off early. I'm working overtime every day this past month."

"I'll bet." She reads my negative reply as the coded positive it was. Looking back toward her husband, Jet says in a louder voice, "I need to get back to the tent. Could you bring me a Sprite or something? Paul wants me close today for some reason. Arm candy, I suppose."

"Sure, glad to," I tell her, forcing another smile, but feeling almost dizzy with disorientation. I'm not sure whether her request was serious or she was using it to break away from the queue—and from me. "What's that symbol mean?" I ask, pointing at her necklace.

She smiles, and her brilliant teeth shine against her dark skin and red lips. "Peace, of course. *Salam.*"

"Ah. We could use some of that, all right."

No one but me would have noticed the flash of emotion in her eyes.

"Thanks for the Sprite, Goose," she says brightly, using my high school nickname, which will instantly put distance between us for anyone within earshot. As she turns to walk away, she catches hold of my wrist in a seemingly casual gesture of thanks, but she squeezes so hard that pain shoots up my arm. Then she lets go and recedes into the crowd, her dark shoulders and long neck making her easy to follow to the Prime Shot tent.

Her painful squeeze communicated intense emotion; the problem is, I can't read it. Was she reassuring me of our bond, despite the public charade? She doesn't usually risk that kind of thing. Was she signaling fear? Even desperation? A combination of all three? The moment she touched me, I felt myself getting aroused. I hope my face isn't flushed, but it's hard to control that response when a woman touches you like that—especially the woman you've been fucking every day for twelve weeks.

CHAPTER 10

THE TOUGHEST ACTING job in the world is behaving normally in the presence of someone with whom you're having illicit sex. Most people who find themselves in this situation think they can handle it, but the truth is sooner or later people pick up on intimacy. Even if they don't see it, they feel it. They notice a hitch in the breathing, an altered tone of voice, a difference in the way you deal with space around someone. And, of course, the eyes. Reality abides in the eyes. What keeps most of these situations from exploding is the tendency of the betrayed not to see what their eyes and other senses tell them.

After my surprise interaction with Jet, I have to decide whether she was serious when she asked me to deliver a Sprite to the Prime Shot tent. To do so will mean interacting with her husband, Paul, whom I have known since I was three years old. Also with her father-in-law, Max, who's one of the most powerful members of the Poker Club. Since Paul might have watched us talking in the refreshment line, the best choice is probably to take Jet the drink.

Prime Shot Premium Hunting Gear was founded by Wyatt Cash, a Bienville native who made some money as a professional baseball player, then parlayed it into a wildly successful company that makes everything from custom camouflage clothing to all-terrain vehicles. Most of the Poker Club members on hand today have gravitated to Cash's tent, although I see a couple of older members at the Bienville Southern Bank tent, paying court to its octogenarian founder, Claude Buckman.

"Yo, Goose!" Paul Matheson calls as I approach the Prime Shot tent. "Wassup, man?"

At six feet even, Paul is a slightly smaller version of his father. Blond, gregarious, still muscular at forty-seven. There's no one on earth with whom I have a more complex history.

"Just covering this Chinese fire drill," I tell him. "Jet passed me in the drink line and asked me to bring her a Sprite."

"What a gentleman. We got beer in a cooler back here. Scotch if you're feeling frisky."

"At eleven A.M.? I'll pass."

"Hey, this is a celebration day. All day, all night."

I hand him the Sprite. "Can you make sure Jet gets this?"

"I'll take it myself," Jet says, stepping up from behind me and brushing my cheek with a kiss. *God, this woman has nerve.*

She moves on through the bodies under the tent, stopping to speak to her paralegal, who's talking to one of the Prime Shot girls. Paul steps closer to me. "I heard about Buck, man. I'm sorry as hell. I know how close you two were."

"Yeah. Thanks."

"What do you think happened?"

"Don't know. Guess I'll wait to hear from the police."

Paul snorts. "Like you've never done once in your life. Come on, man."

"I really don't know. Accident seems unlikely. Floating into that snag would be a stretch. That's a wide river."

"Yeah." Paul lowers his voice. "You think somebody stuck him out there? Wasted him, then tried to hand the cops an accident on a platter?"

"Buck wasn't going to win a popularity contest during this past week."

"No shit. I sure hope it was an accident."

"He didn't die where they found his truck," I say, watching Paul from the corner of my eye. "Somebody staged that."

This intrigues him. "You have proof of that?"

"Call it intuition. But your buddy Beau Holland sure seems on edge about the whole thing."

"Fuck Beau Holland," he says with venom. "He ain't my buddy."

"Did you say you want to have sex with Beau Holland?" asks a deeper male voice.

Max Matheson claps his son on the back, then laughs heartily. "Hey, Goose, how's it hanging?"

I nod but say nothing. Back when he coached us as boys, Max would ask this to trigger responses like "Long and loose and full of juice."

"Heard about Buck," he says, then takes a pull from what looks like Scotch on the rocks. "Bad luck."

"Maybe."

Max's eyes linger on mine long enough for him to read my emotions. He's always had that gift, the predator's lightning perception. "That river can kill you quick. You know that better than anybody."

"Jesus, Pop," Paul says. "Shut the fuck up, why don't you?"

Max clucks his tongue. "All right. Guess I'll leave you girls to it."

As he slides away, Wyatt Cash walks up wearing navy chinos and a Prime Shot polo beneath an olive blazer. With his 1970s mustache and bulging muscles, he still looks like a baseball player. The girls in the Prime Shot shirts are watching him with something like reverence. I'm guessing they've all ridden on either his jet or his helicopter. Cash hands me a sweating Heineken and smiles.

"Welcome to my humble abode, sir."

Most people under this tent would prefer me anywhere but here, but Cash is being polite. "Thanks, Wyatt."

He pats Paul on the shoulder, then moves off in Jet's direction. As I follow him with my eyes, I see Jet's left hand wrapped around one of the poles supporting the tent. Not her whole hand, actually. Only three fingers. Three P.M.

Her flagrant flouting of danger makes me dizzy.

When I look back at Paul, he's watching me with his usual lazy alertness. We stare at each other for several seconds without speaking. It amazes me how deeply I can bury the sin of sleeping with his wife while we're together. In this moment he's the guy I played ball with for years, the buddy who saved my life in Iraq. Who am I to him right now?

"Listen," he says, so softly I have to strain to understand him. "What do you think about that guy?" He nods in Jet's direction.

"Who? Wyatt?"

"No, dumbass. The paralegal. Josh whoever."

"Josh Germany? In what capacity?"

Paul raises his eyebrows like, *Come on, man.* "Him and Jet."

The rush of adrenaline that flushes through me after these words makes it hard to hold my composure. "You're kidding, right? The kid's like, what, twenty-five?"

"Exactly."

To mask my gut reaction, I look down the tent at Josh Germany. He's a good-looking guy, blond and fit, but still a boy—not remotely the kind of man that interests Jet. Witness myself, exhibit A. "Dude, there's no way. What made you ask that?"

Paul doesn't answer. His eyes are fixed upon his wife.

Wyatt Cash leans over Germany's shoulder and says something brief, and Jet laughs with obvious enjoyment. "I'd suspect Wyatt before that kid," I add.

"No way," says Paul. "It's a rule."

"A rule?"

"Poker Club rule. Other members' women are off-limits. Period."

"You're not an official member, are you?"

Paul considers this. "That's true. But Wyatt knows how bad I'd fuck him up if he crossed that line. The kid, on the other hand, may not realize the risk."

I need an infusion of morphine. At no time in the three months since I've been sleeping with Jet has Paul even hinted at suspicion of infidelity—not to her or to me. In relative terms, this is an earthquake. Then it hits me: *Is this why she squeezed my wrist and asked for a meeting at three o'clock?*

"For real," Paul says. "If somebody killed Buck, who do you think it was?"

Thankful for the 180-degree turn, I decide to throw out some bait. "Some people have suggested the Poker Club killed him."

Paul's face tells me he doesn't believe this. "Doesn't make sense, Goose. Murder creates problems. They'd have bought Buck off, not killed him."

He's right. Bribery would be the logical move. And maybe they tried that. "There's one problem with that theory."

"You gonna tell me Buck couldn't be bought?"

I nod.

Paul gives me a tight smile. "I may not be an official Poker Club member, but I've learned one thing by being around those guys: everybody has a price."

"You sound like Arthur Pine." Pine, a former county attorney, is the Poker Club member who works every angle of every sleazy deal without hindrance of moral scruples.

"Yeah?" says Paul. "What did that vain old prick say?"

"'We're all whores, we're just haggling over the price.'"

Paul shakes his head. "That sounds like Arthur, all right. King of the Whores."

A shriek of feedback hits the tents, causing everyone to cover their ears. After it fades, Paul says, "Guess they're about to start this gong show. You gonna hang in the tent with us?"

"Nah. I'm going to move back and try to see the big picture."

Paul gives me his sarcastic smile. "Good luck with that. And about that other thing . . . not a word to Jet."

I look down the tent at the woman still carrying my seed from yesterday. "No problem, man."

I FIND A GOOD viewing perch atop a flatbed trailer parked well back from the tents. From here I can observe the main players without seeming too interested. After my exchange with Paul, my mind is flooded with thoughts of Jet and our constant dilemma, which exerts emotional pressure every hour of the day. Only by learning to compartmentalize all she represents have I been able to function in this town. But rather than get caught in an infinite loop of what-ifs—which won't be resolved until our afternoon meeting—I decide to focus on the men most likely to have ordered Buck's murder.

The eternally feuding county supervisors and city aldermen have broken precedent to come together for this show. Thirteen gold shovels wait in a stand before the Azure Dragon tent, which matches the number of city and county representatives, plus the mayor. But the real power in Bienville doesn't reside in its supervisors and aldermen, or even in the mayor. The elected officials in this town are hired hands. They're the ones standing in the sun in their best suits and dresses, but the ruddy-faced men who control them are under the tents, drinking from crystal highball glasses and watching with the disinterested calm

of gamblers who already know the outcome of every race. I've spoken
to a few already. But to truly understand those men, and the power that
they wield, one must understand the unique history of the town where
I was born.

Bienville, Mississippi, began as a French fort built by young Jean-
Baptiste Le Moyne, Sieur de Bienville, one year after he founded
Natchez and one year before he founded New Orleans. Still a year shy
of his twenty-fourth birthday, Governor Bienville initially named the
fort Langlois after his housekeeper, who had overseen the French "casquette girls"—twenty-three poor virgins removed from convents and
orphanages and shipped to Fort Mobile to keep the soldiers there from
taking Native American mistresses. Each casquette girl brought all her
belongings in a single trunk or "casket," and while no one knows their
ultimate fates, their arrival succeeded in preventing large-scale sexual
exploitation of the Indian women at Mobile. Farther north, however,
French soldiers *did* take Indian mistresses, which triggered the Natchez
Indian Revolt in 1729 and the terrible French reprisals that followed.
Four years later, Sieur de Bienville—by then back in France—was asked
to return to La Louisiane and hunt down the Natchez survivors who
had taken refuge among the Chickasaw. During this effort, Bienville
rebuilt Fort Langlois, which had fallen into disrepair, and used it as a
base from which to attack his enemies.

By the time Bienville sailed back to France, both Indians and whites
in the area had taken to calling the fort after its founder. Fort Bienville
and its surrounding town grew steadily, and in 1763 it came by treaty
under British rule, as did Natchez to the south. Bienville proper began to grow along the pristine bluff above the Mississippi River, and
generous land grants by King George created large inland plantations,
which produced tobacco and indigo. After sixteen years of British rule,
Spain took control of the town, but Charles IV held it only as long as
King George. In 1795, Bienville was ceded to the United States, where it
became the far edge of the American West. This cosmopolitan history
left Bienville perfectly positioned to exploit the cotton gin, which had
been developed in 1793.

As the new century clattered to life like a great steam engine,
Bienville joined a cotton boom that brought spectacular wealth to
the Lower Mississippi Valley, all on the backs of African slaves, who

had proved easier to control than enslaved Indians, who knew the land better than their putative masters and had homes to run to when they managed to escape. The moonlight-and-magnolia dream of the Anglophile whites—and the nightmare of the black Africans—lasted only sixty years. By 1863, Ulysses Grant and an army of seventy thousand Yankees were camped four miles outside Bienville, aiming to conquer Vicksburg, forty miles to the north. Bienville waited in schizophrenic expectation, its anxious planters hoping to surrender, its workingmen and planters' sons ready to fight to the last man.

Bienville's Civil War history usually fills a bloody chapter in books on the Vicksburg campaign. All that matters now is that on June 7, 1863, General Grant decided that, despite fierce Confederate resistance that had originated there, Bienville—like Port Gibson to the east—would not burn. Grant's decision ensured the survival of more than fifty antebellum homes, many mansions that would draw enough tourists during the Great Depression to bring the city back from the dead. The history of the years that followed was as troubled as that in the rest of the South, and it ensured that by the 1960s a crisis would come. Bienville weathered those racial troubles better than most of its neighbors, but the deepest issues were never fully addressed, setting the stage for a reckoning that by 2018 still has not come.

The reason it has not bears a name: the Bienville Poker Club.

When I was a boy, I sometimes heard references to a "poker club," most often when I was visiting Paul Matheson's house. Back then, I thought the term referred to a weekly card game Paul's dad played in sometimes. At that age, I couldn't have imagined its true nature or function, and my father certainly never talked about it. Dad had to have known about it, of course, for the Bienville Poker Club was founded seventy years before he was born and had exerted profound influence over this area ever since. But though my father published many scathing editorials about Bienville politics, he never once wrote about the Poker Club as a political force. To this day, I'm not sure why.

Thanks to the Poker Club, while the other Mississippi River towns withered during the final quarter of the twentieth century, Bienville continued to grow. Up in the Delta, there are drug dealers living in the mansions of former cotton planters. In Natchez, forty miles downstream, commercial real estate values have been eroding for two decades. But in

Bienville business is on the march. Quite a few observers have speculated about the reasons for this. Some tout the foresight of Bienville's
leaders. Others point to economic diversification. One particularly naïve
journalist wrote a piece about Bienville's "uniquely congenial" race relations and cribbed from Atlanta's old pitch as being "the city too busy
to hate."

All that is bullshit.

The Bienville Poker Club was founded shortly after Lee's surrender
at Appomattox. The original members—most of whom were ancestors of the twelve present members—created the shadow organization
to defend themselves against the depredations of the "carpetbaggers"
who swarmed south like boll weevils to plunder what remained of the
Confederacy. Since the Yankees saw Southern gentlemen as habitual
gamblers who loved wasting time indulging in whiskey and cigars away
from their family homes, nightly poker games provided credible cover
for more subversive activities. While men in other towns formed parties of night riders that would soon become the Ku Klux Klan, the pragmatic businessmen of Bienville employed more Machiavellian methods
of resistance. Rather than fight under an ideological banner of violence,
they worked relentlessly to keep their hands on every lever of power still
within reach. They collaborated with the Yankees when necessary, but
betrayed them when they could. They employed cardsharps, whores,
and criminals to control the carpetbaggers and Negro politicians of the
new inverted world, and by the Compromise of 1877—which mandated
the removal of the federal troops that enforced Reconstruction laws—
the Poker Club had most of the town's institutions firmly in its hands.

It is testament to the vision of those men that 153 years later, I stand
in the shadow of a bluff that still supports their mansions, witnessing
their descendants consummating what the *Wall Street Journal* dubbed
the "Mississippi Miracle." Down in front of the Azure Dragon tent, the
governor of Mississippi has introduced a Chinese man in a tailored suit.
He takes the microphone with Bienville's mayor at his side, a local sidekick grinning like an organ-grinder's monkey. The company man has
a Chinese accent, but his vocabulary is better than the mayor's. When
the mayor leans out and calls the aldermen and supervisors forward
to the line of shovels to play out their charade for the cameras, I shift
my gaze to the Prime Shot tent, where most current members of the

Bienville Poker Club stand watching, expressions of mild amusement on their faces.

The 2018 iteration of the Poker Club isn't nearly so rich as the original group prior to the Civil War, when they ranked only behind New York, Philadelphia, and Natchez in banked millions. But the war gutted those fortunes, and that kind of damage takes a long time to make up. Today's club controls something north of a billion dollars among the twelve members. That's a long way from New York rich, but in this corner of Mississippi, it's enough to mold the shape of life for all.

Blake Donnelly, the oilman, is worth more than $200 million. Claude Buckman, the banker, is in the same league. Donnelly's in his mid-seventies, though, and Buckman's over eighty. Max Matheson made his fortune in timber, and together he and Paul run a huge lumber mill north of town, plus the Matheson Wood Treatment plant near the sandbar to the south. They also manage hundreds of thousands of acres of timber all over the state. I'm not sure how much Wyatt Cash is worth. I do know he owns one river island outright, which he operates as an exclusive hunting camp—one frequented by NFL players and college coaches, most from the SEC.

Beau Holland, the asshole I met down on the road with Tommy Russo, is the hungry jackal among the lions of the club. From what Jet tells me, Holland has used inside information to exploit every aspect of the new paper mill, bridge, and interstate. Until last year, Beau had a junior partner named Dave Cowart working for him as a contractor. Cowart built most of Belle Rose and Beau Chene, the two residential developments at the eastern edge of the county. But last year, Jet went after Cowart with a lawsuit alleging rigged bidding on a project partly funded by federal dollars. As a result, Cowart and one alderman ended up doing time in federal prison. This did not endear Jet to the remaining club members, but since she's Max Matheson's daughter-in-law, there was little they could do except bitch on the golf course.

The other members span the professions. Tommy Russo has his casino. Arthur Pine handles the legal paper. Warren Lacey is a plastic surgeon and nursing home king whom Jet nearly sent to jail over bribery of state officials. (Dr. Lacey ended up with a suspended sentence and a one-year suspension of his medical license. He'd happily inject Jet with a lethal drug cocktail if he could.) Then there's U.S. senator

Avery Sumner, the former circuit judge whom the Poker Club some-how got appointed to the seat recently vacated by the senior senator from Mississippi for health reasons. Sumner flew in for today's event on a CitationJet owned by Wyatt Cash's company. The jet's livery features a large circular view through a riflescope, with buck antlers centered in the reticle. The other three members of the club I know little about, but they surely fulfill their function of greasing the wheels of commerce while pocketing whatever they can skim from every transaction or building project.

What must those men feel as they watch the local elected officials—nine whites and four blacks—lift the gold shovels from the stand and spade them into the pre-softened earth? The aldermen and supervisors are mugging for the cameras now, trying to look like Leland Stanford at the golden spike ceremony in 1869. A paper mill is no transcontinental railroad, but any project that brings a new interstate to a county containing only thirty-six thousand people comes pretty close to salvation.

When the photographers stop snapping pictures, the ceremony is over. The crowd disperses quickly, and crews miraculously appear to break down the tents. As the governor's motorcade roars up Port Road, Jet and Paul give each other a quick connubial hug, then separate to find their respective vehicles. *Was that hug for show?* I wonder. Max and Paul walk side by side to a couple of Ford F-250s, while a few yards to their right, Beau Holland climbs into a vintage Porsche 911.

I half expect Jet to text me, but she doesn't. She and Josh Germany climb into her Volvo SUV—Jet behind the wheel—and pull onto Port Road, heading toward the bluff without even a glance in my direction. Suddenly Paul's suspicion doesn't seem so absurd. As I follow the Volvo with my eyes, I notice something I missed when I arrived: a small fleet of earthmoving equipment parked in the shadow of the bluff, under a line of cottonwood trees. As Jet's XC60 vanishes at the top of the bluff, black smoke puffs from a couple of smokestacks, and then the low grinding of heavy Caterpillar engines rolls toward me. I had no idea they intended to start work so soon. In fact, I'm pretty sure they didn't. Nobody made any mention of it today.

They're going to wipe out all traces of Buck's digging, I realize. *And maybe of Buck himself.* Suddenly I'm as sure as I've ever been of anything that Buck was murdered here last night.

A chill races over my skin as the big yellow monsters crawl out of the shadows. I'm not sure what I can do to stop them or even slow them down. As I ponder this question, I hear a much higher sound, rapidly increasing in amplitude. It's the hornet buzz of a drone, the same buzz I heard this morning. Looking up, I see the familiar silhouette of a DJI quad-rotor flying what appears to be a precise grid pattern over the paper mill site.

I want to cheer out loud. Denny Allman didn't wait for the appointed time to meet me here. He came straight to the site and got down to business as soon as the crowd broke up. For a few seconds I worry that the equipment operators will get suspicious and call someone about the drone, but in all likelihood they can't even hear the damned thing above the roar of their big diesel motors. Even if they do, they'll assume that Beau Holland or some other Poker Club member—or even the Chinese—is using the drone for a commercial purpose related to the site. As I glance over at the Flex, trying to decide what to do next, my iPhone pings.

Piloting from the woods, reads Denny's message. *Can you pick me up on top of bluff in 20 mins?*

Will do, I reply.

Any place need special attention?

Look for disturbed earth. This is our only chance before those graders and dozers tear it up. I remember Buck telling me that he unearthed the largest Poverty Point fragment near one of the foundation piers of the old electroplating plant. *Don't fly too low,* I advise Denny, *but get good coverage of the footprint of the old plant. The foundation especially. Understand?*

10-4, comes the reply.

C u in 20 mins, I type, walking rapidly to the Flex.

I don't need to hang out here on the flats, drawing attention. Where to go? Beyond the twenty-foot-high levee that protects the industrial park from the Mississippi River should be a thirty-foot slope to the water. That would put me out of sight of the equipment drivers. They might know I'm there, but out of sight is usually out of mind.

From the moment I saw Buck's shattered skull through Denny's drone camera, I've had a sense of disparate threads coming together, of a hidden pattern revealing itself. A town like Bienville is like the river it was founded on, filled with deep and conflicting currents. Most times, the only way to detect such a current is by seeing something unexpected shoot to the surface. Buck's corpse might be that surprise. There is another way, of course, but it's usually fatal.

Fall in and get sucked under.

CHAPTER 11

YOU DON'T GROW up thinking you'll sleep with someone else's husband or wife. But life has a way of taking us places we never planned to go, and the moral restraints we absorb as children tend to fall away in the face of protracted frustration and desire. Many a man or woman has awakened from a months-long oxytocin high and realized that they've put their spouse, their children, or even their life at risk in a blind quest to regain a purity and intensity of experience allowed only to the young. Sometimes we're chasing reflections of romantic ideals unconsciously implanted in us by our parents. Other times we stumble into someone who carries a key that could open or close a door on some formative trauma we might not even remember. Whatever the trigger of our passion, we cross a line that we once believed inviolate, and by so doing throw the world out of balance in such a way that it must eventually right itself, regardless of human casualties.

Ironically, our passion blinds us to our true motives in these cases. Often we perceive our personal world as out of balance and seize on the notion that another person will somehow right the ship, restoring the "happiness" we crave. The mind-altering ecstasy of sexual union further distorts our perception, making it infinitely harder to navigate the maze we have created for ourselves. This self-induced blindness pushes us to take insane risks. I've had to restrain Jet more than once during the past three months. The compulsion to be "free" from a perceived trap can be overwhelming, and many a human being has gnawed off more than an arm or leg in their desperation.

I began my affair with Jet with both eyes open. I wasn't driven by sexual compulsion to possess her body, which I had come to know intimately as a boy. Nor did I crave the thrill of forbidden assignations, which can amplify sex into a druglike addiction. What I wanted from Jet was everything: her present and all that remains of her future. She wants the same. Our general plan is simple: After my father dies, I'll return to Washington, with or without my widowed mother. A month or two later, Jet will tell Paul that she believes they need some time apart. This will lead to a trial separation, then to discussions of divorce, while I—the cause of this action—will have long been out of the picture. At some point during this phase they will deal with the issue of their son, Kevin, whom Jet wants to bring to Washington to live with us.

The plan is sound, as such things go. The problem is that, for Jet, that final matter is a deal-breaker. She will not leave Bienville without Kevin. Yet she insists that Paul and his father will break every law on the books to ensure that she never takes him away. Since the Poker Club exercises absolute control over the chancery judges in Bienville, Max Matheson can dictate the terms of Jet's divorce. Yet somehow, we've allowed ourselves to ignore this fact. Since my father has not died, we've contented ourselves with stolen hours, pretending the risk is minimal. For three months, we've drifted along on a tide of bliss, believing our plan must eventually come to fruition of its own accord.

Paul's suspicion under the Prime Shot tent showed me in one gut-wrenching minute how blind we have become. Our long-range divorce plan is meaningless now. Paul already suspects Jet of infidelity. If we keep taking these risks for even a week, he'll discover the truth. But if we stop seeing each other, what then? My father could die tomorrow, or he could live another six months. Can we go six months under conditions of absolute separation? Can I live every day as an actor in a theater of the absurd? Can Jet?

Could we live six months without water?

YOU THINK YOU KNOW everyone in a small town, but you don't. Besides, Bienville isn't that small. Not like Soso or Stringer or Frogmore. When I was a boy, Bienville proper had twenty-four thousand people in it, and outside the city limits the county held another fourteen thousand. That meant a school system big enough to make a certain amount of anonymity possible. If you went to a private school, for example, there were always kids at the public school you didn't know. I knew most of the boys in town, of course, from playing ball and riding bikes and swim team and a dozen other things. But the girls—especially the girls at the public school—were mostly a mystery to me.

Several boys in my neighborhood still went to public school, and one—John Hallberg—was a good friend, though he was a year older than I. One weekend John took me to the movies with him, to sneak into *Highlander*, which was rated R. When we arrived at the cinema, we found three public school girls he knew waiting in line for *Pretty in Pink*, which was the movie we were pretending to go see. Two were the ubiquitous archetypes of my childhood, freckled and blue-eyed, one with dirty-blond hair, the other with light brown curls. But with them was a girl unlike any I'd ever seen. Her skin was as dark as a summer tan, though it was only March, and her jet-black hair reached almost to her behind. She was tall for her age, but what captured me from the first moment was her eyes, which were huge and dark above angular cheeks that descended to the dramatic V of her chin. And they took in everything.

John introduced this exotic creature as "Jet," which I assumed was a nickname, albeit an unusual one for a girl. I would learn later that her given name was Jordan Elat Talal. "Jet" was an acronym coined by her aunt, one that even her mother used. And though this "Jet" was the same age as her friends, she seemed at least a year older, probably because she didn't giggle or blush or cut up the way they did. When one of her friends invited Hallberg to skip *Highlander* in favor of *Pretty in Pink* and John said no, it was the dark-haired Jet who suggested the girls try *Highlander* instead.

One of the blessings of my life was that I wound up with Jet Talal sitting on my left in that movie theater, my nerves singing with excitement. This only happened because both other girls wanted to sit beside John, which left Jet little choice but to sit beside me. We didn't talk much during the movie, but we stole several glances at each other, some I remember to this day. They were searching glances of curiosity and, after an hour or so, longer looks of recognition.

After the movie we all went to the nearby Baskin-Robbins and ate ice cream, which sounds corny today, but which in fact was pretty damn great. While John talked about the swordfights in the movie and the girls gossiped about junior high, Jet told me she'd actually wanted to see *Salvador*, a film about journalists covering some Central American civil war. I had no idea what she was talking about, but I faked my way through, and by ten that night I'd squeezed out every drop of information my father possessed on the subject. The other girls made fun of Jet for her comment, but she endured their teasing with impressive equanimity. Hallberg later told me that the public school kids called Jet "the Brain" because of her freakish abilities in math and science. But that mildly pejorative epithet failed to marginalize her, because her beauty was undeniable, and at that age (as at most ages), beauty was the currency of popularity.

I spent ten days trying to get up the nerve to call her, and when I finally did, her father answered the telephone. The sound of his heavily accented voice paralyzed me. Joe Talal was "that Arab scientist from the plating plant," but most of the fathers spoke of him with respect. I would learn later that Joe Talal laughed a lot, but back then, my heart stuttered when his brusque baritone asked who I was. When Jet finally came on the line, a different kind of panic gripped me, but somehow, through the painful pauses, she made it all right.

During the final month of school, we met a few times at the Baskin-Robbins, each riding our bikes there, and we grew closer with every meeting. Soon I was waiting outside old Mr. Weissberg's house during Jet's violin lessons, reading *The Prince of Tides* and trying to think of something interesting to say to her. I wasn't sure I ever did, but when summer finally came, I learned that I had.

I know now that I was blessed in another way to be from Bienville, because my boyhood summers in the 1980s were more like the summers the rest of America lived during the 1960s and '70s. When school let out in May, we hit the door barefooted and didn't return home till dark. Not a house on our block was locked, and every one had a mom in it. Many of those mothers made sure we had food if we wanted it, and all were free to discipline any child who required it. Our playground was all the land we could cover on our bicycles and still get home before full dark (around nine P.M.). That was about forty square miles.

Jet and I made the most of that freedom.

We usually met in the mornings, riding our ten-speeds to LaSalle

Park, then spent the entire day together, pedaling all over Bienville, even way out on Cemetery Road, into the eastern part of the county. We had little contact with other people during this time, but we didn't want it, and nobody questioned our behavior. In retrospect, I believe we entered a sort of trance that May or June, one that would not be broken until the following September. Our trance had phases, each one a level deeper, as though we were descending into a warm pool, a shared fugue state where we existed as a single person, not distinct bodies or personalities.

The first descent occurred on the day we turned north off Cemetery Road and pedaled deep into the woods, following what appeared to be a deer path through what had once been the Luxor Plantation. Luxor's "big house" had burned in the 1880s, and the Weldon family, who owned it, had moved into the slave quarters. As a younger boy, I and my friends had discovered an old cypress barn that stood on the property, partly collapsed and surrounded by a thick stand of trees. The disused barn made a wonderful fort and an ideal base from which to explore the woods. On the day Jet turned down the path that led to the Luxor barn, I hadn't been there for a couple of years, but I was glad she'd done it.

Until that day, when we rode our bikes, we talked endlessly. But on the day we entered the Luxor barn, we stopped talking. The ground floor was heavily overgrown with ragweed and poison ivy, and it looked snaky. But a ladder led up to the spacious, tin-roofed second floor, which was open to the forest at both ends. As I followed her onto that high platform, I remembered standing along the edge with my friends, aiming golden arcs higher than our heads as we competed to see who could pee the farthest. I'd learned that day that a ten-year-old boy can piss fifteen feet laterally before his urine hits the ground—at least from a ten-foot elevation. But I quickly forgot that detail as Jet walked over and stood beside me, then took hold of my arms and turned me to face her.

My stomach flipped as she leaned toward me. The kiss that followed lasted close to an hour. There were breaks, of course. Brief ones, for air. But during that hour we passed out of whatever place we'd existed in before, into a country where words were superfluous. We went back to that barn the next day, and the next. By the third afternoon, our hands began moving over each other's bodies, seeking what they would. I've never forgotten the succession of shocks that went through me when my hand slipped inside the waistband of her jeans. The hair down there was abundant, thick and coarse, which stopped me for a moment. The next shock came when my fingers went between her thighs. She was so slippery that I wasn't sure what I was touching—a world apart from the classmate who'd let me finger her outside a traveling carnival one night. But even that shock dimmed when I felt Jet reach down and unsnap her jeans so that I could reach her without straining. My face suddenly felt sunburned, and I got light-headed for a couple of minutes. Then she put her mouth beside my ear and whispered, "That feels good."

That feels good . . .

All my life I'd been conditioned to believe that sex was something girls didn't want, but submitted to only after a long siege by a boy who felt and vowed unending love. To hear this sublimely feminine creature tell me that it felt good for me to do something that her father would have killed us both for doing was almost more than I could bear. But I didn't stop. The next day, while rain beat endlessly on the rusted tin roof, Jet reached down, placed her hand over mine, and began guiding my movements. It was then that I discovered what pleasured her most wasn't on the inside at all.

For weeks we rode our bikes to that barn. We spent whole days on that second story, living in our world apart. As the summer sun rode its long arc across the sky, the light would change until the barn became a cathedral. Golden shafts spilled through openings in the roof, and dust motes hovered and spun around us as though suspended in liquid. The things we did in our cathedral we did standing, for some reason. Perhaps we knew that if we lay down on those old dry barn boards, we would cross the only boundary that remained uncrossed, and we were too young to deal with the consequences of that. If we had, I'm not sure we would have ridden home as darkness settled over the woods.

That phase of our trance ended on the day I heard a noise from the floor below us. It wasn't a footstep or a voice, but it was a distinctly human sound. A cough maybe, or a wheeze. As quietly as I could, I climbed down the ladder and made my way through the fallen boards that lay tangled in vines and thorns. As I neared an old, broken-wheeled wagon parked under the second-floor joists, I heard weight shift on wood. I froze, my heart pounding, then took three quick steps forward and froze again. I was looking into the eyes of an old black man with a grizzled salt-and-pepper beard. He was lying in the wagon on a pile of big green leaves, a dead cigar stub in his mouth.

Instinct told me to bolt back the way I came, but something stopped me. Maybe it was that he lay supine in the wagon and showed no inclination to rise. Perhaps it was the look of amusement in his features or the weariness in his eyes. As we stared at each other, he lifted a small paper bag and took a swig from the dark bottleneck protruding from it. Then he wiped his mouth with his sleeve and gave me an avuncular grin.

"You been up there two hours and I ain't heard that girl holler yet," he said. "What you doin' up there? Readin' the Bible together?"

"What?" I asked dully.

"I said, what you *doin'* up there? I shoulda heard that girl holler two, three times by now. She old enough."

"Whuh—who are you?" I stammered.

"I ain't nobody. Who *you?*"

"Marshall McEwan."

"You ain't a Weldon?"

"No, sir. I'm friends with Pete Weldon, though." The Weldons still owned the land the barn sat on. "Who are you?"

"Name's Willis. I work for Mr. Weldon."

I weighed this answer. "Mr. Weldon pays you to sleep in his barn?"

The man scowled. "Don't get smart now, Marshall. I wouldn't want to have to get up and teach you a lesson."

By this time I had studied "Willis" a bit. He was a lot heavier than I, and he looked pretty strong, but I was sure I could outrun him. Of course, Jet was upstairs. She could probably outrun him, too. But she would have to get safely to the ground before she could.

"I'm guessing you don't want me to tell Mr. Weldon you were here," I said.

Willis scowled again. "I'm guessing you don't want him knowing you out here, either, smart boy."

I shrugged and tried to look nonchalant.

"Why don't we make a little deal?" Willis suggested. "We'll both just keep our business to ourselves."

I waited a decent interval, then said, "That sounds cool."

"Okay, then. You'd best get back up there and tend to business. That girl prob'ly gettin' nervous by now."

I took a tentative step back. "Are you gonna be here anymore? I mean, after today?"

"I been here other times, too, if that's what you wonderin'. My old lady kicked me out the house, and I ain't got no place to stay."

"You sleep out here?"

Willis nodded. "Right now, anyways."

I thought about this. "Okay, then."

"Hey," he called as I turned to go. "Don't be afraid of it."

"What?"

"Girls ain't made of glass, boy. They want it, same as you. Don't be afraid to work it. And lick it, too. You lick it?"

My face was turning purple. The old man laughed.

"Whatever you been doin', try it 'bout twice as hard. Start gentle, but take it up steady, you understand? That girl'll holler in three, fo' minutes, I guarantee."

"Um . . . I gotta go," I croaked, backing away fast, then turning to run.

His cackling laughter followed me back up the ladder.

I found Jet waiting at the top, looking frightened, but once I explained what had happened, she calmed down. I didn't think we should return to the barn anymore, but Jet thought it was fine.

Two days later, we discovered I'd been right.

On that day, some dopeheads from the public high school showed up at the barn and sat outside in the clearing, getting high. Jet and I hid in silence on the second floor, waiting for them to leave. But when they started building a campfire, we knew we had to go. We tried to slip away unnoticed, but they heard us trying to sneak out the far side of the barn. In seconds they surrounded us and started the usual bullying that older guys love to deal out to young guys as tall as me. It was during this hazing that they noticed how beautiful Jet was.

The conversation that followed that realization scared me in a way I'd never experienced before. These guys didn't look like the potheads I knew, gentle dudes who'd rather lie on their backs staring at the moon than exert a single muscle. These guys looked like what my father called "dopers," needle freaks. As they talked, I saw all the blood leave Jet's face. They were sixteen or seventeen, pale and dirty looking. And they meant to have her. The tallest one told Jet to take off her clothes before it got too dark to see her. If she refused, he said, they would take them off for her. When she didn't move to obey, one guy said he wanted to see what *A*-rab pussy tasted like. I wanted to protect her, but I couldn't see any option other than getting honorably beaten within an inch of my life. I didn't want Jet to know how scared I was, but when I stole a glance at her, I saw tears on her cheeks. That was when I heard a low, dangerous voice speak from the darkness under the barn.

"You boys 'bout to buy yourselves a boxcar full of trouble."

The leader's head snapped left. Like me, he saw Willis coming through the dark barn door, looking pretty goddamn intimidating. I suppose the three older teenagers could have taken that old man, but they didn't look too sure they wanted to find out what it would cost them to do it.

"What you gonna do, nigger?" asked the leader, sounding more petulant than threatening.

Willis regarded him in silence for about ten seconds. Then he said, "What I'm gon' do? That's what you axed? Well . . ." Willis scratched his bearded chin. "I'll prob'ly start by bendin' you over that log there and fuckin' you up da ass. That's how we broke in fresh stuff like you in Parchman. You'll feel just like a girl to me, boy. Tighter, prob'ly."

My blood ran cold when Willis said that, but the threat had its intended effect. The three freaks shared a long look. Then the smallest skittered into the darkness under the trees. The other two followed, though the leader vowed revenge from the shadows. It was hard to believe the situation had changed so fast. It was as though a grizzly bear had scattered a pack of dogs.

"Were you really in Parchman?" I asked, after Jet had gotten control of herself.

"Nah," Willis said. "My cousin was, though. I been in the county lockup a couple times, but not the Farm. I knew that'd scare them dopers, though."

"Man . . . thank you so much."

Jet began crying and shivering—delayed shock, I guess—but she thanked Willis profusely. When I rolled her bike out to her, she said, "What if they're waiting for us on the path somewhere?"

"I'll walk out with y'all," Willis said. "I can't come back here no more anyways. Them boys'll go home and tell their daddies a mean nigger threatened to whup 'em on the Weldon place, and the sheriff'll be out here to run me in. I need to find somethin' to eat anyway."

"I've got twelve dollars in my pocket," Jet told him, digging in her jeans. "You're welcome to it."

Willis smiled. "Twelve dollars'll keep me fed for most of a week, missy. I'll take it."

That was the last day we went to the barn.

We soon found another sanctuary—one equally as isolated and even more beautiful—but it was never quite the refuge that the barn was. It was a spring-fed pool that lay about six miles out Cemetery Road, on the old Parnassus Plantation. Generations of kids had spent summers partying out there, even skinny-dipping, until an accidental drowning and subsequent suicide forced the owner to fence off the hill where the spring bubbled out of the earth. I never saw anything quite like that place again, but I know it remains unspoiled, because Jet and I met there several times before I bought my house outside town.

Thirty-two years ago, she and I spent the last half of July and part of August at that pool, which had gone by many names since Indian times. Our trance slipped a level deeper in its cold, clear water and as we lay on the warm banks in the afternoon sun, like the turtles that were our company. But our time was growing shorter each day. I was scheduled to start summer football practice, and Jet had some sort of mathematics camp to go to. Like many fools before me, I assumed that time was infinite, that we would spend the rest of our school years together, then marry and strike out into the world to do great things—things the people of little Bienville had never dreamed about. To this end, Jet had already persuaded her parents to let her transfer to St. Mark's, despite the extra expense. I couldn't know that within a month, Jet's father would vanish, severing the fragile filament that had bound us like a common blood vessel until then.

The disappearance of Joe Talal shocked all of Bienville. It wasn't one of the garden-variety abandonments that were becoming more common as the '80s progressed. Jet's father was a chemical engineer, seemingly the most stable of men, and his work ethic was legendary. He'd invented a new chemical process at the electroplating plant, something that would have made him rich, had he not done it on company time. But the company patented it and took the money. This would have embittered most men, but Joe Talal took it well, and management rewarded him with what he most wanted, which was acceptance. Joe's brilliance and can-do attitude earned him the respect of the whites at the plant, and their acceptance was naturally extended to his daughter. After all, Jet's mother was white, and a Methodist in good standing. Joe might not have gone to church himself, but any time the congregation needed volunteers to build booths or mow grass, they knew Joe Talal would show up, ready and eager to work.

The cataclysm came the September after our magical summer. Joe had flown up to Connecticut for a continuing education class in electrochemistry. He did that kind of thing every couple of years. Only this time, he didn't come back. Janet Turner Talal initially covered for her husband with a story about a sick relative, so it took a couple of weeks for people to figure out something was wrong. But before a month had passed, plant management was informed that Joe had resigned his position. Two days later, it leaked out that Jet's father had returned to the Middle East, from which he'd emigrated in 1965. Jet had been putting a good face on things at school, but once this news got out, she stayed absent for three days. When she did come back, she was a different person. She had withdrawn into herself, and for the first time, I saw shame in her.

One month later, an explosive revelation swept through Bienville: Joe Talal had another family back in Jordan—a wife and a son. No one was sure about the details. Some folks said Joe had been mixed up in political trouble, Arab craziness, and that his family had been mistakenly declared dead years before. Others claimed he'd been a bigamist all along. In any case, Joe had abandoned his American family to be with his Arab wife and son, and he had no intention of returning to America.

It took me twenty years and a FOIA request to learn the true details of Joe's departure from our lives. As a journalist, I now understand that the tragedy of the Talal family was but a tiny footnote to the Cold War politics of the United States in the Middle East during that era. All that mattered to me at the time was that Jet's father had broken that trance in which she and I existed as one being. Worse, within a month Jet took up with Paul Matheson, who was a year older than we were and one of the least introspective guys I knew. I couldn't understand it, except to reason that after being abandoned by her foreign father, she'd decided to grab the most quintessentially American boy she could find, one whose father's fortune would guarantee security for life—if she could hold on to him. Jet did hold on to Paul, at least until he left Bienville for Ole Miss. They were the golden couple of our high school. Yet by the time Paul left college to join the army and fight in Iraq, things had changed again. But that's another story.

Paternal abandonment is the central fact of Jet's life: it shaped every decision she made afterward. Eight months after Joe Talal abandoned his daughter, I lived through a different version of the same experience—emotional abandonment by a father physically present—and there's no question that it dictated every major decision of my youth. You'd think that shared trauma would have brought Jet and me even closer together. But human relationships aren't symmetrical. The ultimate result of her father's departure was that, after my brother drowned and my father began to blame and isolate me, I faced that situation utterly alone.

Perhaps if I'd still had Jet, I could have weathered the glacial coldness without permanent damage. But I didn't. As the next year wore on, I quit every athletic team, stopped hanging out with former friends, and holed up in my room with the Cure and U2's *Joshua Tree* album. My dad was drinking heavily at this time, so I found it easy to pilfer whatever I wanted from his stock. My mother had been prescribed several drugs in the wake of Adam's death, and I ate those, too. While Jet worked tirelessly to distract herself from her pain, I sank ever deeper into mine, until almost no light from the world above penetrated down to where I existed.

One year to the day after Adam drowned, I drove my mother's car out to the Mississippi River at dawn, stripped off all my clothes, and began swimming toward Louisiana. I was drunk on bourbon, stoned on pills. When I pushed away from the shore, I fully intended to drown myself. As pathetic as it sounds now, I thought about Jet as I stroked toward the middle of the mighty river. I thought about my father, too, how he lived as if I didn't exist. I figured I would do him the favor of making reality conform to his desire. But when I reached the middle of the current, it was my mother who filled my mind and heart. How could I force her to suffer the loss of her only other son? Who would do that to her? *A coward,* answered a voice from deep within. *A gutless coward.* In that moment, an anger unlike anything I'd ever experienced was born within me. And that anger had but one object: the man who had failed me as a father.

Ping, ping, ping . . .

The text tone of my iPhone breaks through my dark reverie like a persistent alarm clock. I'm not sure how many times it went off before it finally registered in my brain, but now I look down at the screen. The text message is from Denny. It reads:

Finished twenty minutes ago! U gonna leave me up here all day or what?

On my way, I type, cranking the Flex and backing it around toward the riprap that lines the last drop to the river. Then I drive over the levee.

The industrial park is enveloped in a vast cloud of dust. The crest of the bluff is barely visible through the thinner dust at the top of the cloud. I point the Flex toward it, but I know that somewhere out there, heavy equipment is scraping and pushing dirt without any regard for me. As I inch along the gravel road that crosses the mill site between the levee and Port Road, another text arrives: *One of the bulldozers blocked the bluff road for ten minutes. I was scared, but it's clear now. U better haul butt.*

A big yellow Caterpillar D7 churns out of the dust to my right, moving toward me. This is how you treat a crime scene if you want to bury evidence. After gauging the movement of the bulldozer, I jam my accelerator to the floor and race for the bluff.

CHAPTER 12

"WHAT DID YOU see?" I ask as Denny opens the Flex's back door and sets a wheeled Pelican case on my backseat. I guess that's how he carries his drone around.

"Check for yourself." He hands a micro SD card in a tiny plastic case over the seat, then comes around and gets up front.

"How about a summary?" I ask, putting the Flex in gear and heading north along the heavily wooded bluff.

"I definitely saw places where someone has been digging."

"By the foundation piers?"

"One of them. Also out in the open ground. But those bulldozers have torn that section up by now."

"I can't believe they've moved this fast. They weren't scheduled to start today."

Denny grins. "The good news is, I have GPS coordinates for the whole flight. I can tell you exactly where to dig to find the places I saw today."

"Can I read the coordinates off the card?"

"If you know what you're looking at."

I hand him back the SD card case. "Why don't you make me a video file and email it to me? Or use Dropbox. Make it a highlight reel with everything marked simply enough for an idiot to read locations."

"You gonna pay me for my time?"

"Absolutely." I take a curve that gives us another broad river vista through the trees. "I appreciate you flying that site, especially coming early."

"Hey, this is what I live for. We're working a real-life murder case, man. We should make a podcast out of this. Like *Serial,* about Adnan Syed."

A chill of foreboding raises the hair on my arms. "There's not going to be any podcast, Denny. This is serious, okay? Buck's dead. Gone. Forever. You saw his head."

"Sure, I get it. But I still don't see why we can't—"

"*No damn podcast,*" I snap. "If I ever go public with this, I'll credit you for your work. But I don't want you taking any risks. None."

"*If* you go public?" he says, looking incredulous. "Why wouldn't you?"

"Because I don't know what we're dealing with yet."

"Sure you do! Somebody murdered Dr. Buck. And they probably did it at the place we just left. Not at Lafitte's Den, where I found the truck."

"What's your evidence for that? Some disturbed dirt on a building site?"

"It's obvious, isn't it? He came back out here to find some more relics, and they deleted him."

"Maybe," I concede. "But we're not going to tell anybody that. Not yet."

Denny looks more than resentful of this restriction. "Isn't there going to be an autopsy or something?"

"Eventually. Depends on the backlog in Jackson. I'm going to speak to the coroner after he's looked at the body. The people who run things around here wouldn't want me to, but I know Byron Ellis pretty well. Also, he's black, which means he might not be as eager to do the bidding of the people who'd like Buck's death to be ruled an accident."

Denny is scanning Instagram on his phone. "So are you gonna go back out there tonight and hunt for evidence?"

"Hell, no. They put guards out there after Buck's first discovery. There's no reason to think they won't be there tonight."

"But—"

"Leave it alone, Denny. Please."

"Just think about it," he says, looking up from his phone. "In their minds, Buck was the threat, right? But he's dead now. And they think they're wiping out all the evidence right this minute. So tonight's the perfect night to go out there and dig."

"Jesus, I already regret getting you involved."

He grins again. "You sound like my mom. Don't worry, that feeling won't last long. Just until you watch my drone footage."

I hope you're right, I think, speeding up so that I can get him home sooner. Into the silence between us flows my memory of Paul Matheson asking me if I think Jet could be sleeping with her paralegal. What the hell? And after Buck's death. It's like four hours ago, the world turned upside down.

We're less than a mile from Denny's mother's house when my iPhone rings. It's Ben Tate from the *Watchman* office. "What you got, Ben?" I ask.

"It looks like somebody broke into Buck Ferris's house."

"Last night?"

"No, today. His wife called the sheriff's office about an hour ago."

"Quinn Ferris?"

"Yeah. She was at the funeral home, working on her husband's arrangements, when it happened. What do you think they were looking for? More artifacts?"

"Bones. They're scared shitless that he found bones. Bones would halt the project. They've got a bunch of bulldozers out there tearing up the mill site right now."

"Can we stop that? Get an injunction or something?"

"Not with what we have now." Up ahead, the mailbox of the Allman house comes into view. "Hey, did you find out who posted the security guards at the mill site on Saturday?"

"No. I've talked to the Chinese, the county supervisors, and any other candidates I could think of. Everybody denies hiring guards. Are you sure they were out there?"

"According to Buck, they were." Nothing about this is going to be easy. "Is there anything else going on?"

"Yes, actually. Quinn called here for you just a minute ago. She wants to talk to you."

"She's probably trying to call me now. Let me go."

"Hang on, man. I heard a rumor that Jerry Lee Lewis might be playing that VIP party on the rooftop of the Aurora Hotel tonight. You hear anything about that?"

Ben's a big music fan. "Something. But don't worry about missing out. This is one of those rumors that doesn't pan out. Besides, the Killer's over eighty now."

Ben laughs. "I hear you. Later."

I start to summarize the call for Denny, but his young ears already picked up both sides of the conversation. He's working hard not to look excited, but I can see the fantasy in his head: a viral reality podcast with web links to drone footage chronicling a "real-life" murder investigation. He could be famous before he enters the ninth grade. As I pull into his mother's driveway, Denny turns to me, his face suddenly serious, his excitement gone.

"If you had a son," he says, trying to sound casual, "would you leave him and stay away? Never come back?"

Whoa. I've wondered if he'd ever ask me something like this. I guess he figures his mom can't give him the answer he needs. I'm not sure I can, either. Trying to formulate a coherent reply, I stare at his mother's transportation, a battered Eddie Bauer Ford Explorer from the early nineties. Its navy-blue panels are dented, rusted through in some places, and the khaki cladding once so prized by yuppies has mostly been ripped away by countless fender benders. Thanks to the father who left long ago, this wreck is the vehicle that carries Denny through the world.

"I had a son, Denny," I say softly. "He drowned in a swimming pool when he was two. My wife and I ended up getting divorced because of it."

"Oh. I'm sorry. My mom never told me that."

"I thought about him today for the first time in a long while. Because of Buck's drowning. My son never got a chance to be a person. Not even a boy, really. I mean, he had a personality. I could see hints of who he might become. But that's all. Still . . . he was happy while he lived."

"He was lucky, then."

"Yeah. Until he wasn't." I look out at the unmown grass in Denny's yard. "When I was your age, there wasn't much divorce among my friends' families. But it accelerated pretty fast. Till now . . ."

"I know, right? More than half of every class at the school has divorced parents. It's not like I'm the only one or anything. But still . . . most of them have dads. Around. Somewhere."

"I know what you mean."

He picks at something on his pant leg. "Wouldn't you think my dad would just be curious?"

I'm tempted to lie, to paint him a rosy picture. But how could that help him? "Maybe I shouldn't give you advice. But I'll say this: if your dad doesn't come around, it's because he doesn't want to. That's got nothing to do with you. He's missing something in his character. Divorce is one thing, leaving a wife. But a man who leaves his children is something else. I've got no respect for a man who does that. A father who leaves his children does damage that can never be repaired. That's why you're hurting now."

Denny nods slowly, then wipes his eyes.

"My father didn't leave our house," I hear myself saying. "But he left me. You understand? He pretended I wasn't there."

Denny looks confused. "How come? Because of the thing with your brother?"

"That's right. He blamed me for my brother's death. Still does. You know who really acted like a father to me?"

"Who?"

"Buck Ferris."

Denny's eyes narrow. "No way."

"Yep. He was my scoutmaster. I didn't even know what depression was, but I was messed up. When Buck saw that my dad wasn't doing his job, he stepped in and picked up the slack. He taught me how to play guitar, how to use tools. That guy was an artist with a chisel. And what a teacher. Hell, I built a guitar when I was seventeen."

"Seriously?"

"Yeah. I've still got it."

"That's so cool. Is that what you've been doing for me? What Dr. Buck did for you?"

The image of Buck being dragged from the river flashes through my mind once more. "Maybe," I concede. "A little bit."

He nods. "Well . . . I like it."

What a day. "Denny, listen. The time may come when your father will be filled with regret and come looking for you. Or he'll call you to come see him, maybe even live with him. When that day comes, you might be tempted to leave your mom."

The boy is staring at me now, hanging on every word.

"I'm not saying you don't talk to him. Do what you need to do. But don't live your life waiting for that day, okay? Don't dream of life with him because you feel like your mother doesn't understand you. She's doing the work your dad should have done, on top of her own. You hear me?"

"Yeah."

"Yes, sir."

"Yes, sir." He looks into his lap. "So what's your next step?"

"Talk to Buck's widow. She lives out on the Little Trace."

"Oh, yeah. The break-in."

"I'll look forward to seeing your video. It'll be a huge help."

"I'm going to go edit it right now. Watch your email inbox."

I give him a firm handshake, and his slim hand squeezes tight. Then he scrambles out of the Flex and unloads his drone.

"Hey," I call through the passenger window. "You got a lawnmower?"

"Uhh, yeah."

"Use it. I don't want to hear your mother had to cut that grass herself or pay somebody else to do it. You hear me?"

He rolls his eyes. "Maybe you're taking this dad thing a little far?"

"You want to be part of this case? Cut the damn grass."

"Okay." He turns and walks into his house.

Before I can back out of the driveway, Denny's mother leans out her door and gives me a weary wave. She looks tired, this woman I slept with thirty years ago because I needed comfort. She generously gave me that comfort, as she did many others. Even from this distance, I see the passage of every year on her face. Three husbands, at least one abortion in high school, a series of crappy jobs, and one precocious son. *What does she think when she looks out here?* I wonder as I back into the road. *Who the hell are we? And why do we do the things we do?*

A quarter mile from Denny's house, I dictate a text to Byron Ellis, the Tenisaw County coroner: *You ready to talk about Buck?* I'm hoping the friendship I've made with Byron while covering the recent spate of shootings in the African American community will prompt him to feed me some inside information. I've sensed deep frustration in the coroner, much of it based on his awareness that the white men who manipulate

Bienville's elected officials have no interest in solving the problems that cause the violence, but only in jailing the perpetrators and minimizing publicity.

My iPhone pings, and Byron's reply flashes up on the Flex's nav screen: *Not yet. Don't call. Give me an hour, maybe less. This is heavy.*

My hands tighten on the wheel. Byron must already be feeling pressure to steer the narrative away from murder. While the implications of this go through my mind, I take out my burner phone. Texting Jet is a risk, but after what Paul said to me under the tent, I don't think I can wait until three. With one hand I type: *Paul asked me if u sleeping w Josh Germany. WTF??? Why he suspicious all of a sudden?*

I've got a twenty-five-minute drive to my next stop. This trip will eat a lot of my day, but Quinn Ferris treated me like a son for two years; the least I can do is fulfill that role when she needs one. I only hope Jet will get back to me before I reach Quinn's house. If Paul is truly suspicious, he might know much more than he revealed to me. What if he's following her? Should Jet even try to get to my house this afternoon? Filled with unexpected anxiety, I drive with the burner phone in my left hand, dividing my attention between the road and its LCD screen. *"Come on, come on,"* I murmur, a desperate mantra.

Nothing.

CHAPTER 13

PAUL MATHESON SAT at the long rosewood conference table on the second floor of Claude Buckman's bank, the Bienville Southern, waiting for more Poker Club members to arrive. This was an informal gathering, one called by Paul himself after the groundbreaking ceremony. Though he wasn't an official member, it was understood that he would one day take his father's seat, and the other members were curious about what had prompted him to ask for a meeting.

Claude Buckman sat at the head of the table, Blake Donnelly at his right hand. Senator Sumner sat on Buckman's left. Next on that side came Wyatt Cash and Arthur Pine. Across the table from Cash sat Paul's father, and to Max's right sat Dr. Warren Lacey. Paul figured Beau Holland and Tommy Russo were the only other members likely to attend. The remaining three were older men—older even than Buckman, who was eighty-three—and rarely attended meetings. There'd been some small talk, but Paul had not taken part. Being seated at the far end of the long table made casual conversation stilted.

The conference room was a temple to antebellum Bienville. The grass-cloth walls were lined with nineteenth-century photographs depicting the booming cotton economy of the pre-war years. Horse-drawn wagons hauling white gold wrapped in burlap from outlying Tenisaw County to the river. Steamboats docked at Lower'ville, so loaded with cotton bales that they looked as though they'd capsize in a mild storm. A big black locomotive shuttling onto the rail ferry that once linked the cotton fields of Louisiana to the market on the Mississippi side of the river. A few photos depicted the war years. Yankee officers stood on verandas owned by ancestors of the men around the table, sipping drinks and watching ladies cavort at badminton on the lawns. For some officers from Philadelphia and New York, the occupation of Bienville had been a welcome reunion with old friends from Harvard, Yale, and Penn. It was connections like those, Paul knew, that had helped Bienville to survive the war mostly intact, rather than winding up a charred ruin, like Jackson and Atlanta.

"Here they are," announced Blake Donnelly, waving at Beau Holland and Tommy Russo, who'd just walked through the door behind Paul. "About time, fellas."

Russo and Holland took seats beside Dr. Lacey, and before Buckman could bring the meeting to order, Beau Holland said, "What's this all about? We've got the Azure Dragon guys in town, and I've got meetings all day."

"Are everyone's cell phones powered down?" Buckman asked in his perpetually hoarse voice. He sounded like a man who had smoked all his life and took pride in telling his doctors to go to hell.

There was a shuffle as a few members switched off their phones.

"Paul has a question for us," Buckman told them.

All eyes settled on Paul Matheson. He wasn't sure how to go about this, but he figured he knew most of these men well enough not to pussyfoot around.

"I'll say it plain, gentlemen. Did we have anything to do with what happened to Buck Ferris?"

Everyone averted his eyes. Suddenly Paul seemed to be the least interesting object in the room.

"Well," he said. "I guess that answers that question."

"Not at all," Buckman protested. "So far as I know, Dr. Ferris had an unfortunate accident. A fall, most likely. Regardless of what speculation the Bienville *Watchman* might be pushing tomorrow."

"Damn right," said Beau Holland, the real estate developer. "I've heard McEwan is out asking questions, implying foul play. That's downright irresponsible with the Chinese in town."

"Irresponsible?" Paul laughed. He couldn't help himself. "Beau, what planet do you live on?"

Holland's eyes flashed anger. He wasn't accustomed to being spoken to that way.

Arthur Pine, the club's in-house attorney, spoke up. "You obviously have a point to make, Paul. Why not make it?"

"You can forget about this playing as an accident," Paul said. "This is a murder case now."

"There's no reason to think that," Buckman countered. "I've been assured the autopsy is well under control. Death by misadventure will be the finding. Ferris was digging up above that cave mouth where he had no business being."

Paul snorted. "You're assured? Who the hell assured you of that?"

No one offered an answer.

Paul looked around the room in disbelief. "You're living in a bubble, Claude," Paul went on. "Like some Hollywood actor. Nobody wants to give you bad news."

"Which is?" asked the old man.

"Marshall McEwan. Marshall's not his old man, okay? He's spent the last twenty-five years in Washington, digging up scandals that shake the Capitol Building. Major Defense Department stuff. He's supposed to be writing a book about racism while he's here, but he was investigating Trump's Russian financial dealings when he came home to take care of his father. Azure Dragon and the paper mill are bush-league for him. Do not kid yourselves. Whatever rocket scientist decided to kill Buck Ferris has got Marshall after his ass now. You'd better get ready for some shit to hit the fan."

Beau Holland leaned back in his chair, his usual smirk pulling at his mouth. "McEwan's a friend of yours, isn't he? Can't you get him to ease off on the muckraking? At least for a week?"

Paul leaned forward. "Is that a joke? Buck Ferris was almost a father to him. Marshall went all the way to Eagle Scout because of Buck."

"Sounds like sentimental bullshit," said Holland.

"Yeah? See how sentimental you feel when Marshall shoves a proctoscope up your butt on CNN. He's got the cell number of every anchor and producer for every major network in D.C. and New York." Paul looked to the head of the table. "Claude, you want to have the club's finances broken down on *Meet the Press*? McEwan can put you there."

Buckman shifted in his seat.

"If Marshall smells foul play," Paul said, "he'll sink his teeth into this case and shake it like a pit bull. He won't let go. If there's anything to find, he'll find it."

"I don't like the sound of that," said Tommy Russo.

"There's nothing for him to find," Blake Donnelly asserted. "Hell, I liked Buck a lot. But if he ran up on some bad characters and got himself killed, that's nothing to do with us. Maybe he walked up on a drug deal out at Lafitte's Den."

"He didn't die at that cave," Paul said irritably. "Marshall told me that in the tent. Somebody staged things to look that way." He looked around the table, giving the younger members a searching glance.

"What's your problem?" Beau snapped. "You got something to say to me?"

Paul smiled, knowing he'd gotten to Holland. "Whoever was dumb enough to kill Buck Ferris put everybody in this room at risk, and every element of the Azure Dragon deal as well."

"Hey," Holland said angrily. "It's not your place to pass judgment on anything a member might do."

Max Matheson leaned forward and cast his eyes down the table at Holland. "Are you saying you killed Ferris?"

Holland glared at Paul's father, which was not something people with good sense generally did. But Beau had always been an arrogant son of a bitch.

"I'm saying if anybody in this room *did* kill Buck Ferris," Holland replied, "then it's none of Paul's business. Until he's a full voting member, our decisions are above his pay grade."

Paul turned up his left hand and gestured at Holland, as if to say, *You guys see why I'm worried?*

Claude Buckman spoke in a tone that brooked no argument. "This group approved no decision to remove Mr. Ferris, however inconvenient his activities had become. And no individual member is empowered to make such a decision alone, except in extreme emergency. Is that understood by all present?"

A few nods signaled general agreement around the table.

Tommy Russo, the only man in the room without a Southern accent, said, "We know Ferris was digging out at the mill site, right?"

"He was," Wyatt Cash confirmed. "I placed cellular game cameras out there that recorded him."

"And if he found bones, that could have stopped construction?"

"No question," said Arthur Pine. "We'd have had to cancel the groundbreaking."

Russo tilted his head to one side and stuck out his bottom lip, as though gauging the amount of life left in a dog that had been run over. "Hard to see how that guy getting dead is a bad thing."

Senator Sumner sighed in distaste and looked at his watch.

"A delay like that could have caused the Chinese to pull up stakes and go to Alabama," Holland pointed out. "We're not dealing with International Paper or Walmart here. Azure Dragon doesn't tolerate mistakes. They hit a bump in the road, they find a different road."

"Somewhere people know how to flatten bumps?" Paul asked.

Russo chuckled.

"Is there anything else?" Donnelly asked. "I've got a foursome of investors waiting on me out at Belle Rose."

"Paul's point is well-taken," Buckman said. "If anyone has information about Dr. Ferris's death that I need to know, I expect you to come to me. And if anyone has any influence over Mr. McEwan or his father, now is the time to use it to get him to soft-pedal this story. Or at least keep it separate from anything to do with the mill. Duncan McEwan always treated us fairly over the years."

"Duncan's got nothing to do with editorial content now," Paul told them. "Don't kid yourself. Marshall decides what goes in that newspaper."

"Let's buy him off then," Holland suggested. "Justifiable PR expense."

"Great idea," Paul said. "How much you thinking? I know of a Russian oligarch who offered Marshall half a million bucks to kill a story."

"He turned it down?" asked Buckman.

"Yes, sir. Then the oligarch threatened to kill him. Marshall went with the story anyway."

"So he's got balls," Russo said. "That doesn't sound good for us."

"I'm thinking about the *Watchman*," said Arthur Pine. "I'm surprised that rag hasn't closed down yet. I think the father's badly overextended. About eight years ago, he took out a big loan to buy out his brother's stake in the newspaper."

"Who's carrying the paper on that?" asked Buckman.

"Marty Denis at First Farmers. He and Duncan McEwan go way back together."

"Let's look into that."

"Duncan's also carrying a business loan on a new press he bought about the same time," Pine informed them. "Nearly two million, I think."

Buckman's eyes glinted. "Marty Denis have that loan, too?"

"I'm pretty sure he does."

The old banker smiled with satisfaction. "Duncan McEwan never learned his way around a balance sheet. Typical English major. Let's get into it, Arthur, just in case."

"Right."

These guys, Paul thought bitterly. *If they want to destroy somebody, they find a way to do it without even un-assing their chairs. An honest man doesn't stand a chance. And Duncan McEwan, for all his faults, is an honest man.*

"Long as we're in here," Beau Holland said, "what's your wife up to lately, Paul? She still trying to put any of us in jail? Because I heard she drove to Jackson today to take a deposition in a bid-rigging case."

Paul gave Holland a dark look. Had they been alone, Beau would never have dared speak to him that way.

"I asked you a question," Holland pressed.

"He gave you the answer you deserved," Max said, his eyes glinting with an odd light that had moved many a man back a step. "We don't discuss wives and children in this room."

"Maybe not," Holland said. "But your daughter-in-law makes herself impossible to ignore, Max. And a lot of people around this table agree with me."

There was some awkward shifting in the chairs, but nobody spoke in support of Holland. Paul was grateful for his father's defense.

"I hear she works with McEwan on stories," Beau went on. "Feeds his reporters information. And some of that stuff splashes on us."

"Then get yourself a fucking raincoat," Max said. "Bid-rigging sounds like your area. You feeling the heat, Beau?"

Holland's eyes smoldered, but Buckman spoke up before he could shoot back at Max. "Max is right," the banker said with an air of finality. "Wives and children are off-limits. Paul, I wonder if you'd mind excusing yourself now. We have a little housekeeping business to take care of before we adjourn."

There were no groans at this announcement, Paul noticed. Everyone in the room was watching him again, and the air felt brittle with expectation.

"Sure," he said. "No problem."

He slid his chair back and got up, then walked to the door, his eyes on a photograph of stooped black figures chopping cotton in a field. *I know how you feel,* he thought. As he took the elevator down to the first floor and moved through the lobby, he came to a certainty about one thing: *Somebody in that room killed Buck Ferris.*

The only thing he wasn't sure of was whether they'd done it on orders from the club. He thought about waiting for his father to come down, but then the others would see that he'd waited. If Max wanted to tell him anything, he would call.

Three minutes later, Paul's cell phone rang as he pulled his F-250 into his spot down at the wood treatment plant.

"Hey, Pop," he said. "How about Beau Holland, huh?"

"I'm gonna hammer a punji stick up his ass one day."

"Beau might just like that."

Max laughed heartily. "You know he would."

A flatbed truck pulled through the gate stacked with bundles of green pressure-treated fence posts.

"What do you think about the Buck Ferris thing?"

"I think Holland killed him. Unless it was Russo. He's got the history for it."

"Did the club order that hit?" Paul asked tentatively.

"No. But I don't think anybody's upset about it. Buck was a real threat to the mill. You know that."

"Problem is, killing him didn't remove the threat. It magnified it. You guys better walk on eggshells for a while."

"You mean 'we,' don't you?"

"Yeah, sure. But I'm not a real member. And I don't stand to make half as much off the ancillary deals as those assholes do."

"You'll be making plenty. And I'll be making more. You need to keep that in mind if your buddy Goose makes himself a problem."

Paul said nothing.

"You also need to make sure he doesn't get too tight with Jet. The two of them together make a bad combination."

Paul felt his face color. "What's that supposed to mean?"

"Exactly what I said. Just make sure your wife doesn't insert herself where she doesn't belong. And vice versa."

Max's syntax was too tortured to try to unravel, but Paul got the point. "I'm losing you, Pop. You going by the field tonight?"

"Yeah. I know we have that party, but Kevin's pitching good. I'll make it to the Aurora in plenty of time to see the Killer."

Paul got out and walked into his office, the conflicting odors of creosote and chromated copper arsenate following him through the door. As he nodded to the receptionist, he remembered seeing Marshall talking to Jet in the refreshment line down at the industrial park. When she'd lowered her sunglasses to look at Marshall, Paul had seen one thing with painful clarity: she was glowing. Given the complicated history they shared, it would be naïve to expect Jet and Marshall to avoid each other under the present circumstances. But it had been a long time since Jet had glowed like that when she looked at Paul. Years . . .

He thought about the last time he'd slept with her. Nearly a month ago now. He'd felt good going into it, and he'd taken a 50 mg Viagra to be sure he could finish her properly. But while Jet hadn't put him off, she'd submitted to the act as though it were any other habitual duty. Again he saw her face tilt up to Marshall's. Thirty years had fallen away from her in that moment. Hell, she even *walked* different when Marshall was around. A stab of pain hit Paul in the back of his neck, near the base of his skull. He reached into his top drawer and twisted the cap off a prescription bottle, then ground an Oxy between his back teeth before swallowing the fragments. *I should've asked Dr. Lacey for another 'scrip at that meeting,* he thought, shaking the bottle.

"Goddamn IEDs," he muttered. "Sometimes I wonder if you haji bastards got me after all."

CHAPTER 14

THE EIGHTEEN-MILE STRIP of asphalt known as the Little Trace began as a deer path in pre-Columbian times, was widened by Indians hunting the deer, then centuries later was taken over by whites traveling from Fort Bienville to the Natchez Trace, where it crossed the eastern edge of Tenisaw County. In those days outlaws would lie in wait along the trail, ready to ambush travelers unprepared to defend themselves with powder and shot. What irony that Buck, who chose to live along that historic route, would be murdered by modern outlaws exploiting that same weakness.

As I turn onto the Little Trace east of town, I wonder who might have staked out Buck's house, waiting for his grieving widow to depart so that they could ransack the place. But before I've covered two miles, my thoughts return to Jet and her father, and to Paul Matheson, who is quite capable of killing me if he finds out I'm sleeping with his wife. To be clear, Paul isn't simply capable of killing me; he's been *trained* to do it. And unlike a lot of men with that training, Paul has used what he knows—just like his father did in Vietnam. I've seen him do it.

By the time Jet and I began our senior year, Paul had graduated from St. Mark's and left for Ole Miss, and this opened the possibility of a new life to me. Thanks to Buck Ferris—and my failed suicide attempt—I had rejoined the world of the living by then. My home life sucked, but at least Dad had settled into a well-worn groove of pretending I was part of the furniture. My struggle with Adam's death was something I pressed down deep in order to survive. The loss of Jet still stung, even after three years, but Paul leaving town had taken a weight from my shoulders.

During the previous year, my athletic pursuits had forced me into constant contact with him. We'd played football and basketball and even run track together, which meant that we'd spent hundreds of hours in each other's company. We shared locker rooms, showers, bus rides, fast-food joints, team suppers, and crazy stunts in the dead of night. Despite the fact that he'd essentially taken Jet away from me, all this activity allowed our childhood friendship to reassert itself. We parted on good terms when he left for Oxford, but there was no denying the sense of relief I felt as he drove away from my house in the Corvette that had been his graduation present from Max.

To my surprise, when school started I found that I had become something of a star in my own right at St. Mark's. In many ways, "Goose" McEwan seemed a character apart from me, but because he was accepted by all, life was easier when I pretended to be him. My grades had always been the best on the sports teams, and after Paul's class graduated, I suddenly emerged as a replacement for my dead brother—or at least a reasonable facsimile of what everyone's expectations for Adam had been. (To everyone except my father, of course.)

With Paul no longer around, Jet and I found ourselves thrown together almost every day. We were awkward around each other at first, but before long the feelings we'd shared during our magical summer returned, and nervousness blossomed into mutual attraction. In physics class one day an analogy hit me: Paul had stood between us like a lead shield separating radioactive masses. The moment he was withdrawn, Jet and I surged toward criticality.

Paul hadn't broken up with her when he left for Ole Miss, as so many college-bound guys did when dating juniors. He'd promised he would come home every weekend, even though Ole Miss was four hours away. As it turned out, Paul didn't return to Bienville for seven weeks, and that left Jet and me sufficient time to find each other again. We began in secret. That was when she told me that her father had originally been resettled in America by the CIA, for whom he had worked against Gamal Nasser, in Egypt. She also confided that a year earlier, Joe Talal had written a letter asking her to come to Jordan and live with his other family. This request had stunned Jet, and her mother had descended into depression, fearing that her daughter, too, would abandon her. As Jet and I grew closer, she gently probed me about Adam's death. Soon we were comforting each other in places far removed from our classmates.

Then the rumors started finding their way back from Ole Miss. Since leaving Bienville, Paul had apparently been screwing every girl in Oxford willing to remove her sorority skirt, or even hike it up behind the frat house. At first Jet wrote these stories off as malicious gossip. Then she had a confrontation with a drunk girl who'd graduated from St. Mark's three years earlier. The girl ended up yelling that she'd not only slept with Paul at Ole Miss, but had also had him the previous year, while Jet was going around on his arm like the queen of the city.

Two days later, Jet and I properly consummated our relationship. It was a bittersweet experience for me. I'd slept with three other girls by then, but Jet had learned a lot during her years with Paul. I couldn't escape the feeling that he had explored and awakened parts of her that I had been meant to, and only because Jet's father had abandoned her a month after our summer ended. Jet sensed a shadow between us, and eventually she asked me about it. This conversation finally exorcised Paul's ghost for me—her assertion that I was not a substitute for Paul, but rather the reverse. He had been a replacement for me, during a time when she'd been too wounded to trust any emotion that made her feel vulnerable. She'd wrapped herself in a shiny new life with an extrovert jock, rather than a wounded, self-conscious introvert like me.

Paul finally came home in late October, and he expected Jet to pick right up with him. When she refused, he got angry for about five minutes. Then he found another girl and spent the night with her. Despite this public abdication of their role as the school's golden couple, Jet and I kept our heads down. For a week we met out at the spring at Parnassus. With cars at our disposal, we could easily drive out there separately, then relive the afternoons of three years before, only with penetration added to the mix. But it was inevitable that someone would eventually see us behaving like lovers, and they did. When word reached Paul, he went crazy.

It turned out that Jet had shared many details of our first summer with him. Because he'd had far more sexual experience than Jet, she'd used her experiences with me to pay him back in kind for his too-vivid

recounting of previous exploits. This left Paul feeling that no matter
how many times he had sex with her, he would never elicit the purity or
depth of response in her that I had.

I hoped he was right.

The night he heard about our new relationship, Paul demanded to
meet me at the Bienville Country Club the next day. At four P.M. on a
weekday—I still remember that. Through a mutual friend he had called
me out, Old West style. The story spread like wildfire. The next day, he
skipped class and drove four hours to kick my ass.

To my surprise, the country club was closed when I arrived, apparently for remodeling, but a line of cars was parked outside the entrance, a 1980s analog of the mob that watched the "chickie-run" in
Rebel without a Cause. I hadn't known the club was closed, because
my family had never belonged to it. Dooley Matheson, Paul's mean
Jackson cousin, opened the locked gate for me, and I drove in to meet
my destiny. The sky was overcast with steel-gray clouds. Paul stood
out on the practice green, staring off toward the tree line, looking ten
pounds heavier than when he'd left town.

We walked the first five holes in silence, not looking at each other
except for sidelong glances, the way you look at other men in public
restrooms. He stank of sweat and stale beer. I had an eerie feeling that
he was measuring me for the first blow. In preparation for my senior
football season, I'd put on a lot of muscle over the summer. Paul had
been out of training for months, pounding bourbon and Cokes and
chowing down with his frat buddies. I had never seen him show fear,
and I didn't that day. But he seemed to be wondering whether taking
me on might prove more painful than he'd imagined after a few shots
of whiskey at Ole Miss.

As dusk fell over the sixth fairway, he started talking. Not to me exactly, just venting. Strangely, he wasn't talking about Jet. He was mum-
bling that college had turned out to be nothing like he'd imagined. It
was basically an extension of high school, he said, and nobody he knew
had any idea what they were going to do in the real world. A couple of
St. Mark's guys were on track to be doctors. Others claimed accounting was the quickest path to a Beemer and a Rolex and a McMansion
in Dallas. None of that interested Paul. He'd been raised by a father

who was larger than life—an athlete and war hero who could outrun, outplay, outshoot, outwork, outdrink, and outfuck (just ask him) any other man in whatever state he happened to be in at the time. In short, Max Matheson was a tough act to follow, and Paul didn't seem to have any idea how to go about it.

At the ninth-hole tee, he stopped to piss out the beer he'd drunk during the drive down from Oxford. Then, as though taking out his dick had somehow broached the subject we were there to discuss, he said, "You love her, don't you?"

When I didn't answer, he said, "You've always loved her, man. Don't try to deny it."

"I didn't deny anything," I said, still tense with the expectation of violence.

He sniffed, then looked off in the direction of the river, which flowed a half mile to the west. "I know she's pissed at me. I've banged a lot of chicks up there, you know that. But Jet's nothing like them. Not even the hottest ones at Ole Miss. Or the smart ones. She's . . . freaking perfect."

"Perfect's a pretty high bar," I said, but I secretly believed the same thing.

"I used to think so," he said. "But Jet clears it."

He finally looked over at me, and when our eyes met, I saw a guy who was hurting at least as much as I had been for a long time. *Why?* I wondered. *Surely not because of Jet. Maybe it's something to do with his old man—*

"The thing about Jet," Paul said softly, "is that no matter what you do to her, or with her, she stays pure. You know? She's above all that, somehow—even though she's doing it, and *into* it. Right?"

I knew what he meant. He was trying to describe something rare back then, the utter absence of shame in Jet's carnality. But I didn't say so. My mind was running rampant. What did Jet think of him in bed, really? Had she been honest with me? Or had she, out of a desire not to hurt me, pretended that sex with Paul was nothing special? How far had she gone with him? What boundaries had they crossed together?

"If you think she's so perfect," I said evenly, "why do you sleep with half the girls at Ole Miss? Why waste your time?"

"Why do you think?" he asked, looking out toward the river again. "I'm stuck there with nothing else to do. You think I'm going to lie around the dorm studying? You know me better than that."

In truth, I didn't know why Paul had even bothered going to college. It was a foregone conclusion that he'd end up working for his father in the lumber business. I guess he'd expected Jet to put up with a few flings, then be waiting for him when he came home with a report card full of "incompletes," ready to settle into the rut that had always been waiting for him. One thing I knew—Jet had no intention of marrying into that life.

"You're boning her, aren't you?" Paul said, and this time his voice had an edge to it.

I said nothing, but my nerves sang, and the muscles in my arms quivered in expectation of a fight.

"You know," he went on, "I could tell you something that would hurt you. Hurt you bad."

My eyes burned and watered, but I held my silence. I wasn't going to take the bait. I feared what he might say too much.

Paul looked off to the west again. Against the clouds I saw the great electrical tower we had climbed two and a half years earlier, just before Adam drowned. The sight half made me want to fight Paul. Fight somebody, anyway. He saw the tower, too, and maybe the flash of rage in my eyes, because his next words were not what I'd expected.

"Everybody's gonna ask what happened out here," he said. "If I kicked your ass or what."

I was surprised to discover that I didn't care one way or the other. My fear had seeped out of me during the walk, or else the sight of the tower had driven it from me. "If you want to try," I said, "let's get it over with."

"How about we don't and say we did?" Paul suggested. "I need a fucking drink."

The implications of his words washed over me like water in a heat wave. "What do we say out there?"

He shrugged. "Fought to a draw. Got tired of beating up on each other. No girl's worth killing each other over. Not even Jet."

I wasn't sure of this. "No black eyes?"

Paul chuckled. "You want to pop each other once apiece? To sell the story?"

I thought about this. "Not really."

"Fuck it," he said. "Let's get back to the cars. I've got an ice chest in my backseat."

This bloodless accommodation couldn't have been what he had in mind when he drove down from Oxford with his hands clenched on the wheel of his Corvette. But whatever rage he'd felt over Jet's cleaving to me had subsided. Night was falling, and a cold wind blew off the river, making the long walk back to the clubhouse an unpleasant prospect. I asked Paul if he wanted to run it, but he just laughed. Three days later, he dropped out of college and joined the army. Everyone we knew was flabbergasted. When George H. W. Bush gave the go order for Desert Storm, Paul was sitting in Saudi Arabia, waiting for the balloon to go up.

The honk of a horn startles me out of my reverie.

I speed up and wave to the impatient driver behind me, surprised to find myself on the Little Trace and nearly to the turn for Buck's house, which sits well back in the hardwood forest in rural Tenisaw County. I've driven out here so many times that I can do it on autopilot, even after an almost thirty-year gap.

The narrow gravel road arrows away from the black asphalt and runs through tall trees wearing the fresh pale green of spring. Back in those trees, Quinn Ferris sits in a house with a bed that will never again hold the weight of the man who built it. Handcrafted guitars hang on its walls—and a mandolin and a mandocello and two dulcimers— that will never have another note pulled from them by Buck's gifted fingers. All because he threatened to slow down the gravy train of the bastards who run Bienville like their personal fiefdom. I dread facing Quinn in her grief and anger, but what choice do I have? If the Poker Club killed her husband, it's because nobody ever planted themselves in their path and said, "This far, but no farther." Am I that guy? My father never set himself against them. But if my brother had lived, he would have. If only for that reason, I realize, I must do it.

CHAPTER 15

QUINN FERRIS GREW up in West Texas, and she looks more like a Westerner than a Southerner. She wears almost no makeup, even when I've seen her out at night, and she has the sun-parched look of a woman who spent much of her life exposed to a dry climate. Mississippi girls grow up in nearly 100 percent humidity, and they're reared from infancy to baby their skin. They get softer as they get older. Quinn has grown leaner and harder with age. Her pale eyes have an avian intensity, her arms and hands a whipcord toughness. She makes me think of long hours riding pillion on a motorcycle, her sun-bleached hair flying behind her from beneath the helmet.

Four days ago, when I met Buck at the Indian Village to interview him about his find, Quinn took care of the tourists who showed up, keeping watch for anyone who seemed more interested in her husband than the archaeological exhibits. Today she looks as though the shock of Buck's death has burned through whatever reserves of fortitude she possessed. She's standing at her stove, making tea with shaking hands. I'm sitting at their kitchen table, a Formica-topped relic from the 1950s. I ate at this table many times during high school and sat around it playing guitar with Buck deep into the night.

"What does a private autopsy cost?" Quinn asks. "An outside autopsy?"

"Three to five thousand. Unless you want a superstar pathologist."

She takes this in without comment.

"You saw Buck's body?" I ask.

"The sheriff told me not to go to the hospital, but I went anyway. They weren't going to let me see him. I made a ruckus. The security guard came. I think they were going to call the police, but an older doctor heard the noise and came. He made them let me in to see him. Dr. Kirby. Jack Kirby."

"He's my father's doctor. A great guy."

"Well, God bless him. But I saw the wound."

"I'm sorry, Quinn."

She closes her eyes and shakes her head. "You asked me about the break-in."

"It's okay, take your time."

As she makes the tea, she gives me a straightforward account. She'd gone to the Ruhlmann Funeral Home and spent a frustrating half hour on the phone with the sheriff, trying to learn when her husband's body might be returned to her after the autopsy. The sheriff was evasive and made no promises. Then she learned from the funeral director that the autopsy was going to be performed at the local hospital. After finally getting in to see Buck's body, and then recovering herself, she arrived home to find her front door standing open, cold air streaming through the screen door into the yard. Two steps inside, she realized that the house had been trashed. While she waited for a deputy to show up, she spent forty-five minutes "picking the place up." After seeing her husband's body so profoundly insulted, she couldn't abide having her house in disarray.

The deputy who responded to her call pushed Quinn into a state of fury. No matter what she told him, he insisted that the break-in had been carried out by "crackheads looking for something to sell." In his estimation (and obviously that of his boss), Buck's "drowning" had been a regrettable accident, but one that had nothing to do with a simple B&E near the county line, twenty miles away. Quinn pointed out that the offenders had taken great pains to go through her husband's papers; they'd even fanned through every book in his library, as though searching for something specific. "Addicts hoping y'all keep cash stashed in your books," the deputy declared, "like some country people do." I told Quinn I'd expected nothing better.

"You're right about Lafitte's Den," she says, fanning our cups with the flat of her hand. "Buck wouldn't have gone out there, not even if they were handing out free barbecue. If he *did* go, it wouldn't be to dig."

"Could he have gone there to meet somebody?"

"I don't think so. I think the killer caught Buck digging out at the mill site, and that was it." She brings our cups to the table and sets hers opposite me, but remains standing. "I can't believe they'd kill him over a few bones. Why not just warn him off? Threaten him? Tell him how far they were willing to go if he didn't back off."

"They knew Buck wasn't the type to be cowed by any of that."

"You think the killer knew him?"

"This is a small town. And Buck was one of its most colorful characters. I know you think the Poker Club is behind this, but I talked to Paul Matheson about that. He said the Poker Club would have bought Buck off, not killed him."

"Buck couldn't be bought!" she snaps. "You know that, Marshall."

I let the silence drag. "If the offer was big enough, Buck might have worried that you'd press him to take it. I'm talking about real money, Quinn. Five hundred grand. Maybe even a million. What would you have said if they'd offered him that?"

This gets her attention. "I'm not sure. We've scraped by for most of our lives. I hope he would have told me. Given me some input. But I can't be sure."

"It really doesn't matter now. Hard evidence is the only thing that can help us."

Quinn shakes her head helplessly. "They hate him now. All those people he did so much for at one time or another . . . they stopped caring about him. They all wished he'd just disappear. They won't care that he's dead. They'll be glad. All because of that goddamned paper mill." Her lips curl in disgust. "Have you talked to Jet about the Poker Club?"

"I'm talking to her at three o'clock," I reply. "But nobody else needs to know that."

"How does that work, Marshall? Her husband's father is one of the richest members of the Poker Club, yet she's fought their corruption for years."

"I'm not sure it works, actually. I think their marriage is pretty strained."

She nods as if this only makes sense. "She's a firecracker, that girl." Quinn finally pulls out her chair and sits, her eyes settling on mine with what feels like maternal concern. "You still have feelings for Jet."

I force myself to hold eye contact. "I probably always will. First love and all that."

A wistful smile touches Quinn's mouth. "Buck used to think you two would end up together."

"But not you?"

She shrugs. "Jet's special, no question. But she had issues. From her father leaving like that."

"And I didn't?"

"Different issues." Quinn reaches out and touches my hand. "You're not thinking you might still wind up with her?"

Am I that easy to read? "What makes you ask that?"

"Your eyes still change when her name comes up. Your voice goes up a half-step in pitch."

"Really? Well. We went through a lot together. What matters today is that if we try to halt construction of the mill to search for evidence, it'll be Jet who files the papers."

Quinn knows I'm trying to change the subject. Graciously, she allows me this. "I know who to call at the state level," she says, "if that's the way you want to go."

"Does Archives and History have the stroke to override pressure from the governor? Even national pressure?"

"In theory? Sure. William Winter fought off serious pressure during the casino boom. In reality, I don't know. That's why Buck went back looking for bones."

I take a long sip of my tea, which has already started to cool. "Why did he risk going last night, if he knew there were guards posted?"

"No, no. He went in to dig because there weren't any guards. He called and told me that."

This is new information. "What?"

"He drove out and parked well south of the site, then walked up the riverbank. The whole way he watched for lights. He didn't see a single guard."

"That doesn't mean there weren't any. They could have been using night vision."

"To guard a small-town paper mill site?"

"With so much money at stake, it's possible. Quinn, why didn't you report Buck missing when he didn't come home last night?"

She closes her eyes with obvious pain. "Because I knew he was trespassing, and he would stay out there all night if he could. I also knew he'd cache any finds somewhere other than here, to protect me. That would take time. I've cursed myself a thousand times for not saying to hell with it and calling the police. Buck might still be alive—"

"No," I tell her. "The local police and sheriff's department wouldn't have been a source of aid for Buck. Not at the industrial park."

"I guess you're right."

"Do you know if Buck was in contact with anyone outside the city? Other archaeologists? Academics? The government?"

She shrugs again. "You know Buck. He was always talking to friends around the country. I don't know how much he told them about this specific find. He was so excited, but also secretive about it. I think he saw this as his legacy, the great work of his life. By the way, the sheriff told me they didn't find Buck's cell phone. So I don't know who he might have called."

"If they found his phone, they wouldn't have entered it into evidence. Do you know whether Buck dug up anything else at the site? You said he would be caching his finds somewhere other than here. Why?"

Quinn studies me as though making some difficult judgment. "Buck got pretty paranoid over the past four weeks, especially the last two. One night he decided to move some stuff, so it wouldn't be lost if our house happened to catch fire or something. We own a small rental house. He's worked there most nights for the past week."

Before I can even ask, Quinn reaches into the pocket of her jeans and takes out a brass key. "This will get you in, if you want to look."

"Address?"

"Three-two-five Dogwood. There's a renter there, but he's an old friend of Buck's. Jim's gone a lot, but I'll let him know you're coming, just in case. Buck's stuff is in a back bedroom. Should be easy to find. He worked at a drafting table."

"Got it," I say, getting up and taking the key from her.

"Don't go yet," she says, reaching out and touching my arm. "Let's step into Buck's workshop."

We walk out to the garage Buck enclosed after his lutherie work outgrew the extra bedroom where he'd begun it a decade before. It smells of glue and sealer and freshly sawn wood. Some of Buck's finest instruments hang from pegs on the walls. A padded worktable with a sheet of rare Brazilian rosewood still on it dominates the center of the room. Against one wall stands a heating unit and some electric blankets used for bending wood, while the remainder of the space is filled by barrels, stands, and shelves containing wood, tools, fret wire, electric pickups, and machine heads. I can't stand in this room and believe Buck is dead.

"You feel it?" Quinn asks, opening her hands like someone trying to catch raindrops. "His spirit is still in here."

Another person saying this might sound like some new-age flake. Not Quinn Ferris, who's practical to a fault. "I do feel it. I feel him."

"I hope it lasts. But I feel like he's hovering here, trying to say goodbye."

Less than twelve hours ago the man who built the guitars in this room was still walking the earth. Unable to fill the void his loss has opened in me, I turn and pull Quinn to me. She hesitates at first, then relents and lets me crush her in my arms. Her chest heaves a couple of times, but she doesn't sob. After half a minute, she pulls back and wipes her eyes. Then she goes to a drawer and takes out a dark leather bag, which she carries over to me.

"I want you to have these," she says.

"Buck's chisels? These were his prize tools."

"And he'd want you to have them. I want you to take a guitar, too. I'm going to have to sell the rest, but I want you to take one. Any one you want."

"Quinn—"

"Don't argue with me."

I look around the workshop, my gaze moving across the instruments. They're so different from one another. Buck loved to learn about new woods, and he did that by working with them. In this small space I see macassar ebony, East Indian rosewood, American swamp ash, koa, quilted maple, bird's-eye maple, figured sapele, Sitka spruce, pau ferro. The variation in design shapes equals the selection of woods. Buck built parlor guitars, concert models, dreadnoughts—

"I know which one you want," Quinn says. "Take it down."

She's talking about Buck's personal guitar, a baritone acoustic fashioned out of one-of-a-kind padauk, a reddish wood so rare it was harvested after a monsoon laid a whole stand low on the Andaman islands in the Bay of Bengal. Set into the ebony fret board is a beautiful B.F. logo in mother-of-pearl.

"I can't take that, Quinn. That guitar's worth more than any two of the others. Ten thousand, at least."

"I'll sleep better knowing you have it."

"Let me pay you for it."

"Don't insult me. I'll get the case."

While she retrieves the hard-shell case from another room, I take down the baritone, put it on my knee, and pick out a haunting finger-style instrumental that Buck wrote when I was in high school.

"That's why it's your guitar," she says. "Nobody else even knows that song. Just you and me."

The notes of Buck's song hang almost visibly in the air of his work-shop, then die to make way for those that follow. When I finish playing, and the room is silent again, Quinn helps me pack the guitar into the case. After a last look around the shop, she walks me to the front door. The baritone is heavy, but it feels right in my hand, and the chisels in my other hand help balance the weight.

As we face each other across the threshold, Quinn says, "It's wrong to kill a man for trying to do what's right. The past matters, you know? Even if people don't realize it. You'd think Southerners would get that."

"Mississippians are pretty selective about what they like to remember."

She laughs bitterly. "You say 'they' like you're not one of them."

"I left a long time ago, Quinn."

"Most people from here, that doesn't make any difference."

"It did to me."

"Promise me you'll find out who killed him?"

I look back into her expectant eyes. Moments like this one have consequences. "I will. I won't rest until I do."

"And then what?"

I turn up my palms. "Get justice."

"What does that look like, you think?"

"I can't bring him back, Quinn."

She tries to force a smile, but the result is an awful grimace. She reaches out and squeezes my shoulder. "Watch your back, okay? These fuckers are serious."

"I know. You, too."

She gives me a light kiss on the cheek, then turns away.

As I walk toward the Flex, the screen door slaps shut behind me, the main door closes, and I hear the bolt shoot home. Quinn doesn't stand around waiting to smile and wave as I drive off, which is the Southern way. She feels more allegiance to her dead husband than to pointless folkways. Yet the guitar in my hand tells me she's already begun the necessary process of letting him go. She will treasure Buck's memory and avenge him if she can, but Quinn is a survivor.

And life is for the living.

I'M BACK ON THE Little Trace, headed west, when the coroner calls my cell phone. The dozen shades of green in the thick canopy give me the feeling of driving through a rain forest. I take the call on the Flex's Bluetooth system.

"Hey, Byron. Thanks for getting back to me. What can you tell me?"

The coroner's deep bass voice rattles the door speakers. "I only got a minute. And I feel a little funny about this."

"I imagine you're feeling some pressure down there. Certain influential people want this to go down as an accident?"

"You know it." He lets out a cross between a sigh and a groan. "But between you and me . . . Buck was murdered."

"Tell me how you know."

"Shape of the wound, for one thing. Blunt force trauma by an object with linear edges, not something irregular like a rock. Second, I found dust down in the wound, in both the skin and the brain matter. All I had was my magnifying glass, now."

"What kind of dust? Not sandstone?"

"Not sandstone. Brick dust, I'm pretty sure. Those old Natchez bricks. Reddish orange."

I think about this. "You don't think Buck could have fallen from a height onto one of those bricks?"

"Oh, he *could* have. Thing is, they ain't *got* any bricks like that at that pirate cave. No bricks at all. Nothing ever got built out there. It's just loess soil and Catahoula sandstone."

"I guess there *could* be bricks out there, right? Taken out there by somebody? To bank a campfire or something?"

"Sure. But what are the odds that Buck would fall from a height onto one of the only couple of bricks at that whole place?"

"You're right. I'm just playing devil's advocate."

Staticky silence stretches as I drive down the narrow asphalt line, which cuts like a cable through trees rising eighty feet on both sides of the road. "What are you thinking, Byron?"

"I been thinkin' 'bout places where they *do* got them bricks. Lots of 'em."

"I know one," I tell him, remembering my childhood.

"The old electroplating factory, right? The paper mill site where Buck found that Indian pot you wrote about."

"Yep. Have you told anybody about the brick dust?"

"Not yet. Autopsy's not my job. That's s'posed to be done in Jackson."

"I hear something in your voice, Byron. What's going on?"

"I don't know if you know, but sometimes autopsies get done right here in Bienville, if the hospital has a pathologist on staff. That's on and off in this town, but right now we got one. 'Locum tenens,' they call it. Temporary. I just got told he's gonna do the autopsy."

My pulse quickens. "Who told you that?"

"President of the county supervisors. I got the first call as I was driving the body up from the river. But I just got confirmation."

"Jesus, Byron. You think they're going to dictate the result they want? Or buy it?"

"Why else change regular procedure? They sure ain't in no hurry to get the real result. So if they're rushing it, they must already know what the report's gonna say."

"The fix is in."

"Yeah. And I don't know what I can do to stop it."

"Nothing, if you want to keep your job. We're going to need an independent autopsy. I just spoke to the widow. I don't think it will be a problem, except for the cost. But I'll cover that. The only problem is time. They're moving fast."

"Man, I hate to say this," Byron says in a portentous tone, "but I been thinking 'bout something else."

"Yeah?"

"This job means a lot to me. I'm the first black coroner in Tenisaw County. But it's not just that. I like the work. The science of it, figuring things out. And I treat the dead with respect. Especially these kids that kill each other like it's Sierra Leone. They deserve respect, even if it's the only respect they'll ever get."

"I understand, Byron. You do great work. I've seen it."

"Lemme finish. If I see things like this here today, and I don't speak up—what does that say about me?"

"It says you need your job."

"Yeah. But I'm a deacon in the church. That ain't just a title to me. It means something. And what them fellas do, that Poker Club . . . it galls me. I been watching them rich white men run this town since I was a boy. In the old days we had to take it. Didn't have no choice. But now . . . I don't know."

I feel my heart beating in my chest. "Tell me what you're thinking. Spell it out."

"I'm thinking you run a newspaper. And I got some news."

A bracing burst of adrenaline shoots through my system. Men of integrity and courage are rare these days. I've known a few, but it's been a long time since I ran into a genuine Christian, one who makes difficult choices based on his faith and then follows through. "Are you talking about anonymous information? Or being named as the source?"

"If I say something, I put my name to it."

Even though I'm driving, I close my eyes in gratitude. "Okay, brother. I'm ready. Tell me what you want to say."

When Byron Ellis starts talking, I feel the rush I used to feel in Washington when a whistle-blower started giving me a world-class story. The rush is no less intense because I'm in the small town in which I grew up. The coroner's words are going to ruin tomorrow morning for a lot of powerful men, and that, in the end, is what I got into this business to do.

BUCK FERRIS'S RENTAL HOUSE stands in a neighborhood built in the 1940s for the workers employed at the Bienville fiberboard plant. The small frame houses were modest even for that period, but the carpenters back then were such craftsmen that the homes are considered desirable now and sell for about a hundred grand apiece. There's no car in the driveway of 325 Dogwood, but I drive the length of the street anyway, checking for signs of surveillance. After satisfying myself that I'm clean, I park in front of a mailbox two houses down from 325. Then I walk fifty yards up the street, cut around back, and try the key Quinn gave me in the patio door.

After a couple of jiggles, it works.

The interior of 325 looks like the abode of a single man, and the books and records on the shelves tell me he's over seventy. I move to a small hall that leads off the den. The house has only two bedrooms, and the one on the right contains a drafting table. Other than the table, the room holds two filing cabinets and some map tubes. Tacked on the wall above the drafting table is an enlargement of what looks to me like B. L. C. Wailes's hand-drawn map of what is now the paper mill site. Scotch-taped to the drafting table is a smaller map labeled POVERTY POINT SITE.

Kneeling before the file cabinets, I find they're only a quarter full, but along with papers they contain several small boxes of pottery fragments, beads, tiny figurines, and what appear to be spear points about three inches long. Rather than try to skim through everything, I transfer the papers into the file drawer with the artifacts, then remove the drawer from the cabinet. If I'm going to meet Jet at three, I can't sit around here for an hour. The map tubes present a problem. In the end, I tape them together and get them under my left arm, then pick up the file drawer and make for the back door.

Crossing the open space between the rental house and the Flex, I notice a woman watching me from the carport of a house across the street. She's holding a cell phone to her cheek. Should that worry me? Half the people I see these days are on their phones. As nonchalantly as possible, I load the file drawer and tubes into the cargo area of the Flex, then head back to Highway 61.

I should stop by the *Watchman* office before I head home. But if I go to the rooftop party at the Aurora tonight with Nadine, I can stop by the newspaper afterward, while they're finalizing tomorrow's issue. Instead of going downtown, I point the Flex east and take out my iPhone. As I drive, I dictate a draft story about the coroner's findings, then email it to Ben Tate. I tell Ben not to post it on our web edition until I've had time to ask some Poker Club members for comment.

Less than five minutes later, Ben calls me to complain. I let him vent his frustration, but when he finally takes a long breath, I say, "Don't post it till midnight, Ben. End of discussion. I've got something else for you to do. Call the locum tenens pathologist at the hospital and ask him twenty questions about Buck Ferris's autopsy. Why the rush? Why break from procedure and do it locally? You know the drill. I want you to scare him. Tell him we're going to be all over the cause of death in that case. And let him know you've already heard the family intends to pay for a private autopsy."

"You're trying to intimidate him into an honest result?"

"He'll find it tough to lie if he thinks Michael Baden will be coming along behind him to repeat the post. And do it now. He might have already cut Buck. He could be dictating his findings as we speak."

"What if I can't get him on the phone?"

"Drive to the hospital. Push him hard, Ben."

"Understood."

As I end my call with Ben, my burner phone pings. I snatch it off the seat with a frantic motion. Jet's texted reply reads: *You're right. Paul and I just had a fight. He's suspicious. Focused on Josh but he did mention you. Don't know where this is coming from. I'm still planning to come this aft but won't if I'm not certain I'm clean. I love you. Stay calm and deny everything if confronted. If it all blows up, I know that's not what we planned, but all we can do is deal with it. For the time being, deny. See you soon I hope!*

I feel like that burner phone is wired to my limbic brain. My autonomic nervous system is firing nonstop, and it's all I can do not to piss my pants. For three months we've been gliding under the radar, knowing there was danger yet somehow feeling invulnerable. That changed today.

Three o'clock is forty minutes away. I fight the urge to speed and force myself to pay attention to the traffic. The last thing I need is a fender bender to prevent me from seeing Jet in private during this crisis. Who knows when we'll get another chance?

Her text made it clear that she has no more idea than I do about what triggered Paul's sudden suspicion. We may never find out. The "six degrees of separation" principle applies on a global scale. In a town like Bienville, few people are even one degree removed from everyone else. A huge percentage of residents know each other directly, and not only by name, but by entire family histories. *My mama went to school with her daddy, and my grandfather hunted with his, and I've heard tell that four generations back, we might even have come from the same Civil War colonel.* The idea that two well-known citizens could carry on an illicit affair in this kind of matrix without being discovered is preposterous.

Yet people try it every day.

What strikes me as I drive out Highway 36 is that Paul and I have always been rivals for Jet's affection. There's no mystery about that. Even after he married her, he knew I still lived within her heart, the way she lived in mine after my marriage to Molly. But something has made him fear a physical manifestation of our feelings. A present-day resurrection of the sexual relationship that he knows far too much about to sleep easily. And if he truly fears that, then what will he do about it?

Paul Matheson is capable of extreme behavior. No one knows that better than I. I made him famous by writing about his courage, skill, and daring, but also by omitting the truth about his terrifying lack of restraint when under threat. Had I told the truth about all I have seen, Paul would be viewed as a different man today. Celebrated by some, surely, but reviled by others. Most of us are never tested the way Paul has been. A few unlucky civilians endure horrific experiences, violent crimes, or terrorist acts. But apart from survivors of sexual assault, almost no one faces the stress levels present in that soul-killing zone of conflict called war. And the relationship between Paul and me cannot be understood without knowing what we went through under fire together.

Not even Jet knows the truth.

CHAPTER 16

IN JANUARY 2004, I left Washington to embed with a company of marines in Afghanistan. Before I left, I reached out to Paul to ask for tips on surviving in combat conditions. To my surprise, I got Jet instead. Newlywed Paul had left Mississippi at the age of thirty-one to begin working as a military contractor in Afghanistan. This shocked me, but Jet explained that 9/11 had tripped a sort of reflex patriotic fervor in Paul. He'd wanted to re-enlist in the Rangers, but this turned out to be more complicated than he'd hoped. Then he heard from some old Ranger buddies who'd been hired as private military contractors. They told him tales that sounded like a cross between the Old West of Hollywood and *Lawrence of Arabia,* complete with horse cavalry charges.

Paul boarded the next plane to Kabul.

After two ninety-day rotations in Afghanistan, he shifted to Iraq, where he quickly realized that military contracting was the new growth industry. All you needed to get a fat government contract was a couple of armored vehicles and a football team's worth of vets who didn't mind getting shot at. Paul already knew the veterans, and the Bienville Poker Club was happy to provide the capital to field an armored unit in Iraq. What better bragging rights could Mississippi businessmen have at every golf course, hunting club, and cocktail party in the South than being able to say they had their own Special Forces team slinging lead at the ragheads in America's far-flung war zones? I wasn't sure Paul would get his venture off the ground, but that was his problem.

I flew to Afghanistan and embedded with regular marines. I got to spend a little time with some private contractors, but I came to know only a couple well. They were former Delta operators—very different from the contractors I would come to know in Iraq. I learned a lot about war in eight weeks. Combat answered the questions I'd pondered while reading Hemingway and Conrad and le Carré and Michael Herr. The eternal male questions: Will my nerve hold when the bullets start hitting around me? When the guy next to me gets blasted into big wet pieces? If I'm asked to pick up a weapon and help, will I acquit myself competently? Honorably? The answers to the first two questions proved affirmative. But in Afghanistan I was never asked to pick up a weapon, not to fire in anger anyway. That would come later.

In Zabul Province I bonded with young men whom I would never have met back in the world. The America those boys had grown up in was far different from mine, though I was only ten or twelve years older than most of them. Their notions about war were alien to me—I who had been nursed on *Paths of Glory* and *The Bridge on the River Kwai* by my father. Those kids had a kind of nihilistic enthusiasm about combat, one bred from later war films and first-person shooter video games. They'd come to Afghanistan expecting an adrenaline-churning synthesis of *Rambo* and *Apocalypse Now,* but one fought behind an insulating layer of technology, as in *Doom, Halo,* and *Call of Duty.* They seemed to understand that they'd been posted to the graveyard of empires, but this awareness was hidden behind the ironic distance they wore like an extra layer of armor. They'd evolved this armor as children, to protect themselves from the pain of disintegrating families. They'd never been infused with the unified, idealized image of America that still lives within me. Nevertheless, they fought with remarkable bravery, and they made sure that I was as safe as possible under fire.

Iraq was different.

I hadn't even planned to go there, but in March 2004, something happened that shook the public and private masters of the American military effort. In Fallujah, four contractors employed by Blackwater USA were ambushed, killed, and mutilated. I felt the reverberations 1,400 miles away, when a team from DynCorp, a Blackwater competitor, described to me how the four operators had been dragged naked through the streets of Fallujah. This atrocity sparked outrage among the contractors, which was easy to understand. What surprised me was the fury that surged through the ranks of the regular military, right up to the generals. Instinct told me that the Blackwater ambush would not go un-answered, so I started reaching out to everyone I knew working in Iraq.

All agreed that some kind of payback was imminent, but no one knew where the hammer would fall. At that point, I decided to call Paul Matheson. I hadn't spoken to him since deploying to Afghanistan, and I didn't reach him right away. But I did reach Jet in Mississippi. As it turned out, my old quarterback had succeeded in starting his own de-fense contracting outfit, which he'd christened ShieldCorp. At that time he had two teams in Iraq: one escorting supply convoys from Baghdad Airport to the Green Zone; the other in a town called Ramadi, near Fallujah, protecting dignitaries for the Coalition. Jet gave me a satel-lite phone number, and fifteen minutes later, I was speaking to my old teammate.

Paul sounded like a starving gold prospector who'd just seen a buddy scoop plum-size nuggets out of a stream: "Something's about to happen here, Goose. No more Somalias, that's the word. The Penta-gon's gonna punish somebody. Afghanistan's about to become a side-show. Iraq's gonna blow. You'd better hop a plane and get your ass down here." I asked him how his business was going. "We're just getting off the ground, but we're doing good. I've got two contracts worth $4.1 million, but there's a lot more coming. I can smell it. It's about to be boom times for PSCs. I gotta run. Call me if you come down. You can ride some convoys with us. It's like *The War Wagon* with IEDs."

I still remember Paul's wild laughter as he broke the connection. It unnerved me a little, the idea of war as a business opportunity—especially one that a ragtag start-up like Paul's could play a part in—but I got on a plane and headed for old Babylon.

Iraq was a world away from Afghanistan. For one thing, it was ur-ban warfare. It also attracted a different breed of contractor, probably due to rapidly escalating demand. While many contractors in Iraq were ex-soldiers, far fewer were former-JSOC guys. To my amazement, many were ex–police officers or sheriff's deputies from tiny American towns, a majority from the South. ShieldCorp's meager ranks exemplified this demographic. Contracting was the only hope most of them had to earn more than minimum wage. They'd gone through a dusty "training school" Paul ran outside Laurel, Mississippi—thirty acres of overgrown piney woods and a half acre of asphalt for driving school. But unlike

Navy SEAL training, where only 6 percent of an experienced applicant pool is accepted for training and 75 percent of those fail to make the grade, about 80 percent of the semi-desperate applicants to Paul's new company had been accepted. This, I learned, was true of most other private outfits in Iraq as well. I don't mean to say that Paul didn't have some good people. He had eight Rangers who'd served with him in Somalia in the '90s. He had one ex-Delta operator called "Rattler" whom he exploited heavily at recruiting time (though I had to wonder why, with Delta credentials, Rattler hadn't signed on with one of the blue-chip companies; I never found out).

There was another difference between Afghanistan and Iraq— one that would become critically important to me. In Afghanistan, the contractors knew the rules about enemy contact, and they were grim. If you were wounded, you had no instant medevac—no real medical care to speak of, in fact—and certainly not the lifelong benefits so critical with war wounds. Worst of all, if captured, you had little hope of rescue. If you were hit on the wrong side of the Pakistani border and couldn't haul yourself out, you were stuck. You weren't even going to be acknowledged. The "leave no man behind" ethos had been left behind with the regular military. In Afghanistan, contractors were expendable.

In Iraq, though, the contractors always assumed that if things got really bad, they could count on the Marines or the army to bail them out of a jam. The reason was simple: the regular troops knew the contractors provided many of the supplies they needed to live, so they felt enough pragmatic self-interest to offer what help and protection they could. Marines would quietly pass the contractors grenades and extra ammo, to be sure they had the best chance of survival in a crisis. Nobody anticipated things getting so hot that the regular troops would be fighting for their lives and wouldn't have time for the cowboys who worked for bigger bucks.

That was what happened in Fallujah, only a stone's throw from Ramadi, where I was embedded with one of Paul's teams. I'm not sure why Paul had his guys there, when their job was protecting a German engineer employed by the United States in Fallujah. I suspected that Paul didn't want his guys living too close to the bigger contracting outfits. Maybe he didn't like the way his men stacked up against the competition. They were underequipped, for one thing, though Paul was bringing more gear and assets online every week. At that time ShieldCorp owned two Mambas—armored South African vehicles that mounted a light machine gun and had gun ports for the operators riding inside. ShieldCorp also owned six regular cars, which served as escort vehicles. But the company's pride and joy was its Little Bird, the small but doughty helicopter originally designed by Hughes Aircraft, now fitted out as a gunship that could also serve as medevac in a pinch. Paul occasionally flew the Little Bird himself, but for the hairy stuff he had a former Special Forces pilot on his payroll, from the 160th SOAR out of Fort Campbell, Kentucky. The guy was a bit long in the tooth, but he could fly that chopper through a parking garage if you paid him enough.

I started in Iraq by riding along on three separate convoy escorts with ShieldCorp's first Mamba team—Sierra Alpha—from Baghdad International Airport to the Green Zone. During those runs, our Mamba took dozens of rounds of machine-gun fire, several sniper rounds, and survived one IED detonation. After that near miss, I had the distinction of being able to say I'd been "blowed up" in Iraq. I also saw two Iraqi civilian passenger cars destroyed by Sierra Alpha for getting too close and not backing off after warning shots were fired in front of them. This happened in reasonably heavy traffic, and it reset my whole idea of America's war tactics. What I'd witnessed was private U.S. citizens shooting Iraqi civilians *prophylactically,* without ever being fired upon. Such was the anxiety created by previous insurgent suicide attacks that the military was willing to overlook contractors killing civilians for getting too close to their supply convoys on civilian highways.

Paul's second team—Sierra Bravo—had been providing security for the German engineer in Fallujah and Ramadi. Protective detail work was different from airport escort duty. In that situation, a ShieldCorp team worked what was called a "diamond" around a VIP. In case of attack, the team's primary responsibility was getting the protectee "off the X" and to safety. The team could return fire defensively, but its main mission was to avoid escalating contact.

During its first six weeks of duty, beginning in February 2004, Sierra Bravo's coverage of the engineer had gone smoothly. There'd been a couple of incidents with thrown rocks and bottles, but the team had evacuated its VIP in seconds with no shots fired and no casualties.

However, the general situation in Central Iraq had begun deteriorating. That same month, disgruntled veterans from Iraq's disbanded army had ignited a nationwide insurgency. On February 12, in Fallujah, they launched an RPG and machine-gun attack on U.S. commanding general John Abizaid and Eighty-Second Airborne general Charles Swannack. Eleven days later, they simultaneously attacked three Iraqi police stations and freed close to ninety insurgent prisoners. The situation was spinning out of control so rapidly that General Swannack placed al-Anbar Province under the direct authority of a Marine Expeditionary Force. On March 27 a U.S. special operations surveillance team was flushed out of hiding and had to fight its way out of Fallujah. Four days later, a massive roadside bomb killed five soldiers of the First Infantry Division as they worked to clear a supply road used by private contractors.

All this was only prelude to the March 31 ambush that wiped out the four Blackwater contractors. It was then that I arrived in-country. After my "initiation" riding with the airport convoys, Paul invited me to Ramadi to live with the Sierra Bravo protection team. Compared to the *War Wagon* gauntlet of the convoys, protective duty seemed almost soporific.

Until it didn't.

On April 4 U.S. forces launched punitive surgical strikes into Fallujah. By the next morning, they'd surrounded the city, and tension across the country rose to an ominous pitch. The climate in Ramadi, which had seemed calm only days before, suddenly made us feel like a lone outpost on the edge of civilization. Ninety percent of the Iraqis who walked past the house Sierra Bravo used as its base scowled openly at us, and the two Iraqis employed by the team—an interpreter and a cook—got so nervous that they couldn't sleep.

I wondered why we didn't just evacuate until the battle for Fallujah ended, but Paul took his orders from the Pentagon, and that meant staying put. In a matter of hours, one-third of the population of Fallujah fled the city. The insurgents who remained were armed with RPGs, heavy machine guns, mortars, and antiaircraft cannons. Once American forces attacked Fallujah in earnest, all Central Iraq exploded into chaos. The Mahdi army declared itself and began attacking Coalition targets, and in Ramadi, a full-on Sunni rebellion sparked to fire. As chaos erupted around us, Paul moved the German engineer out of his private house and in with the protective team. Paul's sources told him that many Iraqi national police officers had turned on the Coalition and he shouldn't look to anyone in a police uniform for aid. With no other option, we hunkered down to wait out the fighting.

The Ramadi insurgents had a different idea. They'd known about the Sierra Bravo house for months, and they had no intention of giving us a pass. At two P.M. on April 8, a hundred Iraqi men gathered in the street in front of our house, and half of them carried either Kalashnikovs or American M4s donated by the Iraqi police. Inside the house, we had eight ShieldCorp contractors, two Iraqis (the cook and the interpreter, both males), the German VIP, and me—the embedded journalist. By Paul's calculations, we had enough food and water to last three days and enough ammunition for about the same, depending on the intensity of any assault. If the insurgents brought up mortars or antiaircraft guns, of course, the equation would change radically.

Paul's biggest regret was that our team's Mamba had not been on site when the rebellion broke out. It was being serviced in Baghdad, which was two hours away on a good day. By the time Paul called Team Sierra Alpha to rescue us in the other Mamba, the insurgents had sealed off our section of Ramadi with roadblocks. A call to the Joint Task Force brought a similar answer and some free advice: *Keep your heads down until we take Fallujah. Then we'll escort you back to the Green Zone.* The army didn't seem to realize that regaining control of Fallujah might take more than a few days. (In the end it took six months.)

The first shots near our house went off around 4:00 P.M. It was sporadic fire, directed skyward, but it rattled the hell out of me. Paul ordered his men to hold fire. Ten minutes later, the first clips were emptied against the windows and front wall of our house. Concentrated bursts chipped away huge chunks of brick and stone and shredded the plywood that Paul's men had used to barricade the windows. Paul was on the first floor with me. He shouted that everyone's guns were "cleared hot," but they should still hold their fire to the last possible moment. The ShieldCorp guys had cut gun ports in the plywood with a jigsaw, and they'd posted their three best snipers on the roof of the two-story house. But all obeyed Paul's order and silently watched the insurgents blast the face of the building without letup. As the walls shuddered around me, I realized that unless a JSOC team dropped out of the sky in a couple of Black Hawks, this was the Alamo.

When Paul finally shouted the order to return fire, the Iraqis in the street began dropping three and four at a time. There's nothing quite like watching the effect of automatic rifles in the hands of skilled soldiers with good fire discipline. Team Sierra Bravo cleared that street in less than two minutes. The problem—as we all knew—was that the Iraqis had virtually unlimited replacements in Ramadi, while we had none. We couldn't even replenish our ammunition. I wasn't firing, of course, but I was absolutely part of the group. We were going to live or die together.

After the street emptied out, Paul called a quick conference in the kitchen. So far as he knew, we had no hope of rescue. Sierra Alpha couldn't reach us, and the army and the Marines were too hotly engaged elsewhere to bother with us. The German engineer asked about ShieldCorp's Little Bird, which sounded like one of God's angels at that moment. *Surely,* I thought, *with enough covering fire, it could pluck us off the roof and whisk us to safety.* Of course, with a crew of two, the helicopter could hold only six passengers, but I felt the logistics could be worked out. Maybe we could divide into two groups and escape in two runs. Paul explained that CENTCOM had grounded private aircraft in this zone, at least for the time being. Cobra gunships and low-altitude ScanEagle drones were swarming over the flat roofs of Fallujah, and the Joint Task Force didn't want any confusion created by pilots not under its direct command. We were, Paul announced, going to have to hold out through the night.

Silence greeted this assertion. Then one contractor, an older Ranger named Eddie Curtz, said, "Just another day in paradise. Let's go earn our money."

Paul quickly outlined his defense plan, which included three-hour slots for pairs of men to sleep. He also issued weapons to the German, the cook, the interpreter, and me. To my surprise, the cook refused to arm himself. He was so afraid of what might happen to him in the hands of the insurgents that he was barely functioning. The interpreter accepted a 9 mm Glock pistol. Paul handed me an M4A1 rifle.

"It's set on semi mode," he said, showing me the selector switch. "But if they get within ten yards of the building, flip it to rock and roll."

The weapon was heavier than I'd expected it to be.

"The second wave will be coming soon," Paul told me. "About dusk, I imagine. I want you to stay with me on the ground floor." As we walked into the room he'd been covering before, he leaned in and whispered, "You scared?"

"Shitless, buddy."

He laughed. "It's just like being on the kickoff team back in Bienville. Only with guns."

"Those kickoffs were over in twenty seconds, max," I said through gritted teeth. "This is going to last a lot longer."

"Maybe," he said, and I saw then that Paul believed we might well die in the next few minutes.

"Where's the German?" I asked.

"Upstairs, center of the building. He's too valuable to expose."

We each sat at a boarded-up window and waited, staring through our firing slits like hunters in a duck blind. About twenty minutes later, as shadows slid across the street, our cook made a run for it. We knew because one of the ShieldCorp men shouted it from the kitchen.

"Dumbass," Paul muttered, and I wasn't sure whether he was talking about the cook or the contractor. Thirty seconds later he said, "See?"

Two insurgents shoved our cook into view across the road, while keeping behind cover themselves. They shot him in the stomach first. After he screamed and fell to his knees, they stood him up straight and shot him in the face.

I felt like I was going to vomit, but I held it down.

"No chance of the Alpha team breaking through to get us?" I asked.

"I've been texting them," Paul said, not taking his eyes from his slit. "But they'd have to fight their way through two roadblocks. Burning tires, RPGs, overwhelming odds. Our best bet is the Little Bird. But if I disobey Joint Task Force command, they could kick us out of Iraq for good."

"Who gives a shit?! You'd be alive at least."

Paul grinned. "I hear you, Goose. Let me see if I can get us some help breaching a roadblock."

Goddamn it, I thought angrily. *We're in the fucking Alamo, and this idiot's trying to save his business—*

"It's funny, isn't it?" Paul said in a softer voice, alternating between his cell phone screen and his firing port. "Jet's father was from this part of the world. Yet we're over here fighting, maybe dying, and she's back in Bienville, safe as houses."

Bringing up Jet should have been awkward, but it seemed the most natural thing in the world.

"So what the fuck are we doing here?" I asked.

Paul laughed. "I'm making a buck. You're telling a story about me making a buck. Any questions deeper than that, I don't ask. That's your department."

"I hope I live to answer them."

He looked over at me then, without guile or intent. "Let's hope one of us makes it back. If not, Jet'll have to start over again with God knows what loser."

The second wave came as Paul predicted, when the whole street had fallen under the shadow of oncoming night. Team Bravo knocked down twenty more Iraqis in the first two minutes, but the hajis—as the ShieldCorp guys called the insurgents—were getting smarter about cover. They'd also brought up some real shooters this time. Ten minutes into the second fight, we lost two guys almost simultaneously. One had a sucking chest wound; the other caught a 7.62 round in the forehead. After that, Paul had to take over one of the dead guys' positions, leaving me to cover our room alone. Before he left, he drew a small automatic pistol from an ankle holster and passed it to me.

"You know what that's for," he said in a taut voice.

"No way," I told him.

"Goose." He looked hard into my eyes. "A .380 round beats the shit out of having your head sawed off and your parents watching it later." He squeezed my shoulder. "I love you, brother."

I nodded, my throat sealed shut with fear.

Then he left me.

In that moment, the terror of every nightmare I'd ever had came to vivid life. I was utterly alone, surrounded by men bent on killing me—or, worse, hurting me very badly, *then* killing me, and doing it all on camera. Worst of all, I wasn't trained for the situation. I had only the vaguest notion of how to defend myself. My only consolation was that a lot of the insurgents outside probably knew less about guns than I did.

I was visualizing the Little Bird landing on our roof like the angel Gabriel when the hajis rolled an antiaircraft cannon into the street before our house. The mere sight of its gaping muzzle loosened my anal sphincter. What remained of our shelter could not possibly stand against that weapon.

The first round from the cannon blasted our front door into metal splinters, announcing the terminal phase of the battle. A Bravo sniper on the roof killed several hajis in succession as they manned the gun, but the fourth gunner finally obliterated our sharpshooters. Then the cannon opened up in earnest. When the front wall had so many holes in it that collapse seemed imminent, the insurgents charged across the street.

At that moment, my conscious mind departed the proceedings. With weird detachment I watched my right thumb flip the selector switch to AUTO. Then I shoved my muzzle back through the slit and emptied a clip into the mass of charging bodies. For three dilated seconds the rifle shuddered against my shoulder. Blood and tissue exploded into the air, men screamed like women, and I saw my fire stagger the charge. Then my clip ran dry. The insurgents recovered, and they kept coming.

Whoever was still alive on our upper floor kept knocking men down, but the outcome was a foregone conclusion. Seeing an extra magazine on the floor at my feet, I ejected the clip and reached for it. Then something slammed into the side of my head, and the lights went out.

I WOKE UP TO find myself lying on the table we had eaten at, with four wild-eyed Iraqis standing over me. I didn't know how much time had passed, and no one would tell me. So far as I could tell, only one spoke any English, and all he would say was that my comrades were dead. When I protested that I was a journalist, they laughed and held up the M4 I'd used against them. A haze of unreality descended over me. My limbs went numb. My heart slammed against my sternum, yet I felt disconnected from my body. I don't know if my blood pressure was crashing or at stroke level, but I remember thinking, *If they cut my throat, it's going to spurt ten feet.*

I wanted to ask if Paul was really dead, but it seemed pointless. They didn't know who Paul was. And if he was alive, admitting I cared about him couldn't possibly help either of us. One of the Iraqis was shouting into his cell phone, and I got the idea that he meant to deliver me to someone higher up the chain. Or maybe that's what he was being ordered to do, while he preferred to kill me on the spot and film it with the iPhone one of his buddies had aimed at me.

They went back and forth about this for five minutes, and during that time I pissed myself. I don't like admitting that. I felt strangely ashamed in the moment. I remember thinking that John Wayne and Robert Mitchum never pissed themselves in this kind of situation. At least not in the movies. I felt I was regressing to infancy in the presence of men who already despised me. I suppose I was. I thought of my mother and how she would mourn me, her second son, who had also died before his time. I also wondered what my father would feel, hearing of my death while on assignment. Would he finally respect me? For dying in pursuit of our shared profession?

I never found out.

As I lay there grieving the brief flicker of warmth and light that had been my mortal existence, Paul and an ex-Ranger named Gary Inman hurled two flash-bang grenades into the room, blinding and deafening everyone in it. Five seconds later, every man but me had been shot through the head.

"CANYOUWALK?" Paul shouted in my ear.

"Paul?" I blubbered, tears streaming from my eyes.

He jerked me to my feet. *"Come on, Goose! MOVE!"*

"Where?" I gasped, staggering like a blind drunk.

"Grab my fucking belt and stay on my ass!"

I jammed my hand into his pants and hung on like a baby monkey clinging to its mother. The gunshots had triggered pandemonium in the house. No Iraqi was sure who was shooting or why. In the midst of this chaos, the skill set possessed by Paul and his buddy proved to be a force multiplier of astonishing lethality. I saw Paul shoot two men in the face while they tried to figure out who he was and where he'd come from. When another insurgent threw up his hands in defense, Paul shot him through his hands. Barely functioning, I hung on to Paul's belt as he swept through the house, killing all before him.

Inman kicked open a door that led into a narrow alley I remembered from our previous life, which seemed a thousand years ago. We darted left first, but a Toyota pickup with a bed-mounted machine gun shrieked to a stop just past the opening. That armed Toyota—known as a "technical"—would back up any second to finish us off.

Paul veered right and charged down the alley. We'd almost reached the other end when the technical opened up. Heavy-caliber bullets ripped into the masonry wall to my right, and either a bullet or stone shrapnel knocked down Gary Inman.

"LEAVE HIM!" Paul shouted, after a momentary glance.

I did.

The next street was hardly more than an alley itself. Paul started left again (as though he had a specific destination), but the familiar whine of an engine told us the Toyota was coming back to head us off. Paul skidded to a stop, jerked my arm, and led me back the other way.

Twenty yards up the alley, a Honda Accord had stopped, facing us. It sat idling, headlights off, as if waiting for us to commit to a move. The street was so narrow that we couldn't slip around the car. I tried to see through the dark windshield. A bearded man sat behind the wheel, and beside him I discerned what looked like a white hijab.

The squeal of brakes sounded behind us. *The Toyota—*

The driver of the Accord screamed, and the hijab beside him flared white. Then their windshield exploded in a hail of bullets. I whirled left. Paul had raised his M4 and was riddling the car. The sight of that windshield shattering into a hail of glass and blood paralyzed me.

"FOLLOW ME!" he shouted.

Paul ran right over the hood and roof of the Accord, his boots smashing dents in the holed metal, then dived onto the cobblestones beyond the trunk. I know I followed him, because I looked down through the missing windshield as I climbed over the car. Inside lay a man and woman. The man had jerked the woman into his lap to shield her with his body, but his effort had gone in vain. Both bodies were covered in bright red blood. The man's head had been smashed wide open by a bullet.

As I leaped off the trunk, I heard a child crying behind me. I started to turn back, but Paul dragged me to the ground as the technical opened up again. While the machine gun chewed the Honda into scrap metal, we belly-crawled to the end of that alley.

Waiting in the next street like a golden chariot was the Mamba belonging to Paul's Alpha team. Beside it a ShieldCorp contractor named Evans stood like a bored chauffeur. "Does this complete your party, sir?" he asked with a grin.

"We're it," Paul said. "Get the fuck out of Dodge. There's a technical right behind us."

"Rangers lead the way, motherfuckers!" yelled Evans, and then he shoved us inside and climbed in after us. Four ShieldCorp contractors carrying MP5 submachine guns grinned back at me.

I'll omit the details of our escape from Ramadi. There were more casualties, but lying inside that South African armor, the only thing I wanted to know was where Paul had been during those awful minutes I was a prisoner. As it turned out, while the insurgents overran the house, Paul and Inman had climbed over the edge of the roof and dropped down into a ten-inch gap between the ShieldCorp house and the one next door. Because the walls were so close together, they'd needed no ropes. They simply wedged themselves between the two buildings and slid halfway to the ground. Before long, they picked up what was going on inside the house.

While in this stone sandwich, Paul sent out an emergency text to the Alpha team, which was parked near one of the roadblocks. Upon hearing that Paul was in imminent danger of being killed, Alpha team used RPGs and their Mamba's machine gun to smash through the roadblock, then drove to the street Paul had named in a previous text. One thing I didn't learn until later was that Gary Inman had wanted to run straight for the Mamba. The German engineer was already dead—killed by a random shot during the final charge—so their mission was a failure. But Paul had insisted they go back for me. In fact, another ShieldCorp guy later confided to me that Paul told Inman if he didn't go back for me, Paul would shoot him and leave his corpse stuck between the buildings.

As dramatic as all that was, the defining moment occurred later, when I was writing about our experience. I was haunted by those Iraqis in that Accord. *Why didn't Paul just run right over the car without shooting the people inside?* I wondered. But of course I knew. They could have been insurgents themselves, and Paul wasn't going to take any chances. *But why not at least fire warning shots, to back the Accord down the alley?*

That's what his teams did during convoy escort duty. Again the primal voice in my head answered: *If Paul had done that, we'd have been trapped on the wrong side of the Accord when the technical opened fire . . .*

These justifications meant little in the dead of night when sleep escaped me. Because I was so haunted by that Iraqi child's cry, I wrote two drafts of the chapter about my rescue. One included the Accord, the other didn't. As the drop-dead date approached during the copyediting phase of my manuscript's production schedule, I heard that Paul and one of his teams had gotten into some trouble, this time in the Jamhori Quarter of Ramadi, during the *Second* Battle of Fallujah.

Paul had a third team operating by then: Sierra Charlie. Apparently, Charlie team—with Paul along—had gotten pinned down during a protective detail, and things got very hot. Paul called in the Little Bird for evac, but the helicopter took so much fire that it had to peel off. Left on its own, the ShieldCorp unit had gone into offensive mode and shot its way out of the neighborhood. It went through some houses to do so—several contiguous structures—and civilians were killed. A fire had broken out as well, which caused more casualties.

I could see how it happened. If Paul had lost another VIP principal under his protection—and brought out nothing but the man's passport and wedding ring, as he had with the German engineer—his business would have dried up overnight. But even the military officers assigned to quietly investigate the incident agreed that Paul's unit had shot people without cause. Two kids were seriously wounded. One lost a leg. Complaints were filed, legal action threatened. The Hague was mentioned. A couple of generals wanted Paul tried as an example to all "cowboy contractors." But because there had been a long series of kidnappings and executions in the wake of the first Fallujah operation, the Pentagon wasn't feeling too charitable toward the Iraqis just then. Still, Paul's unit had made a hell of a mess.

Given what was at stake for Paul, I decided to omit the Honda Accord from my public retelling of the night of April 8 in Ramadi. I didn't lie to myself about what I was doing. Without the Accord incident, it was a different story. It wasn't reality. But it would become history. With that omission, I edited the truth into something like an Arnold Schwarzenegger movie, and I never forgave myself for it. When Hollywood came calling five months later, I declined to option my book. That was my self-inflicted punishment, meager as it may seem now. I neither wanted nor deserved that money. That said, I did not turn down the Pulitzer Prize I won for the same book, which covered all my time in Afghanistan as well as Iraq. And I have reaped untold benefits from that Pulitzer. Every time I'm introduced on television, they mention it. In every bio in every pamphlet handed out before I give a speech for $20,000 or $30,000, that Pulitzer leads my list of accomplishments. For years I've prayed to win another, to wipe the shadow of false pretense from my life. But while I've made the list of finalists twice more, I've never again won the award.

Paul's outcome was very different. He wasn't tried or officially punished for any action he took on the day he and his men shot their way out of the Jamhori Quarter. But he was ordered by Joint Task Force command to leave Iraq, and ShieldCorp had all its government contracts canceled. Worse, Paul was personally barred by both the State Department and the Pentagon from returning to either Afghanistan or Iraq. My book made him a hero to a lot of people, but less than a year after he saved my life, Paul watched his business condemned to oblivion. He returned to Bienville, Mississippi, to work for his father, and within three months, he relapsed into heavy drinking.

Thirteen years later, I would return to Bienville and start sleeping with his wife. It sounds low, I know—perhaps unforgivable to some. But here's the thing: I loved Jet first. She loved me first. More to the point, I'm not sure Paul ever loved her. He *wanted* her, sure, but that's a different thing. I wouldn't be alive today if Paul had not gone back into that house to save me. And I would probably be dead if he hadn't shot those people in the Honda Accord. But there's also this: if I had written the truth about the people in that Accord in my book—while the Pentagon was making up its mind about ShieldCorp's bloody escape from Jamhori—then Paul might have gone to federal prison for the second incident, and the fame that my book brought him as a fearless warrior would have been forever tainted.

The way I figured it, we were even.

CHAPTER 17

WHEN I FIRST moved back to Bienville from Washington, I rented an apartment downtown, just a short walk from the *Watchman* building. I knew I couldn't live in my parents' house, and there was nothing to rent in their neighborhood. They're still in the tract house Adam and I grew up in, a 1950s ranch-style with pleasing touches of midcentury modern, set in a wooded subdivision that was filled with kids when I was growing up but is now inhabited by old people, many widows living alone.

The downtown apartment worked well until Jet and I started sleeping together. After that, it was too risky. I needed a secluded refuge that could give us real privacy while we worked out what the future was going to look like for us. To that end, I bought an old farmhouse on six isolated acres east of town. The place had sat on the market for two years. Only fifteen minutes from downtown, it's bounded by woods on all sides, and there's only one entrance by road.

It was 2:50 when I reached home after my raid on Buck's rental house. Jet had set our rendezvous at three, but because she must evade not only her husband but also anyone else she might run into before meeting me, it's not uncommon for her to be an hour late. As soon as I walked in, I called Nadine Sullivan and told her I would love to attend the party on the roof of the Aurora, if she would still have me. Nadine replied that she was glad to have the company and was looking forward to it. Then I opened a Heineken and walked out to my back patio, which looks onto four acres of woods.

Lying back on a teak steamer chaise, I checked my email on my iPhone. I felt guilty that I wasn't rifling through Buck's files and maps without delay, but given that I hadn't found any bones at the rental house, I didn't think the task was urgent. There would be time to go through the stuff after Jet left and before the party. I did watch Denny Allman's edited drone video, which was a masterpiece featuring superimposed GPS coordinates, and I made a note to pay Denny well for that footage. I wasn't sure what I could do with it, other than go out to the mill site in the middle of the night and risk being killed to try to unearth evidence that an army of technicians would be unlikely to find. Publishing the video to the *Watchman*'s website might be an option, but the video on its own proved little. I took another swallow of Heineken and watched the tree line.

The first sign I usually see is Jet walking out of the shadows beneath those trees, sixty yards away. A few times she has driven her car across the grass and right up to the patio, but leaving her car visible beside my house is too dangerous, even with my security gate. Though only Jet and I know the code required to open the gate, a single electrical glitch could allow a mailman or UPS driver to ride up to the house and recognize Jet's Volvo. When it comes to risk, we've pushed the envelope a few times, but in general we've worked hard to eliminate any chance of disaster.

That's the only way we're going to get what we want.

Most extramarital affairs begin with the understanding that they're not going anywhere. This pragmatic truth isn't generally stated, but both parties—even first-timers—usually grasp the unwritten rules of the game. *We're not in this to blow up our families.* They may be deluding themselves, of course. One may be acting out of desperation, grabbing for a ripcord to escape a marriage they've become convinced is a trap. Another might have fallen truly in love, or at least under the grip of romantic delusion, which becomes the equivalent of a ticking bomb.

Jet and I are different. We're not playing a game. We wanted each other long before I moved back to Bienville, and not simply to consummate the desire that had gone unfulfilled for so long. The love that bloomed when we were kids had survived a nearly thirty-year separation during which we were alone together only twice. If I were self-indulgent, I might call us star-crossed lovers, but the truth is much simpler:

I was stupid.

The first time I saw Jet alone after I left Bienville for UVA was during her senior year of college. She was finishing a year early at Millsaps, a small liberal arts college in Jackson, Mississippi, and she'd flown up to Washington to tour Georgetown Law School. Without telling anyone—including me—she made a quick side trip to Charlottesville. We spent the whole day together, and we slept together that night. Only in the morning did she tell me that she'd been seeing Paul on and off since he'd gotten back from Ranger duty in Somalia. This revelation—along with the shaved-to-stubble pubic hair that greeted me when she wriggled out of her pants—told me that much had changed in her life. I felt sure the grooming choice was Paul's preference, though she denied it.

I had no right to be angry. When I left Mississippi, I left for good. Except for a few Thanksgivings and Christmases, I hadn't been home. Paul, on the other hand, had left the army and was working for his father, only forty miles from Millsaps. When I asked Jet what the chances were that she would choose Georgetown, she told me zero—she couldn't afford it. She'd only come up to see me. She would be entering Ole Miss Law School in the fall.

After that, she and Paul saw each other in a hit-or-miss fashion, at least for some years. But after Jet got her law degree, she took a job with a firm in New Orleans, and they eventually got back together for real. Eight years after our UVA rendezvous, in 2001, she called me from the Fairmont Hotel in Washington, D.C., where she was attending a National Bar Association conference. I met her in a restaurant a few blocks from the hotel, and this time she was straight with me about why she'd come. She'd been dating Paul exclusively for two years, and she sensed that he was about to propose marriage. Before that happened, she wanted to give me a chance to say anything that I might feel needed to be said.

This pragmatic offer stunned me. I was in no position to ask her not to marry Paul. I'd taken a leave of absence from the *Post* to get a master's in international relations from Georgetown. I was also dating one of my professors, a French economics expert named Chloe Denard. But it was less my relationship with Chloe that kept me from admitting my feelings for Jet than my resentment at how close Jet had gotten to Paul. If she could sleep with Paul for years without calling me, why the hell was she coming to see me only days before he proposed to her?

I didn't say that to her, of course. Too many years had passed without me facing hard truths about myself. So I talked around the truth, and she let me. The unspoken fact was that I'd always loved her, and I'd let the gulf between my father and me keep me a thousand miles away from her for eleven years. Jet understood that, I think. But she left it unspoken, too. We drank a lot of wine, and we slept together for the second time in a decade. That one night was better than all the nights I had slept with Chloe Denard, or any other woman.

I didn't tell Jet that, either.

She married Paul six months later, shortly before 9/11. I was invited to the wedding, but I didn't attend. After I returned from Iraq in 2004, and The Hague was considering charging Paul and his fellow ShieldCorp contractors with war crimes, she and I spoke privately again. Jet was deeply upset, not only because of Paul's legal jeopardy, but also because she was afraid that he and his men had really murdered civilians. On top of this, Paul had become depressed and was drinking heavily. She feared he might be suicidal. She wanted my best guess as to whether Paul and his men were guilty. She also wanted to know about my experiences with ShieldCorp in Ramadi.

As I'd done in one draft of the manuscript by that time, I omitted the story of the bullet-riddled Honda from my description of Paul's rescue. I couldn't see that any benefit would result from telling her the truth, other than driving her away from her husband. And by then I didn't see that as a positive. I'd gotten engaged to Molly McGeary two weeks after returning from Ramadi, and we were set to be married three months later. Hearing the strain in Jet's voice probably weighed heavily in my decision to omit the Accord story from my book. I've never told Paul that. Sometimes I wish I had. In any case, he managed to escape prosecution, and their lives moved on.

I had no contact with them for the next thirteen years, unless you count a sympathy card I got after my son drowned. Dad was diagnosed with Parkinson's in 2010, but he was angry and defensive about it, and Mom thought I should let her try to handle him alone as long as possible. His initial disease progression was slow, so it was 2016 before I started making trips back to Mississippi. And it was only after his rapid slide began in 2017 that my trips became regular. I was bound to run into Jet eventually, but it didn't happen until Christmas 2017. Five months ago.

Last Christmas Eve, I tried to have a frank discussion with Dad about his medical prognosis. I also tried to talk to him about the future of the *Watchman,* which carried enormous debt and was losing more money every month. Dad was combative, and he might have gotten violent if I hadn't decided to take a break and buy Mom a Christmas present while she tried to settle him down. I was standing in the checkout line at Dillard's department store (with an expensive glass tub of moisturizer in my hand) when Jet tapped me on the shoulder, then laughed out loud when I turned and became a cartoon caricature of surprise.

Her eleven-year-old son, Kevin, stood at her side. The boy was handsome, like his father and grandfather (and his asshole cousins). The Matheson traits ran deeply in him. He had the strong jaw and high cheekbones, the vaguely Aryan look. But Jet had left her mark in his skin, which was darker than Paul's had ever been, and in his eyes, which were large and brown. Also, Kevin was tall for eleven, which I suspected had come more from Jet than from Paul.

Jet herself amazed me. Buck's description of her as an Arabic Emmylou Harris had proved prescient; she'd aged every bit as gracefully as the singer. She was forty-five then, but except for a few tiny lines around her eyes and mouth, slightly wider hips, and a heavier bosom, she could have been the girl I spent the summer riding bikes with in 1986. We traded small talk while we checked out, but then she told Kevin to go look for some new tennis shoes. As soon as the boy vanished, her mask slipped. She asked about my father again, and I gave her a more honest assessment. Then I asked how she was really doing.

"It's hard," she said softly, averting her eyes. "Paul's been unhappy for a long time."

"Unhappy with what? Life? You? What?"

"All the above." Then she looked back at me. "How are *you* really doing? I wrote you a long letter after . . . you know. But I didn't mail it. It was too personal."

She meant my son's death, I supposed. I waved my hand to move the conversation along.

"So you're divorced," she said.

"Mm-hm."

"And very popular, I'm sure. Are you seeing anyone?"

I shrugged. "There's somebody."

She forced a smile then. "Serious?"

The silence that followed this question was one of the most pregnant moments of my life. "Define serious."

She held up her left hand and tapped her wedding ring with her painted thumbnail.

"No," I said. "Not soon, anyway. Your son looks really great, by the way," I told her, trying to change the subject. "He looks like you."

"Oh, he's something. Paul and Max already have him playing every sport ever invented. They send him off to special camps, and he's on a traveling baseball team. I think he's too young for all that."

"He is a Matheson," I pointed out.

She let out a long sigh. "About three-quarters Matheson, I'd say. I may have a quarter of him. That's what keeps me sane."

In that moment I saw the deep pain working inside her. "Do you have a friend?" I asked. "A good one?"

She gave me a wistful smile. "Not really. Not a close one. You know me. Too private."

"Does Paul realize how unhappy you are?"

"If so, he doesn't do anything to help. I think he knows he can't. Not where it counts. His mother's been kind to me. Sally. She has some sense of the position I'm in. Being Max's wife all these years had to be tough. She's empathetic. But the rest of them, Max and their redneck cousins from Jackson—"

"I remember the cousins," I said, thinking of the night we climbed the electrical tower.

"They were there when Adam drowned, weren't they?" she asked. "In the river?"

I nodded, forcing my mind away from Dooley and Trey Matheson.

"So will you be coming down more often? To help take care of your dad?"

"I think so. More to help with the paper, really. It's been going down fast."

"I'm sorry. It has gotten a little . . . rickety. But I'm not sorry to hear I might see more of you."

And there it was.

After that day, I knew that if I came back to Bienville, Jet would come to me. Even if I didn't ask her to. Even if we resisted consummation, fate would unfold in that direction. And from that moment, this knowledge began to work on me. I felt like Jay Gatsby staring at the stupid green light across the bay. The truth I had denied for decades finally rose to the surface and would not be denied any longer.

I had wanted her for so long. Even during the first year of my marriage, when my new wife filled most of my conscious mind, a faintly glowing anima remained in the dark chamber where Jordan Elat Talal had resided since I was fourteen years old. The farthest I ever got from Jet was probably the two years that my son was alive. Baby Adam soothed the unquiet ghosts of my youth, stilled the restless desire that no other woman but Jet had quenched.

But after he died, my world emptied out, as though all life had been poured from it. I became a ghost myself, moving noiselessly through my days, hardly noticed, noticing nothing. To my surprise, as I retreated inward, I discovered that the inmost chamber of my mind still had its tenant. Even more surprising, that chamber held warmth as well as memories, and life was so cold then that I was glad to huddle inside it. Eventually, my work brought me back to the world. Yet somehow, during every relationship I pursued, Jet was always there, a silent measuring stick for every woman I got close to.

Yet I never reached toward her. Before marrying Paul, she had made two pilgrimages north to try to save me from myself—and to save herself from compromise. Both times, I let pride stop me from seizing the chance. I'd never seen myself as a passive person, but after feeling the surge of life that hit me in that Christmas checkout line, I realized that my lack of initiative with Jet was probably a clue to why I'd spent my life reporting the news rather than making it.

By the time I got back to Washington after that Christmas trip, I'd resolved to move back to Bienville. I had a hell of a rationalization to obscure my baser motive. Trying to both care for Dad and run the *Watchman* had worn my mother down to a shadow of herself. If my brother had been alive, he would have moved home at least a year earlier. In fact, Adam probably would have moved home as soon as

Dad was diagnosed. But I've never had Adam's impulse for sacrifice. Even with the situation critical, the decision was tough for me. To leave Washington for an extended period, I would have to unwind my TV deal with MSNBC and take a leave of absence from the *Post*. The sources I'd cultivated over decades—who were paying off in spades during the Trump administration—I would have to pass off to trusted colleagues and, in one case, to a competitor. With my career plugged into the 220-volt main line, I was going to have to short-circuit my professional dream, probably for months and maybe a year. I might never regain that kind of juice again. But I had to do it. *For my mother,* I told myself.

Jet and I held out for two months after I arrived. During that time, I learned just how she'd kept herself busy—and sane—in our old hometown. Despite marrying into money, she had diligently practiced law since her return, usually representing underdogs against corporate employers or insurance companies. She'd also founded the most successful charter school in Mississippi. And not a typical one. Reliant Charter was no public school for white kids, but rather a highly effective institution that was being used as a model by three other Southern states.

The first time Jet and I were alone after my return, I was interviewing her about a proposed expansion at Reliant. As she faced me across my father's desk at the *Watchman,* we acted out a scene of platonic friendship, avoiding eye contact and blushing whenever other people walked into the room. The second time—when she came over for a follow-up story two weeks later—it was in the same office, but later in the day. The paper was a little quieter. After an awkward, stammering couple of minutes, Jet turned and locked my door, then walked around my desk and kissed me.

I kissed her back. The voices from the newsroom outside faded. Thirty seconds later, I unbuttoned her blouse and began kissing her breasts. With every second that passed, a year fell away. A low purling sound came from her throat, and she took hold of my hand and pressed it between her legs. Her slacks were soaked through. In that moment we were fourteen years old again, standing in the Weldons' barn. My office ceased to exist. I slid my hand up, then down under her waistband, and a familiar shock went through me. There was the coarse, abundant hair I remembered from the barn and from senior year. I pushed my fingers into the thick tangle and squeezed, pulling the hair away from her skin.

"I grew it out for you," she whispered.

"When did you start?"

She bit my earlobe and grabbed my belt buckle. "That night at the department store. Last Christmas."

After that, we were lost. Since that afternoon, we've hardly gone a day without making love. I let my Washington connections wither to nothing—on both the professional and romantic fronts—while Jet began exploring the practical realities of divorce. The problem, as is so often the case in Bienville, is the Poker Club. Divorces and child custody decisions in Mississippi fall under the jurisdiction of chancery judges. Tenisaw County has two. And the chance of Max Matheson allowing either one to grant Jet the right to move his grandson to D.C. is zero. Jet is a brilliant attorney, but even she has found no way to cut the knot that binds her to her old life.

At a quarter till four, Jet walks out of my woods with her usual long-limbed grace. She's no longer wearing the sundress she had on earlier, but dark slacks and a white blouse. I'm not sure at first whether she realizes I'm watching her from the patio. The steamer chaise sits lower than my other chairs, which probably does a lot to conceal me. But she knows. She announces this by unbuttoning her blouse as she crosses the grass, then shrugging it off her shoulders and letting it fall as she walks on. Ten steps farther across the freshly mown field, her bra drops to the ground. I assumed she would show up in a very different mood, ready to comfort me for the loss of Buck and discuss the implications of Paul's suspicion. She may do that yet. But if so, she means to do it naked. By the time she's ten yards from the patio, she's wearing nothing but the silver pendant necklace and sapphire earrings I saw at the groundbreaking.

"Sorry I'm late," she says, standing over the chaise with an expression I cannot read. "I had a couple of issues."

"It's okay," I reply, starting to get up.

She holds up one long-fingered hand in a *stop* gesture. "Did I make a mistake with my clothes?"

I shake my head, reach up with my right hand.

Instead of taking it, she turns away, cups the cheeks of her bottom in each hand, and pulls them apart. The sight is shockingly erotic. "Are you going to invite me to sit down?" she asks.

"Please sit down."

She looks back over her shoulder and smiles at last. "Why don't you get those pants off first?"

CHAPTER 18

TEN MINUTES AGO, Jet sat astride me on the steamer chaise and worked with focused intensity, reaching her first release in two minutes. Then, with barely a pause, she started again, the second time making sure that I fell into rhythm with her, so that I would finish when she did. A sheen of sweat shone on her dark chest, and her eyes dilated as they sometimes do, losing focus as she approached her second orgasm. Her hands gripped my shoulders, her nails dug painfully into the skin, but I made no sound of complaint.

Afterward, she fell forward and nestled her face in my neck without speaking. Given Buck's murder, this isn't what I'd expected of our first few minutes alone, but it's what I needed. Talking to Quinn took a lot out of me, and the last thing I wanted from Jet was more talk. For her part, carrying on an affair in her hometown is exhausting. Each rendezvous requires a carefully planned escape from the tyranny of routine, involving excuses, outright lies, occasional car changes, and constant vigilance. Unexpected crises like Buck's murder only add to the burden. But why talk about it? Words become superfluous when every cell in your body is telling you to leap into the frantic fusion of sex and discharge all your anxiety in one frenzied rush.

After breathing into my neck for a couple of minutes, she says, "Are you really okay?"

"I'm kind of freaked out, honestly."

"Because of Buck? Or Paul?"

"Both. But seeing Buck pulled out of that river started it."

She flattens her hands on the frame of the chaise and presses herself up far enough to look into my eyes. "You saw his body?"

I nod.

"Bad?"

"Bad enough."

She lowers her head and kisses my forehead. "I never told you this, but when Paul and I first moved back to Bienville, I ran into Buck one day at LaSalle Park. We sat on a bench and talked for a while, just him and me. This was before I'd had Kevin. In his shy and courtly way, Buck told me that he'd always believed you and I would end up together."

"What did you say?"

"I told him that I'd always loved you, but it just wasn't in the stars." Jet laughs, her eyes shining. "How's that for cliché?"

"I guess Buck was right after all."

"You bet your ass he was. And I've never been happier to be wrong."

"I thought you were never wrong."

She pinches the soft flesh inside my left thigh, and I curse in pain. Before I can pay her back, she flips off the chaise and scrambles to her feet.

"Shouldn't we talk about Paul and your fight?" I ask.

"We will. I need to pee. Do you want me to come back out here?"

"No, I'll come with you."

I follow her to the master bathroom, meaning to tease her a little, but as we walk down the narrow hallway, I see her transitioning from postcoital languor to purposeful intent. It's in the straightness of her back, the level set of her shoulders. She's got murder on her mind now.

My back bathroom is larger than what usually comes with an older house. The elderly couple who owned the place before me expanded the room so that the husband, who was wheelchair-bound when I met him, could shower in it. As I pick up a couple of stray socks, Jet begins urinating behind the small partition that shields the commode.

"Hey," she calls. "You feel like putting on some coffee? It's going to be a long night with that party."

"Sure."

I pull on jeans and a T-shirt, then walk back to the kitchen and pop a K-Cup into the Keurig. For the first time since this morning, the weight of Buck's loss has lifted slightly from my shoulders. Spending myself in Jet has reset my neurotransmitters, at least for the moment. Had I been able to see her alone this morning, I might not have been sucked into the whirlpool of flashbacks that Buck's death triggered.

A thin stream of coffee begins to drip from the Keurig, and the welcome scent fills the kitchen. I wonder at her ability to heal me this way. For three months I have felt this peace, after decades of yearning for her. What is the essence of that connection? A thirty-year-old fold in my cerebral cortex? Is the first neural imprinting of love and sex so deep that nothing ever supplants it? Like the music you listened to during those years? No matter how I analyze it, this reality remains: being with Jet is a necessity, an involuntary compulsion like breathing. Except that I managed to live without her, with only the memory of air, for nearly three decades. I held my breath and pretended to live. Somehow, the memory of this woman sustained me, even through my grief over my son. Now that I have her once more, I don't ever want to stop breathing again.

Jet's sock feet hiss on the hardwood of the hallway. Wearing my ancient orange Cavaliers T-shirt, she pads over to me, kisses my shoulder, then leans back on the kitchen island to wait for her coffee.

"Three things," she says. "First, Paul asked me about last Thursday."

I shake my head blankly. "Last Thursday?"

"Yesterday he ran into Claire Maloney, who I was supposed to have run with last Thursday. I was out here, of course. Claire's kind of ditzy—that's why I used her for my excuse—so I got away with it. But Paul noted the disconnect. I realized I had really pushed the envelope."

"Are you sure he believed you?"

"I think so. But that wasn't all."

My mouth goes dry.

"Breathe," she says, looking up at me. "The second thing was Josh, which is just ridiculous. Paul didn't have any specific reason to suspect Josh. I think he's just picked up that I've emotionally checked out of the marriage, and he knows I spend hours a day with Josh—even out of town. So he's the first target of suspicion."

"You said he mentioned me."

She shifts uncomfortably. "Yeah. This is the sticky part."

"Tell me!"

"He asked why I'd grown my pubic hair back all of a sudden."

"All of a sudden? Didn't you grow it out before I moved back?"

"Just before. So I've had it back for six months. But I kept it shaved for twenty years. From Paul's point of view, that's sudden."

"How long has Josh worked for you?"

"Five months. I hired him in January."

"Okay." I think about this.

"It gets worse. Paul associates you with me being natural down there."

"Why?"

"Because he's the one who likes it bare. And at some point back in the mists of time, I admitted to him that you liked it the other way."

"Jesus."

"I know, it was stupid. But he was always asking me about us, so I told him to get him off my back. I couldn't possibly have foreseen that a day like this would come."

I'm trying to get my mind around Paul spending hours obsessing about this. "So he thinks you might have grown your bush back for me."

She shrugs. "I did. So, sure, he's thinking that. He's in paranoid mode."

"We're so screwed."

The tension in Jet's face is plain. "It's not ideal."

"Far from it."

"Hey, the coffee's ready." She takes a painted mug from the Keurig and tries a scalding sip. "There's something else," she says, sucking air across her lips.

"What?"

"My mother-in-law's acting weird."

"Sally?"

"She is my only mother-in-law."

Sally Matheson is a Bienville native and archetypal Southern belle. One of the town's great mysteries is how a saint like Sally ever stayed married to Max. "What did Sally do?"

"She asked to talk to me today, in private. I'd gone by her house to drop Kevin off. He was supposed to do some batting practice with Max on the machine. After he got out of the car, Sally asked if I had time to come in. I saw something in her eyes—something off, I don't know what. But she gets that look when there's some serious family matter that needs dealing with. Anyway, I was worried she might have heard something about you and me."

"What did you do?"

"I went in, of course." Jet takes another careful sip of coffee. "Sally fixed some tea. We were trying to find an excuse to get Kevin out of the kitchen when Max called and said some famous baseball player had shown up down at College Sports. He asked if I could run Kevin down there to meet him. Kev got all excited, but I told Sally we could wait ten minutes. I wanted to know what was worrying her. But she waved me off and said to take Kevin right down to the store. We could talk another time."

"That's it?"

Jet arches her eyebrows. "It may not sound like much, but I know Sally. She doesn't ask for tête-à-têtes unless it's important."

"What do you think it was?"

Jet takes a deep breath, exhales slowly. "I'm worried someone busted us without our knowing, then went to her about it."

My heart kicks again. "How careful were you coming out here today? You said you had issues."

"Just logistical complications. Nothing to do with Paul." She takes the K-Cup out of the Keurig and drops it in the trash can under the sink. "I know for sure he's out at the baseball field right now with Kevin and the team."

I sigh with relief. "Okay. But I'd better not go to that party tonight."

"The Aurora party? Were you invited?"

"No. But Nadine Sullivan asked me to be her plus-one."

Jet's eyes flicker with interest. "Really. You told her you'd go with her?"

"I did, actually. Are you okay with that?"

"Well . . . sure. I'm just surprised."

"Why? I thought it was good cover. I want to look over the Poker Club guys, see how they're acting after Buck's death. Maybe question them a little bit."

Jet is giving me a sidelong look. After a few seconds, she clucks her tongue and says, "You're right. You showing up with Nadine could be the best possible move. She's a credible love interest for you."

This makes me laugh. "What does that mean? One who can compete with you?"

"You tell me."

"Are you jealous? Seriously?"

She looks back at me for a while without speaking. In the dim light of the kitchen, her dark eyes appear luminous. Against her brown skin, her sapphire earrings look like stones taken from the eyes of some idol in a distant land. Just as I feel the impulse to reach under her T-shirt, I wonder whether she bought the earrings herself or if Paul dropped ten grand on them one night while surfing the web.

"What are you thinking?" she asks, reaching for the button of my jeans.

"Maybe you should head on home. Just to be safe."

Her unblinking gaze deepens. "You say that like I won't be coming back for a while."

I'd like to argue with her, but the idea that Paul might know about us has profoundly altered my view of our situation.

"If Paul knows," she says, "I'll know it tonight. I'll feel it."

"When he throws you off the roof of the Aurora?"

"Let's hope not." She drinks a big swallow of coffee, then looks toward the back door. "I bought new burner phones at Walmart. They're in my pants, out in the yard."

Now I remember her clothes strewn across the grass. "You paid cash?"

Her eyes say, *Do you think I'm an idiot?* But her mouth says, "Of course."

"Jet . . . we can't keep doing this. Not with Paul acting paranoid. If he's looking for clues, he's going to find them. Just you peeling away from your normal life every day is dangerous."

"Not while they're at baseball practice."

"Paul could get someone else to follow you easily. He's got dozens of employees."

"I know. Are you really saying we need to stay separate for a while? Because that will *suck*."

"I'm saying more than that."

Fear flashes in her eyes, but she waits for me to go on.

"Our whole plan—me going back to D.C. first, then you working toward divorce—that's just not realistic anymore. No matter how much we try to delay or ease the pain, there's never going to be a good time to tell Paul. Whether I'm in Bienville or D.C. doesn't make much difference."

"I think you're wrong about that. Plus, the issue isn't simply divorce."

I take hold of her arms. "It's custody, I know. But this is the flaw we're ignoring. You were always going to hit the wall of Max's control over the chancery court. How the hell can you ever really hope to get custody of Kevin?"

She looks at the floor and sighs heavily, and I worry that I've pushed her too far. But then she looks up with a new light in her eyes. "I've been working on that," she says cryptically.

"What do you mean?"

"I don't want to talk about it yet. Let's just say I've focused my not inconsiderable abilities on finding a way to neutralize Max's power."

"The whole Poker Club's power? Or just Max's?"

"Just Max. If I discredited him with the club, they wouldn't lift a finger to interfere in my divorce."

"Why won't you tell me what this involves?"

"Because it's a little dangerous. And it's not strictly legal. I'm still working on the logistics. I just want you to know that I'm not living in a dream world. I know what the obstacle to our being together is, and I intend to remove it."

Pushing her isn't going to get me the answers I want.

"I hate to ask this at this moment," she says, "but how is your father doing?"

"A little worse, actually. His heart, not his Parkinson's. But there's no way to predict how he's going to do in the short run."

"Please don't get the wrong idea," she says. "I don't want Duncan to die at all. And if my little project works out, my divorce won't depend on you going back to Washington first."

"You're starting to piss me off now. Giving me hope, but not being specific."

She pops up on her tiptoes and kisses my mouth. "I like to promise small, then overdeliver." She bites my bottom lip, then gives my groin a firm squeeze. "You want to go again?" She looks at her watch. "Five minutes or less. I can bend over the counter."

As much as I would like to, I want to question her further before she leaves. "We haven't talked about Buck."

"I'm listening."

I quickly catch her up on the temp pathologist and rushed autopsy. "I'd say 'accidental death' has already been bought and paid for."

"Where'd you get that?" she asks.

"The coroner. Byron Ellis. He also told me he found reddish-orange brick dust in Buck's skull wound. One of those old Natchez bricks. He's going on the record in tomorrow's paper."

"Wow. That'll ring some alarm bells downtown. What's the significance of the Natchez brick?"

"There aren't any at Lafitte's Den. But there are plenty out at the mill site. The old electroplating factory was built from them. Byron and I think somebody caught Buck out there digging last night and killed him."

Jet bites her lip as she races through mental scenarios. "I noticed that earthmoving equipment starting up as I left the site today. Were they destroying evidence?"

"Probably."

"Should we go out there tonight and see what we can find?"

"How the hell would you do that? Can you get away from the house?"

She sighs in frustration. "Not tonight. Too late to cook up a business trip."

"I've got some maps Buck made, also some drone footage that shows where he was probably digging. I'd like to go out there, but there could still be guards. Although Quinn says Buck told her there were none posted last night."

"Too dangerous," she says, squeezing my left hand. "You're worried about my clothes being outside, aren't you?"

"I don't know why, considering we're locked behind the gate. But yeah, it's on my mind."

She tilts her head toward the door, and we walk outside together. Her clothes lie like little islands in the green sea of grass between the patio and the woods. Any other day I would laugh, but not today.

"Killing Buck was a big step," she says, stopping at the edge of the patio. "I think there's something really dark behind that paper mill deal. Really dirty."

"Dirtier than the corruption we already suspect?"

She nods. "Drop all lesser questions about the mill deal and ask the big one: Why did Azure Dragon come here? If I'd been on their site selection committee, I'd have picked six other cities before Bienville. Maybe ten."

"The city and the state sweetened the hell out of their offer."

"Not enough to top Arkansas and Alabama."

She has a point. "They're routing I-14 through here, pretty much solely for Azure Dragon. That's big, Jet."

"The public schools are still crap."

"Not your charter school."

"Which only handles a fraction of the city's students." She shakes her head, and I sense her mind churning. "I'm telling you, there's something rotten at the core of this. Not just garden-variety graft, or even mega-graft. Something so big they couldn't risk Buck causing delays or bringing in state authorities. And I'm going to find out what it is." She clicks her tongue three times fast, then looks out over the backyard. "Let's get those new phones. I need to go."

I catch hold of her arm before she can start walking. "Hang on. Say you do that. Say we go out there tonight and find Indian bones, or even evidence that Buck was murdered for threatening the mill. But to use it, we have to blow up the paper mill deal. Do we do that?"

She looks at me like I've lost my mind. "Isn't that what we've been trying to do all along? Get the bastards who rule this town by breaking whatever laws it suits them to break?"

"Of course. But if the town loses the mill, the dominoes will start to fall. The new interstate, the bridge. A lot of people who've done nothing wrong will be hurt badly. Some we know, others we don't."

"Is this you talking, or Nadine?"

"She did pose the question this morning."

Jet gives me a penetrating look before answering. "You're right about the cost. But we won't be living here, so it's not our problem. And if they murdered Buck, then I say, 'Let justice be done, though the heavens fall.'"

This woman was born to be a prosecutor. "You know, we usually talk about the Poker Club like a monolithic entity. I want you to break them down for me. Tell me who's the most dangerous."

"How do you mean? Arthur Pine's dangerous, but only in a courtroom, not a dark alley."

"I'm talking about violence. Like killing Buck. Which members might go that far, or have the connections to have someone else do it for them?"

Jet looks at her watch again. "Let's talk while we walk. Prepping for that party might make Paul leave practice early."

She starts across the grass, and I have to hurry to catch up.

"Only nine of the Poker Club's twelve members are really active," she explains. "Of those, I'd say Tommy Russo is the most violent. He's from a Jersey mob family, and I've heard some sick stories about him."

"Such as?"

"His brother fed two guys into a wood chipper in Voorhees State Park. While they were alive. Tommy was supposedly there."

"That sounds like an urban legend."

Jet bends and hooks her panties off the grass with one finger. "Tommy's brother fled the country before the FBI could arrest him for it. Tommy also told Max that he'd pushed an informant out of a Beechcraft once."

"Jesus. Max told you that?"

Jet shakes her head. "He told Paul. Paul told me one night when he was drunk."

I guess I shouldn't be surprised that a casino owner has murder in his past. Still, when I think of Tommy walking along the Port Road in his expensive suit, it's hard to picture him shoving a guy out of an airplane. "Who else?"

Jet stops and picks her pants up off the grass. "Wyatt Cash."

"Wyatt? Really?"

She steps into her panties and pulls them up, then does the same with her slacks, wriggling them over her hips, then zipping them tight. "Wyatt's not just a hunter, he's a military groupie. He uses former Special Forces soldiers as paid endorsers for his hunting gear."

"Great. Who else?"

She looks into my eyes. "Max, of course."

"No shit. I would have put Max at the top of the list. He did some bad stuff in Vietnam."

"I forgot. He used to brag to his players, didn't he? I don't even want to think about it. Oh, and there's Paul, of course."

"Paul's not a member of the club."

"He's the heir apparent to Max's seat. And he's tied inextricably into a lot of Max's investments, not to mention the lumber company."

"Paul liked Buck," I say, even as a disturbing thought rises in my mind.

"He did," Jet agrees. "Paul always contributed to his causes, the Indian powwows and stuff. On the other hand, business is business. And Paul has the connections to farm out violence if he wants to."

"ShieldCorp?"

She nods and leads me toward her bra. "He stays in contact with all those guys."

"Jet, does it strike you as strange that Paul suddenly tells me he's suspicious about you having an affair within hours of Buck dying?"

This question sends her into that state where her mind is working at a speed beyond my capacity. "Because you're the most likely to dig deep into his death," she says. "He throws out a shiny object to distract you."

"Right."

"For him to expect that to work, he'd have to know you and I are in fact having an affair."

"What if he does know?"

She shakes her head, but in her eyes I see a shadow of doubt. Still looking concerned, she bends to pick up her bra, then slips her left arm into the strap. "You want a last look before they're gone?"

"Don't need one. They've been imprinted on my mind since I was fourteen."

She gives me an appreciative smile. "They're a little different now. Gravity sucks."

I look down at her breasts, at the dark nipples that have captivated me since I was a boy. "Not so different."

"White lies." She fastens the bra, then skips ten feet ahead of me to retrieve her blouse. After she buttons it, she reaches into her pants pocket and takes out a nondescript black cell phone.

"This one's yours. The number to mine is already programmed on speed dial."

"When did you do that?" I ask, taking the phone from her.

"Sitting at red lights on my way out. I've gotten pretty good at it."

Just like everything else. "About tonight," I say hesitantly. "The party."

"What?"

"We need to do the best acting of our lives. No secret touches, no freighted glances, no double entendres—not even if we pass each other in an empty hallway."

"You think you need to tell me that?"

My warning obviously irritated her. "I wouldn't usually. But something changed today. I feel like the world has suddenly spun off track. It isn't just Buck, or even Paul. This whole day, memories have been flooding over me, things I haven't thought about for years."

Her expression softens. "Me too, a little bit. But all Paul has on his mind right now is Jerry Lee Lewis. So relax. You know I'm not going to do anything stupid."

With that, she kisses me lightly on the lips, then walks swiftly across the grass and into the trees.

CHAPTER 19

THE AURORA HOTEL may be the most unique building in Mississippi. In a city filled with Colonial, French, Spanish, and Greek Revival architecture, this art deco temple rises above all that like a shrine to the early twentieth century. The millionaire who built it was a victim of the Egyptomania that swept the world in the wake of the discoveries in the Valley of the Kings, and the interior of the Aurora reflected his obsession. Only the name of the hotel broke the pattern, and that was no riddle. Aurora was the owner's daughter, so Bienville got the Aurora Hotel rather than the Isis or the Nefertiti.

A gay Bienville wag once famously said the interior of the Aurora looked as though an archaeologist had discovered a pharaoh's tomb and set off a bomb in it rather than loot it for a museum. On the day it opened in 1928, the Aurora's lobby had a twenty-eight-foot ceiling, and its huge brass doors were flanked by enormous marble obelisks. You couldn't stand in any part of the hotel without seeing a pyramid, a Sphinx, a sarcophagus, scarabs, ankhs, or even canopic jars. The lobby walls were clad in relief panels with Egyptian motifs, and the walls of the upper floors were decorated with hand-painted hieroglyphics.

The main restaurant was called the Luxor, and its ceiling was supported by columns modeled after those at Karnak. In the late 1930s, the grand Osiris ballroom hosted Glenn Miller and Duke Ellington, and in 1948 the rooftop Nefertiti Lounge heard Billie Holiday sing "Strange Fruit." Ten years after that, local rock and roller Jerry Lee Lewis belted out "Whole Lotta Shakin' Goin' On" in the same space. And if the rumors are true, tonight the town might get a repeat performance.

"Have you ever been inside this place?" Nadine asks as we pull into the three-story parking garage adjacent to the eight-story hotel.

"Oh, yeah. When I was a little boy, I thought the Aurora was the coolest building on the planet. My parents actually had their wedding reception here, up on the roof."

"They didn't want to come tonight?"

"You think they'd be invited? After all my dad's caustic editorials about the new fascism?"

"I guess not."

"Dad's not in any shape to come anyway."

"I thought you told me he was doing about the same."

Guilt pricks at my conscience. Though Nadine and I have gotten close over the past months, I've tended to minimize the physical toll of my father's illness when I'm with her. I don't know why. Maybe out of an irrational fear that I'll inherit the disease from him. "He can still walk, but his body's board-stiff. If he went into a crowd, he'd fall and break his hip."

Nadine takes my hand and squeezes it. "Why do you hold back when we talk about that?"

"I don't know. It's pretty rough."

She looks up at me, her eyes nakedly sincere. "I can handle rough. I nursed my mom for two years, right to the end."

I nod, finding it hard to speak. "He can't control his bladder anymore. His bowel problems are a nightmare. He has to sleep in a diaper. It's killing his pride, and its wearing my mother down fast, even with sitters."

She leans her head on my shoulder and clenches my hand. "I'm so sorry. I know it's hard. And I know you're a help to your mom."

"I don't know about that. But they did love this place. Dad used to bring us to eat at Luxor restaurant on Sundays, when Adam and I were kids. But they closed the hotel in the late seventies, I think. I never saw the interior after that."

"Nineteen seventy-eight," she informs me as we walk through the low-ceilinged garage to the side entrance of the hotel, which has been strung with white Christmas bulbs. Two couples wearing tuxedos and evening gowns walk about fifty feet ahead of us. I'm only wearing a gray suit, and Nadine, a black sleeveless V-neck cocktail dress.

"I talked to Lenore at the historical society," she goes on, swinging a black clutch. "The Aurora was closed two other times: from '29 to '33, after the crash, and from 2008 till 2015. In 2015, Beau Holland went in with Tommy Russo and bought it as part of the EB-5 visa program. That's the scam where rich foreigners can basically buy green cards by investing in U.S. property."

"That sounds like Poker Club bullshit, all right."

"Since the paper mill deal, they've been secretly restoring the whole thing, to reopen it as a hotel. Even Claude Buckman and Blake Donnelly have money in it now. It's going to be spectacular."

"Will we see the renovations tonight?"

"I don't think so. Was the Egyptian décor still intact when you used to eat here?"

"Yeah, but it was run-down. Peeling gold paint everywhere."

Beyond the side entrance, we find gleaming brass elevators and carpet that looks like no one has ever walked on it. A huge Eye of Ra motif lies beneath our feet. Heavy plastic sheeting has been stapled to the walls, blocking the hallways leading left and right. The owners obviously don't want anyone taking a premature peek at their new crown jewel.

We enter an elevator with two other couples and take a pleasantly swift ride to the roof. The Aurora rooftop once boasted a luxury penthouse apartment and the Nefertiti Lounge, which I'd like to see; but once again, the halls leading away from the elevators are screened with heavy plastic.

As we walk through the double doors leading to the roof, a bracing breeze hits my face, and we're instantly sucked into a whirling mass of tuxedos, evening gowns, crystal glasses, and flashing jewelry.

"We're underdressed," I observe, dodging couples dancing to big band music coming from a PA system.

"Nobody's going to kick us out," Nadine says with a smile. "Let's find the bar."

Above the glittering crowd, a yellow gibbous moon hangs in a sky filled with stars. The deep forests of Mississippi lie just beyond the lights of the town, and the black farmland of Louisiana stretches for miles across the river, but up here it feels like New York or Chicago in the 1920s.

"This is like *The Great Gatsby*," Nadine marvels, still dodging dancers.

She's right. Some of the men are actually wearing white tie. That's not unheard of in Bienville, but tonight there's no hint of camp, as there is during Mardi Gras balls. These people have come to celebrate an economic triumph, and they mean to honor the occasion by looking like they deserve the good fortune that has come their way.

"Don't forget how *Gatsby* ended," I remind her.

I point through the bodies to a large table that's been set up against the southern balustrade of the roof. Two older black men in white coats are serving hard liquor and champagne as fast as they can move. As we pick our way through the bodies, I notice a pattern to our progress. The sight of Nadine triggers broad smiles and hugs from the partygoers, but once they see me, the light in their eyes fades, and the smiles either freeze in place or shrink to scowls. In this euphoric gathering, I'm a potential spoiler, the buzzkill of all time. I try to ignore their ill will, and if Nadine notices their silent curses, she hides it well.

Every few years, one social event ends up bringing out what people call "Old Bienville." This term refers to the generation that moved and shook this place from the late 1950s through the mid-1970s, when the town was rolling in oil money and there were four major industries working at full capacity on the river. Back then Bienville had a vibrant middle class with enough income to travel widely and support downtown retail. Civic organizations were powerful, and the ladies' clubs filled with educated women who gave all their energy to promoting tourism. The black community lived mostly apart—and at a profound economic and political disadvantage—but there was so much money flowing through the city that it raised all boats. Perhaps most important, both black and white communities were tightly knit by extended families, and divorce was rare.

Those people are in their seventies and eighties now, but tonight the survivors of that affluent class have left the sanctuaries of their homes on the off chance that they'll hear one of their contemporaries perform live one last time, before the opportunity vanishes forever. They remember parties from the glory days of the Aurora, when liquor flowed on this rooftop until dawn crept across the city and broke over the river.

White elbow gloves and pearls were de rigueur for the ladies then, and every gentleman owned a tux.

"Here you go, Nick." Nadine shoves a sweating gin and tonic into my hand. "Look at that sky, would you?" She spins in place, taking in everything around her. "You can see to Texas from up here. Look at the river!"

Six hundred yards to the west, the Mississippi shines like a black mirror, reflecting the lights of the old bridge stretching to Louisiana. As I gaze north to south, I realize that the hotel is further from being finished than I'd thought. The party's hosts have done what they could to mask it, but there's a big yellow forklift parked by the wall of the old penthouse apartment, and behind the bar table at the southwest corner, the balustrades don't actually meet. A sawhorse blocks the three-foot gap, and yellow warning tape has been stretched across it to remind the bartenders not to take two steps backward and fall to their deaths.

"Oh, my God!" cries Nadine. "Look at the swimming pool! People are dancing in it."

Through the sea of revelers I see the heads and torsos of dancers in the shallow end of a newly built swimming pool.

"The original hotel didn't have a pool," I tell her. "I know that much."

"Beau Holland wanted to copy the Monteleone in New Orleans," she replies. "It must have cost them a mint to put that thing up here."

While Nadine continues her visual survey, I look more closely at the crowd. Most members of the Bienville Poker Club seem to be here, even Claude Buckman, the powerful banker who serves as the éminence grise of the group. Blake Donnelly is here, too, the $200 million oilman. In the solar system of this party, Poker Club members function as large planets, while various satellites orbit around them. Beau Holland appears to be surrounded by male acolytes, while Max Matheson entertains a mixed group in their forties and fifties, probably with one of his off-color stories. Max's wife, Sally, stands at a small cocktail table with Blake Donnelly's second wife. Blake's trophy wife is a quarter century younger than Sally, but Sally is still the beauty of that pair.

Paul stands in line at a second bar table with Wyatt Cash. As I watch them, Tommy Russo walks up and slaps Cash on the shoulder. Along with Beau Holland, Cash and Russo represent the younger money in the Poker Club. I can't look at Russo now without thinking of wood chippers. Beyond those men, I see Jet and a group of younger women drinking champagne near a makeshift stage that holds a very lonely-looking grand piano. The star of this party has yet to arrive.

"I wonder how they got that grand piano up here," I muse. "That's a big one."

"You won't believe it," Nadine says. "They couldn't fit it into the service elevator, so Paul Matheson hitched it underneath a lumber company helicopter and airlifted it up here this afternoon. That would have made a hell of a picture for the newspaper."

"That sounds just like Paul," I say, laughing.

"Look!" Nadine points at the stage. "Is that Jerry Lee Lewis?"

A stooped man with dyed-black hair is climbing onto the risers that hold the grand piano. He's old enough to be Lewis, but he's not.

"No, I remember that guy. That's Webb Westerly, who owns the music store across the river. He's a damn good piano player in his own right. I guess he's going to keep the crowd warm till the Killer gets here."

Nadine grabs my arm and pulls me across the rooftop. Ahead I see some of the wealthier guests at the party.

"Where are we going?" I ask.

"Charity Buckman just motioned me over. She's a great customer, and she was part of my mother's book club."

This is my chance to question a few members of the Poker Club. Sure enough, as we near Claude Buckman and his wife, Blake Donnelly and Beau Holland move in the same direction. Max and Paul Matheson aren't far behind them.

These guys want to question me, I realize. *They want to know what we're going to print about Buck's death tomorrow.*

"Nadine Sullivan!" gushes Charity Buckman, a woman of eighty who's had a couple hundred grands' worth of plastic surgery. "You look just *darling.* I wish Margaret could have seen this party. She would have *loved* it."

"She would have," Nadine agrees.

"Your escort's mighty handsome," Charity adds with a wink.

"McEwan," croaks Claude Buckman, offering his hand.

I reach out and gently grasp fragile bones wrapped in skin like parchment.

"Goose!" cries Paul, clapping me on the shoulder. "How you like the party, man?"

"I'll like it fine if I get to hear Jerry Lee Lewis."

"Damn right. We only got him because Blake knows him from the Blue Cat Club down in Natchez. *Way* back in the day."

"And Lafitte's Den, right here," adds Donnelly himself. The oilman is actually wearing a tall gray Stetson. "Jerry Lee used to tear up those little honky-tonks when he was just a boy."

Before Donnelly can wax poetic about the birth of rock and roll, Beau Holland slides between Paul and Donnelly and fixes me with a basilisk stare. "What's your take on that accident on the river this morning?" he asks. "That archaeologist who drowned."

"Wasn't that awful?" Donnelly says with what sounds like genuine regret. "Buck was a good fella. Picked me up out on Highway 61 once, when my old Dodge quit on me."

"That was Buck," agrees Max Matheson, stepping up to Claude Buckman's left. "He'd give you the shirt off his back. Damn shame."

Beau Holland has no interest in this informal eulogy. His stare has not wavered, and he looks like his blood pressure is in the lethal zone. "Is there going to be a story about it in the paper tomorrow?"

"I imagine so," I say with a shrug. "That's really up to my editor. I'm only the publisher."

"Oh, bullshit. You're just like your old man. You decide what goes into that rag."

"Now, Beau," Donnelly says in a tone of mild reproof. "You're not being very neighborly."

"What do you expect? McEwan here isn't very neighborly to his hometown."

I would have thought Beau Holland would be reluctant to backtalk Blake Donnelly, but anger seems to have gotten the better of him.

"Shut up and get yourself another drink, Beau," Paul advises.

Holland gives Paul a scorching glare. As they stare at each other, I

realize that more Poker Club members have moved up to the periphery of our circle. Wyatt Cash, Tommy Russo, and Arthur Pine, the
unctuous attorney. Behind Pine, I see Senator Avery Sumner.

"Some people are saying Buck Ferris didn't drown," Holland goes
on. "That he was killed before he went into the river."

"Who's saying that?" Russo asks over the head of Donnelly's wife.

"Just people," Holland says sullenly.

"Is that so?" Buckman asks.

Holland nods, his face red with whiskey or fury. "And a fake-news
story about a murder is the last thing this town needs this week. The
Chinese don't need to see that! Let's talk straight. McEwan wasn't even
invited to this party. But since he's here, I want him to tell us what he's
printing tomorrow."

"As it turns out," I say in a conversational tone, "Buck's skull was
crushed by a brick. And it's looking more and more like he wasn't killed
where his truck was found."

The men's faces go pale at this news, but Beau Holland turns scarlet.
"Will the word 'homicide' appear in the *Watchman* tomorrow? That's
all I want to know."

"Well, a black kid was shot with an AR-15."

"Nobody gives a damn about that. You know what I mean."

The men around Holland look distinctly uncomfortable, but I'm
not sure about the reason. "Why don't you spend fifty cents on a paper
after you come to in the morning?" I suggest.

Holland lunges at me, but Max Matheson plants a splayed hand
on his chest and stops him cold. "Marshall's always invited," Max says
evenly. "He's family. *Get yourself another drink, Beau.*"

Into this minor melee steps Sally Matheson, one of the most gracious women in Mississippi. Some people say it's only her charm and
elegance that extricated Max from quite a few scrapes over the years.
While Beau Holland struggles to get control of his temper, Sally looks
at me as though he doesn't exist.

"How's your father doing, Marshall?" Her gentle Southern accent
hasn't changed since she came out as a Bienville debutante five decades
ago. "It's so hard to imagine Duncan being down like he is."

"He's holding his own, Mrs. Matheson."

"I'm so glad. I know Blythe will get him back in the pink. Your mother's a saint, Marshall. All those years you and Paul were growing up, I was so jealous of Blythe. She just had a *natural way* about her. She could deal with anything. It's a gift."

Arthur Pine shakes his head with feigned empathy. "Tell Duncan I said hello. I miss seeing him on the street."

"You mean in Dizzy's Bar," says his wife, a bejeweled blond standing two steps behind him.

"There, too," Pine says with a sheepish grin.

To my surprise, Sally reaches out and takes Nadine's hand, then leans forward and whispers something in her ear. Nadine giggles, surprising me even more. I don't think I've ever heard her giggle. Then Sally leans back and looks me from head to toe, as though taking my measure.

"Marshall, I've known you since Hector was a pup, and I'm telling you now, you'd better grab hold of this girl with both hands. They don't come any better, east or west of the Mississippi."

I'm so taken aback by this advice that I just stare back at her, mute.

"You two make a lovely couple," Sally goes on. "Plus, Nadine's about the only lawyer in this town who'd stand a chance against Jet in a courtroom. And I'm including *you*, Arthur."

As Pine gives an obsequious laugh, I realize Jet is one of the few members of this set who hasn't drifted over to listen.

"Oh, Sally," says Nadine, "Marshall's just using me as his ticket to see Jerry Lee Lewis. No romance here."

Sally shakes her head like a matchmaker of long experience. "You can't fool me. Go ahead, play charades if you must. But I'll have the last laugh when I throw rice at your wedding."

In the surprised pause that follows this pronouncement, it strikes me how odd it feels to think of this group as a gang of killers. But that may be the reality. The men in this genteel cabal may have met over a card table and condemned Buck to death without a moment's hesitation.

"So," I say to Paul, "is Jerry Lee coming or not?"

He grins and pumps a tanned fist. "You better believe it! His driver just pulled up with him. I just got the text. We're about to hear some bona fide boogie, boy. I'd better run down and bring him up here."

"Hot damn!" exults Blake Donnelly. "I brung him a special bottle of Calvert Extra. I'm gonna go get it."

For two minutes the orbiting planets came together, and now they fly apart once more. Paul squeezes my shoulder like he used to on the basketball court, then he and Max spin off in Blake Donnelly's wake. Wyatt Cash and Tommy Russo fade a few feet away and begin talking among themselves. Only Arthur Pine moves closer to me. The tanned, gray-templed attorney leans in and says, "It really would be regrettable to publish anything that could upset the Chinese at this juncture. Don't you agree?"

"Mr. Pine, the *Watchman* is a newspaper, not a propaganda organ. We don't consider public reaction when making editorial decisions."

Pine actually laughs at this. "You've obviously forgotten how well I used to know your father."

My back stiffens. "What do you mean by that?"

"Only that Duncan knew part of the job of a small-town daily is boosterism. That's always been the deal, in every small town in America. It's part of the compact of capitalism."

"Is that so?"

Pine nods with unreflective confidence.

"Well . . . I never signed that compact."

With Nadine still talking to Sally Matheson, I turn and move back into the crowd. Five seconds later, Jet brushes against me as though by accident, then laughs and catches my wrist. She chose her spot well: we're surrounded by a ring of people three bodies thick.

"We need to talk," she says softly, leaning in close.

Her breath carries the sweet scent of alcohol, and she's wearing the same sapphire earrings she had on this afternoon, though the silver pendant has disappeared.

"Should we dance?" I ask.

"With Paul here? Check your *phone*."

Then she's past me, swept onward by another current of the party.

After a backward glance at Nadine, I take out my burner phone. Jet's text reads: *We have to talk. Meet me by the wall of the penthouse. Not many people that side of the roof. See if Nadine can run interference 4 us. If Paul moves our way, she can head him off for a minute or two. Maybe dance with him. If she loses him, she should text us a warning.*

"Sure," I mutter. "Nadine would just love that. Jesus."

But Jet wouldn't have asked me to risk a public conversation unless not talking would pose a greater danger. I see Paul in my mind, laughing as he talked about Jerry Lee Lewis. And Max defending me from Beau Holland's drunken assault. They can't possibly know about Jet and me. Where is the danger at this moment?

We have to talk . . .

Christ, I think, looking around for Nadine. *The things you do when you're in love.*

CHAPTER 20

WALKING THROUGH THE crowd toward Nadine and Sally, I hear a commotion over by the Aurora's double doors. Voices rise, then spontaneous applause rolls across the rooftop. The star attraction must have arrived at last.

"What was that about?" Nadine asks, suddenly at my side again. "I saw Jet go after you."

"She needs to talk to me about Buck's death. Do you think you can run interference for us for a couple of minutes?"

Nadine opens her mouth but no sound comes out. From her eyes I can see that I've profoundly disappointed her, maybe even hurt her. So far as I know, she suspects nothing about Jet and me sleeping together, at least not in the present. She does know we had a relationship during high school.

"Listen," I start, but she shakes her head and says, "Just make it quick, okay? We don't need a fistfight up here tonight. You and Beau Holland came close enough."

"There won't be any fight," I assure her.

"Then why do you need me 'running interference'?"

I concede her point with a silent plea for understanding.

"Is Paul Matheson on the wrong side of Buck's death?" she asks. "Potential suspect?"

I glance over at Paul, who has reappeared beside the stage and looks to be pounding straight whiskey with Blake Donnelly. "I hope not. But I honestly don't know. He's acting a little paranoid today."

"I can't *imagine* why," Nadine says with a hint of Dorothy Parker in her voice. "Just be quick, Marshall. Seriously."

"I will. Text me if he gets away from you, okay?"

She shakes her head in frustration. "Just get going."

As casually as possible, I make my way over to the old penthouse suite and walk around the corner. Jet is waiting there, twenty yards away, leaning on the balustrade of the roof.

"Here you are," she says, turning back over her shoulder.

As I walk closer, she looks past me, then pops up on tiptoe and kisses me on the mouth.

I pull away. "Shit, are you drunk? Anybody could walk around that corner."

"A little tipsy. But I have a surprise for you."

"Good or bad?"

She points to a forest-green door set in the stucco wall. "That leads into the penthouse. They're using it to store booze for the party."

"So?"

"I want to see the rest of the hotel."

"Jet . . . you're crazy. This isn't the time. Besides, they've got it sealed up tight."

She rolls her eyes like I'm being a spoilsport. "Come on! Just the lobby. I've heard it's unbelievable, all the Egyptian stuff."

I wonder if somebody slipped a drug into her glass. "The lobby's seven floors down," I remind her. "Even if we were crazy enough to go, it would take way too long."

"The Nefertiti Lounge, then. It's right in there. Just a few yards away."

"It's blocked off, Jet. Everybody wants to see the reno—" Another roar of applause drowns my voice, then rises into the night sky.

"I'd say the headliner just hit the stage," she says with a smile. "Come on!"

"What happened to playing it cool tonight?"

"Screw that." She grabs my hand and pulls me toward the door. As we go through, I hear a drawl that sounds like Blake Donnelly's over the PA.

"*Sixty years after he last played this rooftop, here's Jerry Lee Lewis, the Killer, from FERRIDAY, LOUISIANA!*"

Another roar goes up, but the door shuts behind us before I hear even one piano chord. A middle-aged black man holding a case of champagne looks up in surprise.

"Can I help you folks?"

"No, thank you," Jet replies. "We just need to check something for Beau Holland."

And with that we're past him, moving through a penthouse smelling of wet paint. Jet leads me through another door, outside of which is a small service elevator. As soon as we're shut into the small cubicle, she takes my face in her hands and rises for another kiss.

"What the hell's going on?" I ask, holding her away from me as the elevator descends. *You're acting like this is high school,* I want to add, but I don't. Jet never acted like this in high school.

"Sally was right," she says irritably. "You and Nadine look *much* too much like a couple for my taste."

I start to laugh, but there's genuine jealousy in her eyes. I didn't realize Jet had been standing close enough to hear Sally's remark.

"Are you getting a taste for younger women?" she asks.

"Are you serious? Nadine's only eight years younger than we are."

Jet's eyebrows arch. "I'd give a lot to be thirty-eight again."

"Really? I wouldn't."

As the lights on the brass panel above us tick off the floors, I hit M to stop us on the mezzanine. The lobby should be visible from there, and we're less likely to be seen by anyone who might have sneaked into the lobby from the first-floor entrance. Jet starts to complain, then nods approval as the car grinds to a stop.

Before the door opens, she steals her kiss, a quick, urgent probing of the tongue that makes clear she wants more. This new incarnation of my lover has thrown me, and I feel a strong impulse to go straight back to the roof before we get into real trouble. But Jet is already dragging me from the elevator.

"Look!" she cries, pointing down a narrow corridor toward a polished brass balcony rail. "I'll bet that's it."

Even before we reach the rail, I see the points of the great marble obelisks that bookend the lobby entrance. Jet gasps when she reaches the rail, then pulls me to her side. Even in the half-light of security lamps, the lobby is something to behold. Scaffolding and drop cloths cover several areas, but the Egyptian art and hieroglyphics have obviously been restored, and a massive Sphinx gazes silently over the room, sitting atop a fountain that at this moment is completely dry.

"That fountain was inspired by one in Paris," Jet says. "This is going to be so great for the city. That EB-5 scam would have been a disaster."

"Jet, seriously, why are we down here?" I take her by the shoulder and turn her so that she must look into my eyes. "You don't care about this kind of crap."

"Sure, I do. I just don't usually have time to focus on it."

"But tonight you do? Of all nights? I thought you wanted to talk about Paul. Or Buck. I've been thinking we should file a legal challenge to temporarily halt construction at the mill site."

"You need *bones* to do that. Not pottery."

"But with the coroner's statement—"

"Byron Ellis isn't a pathologist. He's not even an M.D. Can we please just drop all that for tonight? Let's finish what we started this afternoon."

She reaches between us and gives my penis a hard squeeze. I'm not shocked by her directness, but by her ignoring a subject that on any other night would be obsessing her.

I catch hold of her wrist and push her hand away. "Come on, Jet. Paul's bound to be looking for you by now. He'll want to dance with you."

"Oh, bullshit. He's watching Jerry Lee Lewis."

"Jet—"

"And there's Na*dine*, remember?" she says in a singsong voice. "Paul will be happy to spend ten minutes dancing with that little number." Jet grabs my cock again, and this time she hangs on, pulling steadily. "Besides, I don't want you going back to her until I've marked my territory."

"You marked it this afternoon."

"Did you shower before you picked her up?"

"Did you snort coke or something?" I grab her hand and yank it up between our chests. "Listen! You're going to take that service elevator back up to the roof. I'm going to wait here five minutes, then get on the main elevators. Find Paul and make him dance, so you're busy by the time I walk back into his field of vision."

She looks longingly down into the lobby. "You're no fun tonight. You need some inspiration." Without further conversation, she turns to the rail, leans against it, and hikes her skirt over her hips. "Come on," she says. "Just go in. I'm still wet from this afternoon." Her derriere is nut-brown and practically bare thanks to the thong she's wearing. Another departure from character—she never wears thongs.

Not for one instant do I consider plunging into her. The absurdity of the scene comes home to me in a sickening wave of anxiety. This woman is smarter than any I've ever known, yet here she stands, leaning against a balcony rail with her dress over her hips, visible to anybody who might be in the dark lobby below. A security guard, for example. Or surveillance cameras. With a shudder of fear I scan the high corners but see no evidence of cameras. While she waits for me to enter her, I walk ten yards up the carpet, toward the main bank of elevators.

"Get back up to the roof," I say in an urgent whisper, turning around for only a moment. "Right now. And think of a good story about where you've been."

Very slowly, Jet straightens up from the rail, then pulls her dress down and presses it flat. "Please come back," she says, looking at the floor.

Her voice is so lifeless that I walk back to her.

"Jet, what the hell? Has something bad happened? Are you afraid to tell me?"

She takes a deep breath, lets out a long sigh. When she looks up, there are tears in her eyes. "I think I'm losing it a little," she says. "Maybe more than a little. I feel desperate. I've always known that my chance of getting custody of Kevin is nearly nonexistent. Buck's murder was like an exclamation point on that. The power they have. Because they're going to get away with it. Aren't they?"

"Not if I have anything to do with it." I take hold of her right hand and pull her away from the rail. "What about that plan you mentioned to me?"

She shrugs. "You'll probably think it's too dangerous. I'll tell you about it tomorrow. I'm drunker than I thought." She swallows hard, then wavers on her feet. All I can see in my mind is Paul combing the roof for her. "When I saw you walk in with Nadine tonight," Jet goes on, "that hit me hard. Took my breath away, actually. It drove home how *stuck* I am. And you're not. You and she could leave for New Orleans tonight, or Paris, and I'd still be trapped in my marriage."

"That's not going to happen," I assure her. "Nadine and I are friends, that's all."

"But it *could*. That's my point. It's the natural thing. You're single, she's single . . . she's great, and she deserves somebody like you. *Fuck!*"

After looking to my right and left to make sure no one can see us, I pull Jet tight against me. "You've got to calm down. We're going to find a way out of this. Buck's death might even be it. If the Poker Club is really behind that, then Max could go to prison."

Jet tries a smile, but it fails. The strain in her face is telling. She doesn't believe she will ever get custody of her son.

I gently kiss her forehead, as she did mine this afternoon. "Come on," I say softly. "You're tougher than this. You've spent your life tilting at windmills. If anybody can nail those bastards, you can. We'll talk tomorrow on the burner phones."

She reaches up to wipe mascara from her eyes but succeeds only in smearing it.

"Wait, let me do that. Crouch down."

Jet kneels on the carpet. Pulling out my shirttail, I carefully wipe the mascara from the orbits of her eyes. "There. That's the best I can do. Now, get back up to that roof. I'll be five minutes behind you."

She closes her eyes for a moment, resetting her nerves. "I love you," she whispers. "I'm sorry I lost my shit."

"You're allowed. I love you, too. Now go."

This time her smile has life in it. She turns and walks swiftly back to the service elevator that leads to the penthouse. As I watch her disappear into it, I hear something shift in the lobby below. Whirling to the rail, I look back over the great dark room. I see no one. If there was anyone down there, I missed them.

WHEN I STEP BACK onto the Aurora's roof, I half expect to find Paul Matheson waiting for me. All I see is drunk revelers thrashing like penitents on the floor of a Pentecostal church while Jerry Lee Lewis bashes his grand piano into joyous submission on the little rooftop stage. Lewis may be over eighty, but he's in constant motion, his slicked-back, dyed-black hair glinting under a makeshift spotlight while women who saw him when he was a wild-haired blond of twenty heave and gasp before the stage. As "Mean Woman Blues" rings out into the night over Bienville, I scan the churning bodies for Nadine. I see no sign of her.

"Looking for somebody?" Lauren Bacall asks in my ear.

I turn to find Nadine looking quite pleased with herself at having fooled me for even a second. "You promised you'd be quick," she scolds. "That was *not* quick."

"Jet's drunk."

"I noticed. Did she get what she wanted from you?"

"She just wanted to tell me some things."

"I see that." Nadine is looking down at my waist, where a fold of my shirttail hangs over my belt. The black stains on it are obviously mascara. "That must have been an interesting conversation."

"That's not what you think. I'll explain later. Let's dance."

Nadine hesitates a moment, but then she takes my proffered arm and twirls us both into the whirl of flesh and flying jewelry. Around us people are jitterbugging or doing what my mother always called the "dirty bop." Just as we find sufficient space to dance, however, "Mean Woman Blues" crashes to an end, and Lewis starts into "That Lucky Old Sun," an elegiac number about nature being oblivious to the travails of the workingman.

"Are you up for a slow song?" I ask.

Nadine looks uncertain once more, but there's a defiant glint in her eye. Just as I think she's about to lead me off the dance floor, she slips into my arms like she's done it a thousand times before. Most nearby couples are gently swaying to the piano, while a few move gracefully through the rest of us, doing dance steps I can't name, with a fluidity that suggests they've either been together for many decades or have the genes of mating serpents. A few feet behind us, maybe twenty couples turn slowly in the empty swimming pool. The joined bodies silhouetted against the bright blue walls have the look of a surrealist art exhibit. Thanks to my height, I can see Jerry Lee a lot better than Nadine can. The old legend looks utterly absorbed in his performance and sings every word with conviction. As I watch him, I realize Jet is dancing with Paul only three feet from the stage. She's looking right at me.

Her eyes are those of a trapped animal.

Breaking eye contact, I murmur, "He does that song better than anybody ever did. Even Ray Charles. There's a lot of suffering in that voice."

Nadine nods against my shoulder. "Did you read Rick Bragg's biography of him?"

"I haven't."

"Lewis lost a two-year-old son, exactly the way you did. The boy drowned in a swimming pool near Ferriday, just downriver from here."

A strange numbness comes over me, and I pull back, looking into Nadine's eyes. "Really?"

She looks worried that she might have crossed a line. Seeing that she didn't, she says, "He also lost a brother when he was young."

This coincidence stops my feet altogether. "The brother didn't drown, too?"

She shakes her head. "Run over by a drunk in broad daylight."

"I had no idea."

"But you recognized the suffering in his voice."

As I look back at Jerry Lee's head bowed over the microphone, Nadine lays her right cheek against my chest, and we gently turn in the warmth of the swaying crowd. Holding her like this feels surprisingly natural, with none of the awkwardness I usually feel dancing with someone for the first time. In the midst of my dark reverie, a sudden cacophony cuts through a flamboyant piano solo.

By the time I look up, a wide circle has opened on the dance floor, as though someone emptied a bag of rattlesnakes there. Sally Matheson and her husband stand in the center of that circle, facing each other as though about to engage in mortal combat. Max looks more flustered than angry, and I can see why. His wife, who all her life has been a model of Southern gentility, looks like a spitting cat with its tail in the air. As the crowd gapes, Max looks around at the ring of faces, then moves cautiously toward his wife, who empties a full drink in his face with stinging force.

Everyone gasps, and Nadine clenches my left arm hard enough to hurt. Max wipes his face on his jacket sleeve, then leans forward and says something in a low tone to Sally, who takes the opportunity to slap him like a drunken sailor. Half the crowd cries out, so alien is this behavior to the image they have of the Mathesons.

Suddenly Paul enters the circle and goes to his mother. He takes her by the shoulders, speaking softly to her. Max tries to join them, but Paul shoves him away. Then Sally yells, "Get away from me! Bastard! I've taken all I'm going to take. You said *never again!*"

"All *right* now!" Jerry Lee shouts from the stage. "I'm the headliner tonight! Let's get this show back between the ditches!"

And with that he breaks into "Whole Lotta Shakin' Goin' On." The crowd stands paralyzed, unable to recover. The confrontation between Max and his wife was like a lightning strike at the center of the roof, leaving scorched tar and the stink of ozone in its aftermath. But after eight bars of Jerry Lee pumping that grand piano, couples at the edge of the crowd begin jitterbugging again. This trips some psychic switch, and suddenly the circle closes, the crowd begins writhing, and Paul leads his mother toward the exit while Max stands looking like a man who just got sucker-punched at his own wedding.

"What the hell just happened?" Nadine asks.

"I've got no idea."

Some drunks in the empty swimming pool start swinging yellow pool noodles around like light sabers, and it hits me how smart the hosts were not to fill that pool with water tonight.

"I don't think I've ever heard Sally Matheson cuss in public," Nadine says, still flabbergasted. "Much less smack somebody. Max must have really messed up."

"Max has messed up his whole life. When it comes to chasing women, anyway. This must be something worse. Wow."

While couples spin around us, Nadine and I come back together and begin a sort of hybrid version of the Shag. As we spin through the crowd, I catch sight of Jet standing where Max and Sally argued. Max is gone now, but Jet is still staring at the spot where Sally slapped him. She looks nothing like she did three minutes ago. I only see her in quick flashes, but she's not moving. She's replaying the scene in her mind, trying to figure out what just happened in plain sight.

"Hang on," Nadine says, stopping in my arms. "Just a second."

Her cell phone appears in her hand.

"I've just had a break-in at my shop," she says, sounding puzzled. "Wow. First time since I've opened."

"It's probably a false alarm, right?"

"Maybe. But the cops are on their way. Do you mind if we go check it out? You can stay here if you'd rather."

"No, no," I tell her, glad for an excuse to get out of this crazy gold-fish bowl. "Let's go make sure everything's okay."

Nadine smiles with gratitude. "Thank you."

As I escort her toward the rooftop doors, I risk one backward glance. Thanks to Jet's height, I can see her eyes between the heads on the dance floor. She's no longer looking at the spot Sally was standing in a minute ago.

She's watching Nadine and me leave.

As I pass through the doors with Nadine's hand clasped in mine, I realize how true Jet's realization was down on the mezzanine balcony. She's tied to Paul and his family by more than paper. The bond that binds her to the Mathesons is blood—effectively unbreakable. I've always known this at some level, I suppose, but in my euphoria at possessing Jet again, I let myself believe that some magical solution would reveal itself later. But *later* has become now, as it always does, and I see no solution. Not even the hope of one. And as for Buck's death, at this moment, nothing links the Poker Club to it other than their collective relief that he's dead.

And there's no law against that.

CHAPTER 21

ONLY ONE CITY police officer responded to the alarm at Constant Reader, and he found both the front and rear entrances locked. The alarm had been triggered by a motion detector on the ground floor. After a quick search, Nadine discovered that a second-floor window had been forced. Oddly, that window was fourteen feet above the pavement of the rear parking area. To gain access that way, the intruder would have had to either bring his own extension ladder or do some creative climbing and risky acrobatics—wasted effort employed in the robbing of a bookstore.

All Nadine can find missing is the tower unit of her computer server. The cash register hasn't been disturbed. We stand with the cop in the midst of the bookshelves, trying to figure out why someone would steal her computer. The cop has already grown impatient. He seems resentful about having to fill out a report.

"Are you sure that's all that's missing?" he asks.

"I think so," Nadine says. "I mean . . ."

"What have you not checked?" I ask her.

She purses her lips, bemused, and turns in a circle. "Nothing. I mean, unless . . ."

"What?"

"The safe?" she asks, almost humorously.

"Check it."

She goes into a small office tucked between the bookstore and café portions of the shop, and I follow. The safe appears to be undisturbed.

"It looks okay," she says.

"Open it," I advise her. "Just for kicks."

She looks back to make sure the cop can't see, then spins the dial right, left, and right again. When she opens the door, I hear a long sigh.

"Well?"

"Somebody was in here," she says. "Shit."

"What's missing?"

"A couple of external hard drives."

"What was on them?"

She's shaking her head in silence.

"Nadine?"

"The backups of my business software, plus my financial records for the past two years."

"That's all?"

"That's *all*?" She looks over her shoulder, her face taut with frustration. "I am *so* fucked."

"How so?"

"It'll take me weeks to get back up and running. Back up to speed, I mean. I have my basic software on disk, but I've lost so many transactions, records . . . God, what a nightmare. And before you ask, I kept those drives here because this is a fire safe. I don't have one at home."

The cop's voice comes over my shoulder: "So that's all of it, ma'am? A computer and two hard drives?"

"Looks like it, yes."

"It's just . . . sometimes people have firearms stolen, and since they're not licensed, they don't like to report it."

"No," Nadine says wearily. "No gun."

"All right. If y'all are okay, I'm going to head out. There's been kind of a rash of these things tonight."

"What things?" I ask. "Break-ins?"

"Yeah."

"What else got broken into?"

The cop pauses halfway to the door. "Couple of law offices downtown."

Nadine and I share a puzzled look. "Law offices? What was taken?"

"Same thing. Some computers. Disks and files and such."

What the hell? "That's pretty unusual, isn't it?"

The cop shrugs, then takes out his cell phone to check a text message.

"I guess. We get all kinds of crazy stuff in this town. Last week some guys backed a truck through a brick wall to rob the fishing store."

Nadine rolls her eyes at me.

"Okay, well, I think we're fine," I tell him. "Thanks for responding to the call."

After walking the cop to the door, I come back and find Nadine sitting at one of her café tables.

"How do you feel?" I ask, just to get her talking.

"Violated."

"It's always that way with burglaries."

She looks around the store with what seems like hopelessness. "What the hell, Marshall? What do you think?"

"I think it's pretty damn weird that they broke into your safe. Even weirder that they didn't bust it open with an ax. Somebody cracked it. A pro."

"Are you sure?"

"Had to be. Somebody's looking for something. Breaking into law offices around town?"

"I'm not a lawyer anymore."

"Have you done anybody a favor? Legally, I mean. Like someone gave you a tape of their husband having sex with his secretary, something like that?"

She looks like she's about to laugh. "God, no."

"Well. Until we get this figured out, you don't need to sleep at home."

She starts to object, but then she realizes I'm right. "I have a friend I could stay with, but it's a little late to call."

"You can stay with me tonight. I have an extra room."

She gives me a long look. "You sure?"

"Of course."

Her eyebrows go up. "Nobody would mind?"

"Hell, no. It's just me."

"Okay, then. I'll need some clothes. Toiletries."

"We'll run by your house. I'll go in with you."

"Let me lock up here. Or should I say, shut the barn door after the horse has bolted?"

"That's about it. Hey, can I grab a muffin from the case? I didn't eat any hors d'oeuvres at the party."

"Grab me one, too. Cranberry."

NADINE LIVES IN HER mother's house on Hallam Avenue, in the Garden District. It's a tall blue Victorian covered in gingerbread, with a whimsical turret at one end of the porch. It's here that Nadine hosted her popular book club during the two and a half years her mother lived with cancer. While Margaret Sullivan was alive, Nadine lived in a small house nearby, but as the end approached, she sold that and moved into the home in which she'd grown up.

"Do you have a security system here?" I ask as she unlocks the door.

"No. Always meant to get one, but I never have."

"It's time. Do you have a gun?"

She switches on the lights, revealing a house that appears to be in perfect order. "I do. It was my mother's. Or my father's, actually. He left it behind."

"Get the gun when you get your clothes," I advise. "You don't want it stolen if somebody does hit this place."

"Aren't you coming upstairs with me?"

"Absolutely."

After we go up, I check the bedrooms for signs of being searched. I see none. Nadine grabs a gym bag and throws in some clothes, then packs a hanging toiletry bag.

"Ready," she says.

"The gun?"

"Oh, yeah." She goes over to her bedside table and takes a small black semiautomatic from the drawer, then starts to put it in her bag. It looks like a .32 caliber, a traveling salesman's gun.

"I'll take that," I say, walking to her. "In case we meet anybody on our way out."

She passes it to me, then follows me out and switches off the light behind us. While she locks the front door downstairs, I scan the yard, which at this hour is a dark jungle filled with azaleas, oak trees, and huge Elaeagnus shrubs.

"Everything okay?" she asks.

"I think so. Let's get to the Flex."

Not a car moves on Hallam Avenue, which is normal at this hour, but I feel strangely alert. I crank the SUV quickly, then head east, away from the Garden District and the river.

"Didn't you say you needed to stop by the newspaper?" she asks.

"I can handle it by phone. Ben's there late tonight."

"You're welcome to call him now."

"I'll do it when I get home."

Soon we're passing through the outer sprawl of Bienville to the outlying subdivisions.

"Who could do that?" she asks in a distracted voice.

"What? Kill Buck?"

"No. Get into my safe like that. Without damaging it. You said a pro. What kind of professional does that?"

"Some of the Poker Club guys have connections who could do that. Tommy Russo for sure. Wyatt Cash has Special Forces guys who endorse his products. And Paul has buddies who served with him in Iraq. They worked for ShieldCorp, his private security company."

Nadine lays her fingertips on the window and slowly drums the glass.

"Did you notice how angry Beau Holland was when he lunged at me during the party?" I ask. "He looked like he was about to pop a blood vessel."

"I've been thinking about that. He's been in my store quite a bit. Most of those Poker Club guys have, for coffee or breakfast. I've learned a fair bit about them."

"What do you know about Holland?"

"My guess is he has the most to lose if the paper mill deal were to fall apart."

"I figured that would be Buckman or Donnelly."

"Those guys are rich enough to take a licking and keep on ticking. Beau Holland comes from a proud family that was short on cash. He's bound to be overextended. He owns the biggest piece of the Aurora, for starters. Russo's deep in that with him. And Holland's the main investor in the white-flight developments out by the county line. Also in the new outlet mall, plus some land grabs near the industrial park. God knows what else he's got cooking. If the Chinese pulled out at this point, Beau could be ruined."

"That makes sense." I still recall Holland's red-faced fury, and how Max stopped him with his flattened hand.

"Why does Warren Lacey hate Jet so badly?" Nadine asks.

"Before you can open a nursing home or surgical center in Mississippi, the state has to issue a certificate of need. They're worth more than gold mines. Lacey was trying to fiddle one in Jackson, for a city where there's no legitimate need. A state official ended up going to jail over it. Lacey kept himself insulated enough to stay out of prison—barely—but Jet almost got his medical license revoked. He's never forgiven her."

"I think he'd strangle her if he could."

"He won't. You don't bite off a piece of the Mathesons if you plan on living the rest of your life outside a wheelchair."

"So . . . Max protects Jet?"

"That's the only explanation I can figure for why she's not dead."

Nadine looks over at me for several seconds. "Max is a real son of a bitch, isn't he?"

"You know the stereotype about Vietnam soldiers committing atrocities? Ninety-nine-point-nine percent never did. But Max did. Worse, he's proud of it. When I was playing football at ten years old, he told us, 'War is hell, boys, so I made it as hellish as possible. That's the way you win.' When I was younger I thought that was just Patton-type bluster. But later I found out he meant it."

Nadine is nodding. "He's hit on me a few times in the store."

"Really?"

"Oh, yeah. I've seen him flirt with other women, too. He's got an instinct for weakness."

"I know. We're about five minutes from my house," I tell her, hoping to change the subject.

"Is Paul an alcoholic?" Nadine asks.

"Yeah. Has been most of his life."

"I feel like his public persona is a mask. Like underneath, he might be a little nuts."

"He might be. But he's basically a good guy. At least he used to be. He's not living the life he hoped for."

She gives the windshield a pained smile. "Are any of us?"

I shrug. "I figured you are, if anybody is."

She doesn't reply for some time. We're on a lightless stretch of Highway 61, a black ribbon of asphalt stretching through thick forest on both sides of the road. There's not much to see.

"This isn't where I thought I'd open my bookstore," she says at length. "But it's been interesting. The social life leaves a bit to be desired, though."

"You do more than your share to make the town interesting."

"I try." Her fingernails tap the window glass again. "Are you sure I'm not putting you out? Staying at your place?"

"I'll sleep a lot better knowing you're safe."

"I can move to my friend's house tomorrow."

"Whatever you want. You're always welcome."

She smiles. "You gonna tell me about that shirttail?"

"Oh. Jet was crying. She's afraid Paul might be mixed up in Buck's murder. I wiped her face with my shirttail."

Nadine nods slowly. "Did she notice something suspicious about Paul?"

"Not specifically related to Buck. But she's around those Poker Club guys a lot."

"No kidding. It's hard to believe she'd be surprised that her husband might be involved."

I suddenly feel defensive about Jet. "She's done more than anybody else to punish them for illegality."

Nadine watches me expectantly but says nothing.

"I think she sort of wears blinders when it comes to her husband," I venture.

"Maybe they both do."

I look back at her, but Nadine is staring through the windshield.

Three minutes later, I click us through the security gate with my remote and drive the long road through the woods to my house. Nadine seems to like the isolation, and once we get inside the house, I show her to my spare room. It's nothing special, just a queen bed, a dresser, and a chair that came with the house.

"Bathroom's in the hall, I'm afraid, but I have my own in the back. So nobody will be knocking on the door while you're in there."

"Thanks. Hey, is that your guitar by the wall?"

I'd forgotten I moved Quinn's gift to the spare room before heading for the party. "Um, I guess it is now. That belonged to Buck. Quinn gave it to me this afternoon."

"Wow. Which one is it?"

I shouldn't be surprised that she's curious about Buck's guitars, especially after we played at her store. Nadine isn't merely a music fan, but a promoter. "That's Buck's personal guitar. One he built himself."

"The baritone?"

"That's the one."

"I love that guitar! It almost sounds like a cello."

This brings a smile to my lips. "That's what Buck used to say."

"Will you play it for me tomorrow?"

"Sure, yeah." I step back into the hall. "Hey, did that muffin fill you up? Or do you need some food before bed?"

She laughs. "You going to cook for me?"

"You've done it for me enough. I can scramble eggs. Huevos rancheros?"

"Maybe for breakfast. I need sleep now."

I nod, then take her father's pistol from my pocket. "I want you to keep this close."

Her face darkens. "I'd rather you hold on to it."

"I have one in my bedroom. But if anybody sneaks up this hall, they'll get to your room first. Better safe than sorry."

She reluctantly accepts the handgun.

"I'll see you in the morning," I tell her.

As I start down the hall, Nadine leans out and calls, "Did I weird you out when I mentioned Jerry Lee Lewis's son drowning in the swimming pool?"

"No. It's fine. Hard to believe, really. That and losing his brother, just like me."

"Truth is stranger than fiction, right?"

"Always." I wait to see if she has anything else to say. I feel like she does.

After a few seconds, she says, "Have you given any more thought to what I asked you this morning?"

"You asked me a lot of things."

"About whether, if you had the power to punish Buck's killer and unravel the corruption behind the paper mill deal, you would do it? If it meant the town losing the mill and all that comes with it."

"I have thought about it. I asked Jet the same question this afternoon."

"What did she say?"

"She'd blow it up without a second thought."

Nadine nods thoughtfully. "Well . . . she can afford to, can't she? She married well, as they say. At least in an economic sense."

"What about you? What would you do?"

"I understand the temptation to blow it all up. Especially after what happened to Buck. But it's like that Vietnam-era saying: 'We had to destroy this village in order to save it.' That's the real dilemma in all this."

"I know. It's just hard to take the macro view when you know somebody beat Buck to death over it."

Nadine is watching me carefully. "Well . . . anyway. I just wanted to make sure I didn't cross a line before."

"No. We're good."

"Night." With a small smile she closes the door.

I check the doors and windows to be sure they're locked, then go back to my bathroom and brush my teeth, glad for quiet after the night's craziness. It's strange to have Nadine under my roof, but not at all unpleasant, and it's absolutely necessary. The break-in at her store was not normal. A skilled criminal was looking for something in her safe. Something specific. The same burglar probably hit at least two other law offices in town. What I don't understand is how Nadine could have no idea what they might be looking for.

Using earbuds, I call Ben Tate to make sure I know the thrust of the stories he'll be running tomorrow. While we talk, I open my top dresser drawer and remove the Walther P38 I borrowed from my father after I moved back home. I was living downtown at the time, and street crime was common enough to warrant keeping it in my car. The gun was made in Germany in 1957, and Dad bought it while serving there in the early 1960s. After hanging up with Ben, I set the Walther on my bedside table, then lay my iPhone and the new burner Jet brought this afternoon beside it. I've yet to take a call on that burner phone, but something tells me that whatever comes over that illicit connection over the next few days could determine the course of the rest of my life.

As I lie in the bed, waiting for sleep, I see Jet on the mezzanine of the Aurora after dragging me down there in a fit of recklessness. Suddenly I understand what triggered her atypical breakout. From the moment she kissed me on the roof to the moment she hiked up her dress, she was trying to get us caught. The months of secrecy and tension took one kind of toll, but Paul's suspicion means we must stop seeing each other, at least for a while. The only rational way forward is for her to ask him for a divorce, one that will never be resolved in her favor. Even for a woman as resolute as Jet, the prospect of fighting an unwinnable battle must bring on something close to despair. How much easier—or so it probably seemed while drunk—to blow up her marriage and let the shrapnel fly where it will. A month ago she would never have done what she did tonight. *Yeats is always right,* I reflect. *Things fall apart. The center cannot hold.* As sleep finally takes me, and the awful weight of this day begins to slip from my shoulders, a sense of foreboding awakens in my mind, too shapeless to define, yet real enough to prevent my descending into true oblivion.

MY IPHONE WAKES ME at 1:40 A.M.

Blinking in confusion, I see that it's Ben Tate, calling from the paper. It's been two hours since he and I finalized tomorrow's stories. I can't believe he's still at the office. I press ANSWER and lie back on my pillow.

"Ben? What's going on?"

"Thirty minutes ago the police scanner went crazy. Something happened at Max Matheson's house, in that ritzy neighborhood out in the county."

"Like a break-in or something?"

"I don't think so. Carl got word from a source in the sheriff's department that Max's wife had been shot."

I sit up and turn on my bedside lamp. "That can't be right."

"That's what I thought, too. But Carl's guy said that when the responding deputy got there, Mrs. Matheson was dead in the bed with her husband, and Max was out of his mind. The gun was in the bed with them, and the sheets were covered in blood. Like a slaughterhouse, he said. She was shot through the heart."

"*Sally Matheson* is dead?" I ask dully, seeing an image of Sally dressed to the nines on the Aurora rooftop earlier tonight. "Is this for real, Ben?"

"I know it sounds crazy. It's like even the cops can't believe it. But it's real."

I rub my eyes and shake my head, as if that could clear my mind. "Actually, the Mathesons had a very public argument at that party on top of the Aurora tonight. Everybody saw it happen. Sally called him a bastard and threw a drink in his face. I've never seen her do anything remotely like that."

"Are you coming down here?" Ben asks.

Nadine rises in my mind. "I don't know. I may wait and monitor—"

My burner phone is ringing. I don't recognize the number, but I never do until I've had a burner for about a week. It's got to be Jet. "I've got to run, Ben. I'll work my own sources and call you back later. Keep me updated."

I hang up before he can reply, then answer the burner. Despite what Ben said, the news I'm braced to hear is what I've feared for the past three months: *Paul is headed to your house with a gun*—

"I'm here," I answer.

"I only have thirty seconds," Jet says, panic crackling in every syllable. "Wake up and listen hard."

"I'm up. Was Sally shot?"

"Yes. She's dead, Marshall."

"The news is already out. Did Max shoot her?"

"That's what it looks like. The police are over there now. Sheriff's deputies, actually. Paul went over. I have Kevin with me at home. My God, this is the last thing in the world I could have imagined."

"Is Max going to be arrested?"

"I don't know. I guess he might be. It's all so unbelievable."

"I saw their argument at the Aurora. Have they been doing that a lot recently?"

"No! Not that I've seen, anyway."

"You told me Sally was acting weird today, that she wanted to talk to you."

Jet is silent for about three seconds. "That's right. You know . . . wait—"

She blocks the mic on her phone, and I hear her muffled voice speaking to her son.

"I've got to go," she says with sudden clarity. "I'll know more after Paul gets home, but I won't be able to call you. And don't call me. Not under any circumstances."

The phone clicks, and she's gone.

I sit naked on the edge of the bed for a minute or so, stunned beyond belief. The image of Sally Matheson, the archetypal steel magnolia if ever there was one, lying beside her husband on their bloody bedsheets is something my brain simply refuses to accept. It's like hearing that Sally Field got her brains blown out. Of course, Sally Field never married a man like Max Matheson. Burt Reynolds and Max probably shared more than a few traits, but so far as I know Burt never killed anybody. Yet despite all I know about Max, I've never heard a whisper about him raising a hand against his wife. In his own way, Max worshipped Sally.

A tentative knock sounds at my door.

"Hello?" I call.

"It's me."

For an instant Jet flashes in my mind, but Jet can't be standing at my door. It has to be Nadine. Getting up, I pull on a pair of Levi's, then go to the door and pull it open.

Nadine stands there in a long T-shirt and wire-rimmed glasses, nothing else.

"The house phone rang," she says. "You didn't answer, so I got up and checked it. The caller ID showed it was from the *Watchman* office. As I was walking back to my room, I thought I heard your voice. You sounded upset. Is everything okay?"

"No. Sally Matheson has been shot. By Max, apparently."

Nadine stares at me without blinking. "Shot dead?"

"That's what my editor told me."

"That's . . . it seems impossible. Crazier than Buck getting killed."

"I know. But it's happened."

She walks past me and sits on the edge of my bed, looking shell-shocked. "My God. She was so nice to me tonight."

"She really was. It truly doesn't seem real."

Nadine looks up. "What are you going to do? Do you need to go down to the paper?"

"I should. But I don't feel like it."

"What do you feel like doing?"

An image of Denny Allman flying his drone fills my mind. "To tell you the truth . . . something crazy."

"Like?"

"Every cop in this county, municipal or sheriff's deputy, is going to have only one thing on his mind tonight: Sally's death. This is the best chance I'll ever get to sneak onto that mill site and do some digging. I mean literal digging—with a shovel."

Nadine's eyes widen, but she looks more intrigued than afraid. "What would you be looking for? Evidence that Buck was murdered there?"

"That, and Indian bones. And thanks to little Denny Allman, I know just where to look."

Nadine covers her mouth with a fist while she transitions from shock to action. After a few seconds, she says, "I sure don't see us getting back to sleep tonight. What the hell? Let's do it."

"The last guy who tried this wound up dead."

She winces, but I can see she wants to forge ahead. Anything seems better than sitting around uselessly in the wake of tragedy. "We shouldn't sneak down there," she says. "Let's put on the clothes we wore to the party, take a bottle of wine and a blanket with us. We'll act like we drove down there to make out by the river. If there's a guard, we'll have a good excuse to be there. If not, we dig."

"That's a damn good idea."

She nods and stands. "I'll be dressed and made up in five minutes."

"I'll see you in the kitchen."

Nadine spins and pads quickly down the hall, then turns into the guest room. I'm starting to see why she was such a good lawyer.

She's a force of nature.

CHAPTER 22

BEN TATE DROPPED the Buck Ferris murder story into our web edition
at 3:30 A.M., and it was like kicking over a hornet's nest. Suggesting that
Buck had been murdered was bad enough in the eyes of the town; backing up that implication with an opinion from the coroner was worse.
But speculating that Buck had been killed at the paper mill site, then
dumped upriver to hide that fact, made people crazy. Our main switch-
board started ringing off the hook at 5:30 A.M., as the print subscribers
began calling in to voice their displeasure. By 8:30 there were 336 reader
comments beneath the story, and I'd received sixty-seven emails at my
Watchman account.

None of that surprised me, and I was too tired to care anyway. By
the time I limped into my office this morning, I'd only slept two hours,
having spent the middle of the night at the paper mill site with Nadine,
digging in the dark in my suit and dress shoes. After driving down to
the industrial park, we parked beside the foundation of the old electroplating plant and waited to see if any guards would challenge us. None
did. After ten minutes of ticking silence, I got out my small shovel and
a handful of trash bags and started hunting for the concrete footing
where Buck had found his Poverty Point–era pottery samples. Nadine
stayed in the Flex to keep watch. If she saw anyone approaching, she
was to switch on the headlights and speed-dial me. I would dump my
tools and walk back as though I'd simply left the SUV to take a leak.

The GPS coordinates Denny had emailed me helped, but they required that I use an unfamiliar app on my phone to exploit them. I
felt like a World War I soldier crossing no-man's-land with a lighted

cigarette as I carried that phone around the mill site. The whole time, I wished I'd stuck my father's Walther into my waistband instead of leaving it under the seat of the Flex, but I didn't want some sheriff's deputy catching me out there carrying. Eventually I figured out the GPS app, and I ended my search by sliding down into a trench beside the exposed concrete footing of a foundation pier.

I know nothing about archaeology, but with the LED light from my phone, I saw what looked like defined soil strata on the face of the five-foot-deep hole. As quickly as I could, I scraped shovelfuls of dirt from the lowest two feet of the trench and dumped them into doubled Hefty yard bags. After collecting about twenty pounds of dirt, I hauled that bag over to the Flex and loaded it into the back. Then we drove to the next set of coordinates, which turned out to be two plots of turned earth in the middle of a patch of Johnsongrass. I figured this work would be in vain, but for Buck's sake I dug up another thirty pounds of dirt and bagged it.

As I started back to the Flex, my right foot kicked something hard, and I cursed. Shining my light down, I saw a brick protruding from the soil. On closer inspection, it appeared to be one of the reddish-orange bricks that Byron Ellis had referred to as "Natchez brick." Turning in a circle with my phone light, I saw three more—fragments rather than whole bricks. Setting down my Heftys, I untwisted one plastic neck and dropped in the bricks. Then I slung the heavy bags over my shoulder and humped them back to the Flex, which was parked thirty yards away, on a strip of Johnsongrass.

"Somebody's coming down Port Road," Nadine hissed as I tossed the bags under the hatchback. *"Headlights just hit the bottom of the hill."*

Looking up, I saw the lights, and my pulse kicked into overdrive. I started to hide my shovel under the trash bags, but on impulse I shut the hatchback, took the shovel by its handle, and hurled it as far into the dark as I could. By the time the sheriff's cruiser pulled up beside us with its red lights flashing, Nadine was lying across my chest, kissing me deeply. The shock of her cool tongue in my mouth blanked the cruiser from my mind, until I heard a male voice over a PA ordering us out of the *vee-hickle.*

Nadine broke the kiss, squeezed my shoulder, and said, "Play it cool." Then she winked.

I got out, holding both hands up in clear sight. A flashlight beam blinded me, and my heart began to pound as I remembered the ghastly wound in Buck's skull. Then Nadine got out, making a show of straightening her cocktail dress.

I didn't know the deputy, but after he got a look at Nadine, it didn't take much effort to sell our story. Once he recognized my name, he felt compelled to tell me about the murder at the Matheson house. I feigned ignorance to give him the pleasure of shocking me with a bloody tale. We were lucky. If we'd gotten a different deputy—or, worse, a private security guard who knew my connection to Buck— things would have gone differently. This deputy did shine his flashlight into the Flex, but he didn't question the trash bags. I wondered if the shovel would have triggered more suspicion or if I'd made a mistake by tossing it into the dark. But since the deputy let us go, I made myself forget about it.

As we drove up the face of the bluff—ten car lengths ahead of the cruiser—Nadine joked about the deputy staring a hole through her chest. I wasn't quite ready to laugh. If he called in my plate to the wrong person, he might still pull us over and arrest us for trespassing. But when I peeled off eastward at the top of the bluff, he continued north into the city, and my pulse returned to normal. Nadine and I went back to my house and took a cursory look at the soil samples I'd collected. They were full of fragments, some of which were clearly charcoal, while others appeared to be pebbles. In the bag of dirt taken from beside the pier, I found three spheres that looked and felt like baked clay. They weren't uniform in size, but each fit easily into my palm. A few small fragments from that bag had the feel of bone, that damp, ossified roughness of something that might once have been alive. But even if they were bone, we had no way to know if it was human. We also discovered two teeth that looked human, but I'd seen hog teeth that looked like they came from people, so I encouraged Nadine not to jump to conclusions. Our ultimate judgment was that we weren't qualified to make any sort of valid analysis of those samples.

We were walking back to our respective rooms to get what sleep we could when she said, "Sorry about the kiss. I figured that was the best play."

A smile came to my lips. "It wasn't exactly hardship duty."

Nadine smiled, too. "No."

"Well, good night. For the second time."

"Night."

I waited for her door to close, then went into my bedroom. I needed a shower but was too exhausted to take one. As I kicked off my shoes, it struck me that I was living in a different world from the one I'd awakened in that morning. In the span of seventeen hours, I had lost two pillars of my childhood to violent death. Strangely, Sally Matheson's death unsettled me most. Unlike Buck, who had pushed his luck past the point of prudence, Sally had seemed beyond the reach of violence. Untouchable, like a TV actress from my youth. And yet she was dead. For five months I'd been waiting for my father to die, and suddenly Paul's mother had preceded him into the grave. As I lay in bed and tried to sleep, I saw the dancers on the Aurora roof opening up a circle as though fleeing a suicide bomber, only to reveal Max and Sally arguing viciously while a rock-and-roll legend watched them from his stage. God only knew what wild rumors that scene would inspire.

Before Nadine and I headed for town this morning, I gave her a key to my house and the code to my gate—2972 (Jet's birthday, but Nadine doesn't know that). I told her that if anything felt wrong during the day, if she sensed even the slightest danger, she should consider my house a refuge. If the drive seemed too far, she could come to the *Watchman* building. A few minutes ago, she texted to let me know that while her customers are obsessed with the shooting of Sally Matheson, our story suggesting that Buck was murdered at the industrial park is running a close second. And while public opinion seems split on Max's guilt, it's running 100 percent against me, Ben Tate, the coroner, and Buck himself.

After dropping Nadine at her shop this morning, I delivered half the dirt I'd collected from the paper mill site to Byron Ellis's home. The coroner figures the county might fire him today, but he has a lawyer and two well-known black activists ready to protest any such move. In the meantime, he's glad to have the soil samples to distract him from the politics. Byron's no archaeologist, but he feels confident that he can determine whether the samples contain any blood or bone. Quinn Ferris is picking up the rest of the dirt later today. Quinn assures me she can get the samples to an expert at LSU in Baton Rouge, who can tell us exactly what Buck was digging into when he was murdered.

Since my texts with Nadine, I've been trying to settle on my next move. Thirty minutes ago, one of my reporters told me Max Matheson was due to be arraigned soon. I've put off dealing with in-house issues until I hear how that went. I've also kept my burner phone close, but I've heard nothing from Jet since last night. And though it's been tough, I've obeyed her order not to try to reach her. I'm hoping Ben Tate's forceful inquiries made the locum tenens pathologist nervous enough to do an honest autopsy on Buck, but I won't know until I get a look at the report, which I might not see until the afternoon.

When my iPhone rings, I curse, wishing it was the burner. But at least it's Carl Stein, the reporter covering Max's arraignment.

"How'd it go, Carl?"

"The judge just granted Max bail."

"How high?"

"A million bucks. For a hundred grand cash, he gets to walk free till trial."

A hundred grand is pocket change for Max, but I expected this. "He's a lifelong Bienville resident, a war hero, has gainful employment and no criminal record. Plus, the Poker Club has a lot of sway over the judges in this town, both circuit and chancery. Probably even federal."

"I hear you, but that's not why I called."

"Something else happen?"

"You could say that. I called about his lawyer."

An odd note in Carl's voice gets my attention. "Arthur Pine?" I say, thinking of the de facto attorney of the Poker Club.

"Nope. Pine sat in the back row during the proceeding."

"Who did Max hire?"

"*Jet,* man. His daughter-in-law. Can you believe that shit?"

I feel as though the earth just paused in its revolution around the sun. "No. Are you serious?"

"I knew that would freak you out. I still can't believe it myself."

Everyone who works for me knows Jet and I often collaborate on stories, and she's given all my staff reporters help at different times. On matters of education or civic corruption, she's the most reliable source in the city. But I'm not sure quite what to say to Carl Stein in this moment.

"Did the judge set a trial date?" I ask in a dazed voice.

"Not yet."

"Did Jet post bond for Max?"

"Pine had the money. The bag man."

My mind reels at the implications of this. "Is Jet still at the court-house?"

"No, she cut right out."

"Was Paul Matheson there?"

"Uhh, yeah."

"Did he leave with his wife?"

"Don't think so."

"Okay, Carl. Good work."

Before I can second-guess myself, I take out my burner phone and speed-dial Jet. Her phone rings five times. Then she picks up.

"I told you not to call me," she whispers.

"Yeah, well, I just heard about your courtroom appearance."

"What about it?"

"You're going to defend Max? I thought you hated him."

"Like I have a fucking choice? *Damn* it, Marshall. This is family I'm dealing with."

Like I don't know that? "Where are you now?"

Silence.

"Jet!"

"Look, how about I come by the paper and explain in person why I can't give you an interview?"

She's laying out the excuse she'll give Paul for the visit. "Whatever works."

"I'm still downtown. I'll be there in five minutes."

The phone clicks, and she's gone.

I'M NOT SURE WHAT I did for the five minutes it took Jet to get to my office. I must have sat at my desk in a trance, trying to figure out how she's rationalized serving a man she's hated and despised for most of her adult life. When my door opens, I'm shocked yet again. She walks in wearing the standard uniform of a corporate lawyer in Jackson, Mississippi: navy skirt suit, cream silk blouse, Christian Louboutins, a Prada purse, a string of small but fine pearls, and the sapphire earrings she wore yesterday. Jet almost never dresses this way, even in court. *What the hell is going on?*

She closes the door softly behind her, then takes a seat on one of the two chairs before my desk. She sits with an unusual rigidness, as though she's been summoned for an interrogation. No one watching this conversation would guess that we are lovers.

"Max asked me to represent him at his arraignment," she informs me. "He asked me through Paul. Paul asked me in front of Kevin. I couldn't say no, all right? He's family."

"Isn't that the very reason to say no?"

"Not in the Matheson family."

"Surely there must be an ethical conflict? A rule violation?"

"Would you let me finish? There are rules, and most of them don't prevent me from representing Max. However, I'm likely to inherit money from Sally, and that will get me out of having to defend him at trial."

"Would you even have considered doing that?"

She exhales slowly, as though restraining herself from snapping back at me. "After I consulted with Max this morning—at the jail—he asked me to represent him at trial. Begged me, actually."

I'm shaking my head in disbelief. "Jet, what the fuck?"

"Please let me finish. This is difficult enough as it is. It's no mystery why Max wants me to defend him on this murder charge. I'm a woman and a family member. Even though someone else will almost certainly end up defending him at trial, my handling the early phase says more to potential jury members about his innocence than anything else could."

"Oh, I know why he wants *you*. But why have you agreed?"

She closes her eyes and takes a long breath. "Surely you've figured that out."

"Uhh, no."

Her voice drops to an angry whisper. "What's the one thing in life I need? Custody of my son. That's the only way I can be with you and live with myself."

"You think representing Max will—"

"*Yes.*"

This is wishful thinking. "Jet, I don't care what Max has promised you, he won't live up to it. Not once you get him off."

"He will. I've made sure of it."

I'm sure she's bound him to some kind of agreement, but I still see a problem. "Does he realize that rules might prevent you from defending him at trial?"

"Not yet. And by the time he finds out, it won't matter. He's providing me a sworn affidavit saying that I deserve to be Kevin's sole custodial parent. He'll describe Paul's years-long depression, his alcoholism, even his suicide attempts."

"Suicide attempts?"

She nods. "There are still a few things I haven't told you."

"Apparently so."

"Max will not only assert my fitness as a mother, but also his opinion that I'm an ideal role model for Kevin. We agreed on all these points before I handled the arraignment this morning."

Her controlled delivery leaves me speechless. I've always known that Jet had a calculating side, but her use of Sally's murder—and Max's likely guilt—as leverage to gain favorable divorce terms takes my breath away.

"I told you last night that I'm desperate," she goes on. "If defending Max for a couple of weeks gets Kevin and me clear of my marriage, it'll be the noblest work I've ever done. Hell, I'd defend him at trial to get that result. I can't help Sally now."

I reflect on this for a bit. "What did Arthur Pine think of you standing up for Max?"

"Arthur was surprised. When I got to the jail this morning, he was sitting outside looking very unhappy. I think the Poker Club sent him over."

This is worth thinking about in detail, but not now.

"Are you and I okay?" Jet asks. "Because I really don't want to discuss this anymore. It's going to be bad enough having to defend Max without you questioning my morality every step of the way."

"Did Max kill Sally?"

Jet takes no time with the question. "He insists he didn't. I honestly don't know. I'm not even sure I want to know."

"From what I've heard, it's hard to imagine that anyone else did it."

"What did you hear? That there were only two people in the room?"

"As far as the police could tell."

She gives me a forced smile that tells me she may be in possession of private information. "What I'm about to tell you goes in the vault," she says. "This is you and me, like we're in bed."

"All right."

"Max says Sally did it."

Once more, the world stops dead in space. This claim seems absurd on its face. "He says Sally killed herself? Shot herself through the heart? Is that what you're telling me?"

Jet nods. "While she was sitting on top of him."

"Like having sex?"

"No. He was asleep, and she climbed on top of him to shoot herself."

"I don't believe that for a second."

Jet shrugs. "Nevertheless, she had a good motive."

"Being married to Max? She's had that motive for forty-six years."

"You saw the argument they had at the Aurora last night."

"Half the town saw it. So?"

"Several years ago, Max had an affair with one of Sally's best friends. Probably her best friend. Sally only just found out about it. Day before yesterday. She was distraught. That must have been what she wanted to talk to me about yesterday."

Though this comes out of left field, it seems plausible. "Who was the friend?"

Jet touches her forefinger to her lower lip. "I'd prefer to keep that to myself for now."

Her stopping short of full disclosure shocks me, but I try not to show it. "Okay. So that's your pitch? Finding out Max screwed some friend of hers years ago was enough to make a seventy-year-old woman *shoot herself*?"

"Sally was sixty-six."

"Oh, that makes all the difference."

"Marshall—"

"Seriously, Jet. Max was a serial philanderer. Everybody knows that, and no one better than Sally."

Jet runs her fingers back through her dark hair. "Sometimes one straw breaks the martyr's back. Sally was drunk last night. Really drunk. That's unusual for her. She may have been taking pills as well. Max was drunk, too. He claims Sally had threatened to kill herself several times over the past thirty-six hours, including on the way home from the party last night."

"Suicide by gun is unusual among women."

"I know, but it happens. And the numbers have been rising."

"Among wealthy sixty-six-year-old white women?"

"I honestly don't know."

I'm trying to fit what Jet's telling me into my larger picture of the Matheson family, but I can't do it. "Yesterday you were worried that Sally might have found out about you and me."

"I don't think that's it anymore. It certainly doesn't matter now. We'll never know."

"Of course it matters. If Sally found out about us, that means someone else knows about us and told her. Plus, if she knew, she might have mentioned it to somebody else. Max, or even Paul."

"Sally wouldn't do that."

"No? I don't think she would shoot herself, either. Not over some affair. I've known Sally since I was three years old, and I'm sure of that. And what about Paul's sudden suspicions about you? Man, this stinks. It stinks all over."

Jet picks up her purse and stands. "Let's not have this conversation here."

I want to keep her here with me, but my mind is spinning. "I figured Max would claim there was a home invasion or something. Meth heads or crazy black kids. The whole town's going to go nuts over this, Jet. One of the richest guys in the county, and his wife shoots herself while sitting on top of him in bed? This is a TV movie, at the least."

"I know. But I don't have a choice. This is the price I pay for custody of Kevin."

"Oh, Jet. You *can't trust Max.*"

"I don't. But for once, I have him by the short hairs. And I'm going to pull *hard.*"

"I still think he killed her."

She blows out a rush of air and takes two steps toward the door. "He may well have. But Sally's gone, and Max's punishment isn't my primary concern. *Being* Max is sufficient punishment, in my view—second only to living with him."

Jet's barely holding herself together. I can't imagine the stress she must be under. "What kind of shape is Paul in?"

She reaches for the knob, then hesitates. "He's close to losing it. I don't think he understood how dependent he was on his mother. Sally loved him. Max . . . he doesn't know what love is."

"No. That's the awful truth."

"Kevin's not doing well, either. Sally doted on that boy. She was so protective of him."

"I'm sorry you're having to deal with this. I know that's inadequate, but . . ." I get up and walk around my desk, but Jet motions for me to keep my distance.

"This is all going to get worse before it gets better." Her hand is on the knob now. "I don't know when I'll be able to see you again. Maybe not for days. After the funeral, probably. I'll need to stay close to Kevin."

"And Paul," I say automatically.

A strange deadness comes into her eyes. "I'm not exaggerating about his mental state. We have to put a wall between us for the time being."

"What if I *have* to get hold of you? A real emergency?"

"I'll keep my burner on silent and try to check it every two or three hours."

"Once an hour would be better. There's no telling how things could break during all this."

"I'll try." She stands poised at the door, her resolve finally crumbling. "Are we really okay?"

"Always."

Her eyes close for a moment. Then she blows me a silent farewell kiss and walks out into the newsroom.

CHAPTER 23

AFTER JET LEAVES my office, I have no desire to wait for my reporters to find excuses to come in and ask what she was doing here. By now the whole staff knows she's defending Max. Before they start filtering in, I grab my keys and phones and head out early for my coffee at Constant Reader.

After starting the Flex, I try to find something calming on Sirius. As I tap the preset button, my eyes are drawn to an irregular line on my steering wheel. I jerk back, thinking it might be a roach or something. But it's not a roach.

It's a flash drive. A black USB thumb drive, 64 GB.

Someone has affixed it to my steering wheel with Scotch tape. The drive is a Lexar, available at any Office Depot. Taking out my iPhone, I text Nadine at the bookstore: *Have you replaced your computer yet? I need to borrow one.*

While I wait for a reply, the hair rises on my neck and arms. The Flex was locked when I came outside. I had to use my key fob to get in. That means somebody broke into my vehicle, left the flash drive, then locked the Flex again so nothing would seem odd as I climbed in. This is like the cracked safe at Nadine's store last night. Too smooth by half.

My iPhone pings. Nadine's reply reads: *I have a laptop here.*

I feel confident that her laptop will be an older model with at least one full-size USB port. *I'll see you in a couple of minutes,* I type.

Come in the back door, she answers. *Late breakfast crowd still here. Hostile to u and ur staff. I'll bring ur coffee to the back.*

Understood. I add a thumbs-up emoji and a coffee cup. Juvenile, maybe, but effective. This is what American communication has come to: adults sending each other cartoons.

NADINE'S OFFICE AT CONSTANT Reader is between the customer area and the back, where she stores inventory and café supplies. But when I slip through the back door off Barton Alley, I find a silver Mac-Book sitting on a large Formica-topped table, surrounded by stacked and flapped copies of *A Land More Kind Than Home,* by Wiley Cash. The North Carolina author must be coming to autograph books in the next day or two.

As I sit at the laptop, a door opens and shuts to my right, and Nadine appears with a steaming mug of coffee. She's wearing black capri pants and a tight-fitting navy top.

"You have a power outage at the paper or something?" she asks. "Why do you need my computer?"

I take the flash drive out of my pocket and hold it up. "Somebody left this taped to my steering wheel. In my locked SUV. I didn't want to go back into the office to open it."

"Why not?"

"Jet stopped by to see me this morning. She represented Max at his arraignment. I didn't want people questioning me about her reasons."

"I already heard. It's all over town. What are her reasons, by the way?"

"Family." I sigh. "Let's just leave it at that for now. I still can't get my head around it, to be honest."

Nadine watches me for a while before commenting. "Max's murder trial is going to be the biggest circus this state has seen in years. It's *Midnight in the Garden of Good and Evil,* Mississippi style."

I shake my head, shoving that image out of my mind. "Let's see what the flash-drive fairy left in my ride." I slide the drive into the USB socket, then take a careful sip from my coffee mug. "Oh, I needed that."

"I've got to get back up front," Nadine says. "Big crowd this morning."

"They're pissed about our story on Buck?"

"They'd tar and feather you if they could get away with it."

"I don't know who would stop them."

She gives me a quick smile. "That's why I told you to come back here. See you in a minute."

This courtesy is typical of Nadine. She'd give her eyeteeth to see what's on the flash drive, but she's going to let me check it first.

The Lexar appears to contain only a single file: a JPEG image. With my fingertip poised over the track pad, I freeze, suddenly certain that I'm about to open a digital photo of Jet leaning against the balcony rail of the Aurora Hotel, her dress hiked over her waist. Or worse, sitting astride me on the steamer chaise on my back patio. Anybody standing in the woods could have shot such a picture with a cell phone, though they would have had to zoom the hell out of it. With a smartphone, they could've shot video of the whole act. If I wait any longer to check, Nadine will reappear. Better to find out now.

I tap the track pad and wait the fraction of a second it takes the image to coalesce on Nadine's screen. I'm not sure at first what I'm looking at. It appears to be a night shot, a low-resolution image like those I've seen taken by wild game cameras. Hunters and curious landowners fasten these motion-triggered cameras to trees to keep track of nocturnal game movements on their property. Old friends from high school have shown me shots of huge bucks as well as coyotes and even a black bear captured on the devices.

Enlarging the image a little, I see two adult men facing each other across three feet of empty space. They're not centered in the frame, but stand to the right. With a couple of clicks, I zoom the image more, then move it laterally to center the faces.

A chill goes through me. The man on the left is Buck Ferris. Even in the pixelated low-res image, I see his ponytail hanging down his chest. The other man is shorter than Buck and more heavily built. Zooming the picture another 20 percent, I get only marginal improvement. I'm at the limits of the camera and the viewing program. Staring intently at the second man's features, and the way his head sits on his shoulders, I recognize the face of one of the men with the Poker Club guys at the groundbreaking ceremony. He was standing just outside the Prime Shot tent, drinking a beer from a bottle. It's Dave Cowart, the contractor Jet got sent to jail for a year. Cowart works for Beau Holland, the man who tried to assault me on the roof of the Aurora Hotel last night.

"Thank you, whoever you are," I murmur, wondering who could have broken into my vehicle and taped the drive to my steering wheel. I search the background of the image for landmarks but see none. Only darkness.

Then I go still. The image has a time and date stamp in its bottom left corner. Because I've always seen these on game camera photos, I didn't think anything about it. But on this photo, it means everything. This photo was shot two nights ago, at 1:17 A.M.

Buck was murdered two nights ago.

"Don't tell me," Nadine says, backing through the door with a box of books. "Some local hottie left you nude selfies."

"Take a look," I say, leaning back to give her room. "A lot better than selfies."

She leans forward and studies the screen for fifteen seconds.

"That's *Buck*," she says softly. "I see his ponytail!"

"Yep."

"Who's the other man?"

"Dave Cowart. The contractor Jet sent to jail for rigging bids. He works for Beau Holland. And that time stamp says this was shot on the night Buck was killed."

Nadine turns slowly to me, her eyes flickering with excitement. "What are you going to do?"

"Copy it onto your hard drive first, if that's okay."

She nods. "After that?"

"Make about ten more copies, then give one to the police."

"They won't do a damn thing with it."

"Probably not. But I have to give it to them." With a couple of clicks I save the image to Nadine's desktop.

"Are you going to print it in the paper?" she asks. "That's what I want to know."

"Oh, I think you can count on that."

"Who the *hell* shot that picture?"

"I think it was captured on an automatic game camera. A trail camera. Someone must have put some up to cover the mill site. I didn't see any last night, but then I didn't see much but dirt and bricks."

"So there could be pictures of you from last night? Of us?"

A ripple of fear goes through my chest. "There could be."

Almost of its own accord, my right forefinger moves toward the image, then hovers, moving up and down. Something's coming to me . . .

"Marshall?" Nadine says. "What are you doing?"

"This is why there were no guards out there the night Buck was killed. They replaced the human guards with automated trail cameras. Somebody saw Buck on a picture like this, taken on a game camera. And they knew they could go out there and kill him."

"In real time, you mean?"

"I'm pretty sure some of those cameras can send images to your cell phone. The newer, more expensive ones."

"Are you saying someone lured him out there?"

"Removing the security guards would have given Buck a false sense of security. When he didn't see any guards, he felt secure enough to trespass and dig again. But they still had live surveillance. The early trail cameras, you had to go out and physically remove the SD card and then view the pictures at home. But the new ones have SIM cards. If that's what happened, the killer could have been sitting in a bar, gotten a JPEG over his phone, and had plenty of time to drive out there and kill him."

"So . . . there might be pictures of the murder?"

"If I'm right, there could be. These cameras are triggered by motion. Maybe heat as well, I don't know. It all depends on whether Buck was killed within view of one of those cameras."

"How many pictures would the camera have shot?"

"As few as one, but maybe dozens. I don't know enough about them. I'll have to do some research. The question is, who broke into the Flex and left it for me? I was thinking it must be the person who cracked your safe. But . . . it can't be. This person is trying to *help* me."

Nadine bites her bottom lip and shakes her head. "Maybe the whole town's *not* against you."

"I wish my secret ally would come out of the closet."

"How do you know it's a he?"

"I don't. I suppose I just associate game cameras with men."

As we stand hypnotized by the image, my iPhone rings. Taking it from my pocket, I see the caller is my mother. She doesn't usually call at this time of day.

"What's up, Mom? Everything okay?"

"I don't know, Marshall."

My stomach does a slow roll. Mom doesn't get excited over trivial problems. "Tell me."

"Dr. Kirby called a few minutes ago. He did some tests on your father last Friday, and he's gotten some of the results back. Liver tests, mostly. He wants to talk to us about them. He asked if you could be here when he comes by this afternoon."

Jack Kirby has been my father's physician for more than fifty years, so house calls are not unusual. But asking that I be present for one is.

"What time's he coming over?"

"Four thirty."

"I'll be there, Mom."

"Thank you. I hate to interrupt your work. I know how much you have to do to hold everything together down there."

"It's no problem, Mom. Really."

"I saw the story about Buck Ferris," she says. "People are bound to be upset about that."

"No bricks through the front window yet."

"I'm glad to hear it!"

Normally, she would have tacked a chuckle on to that statement. But not today. She's deeply concerned about Dr. Kirby's visit.

"Are you where Dad can hear you?" I ask.

"No, I'm in the kitchen."

"What are you most worried about?"

"His liver and his heart. The Parkinson's symptoms are worsening, but apart from the hallucinations and the panic that follows, I can handle them. But he's still drinking. Jack told Duncan six months ago that his liver couldn't keep taking it. Plus, his heart's been on the verge of congestive failure for a while."

"All right. We'll see what Dr. Kirby says."

"I'll see you this afternoon, son."

When I hang up, I notice Nadine watching me with empathy.

"I feel like I'm looking at myself two years ago," she says.

"Yeah."

"Bad news?"

"Don't know yet. Doctor's coming by this afternoon. Wants me there."

She gives me a "Hang tough, it'll be okay" smile, but mercifully, she doesn't say anything more about it. She knows all too well what this kind of visit can mean.

"Do you want anything from the café?" she asks.

"No, thanks. I'd better duck out before anybody sees me. Did you talk to your friend about staying with her tonight?"

"Who said it's a her?"

This stops me. "It's a guy?"

"Yeah. Is that a problem?"

I shrug, fighting the urge to ask who it is. "No, it's fine. It's none of my business. I just assumed—"

"One kiss and we're exclusive?" Nadine looks indignant for a couple of seconds, then gives me her gamine smile. "You're better off not assuming anything with me."

I pull the flash drive out of the computer and slip it into my pocket, then take out my wallet.

"Coffee's on the house, moron. Call it rent for last night."

"Thanks." I walk to the back door and push it open.

"Hey," Nadine calls.

"Yeah?" I ask, turning.

"My friend's gay."

For a couple of seconds I don't know what to say. When I do speak, I sound like an idiot. "Uh . . . okay. I just wanted to make sure, you know . . . you had somewhere safe."

She nods once, still smiling.

And then I'm out the door.

CHAPTER 24

I'M SITTING QUIETLY in the kitchen of the house where I grew up, waiting for Dr. Kirby. My mother's in the den with my father, who might sense an ominous portent in the coincidence of my visit with that of his physician. The house smells different than it did when I was a boy. The sweet scent of Maker's Mark is familiar, but the tang of rubbing alcohol is new, as is the odor of liniment and the melted wax Dad uses to soothe his arthritis. But below these smells lives a sour stink of fermented urine that no disinfectant will quite eradicate, no matter how many times Mom scrubs the furniture and floors. Dad keeps blue plastic urinals beside his chair and bed now, so that he won't have to make the risky journey to the bathroom every hour, which I certainly understand and will probably do myself someday. But the cumulative result of all this alters the house so fundamentally that it doesn't feel like the same one I ran hell-for-leather through with my big brother when he was still with us.

The hours since I left Nadine's this morning have been full. Just after midday, Byron Ellis called to let me know that the locum tenens pathologist had declared Buck's murder to be death by misadventure—an accident. Most likely a fall, precipitated by digging above a cave mouth. Worse, Sheriff Joe Iverson claims to have found the very brick that Buck's head impacted when he fell, a brick that Iverson's deputies supposedly discovered near the river at Lafitte's Den. This brick supposedly lay directly under the drop from the sandstone shelf above the cave. This scenario is preposterous, of course, and most townspeople will realize that. Few will believe that Buck cracked his skull wide open in a fall, then crawled into the Mississippi River to drown himself.

But no one will protest.

The coroner also informed me that he'd found bone fragments in the soil samples I brought him from the mill site—specifically from the dirt scraped from the wall of the trench beside the factory pier. Better still, he'd detected blood on one of the brick fragments from the other area where Buck had been digging. This discovery left Byron Ellis with a dilemma: Should he make these further findings public and try to weather the political fury that will result? Or keep his head down and let the locum tenens pathologist push the party line?

"The county supervisors are already talking about trying to unseat me," he told me on the phone. "That's not easy, because I was elected by the people. But if the past is any guide, they'll find a way. That damn Arthur Pine can twist the law inside out to screw anybody who bucks them."

I assured Byron that I understood the danger and admired him for what he'd been willing to do so far.

"Whole town's up in arms at me already," he said. "That's what I hear. If I go on record about the bone and the blood, and the state comes in here and stops construction, folks'll run me out of town on a rail. Not just white folks, either."

"I'm not going to pressure you, Byron."

"Let me get back to you later," he said. "I'm talking to my lawyer, and also those activists I told you about. They're about ready to challenge that Poker Club. But they don't want to risk stopping the mill from coming in here. Too many of my people will get jobs behind that."

"I understand. Let's talk later today, or tonight."

I haven't heard from the coroner since, but I have hope that he'll come through. After talking to Byron, I decided to delay handing over the flash drive to law enforcement until after I publish the image it contained. Given the influence of the Poker Club over the police and sheriff's departments, showing them the photo of Buck Ferris and Dave Cowart together on the murder night would only invite pressure not to run it in the paper. They can't legally stop me, of course. But if the

Poker Club murdered Buck, they might be willing to go to extremes to prevent my pointing a finger at one of their minions.

"Marshall?" says my mother, leaning through the kitchen door. "Jack Kirby just texted me. He'll be here in five minutes."

"Thanks, Mom. You need any help in there?"

She gives me a resolute smile. "No, thanks. You greet Dr. Kirby. He usually comes to the side door."

Blythe McEwan is ten years younger than her husband. She has stood staunchly beside him through fifty years of alcoholism, fifty years of unrelieved grief, and now the long degeneration of his body. What reprieve can she be hoping for today? "Will do, Mom."

She nods and goes back to my father.

I push all thoughts of Buck Ferris and Sally Matheson out of my mind. If Dr. Kirby has bad news, Dad will not take it well, and if the past is any guide, he might get combative. I'm not the right person to soothe him in that instance; in fact, I usually have the opposite effect. But Mom wants me here, so I will remain, to be of whatever use I can. To an outsider, my attitude toward my father and his plight might seem cold, even cruel. But that attitude would be based upon ignorance.

How deep is the rift between my father and me?

He never met my son. Not once. Adam was born in 2006, two months after one of the most embarrassing experiences our family ever endured. In April of that year, I won the Pulitzer Prize for my book on Afghanistan and Iraq, and the award ceremony was scheduled for May. My parents only flew up because the committee had specifically invited Dad. He and I were the first father and son to have won the prize for journalistic work—his for Editorial Writing forty years earlier, mine for Letters (General Nonfiction). James and Franz Wright had won for poetry in 1972 and 2004, respectively, but the story of an award-winning multimedia journalist raised by a newspaper legend had caught the interest of the media worldwide.

In the annals of Pulitzer award dinners, our ceremony became a legendary disaster. Before the great Duncan McEwan got around to presenting my award—which the committee had graciously invited him to do—he ranted for three and a half minutes, excoriating the modern press, the George W. Bush administration, and, most of all, his nemesis: television news. Dad made it plain that he'd lived through the golden age of journalism and that the lowly hacks who tarnish the art today aren't fit to polish the boots of Robert Capa, I. F. Stone, or Stanley Karnow. He called me up to the dais only as an afterthought and handed down my Pulitzer certificate with a curt nod.

Eight weeks after that dinner, my son was born, ten days before his due date. A few hours after Adam entered the world, my mother got on a plane and flew up to D.C. alone. She told us that Dad had been too busy to leave Bienville on short notice, but even my wife knew this was a pathetic excuse. Still, we pretended it was true, for my mother's sake. Mom later admitted to me that Dad had started drinking as soon as he heard that Molly's water had broken, and he was in no shape to travel by air. I certainly had no desire to swallow my pride and carry Adam south to meet his grandfather, like a supplicant seeking the approval of his paterfamilias. (I'd already gathered that he wasn't happy with our naming the baby after my lost brother.) Besides, the prospect of putting Molly —who was already suffering from postpartum depression—in a room with her alcoholic father-in-law when he was likely to act like an asshole was something not even my mother could face.

I don't know how Dad reacted when *my* Adam drowned. I imagine he drank even more than usual, probably until he was comatose. By that time, I didn't care. My father had cut the cord binding him to us, and I felt no obligation to mend it. If my son's death gave me a better understanding of the pain he'd endured after losing two children, it did not incline me to excuse his past behavior.

A soft rapping sounds at the side door of my parents' house. I pop up from the chair and let in Dr. Jack Kirby, a bald, deep-voiced man who always reminds me of Lloyd Nolan, the doctor on *Peyton Place*. Jack's defining quality is gravitas, which you tend to find in physicians who've practiced nearly fifty years.

"Afternoon, Marshall," he says, shaking my hand as the smell of cigarette smoke wafts in with him. "I'm going to tell Duncan about his tests first, but I'd like you to stick around afterward, if you would. No matter what happens. I want to tell you something about Sally Matheson."

This takes me off guard. "Sally Matheson?"

"You'll understand when I tell you. Let's get this over with first."

WE FIND DAD SITTING in his worn La-Z-Boy recliner, which is aimed at the fifty-five-inch television he uses for target practice every day. Even now, CNN is running in the background, its anchor and pundits muted. Dr. Kirby chooses a chair far enough away from Dad to avoid any thrown object that might come his way.

Dad's face is expressionless, immobile, a classic example of what doctors call the "Parkinson's mask." He developed this quite early, according to my mother, and she finds it one of the most difficult manifestations of the illness to cope with. Even on the rare occasions when Dad feels pleasure or happiness, he cannot smile in a way that can be recognized by anyone but her. Thanks to expert administration and monitoring of his medications, he experiences very little in the way of tremors or jerks, and this has been a blessing to them both. I think Dad would have withdrawn completely into their house had he suffered those classic symptoms. Even so, the less visible complications have come close to breaking his will. Difficulty swallowing, sexual dysfunction, insomnia, hallucinations . . .

Even with his masklike face, Dad appears to be glowering at his old friend Dr. Kirby. Red eczema blotches mark his parched yellow skin, and his shock of white hair looks almost wild, which tells me he hasn't let Mom cut it in a while. The yellow tinge to his skin has been there for the past three months, but looking at him in the late-afternoon light spilling through the window, it seems to have worsened.

"Duncan," Dr. Kirby begins, "you're not going to be happy about this visit. But I've given you all the rope I can. I got your latest liver enzymes back today, and there's no good way to put this: you've crossed into end-stage liver disease. You keep drinking, and your liver will kill you long before the Parkinson's lays you low."

Dad takes this with the stoicism he always displayed when I was a boy—as though he's heard nothing that must be acknowledged, much less attended to immediately. Jack Kirby understands him well enough to know that the prognosis was heard. Now he drives it home, as my mother sits silently on the sofa, wringing her hands.

"I've known you since we were boys," Jack goes on. "And I've been practicing medicine long enough to realize that your intended goal may be to die from cirrhosis before the Parkinson's reaches its final stage. But let me tell you why that's a bad plan. You've been living with heart failure for a while now. Combined with that, liver failure might not give you the result you want. It might cause your kidneys to fail. Or all your issues together might stress your system badly enough to trigger a stroke, or even a series of them. You might have to sit in a wheelchair all day. You might be permanently bedridden. Then you wouldn't be able to drink unless Blythe held the bottle and let you suck it through a straw. And I know she'll draw the line there."

Dad still has not acknowledged his friend's words. He's watching Wolf Blitzer give some paid flack airtime to canonize his employer. Sometimes I wonder whether Dad's reticence is the result of shame over what the disease has done to his formerly powerful voice. The resonant baritone that once steadied *Stars and Stripes* reporters in Korea, pushed back Ku Klux Klansmen in 1960s Mississippi, and delivered heartbreaking eulogies over friends has been reduced to a reedy whisper, a ghost of its former self.

"You could live quite a while that way," Dr. Kirby continues. "The Parkinson's would continue to progress, but your lovely bride would be feeding you by hand and wiping your butt twenty-four-seven, and for a long time. That's not right, Duncan. Not if it's in your power to prevent it. You know that."

Dad sits with unusual stillness for several seconds. Then without looking at Kirby he whispers, "She put you up to this, didn't she?"

"No, damn it," Dr. Kirby says firmly as my mother closes her eyes. "About the only thing Blythe ratted you out for is living on ice cream. I know it's tough for you to swallow, but you've got to eat some mashed-up vegetables to survive. You've lost nearly fifty pounds since my original diagnosis, and we don't want to add diabetes to your list of problems."

"I want to see those tests," Dad demands, his head jerking suddenly. "I want to see if they're as bad as you say."

With his jaw set in anger, Dr. Kirby pulls a folded sheaf of paper from his inside coat pocket, carries it over to the La-Z-Boy, and drops it in Dad's lap. "There you go, you hardheaded son of a bitch. You don't know enough chemistry to read them, but you can see the red warning highlights, with *low* or *high* screaming off every line."

With quivering hands, Dad struggles to hold the papers in his grasp. Dr. Kirby mutters something and does it for him, even though he knows this is a pointless charade.

"Did you see what Trump said today about the *New York Times?*" Dad asks as he studies the quivering papers before his face.

"I don't give a goddamn what he said. I stopped caring a long time ago."

"Not caring is the same as begging for fascism," Dad grumbles.

Dr. Kirby stares down at him for a while. Then he says, "I tell you what, Duncan. I'm going to have a word with Marshall outside. I need to talk to him about something for the newspaper. A Medical Society statement on Medicaid expansion. I'll look back in before I go, after you and Blythe have had a chance to talk."

"Go right ahead."

The doctor motions for me to follow him back to the kitchen, but even there, we're too close to my father for comfort. At Kirby's suggestion, we step out onto the small redwood terrace that overlooks the wooded backyard.

"Poor Blythe," Jack says. "I see it all the time. All the men I grew up with act like kings in their dotage. They expect to be waited on hand and foot, regardless of how obstinate they are or what silly whims they come up with. I've seen a man send his wife and children thirty miles in every direction to find him a goddamn Nehi soda."

"I can imagine."

The doctor sits on the redwood bench against the rail and squints up at me. "Marshall, before I speak, I want to be very clear that everything I'm about to tell you is off the record. Is that understood?"

"Absolutely."

"I'm about to break a bunch of HIPAA regulations, or laws, and you're going to keep quiet about it."

"Yes, sir."

"And please don't call me 'sir.' It's Jack, all right?"

"All right, Jack. Off the record."

He takes out a cigarette, a Winston, and lights it. After blowing out a long stream of blue smoke, he holds up the cigarette and says, "Do as I say, not as I do."

"Noted."

"All right. In the next day or two, an autopsy on Sally Matheson is likely to say she was healthy when she died. But in truth, she was ill. Very ill."

My reporter's radar throws back a hard echo. "Really? If she was that sick, why won't the autopsy pick it up? Are they getting that local pathologist to do it? Like they did with Buck Ferris?"

"I don't know who's doing the post, but medical fraud isn't my worry. About four months ago, I diagnosed Sally with a rare condition called amyloidosis. It's a blood disease. A progressive one. You've probably heard of amyloid proteins—they're what's deposited as plaques in the brain in Alzheimer's disease. But there are different types of amyloidosis. Some you can live with a long time, others you can't. Sally had an incurable type."

"Did she know that?"

"Oh, yes. But she told me she didn't want anyone to know she was ill—not even Max and Paul. She was adamant. And my policy with longtime patients like Sally is to honor their wishes. At least until it becomes a serious risk to them. Of falls, et cetera."

"Were you treating her for this condition?"

"Symptomatic treatment. There's really no treatment for the disease itself. Not for her type. She was a borderline candidate for a bone marrow transplant, but she ultimately decided against it."

Jack's revelation has already altered my perception of both Sally's death and her husband's alibi. "You still haven't said why the autopsy won't pick up her illness."

"The disease is subtle, at first. And they won't be looking for it. Tests involve collecting twenty-four hours' worth of urine, doing skin fat tests, things like that. Depending on the extent of organ damage at this point, a first-rate pathologist might detect it, but my guess is it'll slip through."

"How bad was her prognosis?"

"With her type . . . pretty grim. For a proud, beautiful woman like Sally, it would be tough to endure."

In some fraction of a second I recall with perfect clarity Paul's

TV-pretty mother teaching us to gut, clean, and fry fish at Lake Co-meaux. "How long would she likely have lived beyond last night?"

Dr. Kirby scratches his chin. "Hard to say. I learned long ago that physicians make poor oracles. As long as a year, but more likely seven or eight months. Possibly less."

"Christ. This is some kind of week we're having."

Kirby's eyebrows go up. "We?"

"Everybody. The whole town."

"I'd have to agree with you there."

"Why have you told me this, Jack?"

Dr. Kirby takes a long drag on his Winston, then lets the smoke out slowly. "I read your story on Buck Ferris. I'm glad you wrote it, but I'm probably one of the few. And I was worried that if you wrote about Sally's death in the same way, you might get out ahead of your skis, suggesting it was murder."

For a few seconds I wonder if Dr. Kirby has come here at the behest of Max Matheson or someone else in the Poker Club. But Jack Kirby is no great friend to the Poker Club, and he's certainly not a member of their little cabal. "You're saying Sally might really have killed herself. And not because of any affair Max had. Because of this illness."

Kirby shrugs. "In my experience, when patients kill themselves, it's not usually a single stressor that causes it. There's preexisting depression, which Sally didn't have for most of her life but did after this diagnosis. Then something else pushes them over the edge."

"Like the betrayal of an old friend?"

"Possibly. I've heard the rumors, of course."

"Have you heard a name?"

"Three or four. Some more plausible than others. I don't want to dignify any of them. But with Max they could all be true. He's a legendary pussy hound."

Dr. Kirby's casual use of this term reminds me that his courteous manner is a veneer he preserves for business hours and mixed gatherings. At heart, he's a Southern male who spends his holidays and summers in hunting camps and fishing cabins. He sees life as it is, and he's quite capable of speaking with crude candor.

"I understand, Jack. I appreciate you telling me this."

He nods and takes another drag off the Winston, quickly burning the cigarette down to a stub.

"Are you going to tell anybody else this information?" I ask.

"I think I'm pretty much obligated to pass it on to the police. Don't you?"

"Yeah. I faced a similar dilemma earlier today. Someone left a photograph in my car, a tip having to do with Buck's murder. I'd like to keep it to myself, but I'll give it to the sheriff just before I publish it."

Dr. Kirby rolls his eyes. "For all the good it will do, right?"

"With our sheriff? You're right."

"Can you tell me who the photo implicated?" he asks.

"I shouldn't."

"I shouldn't have told you about Sally."

I give him a wry smile. "What do you know about Dave Cowart?"

The doctor scowls. "A belligerent redneck. Some of the crooks in this town are old-time rogues, you know? Best drinking companions you could hope for. Not Cowart. He's stupid and greedy and doesn't have a lick of moral sense."

"Well, I'm about to make an enemy of him. Probably his boss, too. Beau Holland."

"Another prize ass." Kirby throws down the cigarette butt and grinds it out with his patent leather shoe. "Beau Holland comes from a long line of arrogant, effete bastards."

"It shows."

"Do you carry a pistol?"

Dr. Kirby asked this as casually as he would inquire if I carried a pocket watch. "I started last night."

"Good. Wear it night and day. If you're going to make enemies of Cowart and Holland and their pals, you need to keep your head on a swivel."

The doctor's matter-of-fact warning sobers me. "Sounds like you know some firsthand information about them."

Kirby looks off into the trees. "I've lived in this town a long time, Marshall. That Poker Club's a unique little organization. When they want things to happen, sooner or later those things happen. Sometimes you can trace it back to direct action by a member, but more often you can't. Take civil rights. I know of no direct ties between the

Poker Club and the Klan or even the White Citizens' Council. In fact, I don't think the members give much of a damn about skin color. If you've got the money to live where they live, you're mostly welcome— schools being the exception. They don't like their kids going to school with blacks. They don't mind a few black football players peppering the teams, but they don't want their daughters dating them."

"The old miscegenation bugbear is still alive and well."

"Yes, indeed. But the Poker Club has funneled enough money to black leaders in this county over the years that things have stayed just how they like them. And if a few colored boys got killed back in the day for not knowing their place, well . . . nothing led back to the Poker Club."

"That was a long time ago, Jack."

"Not to me. But if you want more recent history, I can think of five or six men who ran afoul of the Poker Club in the last twenty years and wound up ruined or dead."

"Murdered?"

Dr. Kirby turns up one palm. "It's never that cut-and-dried. One-car crash. Hunting accident climbing through a fence with a rifle. Another guy got caught up in his own bush hog, bled to death."

"And nothing traced back to the Poker Club?"

"Never." Dr. Kirby looks back at me. "Sounds a lot like Buck Ferris drowning in the Mississippi River, doesn't it?"

"Now that you mention it."

"Remember what I said about your pistol. Make sure you don't have any accidents."

"I hear you."

The doctor gets to his feet with a groan. "I'd better get back in there and take a last stab at your father. I've still got one more house call to make."

I smile at him. "You've got some lucky patients, Jack."

A shadow passes over his face. "In general, if I'm going to see some-body at the end of my day, they're pretty unlucky. But that's life, son. Enjoy it while you're still young."

I walk to the side door with him but don't go in myself. "I don't feel too young these days, Jack."

He stops and turns back to me. "Then you're blind. If you could see yourself from eighty-three, where I'm standing, you'd know different. Get yourself a pretty girl and make some babies. That's all that matters. You can use that Pulitzer of yours for a doorstop in the nursery."

Like a lot of people, Dr. Kirby mistakenly assumes that the Pulitzer Prize is a statue, like an Oscar. "I'll try to do that," I tell him. Then I stick out my hand, and he takes it, his grip surprisingly firm for his age.

His wise eyes find mine once more. "I told your father the truth, Marshall. If he keeps drinking, he'll be dead in a month. Maybe even a week. His liver could quit any time. His heart, too. You need to prepare your mother for that."

"She's pretty tough, Jack."

The doctor releases my hand but not my gaze. "Not as tough as you think. Southern women don't show their pain to anybody. They aren't raised that way. But they feel it. So, as unpleasant as Duncan has made the back end of her life, Blythe is still going to shatter when he goes. She's suffering from severe sleep deprivation right now. Depression, too." Kirby glances at his watch. "Will Duncan leave her pretty well fixed financially?"

I shake my head. "If he'd sold out six years ago, when values were high, he might have got eight or nine million. Today we'd be lucky to get ten percent over the real estate value. That's how fast the business has changed."

"Damn. That's the world now, isn't it? I'm glad you'll be here to help Blythe pick up the pieces."

I look back in silence, absorbing the message he clearly intends for me to get: *Don't plan on flying out of here the day after your father's funeral . . .*

"Thanks for your frankness, Jack."

He gives me a quick salute, then marches back into our house. But he's already thinking about the next house he'll visit, the next family living under the shadow of death.

CHAPTER 25

TO MY AMAZEMENT, Jet calls my burner phone at 6:20 P.M. and tells me she's five minutes from my house. I go out to wait for her on the patio as I did yesterday, but not on the steamer chaise. If we have sex, we're going to do it inside. There'll be no more tempting fate, not with things as they now stand.

Once again, Jet appears from the trees across the mown field and walks steadily toward me, only today she keeps her clothes on. The sky has turned deeper blue as the sun moves toward the western horizon. Jet has changed out of her courtroom attire; she's wearing jeans and a sleeveless top. As she nears the patio, I step into the grass and give her a long hug.

"How did you get away?" I ask.

When she pulls back, I see that she's wearing more makeup than usual, and her eyes are bloodshot. "They're practicing baseball, believe it or not. The traveling team. Max said it was the best thing for Kevin, and Paul agreed. They're over at the Baptist church field. They'll be at it till seven thirty, but I need to leave in thirty minutes. We can't take even the slightest risk right now."

"Agreed. Let's get inside."

After a brief kiss, I lead her into the house. Jet walks over to a cabinet and removes an opened bottle of pinot noir, then pours herself a glass and takes a long sip.

"What's it been like over there?" I ask. "How's Kevin doing?"

"He's in shock. Everybody is. Even Max, which is hard to believe. Sally's death has blown a hole in that house."

"Paul?"

"Even worse than I feared. He's a rudderless boat in a storm."

This doesn't surprise me. "Sally was the only real counterweight to Max in that family. I don't know if Paul can deal with Max off the chain."

Jet closes her eyes and sighs. "Deep down, Paul knows there's nothing left in me. Not for him. Sally's death may finally make him face that."

"Or he might shove it down so deep he'll never have to."

"That's what he's been doing for years."

Jet sits at the kitchen table and stares into her wine. I've rarely seen her morose, but given that she's accepted the burden of defending Max, I'm surprised she's not in deep depression. "What have you spent the day doing?" she asks, sounding preoccupied.

My visit with Dr. Kirby rises into my mind, but I'm not ready to broach that subject yet. I ought to summarize my receipt of the flash drive and my interaction with the coroner, but I don't feel like going into that, either. In the end I mumble a boring evasion.

Jet slowly runs the tip of her right forefinger around the rim of her wineglass, as though trying to get it to resonate. I watch her for a while, wondering whether she's come here out of habit or has something on her mind. After a couple of trancelike minutes, she lifts her finger from the glass and says, "Sit down. I need to tell you something."

Her ominous tone makes me swallow hard, but I sit opposite her and wait.

She says, "I've been thinking about what you said, about not being able to trust Max."

"And?"

"I have a backup plan to get custody of Kevin. Two plans, actually. One you know about, one you don't."

"Which one do I know about?"

My iPhone begins to ring. The screen tells me it's Nadine. I click DECLINE and put the phone back in my pocket.

"Who was that?" Jet asks.

"Ben Tate," I answer, inexplicably lying for the first time since we began our affair. "I'll call him later."

"Thanks. Do you remember when I told you that I thought both

Max and Paul had committed felonies related to their businesses? Tax fraud, for one thing, but also improper disposal of the toxic waste produced by the wood treatment plant? Both arsenic and hexavalent chromium."

"Sure, I remember. But you didn't have proof."

"Now I do."

The coldness in her voice is unnerving. "How did you get it?"

"I went through Max's office this morning, while he was in jail. With Sally dead, there was nobody to question what I was doing. The evidence against Paul I found about three weeks ago."

"Okay. So, to sum up: you're suggesting that the best way to get custody of your son is to put your husband and father-in-law in prison?"

Anger flares in her eyes. "Obviously that's not the ideal solution. But it might be the least dangerous one. Would you have scruples about me doing that?"

"Not because of Max. But Paul . . . yes. Plus, I'm not sure Kevin would ever forgive you for that."

"That's my hesitation, too."

"What's this second option? The one I don't know about?"

She bites her lip and studies me, searching for something I'm not sure she'll find. "It's more complicated," she says. "But it would only affect Max."

"Let's hear it. You're running out of time."

"It has to do with the Poker Club and Azure Dragon Paper. I don't know all the details of the deal that brought the Chinese here, but I do know money and favors changed hands over site selection. I'm not sure who got what, but I know from things Max and Paul have said that it happened. I decided to exploit that to get leverage over Max, with the goal of discrediting him with the Poker Club."

"How?"

"About eight months ago, my father sent me some money from Jordan. I didn't tell anybody about it, not even Paul. I ran it through my law practice. Apparently, my father's felt guilty all his life for leaving me. He's sick now. Anyway, knowing I had that money, I decided to create a little alternate reality."

"For whom?"

"The Poker Club."

"I like the sound of this, but you're scaring me a little. What have you done, Jet?"

She looks reluctant to continue, which tells me that her plan must be pretty extreme.

"I'm over at Max and Sally's house a lot," she says. "Obviously. I've gotten into Max's office quite a few times alone. I've never figured out his computer password, but I do have some of his banking information. Using that, I set up an overseas account for him in the Seychelles, which I've heard him mention as a haven for illegal money. Then I took the money I got from my father and bought Bitcoin with it."

She's losing me. "Bitcoin? What the hell?"

"You'll understand in a minute. I held that for a couple of weeks, then deposited it in a Chinese bank under an alias. That was the hardest part, but I managed it. It helped to be a lawyer. Anyway, my last step was transferring the money from the Chinese bank to the Seychelles account in Max's name. Do you see where I'm going with this?"

It takes me about twenty seconds to work it out. "You want Max's partners to think he's double-crossing them. That he's taking money on the side that they don't know about."

She nods, still waiting.

"If Max's partners believe that . . . it won't just discredit him. They might kill him."

"They might," she says. "Someone like Tommy Russo might. But I don't think it would go that far. I don't think the others would let that happen."

Her words sound sincere, but her eyes betray such savage intent that I feel a shudder of revulsion. "I don't think you're being honest with yourself."

"Marshall, I told you I'm desperate. If I execute this plan, Max will lose the protection of his partners. He'd also lose his influence over things like cops and judges. The Poker Club wouldn't lift a finger to help him with something like my divorce."

"Maybe not. But the first thing they would do is confront Max with whatever evidence you leaked to them. And Max would deny it."

"They wouldn't believe him. The evidence is undeniable. Oh, Blake Donnelly might take up for him. But it would only take a couple of malcontents to create chaos in their ranks. Max would never be trusted again."

I let her suggestion hang in the air, hoping she'll recognize the dangers inherent in it. But Jet only watches me, hoping I'll tell her to put her plan into motion.

"You're forgetting something," I tell her. "The Poker Club members might believe Max screwed them. But *Max* would know he was innocent. And it wouldn't take him long to work out who had put him into that trap."

Jet nods like a queen who has already accepted death as the risk of victory in war. "I'm willing to take that chance."

A wave of apprehension rolls over me. Schemes like this end up getting people killed, or at least locked into prison cells. Instead of arguing with her, I reach out for her wineglass. As I drink the remaining contents, an even more frightening possibility hits me.

"Jet, will you swear you haven't put this plan in motion already? You haven't told the Poker Club about this fake Seychelles account, have you?"

She smiles strangely. "It's not fake."

"You know what I mean."

She sighs in what sounds like frustration. "This isn't an Alfred Hitchcock film. I haven't *done* anything, except set up that account. What makes you think I've already set it in motion?"

"Sally was murdered last night. How about that? I'm worried the Poker Club might have sent somebody over there to shoot Max, and they got Sally instead."

"Oh, that's ridiculous."

I'm missing something, I can feel it. "Why today, Jet? Why are you suddenly telling me about this setup that was weeks or months in the planning?"

She gets up and retrieves the wine bottle from the counter, then sits beside me and pours another glass. "I didn't tell you because this was risky to set up. I didn't want you worrying about me every minute. I also hoped I wouldn't have to do it. But now . . ."

"Jet, you've done a one-eighty on Max since this morning. What changed your mind about your plan?"

She takes a sip of wine, then turns to me and lays both hands on my knees. "Sally's physician delivered a little bombshell down at the sheriff's department this afternoon."

Not wanting to betray my promise to Jack Kirby, I act like I know nothing about this. "What bombshell?"

"According to the doctor, Sally had a terminal illness."

I try to look appropriately shocked. "And nobody knew about it?"

"Nobody but Dr. Kirby. Sally didn't want anyone to know."

"Cancer?" I ask.

Jet shakes her head. "Some kind of blood protein disorder. She had the worst form of it. Terrible prognosis."

I take another sip of wine and consider how this must have affected Jet's calculations about Max. "I understand now. Max's claim that Sally killed herself just became easier to sell to a jury."

"A hundred times easier."

"Max thinks he can get acquitted without your help. So he won't honor any promise to stay out of your divorce."

"I never said you were slow."

"I'd say Max's fate depends on the jury. The crime scene was pretty damning. Max could still go to jail for life."

"In this county?" Jet gets up and walks to the back window. She speaks without looking back at me. "Marshall . . . how would you feel if the Poker Club killed Max?"

In all the years I've known her, I have never heard this tone in her voice. Something has snapped. "I'm no fan of Max's," I say warily, trying to stall as I adjust to this new perception. "I never was. But you're talking about murder. Potentially. Remote-control murder."

"Hey—" She's still looking out the window, and there's a new rigidity in her posture. "I thought I saw something move in the trees."

"Probably a deer. They hang out at the edge of the woods this time of evening, using the tree line for cover when they venture into the grass."

She raises her hand to the window and squints. "Do you know how much better off Paul would be without Max riding him every day? Max has spent his life crippling Paul emotionally. Beating him down."

"Granted. But the penalty for being a shitty father isn't death."

At last Jet turns from the window. "I also believe there's a strong probability that Max shot Sally, no matter what Dr. Kirby says about her prognosis. Sally was genuinely religious. Not churchy—truly devout."

"Maybe you shouldn't be defending him."

Jet watches me in silence for half a minute. Then she reaches into her cropped pants and takes out what looks like a necklace with a jewel pendant.

"There may be one more way I can neuter Max," she says.

"What's that?" I ask, pointing to the pendant in her hand.

"A sapphire necklace. Art deco. It belonged to Sally." Jet hooks her fingers through the chain and swings the pendant slowly back and forth like a Hollywood hypnotist. Light from the window flashes blue from the stone, which appears to be surrounded by diamonds. "It was made in Moscow in 1930. Sally's father bought it in Berlin in 1947, when he was in the air force. It's a family heirloom."

"And?"

"You know sapphires are my favorite stone. Sally always told me that after she was gone, this would be mine."

"Okay."

"This morning, while Max was in jail, I didn't just go through his office. I wandered around the house thinking about Sally. I went into her bedroom. I could smell her, see the clothes she'd worn the last couple of days. I also went into her bathroom and looked through her jewelry box."

"And you took the necklace."

Jet nods.

"What's it worth?"

"I don't know. Maybe fifty thousand. You're missing the point. It's not just a necklace."

"What do you mean?"

"There's a white sticker on the back, and there's writing on it."

"What does it say?"

Her eyes flash. "It's passwords, Marshall. A five-digit one on top. Then a longer one, a word followed by numbers."

"Passwords to what?"

"I don't know. I tried Sally's computer—no luck. Same with Max's laptop and desktop. The police have her iPhone, but I think she would have foreseen that. Whatever these passwords open, I think she put them where she knew I'd find them—not right away, but sooner or later."

"What's the word part of the second password?"

"Mai Loc. The whole password is MaiLoc1971."

"My lock?" I ask, incredulous.

"It's not English words," she explains. "It's M-A-I, L-O-C. I googled it. Mai Loc is a village in the central highlands of Vietnam. The U.S. Army Fifth Special Forces Group established a camp there in 1968."

"Holy shit. That's Max all over. Green Beret. But he was still in high school in '68. Was the camp still there in '71?"

"Yes. Wikipedia says the Special Forces had pulled out by then, but there was a sizable operation near there in '71, and Max could have been part of that. He reached Vietnam in 1970, and I know he served in that area in '71. Quang Tri Province."

"Was the name of the operation 'Mustang'?"

"Montana Mustang."

"Max played some role in that. I heard him talk about it in high school. Those have to be passwords, at least the second one. The pun is so obvious. *Mai Loc?*"

Jet nods, her eyes filled with the primal excitement I've seen in men's eyes before a hunt. "Sally left these passwords for me. But unless I can figure out what they open, it won't help us."

"Do you think Max killed her over whatever those passwords protect?"

"Maybe."

"What could it be?"

"I think the first number is a cell phone password."

Suddenly I see her intent. "You're going to try to steal Max's phone?"

"Given the stakes, I'd say it's worth it."

"You couldn't get to it at the jail this morning?"

"I tried, but they wouldn't give it to anybody but Max. The Poker Club owns that department, Marshall."

I'm tired of hearing about everything the Poker Club controls.

"One more thing," she says. "Two days ago, Max asked me about some manila folders he claims were stolen from his home office."

"Why didn't you tell me?"

She shrugs. "I didn't know anything about them. I didn't take them. It never occurred to me that Sally might have. I figured Tallulah mislaid them."

"Jet . . . I need to think about all this. But you remember one thing: you can't put that Seychelles plan in motion. In fact, I'm telling you not to. It's tantamount to murder."

She studies me for what feels like a long time, not challenging me, but seemingly trying to understand my decision. "You realize it might be the only way for me to get out of this town with Kevin? Without hurting Paul."

I'm on dangerous ground here. "I don't think so. I think that after this craziness settles down, there'll be a way to tell the truth—or some less cruel version of it—and still get what we want. Without damning ourselves for all time."

In the silence that follows this exchange, I look back at the woman who at fourteen appeared to me as an earthbound angel. She's almost as beautiful now as she was then, but I no longer see an angel. Of course, angels don't exist. They're the personification of wishful thinking by desperate humans. And that's what I see before me now—a woman at the end of her rope.

My iPhone pings. Taking it out, I see a text from Nadine. It reads: *I'm outside. Someone broke into my mother's house. I freaked out and came here. I tried to call but you didn't answer. Was going to use the key, but I heard voices. Should I leave?*

"What is it?" Jet asks.

There's no point lying now. "Nadine Sullivan's outside."

Her eyes widen. "At your gate? Or right outside the house?"

"The house, I think."

"She has your gate code?"

"I gave it to her last night. Somebody broke into her store during the Aurora party, so she stayed here."

Jet sits utterly still, but she's sifting through the possibilities. "Nadine can't see me here," she says finally. "Not today."

"No."

"If I hide in the back bedroom, will I be okay? Or should I slip out?"

The coldness in that voice . . . the underlying pragmatism. "You'll be okay. Hide in the bedroom."

Her tongue skates along the edge of her top teeth as she thinks my answer through. "Okay." She gets to her feet. "We'll finish this conversation after she goes, if I'm still here. I can't get stuck."

"I don't think she'll be long," I reply, then instantly regret it. I have no idea how long Nadine will stay, or expect to.

As Jet walks toward the hall, her wineglass in her left hand, I text Nadine to come to the garage door.

"If we don't talk again," Jet says, "wait for me to contact you. Don't risk calling me."

"I know. And you don't do anything crazy. About the Seychelles or Max's cell phone. Okay?"

She holds up her free hand in a limp wave that communicates deep sadness. Then she turns and walks down the hall.

CHAPTER 26

WHEN I OPEN the garage door, I find Nadine standing very straight but looking harried and pale. She has her mother's pistol in one hand and her cell phone in the other.

"Did I mess up?" she asks. "You told me I could come if I felt afraid. I don't trust the damn police in this town."

"You didn't mess up. Come in."

I step back and she slides past me, then glides into the kitchen.

"I thought I heard voices," she says. "I thought somebody was in here with you. I didn't see a car, though."

She must not have seen Jet's Volvo parked in the woods. "I was talking to Jet on speakerphone. That's why I ignored your first call."

"Oh." Nadine nods to herself. "What's going on with her? If she's defending her father-in-law for killing his wife, I guess she's having a busy day."

"She just wants to be kept in the loop on Buck's murder. How do you know somebody broke into your mother's house? You went over there?"

"About forty minutes ago."

"Alone?"

"Yes. I took the gun and some pepper spray."

"Christ, Nadine. You know better. What did you see?"

"The house wasn't torn to pieces or anything. But somebody had been there, I could feel it. They'd been through the drawers, looked under the mattresses, gone through the books."

"I don't get this. What are they looking for?"

"I have no idea."

"Well, they think you have something. They obviously know you're living at your mother's house. So either they know you, or they've followed you home before."

A little fear shows in her eyes. "May I have a glass of that wine?"

"Sure." I pour her one, recalling Jet taking her glass with her when she went to the back. "I think you'd better stay here again tonight."

"Oh, I called my friend. He's got a bed ready for me."

"You're safer here, behind my gate and with no neighbors nearby. If we see somebody prowling here, we know they mean us ill. That's not true in town. You might be reluctant to shoot to defend yourself there."

She accepts the glass and takes a small sip. "Do you really think it's going to come to that? Shooting somebody?"

"Two people we know have died this week. Do you have some special immunity to bricks or bullets?"

She answers in a tone of surrender. "No."

An audible *clunk* comes from the back bedroom. Nadine's head pops up. In her anxious state, she's hypersensitive to every stimulus.

"What was that?" she asks.

Jet just left the house. That *clunk* was the exterior door in the master bedroom, which sticks about half the time you try to open it. "The bedroom AC makes a loud noise when it kicks on back there. I haven't done much to improve the place."

She watches me for a couple of seconds, then looks away. "I'm surprised you live so far from town. You know, from the newspaper."

"I like the isolation. It's turned out to be a good thing, given public reaction to my dad's editorials."

"I guess it would be." She takes another sip of wine. "Can I have something stronger?"

"Sure, what do you want?"

"Vodka?"

I go to the freezer and grab a bottle of Crater Lake, pour three fingers into a glass. Nadine walks over and drinks off most of it in one gulp. "*Yes,*" she says with obvious relief. "Thank you. Look, there's another reason I came out here."

"What's going on?"

"Has Jet told you anything about Max's alibi? About the woman he supposedly slept with? The friend of Sally's? The paramour, as they say?"

"No. I asked, but she wouldn't tell me who it was."

"I'm glad to hear that. But the name's gotten out somehow."

"Who is it?"

"Max claims it was my mother."

A sense of unreality descends over me. "*Your* mother?" I don't believe that. Margaret Sullivan? And *Max*?

Nadine nods hopelessly.

"Where did you hear that?"

"It's all over town. It's probably on fucking Facebook by now. Three or four women have been mentioned as the possible alibi, and Max probably screwed them all. But my mother's name was on top of the list. And twenty minutes ago, a friend of mine heard a deputy's wife confirm it. Max named my mother in his initial interview."

I can't imagine the furor this must be triggering in the social circles of Old Bienville. "I just . . . I don't know. Max might have told them that, but do you believe it's possible?"

Nadine points at the vodka bottle, and I pour her another glass.

"Possible?" she echoes, swallowing another shot. "Sure, it's possible. It's sex, right? You know how these things happen. A lot of husbands want to nail their wife's best friend. A lot of divorces start just that way."

"I can't see it. Your mother and Max."

"Diametric opposites, I know. But you know what they say . . ."

"This whole mess is getting crazier by the hour. Did your mother ever give you any hint that something like that had happened?"

A look of uncertainty comes into Nadine's face. "Not directly, no."

"But?"

"There was a short period when Sally stopped coming to Mom's book club. Three or four weeks in a row, she always had an excuse. The first two weeks, no one paid any attention. Then the other women noticed."

"Did Sally eventually come back to the meetings?"

"She did. I checked my old club schedule. Yes, I'm OCD like that. Sally came back the fifth week."

"Do you know whether the two of them talked privately before she came back?"

"No. But I wouldn't necessarily have known. They could have spoken on the phone, or Sally could have come by when I was out shopping or even out of town for a day. Now and then our old maid would come over and stay with Mom and give me a night in New Orleans."

"I see."

Nadine starts pacing around the kitchen and table. "I've been thinking about the last couple of weeks before Mom died. She went through a period of deep depression. She cried a lot. Mom and Sally had been close since they were little girls. When I asked about her crying, she talked about forgiveness. How hard it was, and how rare. She said very few human beings ever forgive anything. They just shove the hurts down deep and pretend they never happened. And they stop trusting."

"Do you think she was talking about herself and Sally?"

"I didn't at the time. She also said something about men bringing out the weakness in women. At the time I assumed that had to do with my father. But now . . . I suppose she could have been talking about Max."

"But from what you've told me, whether Sally forgave your mother or not, it sounds like she knew the affair had happened."

"I guess so."

"If she did, that means Max's suicide story is bullshit. Sally didn't just find out that your mother had slept with Max. She would have known for, how long? Two years?"

"At least." Nadine nods thoughtfully. "I suppose Sally could have brooded over it all that time. But still . . . that's not Max's alibi, right? He's lying about an affair being the suicide trigger. At least about my mom."

"Oh, he's lying. I'd lay a million dollars on that."

"But why would he risk that? If Sally already knew about the affair? Why not find a better lie?"

"Maybe Max didn't know Sally knew."

"You think Sally wouldn't have given him hell for sleeping with my mother if she'd known about it?"

"She might not have wanted to give Max the satisfaction. Maybe by ignoring it she spared herself getting down in the mud with him."

"Maybe."

"Think of it this way. Sally was sixty-six. And your mother, what?"

"Sixty-four when she died. Same age as Sally, same school class for fourteen years."

"Max has been cheating on Sally since their honeymoon. God knows what hell she'd been through all these years. Your mother was her best friend. Max would have known just how to manipulate your mom into sleeping with him, and Sally would know that. I can imagine a situation where Sally saw your mother as a victim as much as a transgressor."

"You're just trying to make me feel better."

"No. I want to get to the truth. You said Sally stopped coming to book club for a month, right? Then she came back. So she agonized for a month. But then she and your mom made up."

Hope shines in Nadine's eyes. "You really think so?"

"Your mother was terminally ill. Sally had no illusions left about the man she'd married. I'll bet all she cared about in the world by then was Paul and her grandson. Not where Max dipped his wick."

"God, I hope you're right."

"I am. The problem is we can't prove any of that. Not unless we turn up a long-lost diary or something."

"That won't happen. Mom never kept a diary."

"Something just hit me," I murmur. "What if these break-ins don't have to do with you, but your mother?"

"The break-ins? What could my mother have had that anybody would want?"

"I don't know. But if she had a secret relationship with Max, then who's to say? Maybe Max asked Margaret to keep something for him."

"No way. Mom might have slept with Max once or twice, but she didn't *like* him. Or even trust him. In fact, in a lot of ways she despised him."

"I'm sure. But this makes a lot more sense than you having something the Poker Club wants."

Nadine looks up sharply. "Why do you think the Poker Club is behind the break-ins?"

"There's something going on under all this that we don't understand. Buck's death, I get. But Sally's? No. The break-ins at your store and house? And at other lawyers' offices? I don't get that, either."

"They don't all have to be connected. Do they?"

"In one little town? Sure they do. There's one other thing. Your mother wasn't the only one who was sick. It turns out Sally had a terminal illness, too. Dr. Kirby told me in confidence this afternoon, and he went to the police after that."

Nadine stops pacing. She looks overwhelmed by this revelation. "Who else knew about that?"

"Only Sally and Dr. Kirby. She didn't want anyone to know. Not even Max."

"But . . . you think she really killed herself, then?"

"The illness is certainly grounds for a depressive state."

"How long had she known she was ill?"

"I'm not sure. But she wouldn't have known about it while your mother was alive. What are you thinking?"

Nadine is hugging herself, her brow knit with worry. "Knowing that makes me wonder if my mother being with Max might have been a trigger after all. If she was already depressed, I mean. Maybe Max taunted Sally or something. You know how cruel couples can be when they fight."

"I guess . . . I see your point."

"What does Jet think?" Nadine asks. "And why is she even defending that son of a bitch?"

While I try to think of a suitable answer, a loud banging echoes up the hallway. Three hard raps. Then a fourth. I was sure Jet slipped out by the back bedroom door. *Has she come back?*

The rapping sounds again, harder this time.

"That's the front door," I say, wondering who the hell it could be and how they got past my gate.

"You're not expecting anybody?" Nadine whispers.

"Hell, no. And the gate's locked."

With my heart racing, I grab my pistol from a kitchen drawer. Nadine watches me with a deer-in-the-headlights look. *That's got to be Jet,* I think, reaching instinctively for the burner phone in my pocket. But I don't take it out in front of Nadine.

This time the knocking rattles the front wall of the house.

That's a man's hand, I realize. *Paul's?*

"Open up, McEwan!" shouts a muffled voice that could be Paul's. *God, I hope Jet got away clean.*

Walking to my little front foyer, I call, "Who's out there?"

Nadine touches my shoulders from behind, and I jump.

"Max Matheson!" comes the reply. "Your best friend's old man! Your ex–assistant football coach."

Nadine spins me around, her eyes asking the same question I am: *What the hell is Max doing here?*

"Open up, Marshall! Goddamn it. I'm not armed."

I grab Nadine and fast-walk her up the hall, whispering as we hurry toward the back bedroom. "I don't know what Max is doing here, but I'm going to find out. I don't want him even laying eyes on you. Either he broke in through my gate or he walked in from the woods. Either scenario's bad."

We move into the bedroom.

"Should I slip out the back door?" she asks.

"No. We don't know he's alone. Hide in the bathroom with your pistol. You'll be locked behind two doors."

Max bangs on the front door again.

Nadine lets me lead her into the master bath.

"This is it," I tell her. "Lock the bedroom door after I go out, then come in here and lock this one."

"I will." She catches my wrist. "Ask Max who told Sally that he slept with my mother. If it really was a recent revelation, the bastard ought to know that."

Nadine's eyes are flashing with anger and determination.

"I will," I promise. "Now focus. If anybody tries to force open this door, shoot them."

Her eyes go wide. "Seriously?"

"Max is out on bail for murder. We don't know what's going on, and we can't take chances."

She nods uncertainly, her face pale.

"Can you do it?" I press. "Can you shoot through a closed door?"

Nadine nods once more, her jaw set tight.

I almost believe her.

CHAPTER 27

WHEN I OPEN my front door, I find Max Matheson standing in jeans and a bright red button-down shirt with a crawfish embroidered on the pocket. Though I'm an inch taller than Max, his cowboy boots put us at eye level. I've known those eyes since I was a boy, and in this moment they are reading my soul.

"You gonna ask me in or what?" he says with a friendly grin.

"How did you get into my place, Max?"

"Parked at the gate and walked. I wanted to observe the property in its natural state." The light dancing in his eyes is hard to describe, but it makes plain that he's enjoying himself.

"I don't know what we have to talk about," I tell him, not moving out of the doorway.

"Oh, I think you're gonna be surprised, Goose."

And with that he turns sideways and pushes between me and the doorframe, then walks toward my kitchen. My only options are to fight him or let him stay, and at sixty-six years old, Max could beat the hell out of most men I know in their forties. He doesn't spend his time in the gym or running marathons. He's simply a natural athlete who has remained active all his life. From a distance, his rangy frame and long muscles give him the look of a much younger man, and this, along with the handsomeness that marks all his family, is surely part of what has pulled so many women to him. But what makes me engage with Max today is my need to know what he knows—and what he wants.

I find him standing by my kitchen table with one hand on the back of a chair. "Well, you're in here," I tell him. "Let's hear your pitch."

He smiles, a poker player holding all the cards he needs to win. "Gratitude's a rare thing, Marshall. Like loyalty. And to my surprise, you've turned out to have neither."

"How do you figure that?"

"Paul saved your life in Iraq. Everybody knows that. Hell, you wrote a book about it. Yet you come back home, and what do you do? You start fucking your best friend's wife."

His words cut right through my meager armor, but I try not to let him see it. "Max, you don't know what the hell—"

He stops me with an upraised hand. "Spare us both the indignity of denials. I just shot a nice snap of you two hugging out back. Zoomed in real good. These smartphones are amazing."

So the "deer" that I thought Jet saw at the edge of the woods earlier wasn't a deer at all. It was Max with his camera phone. "Let's see it."

He reaches into his Levi's and takes out a Samsung Galaxy, then presses a button and holds up the large phone. Though I'm ten feet away, I can see enough to know he's telling the truth.

"Hugging's a long way from sex, Max."

He laughs. "You've got a point, Goose. But I also watched you fuck her on the patio yesterday. *That* scene didn't leave much doubt about penetration."

His words drop into my mind like a paralyzing poison.

"Actually," he says, "it seemed more vice versa, to tell the truth. You made Jet do all the work. Not much of a farmer, are you? Don't like plowing?"

My feet feel nailed to the floor, but my heartbeat's accelerating like a train gathering speed. As I stare helplessly, Max drags the chair from beneath the table to the corner by the back window. As he sits, the left leg of his jeans rises enough to reveal a black Velcro ankle holster. The burled handle of what looks like a nickel-plated .380 automatic juts from the holster.

"Keep it copacetic, Marshall," he says. "Don't stroke out on me. I could've shown Paul that fuck pic yesterday, and I didn't."

"You have pictures from yesterday?"

"Well, sure. Got a video. It's a little blurry, but Jet's clear enough. That hair, you know? And that dark skin. And that miraculous ass. You're lying flat, so I don't have your face, but it's your house behind her, so it must be your cock she's riding. I'm sure Paul will make that leap pretty quick."

We're dead, I realize, dreading the moment I tell Jet about this meeting. "Did you stop Jet on her way out today?"

"Nope. Let her strut right out of your woods in blissful ignorance. Dumb and full of come." Max leans forward, sets his elbows on his knees. "Marshall, I've known you since you were a baby. I don't want you buried out by that statue of your brother. That'd be a downer of an ending."

"What do you want, Max?"

"I'll tell you in a sec. First, you need to understand the bind I'm in."

"I'm listening."

He works his tongue around like a man trying to find a pesky sesame seed from his lunch sandwich. "My wife killed herself, son. That's a plain fact, and a hard one, but I could've lived with it. But she *also* framed me for murder."

"Why would Sally do that?"

He ignores the question. "She painted a target on my back, Goose. A big-ass target."

"Why?"

"She wanted to nail me to the barn wall."

"Because you were cheating on her?"

"Don't worry about why. That's between Sally and me."

"What do you want from me, Max? Why are you here?"

"Sally wasn't content just to frame me, Marshall. She left something behind that would *ruin* me. And my partners."

Something splashes deep in my mind, like a pebble dropped down a well. "What did she leave?"

"Documents. Files, emails, recordings. Digital stuff. Sally was a hell of a lot sharper than I am about that kind of stuff."

An image of Sally's sapphire pendant rises in my mind, and Jet's theory of the passwords stuck to the back of it. "What's in these files, Max?"

"Business dealings." He tilts his head forward. "Poker Club business."

"Why are you telling me about it?"

He gives me the smile of a magician pulling a coin from my ear. "Because you're going to find it for me."

"Why would I do that?"

"Because you're fucking my daughter-in-law. And if my son finds out, he'll kill you. You know that better than anybody."

I stand mute, knowing I have no choice but to at least pretend to agree to his demands.

"It won't be like that time when you were a senior in high school, either," Max goes on. "Out at the country club? When Paul let you off without an ass-whipping?"

"How do you know about that?"

He chuckles. "Not much happens in this town I don't know about, in the high school or the old folks' home."

This is probably true. "Why do you think I can find this stuff if you can't?"

"Because people see you as a crusader, just like Jet. They'll trust you, confide in you. They'll think you're lined up against me, when in fact you'll be working *for* me." Max straightens up in the chair. "So that's the deal, Goose, plain as I can make it. I need that cache of digital dynamite degaussed and burned in a hot fire. And you're gonna find it for me."

"That's all you want? Nothing else?"

"Well . . . there is one other codicil to this contract. Once I have what I need, you're gonna move back to Washington. You've had a good romp with Jet, but you've boned that bitch for the last time. You can come back for your father's funeral, but that's it. I don't figure moving back to D.C. will cause you much pain, since you never cared much for your daddy after your brother died."

I look at the floor, trying to force my whirling thoughts into some kind of order. All I can see is a blurry path toward survival. "If I agree to find this data cache, you'll destroy those pictures? And your video? All copies?"

Max smiles with good humor. "Well . . . I might keep one for myself, to beat off to now and then. Jet looks pretty damn good naked. Especially for her age."

This is the Max Matheson I've always known, joking about "gettin' pussy" when he coached us as twelve-year-olds, telling us bloody tales from 'Nam and reveling in all the naïve hero worship that resulted. Max is the first man I heard say, "Old enough to bleed, old enough to butcher." Knowing that this man has total power over Jet and me—

"Listen, Goose," he says, like we're still on a high school football field. "There's nothing wrong with tasting whatever you get a craving for, long as you don't get greedy about it. A slice off a cut loaf's never missed, right? I think that's in the Bible." He laughs heartily. "At least I know a few preachers who think it is. Anyway, I tap quite a few wives around here nice and regular. I like to catch 'em in their late thirties, early forties. That's the best age. They want it bad, and they know what they're doing. They've finally put to rest whatever hang-ups their mamas stuffed into their heads. Of course this new generation ain't got no hang-ups at all."

Sometimes I wonder whether Max's sexual obsession is genuine or part of a shtick he uses to distract people. Probably both. "Tell me about this data cache. Why can't you find it? Where could it be?"

"If I knew that, would I be here? But I need to find it quick. If I don't, I'm a dead man. Sooner rather than later."

"That doesn't sound like a negative outcome to me just now."

He gives me a wolfish grin. "I bet not. But if I go down, you do, too. Rest assured of that."

"Who would kill you, Max? Who would be so brazen?"

"Any of my more nervous partners. There's a code in the Poker Club, unwritten but absolutely understood. You never put another member at risk. You never take food from another's mouth. And you never fuck another man's wife. That's in order of priority. If I don't neutralize this threat to the club, then one of my partners is going to neutralize me. It's that simple."

"If you become a target of your partners, does Jet lose the protection you've been giving her for the past few years?"

His grin is almost paternal. "You figured that out, huh? What can I say? Jet's family. She's not *blood,* but she's the mother of my grandson. And he's a pip, boy. So, the short answer? Nobody fucks with the Matheson family. End of story."

"But if you go down, Jet does, too?"

Max weighs his answer like a gambler calculating odds. "I'd have to say yes, that's a lock."

"Don't you think you ought to warn her about that?"

"Nah. Jet's a survivor, Goose. She doesn't need to be told something like that. In case you haven't noticed, she goes cold as an undertaker when she's looking at a problem. You probably see her through rose-colored glasses. Always have, I guess. But she's no Pollyanna."

He's right about that, though I don't like to dwell on it.

"Max, nobody's more of a survivor than you. Surely you know more about the crimes of the Poker Club than anyone but Claude Buckman. It would be nothing for you to set up a MAD situation with them."

"Mad?" He looks confused for but a moment. "You mean mutual assured destruction?"

"Exactly. Make your own cache. Let your partners know that if they hurt you, they'll all end up in prison. If you have to use your cache, you can cut a deal with the prosecutors."

He laughs at my apparent naïveté. "That's a nice idea, Goose. And if my partners were all old-timers like Buckman and Donnelly, I might try it. But you're forgetting Russo and Cash. Russo's brother's a made guy. And Wyatt has six Special Forces operators on his payroll. You don't threaten guys like that. They'd lock me in a deer freezer on Wyatt's island and dissect me with a dull pocketknife. I figure it'd take 'em about an hour to find out where I hid whatever cache I'd created. They'll do the same to whoever Sally left hers with, once they find out who it is."

Max's fear is contagious. "There's been a rash of break-ins downtown. Lawyers' offices. And Nadine Sullivan had her shop broken into. They cracked the safe there. Was that you, looking for this data cache Sally made?"

He's no longer smiling. "Yeah, that was me. A guy I hired, anyway. But it wasn't this cache I was looking for. I mean, I didn't know last night that it existed."

That's one mystery solved, at least partly. "What do you mean? What were you looking for?"

"Somebody stole a couple of manila envelopes from my office. Dangerous information. I questioned Jet, and it wasn't her. Sally denied it, too, but something told me it might be her, so I searched the house. Didn't find anything. Then I made a list of lawyers she might have given the stuff to. I figured she might be planning to divorce me."

Now I get it. "Why did you put Nadine on that list?"

"Because her mother and Sally had been so close."

"What would you have done if it turned out Nadine had your stuff?"

Max's motionless face tells me all I need to know. "She didn't," he says. "Let's just leave it there."

"Well, your guys broke into her house today. How about you put a stop to that? She doesn't have anything."

"Sure, no problem."

Max's willingness to kill over information that could hurt him reminds me that people in the normal world constantly underestimate the danger of poking into matters we don't understand. You'd think a journalist would have learned that by now. Maybe the fact that I know all the players in this situation is what blinds me to the danger.

"So you just found out about this cache Sally put together?"

He nods. "Arthur Pine told me about it this morning, at the jail."

"How did Arthur know about it?"

"Sally called Claude Buckman sometime last night, before killing herself. I don't understand it, man. She must have hated me at the end. She wanted to destroy me."

He's sticking to the suicide story. "And it's all Poker Club stuff?"

"Most of it involves the paper mill deal."

"Did you screw Nadine's mother, Max?"

He looks amused by the question. "Margaret? Every way you can think of, boy, plus ten more. Her husband ran out on her, so she needed it. She'd got tired of him even before he took off, though. He wasn't up to her level. Margaret was smart as a whip, just like her daughter. I'd like to hit *that* once or twice. Just to see if the blood runs true."

Seeing my face, Max guffaws, enjoying himself immensely. "Yeah, I saw Nadine drive up here and send Jet running. Where's she hiding? Back bedroom? Should I pay her a visit? Is she decent? Or is she better than that?"

I come to my feet at this.

Max only laughs louder. "Take it easy, Goose. I'm not going back there. But *some*body needs to break that girl down like a shotgun. She's got that buttoned-up librarian thing goin' on, like Shirley Jones in *The Music Man*. And I know *you* ain't doin' it justice."

I walk over to the island and lean against it. Max is kicked back in my chair like he has all night to shoot the breeze. Right now I'd like to call Jet and tell her to set her Seychelles plan in motion. If it worked,

Tommy Russo might put a bullet in Max's ear by morning. I'm also thinking of the passwords behind Sally's sapphire pendant. If those are the key to whatever cache Sally put together, then I'd like nothing more than to do exactly what Max has asked me to do—find it.

"What are you thinking, Goose?" Max asks. "Don't get tricky on me."

Nadine's request bubbles up to the surface. "Tell me something about your alibi. Who told Sally that you'd slept with Margaret Sullivan?"

The levity goes out of his face, replaced by the animal cleverness that's kept him above ground and out of jail all his life.

"Come on," I press. "I mean, how many people could have known you were doing Margaret Sullivan?"

He's clearly weighing the pros and cons of answering. "Why do you want to know?"

"What do you care? Unless the whole story's a lie. Even if it is, I don't work for the DA. Plus, you own my ass, right?"

Max nods slowly. "It was Tallulah, our maid. Tallulah Williams."

An image of a tall, heavy African American woman comes into my mind. Whenever I spent the night with Paul as a boy, Tallulah was there until after supper and back first thing in the morning.

"She walked in on Margaret and me one afternoon at my house," Max explains, "when Sally was out of town."

"Tallulah," I say softly, wondering if he's lying.

"Yeah, she's still kicking, though sometimes I think that old Electrolux will get the best of her." Max is watching me like a dog that doesn't trust the human it's sitting with. "Tell me something, Marshall. Tell me I'm not misjudging you. Tell me you don't already have this cache of Sally's. That you're not planning to print it in your daddy's newspaper tomorrow. Because that would be a historically bad move, survival-wise."

I flash on the photo of Dave Cowart with Buck Ferris that my secret source left me on that Lexar thumb drive. The Poker Club won't be happy to find that in the *Watchman* tomorrow—or on our website tonight.

"If I did have it and I printed it," I think aloud, "then you'd be dead. Right?" I give him a crocodile smile. "Maybe it's worth the risk. Once the truth is out, it's out. Hurting me wouldn't help you at that point."

Max looks deeply disturbed, so much so that it feels like a stranger has taken his place in the chair. "You know, I didn't want to do this," he says. "But you're not leaving me any choice."

"What are you talking about?"

"As a general rule, a man can push things pretty far in this life and still make out all right. Hell, I've spent my whole life pushing that old envelope. But when you go *too* far, when you test that outside edge too many times, nature balances things out. You get slung off the road, or you augur in from the clouds. That's what your daddy did."

A dull ringing has started in my ears. "What do you mean?"

Max stands and walks to the window, glances out, then looks back at me. "You know your problem? You went up north and turned into a superior son of a bitch. That's one thing your daddy never was. Duncan could be righteous, but he wasn't a hypocrite. And he wasn't *smug*. Hell, you probably don't know it, but your father was asked to join the Poker Club back in 1960. My daddy told me that. Duncan declined—he's the only man who ever did—but nobody held it against him. Because he always cut us plenty of slack in the paper. Oh, he'd go on a tear every now and then, about civic responsibility and maybe even corruption, but he never stung us. Gave us a pass."

The anger I feel is so all-consuming I can hardly raise my voice. "I don't believe you."

Max barks a laugh. "Ask him, then! Are you two speaking now?"

"Get to it, Max."

"Duncan's only problem was when he got the civil rights bug up his butt. Back in the sixties, before I shipped out. Ol' Duncan wouldn't let that shit go. He loved him some colored folks. And it made him famous, for a while. The 'Conscience of Mississippi,' remember that? But . . . he kinda lost his fire after that car wreck, didn't he?"

My anger has leveled off and begun cooling into dread. "Are you saying the Poker Club had something to do with that wreck? With the deaths of his first wife and child?"

Max smiles strangely. "Did I say that? No. The Poker Club never got involved in nigger trouble. And we sure didn't whack newspaper publishers."

"Then what are you saying?"

"I'm saying that Duncan was warned by some *different* boys, and he ignored the warning. And, well, they done what boys like that always did back then."

"They caused the wreck?"

Max turns up his big hands. "One-car accident on Cemetery Road? Come on."

"It's happened before, and since. That's a bad turn."

"Sure it is, if you try to take that dogleg at eighty miles an hour. You think a mama with a baby did that? In the rain? Hell, no."

The ringing in my ears has risen in frequency. "They murdered his wife and baby? For what? To punish him?"

"No, no, they thought it was *him* in the car. See? Your old man was working late that night, and his wife had brought him some home-cooked food. She left about the time he would have driven home, but Duncan stayed to keep working. In the rain, those old boys couldn't see it was a woman behind the wheel. They ran her off the road, right down into that gully. Car flipped, and they drowned in the runoff. Three feet of water."

In my mind I hear Dr. Kirby telling me that people in Bienville have died over the years without their deaths ever being recognized as homicide. "You've known that all these years?"

Max smiles again, then raises his chin and scratches his neck. "Didn't I just tell you I know everything that goes on in this town? Why do you think the investigation never turned up anything suspicious? The police blamed that accident on the rain and the dark, and that was the end of it. I don't think Duncan even questioned the accident report."

"Who caused that wreck, Max? Local Klansmen?"

"Not local, no." He hesitates, then seems to decide I can't do any-thing about it after so many years. "It was that bunch from down in Ferriday. The ones behind the murders in Natchez. The Double Eagles."

The name rings a distant bell in my mind. I faintly recall a series of stories by a Louisiana reporter who died chasing the truth about cold cases in his parish. "How do you know it was them?"

Max shrugs as if this kind of specificity is unimportant. "Don't worry about it. I'm telling you this to illustrate a life principle. If you do what your daddy did—get a bug up your ass and start publishing things that'll hurt me or my partners—there's nothing anybody can do to save you. The Poker Club's a goddamn institution. And institutions protect themselves. Your life's in your own hands, boy. Don't throw it away. That's what I'm here to tell you."

"Go fuck yourself, Max."

"Yeah, yeah." He waves off my insult like he knows I have no choice but to work for him. "After you think about what I've said, you'll come to the right conclusion. You're smarter than your daddy was."

"You think?"

"You tell me. Duncan's been a drunk for fifty years. Got a fine son like you and treats you like you don't exist. If he'd just eased up a little back in the sixties, practiced a little live and let live, his wife and baby would've been fine. Course, you and Adam never would have been born. But there's no point speculating about that kind of thing. It's the butterfly and the hurricane, right?"

"I actually spend a lot of time doing that."

Max grins. "Clearly. Like what if Jet would've married you instead of Paul? That's over with, Marshall. That water ran downstream twenty years ago. You can't bring it back. Water don't flow uphill. You need to bury your daddy and get your ass back to Washington, where you fit in."

"It's time for you to go, Max."

He sniffs, then walks toward me from the window. "Do we have a deal?"

It physically pains me to promise this man anything. "I'll try to find Sally's cache for you. But I think you're lying about your wife. I think you killed Sally. I think she knew something about you. Something terrible. And you couldn't risk her turning on you after all these years. You couldn't risk people finding out what you really are. Or maybe you just couldn't stand Sally knowing whatever it is."

Another change has come over him, like a storm cloud passing over a tree. The darkness in his eyes masks his thoughts from me. "All you need to think about," he says in a dangerous voice, "is my son's face when I show him the video of Jet grinding on your cock. Everything else is academic."

"We're done, Max."

"For now. Just remember this: if Paul kills you . . . you deserved it."

"Bullshit. I paid him back for saving my life. I compromised myself to do it."

Max isn't buying it. "Keep telling yourself that. You're only breathing air right now because of him."

With that he turns his back on me and walks to the front door. I trail him to make sure he doesn't veer down the hall to where Nadine is hiding. He doesn't, but as he touches the doorknob, he sings out, *"Nadine! Honey, is that you?"* Then he laughs and walks through the door, slamming it behind him.

Hurrying to the back window, I watch him round the house and stroll across my backyard like he's thinking of buying it. Shame and fear boil through me, but above all, rage. What he told me about my father's first family is something I never even considered. But when I think of Jack Kirby's earlier warnings, it seems obvious. Max's story of their murder typifies almost everything I hate about the South. A few uneducated assholes wrecked a man's life for trying to help those less fortunate than himself. They murdered his wife and child and never paid for it—were never even accused of the crime. The community I was born into tacitly allowed that murder as a punishment for bucking the system. Just as it will allow the murder of Buck Ferris as punishment for threatening the paper mill and the new interstate—

"Mother*fucker*," I mutter as Max vanishes into the trees.

Remembering Nadine, I trot down the hall and call loudly, "It's Marshall! He's gone! All clear! Nadine?"

After about ten seconds, I hear a click through the wall. Five seconds after that, Nadine's voice comes through the bedroom door.

"Marshall? Say something only you would know."

"You kissed me at the industrial park."

The door opens, revealing Nadine standing with her mother's gun in her right hand. "I hated that," she says, her eyes wet with tears of anger. "Hiding like that."

"I'm sorry. Did you hear any of our conversation?"

"Stuck back here? Hell, no. I'd rather have come out and jammed this gun into his balls and demanded the truth."

"Max would have enjoyed that. He'd have given you chapter and verse on your mother's sexual preferences."

"And I'd have blown his balls off." There is steel in Nadine's voice. "I need more vodka," she says, starting down the hall. "Am I crazy, or did I hear somebody sing part of the Chuck Berry song?"

"That was Max on his way out. He knew you were back here. He saw you arrive."

"Was he following me?"

I don't want to get into the issue of Jet. "I don't think so, but I don't know."

"Did you ask about his alibi? Who told Sally that he slept with my mother?"

"Tallulah Williams, he claimed. The family maid."

Nadine stops in the kitchen and turns back to me. "I've met Tallulah. I can see her knowing about an affair. I'm not sure I can see her telling Sally something that would hurt her, though."

"I may go talk to her about it. Tomorrow."

"Did Max tell you anything else?"

"Let's get that drink first."

She goes to the freezer for the Crater Lake, then drinks straight from the neck of the bottle. As I mix myself a gin and tonic, I tell her that Max admitted responsibility for the break-ins at her store and home. Then I give her a quick explanation of Sally's data cache. Finally I tell her what Max said about the murder of my father's wife and daughter.

"These guys," Nadine says, practically grinding her teeth in fury. "Their time is so over. They need to be *erased*."

"I thought you were a bleeding-heart liberal."

She looks up sharply. "Boy, have you got me wrong. I'm for social justice, sure. But I'm for moral justice above all. And those Poker Club bastards belong in jail or in the ground."

She takes another swig of vodka. "Have you told me everything?"

Everything except the blackmail video of me having sex with Jet Matheson—

"Did Max talk shit about my mother?"

"No," I lie. "But he did have an affair with her."

She shakes her head and takes another slug from the frosted bottle.

"Take it easy, now. What do you want to do? Besides get drunk. Are you hungry? I really can fix us something."

A mocking laugh escapes her lips. "No, thanks. My friend's expecting me."

"Well. Let me walk you out to your car. Just to be sure Max isn't out there waiting for you. He could have doubled back."

"Okay."

Pistols in hand, we walk out into the dark and make our way over to Nadine's Acura, which she parked behind some hedges at the side of my house. She gives me a pained smile, then unlocks the car and gets behind the wheel.

"Drive fast to the gate," I advise her. "And keep your pistol in your hand while you're waiting for it to open."

She nods once, looking impatient to leave.

"Are you sure you're all right?"

"I'm fine." She looks down at the steering wheel. "Look . . . I found something back in the bathroom. I thought Max might see them if he went through the house, which I assumed would be bad."

"What are you talking about?"

She sticks her arm through the window, her closed fist turned down. "Open your hand."

I open my hand beneath hers.

When she opens her fist, two sapphire earrings drop into my palm. A rush of recognition floods through me, and color rises into my cheeks.

"I hope you know what you're doing," Nadine says.

Then she shifts the car into gear and drives away over the grass.

CHAPTER 28

AFTER NADINE'S ABRUPT departure, I sit at the kitchen table with my pistol at my left hand, drinking gin and staring at the *Watchman* website on my laptop. Ben Tate has been drafting a couple of stories based on the information I sent him earlier, but I'm not sure how far we're going to be able to go in print. Byron Ellis still hasn't returned my latest call, and without the coroner backing up my assertions about human bones and blood being found at the mill site, we can't publish. If Quinn Ferris's experts come through, we could, but apparently they've gotten wind of the controversy down here and have raised chain-of-evidence questions. But these concerns seem secondary now.

The realization that Max can betray Jet and me to Paul whenever he chooses has fundamentally altered my perception of reality. Max could be right: if Paul is confronted with a video of Jet making love to me, he might well flip out and kill me. After all, I do owe him my life. How big a leap would it be for him to decide he has the right to call in his marker? Before Jet left earlier, she instructed me not to call her. But I have no choice now. After pressing the speed-dial button for her number, I sit and stare at my burner phone without much hope of an answer.

After four rings, she hisses, *"I said not to call."*

"Max showed up after you left."

"What?"

"While Nadine was still here. She hid. Max knows about us, Jet. He took pictures."

"Pictures of what? Us hugging on the patio?"

"Yes, but he was out there yesterday, too. He must have been following you. He filmed us on the steamer chair."

This time I hear only staticky silence.

"Jet?"

"He didn't really . . ."

"I haven't seen the video, but I saw a still shot of us hugging. And he knew details from the patio yesterday. I believe him."

"We're dead," she says flatly.

"No. But we have to start thinking about coming clean with Paul, before Max does."

"Marshall . . . we can't tell Paul now. He just lost his mother."

"Hearing it from Max would be worse. Did you ever really think there was a way for us to be together without confronting Paul?"

"Of course not. But there's a world of difference between hearing that your wife wants to leave you and watching her screw your best friend in living color."

"You and Max agree on that. I don't really think there's much difference."

"With Paul there would be. If he sees me strip-walking across that lawn . . . then riding you? He'll snap."

"You're not giving him enough credit."

"Oh, you don't know. You don't *live* with him. I tell you things, and you just don't hear me."

"What are you talking about?"

"His head injuries, for one thing. Remember those? Blast-induced TBIs?"

"Of course."

"How many IEDs did he survive?"

I have to think about this. "Uhh . . . two direct ones that I know about. He suffered shock impacts from, what, three more?"

"Four more. He gets terrible headaches, Marshall. He's distracted, irritable, depressed. At Kevin's baseball games, he gets violently angry. That's the main reason I don't go. I'm worried he'll charge onto the field and assault a referee."

I have probably tried to minimize Paul's problems in my mind.

"Could Max have shown the video to him already?" she asks.

"He could have, but I don't think he has. Sally apparently created some sort of data cache before she died. A bunch of files that could destroy Max and the Poker Club. Information about the Azure Dragon deal. Has Max told you that?"

"No. Did he say he told me?"

"No. But he's convinced that his partners will kill him over this stuff, and he wants me to find it for him. He's using the video to motivate me."

Jet goes silent as she processes this. "Do you think those passwords I found on the necklace could open this cache, or whatever it is?"

"I do. Max said it was mostly digital files. But something just occurred to me. Why would Sally gather a bunch of damning evidence if she wasn't going to use it? Why go to the trouble if she was just going to kill herself? Or give it to someone else who wouldn't use it?"

"Maybe it was like my Bitcoin plan," Jet suggests. "She considered using it, but in the end she went another way. Or Max killed her before she could."

"For some reason, I don't think that's it. He's really scared."

"Marshall, it's time to stop screwing around. It's time to set my plan in motion."

"Your Seychelles plan?"

"Yes. We leak to the Poker Club that Max cut them out of a bribe from the Chinese, then use the overseas bank account to back up the story."

"But Max *didn't*," I reply.

"He can't prove that. And if Tommy Russo, Wyatt Cash, and Beau Holland know about Sally's cache, then they're already going crazy right now. Even Buckman and Donnelly won't tolerate a threat like that. If they find out Max cheated them while they're in that state of mind, he's dead."

The temptation to cross this line is strong. "I understand why you want to do it. But it feels like putting our heads in the tiger's mouth. We'd be better off finding Sally's cache and using that to keep Max quiet."

"We don't have time. If we don't stop Max now, he'll destroy us. You don't know him like I do. Maybe you did once, but not now. Max can't abide not being in control. He's had me on a choke chain for years." Her voice is cracking. "We *have* to get that video," she says with sudden intensity. "Did Max shoot it on his cell phone?"

"Yes."

"We have to get that phone. Not only for the video, but also because those passwords Sally left might open it."

She hasn't heard a word I've said. "Try to calm down, Jet. Think rationally. And about Max's phone . . . if you try to get that close to him, he'll know what you're doing."

"I don't have to *try* to get close. I'm his lawyer. I'll grab the damn thing and run. If I can't get away with it, I'll destroy it."

"Jet—where are you? Are you home now?"

"Home? Home is with you. Isn't it?"

I close my eyes, feeling something close to shame. "Yes."

"I'm at my house. Kevin's here, and I need to get off. If you somehow find Sally's cache, *don't* give it to Max. Put it somewhere safe. That's our salvation."

"And what do I tell Max when he calls?"

"Leave Max to me."

Two minutes after I hang up, I decide that spending the night at my parents' house might be a good idea. This isolated farmhouse has served me well as a trysting place, but in the present circumstance—with Paul decompensating from grief over his mother's death and obsessed with his wife's possible infidelity—my solitude has become a liability. Max's sudden appearance showed me how useless my security gate is if someone means to do me harm, and sleeping where I'm expected to just seems stupid. Whoever killed Buck surely knows by now that I'm the person pushing hardest for a murder investigation. If they were willing to kill Buck, then surely they would kill me to keep themselves safe. Worst of all, it could be anybody. Someone I've known since I was a kid. So as not to worry my mother, I call and tell her my air-conditioning has gone out. When I ask if I can sleep in my old room for a night, she sounds overjoyed.

My pistol feels heavy, and it's a pain in the ass keeping it in my hand while I pack a weekend bag. But I recall Max's jeans riding up, revealing his ankle holster. I'd be a fool to go anywhere without a weapon at the ready. Dr. Kirby told me as much. *Keep your head on a swivel,* he told me. Good medical advice.

ONCE AGAIN I'M SITTING at my parents' kitchen table, where I waited for Dr. Kirby earlier today. Mom is making sure Dad is settled in his bed. The kitchen smells of burned coffee, because she still keeps a carafe half-full all day. I think my mother has subsisted mostly on coffee since I was a little boy.

"Marshall?" she murmurs, padding into the kitchen in her housecoat. "Can I fix you some food? I have some étouffée in the fridge. Made it myself."

"Where do you find time to cook from scratch?"

She rinses her coffee cup, the ancient one with BLYTHE hand-painted on it, then refills it from the carafe. "Marty Denis brought us a mess of peeled tails today, so I just had to make some for your father. All I see at the store now is those Chinese crawfish, and I don't even consider them *real*."

Marty Denis runs a local bank that competes with Claude Buckman's regional giant, Bienville Southern. He's got Cajun heritage, but he spends most of his time on the country club golf course, not in his home state. "I guess Marty's were seined out of some ditch in St. Martin Parish?"

She slides into the chair across from me with a creak of crepitus. "You know it," she says with a smile. "I can taste the bayou in them."

Looking into her exhausted but still handsome face, I remember Dr. Kirby telling me that she's suffering from sleep deprivation. "You don't have a sitter tonight?"

She waves her hand. "Duncan only likes one well enough to let her help at night, and she needed a night off."

"Mom, you've got to take care of yourself. Money's no object when it comes to that."

She forces a smile. "Let's change the subject."

"All right. Do you know very much about the Bienville Poker Club?"

My question surprises her. "Blake Donnelly and that crowd?"

"I think Donnelly's about the best of the bunch. Some of them are pretty shady."

"Oh, that doesn't surprise me. How many people really do honest work anymore? Blake's just rich enough to live a little straighter than the others."

"I figured Claude Buckman must be richer than Blake."

Mom purses her lips and weighs what information she possesses. "Oh, I don't know. Blake's pumped a lot of oil for a lot of years, collected a lot of mailbox money. Either way, Claude is a slug. Can't keep his nasty hands to himself. Never could. *Ugh.*"

We're silent for a bit, and she sips her coffee in relative contentment.

"What did Dr. Kirby say before he left?" I ask.

She looks unsure whether to tell me, or maybe whether to be completely honest. "I just thank heaven for Jack. He's been so patient. One of those younger doctors would have thrown up his hands over Duncan long ago."

I nod but say nothing, leaving silence for her to fill.

"Jack thinks the end is getting close," Mom says in a church whisper. "Duncan's not going to stop drinking. I could empty all the bottles, but then he'd break his hip trying to get out to the car. Or, worse, run his wheelchair off the porch. I'm sure you judge me for letting him have it, but, Marshall . . . it's the only thing that eases his nerves." She raises her right hand and wipes a tear from one eye. "I know he'll die sooner, but what's the alternative? A few extra months of misery?"

I reach out and take her left hand. "I don't judge you, Mom. You're a saint to have come this far. Dad's going to do what he's going to do."

More tears come, but I pretend not to see them. She takes a napkin from a holder on the table and dabs the corners of her eyes.

"When you're in the house," she says in a wistful voice, "I remember how it used to be, when you and Adam were boys. I don't just remember it. I *see* it, every detail. I can hear your voices, see your little faces while you watched me cook or I worked on schoolwork with you. Not that either of you needed much help. Other than getting you *started.*"

I smile and listen to her weave her memories into words. Mom doesn't usually wax nostalgic when I'm here. I guess the prospect that she may finally be facing life without her partner, whatever his flaws, has her looking backward rather than forward. As she goes on, I recall Max's terrible tale of murder on Cemetery Road. After Mom falls silent and sips her coffee again, I take the opening.

"Mom, this afternoon, Jack Kirby told me about some things the Poker Club was involved with—violent things."

"It wouldn't surprise me. They're all about the dollar. And men like that quickly lose sight of right and wrong."

At the last moment I hesitate, but I've got to know. "Max Matheson suggested that what happened to Dad's first family wasn't an accident.

That some Klansmen from Ferriday might have been behind that wreck. Did Dad ever express any suspicion to you?"

My mother's coffee cup has frozen in midair. Her eyes are wide and locked on my face.

"Mom?"

She sets down her cup and licks her lips. "I've never heard anybody suggest that before. I certainly never heard Duncan suggest it. And I don't want you to ask him about it, either. No good could possibly come of that. Not after all these years. My Lord."

"That's why I'm asking you, not him."

She looks at me for a long time without speaking. In this moment I feel I'm living up to the idea that children are a burden.

"Do you believe there's anything to the story?" she asks.

"Max told me that it was a case of mistaken identity. That Dad was the intended target. The killers were waiting near that hairpin turn to run him off the road, and in the rain they couldn't tell it wasn't him."

Mom closes her eyes, and her lips move as though she's praying in silence. "Dear God, I hope that didn't happen."

"I do, too. But I fear that it did."

She takes a quick sip of coffee the way a prisoner might, as though protecting it from a thief. The gesture makes me strangely anxious.

"When I met your father," she says, "he was a wounded man. Losing Eloise and Emily is what started this whole nightmare of alcoholism."

Eloise and Emily. To me these are but names. To my mother they were real people.

"Oh, he drank before that, but in moderation. I talked to a lot of his colleagues at that time, even to his mother. I started at the *Watchman* as a reporter, you know. I was twenty-two, fresh out of the W. Didn't know a thing."

She means the Mississippi State College for Women. "How many years did you work there?"

"Six. I was working the night of the accident. And nobody ever *suggested* it was murder. Because of the storm, I suppose. But I know this: losing his wife and daughter changed Duncan forever." Her eyes are fixed on the table with unsettling concentration. "Once we started seeing each other, I threw my whole self into healing him. And he came a long way back to the world. After you and Adam came along—

while you were both here—Duncan was whole again, or just about. Then . . ."

"You don't have to talk about Adam. I've been thinking about him a lot over the last two days."

She pushes her cup away and looks into my eyes. "I want you to understand one thing. Losing Adam the way we did sent me into depression, but eventually I was able to work through it. You never get over losing a child—you know that better than most—but you can live with it. If you're lucky. But for Duncan . . . it was different. He'd come so far after that first tragedy, but the wound was still raw underneath. When Adam drowned and was never found, it was like somebody took a knife and drove it into that old wound, then twisted until it severed something."

Mom's face becomes distorted by the pain of recollection. "No matter how much time passed or what I tried, I couldn't reach that part of him. He couldn't heal. It seems incredible to think that thirty-one years wouldn't be enough to get over something, but I've learned that time means nothing in some cases. And the greatest tragedy is that he let it destroy his relationship with you."

"Mom, I understand where he is. It's all right."

"No, you don't," she counters, sounding angry. "You don't understand how proud he is of you."

"Mom—"

"I mean it!" She grips my hand. "I've never bothered you with this, because it's so painful. And I know how skeptical you are. But he's about to be gone. You know that TV in there? That big flat-screen television. Why do you think he bought that? He hates television news. He bought that TV to watch *you*. No other reason."

I heard her words, but I can't find it in myself to believe them.

"You know how tight Duncan is," she says. "But the day you became a regular guest on MSNBC, he drove to Walmart and bought that set for cash money."

This revelation leaves me mute at my mother's table.

"I know it's too late for you two to have a real relationship," she says. "But don't you think you've punished him enough?"

Her question stuns me like a slap across the face. "Me? You think *I've* punished *him*?"

She doesn't answer my question. "If you two could have even one civil conversation before the end, a real talk, where you tell each other how you feel, not how hurt and angry you are—"

"Mom, if he gives half a damn about my work, why has he been the way he has all these years?"

"Envy," she says simply.

"What?"

She squeezes my hands as if trying to physically channel her feelings into my heart. "You've gone so much further in your career than he ever did, it's hard for him to live with it. Every upward step you take reminds him that he refused to get up after fate knocked him down that second time. The stronger you get, the weaker he feels. It's wrong to be that way, but . . . I suppose it's human."

"Tell me something, Mom. Why did Dad never write any stories about the Poker Club's corruption? He didn't hesitate to go after certain kinds of evils. Why not that one?"

She looks genuinely puzzled. "That I don't know. We knew those men socially, of course, or their fathers. But Duncan knew a lot of the men he attacked during the civil rights trouble, and he didn't let that stop him."

"That's what I don't get."

She shrugs wearily. "We're not put on this earth to know everything." The smile that follows this statement must have taken a lot of fortitude to summon. "I'm just glad to have you under our roof. I hope your air conditioner stays broken for a month."

I reach out and squeeze her hand. "I'm glad to be here, Mom."

She rubs the inside of my wrist for a while with her fingers.

"I don't want to discuss this now," she says, "but I suppose the time is coming when we'll have to consider finances."

I feel simultaneous anxiety and relief. For months I've been trying to get her to intercede with my father, but he's clung to control of the books like a man guarding a terrible secret.

She lowers her voice to a whisper. "Do you have any idea what the *Watchman* might sell for today?"

I've dreaded answering this question. "If we're lucky? Ten percent over its real estate value."

Her eyes widen, and then she goes pale. "You don't mean that? I knew values had been falling, but . . . I thought surely it would still bring two or three million."

I shake my head sadly, then squeeze her hand. "Six years ago it would have sold for nine times EBITDA. Today—"

"What's EBI-whatever?"

"Earnings, basically. Nine times annual earnings. I tried to get Dad to sell then, but—"

She holds up her hand. "Water under the bridge. He couldn't give up control. That was the last vestige of his masculinity. And he couldn't let you see what a mess he'd made of things. Today is all that matters."

"The question is debt, Mom. I know Dad borrowed heavily to buy out Uncle Ray."

She shuts her eyes like a woman praying for strength. "The worst decision we ever made. Duncan also bought the new press right after that. That cost nearly two million dollars. What could we get for it now?"

"You can't give away presses today. Consolidation of printing has killed their value."

She takes a deep breath and looks into her coffee cup. What can it feel like, after so much duty and sacrifice, to face this final insult? To confront widowhood and old age in need, when it could so easily have been avoided?

"The trick is to wipe out all the debt we can," I tell her. "But no matter what happens, I'll take care of you. Don't worry about that for even one second."

Relief and despair fight for control of her face. "I don't want you to have to do that."

"I've been hoping you would come up to Washington and live with me."

She clears her throat. "That's very kind. But all of my friends are here."

"Well, you can stay here. I'm not pressuring you."

"You could look after me a lot easier if you lived here, too."

For a couple of seconds I struggle to come up with a reply, but then I see that she's teasing me.

She gets up and washes out her cup. Looking over her shoulder, she says, "Marty Denis told us you had a date to that party at the Aurora last night. He said you took Nadine Sullivan."

"Oh, God. I didn't see Marty there."

"Well, he was." She dries her cup with a rag, then hangs it on a hook beneath the cabinet. "I always liked Nadine's mother, Margaret. A real lady. And Nadine's as cute as a bug's ear."

Why does everyone describe Nadine as if she were nine years old? Of course, the people who describe her that way are about seventy. "Mom—"

"I know, I know. I'm just hoping there are some grandchildren in my future. It's past time."

"We'll see," I tell her, getting to my feet.

"Cute as a *bug's ear*," she repeats, walking into the hall. "And smart. Ten years after you left St. Mark's, she had her picture in the paper for winning all the same awards you and Adam did."

"Eight years," I correct her. "Nadine's eight years younger than I am."

"Even better! She's as smart as Jet Talal was, but not as . . . complicated."

"Mom, that's enough."

"All right." She's actually chuckling now. "You can't blame me for trying."

Without meaning to, I've followed her to their bedroom. Before I can make my escape to my own room, she opens the door, revealing my father lying asleep in his hospital bed. The bed has been tilted up at the middle, putting him at a forty-degree angle. He's lying with his mouth open, his white hair sticking out in all directions. A faint, irregular wheeze comes from his nose or mouth, and his blotchy hands, folded on his stomach, jerk without rhyme or reason.

"I thought his tremors were under control," I think aloud.

"They are, for the most part. But during REM sleep he can jerk violently. That's part of what causes his insomnia."

"I see." I've stood in the room long enough to smell feces. It reminds me a little of when my son was an infant, but it's not really the same. With a baby, caretakers know that they're progressing toward a day of continence and control. Whereas here . . . entropy reigns cruel and supreme. This is a world of constipation, fecal impactions, enemas, and agonizing manual evacuation—

"Watch him just a minute while I brush my teeth," Mom says. "He's asleep. Just stay with him till I get back."

"Mom—"

"I'll be right back," she says, and then she's gone.

Though I've been back in Bienville for five months, I've hardly been alone with my father. Neither of us handles it well. Any discussions inevitably turn to politics and journalism, and while in theory we are of the same mind about the present insanity, our approaches to dealing with it are quite different.

Watching my mother care for this failing shell that was once her proud husband, performing years of menial tasks—and now doing those things that wound and ultimately destroy personal dignity—humbles and even shames me. To do those things and not complain, to stand by your partner come what may . . . that is love. My mother and father endured what my wife and I could not: the death of a son. They didn't survive it whole, perhaps, but they stayed together. I've kept that in mind while Jet and I have fallen ever deeper into what surely feels like love. But where Jet and I are concerned, I know only one thing beyond doubt—

We have not been tested like this.

Looking down at Dad now, trapped in the grim spiral of life's last unwinding, I'm confronted by the essential fact of our relationship. *Were it not for this man, I would not exist.* Surely he and I must have shared happy experiences before my fourteenth year, when Adam drowned and nearly took the rest of us down with him. A few times over the years I've had flashes of memory, déjà vu while doing something with a friend or acquaintance, and wondered if I'd done it before with my father. But somehow, the bitterness that followed Adam's death ruined all that preceded it, like quinine poured into Coca-Cola. Eventually I came to believe that if my father's love for me couldn't survive the loss of my brother, then it wasn't ever love. I've applied the same ruthless logic to my own life. My love for my wife didn't survive the death of our son, ergo I must not have truly loved her. Whereas my son . . .

"I'm back," Mom says, laying her hand on my forearm. "I'll take over now. You get some sleep. I think we have a difficult few days ahead."

"Yes, ma'am."

I look down at this woman who bore me—worn down to 120 pounds and standing a head and a half shorter than I—and know without doubt that her courage dwarfs my own. Despite Dr. Kirby's caution to the contrary, her strength seems immeasurable. I pull her close and hug tight, feel her shaking against me.

Then I leave her to face the night alone.

CHAPTER 29

IF PUBLISHING YESTERDAY'S edition of the *Watchman* was like kicking over a hornet's nest, then publishing today's was like detonating a bomb. Above the fold we printed the trail camera photo of convicted felon Dave Cowart facing Buck Ferris on the night he died. Beneath the photo we reported that the county coroner had detected blood on a piece of brick taken from a spot where Buck was known to have been digging for relics on that night. We also reported that fragments of human bone had been excavated from a trench on the paper mill site, a trench clearly marked as a digging location in Buck's personal notebook. We got these facts into the paper only because, twenty minutes after I lay down in the bed of my childhood, Byron Ellis called and told me that after consulting his attorney and two black activists he trusted, he was ready to tell the truth about how Buck died, regardless of the consequences.

The obvious implication is that the Tenisaw County sheriff has been lying about Buck's death and that deputies fabricated or tampered with evidence by moving a brick from the paper mill site to Lafitte's Den. As a deterrent to further police misconduct, we revealed that some bone fragments and teeth were on their way to a lab at Louisiana State University in Baton Rouge. We also pointed out that the discovery of human remains requires that the sheriff halt construction while the Department of Archives and History decides whether to declare a preservation easement on the mill site. In the hope of avoiding being charged with felony trespass by an angry sheriff, I held back the identity of the "amateur archaeologist" who had recovered those bone fragments. I had hoped to announce that the artifacts bolstered Buck's theory of the mill site, but the archaeologist that Quinn Ferris trusts most at LSU has been out of town and won't be able to examine what I dug up until this afternoon.

Nevertheless, our story resulted in a flood of obscene email to the newspaper, much of it to my inbox. But at 8:40 A.M. I received a different kind of message. The heading read: PERSONAL FOR MARSHALL MCEWAN, NOT TROLL MAIL. The sender was listed as "Mark Felt." Mark Felt was the real identity of "Deep Throat" during the Watergate investigation. Intrigued, I opened the email, even though it had a file attached. The file turned out to be a lengthy PDF containing more than fifty different documents. A ten-minute perusal told me either I had been sent part of Sally Matheson's data cache, or a member of the Bienville Poker Club had gifted me priceless evidence. The former explanation seemed far more likely. Had the person Sally entrusted with her most dangerous bequest finally decided to make a move? If so, why?

I stored the PDF in my personal Dropbox folder, which moved a copy of the file to a server farm somewhere in the cloud. Then I used my personal office printer to produce a hard copy, which covered several different matters that would certainly result in scandals, if not legal indictments. Finally, I called in our IT guy—a twenty-four-year-old Texan named David Garcia—and asked him to trace the source of the email that had delivered the PDF.

While Garcia worked at my computer, I sat in the corner and read through the hard copy. The first twenty-six documents detail a scam that exploited advance knowledge of Bienville's site selection for the new paper mill to defraud more than three dozen homeowners of their property. These citizens of Bienville and Tenisaw County had lived in three areas: on land contiguous to the industrial park, along a secondary road that leads to the industrial park, and along the proposed corridor of Interstate 14. On the day the governor announced that Bienville had won the Azure Dragon mill site competition, all that land tripled in value.

The emails and deeds contained in the PDF establish that real estate developer Beau Holland coordinated the effort to buy those homes and lots for bottom dollar. The last home to sell closed thirty-four days prior to the governor's public announcement. Some of those houses are only a mile from my own, but at the time of these sales, I—like everyone else—merely assumed that cash-rich investors were taking a gamble that Bienville would get the new interstate. Emails in the PDF file prove that Beau Holland and at least seven other Poker Club members knew four months before the official announcement that Bienville would get both the paper mill and the interstate. The primary investors in Holland's scheme are Claude Buckman, Tommy Russo, Dr. Warren Lacey, Arthur Pine, and Max Matheson. Astonishingly, their source of information about both site selection and the interstate decision was a "Mr. Chow" from "Mai Loc Incorporated." That last name hurled me back to Sally Matheson's sapphire necklace with the "MaiLoc1971" password stuck to its backside.

The second set of documents includes emails between Wyatt Cash, Tommy Russo, and Max Matheson. The exchange discusses problems surrounding the hiring of illegal immigrant workers for specific jobs at the companies belonging to those men. All apparently use illegal workers on a regular basis, and pay them far below minimum wage. A couple of "Mexican troublemakers" are mentioned frequently in the correspondence—labor brokers, apparently—and Wyatt Cash refers to a private detective agency being hired to surveil those men. Tommy Russo makes reference to having "some of my guys straighten those goddamn beaners out."

But the most explosive set of emails reveals behind-the-scenes machinations that helped get former Tenisaw County circuit judge Avery Sumner appointed to the U.S. Senate seat vacated by the senior senator for Mississippi. The writers of these emails used coded language when describing political moves, but the messages are filled with personal insults about three other candidates favored by the state Republican Party. Most damning, there are multiple references to Avery Sumner being "malleable" and "enthusiastic about pursuing our private agenda." One sentence in a message from Arthur Pine to "Mr. Chow" sticks with me. It read: *Avery fully understands the debt of gratitude owed to your friends, and also the principle of reciprocity.* The "Avery" referred to in that email is now a U.S. senator. In the same email was a reference to the Royal Bank of Seychelles.

As I reflected on all this, it struck me that the Azure Dragon paper mill deal has become a scandal of national proportions.

"Marshall?" David Garcia said from behind my desk. "Whoever sent this PDF used the Proton mail program. I don't have the technology to penetrate to the original source."

"Does that mean the sender was some kind of hacker?"

Garcia looked up from my computer. "No. You can get hold of that program commercially."

"Is there anybody who could trace the sender for us?"

He shrugged. "The NSA."

"Anybody *local?*"

Garcia laughed. "No way."

I thanked David and asked him to keep quiet about the PDF and the work he'd just attempted. After he closed my door, I went back to my desk to think long and hard about what I'd read.

Except for the mention of Avery Sumner's Senate seat, none of the potential crimes described in the PDF involve either Azure Dragon Paper or city, county, or state government officials. It's as though whoever sent me the file was giving me ammunition to hurt members of the Poker Club while risking as little damage as possible to the paper mill deal itself. The "Mr. Chow" correspondence hints at some sort of tit-for-tat arrangement between Avery Sumner and the "friends" of Mr. Chow, but nothing is spelled out in sufficient detail to prove a crime. I know reporters in Washington who would cream themselves over a lead like that, but right now I'm more interested in the fact that Max Matheson figures in all three sets of documents. Beau Holland does, too, but I can't imagine anyone related to Holland leaking damaging information about him. Sally Matheson, on the other hand, put together information exactly like this in order to destroy her husband. And it's Max who holds my future—and possibly my life—in the palm of his hand.

Am I looking at part of her final cache? I wonder.

A quick soft knock sounds at my door. Lucy Hodder, our receptionist, steps in, looking worried.

"You've got a visitor," she says. "And you might not want to see this guy."

"Who is it?"

"Mr. Holland, the Realtor. And he is *not* happy. I told him I wasn't sure you were here. But I didn't want to send him away unless you told me to."

I start to beg off, but something stops me. Two nights ago, Beau Holland had to be physically restrained from attacking me. Has he come back to finish his assault? Given what I saw in the PDF file, I can't say I'd be surprised. But what would be the point?

"Send him in," I tell Lucy, wondering if Holland could be under enough financial strain to walk in here and shoot me. Surely not—

"I'm already in, you son of a bitch," growls a prissy male voice.

Beau Holland pushes past Lucy and plants himself before my desk. "And I'm not alone."

As I slip the hard copy of the PDF file into my top drawer, Tommy Russo steps into my office, wearing his usual tight-fitting suit.

Lucy looks at me with flushed cheeks. "Should I call somebody?"

I'm about to say no when Dave Cowart pushes in behind the other two. The pilled red Izod shirt he's wearing makes him look like a human fireplug, and the contractor's sunburned face is only slightly less red than his shirt. Holland glares at him and says, "I told you I'd handle this."

"I was smoking outside," Cowart says. "But when I saw Tommy come in, I figured I'd put in my two cents. I'm the one already got fucked by that Matheson cunt."

I catch Lucy's eye, but before I can speak, Russo says, "No need to call the police, hon. I'll keep these gentlemen in line."

"I'm all right, Lucy," I tell her, but she exits with a doubtful look.

"How can I help you guys?" I ask, leaning back in my chair and folding my hands across my stomach.

"You could get hit by a truck," Cowart says. "Man, what's with you? You print that goddamn photo like you're bulletproof or something."

"I'm confused, Dave. Did you not get enough of prison last year?"

He closes his big fists and steps toward me. "Come out from behind that desk and find out."

"Oh-kay," Holland says, taking Cowart by the arm and pulling him back two steps. "I think he got your message, Dave."

Cowart's eyes show fear as well as anger. "I'm on probation, damn it! This piece of shit's gonna get me thrown back in the can."

"That could happen," I tell him, thinking of Buck's body being wrestled from the river. "You want to tell me what you were doing out at the mill site with Buck on the night he was killed? On the record?"

"Don't say a word," Beau Holland advises. "Anyway, who says that photo you printed was taken at the mill site? Your story didn't say that."

"That's true. We can't prove where it was taken. Yet. But whoever sent it to me could probably provide that information. We'll see what else he sends me."

All three men freeze for a moment. Then Holland leans forward and lays his hands on my desk. "I don't think the police or the sheriff's department will be picking up Mr. Cowart based on your reporting."

"No. But the FBI might. We're making sure all evidence related to Buck's murder gets sent to every agency that might have jurisdiction."

Tommy Russo has been leaning calmly against my office wall, chewing gum. But at my mention of the FBI, he makes a face like he just bit into something bitter.

"You have no idea what you're doing," Holland says. "You're interfering with people's lives, their businesses. With this whole town's future."

"Am I? I thought I was just trying to solve a murder."

Cowart grimaces, then shakes his head like all this talk is a waste of time.

"You're about to get an education," Beau Holland says with relish. "You keep printing stories like the one I read today, you're going to find out exactly where you stand in the food chain around here."

"The bottom, is it?"

Beau gives me his superior smile. "Another thing. Keep this up, and we'll sue you into bankruptcy. It wouldn't take much, from what I hear. We'll own this rag, McEwan. And the day we do, we'll chain the door shut."

Russo is watching this scene with his usual expression, that of a languid predator at leisure. Given his background, Holland's threats must seem about as tame as those from a kindergarten playground.

"I think you're overestimating your influence, Beau," I say calmly. Leaning forward in my chair, I turn and point to a tall picture frame on the wall. Under its glass is a copy of the first Bienville *Watchman* ever printed. "This rag, as you call it, has been published continuously since 1865. Through world wars, depression, civil rights battles, and hurricanes. I think we'll survive you and the Bienville Poker Club."

Holland gives me an eerie smile that promises undreamed-of revenge. "Our club's been around since the Civil War, too. We know what makes the mare go. You ignore my advice, you'll be lucky if your fellow citizens don't burn this building to the ground. They know who's on their side, and it's not this fake-news mill."

I let his threat hang in the air, waiting for his smile to fade. When it does I say, "If Dave had come in here alone, yelling and raising hell, I'd have blown it off. But since you two came in with him—a convicted felon—it's pretty clear he's still working for the Poker Club. So whatever he did to Buck, you're all part of it."

A shadow passes over Holland's overbred features, but Tommy Russo still looks as though he wandered in here by accident. Beau straightens up and puts his hands on his hips, a vaguely feminine gesture. "Picking friends is an art, Marshall. But picking your enemies is survival. You'd better keep that in mind."

"Got a lot of friends, have you, Beau?"

"More than you, after today."

I fight to suppress a powerful urge to stick the knife in and twist it. In the end, I can't resist. "I think I know one of your friends," I tell him. "An interesting guy."

"Yeah? Who's that?"

"Say hello to Mr. Chow for me the next time you see him."

Holland blanches. Dave Cowart looks blank, but Tommy Russo has stopped chewing his gum.

"Where did you hear that name?" Beau asks in a near whisper.

I turn up my hands. "Here, there—it's hard to say with the way things are popping since yesterday."

Holland fixes a superior smile on his face. "You have no idea what you're fucking with. You're not long for this world, my friend."

I should keep my mouth shut, but all I can think about is Buck's open skull on Denny's drone video. I want to make Beau Holland squirm. "I think you and your buddies are one jury verdict from the penitentiary. People can't *wait* to give you guys up. This morning somebody told me how you ripped off a bunch of homeowners on the I-14 corridor, using inside information. Somebody else told me about Tommy and Max and Wyatt Cash threatening illegal workers. Best of all, though, is how you jammed Avery Sumner into that U.S. Senate seat. I've got contacts in

D.C. who'll *eat that shit up*. All those insults about the other candidates? We might hijack the news cycle for a full twenty-four hours. So buckle up, Beau. You're about to have a bumpy week."

"I need to speak to Marshall alone," Tommy Russo says softly.

Beau starts to protest, but before he reaches his third syllable Russo says, "Give me the fucking room."

After Holland and Cowart shuffle out, Russo closes the door, then walks up to the edge of my desk. The predator-at-leisure expression is gone. The casino owner looks like a lion that could bare his claws and snatch me up by the throat any time he feels like it.

"You're in the business of printing news," he says, his Jersey up-bringing suddenly evident in his voice. "I get it. You made your bones on some big political scandals. National stuff. But you need to think hard before you take your next step."

"Tommy—"

"Let me finish, Doc. I've only known you five months, but I like you, okay? I respect what you do. We both know the future of this town depends on that paper mill. Also the interstate and the businesses coming in behind it—my new casino, for example. Bienville's gonna be a showplace, while the rest of this state shrinks and sinks. I know a hometown boy like you don't want to hurt the town he came from. What the old neighborhood is for me, this town is for you."

"Tommy . . . I think this town can survive a lot. And I think the Azure Dragon deal can survive you guys taking a few hits."

He sniffs and looks around my office. "Yeah? Well, maybe what you don't know is a lot. What you got in your pocket? Some emails?"

"Yeah. Plus bank transfer records, deeds . . . It's impossible to ignore."

"That sounds like private information to me."

"I didn't steal it. A whistle-blower sent it to me. Fair game."

"A leaker, you mean." Russo makes an expression with his mouth that looks copied from Robert De Niro, circa 1974, then tilts his head to one side. "Sounds like maybe I need to call a plumber."

"I'm not your problem, Tommy. Whoever's throwing you to the wolves is. I think it's one of your Poker Club buddies. Now, I need to get back to work."

He stares down at me awhile longer, then walks to my door and opens it. Before he goes out, he looks back and says quietly: "I don't fuck with a man's livelihood if I can help it. I'm in a competitive business, but I don't hurt nobody unless they come at me first. You've come to a fork in the road, my friend. You go one way, life is good. You see your old man out in style, sell this newspaper, head back to the city. But—you take the other road, things maybe don't turn out so good."

Russo rotates his flattened hand back and forth. "Anyway, the point I want to leave you with is this: It's up to you. I'm not telling you which road to take. I'm just saying that whatever happens at the end of it, you got nobody to blame or thank but yourself." He interlocks his fingers and cracks his knuckles so loudly that I start in my chair. "You have a good day now, Doc. I'll see ya round the place."

Then he closes the door.

Tommy Russo should record a master class on how to threaten people. Three minutes after he leaves my office, I still feel like I might throw up.

When the door opens again, I jump. But it's only Ben Tate. "What the hell did those guys want?"

"You don't want to know."

"Did they threaten you?"

"Be glad you didn't hear it."

"That short guy looked like he wanted to strangle you with his bare hands."

"He was the comic relief. Look, I want you to find out everything there is to know about Tommy Russo. His crime family links. Actual crimes he's been tied to or suspected of."

"I'll get on it. Has your secret admirer delivered any more goodies today? More trail camera pics?"

I think about the PDF sent to me by "Mark Felt." Then I remember Russo's expression as he talked about the fork in the road. "I haven't been out to my car yet. I'll know when I get coffee."

Ben has the gleam of ambition in his eyes. "We need to keep this story going, man. People are sharing it all over the place. It could go national."

"I don't think there'll be any shortage of developments today. We'll talk later."

He takes the hint and closes my door.

Things are happening so fast that I can hardly wrap my head around the implications. Two days ago, Buck was murdered by power brokers I would have sworn were untouchable. Now somebody's feeding me information that could send them to prison. But the price of using it could be death at the hands of a New Jersey–born casino owner. Of course, for Tommy Russo to kill me, I'd have to live long enough to print the story that would make him mad enough to do it; and with Max threatening to show his son the video of me making love to his wife, even that lifespan isn't guaranteed.

As I lock my hard copy of the PDF into my filing cabinet, I think of Sally Matheson. She's lying on a cold slab somewhere, or in a refrigerated drawer. But the cache that she created holds the power to dictate the future of every man in this complex equation. I may already possess part of the data she gathered, but surely there's more. If so, I need to find it. If I don't, I may have to consider letting Jet put her plan against Max into motion. Because despite Tommy Russo's pragmatic threat, it's Max who has the power to turn Paul against me. And unlike Russo, Paul would not react rationally. That said, I have a paradoxical feeling that Paul Matheson could end up my only reliable ally in what is fast shaping up to be a war. Yes, I have betrayed him. But at some level I feel bound to Paul in a way that excludes even Jet. He knows me as well as anyone ever has, and at bottom he knows I mean him no harm. Logically that makes no sense, I know.

But since when has human behavior ever followed logic?

CHAPTER 30

AT TEN FORTY A.M., I walk out to the Flex to head for my morning coffee at Nadine's store. Crossing the open space between the building and my vehicle, I turn in all directions, looking for threats. I spent the previous ten minutes briefing reporters on what they'll be doing today. This was tricky, since I don't want to reveal the existence of the mystery PDF file yet. To cover, I told them that I have suspicions about the "land grabs" near the mill site and along the I-14 corridor and gave them a list of former property owners to interview. I also asked Ben Tate to have somebody assemble everything there is on the selection of Avery Sumner to fill the Senate seat he assumed only five months ago.

Even before I open the Flex's door, I see another USB flash drive taped to my steering wheel. This one is bright orange. Once inside, I find it's another Lexar—32 GB this time. Slipping it into my pants pocket, I back out of my space and pull onto High Street. Nadine's is only five blocks away. Driving the lightly traveled streets, I curse myself for not installing a wireless video camera to cover the back lot of our building yesterday. If I had, I might already possess the identity of my secret benefactor.

After easing into one of the tight spaces behind Nadine's build-ing, I slip through the back door and go straight to the laptop in her inventory room. Fifteen seconds later, I'm staring at another photo taken by a trail camera, this one—according to the time stamp—shot thirty seconds later on the same night as the photo we published this morning. But Dave Cowart is only a bit player in this one. In this im-age, *Beau Holland* stands very close to Buck Ferris, shaking a finger in his face. Dave Cowart stands behind Holland, arms akimbo. My pulse pounds as I stare at Holland's angry expression, but what fixes my attention is the background of the photograph. Behind the men, about knee level, a line of concrete stretches into the distance—a line that looks familiar from my excursion after the Aurora Hotel party. It's the edge of the old factory foundation at the mill site. And in the far distance, exactly where it should be, a bright pinpoint of light shines against the dark sky. That light is the beacon atop the electrical tower I failed to climb when I was fourteen.

I don't think I've breathed for the last twenty seconds. *This* is why Holland got so angry back in my office. He was at the mill site with Cowart on the night Buck was killed, and he knows there might be photos that prove it.

After saving the file on Nadine's MacBook, I pull out the flash drive, slip it back into my pocket, and head up front. I'm excited to tell her about the new image, but to my surprise, she's nowhere in the shop. Behind the counter stands a young recent college grad named Darryl. Seeing me coming from the back, he starts making my coffee without asking for my order.

"You want your muffin, too?" he asks.

"Ah, sure. Where's Nadine this morning?"

"She had to run an errand. I'm not sure where. Said it wouldn't take more than an hour. She left thirty minutes ago."

Maybe it's not so odd that Nadine isn't here during my usual visiting time. When she dropped Jet's earrings into my hand last night, it was pretty clear that she assumed I've been sleeping with Jet. Given the unexpected intimacy of our kiss the previous night, discovering Jet's earrings in my bathroom might have soured Nadine on our daily kaffeeklatsch. The maddening thing is that I know Jet left those earrings there solely so that Nadine would find them if she used the bathroom that adjoined my bedroom. They were left there as a test of fidelity.

"Thanks, Darryl."

I take my muffin and walk into the café seating section with the hot mug in my hand. I'm glad to find the tables almost empty. Against the wall to my left sits another couple who look like tourists, though not the same ones I saw two days ago. At the back of the room sits a tanned blond college student wearing tennis shorts. He's facing away from me, so I'm spared the ordeal of trying to figure out whether I should know him or his parents. I choose one of the two-chair tables and eat the muffin while waiting for my coffee to cool. As I chew, I feel anger building at Jet's little earring trap. She's not normally into games, at least in my experience.

I take a sip of coffee, and the caffeine hits me immediately. I welcome the relief. I'm feeling jumpy, and paradoxically, caffeine sometimes settles me down. Relief from withdrawal, probably.

Before I take my second sip, my iPhone rings. As I take it out, I find myself wishing it had been my burner phone. But Jet hasn't called. No surprise, really. The family's bound to be consumed with preparing for Sally's funeral. And yet—the name on my iPhone screen reads *Max Matheson*.

"Shit." I answer and put the phone to my cheek. "What do you want, Max?"

"I heard you've found Sally's data cache."

"That's bullshit." But then it hits me. "You've been talking to your poker buddies."

"You rattled 'em, Goose."

"I don't have the cache, Max. I have a few files some anonymous person emailed to me, that's all. The address is untraceable. That person might have Sally's cache, but I have no way to find out who they are. I already tried."

"You told Russo you're planning to print this stuff?"

"No. But I might have said more than I should have. Beau Holland pissed me off."

"You let that prissy asshole get to you?"

"Yeah. I need to go, Max."

"You bury those files, Goose. Hear me? If you print them, I'll have to show Paul your little amateur skin flick."

"I'll try to bury them," I tell him, stalling for time. "But it won't be easy."

"Find a way. Because Paul may not be your biggest problem. If he kills you, at least it'll be quick. But you've got Russo worried now. And Tommy's the creative type."

"Where are you?"

"At my office at the sawmill. Why? You need to see me?"

I asked because I'm thinking about going to talk to Tallulah Williams, the Matheson maid. "Where's Paul?"

"What's with the twenty questions?"

"Jesus, Max."

"Okay, hell. Paul's at the wood treatment plant. I hope you're not trying to see Jet again. I told you last night, you've hit that pussy for the last time. If I find out you're disregarding my advice—"

"I'm not looking for Jet. I'm trying to find your damn cache."

The tourist couple is staring at me.

"Good survival strategy, Goose. Keep me posted."

I click off and take another long swallow of coffee.

Before I can even reflect on my conversation with Max, my iPhone rings again. I figure it's Max calling back, but the screen says BIENVILLE SOUTHERN BANK. That bank belongs to the most senior member of the Bienville Poker Club.

"Hello?"

"Mr. McEwan?" says a perky female voice.

"Yes."

"I have Claude Buckman for you. Please hold."

Two seconds later, a hoarse, elderly voice says, "Mr. McEwan, this is Claude Buckman. We met on the roof of the Aurora two nights ago."

"I remember. What can I do for you?"

"You've got that backwards, son. I want to do something for you."

"What's that?"

"I'd prefer to tell you in person. Could you come by my bank in half an hour?"

This request is so unexpected that my initial instinct is to stall. "What for?"

"Merely a conversation."

"On the record?"

"I'm afraid not. But you'll be glad you came."

Now I get it. "Is this about a bribe?"

Buckman chuckles. "Not in the sense you're thinking of. This is about making the world a better place."

Those are the last words I could have imagined coming from Claude Buckman's mouth. "Can you be more specific?"

"Only to say that you'll be perfectly safe, and several of my associates will be present. You know most of them, I believe."

So this is to be a meeting of the Poker Club. "I just spoke to Max Matheson, and he didn't say anything about a meeting at your bank."

"Max doesn't know about it. Half an hour, Mr. McEwan. I'll be expecting you."

He hangs up.

"Unbelievable," I murmur.

Like Max, Claude Buckman must believe that I'm in possession of Sally Matheson's cache. What princely sum will the banker offer me to bury it? The most interesting thing Buckman said was that Max doesn't know about the meeting. That tells me there may already be a rift inside the Poker Club. The covert delivery of the flash drives has already suggested as much. If there is dissent in the club, then maybe this meeting will offer an opportunity to turn one faction of the club against Max.

As I ponder this prospect, I sense someone approaching me from behind. I turn in my chair, causing a loud scrape on the floor.

"Sorry," says the "college guy" who a moment ago was sitting in the back of the café. "I didn't mean to startle you."

The man I mistakenly assumed was a college student turns out to be about fifty. Like Max Matheson, he's in such good physical shape that I didn't notice his true age from a distance. Also like Max, he's blond and handsome, though not quite as rugged or rangy. This guy reminds me of Stefan Edberg, the Swedish tennis player. But maybe it's only his outfit.

"Mr. McEwan?" he says. "I was hoping I could speak to you for a minute."

So he knows me. "Look, if you're upset about a newspaper story, I'd rather you write me an email."

He blushes. "Oh, no. I've loved the recent stories. Buck Ferris was a wonderful man. The idea that somebody killed him because of that paper mill is just . . . obscene."

This is so far from the usual reaction I get when people accost me in Nadine's that it makes me curious. "You look familiar. Have we met?"

"A long time ago. I'm Tim Hayden. I coached tennis at St. Mark's for two seasons, back in the mid-eighties."

A rush of good memories spools through my head. "I remember you! You coached Adam."

Hayden breaks into a broad smile. "I did. He was a great player. Really gifted."

"In every sport, annoyingly."

Hayden's smile widens. "I think Adam could have gone pro if he'd . . . you know, had a chance. And if they hadn't made him play football and baseball."

"Nobody forced him."

He laughs. "You're right. Do you have a minute to talk?"

"What about? Adam?"

Hayden's smile vanishes. "Yes, actually. I need to confess: this isn't a random meeting. I'm a friend of Christopher Simms, Nadine's friend. The one she's staying with. He told me that you come in for coffee every day around this time."

"I see. Well . . . I have about twenty minutes before a meeting. Sit down."

Hayden looks uncertain. "Actually, I was hoping we could speak privately."

I look around the shop. "Nadine's courtyard?"

He shakes his head. "Customers out there. There's a little park half-way up the block. I hate to impose. I've wanted to talk to you for a long time, but you've lived away ever since high school. It would mean a lot to me."

Maybe Hayden's request should trip my radar, but something about his manner reassures me that he's not a threat. "Okay, let's go."

I pick up my shoulder bag and walk toward the door. "Have you lived in Bienville all your life?"

"No, no," he says. "I lived in New Orleans for twenty years. I liked it, but it was too violent for me. Katrina gave me an excuse to get out. I've moved around some, but now I'm the tennis pro out at the new country club here. Belle Rose."

"I see."

"The park's just up on the right," Hayden says, pointing.

I remember it now. I drank an eight-pack of Miller ponies with a buddy in that park when I was about fifteen.

I find the little alcove between two buildings. Behind a low wrought-iron fence, two heavy park benches stand on weathered flagstones. The ornate green benches face each other. Tim Hayden takes the right-hand one, and I, the left. Looking into his still-boyish face, I suddenly wonder whether the pitch about Adam was a pretext, and he's my secret source for the Poker Club material.

"This is hard for me," he begins. "Do you remember me from Adam's funeral?"

Something in me goes still. I don't know what he's getting at, but bringing up Adam's funeral puts me on guard. Over a thousand people came to the high school for Adam's memorial. Athletic teams from nearby cities caravanned in on school buses. "I'm sorry, that day is mostly a blur for me."

"I'm sure. Of course."

"What's important about that day?"

"It's not that day, really. I got to be good friends with Adam when I coached at St. Mark's. We were only four years apart in age. I'd just graduated from college, and I helped out there as a favor to my old coach. I wasn't on staff or anything. St. Mark's never took tennis that seriously."

"I know. Same with swimming."

Tim smiles wistfully. "I remember your swimming medals, by the way. If you'd kept on . . ."

I wave my hand. "After what happened to Adam, I couldn't do it anymore."

He looks down at the flagstones and shakes his head. When he looks up, his eyes are wet. "I don't know how to say this. I don't even know if I'm right to say it. But I imagine you've spent a lot of time wondering about your brother, what his life might have been like if he'd lived."

"Sure I have."

"Adam was very confused during his senior year."

"Confused?"

"Yes. He thought he might be gay."

I should have realized sooner where this was headed. My conversation with Russo and Buckman must have knocked me off-balance. But the truth is, I never once suspected that Adam might be gay.

"Should I go on?" Hayden asks.

"Yes. Please."

"Adam got so much attention from girls, remember? And women, too, my God. I think every female teacher under fifty was in love with him."

"Oh, I remember."

"He was lucky because of that, though. All the female attention, plus him being a star athlete, kept everyone from guessing he might be anything but straight. But late in his senior year, he started asking me questions. He sensed that I was gay, and about halfway through the tennis season, he got up the nerve to ask me about it."

I nod to encourage him.

"I told Adam about my own experiences in high school. How tough it had been with the father I had. I was still in the closet, but a small number of people knew. My mother was one, thank God." Hayden shifts his weight on the bench, then winces as though what he's thinking about causes him physical pain. "The thing is . . . near the end of Adam's senior year, he and I had an experience together. Then one more. That was it, just two times. He drowned shortly after that."

A strange numbness is moving through my limbs.

"Adam was eighteen," he goes on, "but I feel very ambivalent about what I did. Technically I was his coach, even though I wasn't being paid. But that's not what I wanted to talk about. I just . . . I feel like there was a side to Adam—not a side, really, but his essence—that no one knew about. On one hand, he was worshipped by everyone, but that didn't mean much to him. Because no one really knew who he was. At least I don't think so. That's why I wanted to talk to you. To find out whether you knew that side of him. Or even suspected it."

I'd like to be able to tell Hayden that I knew, that Adam had trusted me with his secret. Or failing that, that I'd known my brother well enough to figure it out on my own. But I hadn't. I remained at the same distance as the other mortals. Perhaps a little closer . . . but not close enough.

"I didn't know, Tim. I had no idea. He dated Jenny Anderson for two years, and I just assumed—"

"Everybody did." He nods and smiles wistfully. "Their relationship wasn't sexual, believe it or not."

"I can't believe I was that blind. I knew how sensitive Adam was, especially for a jock. Not that he was ever a jock, in the simplistic sense. He just had the talent. But there was something else in him. Empathy, I guess. And a kind of magnetism that pulled people to him. Men and women wanted to talk to him, to be around him. Old or young, it didn't matter. Adam was just . . . different."

Tim is nodding, his eyes bright with tears. "This must be strange for you. And hard. I hope I didn't presume too much. I was afraid you might be furious at me."

I shrug, then shake my head. "No point being angry now. Was he confused by the experiences? Or relieved? What?"

"All the above. Adam carried a lot on his shoulders. The hopes and dreams of a whole school, a whole town. And of course your father's, too, heaviest of all."

"Don't I know it."

Tim sits with his head bowed. Dark spots appear on the stones beneath his face. I'd like to comfort him, but I'm not sure how to make him feel better. Sitting mute, I flash back to the night before Adam died, the night we climbed the electrical tower beside the river. All that night, the Matheson cousins ragged us with the usual litany of high school insults. As I watch Tim Hayden crying in this little park, the main Matheson theme comes back to me with painful clarity: *faggots, homos, queers.* Even the stupid "Casey Jones" parody they jeered at me had homosexual references. I took those insults like water off a duck's back, but Adam didn't. For once, the taunts of idiots got under his skin. Was he in the grip of a sexual identity crisis on that night? Was that what drove him to the top of that tower to dance along the light strut like Dooley Matheson, six hundred feet in the air? Was that what pushed him to try to swim the river with me?

No, I tell myself. The tower, maybe. But Adam went into the river to protect me, his little brother. I still remember his words: *If you drown out there, I can't walk in our house and tell Mom and Dad I watched it happen.* He couldn't have imagined that it would be me rather than him who would face that soul-searing ordeal.

"Do you know when I think about Adam the most?" Hayden asks.

"When?"

"When I hear Jeff Buckley sing Leonard Cohen's 'Hallelujah.'"

"Yeah? Well, that's a great song."

"It is, but that's not the reason. Jeff Buckley drowned in the Mississippi River. Did you know that?"

I feel like someone walked over my grave. "I didn't. Where did he drown?"

"Memphis. When I hear Buckley singing 'Hallelujah,' I always hope that his soul and Adam's found each other in that river." Hayden smiles through his tears. "I sound crazy, right?"

"Actually no. I loved him, too. And I used to be a musician."

"I didn't know you could stop being a musician."

This makes me smile. "You're right. You never do." I look at my wristwatch. "I hate to say it, but I have a meeting to get to."

He wipes his face with the flat of his hand. "You've been great about this. It's such a relief after so long. I hope you feel the same, after you've had time to process it."

"I'm glad you told me. This seems to be the week that my whole life history gets explained to me. It's like time is running backwards. I'm living from flashback to flashback."

He gives me a sympathetic smile. "Do you think your parents had any idea about Adam?"

"No. And I wouldn't bring this up to them. In fact, I'll ask you not to. My father couldn't take it, and my mother's got enough to handle without wondering why she didn't see it herself. She'll start thinking that if only she'd recognized that, and nurtured it, Adam might still be alive."

Hayden nods. "I understand completely. I won't ever speak to them about it. I just wanted someone in the family to know."

I get to my feet and reach out to shake his hand, but Hayden pulls me in for a hug. Feeling tears rise, I blink and wipe my eyes after I pull away.

"Thanks for this," he says. "And please find out what happened to Buck. He was a good man."

"I will."

He turns and leaves through the little wrought-iron gate.

Nothing would ease my nerves in this moment more than to sit in this little park and go back over my brother's life, searching for clues I missed while he was alive. But Claude Buckman and the Poker Club are waiting for me. I might as well go listen to their pitch. Shouldering my bag, I walk down Second Street to the Flex. Buckman's bank is only a few blocks away, but I'd rather have my vehicle with me. There's no telling where I might need to go after that meeting, or if I'll need to get there in a hurry.

CHAPTER 31

THE BIENVILLE SOUTHERN Bank is a Greek Revival pile built in the 1880s by Claude Buckman's grandfather. An exceptionally attractive receptionist escorts me to the second-floor conference room, where I find a massive rosewood table capable of seating twenty, but which today holds only five men: Claude Buckman, Blake Donnelly, Avery Sumner, Wyatt Cash, and Arthur Pine. Stripped of their names, I'm facing a predatory banker, an old-time oil tycoon, a newly minted U.S. senator, an entrepreneur with ties to the U.S. military, and a sleazy lawyer. What could possibly go wrong?

"Greetings, Mr. McEwan," Claude Buckman says. "Come up and have a seat with us. There, beside Mr. Pine. I believe you know him."

"I do." I walk up the other side of the table and sit beside Wyatt Cash.

Except for the conference phone sitting at the center of the table, this room could have been furnished in the 1860s. The prints on the walls appear to have been chosen by someone intent on celebrating the pre–Civil War South: Confederate soldiers, racing steamboats, cotton wagons, cotton trains, belles in hoop skirts, and—in almost every photo—slaves. Slaves driving wagons, crewing steamboats, serving drinks to officers; whole black families bent in a cotton field, with children too small to drag a sack sitting in a turnrow, playing in the dirt.

"Are you carrying any recording devices?" Buckman asks as I take my seat.

"No."

"I'd appreciate you taking out your cell phone, switching it off, and leaving it on the table." He waves a hand at his colleagues. All their phones lie before them on the polished wood, all apparently switched off.

Shrugging my shoulders, I partly comply with his request by laying my iPhone on the table.

"Thank you," says Buckman. "Now, Mr. McEwan. I detest pointless talk. So I'm going to be as straightforward as I can. We are businessmen. We make no pretense of being anything else. We exist to earn profits, expand our businesses, and consolidate our power. We create wealth. If the lot of others happens to improve while we do that, that's fine, but it's not our concern." The banker pauses as if to be sure I'm following his lecture on capitalism. "You, on the other hand, are a journalist. Some have characterized you as a crusader. A do-gooder. An optimist, even."

"I'd contest that last assertion. I don't know a veteran reporter who's not a cynic."

Buckman's smile tells me he thinks I'm deluding myself.

"We've brought you here to tell you that today is your lucky day."

I look at the other faces around the table. Blake Donnelly and Wyatt Cash are grinning. Senator Sumner has a guarded look, while Arthur Pine gazes down at the table in front of him. I can't tell whether Pine has no interest in the proceedings or is certain he already knows the outcome.

"My lucky day," I echo. "How's that?"

Buckman lights a cigarette, blows out a raft of blue smoke, then continues. "It's come to our attention that you're in possession of information that could interfere with certain financial endeavors. To wit, the Azure Dragon paper mill and its associated ventures. Because of this, we are prepared to offer you certain considerations in exchange for not using that or any other information to harm our businesses."

"You want to bribe me."

Buckman gives me a tight smile. "I'll let you be the judge. Now, I've reviewed the editorials you've written over the five months since you returned to Bienville. It's clear that you have certain, ah, pet issues that concern you. Public education is one. Would you agree?"

"Sure. Other than Reliant Charter, Bienville has some of the worst public schools in America."

"Just so. How would you feel if Bienville were to have a brand-new public high school? With all the bells and whistles? State-of-the-art computers, smart boards, metal detectors, good teacher salaries, the works."

I look from face to face again. None of these men seems surprised by Buckman's words. "You realize you're talking about forty or fifty million dollars? Minimum."

"Money is my business, Mr. McEwan."

"And you're saying . . . what? You'll build this school? Get it built?"

Buckman settles back in his chair and speaks with utter confidence. "We'll push the votes through, get the tax millage increased, and anything that doesn't cover, we'll cover ourselves. We'll have it up and running in a year."

"That's one hell of a bribe."

Senator Sumner leans forward and says, "Marshall—may I call you Marshall?"

"Why not?"

"Marshall, we're not talking about a bribe. We're talking about solving one of the most crippling systemic problems in the history of this town. The whole state, really. When I was a judge here, I sentenced hundreds of young black men to prison who had no business in a penitentiary. The real crime in their lives was ignorance. They hadn't been educated. Claude is offering you a chance to rectify that problem."

"I'm amazed to admit it, but . . . he did seem to offer that."

Buckman smiles as though he's enjoying this. "You've also written a lot about crumbling infrastructure, particularly drainage and water mains on the north side of town. Bucktown, they call it in polite company."

"We called it Niggertown when I was a boy," Donnelly interjects. "Different time, of course."

"We're prepared to make sure all that gets repaired in a timely manner," Buckman declares.

"Of course you are," I say, scarcely able to believe the turn this conversation has taken. "Since you're fixing the world all of a sudden, how about crime?"

Wyatt Cash catches my eye. "What would you recommend? More police officers? A community development fund?"

"More cops on Bienville's city force, for sure. Higher salaries to attract quality recruits, and to keep them. And a real chief, not the puppet you have in there now."

Buckman smiles. "Done, done, and done."

"You're serious, aren't you?"

"I never joke, Mr. McEwan. I'm told I'm not funny."

I wonder who had the balls to tell Claude Buckman he wasn't funny. Had to be his wife. "Let me ask a question."

"Certainly."

"Why are there only five of you here? I thought the Poker Club always had twelve members."

A couple of the men look uncomfortable, but Buckman doesn't hesitate to answer. "We five are the voices that matter."

"How would Beau Holland and Tommy Russo feel about hearing that?"

Buckman shrugs. "Immaterial. Holland's a junior member, and Mr. Russo is from out of state. He's a sort of . . . provisional member."

"Max Matheson's not from out of state. His ancestor was one of the founding members, right?"

"True."

"And Max isn't just a heavyweight in this town. He's a force statewide."

"All true." Buckman steeples his fingers and speaks with precision. "But Max has been . . . profligate in his personal relations. He has put this consortium at risk, and by so doing has sacrificed both his voice and his vote. That's as clear as I'm prepared to be at this time."

For an old man who smokes too much, Claude Buckman can still bring it. He talks like a character from a John O'Hara novel. I see why Max is scared, too. With friends like these . . .

"Let me get this straight," I temporize. "You guys have the power to do all this—you've always had it—yet you've chosen not to?"

"As I said at the outset," Buckman replies, "we're not in the business of saving the world. That's your department. But at this moment in time, we happen to have a coincidence of interests."

"Unbelievable."

"Could I say something?" asks Avery Sumner.

"Of course, Senator," says Buckman.

"Here's what this comes down to, Marshall. If you keep pushing ahead with these newspaper stories, you're going to wreck a deal that took one hell of a lot of hard work. More important, you'll damage southwest Mississippi beyond repair. This development means salvation to your neighbors. Hundreds of jobs, health insurance, a business renaissance . . . you name it. So why on God's earth would a good man like you want to hurt all those people?"

The answer comes to me without effort. "Because somebody murdered my friend."

Sumner coughs and looks at Buckman, but Blake Donnelly is nodding. "I hear you, son. I knew Buck Ferris, as I told you the other night. He was a damn good man. And if he was murdered, that's an awful thing. But no man in this room had anything to do with that. I give you my word. Now, you've heard the kinds of things we're prepared to do to improve this town. And I think if you put a question like this to Buck, he'd say, 'Do all the good you can, Marshall. Don't look a gift horse in the mouth. The world is for the living.' Don't you think so?"

I wish Quinn Ferris were here to respond to Donnelly, but the truth is he might be right. "He might," I concede.

The oilman smiles to hear his instinct confirmed.

"To summarize," Buckman concludes. "Do you want to torpedo the future of this whole area so that men like us will make a few million dollars less than we otherwise might? Condemn your hometown to eventual poverty and obscurity? Or do you want to bless Bienville with another fifty years of prosperity? I do not exaggerate, Mr. McEwan. Today the decision lies in your hands."

Several responses rise into my mind, but before I can voice any of them Buckman says, "We're not saints, young man. My only virtue is that I've never pretended to be one."

"Look, I appreciate that you—"

"Write yourself a Christmas list!" Buckman says effusively. "All the things I've named, plus your pet projects, plus a community development fund to be disbursed at your discretion."

"A liberal's wet dream," Blake Donnelly says with a grin. "Compliments of the greedy conservatives."

Everyone laughs at this, even Buckman.

"Just to be clear," I say, trying to keep my voice under control. "To get what I put on my Christmas list, I'd have to drop all investigations into anything related to the Poker Club."

"Just so," says Buckman.

"And the murder of Buck Ferris?"

Buckman and Donnelly look down at the table, as though communing with their guiding principles. Then Buckman says, "If Mr. Ferris was indeed murdered on the mill site, then yes, I'm afraid so. Justice is a pillar of social order, Mr. McEwan. But we can't afford to have the mill project derailed. Too much depends on it, and the Chinese can be skittish about public image. To get this deal, you're going to have to leave the Ferris matter to the sheriff's department."

"Who'll bury it."

The old banker gives me a look of perfunctory sympathy. "Not your concern. So, how do you feel about what I've said today?"

"I'd like to have a day to think about it, if I could."

"You have one hour."

His words hit me like a slap. "One hour?"

At last Arthur Pine stirs from his ennui. From across the table he says, "We don't want an embarrassing data dump hitting the *Watchman*'s website tonight. This story has to go away, Marshall. Now. We need that cache."

I have to work to keep my face impassive. "The cache?"

Pine sighs as though he resents being forced to tell me something I already know. "Before she died, Sally Matheson put together a data file containing damaging information. We believe it contains printed documents, emails, recorded conversations, various other materials. We'll need that from you, as a sign of good faith."

"I don't have it."

Every eye in the room focuses on my face.

"That would be regrettable," Buckman says. "And it would invalidate our offer."

"We believe you have it," Pine says. "Or if you don't, that you can get it. So please do that, and contact us within an hour. Do that, and you can make Bienville a better place from this day forward."

It's already occurred to me that the PDF I got via email might be enough to placate them and earn the staggering bribe they've offered.

Buckman stubs out his cigarette. "You're looking through a win-dow of opportunity, McEwan. This market exists now, in this moment, and for the next sixty minutes. But circumstances change. All markets are subject to outside pressures. Fluctuations. Given what you've been offered, I suggest you make a swift decision."

"If I said yes, what proof would I have that you'd live up to your word?"

Buckman looks at me as though puzzled by my question. "I'm no saint, as I said. But I am a man of my word. My word is all I have."

"And about three hundred million dollars."

The banker gives me a tight, patronizing smile. "Closer to five, actually. May I make a suggestion? Ask your father about me. Duncan and I were never close, but he always treated me fairly. He did right by the club as well. Put it to him the way I've put it to you. See what he advises."

"I might do that. One thing I would need is compensation for Buck's widow, Quinn Ferris."

"Did Ferris have life insurance?" Buckman asks.

"I don't know, and I don't care."

"Seven hundred fifty thousand," Buckman says flatly. "All cash, pay-able by five P.M. today."

"A million," I counter.

"Done."

"Damn." I believe I could have asked for more and gotten it. "You guys must be set up for a world record payoff on this deal."

"That's our business, son. We look forward to hearing from you."

"One hour," Pine says. "Don't push it."

CHAPTER 32

I'M PLAYING BUCK'S handmade guitar on an earthen mound built by Indians around the time Genghis Khan invaded China. That's recent construction compared to the site Buck discovered down at the industrial park, but Buck spent a lot of time on this hill, so it seemed like a good place to take stock of my situation. He served as superintendent of these 170 acres, officially called the Snake Creek Site but known locally as the "Indian Village." A lot of Bienville residents come out here to walk, picnic, or run their dogs. When I was in junior high, I had buddies who used to sneak out here at night to get high and lie on their backs staring at the stars. I sneaked out here a few times with Jet during our magic summer, but today that seems a lot further in the past than it once did.

My meeting with Claude Buckman and his buddies left me disoriented. I felt like a protester who'd walked into a boardroom to tell off a bunch of corporate execs and walked out with a thousand shares of preferred stock. I've always felt I had a pretty stable moral compass, but the magnitude of the bribe offered by the Poker Club has set that compass spinning the way an electromagnetic field would. My intention in coming to this ancient site was twofold: first, to ground myself with Buck's memory; second, to have a quiet place from which to make telephone calls. During this brief period when Buckman believes I might agree to his proposition, I feel physically safe, and I'd rather make my calls under the warm May sun than from my office downtown.

I hadn't touched Buck's guitar since picking out that one tune for Quinn, right after he died. The simple act of tuning the big baritone, then playing some of the songs I used to play with Buck, has settled me quite a bit. I've got the Indian Village mostly to myself today, and that's helped, too. About four hundred yards away, an elderly man is walking a golden retriever near a smaller mound. They're my only company now. After about twenty minutes of fingerpicking, I set the guitar in its open case, push my earbuds into my ears, and call my mother.

When I tell her I want to ask my father a question, Mom goes into protective mode. She's worried I might pester him about accounting issues at the paper or even bring up the car accident that killed Dad's first family. When I tell her I only want to know something about the Poker Club, she finally relents. I could have gone to their house to question him, but if Dad's going to make me a target of abuse today, I'd rather it be from long distance. He can't hold a cell phone with any stability, so she puts him on speaker. And because of his speech limitations, Mom acts as his interpreter and megaphone. Thankfully, she mutes the television.

"Marshall?" I hear Dad whisper. "Are you there?"

"Yes, sir. I'm here. I'm working a story, an important story, and I need to ask you a question. It's about the Bienville Poker Club."

He grunts as though surprised. Then he slowly croaks, "Fire away. Beats watching these paid flacks pretend to deliver objective commentary on CNN."

Mom must be holding the cell phone right against his lips.

"All the years you ran the paper," I say, "I can't find any stories where you wrote critically about the Poker Club. I've been all through the morgue, and so far as I can tell, you never attacked them."

This time my mother answers, trailing just behind the hoarse whisper that remains barely audible. "Well . . . I imagine you're right. I think I suffered from tunnel vision back then. Those guys weren't involved in the racial violence, not directly, and that's where my focus was. I didn't realize then that their corruption probably hurt the black community a lot more than a few rednecks with burning crosses. It was those guys, above all—the moneymen who held the power—who maintained the status quo."

"Were they friends of yours? Buckman and the others?"

"Not really. I liked Blake Donnelly all right. Wyatt Cash's father was a decent fellow. But I never had many friends in this town. My buddies were in the army or overseas. Foreign correspondents. The Poker Club actually asked me to join once, but I never considered it."

"Why not?"

Dad hawks and spits with laborious effort, hopefully into a Kleenex. Then my mother says, "Different breed."

"It sounds like you were aware of their corruption, though."

This time the silence stretches for a while. "So that's what this is about," Mom repeats finally. "I read your story about Buck Ferris being killed. And I believe he was. But here's the hard truth, son. Corruption is a part of capitalism. It's a by-product of the system. A necessary lubricant to make the machine work. Given human nature, I mean. Because that's the motive force of capitalism: greed. It's the most pragmatic system there is."

Even after decades of hard drinking, Dad still has a way of reducing complex questions to a few empirical statements. That's why his editorials were always so pithy. "You're saying we have to accept a certain amount of corruption as the price of business getting done?"

"I *used* to believe that. Take this paper mill deal—leaving out the question of whether the Poker Club killed Buck or not. If that mill is built, it will surely rest upon a tangled web of felonies and misdemeanors. You dig around enough, you can probably cut some of the strands of that web, maybe even pull the whole thing apart. But *should* you? The town needs that mill, Marshall, and everything coming with it. Is it right to deny folks employment just so you can stop Claude Buckman banking another few million dollars?"

Would Dad be surprised to learn that he's restated Buckman's thesis for him, in almost his exact words? For a moment I wonder if the crafty old banker just got off the phone with my father. "Probably not," I tell him. "But *damn,* I'd like to take those bastards down."

"Of course you would!" Mom says for him. "That's the newsman's dream. It's Jesus driving the money changers from the temple. John Wayne wading through the black hats with a shillelagh, taking no prisoners. But that's not real life."

"Maybe not. But right now, I have the power to do it. I'm close to it, anyway."

"Are you? I'm impressed. But you know the old saw."

I think for a minute. "With power comes responsibility?"

"Hah! Maybe I did teach you something all those years ago."

"Maybe you did," I concede. *Maybe more than I realized,* I add silently.

"Are we done?" I hear Dad say. "Your mother just changed the channel to *Pravda,* and I have some shoes to throw."

Pravda is one of Dad's nicknames for Fox News. He often refers to CNN as *Entertainment Tonight.* "That's it, Dad. I appreciate it."

"Uh-huh. Over and out."

After Mom says goodbye, I pick up my burner phone and text Jet, typing: *I know you said not to call. This is important. Get back to me ASAP.* Then I set down the phone and pick up Buck's guitar again. Travis-picking in C, I marvel over the clarity and amiability of my father's response. I figured getting him to speak civilly would be like pulling teeth, as it has been on most occasions when I've tried to draw him out during the past months. What explains the change? If anything, I'd expect worsening health to make him less amenable to giving me a coherent answer. And less able. Thinking back on what he said makes Dr. Kirby's dire prognosis difficult to accept. Can a man who speaks with such enthusiasm be that close to death?

Of course he can, answers a cold voice in my head. *An airplane engine can run perfectly until the moment it fails—*

My burner phone is ringing. I snatch it up and hold it to my mouth. "Are you alone?" I ask.

"I've got three minutes," Jet says in a taut voice. "What's happened now?"

"I just met with half the Poker Club at the Bienville Southern Bank. Max wasn't there. They made me an offer. I want your advice."

"What's the offer?"

"Pretty much anything I want."

"Money?"

"Not just money. They said if I want a new public school, they'll make it happen. Infrastructure, done. Community betterment fund, done."

There's a brief pause. "In exchange for?"

"Dropping my investigations into Buck and the Poker Club."

"Of course. What do you want from me?"

"Tell me what you'd do in my place."

Jet is silent for a few seconds. "Have you found Sally's cache?"

"No. That's another thing. They want it. I told them I don't have it, but they assume I'm lying."

"Well, all this is hypothetical then. Without the cache, they won't give you anything."

"Not strictly true. Turns out I have a couple of secret admirers. First, whoever's sending me the game camera photos."

"Photos, plural? You got another one?"

"Yeah. This one shows Beau Holland with Buck. Same night."

"Wow. Who's this other source?"

"I don't know. But I think they've sent me part of Sally's cache."

This time the silence lasts longer. "What's in it?"

"Emails, deeds, bills of sale. It details some scams involving members of the Poker Club."

"Enough to ruin the Azure Dragon deal?"

"It's definitely a start. It might be enough to persuade Buckman it's the cache. But assume I had the whole cache. What do you say? What would you do?"

"Burn them down. Stall them, play along, then rip them to pieces in the paper tomorrow. Crucify them. They deserve it, every one. "

"You didn't take long with that. What about the consequences for the town? Losing the mill?"

"Screw this town. I know that's not how you feel, but I've lived here for the last thirty years. You haven't. You romanticize this place, Marshall. But it's rotten. Think about Buck's murder. Think of all he did for Bienville. But after they killed him, who really gave a shit? They all wished he'd died a year earlier, so their precious new mill wouldn't be threatened."

The bitterness in her voice makes me want to argue, but she's right.

"You said half the Poker Club was at this meeting," she reminds me. "Exactly who was there?"

"Buckman, Donnelly, Sumner, Cash, and Arthur Pine."

"That's the old blood, the old Bienville families. Excluding Max shows they're already worried about him putting them at risk."

"Buckman stated that explicitly. And leaving out Holland and Russo?"

"Beau's never gone out of his way to kiss Claude's ring," she explains.

"Claude hates him. And Claude might know that Beau was involved in Buck's murder, if he was. Also, Russo's an outsider. Mob-tainted."

"Why would Buckman care about that?"

"He probably doesn't. The Italian heritage is probably more of an issue for Claude. Tell me how they put this to you. They said they'd give you anything you want?"

"Buckman told me to write a Christmas list."

"Wow. Wait a second."

My earbuds go empty all of a sudden, and I wonder if I've lost my connection. Then Jet says, "Don't you see? This is our chance."

"For what?"

"To get away clean! This is how we get custody of Kevin."

She's giving me whiplash. "Seriously?"

"Claude Buckman can do it, Marshall, like issuing a royal edict. With Donnelly's support, nobody would dare cross him. Not even Max. No chancery judge, that's for sure."

"Wait. Two minutes ago you said screw the town, crucify them. Now you're saying cut a deal, but make sure custody of Kevin is at the top of my list?"

"I'm saying take all the good things that Buckman offered the town. But make sure custody of Kevin and a pain-free divorce are included. Everybody wins. The town, Kevin, you and me."

"And the Poker Club."

"They always win," she says irritably. "That's practically a law of nature. Their ancestors outsmarted the Union army of occupation."

"What about the video, Jet? Max has a knife to our throats."

"Tell Claude about the video! He's a sleazy old man, he'll get it right away. You tell him to make sure that footage is destroyed, or you'll nuke that Azure Dragon deal like Kim Jong Un. Claude will make Max *eat* that video."

"Jet—"

"I've got to go." Her voice drops to an urgent whisper. "Make it happen, Marshall. Please. We've got swords hanging over our heads, hanging by a hair, and Max is holding the scissors. If he shows Paul that video, not even the Poker Club can protect us."

"You haven't had any luck stealing Max's phone?"

"No. Oh—"

"Jet? Jet . . . ?"

She's gone.

Her breaking off like that leaves me with an image of Paul snatching her burner phone from her hand. She's right: we can't live like this any longer. If Buckman can force Max to destroy that video, then maybe I don't have a choice about whether to accept their offer.

Still, I think, laying down the guitar and walking a circuit of the mound's flat top. I came out here intending to ask for three opinions, and I still want to hear the third. Before I sell my soul to save my ass, I ought to at least speak to someone whose judgment I respect without qualification. Nadine Sullivan is the most objective person I can afford to speak candidly to about this situation.

Though I've used up most of my allotted hour, I text Nadine and ask if she has five minutes to discuss something important. She rings me back thirty seconds later.

"Darryl told me Tim Hayden buttonholed you this morning," she says. "I'm sorry about that."

"No, we had a good talk. I missed talking to you this morning."

"I rode out to Belle Rose and spoke to Tallulah Williams. I wanted to check what Max had said about my mother. I learned some interesting things."

"Like?"

"Later. You should talk to her, though. She's seen a lot out there. Anyway . . . what's going on with you?"

As quickly as I can, I summarize my meeting at the bank. I tell her nothing about Max and his video, of course, but she gets the basic dilemma.

"You know what I think," Nadine says. "Or you ought to by now."

"Which is?"

"You go first. What's your gut telling you to do?"

"Honestly? I'd like to tear the Poker Club apart."

"Why?"

"Because they've ruled this town too long. It's a deep cancer."

"Can you honestly say it's not because you want to be the one to cut it out? You don't want to break a story that could carry you back into Washington with a bang? Chinese money meets American desperation and corruption, a marriage made in hell?"

"Nadine—"

"I mean it. Are you sure that's not it?"

"Yes, I'm sure! It's Buck, goddamn it. They murdered him. Not Buckman and Donnelly, maybe, but the younger guys. Probably Holland and Cowart, maybe Russo as well. They shouldn't get away with that."

"No, they shouldn't. But they're prepared to pay Quinn a million dollars in compensation. Have you asked her what she thinks?"

"No," I admit.

"Maybe you should. Here's my philosophy: the greatest good for the greatest number. That's my mantra. I practiced law for seven years, and I can tell you this: justice is rare and fleeting. This Azure Dragon deal will shower good things on this area for decades. That's its own kind of justice. It's not the moral justice that Buck or his wife deserve, but it's still a blessing."

This was neither the answer I expected from her, nor the one I wanted. "And what about the little matter of betraying my profession?"

"Most people sell their soul in small pieces, my friend. You've kept yours intact long enough to get a high price. Be glad of that. And do it."

"I wouldn't want that on my tombstone."

"Hey, if they put up a fifty-million-dollar public school in this town, you'll earn your soul back ten times over. You hear me?"

This is the Nadine I remember. "Thanks for that."

"Who else did you ask about this?"

"My dad."

"And?"

"He articulated both sides. But if it were up to him, I think he'd side with you."

"Who else?"

"Jet."

"Ah." That single syllable communicates a new tension. "Did you give her her earrings back?"

"I haven't seen her."

"I'm surprised. What did she say about your dilemma? Same as before? Blow up the deal?"

Tell him to make sure that footage is destroyed, or you'll nuke that Azure Dragon deal like Kim Jong Un—"Actually, she agrees with you today. Denying the town all the things the Poker Club offered would be criminal."

"Maybe she woke up on a different side of the bed."

I guess Nadine and Jet are never going to be friends. The conversation of a group of people ordering coffee and pastries comes through the phone. "You sound busy."

"I have a book signing starting in ten minutes."

"Oh, man, I'm sorry. I'll catch up with you later."

"Are you going to accept their offer?"

"I'm close to saying yes. But sitting here now, I realize I've forgotten something. If they build that mill on the present site, they'll destroy the Indian settlement that Buck meant to be his legacy."

Nadine doesn't answer immediately. At length she says, "I get that. Maybe you demand that they move far enough downriver to save the site."

"I have a feeling that'll be a deal-breaker. Buckman's ready to give me whatever he can, but that would be up to the Chinese. And it's bound to be complicated."

"Don't mess this up, Marshall. Save the site if you can, but work it out."

I click off.

I should call Arthur Pine right away. My allotted hour expired two minutes ago. The thing is, I dread giving him the answer they want. I now have more rationalizations than I need to justify saying yes, yet still something stops me. What? Is it my contrary nature? Am I simply too proud to knuckle under? Does it mean that much to me to tell Claude Buckman and his cronies to go to hell?

I pack Buck's guitar back into its hard-shell case, then pick it up with my left hand and start down the narrow wooden steps of the ceremonial mound. With my right hand, I take out my iPhone and search my contacts for Pine's number. I'm pretty sure I have it from a couple of stories where I contacted him for quotes. While I try to maintain my balance on the steps, my burner phone starts ringing in my pocket.

Knowing it must be Jet, I set the case on the grass and dig the phone out of my pocket. "Are you there?" I ask. "You got cut off before. I freaked out a little bit."

"It was Paul. I don't think he heard me. I was in my closet. I heard him open the bedroom door, and I killed the phone and threw it in a drawer just before he walked in."

"God."

"Something has happened, though."

The hair all over my body stands erect, and fear spreads through me in a paralyzing wave. "What is it?"

"Max gave him a photo."

"No."

"Take it easy. It's not the video. It's you and me hugging, from yesterday."

"What the hell? What is Max doing?"

"Jiggling the swords over our heads. He wants you to find that cache."

"What did you tell Paul?"

"The only thing I could say. We've been working on stories together. That was the first time I'd seen you since Buck's murder, and you were upset. That Buck was like a father to you."

"Paul knows that. Did he believe you?"

"He seemed to. But I can't be sure. You'll have to see what you think. He's on his way to the *Watchman* right now. To your office. He wants to talk to you."

All thought vanishes in a wave of heat. "Jet—"

"You've got to deny it, Marshall. Us, I mean. I know you've talked about coming clean, trying to get ahead of Max, but you're kidding yourself. There's only one thing you can say. Do you understand?"

"Jesus. Yes, I hear you."

"If Paul asks you if we've spoken today, say no. Got it?"

"Yes."

"You also need to call Claude Buckman before you speak to Paul. Tell Claude about the video. Max only showing Paul that hugging photo was a gift from God. Claude has to stop Max from ever showing Paul the sex footage."

"Jet, calm down—"

"Me? Will you do all that?" she asks, her voice cold. "Swear to me you will."

"Jet, I'll deal with it. I'll call you when it's done."

"Don't do anything crazy, Marshall. Nothing noble. Think about Kevin. Okay?"

Unbelievably, my iPhone rings while I'm trying to get off the burner phone. The screen says ARTHUR PINE, ATTY.

"Jet, I've got to go. Pine's calling."

"Good. Tell Arthur to get Claude for you."

I pocket the burner and answer the iPhone. "Arthur, I'm sorry. I was on another call, but I was about to call you."

"I saved you the trouble."

"Look, about the club's offer . . . I need to talk to you about one issue in particular."

"You can throw away your Christmas list."

Pine took too much enjoyment in saying that for me to mistake his meaning. "What's happened?"

"The offer's off the table."

"Because I took longer than an hour?"

"That didn't help, but that's not it. Circumstances have changed. Claude told you they might."

"What changed?"

"We've become aware of a certain video."

Oh, hell—

"A video that, if it were made public, could put a very close friend of yours in a homicidal state of mind."

They think they've got me by the balls now. They think they don't have to give up anything, or help anybody, to get their crimes buried. I can't believe I even considered making a deal with these bastards.

"We still need that cache," Pine says. "We need everything you have, as soon as you can get to the bank."

"Go to hell, Arthur."

"Listen to me, Marshall. This is life and death for you."

The only coherent thought I can hold in my mind is that before I do anything else, I need to have the conversation with Paul Matheson that I should have had three months ago.

"Did you hear me?" Pine presses. "Where are you?"

"Go fuck yourself, Arthur."

CHAPTER 33

IT'S BEEN A long time since I felt real fear. In our insulated lives we only brush up against it, usually when confronting medical symptoms that suggest a mortal disease process. Raw, paralyzing fear is something you forget as soon as possible yet instantly recall when it hits again. That's what I feel when I approach my office at the *Watchman*, knowing Paul Matheson is waiting inside to question me about his wife.

The mere sight of his F-250 outside the building sets something thrumming in my chest—not merely the prospect of confrontation, which is certain, but of violence. I feel a sense of foreboding that Max spoke truly in my kitchen: that the fight we avoided on that golf course almost thirty years ago is about to happen. Why? Maybe because thirty years ago, Paul had betrayed Jet a dozen times himself.

Today he's married to her.

The moment I enter the building, I become aware of an unusual quiet, which tells me that at some level my employees perceive some threat, if not outright danger. Ben Tate falls into step beside me at the pressroom door.

"Bad vibes in your office. Worse than those guys from this morning."

I keep walking down the narrow hall. "And?"

"He asked me if I'd seen his wife in the building recently."

Ben was never slow on the uptake. "And you said . . . ?"

"I thought I saw her here after Max was arraigned yesterday, but I might have been mistaken. She's in and out a lot, talking to reporters. Did I screw up?"

"No. It doesn't matter." It's odd how willing people are to cover for you, even if they're not sure why they're doing it. "Can you hold something for me, Ben?"

"Sure."

I take out my burner phone, mute the ringer, then pass it to him. "I use this with only one source. If it rings, ignore it."

"Got it."

"One more thing." I reach into the small of my back, then hand him my pistol.

His eyes go glassy, and both of us stand awkwardly holding the gun. "Shit, man," he breathes. "Is it loaded?"

"Yeah, but there's no round in the chamber. It's all right. Just put it in your office."

After staring at the ugly but functional pistol for a few seconds, he says, "Okay. Good luck." He clumsily stuffs the Walther into the back of his pants, then pockets the phone and veers off toward his office.

I feel a primal urge to run as I reach for my doorknob, but that's a childish impulse. The truth is, as I drove into town from the Indian Village, I felt more and more certain that further deception would be stupid, as well as an insult to Paul. Even if I manage to convince him that his suspicions are groundless today, the truth will eventually come out.

The moment I open my office door and see my old friend sitting slumped at my desk, I realize confession would be a mistake. Paul is forty-seven years old—one year older than I—but today he looks fifty-seven. Only two days ago, in the Prime Shot tent at the industrial park, he seemed to have the glow of youth. He was drinking then, of course, which probably gave him some color, and the midday sun cast a youthful glow. Maybe most telling, I never really focused on him long.

Today there's nowhere to look but at each other. And what I see is a man deprived of sleep and peace, haunted by demons, doubting everything he's ever believed or done. The contrast with his father hits me like a gut punch. Max always looks fifteen years younger than his age; Paul, a decade older. This has the unnerving effect of making them look more like siblings than father and son. More trenchant, though, is my sudden conviction that Paul has not come here to learn the truth, but to hear me deny that I'm sleeping with his wife. There is surely anger in him, but what I sense above all else is fear. Crippling dread.

"What's going on, man?" I ask. "My editor texted me you were here. I'm so sorry about your mom. I don't even know what to say."

Paul waves his hand as though I've mentioned something of no importance.

"Does this have something to do with Buck?" I ask. "Or the Poker Club?"

He shakes his head and stands, his eyes cloudy with drink or confusion.

"Are you okay?" I press.

He laughs as he comes around the desk, but the sound contains no humor. "I'm fine. Not getting much sleep, is all."

"You look rough. You want to talk about it?"

"Did Jet call you?" he asks, sitting on the front of my desk.

"When?"

"Last thirty minutes or so. To tell you I was coming?"

"No."

"You sure?"

"Yeah."

He nods slowly. "Mind if I look at your cell phone?"

Maybe I misread his state of mind when I came in. "Not at all. Here you go." I take my iPhone from my pocket and hand it to him. "My password is 052772."

"Your birthday."

"Yep."

He enters it, then starts scrolling through my recent calls. "You ought to use a tougher one than that."

"Nothing to hide."

Another wretched chuckle. "We've all got things to hide, bro. Mind if I look at a few texts?"

Shit. "Knock yourself out."

As he scans several text threads, I wonder if he's armed. *Of course he is,* I think, seeing how his Levi's ride above his left shoe. He's probably carrying a small automatic in that ankle holster, just like his father. Not that Paul would need that to kill me. He's quite capable of doing it with his hands. After about a minute of studying my phone, he straightens up and hands it back to me. "This your only cell phone?"

"Paul, what is this? You in the CIA now?"

He looks at the floor for a couple of seconds, then takes out his iPhone, presses a button, and holds it out so that I can see a photograph displayed on its screen. The image has the pixelated graininess that results from being zoomed to the maximum, but I can clearly see Jet hugging me on the edge of my patio. This is the image Max shot yesterday from the trees behind my house. Jet's back is to the camera. One of my arms is wrapped around the small of her back, while my other hand cradles the base of her neck. It doesn't look very platonic. If I weren't several inches taller than she, the pose would have looked like a kiss.

"What the hell?" I say. "Where'd you get this?"

I asked the question before I realized the risk. For all I know, Max has given him the whole history of the shot and told Paul that I already know it exists.

"Does it matter?" he asks.

"I don't know. Do you have private detectives following her or something?"

"Should I?"

"Are you serious?"

He smiles strangely. "It's not like we haven't been here before, man. You two were fucking all y'all's senior year. Why shouldn't you be now? Right of re-entry and all that?"

"What?"

"You know what I'm talking about."

"Paul, what the hell? What do you want to know?"

He takes a deep breath and holds it like a man about to throw a punch. "Are you fucking my wife?"

There's only one acceptable answer to this question—at least when you're standing face-to-face with the husband. "I'm not."

"Then who are you fucking?"

"Nobody."

The strange smile returns, and he shakes his head. "Okay, now I'm suspicious. Come on. You're not doing Nadine Sullivan?"

Naturally he would think that. And right now, I'm grateful that Nadine's there to divert attention. "If I was, would that be your business?"

"You are." He nods as though confirming his instinct. "Can't say I haven't watched her walk across that café a time or three. She's got a tight ass, in a good way. Some people say she's gay, though."

The thrumming in my chest has slipped down a gear, but I'm wondering if Paul is distracting me in order to hit me with an unexpected jab. "She's not gay."

"Huh. So, how about you tell me about the picture? That's your house, right?"

"You know it is."

"So what the hell's Jet doing out there?"

I shrug as if the answer should be obvious, almost inconsequential. "She came to talk to me about some stories. She works a lot of cases involving local corruption, and she knew I suspected the Poker Club might have something to do with Buck. I told her that at the groundbreaking—*just like I told you.*"

Paul stares at me without speaking. His wordless gaze is disconcerting, but it doesn't compare with the primal X-ray of his father's stare.

"That's what Jet said," he says at length.

I turn up my palms. "There you go. Two sources." Glib, I know, but I'm riffing. Guilty men don't make light chatter, or, at least, that's what I'm thinking. Maybe that's exactly what they do—like Ray Milland in *Dial M for Murder.*

Paul takes two steps closer to me, into my personal space. It's a tense thing, standing close to another male when a woman's fidelity is being discussed. I feel the energy crackling between us.

"But you love her," he says in a leading tone.

Whoa. "Of course I love her. I always have."

He nods. "And you want her to leave me. To come to you. Go back to Washington with you."

It's hard to lie about this with a straight face. "Paul, what the *fuck,* man? What's gotten into you?"

After a couple of seconds, he looks away, then walks to the small refrigerator in the corner of my office and looks down at it with contempt. "How come you don't keep beer in this thing?"

"Sorry. There's probably some in the break room fridge."

He waves his hand and sits in one of the two chairs that face my desk. Rather than look at me, he bends at the waist and puts his head in his hands, then begins pushing his fingers through his hair with quite a bit of force. He looks like a man suffering from intractable head pain.

"Paul . . . ? Is your head hurting, man?"

"Just give me a minute."

"Sure."

I walk back behind my desk and sit, wondering if the worst has passed. Last night Jet told me his temper has been worsening, giving me the idea he could go off at any moment, like old dynamite. But Paul is more like a man being eaten alive from the inside. And though he does not know it, there can be no doubt that I have played a part in triggering that process.

Does he really not know? asks the cold voice from within. *How could he not?*

As he sits there, massaging his scalp and neck like a man in the corner of an asylum, I ask myself something I've asked a hundred times before. Why do so many people being deceived by their spouses go to absurd lengths to deny what they see? What they sense with their intuition? Even what, in the end, they hear whispered by their friends?

I used to think it was to avoid the pain of betrayal, of facing inadequacy, of confronting a train of mistakes and admitting that their lives are an illusion and that they didn't measure up to their partner's image of them. But that's not the marrow of it. Once a wife or husband begins a love affair, the marriage becomes a brittle, carefully maintained façade, beneath which lies a horror that most humans lack the courage to face. And the horror is this: when your wife or husband truly gives themselves to another person, they haven't done it to hurt you. In fact, they've probably taken great care to avoid hurting you. No, the unspeakable truth is that *you no longer matter to them.* Except as the mother or father of their children, you do not exist. *That* is why people refuse to see. To do so, they'd have to crack the door on a limitless darkness in which they have come to mean nothing to the person who knows them better than anyone else in the world. They must face, probably for the first time, being utterly alone. And that way lies madness.

How many nights has Paul lain awake and wondered if he's losing Jet, or has already lost her? Has he wondered how his son would react to his mother leaving the house? Maybe even leaving the state? Who could possibly take Jet's place? A hundred local women would be happy to move into her house and give their best years to Paul. But how many could fill the massive hole that her departure would create? None of them. I know what it's like to try to replace Jet Talal. I tried, and with a damn good woman. But even she never quite banished Jet from my mind and heart.

"Dying doesn't scare me," Paul says softly, still looking at the floor.

A chill races over my arms. "What?"

"Dying doesn't scare me. In fact, there've been times when I would have welcomed it." He looks up, his face scarlet from hanging his head over like that. "Don't freak out, I'm not about to slit my wrists. I'm just saying, I've seen death up close. You know that. You saw some with me."

"Yeah."

"It's dying *alone*, man."

"Now you're talking crazy."

"Am I? My mother's gone, Goose. She'd dead. My father may have killed her. And Jet? Who knows, man? I feel like she's miles away, even when we're sitting across the table from each other. Even when I'm inside her. She's just . . . not there."

I breathe slowly, keeping my face immobile. "Maybe that's just in your mind."

He shakes his head with conviction. "No! I'm not saying I blame her. I've got all kinds of problems. Head problems, dick problems— which drugs don't always help—but mostly anxiety. And my temper. I can't keep my shit in one sock. Sometimes, I'll be at one of Kevin's baseball games, and some asshole parent will start trash-talking a ref or even a kid. In less than a second I'm one tick from walking over and snapping the dude's neck. It's like my mind goes red, my brain's on fire. I don't carry a knife anymore, because I'm worried I might decapitate some asshole in the time it takes to cover three rows of bleachers."

I get up and walk around my desk, sit on its top. "Paul, you know what that is. PTSD. You've got to talk to somebody."

He looks up with irony in his eyes. "Ain't we talkin'?"

"Yeah. But you came in here to ask if I'm fucking your wife."

"Are you?"

This time his gaze is piercing. I don't even allow myself internal dialogue before I give him a reflexive "No."

His stare doesn't waver. "You used to, though."

"Yeah, in high school. Ancient history, man."

He nods slowly. "You must have tapped it a few times since then. Right? College? She come up to UVA for a weekend? D.C., maybe?"

Did he put Jet through this kind of grilling? If so, what did she answer? "Paul, goddamn it. This is pointless."

At last he breaks eye contact and looks at the floor again. "Don't mind me. I'll get out."

"You don't have to. Tell me about Kevin," I say, hoping to steer him to more solid ground.

Sure enough, when Paul looks up, five years have fallen from his face. "He's awesome, man. Not just an athlete. He's smart, like Adam was. You know?"

"Yeah, I know. I bet the girls love him, too."

Paul's eyes shine. "Oh, yeah. He makes me remember how good we had it back then."

"That's how it's supposed to be."

"Yeah. Only . . ."

"What?"

"I don't know. I shouldn't say this. But he spends so much time with my dad that I don't see him like I used to. This goddamn traveling baseball team? Max is obsessed with it. He bought the team an RV, and he drives it everywhere. And I see all those boys looking at him like some kind of hero—which you and I know he's not."

"No, he's not."

"But they don't know that, see?" Paul's eyes fill with the intensity of a man incapable of expressing some deeply felt conviction. "The problem is I think Kevin senses I'm not exactly stable right now. I feel like he gravitates to Max because he's not sure I'm solid."

What hell has this man been living in? How did Jet ever believe we could move to D.C. and take Kevin with us? Paul wouldn't survive that. We might not survive it, either, if he chose to vent his anger before killing himself. In fact, he would likely kill us to remove the possibility that Kevin could be taken away—

"I'm gonna go," he says, getting to his feet. "Sorry about ambushing you like this. I just didn't know what to think."

"You don't have to worry, man. Not about me."

I can't believe I just spoke those words knowing that Max still possesses the video of Jet and me on the patio.

"Hey," he says. "Just promise me one thing."

"What?"

"I'm not gonna find out a week from now that this was all bullshit, right? That you just didn't want to tell me the truth?"

I feel as though my body has turned to lead. Somewhere deep in my mind, far behind the frozen mask of my face, a rogue impulse whispers, *Tell him. Tell him the truth. The whole truth. Tell him you love Jet, but that you love him, too. Because he knows that's true—*

"Goose?" he says hesitantly.

Even as I answer, I know a moment will come in the future when we face each other again and he'll know that I lied today, as Jet lied— that we did not grant him the respect he deserves. That moment may mean death for us all.

"I promise, man. Now get out of here and go take a pill or something. You've got to sleep. You're going to drive into a bridge abutment."

He laughs again. "If I do, tell Byron Ellis it was sleep deprivation. Get me off the hook."

"Goddamn it, Paul—"

"Just kidding." Without warning he takes two steps and throws his arms around me, hugs me the way he did in Ramadi, after we made it out of the city and climbed out of the Mamba. He stinks of Scotch and old sweat, and though almost thirty years have passed, his smell is as familiar to me as my own, from a hundred dressing rooms, football fields, and basketball courts across Mississippi.

"Thanks, man," he says. "Later."

And then he's gone.

An enervating wave of exhaustion rolls over me. Is this how actors feel after delivering an immortal performance? Jet must be sitting with her phone clenched in her hand, waiting to hear what happened. Before heading back to Ben's office to get my burner phone, I unlock my file cabinet and remove the hard copy of the PDF file I received this morning. Then I carry it down to Ben's office, where I nearly bump into him on his way to the newsroom.

"What's this?" he asks when I hand him the stack of pages.

"Your first Pulitzer. The start of it, anyway. Don't show it to anybody else. We'll talk after you've read it."

He holds my gaze long enough to be sure I'm serious, then walks back into his office and locks the papers in his desk. Opening the bottom drawer of a file cabinet, he takes out my burner phone and the Walther.

"Is there anything else you need to tell me?" he asks.

"You're not in danger, so long as you don't show anybody those papers."

He nods slowly but doesn't speak for a few seconds. Then he says, "You weren't kidding about the Pulitzer, were you?"

"No. But when I won mine, it was mostly for getting shot at."

Ben smiles. "I hope there's an easier way. Just let me know if I need to start carrying."

Before I can ask whether he owns a gun, Ben heads for the newsroom. Since he's left me alone, I decide to call Jet from his office, where there's little chance that Paul could walk in on me, should he decide to come back.

"What happened?" Jet asks as I close Ben's door.

"He bought it. I felt so damned low lying to him. Paul's in bad shape, Jet."

She sighs like someone who just dodged a runaway bus. "And Buckman? Did you reach him?"

"No. That deal's off the table."

"*What? Why?*"

"Arthur Pine called me. They know about Max's video. They must have hauled him into the bank and demanded he give them anything he might have on me."

She's silent for several seconds. "That's not the choice I'd have expected Buckman to make. He's relying solely on that video to keep you from publishing the cache? I figured he'd get the cache from you, then try to welsh on whatever promises he could."

"Jet, that video *will* keep me quiet. Paul is clinging to sanity by his fingernails. I just lied to his face after he begged me not to. Max and the Poker Club own us now."

"Maybe not."

"What?"

"They don't have the video themselves. Max would never give it to them. He might *tell* them about it, but he's too smart to give them that power. If he did, they wouldn't need him anymore."

She's probably right about that. "So we're safe for the time being? Look, I have no idea what our next move is."

"I do."

Ben Tate walks back into his office and motions for me to keep talking. Then he writes six words on the notepad on his desk: *Arthur Pine is in your office.*

"Tell him I'll be right there," I say.

"What?" Jet asks.

Ben disappears.

"Arthur Pine is apparently waiting in my office."

"That can't be good."

"I can handle Arthur. What did you mean? What are you planning to do?"

"I'm going to get that goddamn sex video from Max. I'm not going through another spousal interrogation like that."

"You might get his cell phone, but you won't know if you have all copies."

"Maybe not, but if those passwords from Sally's necklace open his phone, I'll be flipping the script on him. We'll own Max for a change. How does that sound?"

"Be careful, Jet."

"Remember who you're talking to. P.S., I love you."

"You, too," I say, but the words are automatic. The desperation I felt when Paul hugged me is too fresh to feel clean about intimacy with his wife.

WHEN I WALK BACK through my office door, I find Arthur Pine waiting in his five-thousand-dollar suit. Unctuous on his best day, Arthur stands smirking before me with his golfer's tan and perfectly coiffed gray hair.

"Looks pretty busy around here," he says. "I'm surprised."

"We're working some big stories, if you haven't heard. What do you want, Arthur? You here to threaten me not to run any more photos of your poker pals?"

He gives me a patronizing smile. "No, I'm here to inform you that you won't be printing any more stories of any kind."

"What are you talking about?"

The lawyer opens his coat and removes a sheaf of papers covered with tiny type. "I've come to shut down the *Watchman*."

CHAPTER 34

I DECIDE TO take the back way from the paper to my parents' house—Cemetery Road. I haven't yet called my mother, and I wish there were some way to avoid it. The news of what happened to the Bienville *Watchman* over the past half hour could quite literally kill my father. It's probably already broken on Twitter and Instagram, as the kids from our newsroom attempt to deal with the shock of their unexpected terminations. If the news has hit Facebook, even my mother might see it before I reach their house.

As I leave the old grid of downtown streets, heading east, I think back to the pitiful scene that unfolded before I left the *Watchman* for the last time. Standing gobsmacked in my office door, I asked Arthur Pine what he was holding.

"A debt-purchase agreement," he told me. "Marty Denis is an old friend of your father's, I think?"

"Marty Denis?" I said, recalling only that he took my parents some crawfish tails yesterday. "The president of First Farmers Bank?"

"The very man. Marty's been carrying the paper on your father's various loans for a number of years—at considerable risk to himself, I must say. He imperiled his position at the bank. But all that's been resolved now. As of an hour ago, Mr. Denis sold all those loans to Bienville Southern."

Claude Buckman's bank. I wanted to tell Pine I didn't believe him, but he wouldn't have been in my office if his mission weren't a fait accompli.

"We have the right to demand full payment at any time," he went on, "and we're calling the notes today, in full. If you can't pay, we're foreclosing on the property and all physical plant of the Bienville *Watchman* as of five P.M."

"What's the total amount?" I asked, barely able to summon my voice.

"Just under five-point-five million dollars."

I probably wavered on my feet. "That's impossible."

"Talk to your father. You'll find that it's not only possible, but the state of his balance sheet as of yesterday."

I had some idea of the company's debt, but when I used what I knew to express skepticism, Pine quickly disabused me of my illusions. He could do that because my father had kept his longtime "business manager" on the payroll to act as a buffer between me and the true nightmare of our situation.

"Beyond what I've told you, the company pension plan is under-funded," Pine informed me. "You're even in trouble with the state, over payroll taxes. By the way, we're going to allow your parents to keep their house, which is heavily mortgaged, if and only if after severance from this newspaper, you cease all criticism of the Poker Club or any ancillary business ventures."

I walked past the lawyer and stood beside my desk like a dog returning to a house where it had once lived. *How is it that the worst moments of our lives happen without warning?* Only hours earlier the Poker Club had offered me the moon. In response, I nearly sold out everything I'd ever stood for. Now, thanks to a video of me having sex with a married woman, my deal with the devil would not be consummated. And years of financial negligence by my father would allow the Poker Club to destroy the work of seven generations of my family.

While Pine watched with ill-concealed pleasure, I took a sip of coffee from the Styrofoam cup beside my laptop. It had gone cold hours ago. "You're a parasite, Arthur," I told him. "You make ambulance-chasing look like an honest living."

"Save your breath," he said. "And don't try to salve your conscience by blaming us. Your father borrowed and borrowed, throwing good money after bad. The interest kept piling up. Duncan had plenty of offers to buy this paper, but he turned up his nose at all of them. Everybody tried to talk sense into him, but he refused to listen. I know you must have tried."

He was right, but I didn't give him the satisfaction of admitting it.

"There's nothing left of this company but a hollow shell," he concluded. "We've created an LLC, the Tenisaw Newspaper Group. We'll hire new management, let this paper start performing its proper function."

"Which is what? Cheerleading for Poker Club business ventures?"

"And for Senator Sumner. Bienville's a community, Marshall, not a commune. You can put your red headband back on as soon as you land in Washington."

Pine looked around my office like an auctioneer estimating fire sale values. "As to practicalities. There's a sheriff's deputy outside, to be sure this is done professionally. You may remove personal items, but nothing that's part and parcel of the paper's operations. No computers, hard drives, disks, or flash drives. These premises belong to us as of now. Anything you remove will be considered theft."

I asked him how long I had to gather my things.

"You're leaving now. By the way, any work product currently under consideration for publication is the property of the Tenisaw Newspaper Group. You may not publish any of it. And all your employees will be so advised."

"That's bullshit. I know the law in this area better than you. You can't buy facts. Not yet, anyway. Also, you should treat all personal emails on my office computer as my personal property."

"If they're on your office computer, they're ours until you prove otherwise in court."

I pointed at the computer on my desk. "That laptop is my personal machine."

Pine looked dubiously at the computer. "Your personal laptop is a Mac you generally keep at home. That Toshiba machine belongs to the newspaper."

What the hell? I thought. *Somebody in this building has been talking to the Poker Club.*

"Let's get this over with," he said. "Do you plan on taking anything with you? Legitimate personal items?"

I looked around the office, finally settling on the framed front page of the first Bienville *Watchman* ever published. The masthead of the original *Watchman* bore an eagle with a banner in its beak above the name of the newspaper. The banner read *Vincit Omnia Veritas*: Truth Conquers All. "That belongs to my father, not the company."

"Take it, then. You won't be coming back."

I walked over and lifted the frame off its nail, fighting the temptation to crack the lawyer's nose with it. But as I passed my desk, inspiration struck. With the bottom edge of the frame, I tipped the contents of the coffee cup into the laptop's keyboard. Pine didn't immediately realize what I'd done, but about six seconds later, the machine shorted out with a flash and a crackle.

"All right," he snapped. "Deputy!"

A uniformed sheriff's deputy stepped into my office with a gun on his hip. Accustomed to overseeing evictions, his face showed not an iota of sympathy. Thankfully, my burner phone was already in my pocket. After slipping my iPhone into another pocket, I looked at Pine and said, "I shall return, asshole. But for now, let's go."

The lawyer waved me out of my own office.

I walked ahead carrying the big frame, so as not to look like I was being led out by the deputy. But the appearance of law enforcement had done its work. Entering the newsroom, I found the whole staff assembled, their eyes wide, their mouths tight with anxiety.

"Just keep moving," Pine said. "No tearful farewells."

I stopped in the middle of the room and looked at the group I'd led for the past five months.

"Don't let him give a speech," Pine cautioned.

I felt the deputy coming up behind me.

"You guys are as good as anybody I worked with in Washington," I told them. "And this war's far from over. In fact, it just started. You'll hear from me soon. Stay ready."

The deputy shoved my back. "Outside, Mr. McEwan."

"Hey!" Ben Tate yelled. "What the hell, man?"

"Fascist!" shouted Carl Stein. "This is America, motherfucker!"

"Where we have to pay our bills," Pine retorted. "Gather your things, children. Recess is over. You're all fired."

While I stood there in shock, Ben Tate flipped Arthur Pine the bird. Seconds later, everyone else in the newsroom followed suit.

Walking out under the harsh afternoon sun, I thought about the attorney for the Poker Club. When guys like Arthur Pine watched Frank

Capra films like *It's a Wonderful Life,* did they root for greedy old Mr. Potter? As a young man, did Pine dream of accruing wealth by skimming money off other men's work? By foreclosing on anyone he could nudge or lure into financial difficulty? The further along we move in this American experiment, the more Arthur Pines we seem to produce. But Pine didn't show up in person to be thorough. He came to rub my face in the dirt—and my father's, too. The Poker Club doesn't want a newspaper in Bienville; they want a PR rag, preferably a glossy one filled with promotional hyperbole. Standing on the sidewalk, I turned back to Pine, who didn't seem the least discomfited by the mass firing he'd just carried out. In fact, he looked smugger than he had in the newsroom.

"Remember this moment, Arthur," I said with as much restraint as I could manage. "This is the moment when I decided to destroy the Poker Club."

The lawyer looked singularly unimpressed.

"You want to fire those kids?" I went on. "You want to send me home to tell my dying father that his family's legacy is gone? Okay. But get ready to own it. I'm going to send you to prison. Your fat-cat buddies, too, every one. But I'm going to pay special attention to *you.*"

Pine waved off the deputy, then folded his arms across his chest and said, "Aren't you forgetting Max Matheson's video?"

"Nope. That'll ruin several more lives. I'm willing to take the punishment for what I've done. But you? You're a chickenshit. A weasel. You can't take what's coming your way. And you can bet your ass something is coming."

"Knock yourself out," Pine said with a smile. "We'll publish a nice farewell piece when you head back to D.C."

Sarcasm dripped from his voice, but as I turned toward the parking lot, I saw his mask slip. The smile on his lips no longer touched his eyes, which were those of an animal transitioning from predator into prey.

I WON'T DESCRIBE WHAT happened after I informed my mother and father what had transpired at the *Watchman.* There's a shame in witnessing a proud man broken, reduced to penury and forced to confront the fact that he has failed to provide for his wife in her old age, and not only because of his own poor management, but also his misplaced trust in a friend. When you are that man's son, the sight shakes you to the core. I will store my father's breakdown in the same locked vault where I keep the events of the morning that the sheriff walked me into the same house to tell my parents that my brother had drowned.

After the initial shock, Mom had to give Dad a nitroglycerine tablet for his heart, extra meds for his tremors, and a Xanax to try to blunt his anxiety. Yet still he remained distraught. His hands trembled constantly, and his extremities jerked in ways my mother had never seen before. Worst of all, he was crying, something I couldn't remember seeing him do since the day Adam drowned.

"Have you called Dr. Kirby?" I asked Mom.

"He's going to come by after he finishes at his office."

What emerged after Mom and I were able to question Dad in detail was simple and heartbreaking. After I moved home and started running the paper in earnest, Dad began to believe that if I stayed in Bienville, I might be able to turn the business around. His time had passed, he knew, but he thought my passion and experience might be enough to succeed where his had failed. If only the paper could stay open another year, he thought, I might get the *Watchman* back on its feet. What greater legacy could he leave than his family's newspaper back on solid footing, free from the tyranny of any media group? To that end, he'd taken out one more major loan, securing it with the equity in his house and some securities he'd held back for my mother. Marty Denis helped him with all this; Mom had known nothing. Dad hadn't told me, he said, because he didn't want me burdened with financial worries. Of course it was that very attitude that had prevented me from working to save the paper from the day I got back.

Mom couldn't imagine that Marty Denis had betrayed Dad by selling the loans to Claude Buckman, but I told her they'd probably gotten their way with Marty the same way they did with everyone else. Pine told me Denis had "imperiled his position at the bank." The Poker Club would have been happy to bail him out of his trouble. All he had to do to save his own ass was burn Duncan McEwan.

"It's my fault, all of it," Dad whispered, staring dully at the switched-off television. "I wanted the paper to be there for you. I thought you were enjoying the work. I thought . . . you'd come around and want to stay and take it over."

"It's all right," I told him.

"How much could I have gotten?" he kept asking. "Back when you pressed me to sell? That last time, seven or eight years ago."

"It doesn't matter," I said.

"Tell me."

"Nine million. Maybe ten."

At some point after this he became hysterical, but thankfully the drugs kicked in, and he transitioned into a sort of muted daze. He reminded me of schizophrenia patients I'd seen in a Maryland hospital while writing a story on mental illness. He must have mumbled "I'm sorry" a hundred times, like a meaningless mantra he couldn't stop repeating.

My mother kept looking from him to me, then back again. I was afraid she might break, as Dr. Kirby had predicted she would after Dad passed away. The specter of poverty had to be working on her, even though she knew that I'd never allow her to go without. But she didn't break. She merely rubbed Dad's neck and shoulders, as she always did when he became upset. Time passed in near silence, and the afternoon sun moved across the sky, sending a shadow slowly across the den floor. Nadine called and texted me several times, as did Ben Tate and others, but I didn't want to break the calm by answering or returning calls. I was hoping for some word from Jet, but my burner phone remained silent. I texted Nadine that I would get back to her when I could, then muted my iPhone and sat with my parents while the new reality settled over and into us.

After all that's happened, it's strange to sit quietly in the house where I grew up. In the five months I've been back, I've hardly done this. Despite Mom's efforts to reconcile Dad and me, most of my time has been spent helping her do household chores, while my main method of assistance has been paying for professional sitters and taking care of errands outside the house so that she can remain at his side. To see Dad sitting motionless like this is a new and disquieting experience.

In the silent den, I get up and walk along the shelves of the built-in entertainment center, perusing the spines of the book overflow from his study. Propped on one shelf is a photo of Dad and Hazel Brannon

Smith, publisher of the *Lexington Advertiser,* in the newsroom of the *Watchman.* Another shelf contains personally inscribed volumes, an alphabetical treasure trove comprising a who's who of twentieth-century journalism: Agee, Arendt, James Baldwin . . . Jimmy Breslin, Bob Capa, Rachel Carson, Cronkite, Walker Evans, Martha Gellhorn . . . Halberstam, Hersey, Sy Hersh, Langston Hughes, Stanley Karnow, Walter Lippmann . . . Murrow, Gordon Parks, Eric Sevareid, Bill Shirer, I. F. Stone, Curtis Wilkie. Some of these writers were friends of my father's, others mentors. A few simply admired his stand during the civil rights movement so much that they sent him their own work with a thoughtful inscription.

As I walk along the shelf, tapping the spines with my fingers, I find myself recalling some of his fiery editorials from the 1960s. My father's voice on the page was reminiscent of the one Ted Sorensen gave John Kennedy in his greatest speeches. In his prime, Duncan McEwan could summon power and moral authority from sentences in a way that still eludes me after decades of writing.

"You can't let them silence you," says a faint voice.

I whirl from the shelves and see that my mother is as startled as I am.

"Duncan?" she says, rubbing his arm. "Are you all right?"

"Do you have more to print?" Dad asks, not quite focusing on me. "More on those Poker Club bastards?"

I walk back and sit in the dining chair I pulled up next to his two hours ago. "I've got a photo of Beau Holland at the murder scene. And I'm sitting on some data Sally Matheson put together that could hit them pretty hard. There's a lead in there that could hole them under the waterline. If I print, it might just inspire my source to send me even more damning evidence. But we'll pay a price. A heavy one. War with the Poker Club means casualties."

Dad's hand shoots out and grips my wrist. Then his head tilts so that he's staring at me from the corner of his eye. "Get it out there!" he croaks. "I let those guys have their way for too long. Buckman and Donnelly and the rest. You can't let them shut us down."

Dad never speaks of "us" when discussing the *Watchman.* Not since I was a boy, anyway. He's always treated my running the paper as a temporary stewardship until he can get back on his feet. The obligation of a son to his father. Mom is clearly shocked by the intensity of his words, but she nods at me, which I take to mean that I should engage him in conversation, despite the risk of upsetting him further.

"I know how you feel, Dad. But they own the paper now. They've won, at least in the material sense."

"No, no, no, no," he drones. "That's a battle, not the war. Find a way."

"A way to what?"

"Print."

I haven't even considered trying to print anything. "I was thinking of posting a story to the web," I tell him, "just under my own name. If I use our existing social media accounts, they'll probably sue—"

"Screw 'em!" Dad shakes his head violently. "That's not good enough! This town's full of old people, poor people with no internet. You've got to give them what they're used to. A *newspaper*."

"Dad—"

He points a rigid arm at the framed copy of the first Bienville *Watchman*, which I leaned against the wall after showing him I had salvaged at least that. "You've gotta get it into the machines," he goes on. "The truck stop, the gas stations, the supermarkets. Not everybody gets their news off the goddamn computer."

"I understand. But we don't have access to a press anymore. I suppose we could contract with a paper in a nearby town. Somebody might be willing to run off a daily for us, if we throw a little money their way. But not under our name."

Dad's right hand is frantically shaking, as though he can't force his thoughts out through his mouth.

"Take your time, Duncan," my mother pleads. "What are you trying to say?"

"That—won't work. I've burned too many bridges. Everybody's owned by a group now, and they're all Trumpers down here. They'd love to see us beg."

"Surely I can find somebody."

"That you can trust not to call the Poker Club as soon as you hang up? You can't give those bastards a shot at you. They'd find a way to stop you."

"Well, what do you suggest?"

Dad's head jerks to the left, then again. "I've still got the old press out at my barn. More than one. My collection."

"Oh, Lord," Mom says. "Those antiques?"

"They're good machines!" Dad's face has gone red. "And I've paid the Terrell brothers to keep them in mint condition. The old linotype especially."

Linotype? I think. *You want me to print a newspaper on a linotype?*

Mom closes her eyes, looking more worried than she has in the last hour.

"What's he talking about?" I ask.

Dad grabs my wrist again in his clawlike grip. "The barn, at my fishing camp. I've got three different presses out there—four, counting the old ABDick job press. With Aaron and Gabriel Terrell helping you, you could print a paper off any one of them."

Surely he's delusional. "What about electricity? Supplies? Interfaces? Tools?"

"I've got the barn wired for two-twenty," Dad says doggedly. "Aaron and Gabriel have all the tools you need. And the expertise. They're my old press men, for God's sake."

This sounds more like the fantasy ending of a Jimmy Stewart movie than a workable plan, but I don't voice that opinion. To his credit, my father has always been a tinkerer, and mechanically gifted. As a boy I watched him repair and restore everything from old typewriters to a slot machine that a bartender brought him from a Louisiana honky-tonk. Dad's "camp" is a twelve-acre tract of woods surrounding a little pond, about eight miles east of town, between Cemetery Road and the Little Trace. Until his Parkinson's got bad, he puttered around out there with a garden and did some bream and bass fishing from a johnboat.

Despite gentle discouragement from both Mom and me, Dad refuses to drop the idea of printing a paper for tomorrow. His brainwave spurs a burst of physical activity, what my mother always called "thrashing." Dad makes a call to Aaron Terrell, and in no time I have the old press man's cell number and address in my pocket. My initial understanding is that Dad has committed me to ride out to his barn with the Terrell brothers and check the equipment. Then it becomes apparent that he intends to accompany us, which precipitates an argument between him and my mother. This escalates for about five minutes, until Dad faints in the bathroom, which thankfully settles the matter.

As I prepare to leave on my fool's errand, Mom follows me into the kitchen.

"I still handle the household expenses," she whispers. "I stopped paying the Terrells over a year ago. Keeping up that equipment seemed like a waste of money."

"Don't worry. I'll figure a way to let him down easy."

I start to leave, but I can't go without passing on Arthur Pine's warning: my parents can remain in this house only if I cease all activity that could harm the Poker Club or the paper mill deal. If I pursue the course Dad has suggested, this house could soon be only a memory.

"Would they really take it?" Mom asks.

I remember Arthur Pine's face. "They wouldn't hesitate."

She looks back toward the den, where Dad sits clinging to one lifeline: the hope that I'll use one of his treasured old presses to destroy the men who have ruined his life's work. "I can't tell you what to do," she says softly. "Duncan bought this house in 1963. I've lived here since '68. I love this old place. But mostly for my memories, when you and Adam were here. Once your father's gone . . . I can live anywhere."

"Washington, even?" I say hopefully.

She wipes her eyes with her fingertips. "That's a big step. Let's take things one at a time. I just . . . I'd hate to have your father find out he couldn't keep them from putting us out on the street. I don't think he'd survive that."

I take hold of her arms, meaning to promise that I'll find a way to buy the house myself. Before I can, her eyes harden, and she says, "But I don't want you to cow down, either. That's not our way. You *do* have a legacy to uphold, however battered it may be."

Where does it come from, this stubborn resilience? *That's not our way.* Is it the blood of Scots driven off their land generations ago? Old crofters who said, *This far, but no farther?*

"I'll think about what to do while I'm riding out to the barn. But don't worry about the house. I'll find a way to keep it. Dad's going to spend his last day here."

She closes her eyes and lays her head on my chest.

"I won't let you down," I promise.

"Or him," she whispers.

"Or him," I echo.

She pulls back and looks toward the den once more. "I'd better get back in there. You be careful. Remember what Max Matheson told you about the accident on Cemetery Road. Duncan's first family."

"I do."

"No story's worth dying over."

I nod, but then I think of Buck Ferris floating dead in the river, of Arthur Pine standing smugly in my office waving his debt-purchase agreement, and of my father sobbing in impotent rage. And a voice in my head says:

This story might be.

CHAPTER 35

TEN MINUTES AFTER leaving my parents' house, I pick up Aaron Terrell and his brother at their house in Bucktown. Aaron takes the shotgun seat, while Gabriel climbs into the back behind his brother. African American men in their seventies, both worked as my father's press men for nearly fifty years. Both have close white beards and an amazing amount of muscle tone for their age. Neither says much after our initial handshakes. I saw both these men many times when I was a boy, but after Adam died, I rarely went down to the newspaper building, so we don't really know each other.

As I turn onto Cemetery Road, Aaron asks how "Mr. Duncan" is doing, then falls silent after I give him a general report. He could probably tell on the phone that Dad isn't at his best. I figured he'd ask for details on how our family "got screwed out of the paper" (as I heard Dad describe today's events), but Aaron seems content to simply fulfill the favor my father asked of him.

Three minutes after I pick them up, we're rolling over the dogleg turn where Dad's first wife and daughter were murdered in 1966. The gully where they drowned is still there. Two sets of railroad tracks still cut through the asphalt at the lowest point in the road. How easy it would have been, I realize, to run a car off that pavement in a rainstorm and send it pitching down the kudzu-strangled gully.

As we leave downtown behind, I call Ben Tate, who turns out to be drinking at a Lower'ville bar with some of the former *Watchman* staff. I tell him to go outside so that he'll have privacy. Then I ask him if he got

out of the building with the hard copy of the PDF file I gave him before
Pine showed up.

"I did indeed," he says in a game voice.

"You read it?"

"Oh, yeah."

"You think you can write a story from it by tonight?"

He hesitates. "Absolutely. But why? You planning to post it online or
something?"

"Actually, I'm thinking we might put out one last edition of the
Watchman tomorrow."

"No shit? How do you plan to do that?"

"I'm working outside the box. Way outside. But tell me this: If my
plan doesn't work out, do you know anybody in this corner of the state
who might run us off a paper if we throw some money their way? All
the local publishers Dad knows are enemies now and would love to see
him go down."

"You want this printed under our masthead? Our former masthead,
I should say? That would probably be illegal, or at least a trademark
infringement."

"I'm betting that if we bust this story wide open, the Poker Club
will be too busy to worry about suing over Mickey Mouse shit."

"Maybe. But no publisher around here is going to want to risk a
lawsuit."

"You're right. So, can you think of anybody who might help us?"

He takes a few seconds with this. "I know the editor at the *Natchez
Examiner* pretty well. Walter Parrish. He and I supported the bars of
Athens, Georgia, for about four years."

"That's right, you're both Bulldogs. Does he listen to as much
R.E.M. as you?"

"More. You know, the Masters Group does the printing for four
south Mississippi papers now. They added Vicksburg and McComb. You
want me to give Walter a call?"

"Yes, but don't even hint what the story's about. Just tell him we
need it bad. I'll pay him out of my pocket."

"Right. Shouldn't cost you more than seven or eight hundred bucks.
What about our staff?"

"You can't use them."

"Nobody? You told them to stay ready. They're so pissed, they'll work for free."

"It's not the money, Ben. Arthur Pine gave me the feeling he has a mole in our ranks."

"Ahh, okay. So am I just writing a story? Or are we going to reprint some of that PDF file?"

"We're definitely going to reprint some stuff."

"Oh, hell yeah."

"One thing. Did you see that reference in the emails to a 'Mr. Chow'? Related to Senator Sumner? An implied exchange of favors?"

"I did indeed."

"Leave that out of your story until we know more. I mentioned it in front of Holland and Russo, and they nearly shit themselves."

"Understood. I'll head home now and get started."

After I hang up, Aaron Terrell says, "We 'bout three miles from the turn now. You lookin' for a Billups gas station on the right."

We already passed the turn for the barn where Jet and I spent most of the summer of 1986. What lies ahead is a straight shot to the county line. When Jet and I were kids, this stretch of Cemetery Road was un-paved, a plumb line of dirt cutting through trees so tall and stately they might have been standing for a thousand years. I can still see our bike tires cutting through the powdery dust, and fat raindrops slapping into it, making nickel-size black circles as the gray clouds that flung them swept over us toward the river.

I've seen Dad's fishing camp only once, when I drove out to meet the guy who keeps the grass bush-hogged. There'd been armadillo damage to the dam that keeps the pond filled. I know nothing about armadillos or dams, but Dad was going through a tough period, so I handled it. I saw what he refers to as his "barn" that day, but it was padlocked, and I had no way to look inside. What I remember sure doesn't seem like an ideal place to store printing presses.

"What do you guys think about our chances?" I ask. "Of printing a paper off one of the old presses in Dad's barn?"

"Hard to say," Aaron answers. "Your daddy used to pay us to come out here reg'lar and keep the place locked tight, dusted down. We'd even run the equipment once or twice a year. But that's been a while ago now."

"My mother told me she stopped paying you."

Aaron nods philosophically. "I get that. Hard to pay good money to keep up something nobody use."

"I can't believe you guys could put out a paper on a linotype."

Both men laugh heartily. "That linotype jus' a museum piece," Aaron says. "I could probably print a little something on it, as a demonstration. But them old offset presses are like Dee-troit classics."

"Damn right," his brother agrees. "All-metal monsters."

"Your daddy bought that old Heidelberg in 1973. That big girl could *jook*."

"Never shoulda bought that new press," Gabriel declares in a chiding tone. "He quit that Heidelberg in 2010, but she had plenty of life left in her."

"Might just take a little loving care," Aaron agrees. "We'll know in a couple minutes."

When I grunt skeptically, Aaron says, "Sounds to me like you all set up to pay that Natchez group to print for you. Fee-for-service. We just wastin' time out here or what?"

"We're humoring my father," I concede. "But I wouldn't waste your time. What I'm really hoping is that you guys can run me a front page with the old masthead on top. That's all, one broadsheet with a headline. Even if the Natchez group will print a paper for us, they won't do it under the *Watchman* masthead."

Aaron is nodding, a trace of a smile on his lips.

I turn off Cemetery Road where he tells me to, then follow a narrow road to a metal gate that opens to the pond and the barn. The place looks much as I remember it, but it was winter during my first visit, and now it looks like a jungle. Vast curtains of kudzu hang between the trees, giving me the feeling that the whole place will be covered in a year or two. I park the Flex about ten feet from the barn door.

Aaron still has a key. He walks up to the building with confidence, but it takes him half a minute to get the lock to yield. After it does, Gabriel trudges to the side of the heavy sliding door and walks it open. I let the brothers go in first, to assess the condition of the press. What I see from behind them looks like some sort of hardware museum that a Hollywood set designer draped in cobwebs.

A few feet from the door stands a Willys jeep that has to be seventy years old. Beyond that I see a shelf unit lined with typewriters, slot machines, and what might be a photo enlarger. After about ten seconds, my eyes begin picking out the printing equipment. The linotype stands closest to the door. It looks like some steampunk contraption, a relic that belongs in a Dickens novel. Beyond the linotype I see more curtains of cobwebs, dust-caked machine parts, rust on everything. My heart is sinking, but Aaron walks right past this junk to a big machine that looks like an F-150 pickup truck with half its bed sawn away.

"Used to be a tarp on here," he says in a doubtful tone. "Must've come off a good while back. What you think, Gabe?"

"Nothing good."

The Heidelberg offset press is nearly as tall as I am. After walking around it once, Aaron begins pulling cobwebs off the German behemoth. I watch in silence as he and his brother begin exploring the machine with their hands. Aaron squats to look beneath it, while Gabriel climbs onto an attached metal step, leans over, and peers down into the guts of the machine.

"What do you think, guys? Is there a chance in hell?"

Aaron steps back from the press and stands with his hands on his hips. "This front page you're imagining," he says. "Are you seeing colors?"

"Nope. Black-and-white's fine. Just the masthead and a headline. Table of contents, maybe. Teasers. We could start the stories on the front page, but I hate to risk that. I need ten thousand broadsheets. Can you do it?"

Aaron looks at his brother.

"Hell," says Gabriel. "If we can't, we ain't got no business calling ourselves press men."

"Whoa, now," Aaron cautions. "We got some work to do before that kind of talk."

Gabriel spits beside the press. "I didn't say it'd be *easy*. The problem is the folder. Getting that bitch hooked up."

Aaron leans against the press and regards me with interest. "I read that story you wrote about Byron Ellis. I knew Byron back when he drove an ambulance, way before he was coroner. You goin' after them Poker Club fellas, ain't you?"

"Looks like it."

"And Byron's helping you?"

"Yep. He went out on a limb to help."

"Well, then." Aaron reaches into his pocket and takes out a pack of Kool Menthols, shakes one out, and puts it between his lips. "I reckon we better help that brother out."

After he lights up, the three of us stand looking at the press the way all men do who must use inadequate tools to do important work.

"If we can't get her runnin' right," Aaron says, "we can print a single sheet on the old ABDick jobbing press, then fold that around the main edition. We'd better get hold of some eleven-by-seventeen paper while we can, just in case."

"Whatever you need," I tell him. "I'll cover it."

As Aaron nods, my iPhone rings. It's my mother.

"Hey, Mom. How's Dad doing?"

"I'm not sure. Jack Kirby wanted to admit him to the hospital, to be on the safe side, but your father wouldn't hear of it. Duncan insisted that I call and ask you about the presses. He wants to know if one's in good enough shape to get the job done."

I look at the big offset press, standing silent as a mausoleum and showing rust at every seam. "Tell him everything looks great, Mom. Mint condition."

Her voice drops. "Are you sure? I stopped paying Aaron a good while back."

"Tell Dad we're gonna use the Heidelberg. Everything's under control."

"If you say so. He's going to want to see the issue tomorrow."

This is a warning against shining my father on. "No worries, Mom. Try to get some rest."

"All right," she says wearily. "Thank you."

After I pocket the phone, Aaron says, "Duncan ain't doin' good, is he?" The press man's eyes are filled with genuine concern.

"Not really, no."

He grunts in a way that communicates many emotions at once, but empathy above all.

"What can I do to help you guys?" I ask.

Aaron grins. "You ever run an offset printing press?"

"I have not."

Both men shake their heads. "Tell you what," Aaron says. "You go back to town for an hour or two. Get yourself a drink. Finish making your deal to get the main edition printed. Let me and Gabe clean this old girl up, see if we can't get her kickin'."

"Are you sure?"

The old press man shrugs and gives me a lopsided smile. "Ain't got nothin' better to do this evenin'. But tell me this. Say you get this paper printed. Who's gonna deliver it for you? I hear they done fired everybody downtown."

"They did."

"Your regular carriers still gonna stock the machines and stores? Or are you and your reporters gonna ride the routes?"

He's got a point. "I hadn't really thought about that."

Aaron grins. "You better start. But if you don't have no luck, I might have an idea about it."

"I'll get back to you."

"You're also gonna need somebody to wrap our broadsheet around the main paper—*if* we get it printed. Ten thousand copies? That's some work right there. You gonna need a crew in here to do that by two A.M. to be on the safe side."

"Shit, I forgot that, too."

Aaron gives me an expert's rueful smile. "Easy to take that for granted up in the front office."

"What about newsprint?" I ask. "I don't know if I can get into the building downtown."

"Gabe knows where he can find some. But the less you know about that, the better."

I've found my ideal co-conspirators. "Look, you guys need to know one thing. If we publish under the *Watchman* masthead, the bastards who own the paper now are gonna sue me. I'll never give you guys up. I'll say I did all this myself. But they might try to make life as hard on everybody as they can. You have to know that before you do this."

The brothers look at each other. Then Gabriel turns to me and says, "Your daddy paid me a check every week for forty-seven years. Wasn't a big check. But I could count on it. And if I needed an advance, Duncan give it to me, no questions asked."

I wish Dad could have been here to hear that. I figured these men would remember him as a hard, thankless taskmaster—as I do. But they were not his sons, and they knew a different man.

"Your daddy done a lot of hard drinkin' for a lot of years," Aaron says, almost to himself. "A lot like our daddy, really. Life wore 'em both down pretty hard. But I was with Mr. Duncan back in the sixties, when things got bloody. After Medgar was killed, and the movement hadn't got goin' yet. You couldn't *find* a white man to stand up for black folk. Not in public. But old Duncan sat back in that little office with that Remington typewriter, and he set down how it *was*. He didn't care if some white preacher cussed him in the street or a big store pulled their advertising. He said, *The time has come to do what's right.* That might not sound like much today. But back then it was like a stick of dynamite."

I don't know what to say to this.

Aaron turns and looks back at the old press as though listening to a dialogue in his own head. Then in a soft voice he says, "Duncan tol' me he needs a paper out tomorrow. So I reckon we gon' print one. One last time."

"Damn right," says Gabriel. "*Damn* right."

CHAPTER 36

THE SHADOWS HAVE grown long outside the barn, but when I climb into the Flex, I see yellow light spilling from the cracks around the big door. Aaron and Gabriel are already hard at work, and their commitment has inspired me. Yet I don't feel like doing any of the things I need to do. Nadine is waiting to hear from me, but she's not going to like the idea of me going to war with the Poker Club. I should call Ben Tate back to discuss tomorrow's stories, and also Walter Parrish at the *Natchez Examiner,* to finalize a deal for him to print a paper for us. But as I sit in the Flex, looking at the barn where my father must have spent hours fiddling with his old printing presses while swigging Maker's Mark from the bottle, it strikes me that I've been ignoring the obvious.

Back on the street outside the *Watchman* building, I warned Arthur Pine I intended to destroy the Poker Club. By now Buckman and Donnelly and Holland and Russo and the rest know that I made that threat. I'd be a fool to ignore the fact that such men will not sit by while I take steps to send them to prison. After all, they almost certainly murdered Buck, and God knows who else over the years. Anybody who stood in their path got crushed one way or another. And they're not the only threat I face. If Ben and I drop our story on the website tonight, how long will it take Max to show Paul the video of Jet and me making love? An hour? Less?

I'm at that hinge point where characters in films do really stupid things, like sleep at their own house or go to places they're known to frequent, such as Nadine's shop or my parents' house. As much as I'd like to drive home, log on to my computer, and start working with Ben on the PDF file story, that would be an idiot's move. Especially given that Paul seemed only minimally stable this afternoon. The smart thing would be to get out of town for a couple of days. Not all the way back to D.C., but maybe to a hotel in Jackson or even Oxford. I can work on tomorrow's issue from anywhere, so long as I have a computer and an internet connection. The problem is I can't risk leaving Jet behind. If Max shows Paul that video—and I've abandoned the city—Paul might vent all his rage on her alone.

Taking out my burner phone, I punch in a quick text to Jet: *Find a safe place and call me. I need two minutes. URGENT.*

After sending this message, I speed down the gravel road and pull through the gate, then close it by hanging the wire loop over the post. I turn onto Cemetery Road, looking for one of the little winding lanes that runs south between it and the Little Trace. From there I can pick up another cut-through to Highway 36, which runs past the turn to my farmhouse.

I'm on the Little Trace when my iPhone rings. To my surprise, the caller is Arthur Pine. After a moment's hesitation, I answer and say, "Well, Arthur. You feeling the ice crack beneath your feet?"

"Not at all. This is just a friendly call. I know you were upset today. That's understandable. But you made some threats."

"I did indeed," I reply, mimicking Ben Tate's syntax.

"There are different ways to handle problems, Marshall. One way involves men like me. The other . . . well, it's the other way."

"Are you telling me Tommy Russo is going to send a button man to my house? Or are Wyatt Cash and a couple of retired SEALs gonna explain things to me?"

"You have a vivid imagination for a nonfiction writer. Actually, I'd say your biggest worry is going to be your best friend."

"Possibly. But let's talk about you. You're getting closer to Parchman Farm every minute. And I don't think you have the survival skills for that particular environment. Neither do most of your buddies. Let's see how well you sleep tonight."

There's a brief silence. Then Pine says, "We're all vulnerable, Marshall. We all have people we love. And you don't have many allies. I've got the whole town on my side."

"I guess we'll see about that."

"What does that mean?"

"Tick-tock, Arthur. You'd better start researching non-extradition countries. Your bosses will be asking for a list soon."

I hang up.

When I hit Highway 36, I turn east and join the Jackson-bound traffic. After two miles I'll pass Blackbird Road, the turn to my house. I'm tempted to go home long enough to run in and get my MacBook Pro, a change of clothes, and some toiletries. But that could be a fatal mistake. Tommy Russo *could* have a man sitting in my kitchen, waiting for me to open the front door. One silenced round through the forehead, and the Poker Club's problems would be over. Or SEALs paid by Wyatt Cash could pour half a bottle of vodka down my gullet, then hold my head under a full bath, probably without leaving a mark on me.

I don't even slow down as I pass my turn. I can buy a new laptop at the Apple store in Jackson, new underwear and toiletries at Target. Hell, I can buy a computer at Walmart if the Apple store is closed. It'll be a pain downloading some of the software I need, but most of my critical files are in Dropbox, so what does it matter?

A mile past my house, I slow down to scan a great wall of signs that must have sprung up over the last day or two. Where a line of inexpensive ranch homes stood before, the new line of billboards blares: COMING SOON: T.J. MAXX. OPENING 2019: CHILI'S. COMING SEPTEMBER: SUPER TARGET. After that it's all a blur announcing that Bienville will soon look like every other interstate town in America. BED, BATH & BEYOND. MICHAEL'S. BONEFISH GRILL. This, I realize, is one of the strips acquired during Beau Holland's land grab. Most of my fellow citizens look at this development as a blessing, but I see, at best, a necessary evil.

My ringing iPhone startles me out of my funk. It's Quinn Ferris calling. "Hey, Quinn, how are you making it?"

"This still sucks, but karma just shined on us."

"What do you mean?"

"I'm with Buck's friend from LSU. Dr. Jake Barnett. Those little clay balls you found at the industrial park are from a Poverty Point–era site, no question. They're actually called 'Poverty Point objects.' They were used for cooking food underground, sort of like charcoal briquettes. Also for some other purposes. But that find is definitive, Marshall."

I realize my heart is pounding. "What about the rest of it?"

"Bone, for sure. Human. Byron Ellis was right. The teeth, too. Dr. Barnett's going to have to do some dating work, but he says the teeth show no sign of decay, which means they didn't come from corn-eating Indians. He's going to contact the Department of Archives and History in Mississippi. It's a huge find, he says. Momentous."

"Jesus Christ. I'm so happy for Buck. But sad, too. Goddamn it."

"I know. We've got to get those bastards, Marshall."

"We will. Can you send me your friend's contact information? I need Ben Tate to call him."

"Will do."

"Thanks, Quinn. Be careful coming home."

I hang up, but before I can even reflect on what she told me, I hit the brakes. I'm not even sure why. Then I register what my intuition picked up. On the right shoulder of the highway sits a battered blue Ford Explorer. As I get closer, I see it's an Eddie Bauer model, and most of the cladding has been ripped away. Sure enough, Dixie Allman gets out of the driver's seat wearing jeans and a halter top and kicks the back door panel with surprising force.

A tractor-trailer behind me honks angrily as I pull onto the shoulder to park behind the Explorer. Dixie looks back at me with annoyance, but then she recognizes my vehicle.

"Hey, Goose!" she calls as I get out. "Bad luck, as usual."

"That sucks. Is Denny in there with you?"

"Nah, he's home on his computer."

The closer I get, the rougher Dixie looks. Like Paul in my office today, she appears to be in her mid-fifties, not her mid-forties. In three seconds I take in bloodshot eyes, dry skin yellowed by decades of smoking, yellow teeth, and stringy hair that hasn't been washed for a while. Dixie looks emaciated up top, but she has a paunch. Only under her jeans do I see a trace of the muscle tone that made her an athlete in high school.

"Are you out of gas or what?"

"Yep. Happens once or twice a month. My gauge has been reading a quarter full for three years. I try to keep plenty in it, but sometimes I forget."

I give her a smile. "No sweat. There's a station a mile east of here."

"I was about to walk to it."

Looking at the horizon, I figure there's about thirty minutes of light left before full dark. Some drivers have already switched on their headlights. "Jump in. We'll take care of this."

She manages a tired smile. "Hang on, I've got a gas can in back. The last guy who helped me out threw it in there and told me to keep it."

She opens the hatch of the Explorer, and I transfer the sun-faded plastic can to the back of my Flex. Then she climbs in beside me and we merge into the eastbound traffic.

"Where were you headed?" I ask.

She flips her hand like a sorority girl taking a spin in a Porsche. "Nowhere, really."

Nowhere? "Just riding, huh?"

"Pretty much." She takes out a pack of Virginia Slims, then cracks her window and lights up. "Denny said he's been filming some stuff for you."

"Yeah. He's great with that drone. We may post some of it to our website."

My iPhone pings with the contact information of Buck's colleague at LSU. I'll send it to Ben when I can add an explanation.

Dixie holds out her left hand and examines her bright pink fingernails, which are peeling badly. "You gonna pay Denny anything?"

"Sure, of course."

"Good. 'Cause that boy needs some real work."

We reach the service station without further conversation, and I pay to fill the five-gallon can. After I pull back onto the highway, Dixie starts to light up again, but I shake my head and use my thumb to point behind us.

"What?" she asks.

"Gas fumes."

She looks blankly at me for a couple of seconds, then gets it. "Ohh." Frowning, she slips the cigarette back into the pack.

We reach her Explorer in less than a minute, and she opens the gas cap for me to start pouring from the can. While the biting smell rises from the opening, I catch Dixie's eye. "What are you really doing out here? You headed to Jackson or something?"

She sighs with irritation, looks away. "What do you *think* I'm doing? Making a drug deal or something?"

"I don't know, Dixie. I'm just wondering."

"Well, it ain't your damn business, is it? But if you have to know, I'm on my way to work. And I'm running late." Her tone is accusatory, like it's my fault she ran out of gas.

"Where you working now?"

Color rises into her cheeks. "The Show 'n' Tail. What of it?"

My mouth falls open before I can cover my reaction. The Show 'n' Tail is a titty bar on the county line, where drug-addicted girls fresh out of high school dance for truckers and meth heads. Word is the lap dances are bottomless for the right price, and most of the girls turn tricks in the trailers behind the cinder-block club. Several citizens' groups have tried to get it closed, but so far they've failed. I've heard speculation that a powerful silent partner keeps it open.

"Dixie, you're right, it's not my business. But we went to school together for twelve years. Tell me you're not stripping out in that shithole."

She runs her tongue around inside her cheek, then bursts into laughter. "I'm forty-six years old, Marshall! You think they'd pay me to take my clothes off?" She pops a stripper move, throwing her chest forward to emphasize the sagging mammaries under her halter. "Young stuff only out there, bub. I work behind the bar."

This is better than what I feared, which was Dixie making a drug run while her son sits home by himself. Still, a sickening sense of futility settles into my bones. This woman is Denny's mother. She graduated with me, and the best job she can get is working in a joint where every girl on the premises is in desperate straits?

"Listen," I say without thinking. "Today's Thursday. I want you to go home and get some sleep. Tomorrow, get up and come down to the newspaper. I'm hiring you for the advertising department."

She knits her brow, watching me with something like suspicion. "I heard the bank shut down your paper today. Foreclosed on y'all."

I stand in silent shock for a few seconds. Jesus. I'm like a person who speaks of a relative in the present tense, having forgotten that they died earlier in the day.

"You're right," I tell her. "But that's just temporary. I'll have it back up and running in a week. And I'll hire you now for then. I don't want you working at the damn Show 'n' Tail."

"You don't, huh?"

"No."

She nods as though considering my offer. I see shame in her face, but also anger. "Well," she says. "Who died and made you Jesus?"

Her words shock me so deeply that I simply wait for what follows.

"You think you're saving me or something?" she asks. "I don't need saving, okay? And you ain't in any position to save me anyway. You need to save your own damn self."

"What do you mean?"

Her laugh has a raucous, almost mocking undertone. "I read the paper. I hear people talk. You've crossed that Poker Club, haven't you? Tried to get 'em in trouble over Buck Ferris. You even got my Denny caught up in that shit."

The implication that I've somehow led her son astray brings blood into my cheeks. "I'm sorry. I thought you wanted me to spend time with him."

Dixie starts to say something, then looks at the ground as though she's changed her mind. "Why are you so fired up to get those Poker Club guys, Marshall?"

"Because they killed my friend."

"Who, Buck? Do you know that for sure? Can you prove it?"

The gas can is empty. I pull the nozzle from the tank, screw the cap back on, then replace the can in her Explorer. By the time I've closed the rear hatch door, she's lit up another Virginia Slim.

"I'll prove it," I tell her.

"You will, huh?" She looks skeptical. "In case you haven't noticed, this isn't the town we grew up in anymore. People get killed all the time. It's been what, five black boys since January? And more coming, I'm sure. Man, a month before you moved back, some guys locked a girl from the club in her car trunk and set it on fire. Drug debt. You get me? Didn't you pass those big signs when you came this way? You see there's a Super Target coming? Bonefish Grill? At least the Poker Club's doing something to help this town. I'm only working the Show 'n' Tail until T.J. Maxx opens. Joey Peters is gonna be manager, and he told me he'd hire me two weeks before the grand opening. But *you* want to hire me at your nonexistent newspaper. Well, aren't you *special*?"

"Dixie—"

"I don't need your damn help! Neither does Denny. Your high school Boy Scout bullshit won't help Denny in this world we got now." She shakes her head with bitter frustration. "But anyway . . . thanks for getting my gas."

As she throws down her cigarette and stamps it out, a gleaming white King Ranch F-250 zooms toward us, then passes at seventy miles an hour. Without even thinking, I register it as Max Matheson's truck. But what lingers in my mind is the outline of the woman who was sitting next to him in the cab.

Jet.

"What's the matter?" Dixie asks. "You see a ghost?"

I dig out my burner phone and check it. No messages or missed calls. Looking down Highway 36, I see Max's taillights as the Ford speeds away through the falling dusk. For a moment doubt makes me waver, and I think of asking Dixie if she saw Jet in that truck. But something stops me.

"Dixie, I need to borrow your Explorer."

"What?"

"I need your truck."

She looks at the Explorer as though trying to discern something that's been invisible up to this moment.

"Dixie!"

Her face is a study in confusion. "But . . ."

"You can take my Flex. You'll love it, it's practically new."

"What the hell's going on, Marshall?"

"I'll trade you back in a day or two. Do you want it or not?"

She looks back at my shining SUV. Then she shrugs. "Sure. What the hell?"

I exchange keys with her, then climb behind the wheel of her wreck and slam the door. I don't know where Max could be taking Jet, but under the circumstances, her presence in that truck can't be good. Closing my eyes, I turn the key and pray. The Explorer whines, stutters, coughs, then dies. Cursing, I floor the gas pedal and repeat the sequence. This time it ends with the engine rumbling to life.

"Don't scratch my truck now!" Dixie hollers as I jerk the Ford into gear. She cackles as I peel off the worn asphalt shoulder, gunning the old engine in the faint hope of catching Max's $80,000 pickup.

CHAPTER 37

I'M PUSHING DIXIE Allman's rattle-trap Explorer to ninety-five, and I've yet to see any sign of Max's truck. Dusk is coming on fast. The land in the eastern half of the county is relatively flat, but there's a fair amount of traffic on the highway headed toward Jackson. This makes it hard to discern different vehicles far ahead. I can't figure where Max and Jet might be going, unless it's to Max's house in the Belle Rose development, which lies in this direction but ten miles farther east. I can't imagine Jet going there with him, unless . . .

She's trying to get hold of his cell phone.

What excuse would she have used to get him to drive her out into the county? A mobile client consultation? She could have faked car trouble and asked Max for a ride home. But would he buy that? Jet would have called Paul if she needed a ride home. Her husband might not be her first choice, but surely Max would know he would be her last.

Just as the Explorer reaches a hundred, I catch sight of Max's pickup parked nose-out at a tiny store across the four-lane. Rather than hit the brakes, I zoom past the store so as not to draw attention to myself. There'll be a turnaround soon, and if not, I can drive across the shallow median ditch. *Why that store?* I wonder, catching sight of a rutted cut-through a quarter mile ahead. *Did Max need gas? The way he was parked, it almost looked like he was checking to see if anybody's tailing him.*

By the time I get the Explorer turned around, I remember that store sits at the junction of a narrow road that cuts north through the woods to the Little Trace. Max's truck has already vanished when I reach it, but a pair of taillights that look like his flash in the distance, disappearing into the forest. If that's him, all I need to do now is stay close enough to see which way he turns when he hits the Little Trace.

I consider texting Jet to make sure she's all right, but something stops me. I can't imagine that Max means her physical harm. Why go to the trouble of blackmailing us with the video if he intended to hurt her? Also, she still has value to him as his lawyer. No, the best plan is to hang back and be ready to intervene if anything crazy happens. I might be too late to help her if he gets violent, but if Jet were to leap from Max's truck with his cell phone in hand, I could swoop in and rescue her on my borrowed, if battered, steed.

Three minutes on a narrow lane like a tunnel through trees takes me almost to the Little Trace. I use the time to text the contact info of Quinn's archaeologist to Ben Tate, followed by a brief explanation. At the Little Trace, Max turns left, but as I turn to follow, I see him veer right onto another winding lane that leads farther north. Unless the memories of my youth are wrong, that little lane winds through the forest like a creek, eventually intersecting the worn asphalt of Cemetery Road. Which leaves me with a mystery. All three main routes out here—Highway 36, the Little Trace, and Cemetery Road—run east-west. If Max wanted to get somewhere on Cemetery Road, why ride this far out on 36, then cut north through the woods on crummy little roads?

I tap my brake pedal when I see his brake lights flash. Sure enough, he turns right onto Cemetery Road, heading east again. Now I'm in familiar territory. A few miles behind me stands the barn where Aaron and Gabriel are working to produce the front page of tomorrow's gonzo edition of the *Watchman*. Only at the end of our magic summer did Jet and I cycle this far out, when we rode to the spring at Parnassus Plantation, which had replaced the Weldon barn as our private Eden. Parnassus lies about four miles east of here, and once you pass its gate, there's nothing but woods till you hit the county line. Where could Max be headed? Maybe he owns or manages some timberland out this way?

I can already see Parnassus Hill in the distance to my left. Though it would be but a molehill in a mountainous state, locals took to calling the three-hundred-foot hump "the mountain" long ago. The thickly wooded hill is a smudge of dark green against the vivid purple sky, rising like a miniature volcano out of knee-high soybeans. Now that we've broken out of the forest, light seems plentiful again. Two cars separate me from Max's F-250, which suddenly moves into the left lane and begins to slow.

Could he be headed to Parnassus?

A mile farther on, his brake lights flash, and he turns left at the brick-pillared gate of the plantation. The main road beyond that gate leads to a large Greek Revival mansion with two slave quarters standing behind it in the classic fashion. Even before I reach the gate, I see Max veer right off the main drive. About where he turned, a dirt road makes the long run across the empty fields to Parnassus Hill. With a chill of foreboding, I pull through the gate and park in the shadow of one of the great pillars. It's still light enough that if I start across the flats right away, Max will likely see me in his rearview mirror. I've got to wait until he reaches the hill, then race across the fields while he's climbing the back side.

While I wait, it strikes me that you can come to feel you own a place simply by spending time there. Someone else's name may be signed to the deed in some courthouse file cabinet. But once you have walked it, worked it, made love on it, or bled on it, that land becomes part of you. The Weldon barn was that way for Jet and me, until the three freaks trespassed there and left the serpent of fear behind them. That close call drove us out here, to Parnassus.

At the summit of the hill lies a geologic anomaly for this area, a circular, spring-fed pool a hundred yards across. Thanks to the Artesian spring that is its source, the water stays cool all year round. The banks are grassy, but deer generally keep them trampled down enough to access the pool in a couple of places. That pool has a long history, and more names than are known. The Indian name has long been forgotten. The French christened the spring Bellefontaine and used it as a bathing spot. The English used a name I don't recall. The slaves on Parnassus called it "the drowning pool" for some reason lost to history, but the owner of the plantation named it Delphi Springs. The bastardized version became "Delfey Springs" (coined by Confederate raiders who hid out there), and that's what high school kids had called it since long before our time.

As I stare across the fields, Max's headlights finally disappear behind the hill, which is covered with oak, pecan, elm, and pine trees. In a few places only a thin fringe of pines lines the shoulder of the road, and a skid would send your car tumbling down the hillside. But for most of its length Max will be blind to everything crossing the fields below. The sun has dropped well below the horizon now. If I keep my headlights off, the falling darkness might give me sufficient cover to make the run safely even if Max circles the hill before I reach its base.

Jamming the Explorer into Drive, I gun the motor and tear across the flats toward the great dark hump. Forty seconds at seventy miles an hour carries me to the broad base of the hill. I figure Max is five hundred yards ahead of me. The road that climbs Parnassus is barely wide enough for one vehicle, and it encircles the hill the way roads climb the Smoky Mountains. At the crest, the road ends in a small turnaround cut into the woods. From there a narrow footpath leads to the pool. Max will reach the top before me, and if he shuts off his engine—and they get out of the truck—they'll surely hear the Explorer climbing the hill.

Pressing harder on the gas pedal, I begin circling up the hill, keeping my eye on the ragged edge of dirt to my right. About eighty vertical feet from the crest, I stop the Explorer in the road. My first instinct is to back into the trees, but I decide to leave the Ford where it is. I don't want Max racing back down with Jet while I'm climbing this damned hill on foot. The Explorer is wide enough to stop him from getting past, and best of all, Max doesn't know the vehicle. Pocketing Dixie's keys, I get out and look up the dirt road. The underbrush is too thick here to try to climb straight up through the trees. After making sure my pistol is snug in my waistband, I start running up the road.

Using a pace count I developed long ago running track, I cover four hundred yards in a minute and a half. This brings me to within forty yards of the turnaround. Slowing to a walk, I cross the last twenty yards as quietly as I can, in case Jet and Max are sitting in his truck.

The turnaround is empty.

There's no way Max could have driven down the hill without me seeing him. Looking around the clearing, I see a place where the undergrowth has been pushed down by a vehicle. Max must have used his F-250 like a bulldozer and driven right up to the pool.

Instead of walking up on them from the footpath, I backtrack about seventy yards and start working my way through the trees, which should bring me out on the opposite side of the water from Max and Jet. This way, even if they detect my approach, they'll assume the noise is being made by deer or an armadillo. Progress is slow and difficult. The brush under the trees is thick, thorn bushes plentiful. Also, the risk of stepping on a copperhead or rattlesnake is significant this time of year, especially in the darkness under the canopy.

Halfway through the ring of trees that surrounds the pool, I hear music. The truck's radio. It's Creedence, the music of Max's youth, and the last thing Jet would choose. Confident that the music will mask my approach, I push harder through the brush. Another thirty seconds' struggle takes me to the edge of the trees, where ten feet of muddy ground separates the woods from the water.

It felt like night under the trees, but here twilight still diffuses through the clouds, and the water picks it up like a mirror. A hundred yards across the pool, the running lights of Max's truck shine like red beacons. The tree line on the far side looks black, but staring through the dusk I see two figures silhouetted against the white paint of the truck. For a moment I'm confused; then I realize Max and Jet are standing on a little pier that juts out at an angle from the far bank. If it weren't for Max's truck parked behind them, I wouldn't have seen them at all.

It's unsettling to find Max and Jet where she and I spent so many hours together. They appear to be facing each other and standing close together. I can't hear their voices, only John Fogerty singing "Someday Never Comes." A waxing gibbous moon is rising in the southwestern sky. *What are they doing here?* I wonder. *Did she want to be close to water, so that if she can't steal his phone outright, she can destroy it?*

As I stare through the dusk, a sharp cry cuts through the music. The smaller of the two figures runs down the pier and vanishes against the trees. The larger follows, but only at a walk. A sound that must be Max's voice rolls over the water, and then he disappears as well. My heart starts to pound again. If they get back into the truck and drive down the hill, I'm screwed. I can't possibly get back to the Explorer before they reach it. Risking exposure, I step out of the trees and crouch in the mud, squinting through the darkness.

At first I see nothing. Then Jet darts across the whiteness of the truck. Max follows, and suddenly I'm watching a shadow play staged against the backdrop of his F-250. As the song fades, Max bellows something. Three feet away from him, Jet screams back. He moves forward, reaching. Jet lets him take hold of her, pull her to him. They spin in a circle. I can't tell if they're arguing or kissing. Dizzy with confusion, I feel relief as Jet violently shoves him back, removing all doubt. *They're fighting.* I'm rising to my feet when Jet ducks down, then pops back up and raises her right arm as though swinging a tomahawk.

I gasp in disbelief as she drives her arm forward.

Max staggers back, wavers on his feet, then drops to his knees. Jet draws back her arm again, but Max topples over onto his back. Jet falls to her knees and starts grabbing at Max's body like she's going through his pockets.

What the hell has she done? Has she killed him?

Shaken from my trance, I start racing around the pool, but I haven't covered twenty yards before Jet raises her arm again, preparing to slam whatever she's holding into Max's motionless head once more.

"Jet!" I scream. "Don't! Jet . . . ? STOP!"

She freezes, probably looking my way, but it's too dark to tell. For a second she kneels motionless, like a cave woman in some museum diorama. Then she scrambles to her feet and jumps into Max's truck. The engine roars, and two seconds later, she's backing through the woods as though fleeing a forest fire.

If she races down the hill road at full speed, she'll slam into the Explorer. My only chance of stopping her is to cut her off at the road, and I've got maybe twenty seconds to do it. I charge into the trees, bulling through the brush without regard for consequences. Thorns and branches tear at my face and arms, but my only concern is avoiding the trunks.

I burst from the woods as Max's truck rounds the curve above me, accelerating with a roar. Seeing no alternative, I run to the middle of the road and start windmilling my arms like a sailor waving off a fighter jet during a carrier landing. Max's high beams stab my eyes, but I stand my ground. *Surely Jet will recognize me before she runs me down—*

The F-250 shudders to a stop six inches short of crushing me.

I run around to the passenger door and bang on the window glass.

"I'm sorry!" Jet cries in a muffled voice. She hits the unlock switch. "I had no idea who yelled back there! That was you?"

I yank open the door and climb up into the big Ford, which smells like a wet baseball glove. "What did you do to Max? What did you hit him with?"

She reaches down to the floor and brings up a claw hammer with blood and hair on its head. "I stole it from his toolbox."

"Is he dead?"

"I don't think so."

"That's why you were about to hit him again?"

She hesitates, then nods.

"Jet, what the *fuck*? What's going on?"

"I'll tell you, I swear to God, but can we please get out of here?"

"No! We have to see if Max is dead or alive."

Terror lights her eyes. *"Why?"*

"To know what to do next! A lot of people could have seen you riding in this truck with him. Plus, you can't steal this thing. Not after what you did. You have to leave it here, and your prints are all over it."

"How did you even get here?" she asks. "Were you following me?"

"Yes and no. Too long a story. Pull back up to the turnaround."

Terror lights her eyes again. "No! Marshall, please. We have what we need. Look!" She digs a large cell phone from her pocket.

"Is that Max's phone?"

She nods with excitement. "No more video! No more blackmail."

"Great. You've traded blackmail for a murder charge. Jet, back this thing up to the turnaround, or I will."

"Let's just leave the truck!" she yells. "We can talk somewhere else. Anywhere." She grabs my arms. *"Please* get us out of here. I'll throw Max's keys into the woods. If Max dies, he dies. Nobody will ever know we were here."

"Jet—" I reach down and yank the door handle, then push the door open.

Her eyes go wide again. "Where are you going?"

"To check on Max."

She looks like a cornered animal. "Okay, okay . . . *shit.*"

Jet jams the truck into reverse, looks down at the rearview camera, then starts backing around the curve that leads up to the clearing. As we roll uphill, I notice that her blouse is badly torn. She's shoved it up under her bra strap to stay covered.

"Max tore your top?" I ask.

She nods but says nothing. Five seconds later she kicks the brake pedal and stops. "What now?"

"You'd better come with me," I tell her, suddenly worried that she'll bolt while I'm checking on Max.

"Do you have your gun?" she asks.

"Yeah. Does Max still have his?"

"No." She reaches into the console and brings up the .380 I saw in Max's ankle holster yesterday afternoon.

"Bring that," I tell her.

She opens her door and climbs down to the ground. Using the LED light on my iPhone, I lead her along the footpath toward the pool, gun in hand.

"What are we going to do if he's alive?" she asks.

"I don't know."

"You're not taking him to a hospital or anything? He'll lie, Marshall. He'll say I tried to kill him."

Would he be lying? "Let's just see what shape he's in."

We've come to the band of grass that separates the trees from the water on this side of the spring. I see the deep ruts Max left behind when he drove his truck up to the water's edge. Emerging from under the trees, I make out the wooden pier in the moonlight.

What I don't see is Max.

"He's gone," Jet gasps beside me. "Holy fuck, he's not here."

The raw fear I felt when confronting Paul in my office returns, jacked to double intensity. The urge to run blindly is almost irresistible, but instead I focus on the ground. From the marks in the mud, it looks like Max belly-crawled into the underbrush beneath the trees, like a wounded alligator.

"We have to find him," Jet whispers.

After checking the tree line to make sure Max isn't sneaking up on us, I kneel in the mud and shine my LED down on the spot where I think he fell. Blood loss is hard to judge, but there's a lot of bright red on the ground. It looks like somebody kicked over a tester can of paint. *That came from Max's head,* I realize. I can't believe he could move after a blow like that.

"Where'd you hit him?" I ask. "Front of the skull? Or the side?"

Jet looks almost too rattled to function. "Um . . . right side, I think. My right. His left. He was facing me, and I swung right-handed."

"Did you hit him with the ball of the hammer? Or the flat side?"

"Does it make a difference?"

"Ball would probably be worse. He'd have a depressed skull fracture. I know a little about those. He could definitely die."

"I think it was the ball." Her voice has a frantic edge. "When he fell, it sounded like Paul dropping a bag of pool salt on our patio."

"He could have a subdural hemorrhage . . . a cerebral contusion. He could die five minutes from now or tomorrow."

"He can't have gone far," she whispers, her eyes on the trees. "Let's find him."

"No," I say, getting to my feet.

"Why not? He can't—"

"Jet! He can't what? Fight back?" I grab one shoulder and pull her face close to mine. "Did you bring Max up here to kill him?"

Even in the dark I see the whites of her eyes growing. "God, no! If I'd got him up here to kill him, I'd have been in control. I was fighting for my life."

"He attacked you?"

"He tried to rape me, okay?"

This stops me cold. "He tried to rape you? But . . ."

"My *God*," she says. "Not one more word until we're safe."

I nod slowly, my gaze on the tree line again. "Okay. We're going back to town."

"Without knowing whether he's dead or alive?"

"We're sure as hell not going into the woods after him!"

"Why not? We have the guns."

"Jet, Max did two tours of duty in Vietnam. Most of it jungle fighting. He was hit by an AK-47. He fell on punji stakes smeared with shit and survived. So far as we know, he's alive right now. You want to go crawling through that brush in the hope of finishing him off? Max could kill us both before we even knew he was close."

She's staring at the long scar in the mud as though she wants to drop to her belly and crawl after him. Instead of arguing further, I turn and walk back along the path to the turnaround.

"Wait!" she calls. "I'm coming!"

CHAPTER 38

ONCE WE REACH Max's truck, which I approach with great care, we spend two minutes wiping down its wheel, its dash, and the brown leather of its interior. Jet uses the remainder of her blouse, while I use my shirt, keeping my pistol in my left hand. Though it makes the job harder, I also keep the truck doors shut. If Max is still alive, doing this work under the dome light would qualify as suicidal behavior.

"Wipe your fingerprints off Max's keys," I tell her. "We'll toss them in the woods on the way down. Max won't find them tonight, but if he dies, the police eventually will."

"Are you going to call the sheriff or anything?"

As we wipe down the door handles and shifter, I remember what Jet said beside the pool. With this memory comes an image of Max sitting in my kitchen, warning me never to have sex with her again.

"You said Max tried to rape you," I say softly. "Tell me what he did."

"Not till we're safe. We're sitting ducks out here. You said it yourself."

"Okay," I tell her, twisting to pull my shirt back on. "That's the best we can do. Bring the hammer. We'll dump it far from this hill."

After we climb out, Jet cocks her arm to throw Max's car keys into the dense woods lining the edge of the road.

"Not yet," I warn her.

She freezes. "Do you think he's watching us?"

"He might be. Do you feel like you can run?"

"How far? I feel like I might vomit."

"Fifty yards."

"Go. I'll keep up."

Ten seconds of jogging brings us within sight of the parked Explorer.

"*Wait!*" Jet cries as it materializes in the road ahead of us. "Somebody else is up here!"

"That's mine," I explain, reaching for her hand. "Take it easy."

We're both breathing hard, and even in the dark, she looks paler than I've ever seen her. She's staring at the Ford Explorer like it might hold a squad of hit men.

"Whose truck is that?"

"Dixie Allman ran out of gas on Highway 36. I was helping her out when you and Max rode by. I switched cars with her so I could follow you without Max noticing."

"Why'd you block the road?"

"To make sure Max couldn't get away with you while I was climbing up. Come on, this is our ride home." I pull her forward and we run to the Ford.

"We're leaving?" she asks hopefully.

"Not yet. But soon."

The Explorer's doors open with a grating of steel, but the engine cranks readily. *Is Max lying up on the hill somewhere, listening?* I wonder.

"Why can't we go yet?" Jet asks, climbing into the seat beside me and dropping the hammer on the plastic floor mat.

"We need to make sure Max doesn't come walking down this road. And that nobody comes to pick him up."

"How could they? He can't call anybody. I have his cell phone."

"I know. And Max is probably bleeding to death up there right now. But let's just give it a half hour to make sure."

Jet groans with frustration, but she doesn't argue.

"Are you going to tell me what happened?" I ask.

"Are we just going to sit here in the road?"

"No." Shifting the SUV into reverse, I back down the narrow hill road with only the brake lights for illumination.

"What are you doing?" she asks.

"I want to be farther down the hill, and I'm not going back up to the top to turn around. I also want to be on the front side, so we can see the gate. Watch for an opening in the trees where I can get this thing turned around."

"Up there on the left. You already passed it."

I hit the brakes, then pull forward twenty yards, shift into reverse, and back into the opening between an oak and some popcorn trees. The rear end of the Explorer dips, then kicks up hard, but I manage to go far enough back to rotate the steering wheel and get our nose pointed downhill. Shifting into low, I nurse us back onto the road. There's enough moonlight to see under the overhanging branches, but just. We coast forward in the darkness, steadily descending.

"Look for a spot where we can hide but still see the gate down on the flats."

"Thirty yards ahead, on the right," Jet says. "Can you fit through there?"

She's pointing to a narrow gap between two pine trees. It looks iffy, but with careful use of the pedals, I manage to back us off the road and under cover. We end up nose-down about thirty-five degrees, but the trees on the other side of the road are thin enough to give us a clear view of the fields below. A half mile away, a lone pair of headlights moves west along Cemetery Road.

"Do you think Max is dead?" Jet asks.

"Anybody else would be." I kill the engine, then reach over and gently take her left hand. She's shivering. "How did you end up with Max this afternoon?"

"He surprised me in the alley behind my office. After work, when I was going to my car. He said he needed to talk to me about Sally. He was freaked out. He told me his partners were trying to kill him. The Poker Club. Half of them, anyway."

"That might be true."

"He said he was being followed. He was yelling about microphones everywhere. He said he'd swept his truck with some kind of wand, and the truck was the only space he trusted. Even though he was in a wild state, I figured that might be my best chance to get hold of his cell phone."

"That's what I figured."

"The thing is, once I got in with him, he asked me to give him *my* cell. Like a fool I did, because I was so intent on stealing his from him. He shut mine off, wanded it, and slipped it into his pocket. Then he drove us out of town on Highway 36."

"That's where I picked you up."

"He was headed out here the whole time. I think half that paranoia was an act to get me to come out here with him. He wanted me where no one could hear me scream."

Something cold and clinical takes hold of my heart, like a wet latex glove. "Max brought you out here to rape you?"

Jet lifts her closed fist to her mouth and breathes slowly. She looks like she's struggling not to hyperventilate.

"My father-in-law," she says at length, "is obsessed with me. I know you think you know him, but you have no idea, okay? Max is sick. All those business trips he takes to Vietnam? Because of their lumber business? He goes to relive his war years and have sex with fifteen-year-old prostitutes. He's told me I'm the closest thing around here to French-Vietnamese girls, which he claims are the most beautiful in the world. Today's big news? He thinks about me every time he masturbates."

My stomach rolls like it does when a plane hits an air pocket, and a tingling fight-or-flight sensation goes through my legs. "How long has this been going on? His behavior, I mean."

"He's always had a thing about me. But watching you and me make love two days ago pushed him over the edge. He's snapped, Marshall. Halfway up this hill, he took out his cell phone and played me the video of us on the patio. He acted like I'd cheated on *him*, not Paul."

Again I remember Max sitting in my kitchen, casually commenting on Jet's body and talking about wanting to screw Nadine. "I'm not surprised about Max being sexually aggressive. Even Dr. Kirby called him a 'pussy hound' yesterday. But why is he obsessed with *you*? His son's wife?"

Jet cuts her eyes at me but says nothing. This is clearly tough for her to talk about.

"So he didn't talk to you about the case at all?"

"Nothing new. He was just stalling."

"What happened once he got you out here?"

She settles back in her seat and recounts her story in a mechanical voice. "He drove right through the trees and parked by the water. I asked why he'd come here, but he just got out of the truck and told me to follow him. I wasn't sure what to do. I had a bad feeling, but he'd taken the keys with him. Before I got out, I looked around for anything I might use as a weapon. He keeps a tool bag in the backseat, just like Paul. I wanted a screwdriver, but I couldn't get one with-out crawling back there. That hammer was sticking up, though, and I could just reach it. It was too big to hide, so I dropped it on the ground as I got out. At least it would be close in a crisis."

"That was smart."

She nods reflexively. "Once we were out of the truck, he didn't waste time. He walked out on that pier and said we ought to go swim-ming to relax."

"Without clothes, I suppose?"

"Naturally."

How many times did Jet and I do that out here?

"Apart from being scared," she goes on, "all I could think about was his cell phone. If I could get hold of it, I'd have two choices: try to get away with it—which would give me a chance to try Sally's passwords on it—or just throw it into the middle of the pool and at least destroy the video. Getting away with it didn't seem very likely at that point."

"I was watching by then, but it was hard to tell what was happening."

"As soon as I got close to him out on the pier, he pulled me to him. He started talking shit and touching my breasts. He tried to get a hand up under my top. It was like junior high. I tried to play it off as him kid-ding around. Then he pressed my hand against his penis. I jerked my hand back, and that's when he ripped my top."

She shakes her head, obviously reliving each second. "Once it got that far, I knew he wasn't going to stop. But I forced myself to relax, like I was going to submit. He pulled my hips against his. He was hard already, and I let him sort of dry-hump me standing up, until his eyes glazed over. Then I shoved him back and I broke for the truck."

"I saw that happen."

"Did you see how he just *walked* after me?" She shudders in her seat. "It felt like a damned monster movie. He knew he didn't have to hurry up here. Motherfucker. For a second I thought about running out to the road or trying to hide in the woods. But I knew I couldn't get away from him. Besides . . . I was just sick of it all, sick of him. So I picked up the hammer."

"I saw that, too," I tell her, my mind hanging on to something she said. "And I know I can't possibly understand the full horror of what happened back there . . ."

"But?" she says. "I hear a 'but' coming."

I should just let this go. But I've known Jet a long time, and something isn't adding up. She's twenty years younger than Max, and four months ago she was running half-marathons. Since she isn't physically hurt, I figure she'd have had a better-than-even chance of escaping him on this hill.

"You said you knew you couldn't get away from him," I say gently. "So you turned around and picked up the hammer. Was it only the threat of rape tonight that made you do that?"

"What?" Her breathing has become a sort of frantic wheeze. "What are you doing? Playing prosecutor? Are you saying defending myself against rape isn't self-defense?"

"I'm not saying that at all."

"It sounds like you are!" Her answer is almost a snarl, like a blow intended to drive away something she can't face.

"Jet, this is me. I love you. I came here to protect you. That's all I want to do. But to do that, I need to know what's really going on. Last night, you told me about a plan that could end in Max's death. It could have been designed solely with that end in mind. And tonight you hit him in the head with a hammer."

She looks away from me, expels another rush of air.

"I know you wanted his cell phone," I press. "And I understand why. Max is an existential threat to us, no question. He's threatened our lives. That video alone does."

No response. Just when I think she's shut down completely, she says, "Tonight wasn't the first time he tried to rape me."

The cold fist tightens around my heart. A hot wave of shame follows for doubting her initial story. "Will you tell me?"

"He tried it six weeks ago. I stabbed him."

Stabbed him? Six weeks ago, she and I were making love every day. "Where did this happen?"

"My house. He claimed he'd come by to see Kevin, but he knew Kevin wasn't going to be there. And he'd sent Paul on an errand to Jackson."

"Jesus. What did you stab him with?"

"A steak knife."

"Did anybody find out?"

She shakes her head. "He probably got Warren Lacey to sew him up. He saw it coming, and I caught him in the side. But it was enough to get him off me."

I'm so dumbfounded by this story that it's hard to know where to go from here. "Did you and I see each other that day?"

"No. I told you I had business in Tupelo."

I remember that day now. "Last-minute trip," I murmur. "You brought me back that Elvis guitar strap."

A pained smile lights her face for a moment. "I couldn't have seen you without telling you about it. And I just couldn't get into it then. I wasn't ready."

"I understand. Look, I don't want to push you . . ."

"Another 'but'? Go ahead. We're stuck here anyway."

"I still feel like there's something you're not telling me. Maybe a lot."

She looks into her lap, biting her lip like an anxious little girl. "What if it's terrible? What if it's something you can't live with?"

I take her left hand and squeeze it. "There's nothing about you I can't live with. Nothing."

She laughs bitterly in the dark. We're sitting less than a foot apart, yet a gulf has yawned open between us. Can thirty-two years of love not bridge that divide? "Jet . . . a year from now, we're going to be married. But to get there, we have to get through this, whatever it is. Just tell me. There's nothing to fear."

She nods, but her face is filled with torment, as though she's fighting some invisible restraint. "Six weeks ago wasn't the only other time," she says.

I shift in my seat. "Okay. So he tried to rape you before that?"

"No."

I blink in confusion, trying to understand. At first I don't get her meaning. Then I do. The cold I felt earlier spreads through me like a numbing anesthetic. "You mean . . . Max didn't just *try* to rape you? He succeeded?"

She sets her jaw and looks straight through the windshield. "Yes."

I've clumsily driven my dull scalpel through thick scar tissue, exposing a necrotic cyst that threatens life itself. *Max Matheson raped his daughter-in-law.*

"Will you tell me how it happened?" I ask softly.

Jet sits silent in the moonlight falling through the windshield, look- ing out into the dark. She reminds me of crime victims I interviewed as a young reporter, people who had either suffered or witnessed violent acts and were struggling to maintain control. "It was about ten years ago," she says in a monotone. "Sally was sick. She'd had colon surgery. I was help- ing take care of her. Tallulah and me. Tallulah was worn out, so I stayed up for a night and a day without sleep. I was exhausted. Paul was drunk, like he always was back then. He'd passed out in the den."

"This was in Max and Sally's house?"

She nods. "Max offered to spell me, so I could rest. I went to the guest room, but even though I was wiped out, I couldn't fall asleep. I went into the kitchen for something to eat, and Max walked in. When I told him I couldn't sleep, he gave me one of Sally's pills. A Xanax. A big one. Then he went back in with Sally, and I went back to the guest room. The pill knocked me out."

Part of me doesn't want to hear what follows, but I have proba- bly heard worse. In 1993, as a college junior, I interviewed six Bosnian women who had been repeatedly raped in a camp set up solely for that purpose.

Jet wipes her eyes with her torn blouse, then continues in the same lifeless voice. "When I first woke up, I thought it was Paul on top of me. He'd done that before, drunk. This is TMI, but . . . what brought me to my senses was how hard he was. And how rough. Paul was practically impotent by that time. Now and then he would take a Viagra, but he'd never admit it. The whole situation was just . . . *shit*."

"It was Max on top of you?" I prompt quietly.

She nods, still facing forward.

"He did this with Paul in the next room?"

"Just down the hall. Max had seen enough of Paul in those years to know he wasn't going to wake up, not even if I screamed."

"Did you? Scream?"

"At first. Max just clapped his hand over my mouth and kept on ramming me. I could have screamed after that, but I started thinking about what would happen if I did. If Paul woke up and came in there. Would they fight? Would Paul get a gun? If he shot Max, would he go to jail? Or would Max kill Paul and find some way to blame him? Paul was taking drugs back then, a lot of them. Opiates, but some Adderall and other things, too. He bounced back and forth between zoned out and fighting mad. Anyway, as I lay there spinning all this out in my head, it suddenly ended. Max collapsed on top of me, then rolled off."

"Did he say anything?"

Jet purses her lips like someone trying to recall a distant detail from childhood. "No. He didn't even bother warning me not to tell anybody what he'd done. He knew nobody would believe me. Not in that family. He knew I wasn't going to the police. The Poker Club *owned* the police then. They still do, but it was worse then. No rape kit evidence would ever have made it to a courtroom."

The enormity of what she's telling me has overloaded my analytical faculties. All I can do is try to elicit as many facts as possible, to try to make sense of them later. "Was that the only time this happened?"

"Yes, thank God."

"Why, do you think? If you kept quiet about it the first time?"

She slowly shakes her head, as though trying to figure this out herself. "I think that's complicated. You know Max—he always has to be the alpha male. I think he'd been watching me for a long time. He had to have me, to mark me, like a dog pissing on a tree. He saw his chance and he took it."

"That sounds like him, all right." The full horror of Max's act is almost too much to grasp. Yet one obvious question has risen in my mind. Should I shove it down deep and never voice it? Maybe. But if I'm going to spend the rest of my life with this woman, I need to know the answer. "I get why you didn't report it to the police," I tell her. "And I agree that either Paul or Max would have killed the other over what happened. But . . . one thing about this doesn't sound like you."

Jet looks at me from the corner of her eye, mistrust plain in her face. "What?"

"Why didn't you just *leave*? Take Kevin and run. Leave Mississippi. I realize it would have gotten difficult, but it's hard to see how staying in that family would have been possible after what happened. I know you, Jet. I can't see you staying after that."

I expect her to say, *Because of Kevin. He was just a baby. They would have come after me, brought me back.* But she doesn't. She doesn't say anything.

"Because of Kevin?" I lead her.

She looks at me like she's about to confirm that, but then she pulls back, like a parachutist hesitating in the open door of a plane.

"Where was Kevin when this happened?" I ask, sensing something even more frightening in the darkness of what remains unknown to me. "He was, what, two at the time? Was he home with Tallulah?"

She shakes her head.

"He was *in the house?*"

She hesitates, then nods.

"My God. Did he hear any of it?"

"No."

"Well . . . that's good. Jesus, I can't believe Max was crazy enough to try this again now. And more than once? I mean, I *do* believe it. But he's under indictment for murder! He really must have lost his mind."

Jet shrugs, still not looking at me. "Yes and no. He's the same man he always was, only worse."

"How crazy do you have to be to rape your son's wife? And especially you. Knowing you could have told Paul about it? I mean, screw the cops—Paul would have killed Max if you'd told him. I have zero doubt about that."

"Maybe," she says softly. "But that's complicated, too. The physical tension between them. It's always been an issue."

"I know. But even if you told Paul this tonight, ten years after the fact, he'd strangle Max with his bare hands."

She gives a halfhearted shrug. "You're probably right."

A fearful possibility hits me. "Have you ever thought about telling Paul? I mean . . . with intent?"

I see a new tension in her neck and face. My first read is that Jet has considered doing this, but something stopped her. "Hey?" I whisper.

"I can't tell Paul," she says. "And Max knows it."

There's something different in her voice. A new note of fear, even dread. "Why not?" I ask.

"Because Max has something on me."

With that sentence, some of her dread passes into me. I turn in my seat and take her hands in mine. "What are you talking about? The video?"

"No. This is something he's had for years." Before I can speak again, she looks up with tears in her eyes. "Max *knows* I can't tell anybody what happened. Ever."

"Jet . . . what could be bad enough to keep you quiet about a rape?"

She shakes her head, tears pouring down her face.

"Did you have an affair with somebody? Something like that?"

A bark of hysterical laughter escapes her throat. "God, no."

"Jet, there's nothing you could have done that I can't accept or forgive." My mind is spinning out wild possibilities. "Did you hurt somebody? Like . . . run over somebody, and the Poker Club covered it up?"

She looks bereft. "No."

"Then what?"

She wipes her face on her sleeve, then takes a deep breath, as though gathering herself before taking the jump I imagined before. Then she says, "Paul isn't Kevin's father."

I stare back at her, uncomprehending. "But . . . you said you didn't have an affair."

"That's right."

A wave of nausea precedes the truth. But at last it hits me, like a dagger slipped between two ribs. "Are you saying Kevin is *Max's* son? From the rape?"

"Now you've got it!" she says with false gaiety.

Sixty seconds ago I thought I knew what horror was. This is beyond anything I could have conceived. And yet . . . it follows from the preface as naturally as pregnancy follows sex.

"You're not looking at me," she says. "Can't you stand to anymore?"

I snap out of my shock and look into her mascara-smeared eyes. "You said the rape happened ten years ago. Kevin is twelve."

"I know. I'm sorry. I wasn't sure I could tell you the whole truth, so I said ten years. But it was thirteen."

I feel like we're sitting in some actors' workshop, improvising an absurd situation to see how far we can carry it. But we're not. This is real. This happened. To her. And my life is not what I thought it was. A nagging intuition tells me I should be alert for any movement outside the Explorer, but the idea of physical danger seems trivial compared to the threat of shattered trust. My mind is making what it can of the known information, trying to create a coherent or even sympathetic narrative.

"So then . . . just after the rape, you didn't know that Kevin had been conceived. You didn't know you were pregnant. But you knew what Max had done, and that if you stayed in that marriage you'd have to see him every day. So . . . again . . . why did you stay?"

Jet stares through the windshield as though waiting for someone to arrive and spare her from answering my question. "I don't know," she says finally. "I wish I had an answer for you, but I don't. The core of it had to do with my marriage, I think. And with Paul's problems. But I'm obviously not as strong or independent as I once thought I was."

"I'm not judging you," I tell her. "I'm just trying to understand."

"*Look,*" she cries, pointing through the windshield.

"Where?" I ask, scanning the dark road for Max.

"Down by the gate. Headlights!"

CHAPTER 39

SURE ENOUGH, A half mile from Parnassus Hill, a pair of blue-white LED headlights sits motionless where the plantation's gate should be.

"Maybe it's teenagers," I suggest, "looking for a place to make out."

"They've come through the gate," Jet says in a taut voice.

She's right. Far below, the lights are cutting across the field now, moving fast.

"You think Max called the police?" I ask.

"He *couldn't* have. I have his cell phone."

"Let me see it again."

She digs into her back pocket and brings out the big smartphone I saw earlier. "That looks like the Samsung he had in my house yesterday."

"Maybe that's the landowner down there," Jet suggests, still watching the headlights. "Maybe he saw Max's lights earlier, and he's just now checking them out."

"No. Mr. Hales would be coming from the direction of his house, not the main gate. Do you think Max could have had two cell phones on him?"

"No. I went through his pockets."

"Every one?"

"Yes."

"Then he must have had one in his truck."

"We just wiped it down! I didn't see any phone."

I shake my head in anger and regret. "All I know is that Max is shadier than we ever thought about being. If anybody would carry two phones, it's him. I kept the truck doors shut so the light would stay off. Maybe it was down in a door pocket or something."

"Goddamn it!" she curses. "We can't be this unlucky."

The headlights are halfway to the hill and moving faster than any trespassing teenager or poacher would likely drive. While other possibilities certainly exist, all my instinct tells me that whoever is in that vehicle was summoned here by the wounded man on top of the hill. If we're going to get off Parnassus alive, we may have to fight our way down.

The Samsung in Jet's hand lights up as she punches numbers into it.

"What are you doing?"

"What I should have done the second I found the phone. Trying the passwords from the back of Sally's necklace."

"You memorized them?"

She looks up at me like I'm an idiot. It was a stupid question. The public school kids didn't call Jet "the Brain" without reason. She has an eidetic memory for numbers.

"How can this be?" she asks, stabbing the keypad again. "The only possible phone password of the two is the shorter one, and it doesn't work. Now we can't even be sure this phone has the video on it."

"It might not. Instead of using cash burner phones, Max may have kept two identical Samsung phones to fool Sally. A clone phone."

Jet shakes her head and stuffs the Samsung back into her pocket. "That car's got to be some random person, right? Or maybe Hales called the sheriff's department, thinking we're poachers."

"That's better than the alternative. Although a deputy or game warden will call in Max's truck if he finds it abandoned."

"That beats Max running out of the woods yelling that I tried to kill him. I told you we should have finished it back there."

Knowing what I know now, I'm starting to think she's right. "If Max called whoever's in that car, then we know he has another cell phone."

"Which means I went through all that shit for nothing," she says in a grim voice.

"Listen. We're going to sit tight in these trees until that car passes. It could be anybody. Russo and his mob guys. Even Paul—"

"Don't say that."

"It could be, Jet. We're going to get down in our seats. Don't even breathe when they pass."

We hunker down below the doorframes, like teenagers on a lover's lane trying to make themselves invisible to a cop. The headlights have vanished below, which means our new visitor is climbing the hill.

"I know you're freaking out about what I told you," she whispers, finding my eyes in the darkness. "Can you still love me?"

"I still love you. Don't even think about that. It's just . . . it's like everything suddenly went four-dimensional. I can't believe you've carried that secret alone for thirteen years."

"Not alone. I'd welcome carrying it alone. *Max* has known. That's the hell of it."

A dozen new questions rise, but I simply nod in the dark.

"The reason I didn't tell you before," she says, "is because I never wanted you to look at Kevin and think of Max. And I never wanted you to make love to me and think of Max."

"I understand."

"Would you tell me now if you felt different about me? I mean it."

"Yes. I just wish I'd known about this when I saw you swing that hammer. I'd have run over there and helped you finish the mother-fucker off."

She squeezes my arm in the dark, then lays her cheek against my shoulder. I strain my ears, listening for the low note of an engine, but I hear only our ticking motor and the high whistle of crickets in the night.

"Whoa," I whisper, gripping her arm. "The sky just got brighter."

"I see it."

A crazed drummer beats out an arrhythmic solo in my chest. I'm praying that nothing on this Explorer reflects light back to the eye of whoever's behind the wheel of that vehicle. For the first time, I'm glad to be in Dixie Allman's rust bucket. Without being obvious, I reach down and grip the butt of my pistol, then slide it up into my lap.

The headlight beams grow brighter, turning our windshield into a blue-white trapezoid. *An isosceles trapezoid,* I think crazily.

"I can't take this," Jet whispers, clenching my hand hard enough to cut off circulation. "*Fuck, fuck, fuck—*"

At the last moment I slide up in my seat, just high enough to see a sleek red car glide silently across my field of vision.

"Did you see that?" I ask. "I know that car. A Tesla Model S. Bright red. There's only one in the whole town."

"Warren Lacey," she says, sliding up in her seat.

So much for Max dying quietly on the hill. Lacey is the doctor whose license Jet got suspended for a year. He's also a certified Poker Club member. "Max called him," I tell her. "That's the only explanation. He's definitely got another phone up there."

"Damn it! What do we do now?"

"We can't do much. But Max calling Lacey is a good sign. He could have called the sheriff, and he didn't."

"He could still be dead, right?" she asks. "He could have died after calling Lacey?"

"Absolutely. But we can't count on that."

"Marshall, can we please get the hell out of here? If Max leaves with Lacey and they lock the gate, we'll be stuck."

"No, we won't. We can push down some fence posts with this SUV if we have to."

"What if there are more people on the way? You want Russo and his thugs out here hunting us?"

"No. You're right. It's time."

I pull the parking brake release, wrench the wheel right, and let the Ford roll down onto the road. Then I crank the engine and press the gas pedal harder than I should. The wheels spin in the dirt, then catch and throw us forward.

Squinting through the dark, I start down the perpetual curve that circles the dark hill in its slow descent. Beneath the overhanging trees I can hardly track the left edge of the road, but I can't hold myself to a crawl. After ten seconds we're going thirty-five, and in twenty we're careening down the hill like two kids in a teenage death anthem.

"You want me to slow down?" I ask through gritted teeth.

"No!" she cries, bracing her arms against the dash as we fly through the dark.

She lets out a sigh of relief as we land on level ground. On the flats there's enough moonlight to see, and I push the Explorer to sixty, then seventy-five across the bean field. Jet rocks forward and back as though willing the vehicle faster. When we finally shoot through the gate, which is standing open, it feels like blessed deliverance.

"My God," she gasps. "*My God, my God, my God.* We made it!"

I click on my headlights and turn hard right onto the dark line of

Cemetery Road, headed toward Bienville. After thirty seconds, something lets go in Jet. She shudders and sobs beside me. I reach out and take her hand, trying to calm myself as much as her. I haven't felt this shaken since Iraq, and no one has even fired a gun tonight. What can she be going through? The prospect of telling me this secret has probably terrified her since before we got back together. Now she's done it. I should leave her in peace, no question. But nearly everything she told me has raised a question. One flashes like a tower beacon above all the others.

"Jet, can I ask you one more thing? Just one. It's a tough one."

She's still rocking in her seat. "You might as well. We'll see where we stand."

"Why did you keep the baby? Were you sure it was Max's?"

She closes her eyes, and her mouth makes what looks like a painful smile, but she's still weeping.

"Take your time," I tell her.

"How can I explain it so that you'll understand? Paul and I had been trying for so long to have a child. He'd tried suicide, twice. Pills. I found him. You don't know how he was after that mess in Iraq. Your book ended up making him a hero to a lot of people, but the government barred him from the country. He lost everything that was *his,* you know? And that broke him. Working for Max is hell for Paul. And not being able to father a child . . . that was the last straw."

I drive steadily, my eyes on the faded white lines, trying to understand. "Did you know from the start that it was Max who got you pregnant?"

"No. Early on, I didn't think the baby was his. He'd only been in me that one time. Paul had . . . managed to finish in me three times that month. So the math was on his side. I clung to that. But the further along I got, the more afraid I became. I tried to tell myself I was being irrational, that everything would be okay." She reaches out and taps the dash with her forefinger. "But some part of me knew."

I feel her watching my face, searching for the slightest judgment. I do all I can to watch the road without reaction.

"At that point," she says, "I had two choices. Stay and try to make the best of things, or abort the baby and quit. And when I thought about quitting . . . Marshall, I had so much guilt."

"Over the rape?"

"No. Over marrying Paul."

This takes me aback. "What do you mean?"

"I'd married a man I didn't love. Not really. Not the way I knew love could be. But I'd done it anyway."

I know where this is going, but I'm not going to challenge her tonight.

She turns in her seat, facing me full-on. "And when I thought about leaving, I'd think, 'What am I going to do? Start over single at some big law firm? At thirty-three?' In my mind, you were my refuge. But you'd just gotten married."

"Please don't try to put this on me," I say, despite my intention to remain silent.

"I'm not putting it on you. I'm just saying, what was I supposed to do? Abandon Paul in the state he was in? Let him drink and drug himself to death, so I could have an abortion and go somewhere else to start over from scratch?"

There it is. Max's crime had been terrible, yet to Jet, living with the result of it had ultimately seemed the sanest path. *Was it the lesser of two evils?* I wonder. *Or simply the path of least resistance?* Especially as long as she could keep her doubt alive.

"Do you know for sure that Max is the father? Like, DNA sure?"

She nods once. "I didn't intend to get a test. I'd have been perfectly happy never knowing beyond a shadow of doubt. But Max got one done."

"How'd he manage that?"

"He stole some hairs from a baseball cap he'd given Kevin on his first birthday. He had them tested in secret. That's what he told me, anyway."

"You never saw a report? Max could be lying."

"He tried to show me the test results, but I refused to look. I didn't need to, Marshall. I've seen Max in Kevin's face and body ten thousand times. A hundred thousand. And it kills me every time. I think it's driven me close to crazy."

"No one else saw the resemblance?"

"Of course they did." Exasperation has entered her voice. "But why should that bother anybody? To other people, Max is Kevin's grandfather by blood."

A pair of headlights appears in the distance. Totally normal, yet the sight of them nudges up my stress level.

"And Sally? She never suspected?"

"No, thank God."

This I find hard to believe. "She never said anything to you. That's all you know for sure."

Jet is shaking her head. "She never knew, Marshall. Sally would have said something."

Despite Jet's certainty, I'm starting to wonder about Sally's suicide. "Didn't you tell me Sally tried to talk to you on the day before she died?"

She runs her hands back through her hair, then shakes her head with sudden violence. "Are you suggesting she killed herself because she figured out the truth about Kevin?"

I look away from the road long enough to see the last of Jet's emotional fortitude crumble. She bends over as though she might throw up, then covers her eyes with her left hand.

"I'm sorry," I tell her. "I'm just trying to understand it all. Because if Max is still alive, we've got big problems. I need to figure out what he might do. Sally's death never made sense to me, not as a suicide."

"Until now, you mean."

"Well . . . I never believed that bullshit alibi about Nadine's mother. But if Sally figured this out . . . she really might not have been able to live with it."

The headlights are almost upon us, undimmed by the rude driver behind them. The interior of the Explorer fills with light, and Jet shields her swollen eyes with her hand. After the truck roars past, I say, "What if Sally didn't figure it out? What if Max *told* her the truth that night?"

"Why would he? To purposefully hurt her? He's threatened to tell Paul before, even Kevin. But never Sally. Not first."

Yet another epiphany rocks my perception of the situation. "Think about this. If Sally knew about Kevin, why would she kill herself? Why not *Max*? Seriously. Maybe she did try to kill him that night, and they struggled over the gun. Maybe Max killed her out of self-defense. But he can't explain that to anybody without revealing the truth about Kevin."

"Don't say that," Jet whispers. "Don't even think that. I can't deal with that."

As much as she wants to avoid all culpability in Sally's death, that scenario sounds more reasonable than anything else has to me. "There's only one thing that makes me believe that's not it," I think aloud.

"What?"

"The blackmail cache she made. The one that's scaring the Poker Club to death. That shows premeditation on Sally's part. That's the piece that doesn't add up, no matter what kind of math you use. She puts together something that can destroy not only Max but all his partners, then doesn't use it. Why?"

"I can't think about it right now," Jet says in an exhausted voice. "I can't think at all."

"We have to figure this out. Sally gave that cache to somebody else. Why? What were they supposed to do with it?"

"Didn't they send you a piece of it? That PDF file?"

"I don't know who sent me that. It could have been the person with the cache, but I don't know for sure."

Jet is thinking again; I can see it in her rigid posture. "All I know is this," she says. "If Sally really figured out that Max is Kevin's father, the *only* thing she would have cared about was making sure Paul and Kevin never learned the truth. And framing Max for murder wouldn't guarantee his silence. He could broadcast it live from death row if he wanted to. *Farewell world, I'm Kevin Matheson's father!*"

This nightmarish image makes me shudder. "I can actually see Max doing that. You're right. So we haven't got to it yet. The bottom of all this."

We ride in silence for a mile or so, and three cars pass us in that time. We're not far from the eastern edge of Bienville. Before I can even filter my thought, I say, "Paul never suspected that Kevin might not be his?"

Jet turns to me, and this time I see something in her eyes that's hard to look at—her awareness of her husband's weakness and his potential for lethal overreaction.

"If even a germ of that thought was born in Paul's head," she says, "he would crush it. He'd kill himself before he'd admit that's the reality of our lives." She touches a finger to her lips. "Maybe that's what he's been doing all these years."

It's nearly impossible for me to believe that this has been Jet's existence for more than a decade. Since the year before my son was born, she has lived with this lie every minute of every day, knowing that at any moment Max could blow her family apart. I'm surprised she didn't kill him years ago. Or herself.

"I don't know how you've stood the stress."

She sits back in her seat and exhales slowly. "I'm not sure I have. What do they call people like me in war? Walking wounded?"

"Did Max ever let you forget about it?"

She stares into an invisible void between us, the way I saw guys in war zones do after getting bad news from home. "Honestly? For the first eight or nine years, it was fine. Max kept his distance. And Kevin was such a gift that he accomplished the impossible. You know how people say babies can't save a marriage? They don't know what they're talking about. Kevin was literally Paul's salvation. He *redeemed* us."

I recall the miraculous effect my own son had upon me. He was the only tonic that ever eased my grief for my brother. "Believe it or not, I understand."

"I know you do."

She reaches out and takes my hand again. We're in the periphery of Bienville. There are more cars on the road, and I see the first highway lights a half mile ahead. "When did Max start to change?"

"It's hard to say. About three years ago I really started to notice. The more he aged—or the more Sally aged, really—the more attention he started paying to Kevin. And to me. You know women age faster than men. Sally was beautiful, but you can only turn the clock back so far. Max still lives like he's forty."

"The son of a bitch could pass for ten years younger than he is."

"Oh, he's starting to creak a little. He feels the reaper out there in the dark. But during those good years, Max coached Kevin's athletic teams, taught him to hunt—all the things Kevin loves doing now. I didn't realize then what the result of that would be. Max was stealing Kevin from Paul. I'm not kidding. That damned traveling baseball team has taken over their lives. Kevin lives for it. This past year and a half, I've watched Max become more obsessed every month. He *wants* that boy. He wants to be his father. To *live* as his father."

"And he wants you."

Jet nods with what looks like desperation.

A terrifying thought has risen from a dark place in my mind. "Do you think Max has ever thought about trying to get Paul out of the way?"

In the light of the dashboard, I see something chilling in her eyes. "I don't think he's thought of much else for the past year. He said it out loud tonight. He didn't talk about killing Paul. But setting him up in Dallas or Atlanta with a new business and all the money he could ever need."

"Without Kevin or you? Max is crazy if he thinks Paul would ever do that."

Jet looks back at me like someone grieving a death that hasn't happened yet. "He would tell Paul the truth first. To drive him away."

"Push him to suicide, you mean."

She closes her eyes. "That's a short push."

As I wrap my mind around this potential nightmare, a new question comes to me. "If Max had this to hang over your head all this time, why didn't he use it to extort sex from you?"

An eerie laugh echoes off the window glass. "He didn't need me. He had plenty of women back then. And he cared about Kevin way too much to risk messing that up. I think he sensed that if he pestered me that way, he'd destabilize the situation. So he screwed other women and made sure he always had access to Kevin."

"But now . . . ?"

Jet's jaw tightens. "Now it's different."

"I honestly don't see how this situation ends without violence."

When she speaks again, I feel like she's talking to herself as much as to me. "He's been watching me for months. Stalking me, practically. After you and I got back together . . . it was like he could smell you on me. He sensed I was sexually active again. I could feel his eyes on me all the time, even when Sally and Paul were around."

"And you think Sally never saw that?"

"I'm sure she noticed him ogling my ass. But he does that to any woman with a figure. That doesn't necessarily lead to the secret."

"So when Max saw you and me on the patio—"

"He lost it." She takes hold of my wrist. "Seriously, I think he wants to kill you."

"He covered his hatred pretty well at my house yesterday."

"Of course! He's a consummate liar. A *natural* liar. Not a pathological one, because he doesn't lie for the pleasure of it. He lies to get what he wants."

We've entered Bienville proper now. Convenience stores and service stations drift past on either side of the Ford. As we shunt down the dark vein of Cemetery Road, the essential reality of this nightmare finally comes home to me. *Kevin Matheson is Max's son.* Jet's dream that she and I would move away from here and set up a new life in Washington with Kevin was never more than that. A fantasy.

"I always thought Paul was the obstacle to us being together," I say softly. "But if you took Kevin away from this town, Max would hunt us to the ends of the earth."

She answers with solemn intensity. "That's why I hope he dies back there. I hope Warren Lacey tries to save him without going to a hospital, and he dies of a brain bleed."

As more buildings close in around us, Jet says, "Do you want to wash your hands of all this? Of me?"

Instead of answering, I reach for her hand. As I do, my iPhone rings. It takes me a few seconds to get it out, but when I do, I see the caller is my mother. A pulse of fear goes through me, and I remember my father lying helpless in his bed last night.

"Mom?" I say, trying not to betray my anxiety.

"It's me, Marshall."

Something in her voice sets off every alarm in my brain. "What is it? Dad?"

"He's in the hospital. Don't worry, he's not dead. But he's had a heart attack. A severe one."

Sensing my distress, Jet reaches out and grips my knee.

"When did it happen?" I ask.

"About an hour ago. Jack Kirby came by the house after work. He tried to convince Duncan to be admitted to the cardiac unit, just as a precaution. But you know your father. He wouldn't hear of it. I begged, but he just wouldn't go."

"That's not your fault, Mom. Everybody knows how hardheaded he is."

"I don't know. Anyway, about eight thirty he got short of breath, and then the pain started in his back. High up. I called an ambulance. He was unconscious by the time they reached the hospital. Jack's been up here ever since, tending to him. They've used some kind of device to put him into hypothermia, to reduce the chance of brain damage. And they've induced a coma as well."

I suppress the urge to say "My God," but it's clear that Dad is in critical condition.

"They've done enzyme tests, of course," Mom goes on, "but those take time. Jack's sure it was a major heart attack, and he says Duncan's heart failure is worse. He's got a lot of fluid buildup."

"I'm sorry, Mom. I'll come straight there."

"I want to tell you something," she says, and I hear her voice crack. A single sob comes down the line, and my throat goes tight. I know what it costs her to break down in front of me. "Right up until it happened," she goes on, "he was talking about you getting out a newspaper tomorrow. He was so excited. He'd talked to Aaron at the barn three or four times. Ben Tate, too. It seems like everybody's pitching in. Duncan was more excited than I've seen him in years. Today was just too much for him. He felt like he'd let us all down."

"I know. He's going to see that newspaper tomorrow. You hang tough. I'm on my way."

"Hurry, Marshall."

I click END and hit the gas hard.

"Your dad?" Jet asks.

"Major heart attack. I don't think he has very long."

"I'll go with you."

"You can't. Not after tonight. Where's your car?"

"My law office."

"I'll run you there first."

"Don't be crazy! It's too far out of your way. Drop me somewhere on the way, and I'll have somebody pick me up and take me to my car."

"Who?"

"My paralegal. If Josh can't do it, I'll get somebody else."

"With Max's gun?"

Jet's eyes go wide. "And the hammer. Shit, I forgot about that."

As my eyes register where we are, a simple answer hits me. "We're about to come to that turn where the railroad tracks come together.

Roll down your window, and when we get there, throw it all down into the gully. There's nothing but kudzu and rattlesnakes down there. Nobody's ever going to find anything."

"Are you sure?"

"Wipe them on your pants leg just in case. For prints. Hurry."

"Max's phone, too?"

"No, keep the phone. Hide it when you get home."

Jet reaches down for the hammer and wipes it on her pants leg. Then the gun. Twenty seconds later, we enter the turn where my father's first family slid into eternity. I see no other headlights, no pedestrians on the road.

"Do it!"

Jet hurls the hardware through the window while our tires judder over the railroad iron. I don't hear any impact noise.

"Did you make the gully?"

"Yep. They're gone."

Four blocks past the turn, I pull into a black pool of shadow against the curb. Instead of getting out, Jet turns and takes my face in her hands. Hers is a mosaic of dried tears and mascara.

"I never wanted to lie to you," she says, looking deep into my eyes. "I love you."

"I know. I love you, too. Where will you say you've been?"

"My office, I guess."

I wrap my arms around her, hard enough to hurt, then kiss her ear and neck and hair with frantic urgency. Despite all she told me tonight, her skin and hair taste exactly the same. She smells the same. Most of all, her eyes still shine with life. After she shivers against me for a few seconds, I release her, and she vanishes into the dark. When I shift into Drive and press the pedal to the floor, blood suffuses my muscles, and a wild compulsion fills my chest. If I see blue lights behind me, I will not stop.

I must see my father while he still lives.

CHAPTER 40

MY FATHER WAS still in a coma when I reached the intensive care unit. Dr. Kirby and our local cardiologist had used a device called the Arctic Sun to put him into hypothermia, and a propofol-induced coma was part of their protocol. By circulating cold water through pads affixed to the thighs and torso, the Arctic Sun can prevent brain damage from insufficient blood flow. The ICU only allows visitors for fifteen minutes out of every hour, so we've set up a temporary camp in the waiting room. Right now Mom is in with Dad, having given me the first ten minutes of this quarter hour.

After my first silent visit with him, I rode out to Dixie Allman's house to get my Flex back. She'd lost her shift at the Show 'n' Tail and wasn't happy about it. I gave her a hundred bucks as compensation, but she still griped about having to take her Explorer back so soon. As I pulled out of her driveway, Denny ran up to my window and knocked. He'd been proud to see his photos in the *Watchman,* and while his mother has forbidden him from doing any more filming for the paper, he hopes to keep helping out on Buck's murder case. I told him I'd call him if I needed aerial support.

Back at the hospital, I found Nadine in the ICU waiting room with a food basket and a big steel thermos. As soon as she'd learned about Dad's plight, she'd run by her bookstore and gathered up muffins, sandwiches, and coffee. The Bienville General Hospital has no food available after hours, other than vending-machine crap, so Nadine made sure we would want for nothing. I told her she didn't have to stay, but she planted herself beside me on the plastic couch and started reading Twitter and Instagram like she meant to stay all night.

After a while, she asked me about the closing of the *Watchman*, which is apparently the talk of the town. Though she didn't know the inside story, she knew enough to guess that my deal with the Poker Club was never consummated. After some reflection, I told her that Ben Tate was working on getting out a newspaper tomorrow, one that would at least wound some Poker Club members. When her face betrayed concern, I confessed that I'd avoided telling her ahead of time because I knew how she felt about risking the loss of the paper mill. While she thought about that, I described how Arthur Pine shut down the paper and fired our staff, and the effect that had on my father.

"Hit them back," she said flatly. "Jab them with a sharp stick and let them know they're mortal. They have to obey the rules like everybody else, or they go down."

"I thought you'd try to talk me out of it."

She shrugged. "I don't want Bienville to lose the mill. I won't lie about that. But I don't see why taking down some corrupt assholes has to destroy the whole deal. Is the story you're running tomorrow going to hurt Azure Dragon directly?"

"Nothing they can't survive. There was something in the PDF file that hinted at a quid pro quo between Azure Dragon and Senator Sumner—or that's how I read it—but I told Ben to hold that back until we know more. I'm hoping my source will flesh that out with the next delivery. If there is another delivery."

"What alias did you say the source used?"

"Mark Felt."

She looked as though she were trying to recall the name of a song playing on the radio. "Was he one of the Watergate burglars?"

"No, he was Deep Throat, Bob Woodward's secret source."

"Right. Got it." She shook her head, a wicked smile on her face. "Man, oh, man, when that trail camera photo of Beau Holland with Buck hits tomorrow, Beau's going to lose it. He'll be truly desperate. He won't know who he can trust. I'd love to be there when he opens that paper."

We've sat in companionable silence for a while since that conversation, Nadine reading a novel on her phone while I text back and forth with Ben about tomorrow's stories. When a woman of about seventy walks in and sits in a shiny brown chair on the opposite side of the waiting room, Nadine leans close and whispers, "So Ben Tate is editing this issue alone?"

"He's *writing* it alone, for the most part. Building the pages, everything. I'm just giving him a little guidance. I may read the stories before he sends out the final file, but I trust Ben. All but the front page we're contracting to a paper in a nearby city."

"Why not the front page? Legal issues?"

"Bingo. My dad's old press men are trying to run off a front page with the original *Watchman* masthead, but I don't know how much luck they're having. If they succeed, we're somehow going to have to recruit a crew to wrap that page around the main issue, as well as deliver the papers before sunup."

"That sounds like a lot of work. How many papers?"

"Our normal run is seven thousand. But we're going to try for ten thousand tomorrow and just throw them at every house. To hell with the subscriber list."

Nadine looks intrigued. "That sounds like something I could help with, organizing some of that. Or grunt work, whatever. I know how to fold."

"Would you really?"

She smiles. "Sure. I can do whatever those guys need, plus keep you up to speed, since you'll be stuck here."

"I've got to say, I'm surprised."

She laughs. "Hey, I may be pragmatic, but I won't stand by while a bunch of Daddy Warbucks–types subvert the free press."

I can't help but smile. After giving her Ben Tate's contact info, I text Ben that Nadine will be calling him and that he should trust her. While she walks down the hall to talk to Ben out of earshot of the other visitor, I lean back on the hard plastic sofa and wonder how Jet fared tonight. How long did it take her to get a ride to her Volvo? To get home to Paul and Kevin? She hasn't texted me, so I'm guessing things must be tense over there. I'll probably have to wait until tomorrow to get any answers.

My watch shows thirty minutes until my next ICU visit. They've obviously let Mom overstay her allotted time, unless she's in the restroom. I'm so dazed by all that Jet told me on Parnassus Hill that I've found myself focusing on other things, however painful. The last ten minutes I spent in the ICU were nothing like the sixty seconds that Mom left me alone with Dad last night. Last night I could have nudged him awake, brought him back to the present, into the flow of human existence. But standing over him tonight, I knew that if I nudged him, nothing would happen. He's sedated, yes, but he was unconscious when the paramedics brought him in, and Dr. Kirby made it clear to me that he might never wake up. How can it be that only this morning, I called Dad and got a long, well-reasoned answer about why he never went after the Poker Club in print? Tonight he can't even hear my questions. I fear that my mother's dream of Dad and me having a cathartic conversation, one in which forgiveness is at least a possibility, is receding to the unreachable horizon of might-have-been. It may not be too late, of course. But it *feels* too late.

Looking up and down the hall, I see no sign of either Nadine or my mother. Left in relative solitude, I allow the thoughts I've held at bay for the past couple of hours to rush in. Jet revealed life-altering facts back on that hill. Kevin's true paternity was a revelation of such magnitude that a few hours can't possibly suffice to work through all the implications. I can scarcely get my mind around the idea that Jet's been hiding a rape for thirteen years. And not a rape by a stranger, or even an acquaintance, but a family member—one who raped her when she was an adult. Not only an adult, I remind myself, but an *attorney*. Moreover, she's been raising the child of that rape *while the rapist is involved with him*. Everything I know about Jet tells me she wouldn't be able to do that. And yet . . . she has.

The oldest human failing is to assume we know everything about those we love. We may well know more than anyone else on earth about a person. But even if we know 99 percent of their thoughts and history, the remaining unknowns could shatter everything we believe about them. Yet what did Jet's revelations prove? That I don't know her at all? Or that she's as human as the rest of us? I'm certainly guilty of having idealized her. The girl I knew at fourteen could never have survived unchanged through adulthood. Besides, nothing Jet told me implicates her in any way. Max is the villain in that horror story. And yet . . . as I think of her now, a small aberration has appeared in the lens of my perception. The cause of it must be the one question Jet couldn't answer: After Max raped her, but before she knew she was pregnant, why didn't she leave? Throw a bag into the back of her car and run for her life—

"Marshall?"

I jump in my seat.

Nadine walks around from behind me. "People are up in arms about the closing of the *Watchman*," she says excitedly, though in a low voice. Glancing over at the woman in the chair, she sits close to me on the sofa. "I talked to a friend of mine after I spoke to Ben. You'd think people would be glad the paper closed, given how angry they were at Buck, not to mention your dad's anti-Trump editorials. But there seems to be a groundswell of anger about losing the paper. Sympathy for your father, maybe? The black community's especially angry. Alderman Washington went on the radio and tore into the Poker Club right on the air."

"Really?"

"They're supporting the coroner in a big way. Daring the supervisors to try to unseat him. Somebody on Facebook said that come November, the black community may surprise their old-line leaders, the ones who sold out to the Poker Club, and try to elect some new blood."

"Maybe," I murmur. "More likely they'll wait until the paper mill is built and they've gotten all the jobs they can."

Nadine sighs wearily. "You're a buzz kill."

"What else did Ben say?"

"Your dad's press men can use me out at the"—she glances at the woman sitting ten feet away from us—"the place. They've recruited a bunch of teenagers from a church to fold the front page and drive the routes. Literally choirboys and -girls. They need food and drinks and supplies from Walmart."

"Ben thinks they can really do that front page?"

"He seems to. He's fired up." She drops her voice to a nearly inaudible level. "The main printing in Natchez is all set. They're going to run it off about one A.M. Ben's going to pick up the papers himself in a borrowed truck."

"I sure hope the Poker Club doesn't get wind of this. I can see Tommy Russo's guys hijacking Ben's load between there and here. That's a dark highway."

"How many people know this is going on?" Nadine asks.

"I'm not sure. The number's obviously growing."

"Don't worry. Before long it'll be too late for anybody to stop it." Nadine gets to her feet, then takes my arm and pulls me thirty feet down the hall. "Tomorrow's going to be a historic day. People are going to look outside and find a *Watchman* in their driveways when they weren't expecting one. And you're going to be able to take it into that ICU and show your dad."

Even after today's wretched events, her boundless optimism proves infectious. "I've got to admit, that seems like a pretty good prospect right now. You know what I really wish, though?"

"Tell me."

"That I could get the paper back from those bastards."

Nadine nods thoughtfully. "Maybe you can."

"How?"

"Find out who your source is—Mark Felt or whoever—and get the rest of Sally's cache. Then you'd have the Poker Club by the balls. You could demand anything you want."

Something warm stirs in my breast. "*That's* worth working on."

"I'd say. What would Buckman and his buddies have to give you to keep you from printing that cache?"

Something feels wrong about her question, or maybe her tone. "When you put it like that . . . it seems like a messed-up thing to do. To cut a deal with the devil."

Nadine shakes her head. "You've got to get over this choirboy complex. Don't you remember what I said? Most people sell their souls a piece at a time. Whatever they get in exchange, it's lost forever. You do this right, you're going to sell yours for a record price. You can change the world—or at least your little corner of it. I told you once before: you don't destroy a village in order to save it."

In the silence that follows this exchange, my iPhone rings. To my surprise, it's Jet. Why would she call my iPhone and not the burner she bought me? A nightmare image of Paul discovering her burner and grinding it up in the garbage disposal rises in my mind. Or, worse, him finding it and calling the speed-dial number programmed into it. I click my iPhone but say nothing.

"Marshall?" says Jet. "Are you there?"

"I'm here. Are you okay? Are you home?"

"No, I'm at the hospital. Kevin's with me. We wanted to pay our respects to your father. I know we can't get into the ICU, but I want your mom to know we care. I also need to talk to you about the Ferris murder. Can you meet me in the lobby?"

I look at my watch. "Um—"

"Like right now."

Something's wrong. "Uh, sure. I may have to come unlock the front door for you."

"We're already inside."

I look at Nadine in puzzlement. "Okay. Listen, Nadine is here. She brought us food and coffee. I'm going to bring her out to sit with Kevin, if she will. We don't want him hearing a bunch of stuff about his father's friends."

"That's a good idea, if she would."

"We'll see you in a sec."

As I slip my phone back into my pocket, Nadine says, "Jet?"

"Yeah. She sounded weird. She needs to talk to me about Buck."

"I'm happy to sit with Kevin. He's been in my store plenty of times, buying books from his school reading list."

"I appreciate it."

She gives me a smile, but it looks forced. "We should take the snacks. He's twelve, right?"

"Right," I reply, trying not to think of the conversation I had with Jet only hours ago. *And his grandfather is his father—*

As Nadine and I walk down the corridor toward the lobby, she says, "What are the chances that Jet could be your secret source?"

"Zero. She'd tell me if she had Sally's cache."

"Would she? She seems like a good choice. Sally was her mother-in-law, and Jet's an attorney."

"I know, but . . ." An image of Sally's sapphire necklace comes to me. "They had a complicated relationship. Jet doesn't have the cache."

"Well. You'd know, I'm sure."

THERE'S A SECURITY GUARD in the hospital lobby, but he's kicked back in a Naugahyde chair reading *Sports Illustrated* and paying no attention to the mother and son standing by the unattended reception desk. Kevin sights us first. He perks up his head, then nudges Jet, who turns to us with a face so pale that my ears start to pulse. She looks more agitated than she did after smashing a hammer into Max's skull.

Nadine instantly picks up on the tension. She steps forward and extends her hand to Jet with an odd formality. Jet squeezes it lightly, a tight smile on her face.

"Anybody hungry?" Nadine asks, offering Kevin a raspberry muffin.

"Thanks," the boy says in a restrained voice, and takes the fist-sized treat. "I always get these at the bookstore."

"How's your season going?" I ask, trying not to look for Max's features in his young face.

"We're doing pretty good. Nineteen and one, so far."

"Wow. You play, what, second base?"

"Pitcher now."

"On a Bienville traveling team?"

"Nah. The local teams are too diluted now. Too many dads with money. I play on a major league team out of Baton Rouge. That's one level above triple-A."

I glance at Jet, who's clearly waiting for her son to finish so that she can talk to me. "Major league, huh? At twelve? You must be pretty good."

He blushes a little. "I do a'ight."

Having paid sufficient court to Kevin, I ask him to excuse his mother and me for a couple of minutes. Kevin doesn't look too put out at being left with Nadine.

I lead Jet to the automatic doors and wait for them to slide open. I can almost sense her heart pounding. Beyond the doors, the sidewalk recedes into a circle of black asphalt designed for easy entry and egress by wheelchairs. A few shrubs line the circle, apparently to give visitors and employees a place to throw their cigarette butts. We walk out into the industrial glow of sodium-vapor streetlamps, moving far enough from the building for privacy, but remaining within sight of Kevin and Nadine, who are visible through a large picture window with its blinds turned open.

"Where's Paul?" I ask in a low voice. "What's happened?"

"Paul's in the ER."

This can only be bad news. "Is he hurt?"

"No. Don't react when I say this, okay? Be stone cold. *Max* is in the ER. He's the patient. Paul's here for Max. And he could be watching us right now."

CHAPTER 41

JET MIGHT AS well have sucker-punched me in the throat. "Dr. Lacey must have figured he'd die without emergency care," I reason, glancing back at the hospital entrance. "Turn your back to the doors, so I can watch for Paul over your shoulder without being obvious."

Jet turns until I have a clear line of sight to the main doors without moving my head.

"Has Max said anything about the attack?"

"I have no idea. I don't know if he can even talk. Two doctors are working on him now, and they've called the helicopter to take him to Jackson."

"Oh, man. Have you been alone with Paul?"

Jet looks like she's gritting her teeth hard enough to crush a stone. "Not since we got here. He was drunk when I got home, and he drank some more after. We only got the call a half hour ago. I was going to leave Kevin with Tallulah, but she wasn't in her house or Max's. She didn't answer her phone, either. Marshall, I have no idea what to do. What if Max accuses me of trying to kill him?"

"He won't. He'd have to explain too much."

"What if he doesn't care anymore? What if he's ready to blow everything up? The whole family?"

"Jet, he can't. It just hit me: Max can't implicate you in this assault—he can't even use the video he shot of us. It's all a bluff."

"What are you talking about?"

"You've got the nuclear option in this war, not him. If he comes at you with *anything,* you can charge him with rape. Kevin is living proof of his guilt."

Jet opens her mouth, but no sound emerges. Her eyes seem to dilate, as though the prospect of escape from Max's power has intoxicated her. But then she shakes her head. "That's a weapon I can never use. It would destroy Kevin. And Paul."

"I'm not saying you use it first. Or ever. I'm saying it's a deterrent. A neutron bomb. If Max believes you'll use it, then he can't hurt you. Not without hurting himself worse."

She's breathing harder. "I'll lose that game, Marshall. Max can stand more pain than I can. Not me, but . . . you know. I can't watch Kevin suffer through that."

I want to hold her close and comfort her, but I can't do it out here. Looking over her shoulder at the brightly lit hospital entrance, I see Nadine and Kevin sitting on a couch just inside the big glass doors.

"Max isn't going to say anything. It'll be just like when you stabbed him with the steak knife. But *if he does,* you only have one play. And you can't hesitate. Max tried to rape you tonight—you defended yourself. You fought for your life, and not for the first time. Tell Paul about the stab wound. Max will still have a scar from that. Tell Paul you kept all this from him because you didn't want to destroy the family. But now Max has lost his mind. He killed Sally, and now he's obsessed with you."

"I think I'm going to puke," Jet says, looking back at the lighted doors. "Seriously, I can't get my breath."

"You're having a panic attack. Try to breathe slowly. You've been under massive pressure for a decade. You kept an explosive secret all that time. Now you feel it's on the verge of coming out. That kind of stress kills people. It can also make them do self-destructive things. Stay in control, Jet. Stay ahead of Max. Know what you're going to do, whatever move he makes. You're twice as smart as he is."

She's nodding, trying to get her composure back. "As soon as I got home tonight, I showered and changed clothes. I thought about destroying the ones I was wearing on the hill, but in the end I just washed them."

"That might not get the blood off, if you had any splatter on you."

"Okay. I'll burn them. I also destroyed Max's cell phone. I couldn't hack his password, and I didn't want to risk being caught with it."

"Good. I still have some hope the video was on that phone."

"Me, too. Oh, when I was in the ER, I looked through his personal effects for his second phone and didn't find it. Turns out a nurse had already given it to Paul."

"Was it a Samsung, too?"

"I haven't seen it yet. I'm afraid to ask. But if I can somehow get hold of it tonight, I will." She reaches up to her neck, takes hold of a slim chain, and lifts Sally's sapphire pendant from beneath her top.

"You're wearing a fifty-thousand-dollar necklace around town?"

"This is our good-luck charm. Sally left these passwords for me. When I find whatever they open, we'll be able to save ourselves. I'm betting it's Max's other phone."

"Two passwords for a phone?"

"The second could be for a program on the phone."

"Jet, those passwords could be years old."

"No," she says, unshakable faith in her eyes. "The sticker is new, clean and white." She flips the sapphire so that I can see the bright paper, then tucks the pendant back beneath her blouse.

"Don't take stupid risks to get that phone. Let's see how Max plays this—if he lives."

We stand in the sodium-yellow glow like refugees, a desperate couple with nowhere to run. "I'm so sorry you had to find out about Max," she says. "This isn't what you signed up for."

"I signed up for *you*. Okay? Remember that, no matter what happens tonight. I wish I could hug you."

She looks afraid to believe me.

"Oh, I forgot," she says. "A bunch of calls came in on Max's phone before I destroyed it. Three from Beau Holland, two from Arthur Pine, one from Wyatt Cash, and one from Claude Buckman."

"All tonight? What does that suggest to you?"

"Trouble inside the Poker Club. Think about it. Who leaked you that picture of Beau Holland and Dave Cowart with Buck? A lot of people hate Beau, even in the club. Maybe he's scared the club will throw him to the wolves."

Something makes me turn and scan the parking lot. A presentiment of danger? I'm suddenly aware of the hard bulge of my pistol in the small of my back.

"What is it?" Jet asks.

"Nothing. I just felt funny for a second. Like we're being watched."

She looks over her shoulder. "I'd better get back inside. Kevin's probably wondering about this, and the helicopter will get here any minute."

"Will you go to Jackson with them?"

"Probably. To look after Kevin."

As I fight the urge to take her hand, a black city police cruiser wheels into the entry circle and parks thirty feet from us. Two cops get out: one in his twenties, the other in his forties.

"Oh, God," Jet murmurs, losing color fast. "I told you. He did it. Max told them it was me."

The cops are talking to each other across the roof of the cruiser. The older one's holding a cell phone to his ear. "No way," I say. "Take it easy. They're probably just visiting somebody in the hospital."

"You're wrong, Marshall. Max must be awake."

"If he accuses you, then you know what to do. Go nuclear. Incinerate that son of a bitch. Tell Paul everything. I'll support you in the paper, and I'll be waiting for you when the ashes clear."

Now the cops are walking our way. Even so, I feel confident. There's no way Max invited police into the middle of his family soap opera. After trying to rape the mother of his "grandchild"? Jet's back is to the cruiser, and she's standing as stiffly as someone awaiting a bullet from a firing squad.

"Are you Marshall McEwan?" asks the older cop.

"That's right."

As he comes closer, into our pool of light, I see that his name tag reads FARNER. The look on his face makes me acutely aware of the gun wedged against my skin.

"Where were you earlier tonight, sir?"

Jet closes her eyes. She's so pale that I worry she might collapse. In this moment, I realize that I'm going to lie to protect her. "Is there something I can help you with, Officer?"

"I just told you what I need from you. Your whereabouts earlier tonight."

"I've been at the hospital for quite a while. My father had a massive coronary."

"Before that."

Jet opens her eyes, and I see confusion in them.

"I was at my home."

"Can anybody corroborate that?"

Jet nods almost imperceptibly, by which I gather she means for me to use her as an alibi. But I don't want to go that way unless there's no other option. Glancing left, I see Nadine standing at the big lighted window thirty yards away, her face a dark oval against the glass. Kevin Matheson stands just behind her, a cell phone pressed to his ear.

"Officer, do I need to consult an attorney?"

The big cop ignores my question. "I just left the emergency room, where Mr. Max Matheson informed me that you assaulted him with a hammer. He has a skull fracture. That's aggravated assault, which is a felony. You need to come down to the station with us to straighten this out."

Jet's mouth falls open. "Wha—wait," she stammers. "Where and when did this assault supposedly occur?"

"Let it go," I tell her, realizing this could end in worse ways than me under arrest. My first priority is finding a way to tell them about my gun without getting killed. "I'm happy to go to the station with you and sort this out."

"Step out of the way, ma'am," says Officer Farner.

Jet doesn't move. "I happen to be Mr. McEwan's attorney. Where and when did this alleged assault occur?"

"Parnassus Hill, if it's any business of yours. Now, step *back*, lady. That's your last warning."

"Do you know who I am?"

Farner laughs. "Yeah, I know. Princess Muckety-Muck. And I got a news flash for you. Tonight it don't make a fuck."

An alarm goes off deep in my medulla. Did Farner just announce that Jet's protection has been withdrawn?

"Parnassus Hill is outside the jurisdiction of the city police," she points out.

The officer heaves a heavy sigh. "We'll call the sheriff's department on the way to the station, and they can take custody there." Farner turns to me, his eyes weary but belligerent. "Marshall McEwan, I'm placing you under arrest for aggravated assault. Put your hands behind your back."

Jet shakes her head in disbelief. "That's absurd. My client is innocent. He wasn't even there."

"How do you know that?" asks the younger cop. "Were you with
him?"

"Did Max say I was with him?"

"Jet, let it go," I plead. "You can't stop this."

Farner turns back to the younger cop. "Floyd? Cuff him."

"Hands behind your back," barks the younger cop. "You have the
right to remain silent. Anything you—"

"Turn off that camera!" yells Officer Farner.

Nadine is walking swiftly across the asphalt circle with her iPhone
held in front of her. "This isn't Russia yet," she retorts. "I don't see a
body cam on you, and I can film anything I please."

"You can't do this!" Jet snaps, taking a step toward Farner.

"Mrs. Matheson," he says, "both you women are interfering with an
officer in the performance of his duties."

"I'm doing no such thing. This is bullshit."

"Public profanity, Floyd," Farner says. "Add that to her list."

"Jet, please," I implore.

She's not hearing me. Jet is obviously racked with guilt that I'm being arrested for something she did. Max pulled a neat trick by accusing
me rather than her. It gets him lifesaving medical care without bringing
Jet into the equation at all. What I want to know is my supposed motive
for assaulting Max.

"Officer," I say in the most level voice I can muster, "you'll see that
both my hands are in plain view. I need to inform you that I'm carrying
a pistol. It's in the small of my back—"

"*GUN!*" shouts Farner, whipping his automatic out of his holster
and aiming at my chest. His partner does the same, and Jet's shriek does
nothing to defuse the situation.

"*Get on the ground!*" Farner screams, moving around behind me.

This is the overreaction I feared. Most cops in this situation would
have asked me to turn around, then simply taken my gun. I spread
both empty hands wide and look into Nadine's cell phone. "I'm about
to comply with—"

"*NOW! FACE DOWN! BOTH HANDS ABOVE YOUR HEAD!*"

As I kneel in preparation to lie down, Jet says, "Officer, my client voluntarily informed you that he is armed, and he poses no threat to—"

Planting his tactical boot between my shoulder blades, Farner kicks me flat. The impact knocks the breath from my lungs. "Cuff him, Floyd."

The younger cop slaps his handcuffs around my wrists, then yanks my pistol from my belt.

"Whoa! This is fancy. Is this a Luger?"

"Hey!" Jet yells. "What the hell is wrong with you guys?"

"I warned you, Princess," Farner says, throwing up a beefy arm and shoving her three feet backward.

"That's assault!" Nadine shouts. "I'm an attorney, and that was assault."

"Fuck this," Farner mutters. "Arrest 'em all."

Gasping for air, I look up to see Jet fly at the big cop like a wildcat. He looks stunned to be attacked by a woman, but his partner's already got his Taser out.

"Jet, stop!" Nadine shouts. *"Let go of him!"*

Jet breaks contact with the cop, but when she sees the younger cop aiming his weapon at her, she says, "You're going to tase me? Go ahead. Look right in the camera while you do it."

She's lost it. After fearing arrest for hours, seeing me arrested in her place has pushed her over the edge.

"Cuff these bitches, too," Farner says, pointing at Jet. "Her first."

The young cop takes the cuffs from Farner's belt and moves behind Jet.

"Hey!" yells a male voice from the direction of the hospital. *"Hey, that's my wife!"*

Looking left, I see Paul charging across the asphalt from the hospital doors, Kevin trailing behind him. Paul may be forty-seven and drunk, but he's an intimidating sight with his head and shoulders lowered the way they used to be when he hammered running backs as a strong safety. I hope the cops don't shoot him out of reflex.

"Stay back, Paul!" the older cop yells. "You don't want none of this."

"You boys need to stand down," Paul drawls, stopping five yards short of us. "What the hell's going on out here, Jerry? Why's that kid trying to handcuff my wife?"

"She was interfering with our arrest," says the young cop.

Paul grins good-naturedly, but I see anger in his eyes. "She's a lawyer, son. That's what lawyers do."

"She assaulted Office Farner."

"Over what?"

Farner steps closer to Paul. "Me arresting the asshole your daddy says hit him in the head with a hammer."

"Ahh," Paul says in a knowing tone. "Yeah, she gets a little defensive about this particular asshole. Takes things a little *personally* where he's concerned."

I try to catch Paul's eye, but he's taking pains to avoid my gaze.

"You need to get back inside," Farner tells him. "You've obviously had a few."

Paul grins. "More than a few. But that's my normal state, brother. I'm a high-functioning drunk, like Marshall's daddy. But now it looks like mine may beat his to the cemetery."

"Can I get up now?" I cough.

"Slowly," says the young cop. "Damn slowly."

As I struggle to my knees, Farner says, "Mr. McEwan, do you have a concealed-carry permit?"

"Mississippi's an open-carry state," Jet declares.

"Stay out of this, Jet," Paul snaps.

I get carefully to my feet.

"Answer the question," Farner orders.

"No, I don't have that permit."

"Well, I don't see a belt holster. Was the gun in plain view when you walked out of the hospital?"

"It was," Jet says quickly. "I asked him to get it out. I didn't feel safe."

"Goddamn it," Paul mutters. "Would you shut up?"

Jet's head snaps up as though he slapped her.

Farner laughs. "Something tells me you're being less than honest, lady. Well, security tapes will tell us. Mr. McEwan, I'm adding carrying a concealed weapon to your charges." He turns to his partner. "Get him in the car, Floyd. I'll call backup for these other two."

"Bullshit you will," Paul says in a low voice.

Knowing Paul's explosive temper, I try to distract him. "Why am I supposed to have assaulted Max, Paul? What was my motive?"

His head turns slowly from Farner to me, and even the cops seem to be waiting to hear his answer. "You accused him of killing Buck Ferris."

This is the last answer I expected, but it makes sense.

"When Pop denied it," Paul goes on, "you accused him of killing my mother. Supposedly because she wouldn't give him an alibi for the night Buck died."

This is no place to argue Max's lies. For the moment I have to be satisfied that Max turned Paul's focus away from Jet.

"That sounds like you, doesn't it, Goose?" Paul says, stepping closer to me. "You gonna deny it?"

I can smell the alcohol from two feet away. "Nobody here is interested in my denial."

"Imagine that. You know, I've kept my distance tonight because Duncan's close to dying. That's what they said in the ER. But I want to hear you deny what you did to Pop."

Something in Paul's eyes doesn't look right. It isn't just the alcohol. He's not all there. I fight the urge to glance at Jet. Something tells me she's about to confess to being Max's assailant.

"Let's get this show on the road," Farner says, obviously more than a little worried about Paul.

"Backup's on the way," says the younger cop.

It's only because I know Paul so well that I sense his punch coming in time to duck. He still manages to clip my skull above the ear, and white light explodes through my brain. When my vision returns, I find myself lying on my back, staring up into the streetlight, my cuffed hands crushed beneath my pelvis.

"Goddamn it!" Farner bellows. "That's it! Get back, Paul, or I'll arrest your ass, too! What the hell's wrong with this family?"

As Paul stands over me, panting from exertion, the sound of helicopter blades cutting the air rolls over us, growing louder by the second. That distinctive *whup-whup-whup* always carries an overtone of Vietnam, but especially tonight, given the passenger that this medevac chopper has been summoned to carry.

"That's Max's ride to UMC," Paul says. "Jet, come on with me."

"Uh-uh," Farner says. "Not this time. The lady stays."

Paul looks at the cop, then runs his tongue around behind his bottom lip. He points at me. "There's your outlaw, Jerry. Attempted murder. My wife's just a little high-strung tonight. You know how that is."

"We're taking her in," Farner says doggedly, glancing over at Nadine, who's still filming.

"Nadine, turn off that camera," Paul says.

Nadine hesitates, but Jet nods at her.

As soon as Nadine lowers her cell phone, Farner says, "Look, man, if you don't like it, call Mr. Buckman."

Max's umbrella of protection for his daughter-in-law has definitely been removed. I don't think Paul's ever experienced this kind of resistance from Bienville cops. He sighs, looks at the ground for a few seconds, then steps within two inches of Officer Farner. In a voice so low as to be nearly inaudible, he says, "I'll tell you how this is gonna go, Jerry. You can take Marshall there straight down to the pokey, but my wife and son are coming to Jackson with me."

Farner stiffens and tries to step back, but Paul catches his arm and holds him close. The young cop clearly has no idea what to do.

"If they *don't*," Paul goes on, "you're gonna be calling Roto-Rooter to fish your balls out of your septic tank. After I flush 'em down the toilet."

Pale with anger, Farner lays his hand on the butt of his gun.

"Last thing you'll ever do," Paul says, never taking his eyes from the cop's face. "Badge or no badge, I swear to God."

Farner leaves his hand on his pistol for a few face-saving seconds, then pivots away from Paul, catches hold of my arm, and drags me toward the cruiser's back door. The young cop jumps forward and opens it for him.

"We'll have you out first thing in the morning," Jet promises me.

"You leave that to Nadine," Paul says.

As Farner's big hand clamps down on top of my skull and forces me into the stinking backseat, it comes home to me just how dangerous Paul is. He just told a cop—in front of witnesses—that he'd beat the hell out of him if he disobeyed Paul's order. And rather than wait for backup and arrest Paul, both cops decided to let it go.

Not the guy whose wife you want to sleep with . . .

"How you like it back there, Mr. Newspaperman?" asks Farner.

The reality of spending the night in a cell at the mercy of the Poker

Club is settling over me. But not even that can bury the epiphany that hits me behind the metal mesh separating me from these fine officers of the law. Paul didn't slug me because he thinks I hit his father with a hammer. Paul *hates* his father. He hit me because at some level he knows that, despite my denial earlier today, I am sleeping with his wife. He may not know that he knows . . . but he does.

"Hey," Farner goes on as the squad car leaves the parking lot. "A week ago I'd have worried what you'd write about me in the paper. But you ain't *got* no newspaper anymore. There ain't no more *Watchman*. Not now. And when they reopen that rag, it's gonna be under new management. Things are gonna get a little easier around here. A little *looser,* you know? Like the good old days."

I give him nothing.

"I said, how you *like* it back there, boy?"

I should keep quiet, but for the thousandth time I picture Buck being dragged from the river by incompetent deputies. He was probably killed by a guy a lot like Farner.

"How do you like being Paul Matheson's bitch?" I ask mildly.

CHAPTER 42

I'M DROWNING.

The more I gasp for air, the more water I suck down my throat. I've been blinded, and my arms are strapped to my sides. My mind is screaming, my vocal cords locked in spasm. A man is shouting in my ear, but the words make no sense. This nightmare is not happening in Afghanistan or Iraq, but in my hometown jail.

The city cops handed me over to a deputy who booked me, but I was never taken to a cell. The deputy led me, still handcuffed, to a group shower in the basement of the county jail. There I found good old Officer Farner waiting for me. City and county law enforcement usually coexist in a state of cold war, but apparently the Poker Club has the power to bring them together in common cause. Farner showed me that he had my wallet and cell phones. Then he locked me in the shower room, telling me on his way out that we were going to have a good time together soon.

An hour after he left, Farner returned with a second man wearing a hood. The new man wore jeans and a black T-shirt, not a city or county uniform. The two men used ballistic nylon straps to bind my legs, chest, and arms to the long bench. They wrapped a towel around my head and used duct tape to secure my head to the wood—to keep from bruising me, I guess. Then one of them started pouring water down my nose and mouth.

I figured I would hold my breath, but when I tried, they pulled the wet towel close over my face. I knew that when I gasped, there would be no air, and that knowledge drove the breath from my lungs and made me suck in with all my strength.

All I got was soaked cloth and water.

After ten seconds of blind panic, they stopped pouring. Until that moment, I had never understood what waterboarding was. The simplicity of the torture makes it incomprehensible to anyone who hasn't endured it. That's how life is: in the simplest things lie the greatest joy and misery. Ask any hospital patient who can't urinate or defecate without emergency catheterization or a forcible bowel evacuation. Ask someone dying of thirst the value of water.

Ask a drowning man about air.

They did it to me twice before they even asked a question. Until that moment, I believed Officer Farner was simply punishing me. But no, their process had an object. While dripping water onto the towel, a new voice said, "Where is the stuff Sally Matheson put together to blackmail her husband?"

"I don't know," I coughed, trying to place the genteel Southern accent.

"We know you have it."

"I don't! I never had it."

"You're lying. You quoted from it to Tommy Russo this morning."

"No! Somebody emailed me that. Anonymous source. You can look in my phone. Look in my phone!"

"Stop for a minute," said the voice.

Until those words, I'd existed only moment to moment.

The prospect of even temporary cessation of the pain and terror filled me with shameful gratitude. In less than two minutes I'd learned that I would betray anything I knew, everyone I loved. How could it be so easy to break a man? How could it be that some men had held out for days or weeks or months against torture? The only answer I could imagine was that there are degrees of torture. Pain is one thing; terror is another. Pain can be isolated by the mind, objectified, distanced, even befriended. Terror is a wild animal trying to claw its way out of your chest.

"Take that blindfold off," said the genteel voice.

A strong hand yanked the towel from around my head, banging the back of my skull against the bench. Beau Holland stood over me, his golfer's tan dark and rich above a salmon-colored button-down. His eyes contained a mixture of malice and pleasure, and when he smiled, his Chiclet-white porcelain veneers shone in the dim room.

"I warned you this morning," he said. "You didn't listen. Listen now. You had two phones when they brought you in."

"The email I quoted from is in my iPhone. Look at it. You'll see the sender used some high-tech anonymous program to send it. We tried to trace it, but it's impossible."

Holland nodded to the man in the hood. "What's your password?"

"Zero-five-two-seven-seven-two."

"Good boy. You don't like drowning on dry land, do you?"

"Go fuck yourself."

"I would if I could. I'd save myself a lot of time." Another smile. "What's your second phone for?"

"That isn't mine. One of the *Watchman* employees Pine fired gave it to me today."

Holland thought about that. "Who does it connect to? A source?"

"I don't know."

"I guess it's time to play again."

"Damn right," said Officer Farner, picking up the water jug.

"Not yet," said Holland. "Have you found his emails?"

The hooded man answered, "Got an email with a big PDF sent by a Mark Felt."

Holland laughed. "A source with a sense of humor. Whoever sent that is going to be giving me deep throat before they're finished."

He crouched easily beside the bench and looked into my eyes from inches away. "Am I going to have to tell them to keep going? Or are we going to have a civil conversation?"

"What do you want to know?"

"Good boy. I need one name from you, McEwan. Who did Sally Matheson give her cache to? Think hard before you answer. Because these Rhodes Scholars here are going to keep going until you tell them. You might as well start where it's going to end anyway."

"Sounds like you're trying to talk him into giving you a piece of ass," Farner muttered.

"You want severance pay with your pink slip?" Holland asked without even looking at the cop.

"No, sir. I mean, sorry, Mr. Holland."

Beau Holland raised his hand and gave my cheek two friendly

pats. "You heard my question. Now's your chance to answer. Think hard, McEwan."

Fear unlike anything I'd ever known turned my bowels to water. When I crouched in that house in Ramadi, waiting for the final insurgent assault, I never felt this. Back there, at least I had a rifle. I could do something. Even after they captured me, and I lay helpless on the kitchen table while they argued about cutting my throat, something told me that if I died, it would be because I was American. But facing Beau Holland in this stinking basement was the worst torture of all. I didn't have the information he wanted, but he believed I did—which meant that he would drown me for no reason.

"Beau, listen," I started. "I'm telling you the truth. I haven't even—"

"Wrap his head again," Holland ordered, getting to his feet. "Go till he gives me the name."

Farner laughed in anticipation of taking out his hatred of Holland on me. Then he wrapped the cold towel around my head once more, binding it to the bench. I strained my back and neck hard enough to snap ligaments, even break bones, but I couldn't evade the little cascade of water falling onto the towel.

I'M DROWNING AGAIN.

I gasp, breathe water, choke, suck in more water. A man screams questions in my ear, over and over, but I can't give him what he wants. They tip the bench to drain my windpipe, give me a few sips of air, then start again. My chest muscles burn as the animal inside claws between my heart and sternum. My brain feels like it's being squeezed out of my ears. In the epicenter of my terror, a shattering truth blooms like a silent, slow-motion explosion, answering a question that has haunted me for years—

This is what my son felt as he sank to the bottom of that swimming pool. Above him, the surface lay utterly silent, or rippled under a breeze, reflecting the muffled crystalline laughter of women's voices from inside the condo. But at the bottom my little boy endured this horror with no comprehension of what was happening to him.

He knew only that he was alone.

"*WHO SENT THIS EMAIL?*" roars the voice.

"He's not hearing you. He's out of it. Give him a second. We may have to turn him over again."

I've been plunged into the most Kafkaesque nightmare imaginable: being killed for information I don't have.

"Come on! We need to clear his trachea and sinuses!"

Someone twists my neck, and the towel is ripped away again.

"Let's lay the whole bench over this time," says the man in the hood. "He's gray."

As they take hold of the bench and tilt me left, a door opens and slams against a wall, reverberating through the tiled room.

"Sheriff Iverson says stop," says a new voice.

"Stop?" says Farner. "Why?"

"I ain't paid to ask questions like that. Sheriff says stop, you fuckin' stop. Put him in the drunk tank."

"This is absurd," Beau Holland declares. "Iverson said I should stop? Has he talked to Claude Buckman?"

"All I know is Arthur Pine is on his way to talk to this guy. Right now."

"The lawyer?" Farner asks. "That slimy bastard?"

"Judas is what he is," says Holland.

"Get that fool dried off!" yells the deputy. "Throw him in the drunk tank like the sheriff said."

ARTHUR PINE COMES TO the bars of the drunk tank alone. Even at this hour he's wearing a suit, a brown pinstripe. It's plain from his expression that he'd rather be anywhere but here. I'm sitting on a metal shelf bed jutting from the wall, and I don't get up. Ten minutes after they brought me here, I started vomiting water and stomach acid. Most of it I managed to get into the toilet hole, but the rest is on the floor.

"Say what you've got to say," I croak, and my ribs scream in protest. "I won't be getting up."

Pine watches me without saying anything.

"Your minions just waterboarded me."

"I don't know anything about that."

"Fuck you, Arthur. My father's in the hospital, probably dying, and I'm getting waterboarded by your Poker Club brownshirts."

"Then why in God's name did you hit Max with a hammer? Surely you knew something like this would happen?"

I carefully hug my ribs, trying to muffle the pain to a manageable level.

"Were you trying to get that video from him?" Pine speculates. "Seems like a waste, since we already have it."

"Do you? Because I'd be damned surprised to learn that a survivor like Max Matheson gave you his only hole card."

A flinch in Pine's face tells me my guess hit home.

"I'll let you in on a little secret," I tell him. "I don't care about Max's video. Because he can't use it."

Now I have the lawyer's attention. "Why is that?"

"Think about that tonight during sleepy time, okay?"

"If you didn't attack him to get the video, then why? Surely you don't think he really killed Buck Ferris?"

"Beau Holland killed Buck Ferris. Dave Cowart helped him. Maybe Russo, too."

Pine moves to his left, trying to make direct eye contact with me. "What's going on between you and the Matheson family? And why the hell did Sally kill herself? Or did Max kill her?"

"You don't know?"

Pine sighs in frustration. "I know that whatever's wrong at the heart of that family is tied to the cache. It wouldn't have been put together except for whatever this thing is."

I say nothing.

"Does it have something to do with you?"

"Max wouldn't tell you?"

"Max hasn't been particularly helpful."

At last I look up and smile with a confidence I don't feel. "You think I'm going to tell you things I didn't tell Holland and his waterboarding team?"

Arthur Pine looks like he's on the verge of telling me something, but he doesn't. Instead, he studies me the way he might some animal of passing interest during a forced trip to the zoo.

"How long have you guys known about Sally's cache, Arthur?"

He hesitates, then answers, probably figuring I have no way to record him. "Sally called one of us about fifteen minutes before she died. She revealed the existence of the cache at that time."

Now I'm learning something of value. "Why would she do that?"

"I think she was going to kill herself, but she wanted to make sure the cache accomplished what she wanted it to."

"Which was what? Destroy Max?"

Pine shakes his head. "No. Max knows something that would traumatize his family. Something personal—nothing business related. Sally told us we had to make sure he never reveals it. If he does, not only Max but also the members of the Poker Club will be destroyed."

At last, I think. Arthur doesn't have enough information to understand Sally's plan, but I do. At some point she must have figured out that Max had fathered his "grandson" by their daughter-in-law. Sally probably knew it was rape, but rather than confront Jet about something so uncomfortable, she decided to take things into her own hands—to make sure that neither Paul nor Kevin ever learned the truth about Kevin's paternity. By framing Max for her own murder, Sally could prevent him from playing any role in the boy's life—or, God forbid, ever getting custody of him. But Sally also knew her husband well enough to know that making Max rot in prison wouldn't necessarily silence him. To do that, she'd have to put him under perpetual fear of death. She solved that problem with ruthless elegance. By placing every member of the Poker Club at risk of imprisonment, Sally ensured that *they* would keep Max quiet.

It's a miracle they didn't kill him outright, I think, *to remove all risk of him destroying the Poker Club.*

"How," I ask Pine, "do you stop Max from revealing a secret when you don't know what the secret is?"

He smiles in appreciation of the problem. "You let him know he's one cunt hair from being dead already."

"That sounds like Tommy Russo's department."

Pine shrugs. "Tommy knows how to deliver a message."

For a time we simply look at each other, until it strikes me that Pine being here makes no sense. Surely he didn't come for a casual chat. And I was so happy to escape the shower room that I haven't bothered to ask why they stopped torturing me.

"How does this end, Arthur? What are you doing here? Why did Buckman make Beau stop torturing me?"

Pine reaches into his pocket and takes out a cigarette, then lights it and takes a drag like it's the elixir of life.

"Take it easy there, Arthur. You'll blow a lung."

"I allow myself one a day. This seems like a good time."

"So, what are you doing here?"

He takes another greedy hit, then blows the smoke away from the bars. "We've been contacted by your accomplice."

I go still. *My accomplice?*

"He spoke to Claude and provided some bona fides that have altered the situation profoundly."

Who the hell is he talking about? "It's about damn time. Past time, in fact."

"You're probably going to be getting out of here before long."

"At what price?"

Pine shifts uncomfortably. "What happened in the shower room earlier was a mistake. Chalk that up to Beau Holland's account. Rest assured that you'll be compensated for pain and suffering. As you know from our meeting this morning, the club is prepared to be quite generous to acquire Sally's materials."

I make the mistake of shifting on the bed, and my ribs shriek again. "Do you think this is a negotiation, Arthur?"

He gives me the smile of the eternal fixer. He could have been a clerk under Pontius Pilate. "If it weren't, whoever has the cache would already have gone public with it. And you'd be dead. As it is, your accomplice won't deal until he sees you alive."

That's the best news I've heard all year. "What makes Claude and Donnelly think we'll deal once you let me out of here?"

"You were ready to make a deal at midday."

"You yanked that deal off the table."

"That wasn't my call."

"Don't bullshit me, Arthur. You had a vote. This afternoon you thought Max's little porn video would keep me in line. You were cocky enough to shut down the paper and ruin my father based on that belief. Now you want to kiss and make up? What's changed?"

He finishes off his cigarette with one ferocious pull. "Your accomplice has more sensitive information than we first imagined."

"Translation, Buckman's shitting his geriatric diaper."

Pine wrinkles his lips in disgust.

"So, when do I get out?"

"That's not my call, either. But it shouldn't take long."

"Then how about letting me get some sleep?"

"Tell me one thing first. What is this secret Max knows?"

The prurient light in Pine's eyes tells me his interest is purely personal. He wants to know the intimate sins of Max's life. Or is even that a business interest? Secrets are weapons to be hoarded for future use.

When the lawyer realizes that I don't intend to answer, he says, "The club can make you whole again, Marshall. Think about what you're going to need to put all this behind you."

At last I let him see my hatred and disgust unmasked. I should keep my mouth shut until I'm free from this building, but all my instinct tells me they have no choice but to let me out. "What if I need your hide, Arthur? I told you today that I'm going to get you."

"Don't make this personal. It's only business."

"Yeah? Here's how I see it. If my father dies this week, you killed him. You, Holland, Russo, Cowart, Buckman, Donnelly . . . the whole club. And I will balance that out. Think about that while you're driving home."

Pine taps the bars with a manicured nail. "Losing a father isn't easy. I can still feel the pain like yesterday."

"If you were the best he could do, your father was a failure."

He gives me a cynic's smile. "And yours is a drunk with one foot in the grave. That's life."

"Mine did some good in his time."

Pine pushes off the bars and walks to the big metal door. "All this will look different in the morning. You'll want your old life back."

"Maybe. But no matter how this turns out, you're part of the price."

The lawyer turns and looks back at me. "Why me, more than the others? They're the real power in the club."

I struggle to my feet and walk to the bars. Every step sends a bolt of pain through my torso. "I'm not sure. Maybe because you're the soulless drone who greases the track for the fat boys on top. The flunky who brings the devil coffee. You shine his shoes and defend him in court, and on TV. Right now the country's full of empty suits like you. I met them every day in D.C. Buckman and the other big boys will go down in the end. But hacks like you tend to slip through the cracks when payback is handed out. I just want you to know that when that day comes, I'm going to make sure you don't."

Pine looks back in silence for maybe ten seconds. Then he raps on the door, which is opened from without. After he goes through, it closes behind him with a heavy clang.

I don't know how long I'll have to wait for freedom, but there's no point sitting here trying to figure out who my "accomplice" is. I suppose I'll find out soon enough. Half my ribs feel cracked or broken. All I want to do right now is forget what it means to drown in a small room on dry land. Curling into a fetal position on the hard, piss-smelling shelf, I blank my mind to everything I saw or heard over the past twelve hours.

The nightmares that come in the fetid darkness of the drunk tank are horrible. Drowning dreams, drowning and sinking, my brother and my son. Nothing I haven't endured before, only now I have a more visceral understanding of the experience. But at some point, I find myself flying low over the big river at night, like a gliding bird. Ahead, in the moonlight, something floats in the shining water, half-submerged. It's a man, floating faceup. I swoop lower, accelerating as I descend, expecting to see the face of my brother frozen at eighteen, like the young Elvis on his postage stamp. But as I come even with the body, it's my father's face I see staring skyward from the water. His eyes are open but lifeless, or else they're looking far beyond me, to a sight I'll be denied until I, too, undergo the final transformation. Passing above his supine form, I realize that—like Paul Matheson—I know something I did not realize I knew. I know what my mother meant when she asked me if I'd punished my father enough. What I don't know is whether he'll live long enough for me to ask his forgiveness.

CHAPTER 43

COOL AIR HITS me like a spray of water as I push through the doors to leave the sheriff's department. My Flex is parked out front, halfway up the block. A female deputy gave me back my keys and cell phones as I left, both phones powered up. She didn't give me back my father's gun.

My iPhone reads 3:17 A.M. The moon has fallen behind the downtown buildings. Paranoia tells me to power down both phones before I leave this area, but as my thumb moves to do it, a text from what appears to be a blurred out email address pops up on my iPhone. It reads: *There's probably a tracker on your vehicle. Maybe even someone waiting to follow. Shut off your phone. Pretend to go to Flex, then cut through the alley at middle of block. Run it! I'll be waiting. You'll know.*

Unless the Poker Club is about to have me murdered, the text must be from my unknown "accomplice." Instead of standing on the sidewalk second-guessing myself, I walk up the block toward the Flex, switching off my phones as I go. The alley mentioned in the text is ahead on my left, opposite my vehicle. Using my key fob, I remotely unlock the Flex, which also turns on its interior lights. But as I come even with the door, I break left at a sprint.

I can still run. A hundred yards will take me to the end of the alley, and I can cover that in twelve seconds, even in street clothes. Halfway down the alley, I see a car pull across the opening at the end, its headlights switched off. *I guess that's my ride.*

Churning my legs as hard as I can, I recognize the waiting car as a Mazda Miata convertible with its top up. I don't know anyone who drives that make of car, but beggars can't be choosers. I run full-out until my hands slap into the fabric top.

"Get in!" shouts a male voice.

When I open the door, dual shocks of recognition and confusion go through me. The driver is Tim Hayden, Adam's old tennis coach.

"*You?*" I say, astonished.

Hayden grins like a teenager playing a prank on the police. "Every second you stand there you're risking our lives."

I get into the convertible. Hayden guns the motor, which slams the door and pushes me back against the seat.

"*You* have the cache?" I ask, staring at him in disbelief.

His eyes glued to the rearview mirror, Hayden wrenches the Miata through a ninety-degree turn, then slows as if looking for a turn. "I'm about to turn again, then slow down. When I say 'go,' climb through the window. If you open your door, the light will come on. Just go as fast as you can. I'll make sure you don't kill yourself."

"Where am I going?"

He brakes hard, turns sharply left again. "Five seconds. You won't see me again tonight."

"Where are *you* going?"

"To lead a wild-goose chase. Go!"

He slows but doesn't stop. Stuffing my long frame through the small window is no easy task, but I manage it by going headfirst. Hayden brakes just enough for me to land without killing myself. Then his motor whines, the Mazda fishtails, and he's flying down the remainder of the alley.

There's so little light here, he might as well have left me on the seafloor. Somebody has obviously knocked out some bulbs.

"Marshall!" comes an urgent hiss. "Over here."

I can't place the source of the voice. Then a tiny LED flashes like a supernova in the dark. Abandoning caution, I move toward the blue-white flare. As I near it, a soft hand grabs my wrist and says, "Through here."

A vertical bar of light opens in the blackness. The hand pushes me through it and the door shuts behind me. Then the snick of a cigarette lighter precedes the bloom of a candle flame. By its light I see Nadine Sullivan looking up at me.

"Are you all right?" she asks. "Did they hurt you?"

I can just make out the inventory room of the bookstore. "You got me out? You sent that blocked text?"

She nods, her eyes filled with worry.

"How?"

"I sent it from my computer, using a special app."

"No, I mean how did you get me *out*? Free from those bastards."

"With Sally's cache." Nadine gives me an apologetic smile. "I've had it from the beginning."

Of course she has. "Because of your mother," I say softly.

"And the book club. Sally and I got very close during those two years."

"But . . . why didn't you tell me? My God. Didn't you trust me?"

"Honestly? No."

I can't get my mind around this. "Why not?"

"Marshall, I think you're a good person. I like you a lot. But you're also a journalist. A journalist who made his name by breaking big stories. And this story is as big as anything you've ever done."

"Which part? Buck's murder? The Poker Club? The paper mill?"

"It's all connected. But the paper mill is the lights-out scandal. I couldn't risk you ruining the town's future by going live on CNN three hours after you learned the truth."

"Do you really think I'd do that?"

"Are you sure you wouldn't? You don't know yet what's under all this. Think back three days ago, to Buck's murder. How would you have felt if I'd handed you a bomb that could destroy the Poker Club?"

She's right about that. "Okay . . . I get it."

"By the way, you're set to meet with the Poker Club in four and a half hours. At Claude Buckman's bank."

"What the hell? Why?"

Nadine looks at me like I'm an idiot. "Because if you don't, you're as good as dead. They're not going to let you run around loose if they don't think we'll cut a deal with them. Especially after they see the morning paper, which should hit their doorsteps in two or three hours. They are going to freak when they see those stories."

After what happened to me in the jail, this is too much to absorb. "Ben and those old pressmen are really going to get a paper out?"

She nods in the dim light.

"Well, if you didn't trust me a few hours ago, at the hospital, why do you now?"

"I'm sorry about that. I was actually on the verge of telling you I had the cache when Jet called. Three minutes later you were outside with her." Nadine lifts a steaming cup of coffee off a cardboard box and hands it to me. "Maybe this will lessen the sting."

The coffee fills my mouth like a healing elixir, and the first infusion of caffeine makes me shiver with pleasure. "What made you decide to confide in me at the hospital?"

"You told me about the paper you were planning to put out."

"I don't understand. It was you who sent me that PDF file? You're 'Mark Felt'?"

"Of course. And I don't want to hear any damned Deep Throat jokes."

I hold up my left hand. "Not from me."

"I sent you that as a test of sorts. To see how you'd handle the information. And you passed. You're using the material that will hurt the Poker Club members, but you held off on the Mr. Chow stuff, which was potentially more explosive, because you weren't sure what you had. That told me you were willing to proceed with caution, even after they hurt your father. You're not trying to wreck the whole Azure Dragon deal without regard for the consequences."

"Yeah, well . . . I'm not so sure about that now."

"What did they do to you in the jail? Your forehead looks like it has rug burn."

"They taught me how to hold my breath."

"What does that mean?"

"Not now. Have you heard anything about my father?"

"He's about the same. You should call your mother. She's sleeping at the hospital tonight."

I glance at my watch. "Arthur Pine came to see me in the jail. In trying to get me to talk, he told me some things I didn't know. I think I understand why Sally created the cache now."

"Is that so? Why, do you think?"

"If she chose you to hold it, then you must know."

"Actually, I think Sally initially hoped I'd hold the cache without

knowing what was in it. But I persuaded her to tell me everything in
the end."

"What's 'everything'?"

Nadine bites her lip, still struggling with whatever it is she knows.
"The last thing she told me—and it nearly killed her to do it—was that
her husband had fathered Jet's child."

I don't know if it brings anxiety or relief to hear someone else say it
out loud. But if Nadine got close enough for Sally to confide this to her,
then she must know more than anyone else alive—other than Max—
about Sally's death.

"How long have you known about Kevin?" Nadine asks.

"Since about nine o'clock tonight."

"Wow. You must be pretty freaked out then."

I drink some more coffee, then wrap my hands around the cup for
warmth. "You could say that."

"It was Jet who hit Max with the hammer tonight, wasn't it?"

"What makes you say that?"

Nadine leans against a shelf unit behind her. "After the police hauled
you off, I pulled her away from Paul long enough to ask if you'd done it.
She had the decency to say no. That—and the way she overreacted to
that cop arresting you—told me Jet must have done it."

"Max tried to rape her tonight. By the pool on Parnassus Hill."

Nadine blinks but doesn't otherwise react. Nevertheless, I see her
mind working behind her eyes.

"I think she'd have killed him with that hammer if I hadn't been
there," I add. "She hates him."

"I imagine so. She's been living a lie for thirteen years. Not many people could endure that. She snapped tonight when she attacked that cop."

"You don't like Jet much, do you?"

Nadine takes the mug from my hand and drinks a sip of coffee. "I
actually admire her in many ways. I've seen her in court. But I think
she's screwed you up pretty bad."

I hesitate to go further in this direction, but after tonight on the
hill . . . "Do you want to elaborate on that?"

"Let's just say Jet's another reason I didn't tell you about the cache
before now. I knew you'd tell her about it. And I don't trust her not to
use it for personal reasons."

"To get custody of Kevin, you mean?"

She nods.

"How long have you known about her and me?"

A faint smile touches Nadine's lips. "I figure you've been sleeping with her for about three months."

She guessed it nearly to the day. "When did you know? And how?"

"The first two months you came into the store for coffee, you were so pissed off about leaving Washington and watching your career stall that you were hard to be around. Then one day you waltzed in on air. Either you'd started sleeping with somebody or doing drugs."

"How did you know it was Jet?"

She shakes her head, her incredulity plain. "Any time her name came up in conversation, even four tables away, you'd look up from your coffee. Every time you *said* her name the timbre of your voice changed. Even now. Not to mention, your gate code is her birthday."

I feel my cheeks go red. "How'd you know that?"

"After I found those earrings, my mind started working. The code ended in your birth year, but it wasn't your birthday. I have a St. Mark's alumni directory. Took about thirty seconds to find out what Jet's was."

"I guess I wouldn't make much of a spy."

Nadine snorts a little laugh, but then her expression turns serious. "If Paul Matheson doesn't know you're sleeping with his wife, it's because he's worked hard to blind himself to it. He's not my cup of tea, but he's no dummy, either."

"No."

"After what I saw tonight, you'd better be damned careful. If that cop had tried to handcuff Jet, Paul would have hurt him. The other cop would have shot him for it, but Paul didn't care. I don't think he'd hesitate to hurt you, Marshall. Even kill you."

"I saw. He's close to the edge."

The sound of an engine rises in the alley behind the back door. Nadine looks up at a small window set high in the wall, then reaches out and snuffs the flame of the candle.

"A wavering light might look weird," she whispers, "no matter how dim."

"Do you still have your gun?"

"In my purse, on the floor. But I'd rather not shoot a cop if we can avoid it."

I hear my heartbeat in my ears as the engine grows louder. It seems to stop outside the door, but after several seconds, it moves on.

"Why don't we go sit in the banquette up front?" I ask the barely discernible form in front of me.

"Because even with the lights out, it's visible from the street if you press your face to the glass. We'd better stay back here. There's a little bathroom over there. I'll turn on the light and crack the door in a minute."

"Okay. Hey, how did you recruit Tim Hayden to pick me up?"

I sense more than see an affectionate smile. "He and the guy I'm staying with are lovers. I got my friend Chris to call Claude Buckman and deliver the threat that sprung you from jail. Tim volunteered to pick you up and bring you here. If I don't hear from him soon, I need to call and check on him."

"Why don't you call him now? I'll call my mother."

"You can't power up your phone." Nadine's cell flashes to life between us, and I see a snarky look on her face. "Either of them. Use mine."

She dials my mother's cell from her contacts list, then holds the phone to my ear. After five rings, Mom answers in a ragged voice, "Nadine? Have you heard anything about Marshall?"

"It's me, Mom," I say, taking the phone. "I'm out of jail, and I'm okay."

"Thank God. They didn't hurt you, did they?"

"I'm fine. Nadine got me out."

"I told you she's good people. I like that girl, Marshall."

"Me, too. Is Dad awake yet?"

"No. They're thinking about bringing him out of the coma later this morning. I'm trying to stay optimistic."

"I'll check back soon. I wanted to tell you something. I had a sort of epiphany, I guess, while I was in jail. I realized why you asked me whether I hadn't punished Dad enough by now."

"I shouldn't have said that."

"No, you were right. I—"

"Don't tell me, Marshall. Tell him. You're going to get your chance."

I feel my mother's invisible hands pushing me toward forgiveness, and maybe redemption. "I'll be there after it's light, unless you need me sooner. Just call Nadine's cell phone."

"I will. Be careful."

I click END. "I guess you heard all that?"

By the phone's light, I see Nadine smile to herself.

"So . . . are you ready to tell me what's in the cache? Or are you still trying to decide whether you can trust me?"

Her smile vanishes. She looks over her shoulder to the faint outline of her worktable. "Why don't we sit down? Let me get some light on."

She crosses the room in the dark, then turns on the bathroom light and leaves the door cracked, enough to throw a faint wedge of fluorescent light into the room. I take my coffee and sit on the near side of the table. She sits opposite me and absently picks up a pen resting on a notepad.

"There are three main issues," she says, doodling on the pad. "First, what's in the cache. Second, how I got it and what Sally intended should be done with it. Third, what are we going to do with it? A lot of this is going to get very personal for you. But we have to talk about it. Where do you want to start?"

"What's in the cache? I need to know what's at stake for everybody."

"A lot," she begins, tapping the pad like an attorney framing a question in a deposition. "There's a staggering amount of general business corruption. Political manipulation, bribery, tax evasion, you name it. Most of that's local, except the tax stuff, which involves accounts in the Seychelles. There's a local dimension to the paper mill and the interstate and bridge as well. The Poker Club wired those deals every way they could think of, skimmed in ways I've never seen before. All the new infrastructure, the ancillary businesses—every angle has been maximized for graft and spread among the local constituencies, including the black leaders. But all that's *nothing* compared to the central knot. The plum on the wedding cake. It's the crime of the century, Marshall—I kid you not."

"That's enough foreplay."

Nadine mimes disappointment. "Don't deny me my little triumphs. It's been killing me to be the only person who knows this shit. Scaring me, really. This mill deal is like the ultimate expression of Trump's America. It took the new EPA granting an unprecedented exemption to allow construction on top of the old electroplating factory, which was almost declared a Superfund site ten years ago. But who cares, right? It's moneymaking time. And that mill is the golden anchor that made the interstate and the bridge and all the rest possible."

"Jesus, would you tell me the heart of the thing already?"

There's wicked pleasure in her eyes. "Can't you tell *me*? I've been pushing you toward the answer for three days. *Think.* Why did Azure Dragon choose Bienville, Mississippi, for their billion-dollar paper mill? At least five other towns on their list were far superior in every respect."

I throw up my hands. "Why?"

She sighs with disappointment. "Avery Sumner."

"Judge Sumner? The Poker Club member who got appointed to fill the vacant Senate seat?"

"Yes!" She looks as though the whole truth should be self-evident.

"I must be a moron. Explain, damn it."

"God. Bienville was in the running to get the paper mill, but way down the list. It was a cattle call. Most potential site cities sent distinguished delegations to China to make their pitches. Some state governors flew over. Everybody's singing the same song. They compete to give the biggest tax breaks and best infrastructure package, a contest *Bienville* couldn't possibly win. Right?"

"I imagine not."

"But somebody in the Poker Club—I'm pretty sure it was Max Matheson—got the brilliant idea of offering the Chinese something nobody else could."

"Which was . . . ?"

She extends an open hand as though offering me something of immense value. "A U.S. Senate seat."

Avery Sumner. "How could they offer the Chinese Sumner's Senate seat?"

"Not the seat itself. They offered *votes*. Pro-China votes on major pending legislation. Especially *trade* legislation."

I must have been more exhausted than I knew. But now my heart is racing. "The Poker Club guaranteed Sumner would vote pro-China in exchange for Azure Dragon building their paper mill in Bienville?"

"Bingo. For a cool six billion yuan invested in southwest Mississippi, China got a guaranteed Senate vote."

"Christ. But . . . leaving aside the treason, or whatever crime that is, Avery Sumner was only appointed to serve out the remainder of a term. How many votes affecting China will come up in the time he has left?"

"In two years and four months? Enough. I think the Chinese would consider his vote on even two major bills a thousand percent return on their investment."

She's right: the scale of this crime is staggering. It's hubris on the part of the Poker Club, but to Buckman and Donnelly and the rest, the potential payoff must have seemed worth the risk. "And the Chinese government?" I ask. "Were they involved with this? Or was it just Azure Dragon Paper?"

Nadine laughs softly. "That's like asking me if Putin knew his oligarch buddies were involved in election tampering. You think some Shanghai businessman would risk espionage against the U.S. without the sanction of his government? You get a bullet in the back of the neck for that in China."

"All this is detailed in Sally's cache?"

"Painstakingly. Her recordings of the Poker Club meetings contain several discussions about it, and her documentary evidence verifies it beyond doubt."

Though I'm sitting, I feel dizzy, as though I've been whisked a thousand feet into the air. "This is bigger than . . . almost anything I can think of. Selling a U.S. Senate seat to a foreign power?"

Nadine has an almost beatific smile on her face. "If you think about it, U.S. Senate seats have been sold for a long time. Candidates have to spend millions to even have a chance at winning one. The *Citizens United* decision worsened the problem exponentially. And once a senator's in office, lobbyists pay millions to get their votes. How big a leap was it, really, to start selling votes directly?"

"It's not the first time, is it?" I realize. "Governor Rod Blagojevich tried to sell the seat vacated by Barack Obama. Went to jail for it. Fourteen years. Did you ever hear the FBI tape of what he said about that seat?"

She shakes her head.

"*'I've got this thing and it's fucking golden. I'm just not giving it up for fucking nothing.'*"

"He'd have been right at home in the Bienville Poker Club. At least Buckman and his crew are trying to help the city as well as themselves."

Despite my earlier indignation over Nadine's lack of trust, I can't help but fantasize what breaking a story of this magnitude would mean to my career. It's like being the only reporter with the Pentagon Papers story, or Watergate. I feel an irrational fear that I'll be killed before I can write it up and get it out to the world. Or maybe that's not so irrational—

"This crime is actually ancient history," Nadine informs me. "The Romans had a specific law to deal with bribery of senators for their votes. *Lex Acilia repetundarum*. But our situation gets into *ambitus*, as well—all the illegal crap the Poker Club did to get Sumner appointed to that seat. All twelve members pulled every string they could reach to put his butt in that chair."

"Where is the cache now?" I ask.

"A safety-deposit box."

My fear ratchets up three notches. "Not here in Bienville!"

Nadine smiles. "Not a chance. I'll bet there's not a safety-deposit box in this town that Claude Buckman couldn't get opened one way or another. No, it's in Monroe, Louisiana, in a bank with no ties to the Buckman empire."

Monroe is seventy miles across the river. "Okay, good thinking. How long have you had the cache?"

"Eleven days."

We've come to the point where things are going to get personal. But before I can ask my first question about Sally's motive, Nadine says, "What did they do to you in the jail? Come on. I see petechiae under your eyes."

I might as well tell her. "Officer Obie and a black-hooded buddy waterboarded me."

"Shit, they didn't."

"And Beau Holland was asking the questions."

Nadine's eyes narrow, but I can see hatred burning in them. "It's guys like Beau Holland who make me want to use the cache to blow the Poker Club to hell and gone, no matter what it costs the town. How bad was the waterboarding?"

If I were in her place, I'd probably ask the same absurd question.

"Worse than it sounds. The name sounds vaguely related to wake-boarding. They need to rebrand that little technique."

She lifts a finger to her mouth and shakes her head. "I should have gotten you out of there faster."

"You did fine. I survived."

We both jump when her iPhone rings. She checks the screen, then answers and puts the phone in speaker mode.

"It's me," she says.

"Sorry it took so long," Tim Hayden says. "I drove out toward Marsh—toward his house—and a police car followed me. It peeled off at the county line, and a sheriff's deputy picked me up. When I turned back toward town, he stopped me. Searched my car, made me open my trunk. He was furious not to find anybody hiding in back. As if Marshall would fit in that shoebox."

"But he let you go?"

"After he made two cell phone calls. Are you guys okay?"

"Yes. You get home. And thanks. I owe you a big one."

"Glad to help. Even though I don't know exactly what this is about, I feel like I just stuck it to the Man."

"You did, Tim," I tell him. "In a big way. Adam would be proud."

"Then I'm glad."

After Nadine hangs up, we regard each other over the worn table.

"What now?" she asks.

"We've come to the heart of it. Sally's motive. What you know about her plan, and her death."

She looks anything but pleased at this prospect. "You have to meet the Poker Club at eight A.M. You look wiped out. Are you sure you want to go into that now? You could grab some sleep on that couch." She points at a broken-backed relic against the far wall.

"I'm too wired to sleep. And I need to know the rest."

"I know. I'm not avoiding. But I don't think you realize how exhausted you are. You need to be on top of your game when you face Buckman. The future of this town's on the line. Not to mention our lives."

My mind goes to Ben Tate and the Terrell brothers, who are working to produce an edition of the paper that—if everything goes well—will hit the unsuspecting Poker Club like a laser-guided bomb. "Have you been out to the fishing camp?"

Nadine nods. "I took them a bunch of stuff from Walmart. Rubbing alcohol, small paintbrushes. Aaron Terrell texted me a long list."

"How about we make a run out there? Talk on the way?"

She sits back in her chair, clearly surprised by my suggestion. "Do you think it's safe?"

"If we can get across town to Cemetery Road without trouble, we should be all right. Besides, what can they really do to us?"

"Cave in our heads and dump us in the river?"

She hasn't forgotten Buck. "No. For all they know, if we die, the cache automatically hits the internet. They just let me out of jail, didn't they?"

She doesn't look convinced. "They didn't have control of both of us. And just because Buckman says he's willing to cut another deal doesn't mean some other guys in that club wouldn't kill us if they got the chance. Man, I wish I had set up something like that. An insurance policy."

"If the cache wasn't in your safe-deposit box, we'd do it now. But we can't help that. Where's your car?"

"My Acura's parked just up the alley, behind a friend's shop. Why do you want to do this?"

"Honestly? This may be the last edition of the Bienville *Watchman* ever printed. If my father can't be there to see it, then I will. I want to be able to tell him about it tomorrow."

Nadine looks at me for a long time. Then she says, "What the hell. What did Tim say? Let's go stick it to the Man."

"Now you're talking!" I slap the table. "Let's go. And don't forget your gun."

She gets up and retrieves her purse from the floor. "Wouldn't dream of it. It's my new essential accessory."

CHAPTER 44

NADINE GOT US to Cemetery Road without incident. We hardly spoke until she turned east, away from the river. Even then, I sat silent as we rolled over the gully where Jet dumped Max's hammer and gun. Two miles farther on, we passed the turn for my parents' neighborhood, then the overgrown path that leads to the Weldon barn, which is probably buried under a jungle of kudzu by now. When we're almost out of the city limits, I switch on my burner phone in my pocket.

"Think I should cut over to the Little Trace for a few minutes?" Nadine asks. "Less chance of passing a sheriff's car?"

"Nah. We're only five miles from the turn to Dad's camp. I say go for it. Just don't speed."

We've left the only streetlights along Cemetery Road behind us. After we pass a lighted self-storage facility and a small-engine repair shop, full dark closes around the car.

"What do you want to ask me?" Nadine says.

"Do you believe Sally killed herself? Was she trying to frame Max?"

"I think that was her plan. I'm not sure she didn't try to kill him at the last minute instead, forcing him to kill her in self-defense. Or that Max didn't murder her outright, before she could try her plan."

"So when you and I were dancing to Jerry Lee Lewis at the Aurora Hotel, you knew she planned to commit suicide later that night?"

Nadine's head snaps around. "God, no! I had no idea of her real intentions or her timeline. I had to drag what I know out of her over the course of ten days. We had three private meetings in person. At first she told me she was having marital problems and didn't trust Max. She wanted me to hold something for her. She asked me to get a safe-deposit box. I figured she was preparing to divorce him."

"You didn't question her further at your first meeting?"

"Sure, but she wouldn't open up. She seemed afraid, or deeply disturbed. They'd been married so long, I didn't think Max was beating her, but I didn't know. I worried about sexual abuse—of Kevin, I mean—but I didn't bring it up at that meeting."

"She gave you the cache then? At your first meeting?"

"No, the second. And she was a lot more upset at that meeting. I got the feeling she was conflicted about whatever she was thinking of doing. That's when she told me that the cache could destroy not only Max, but all the men in the Poker Club. When I questioned her motive, she told me she'd discovered that Max was a truly evil man. Not merely weak, like most men, but evil. Her word. She'd always known that he cheated with other women. This was different. But she wouldn't tell me how."

"Do you know more than you originally told me about the affair between your mother and Max?"

"No. We never discussed that directly. Sally and I drank a lot of wine at that second meeting. At one point she said all human beings make terrible mistakes, and that she was no exception. When I asked what she'd done, she said she hadn't paid attention to what was right in front of her. She'd taken things for granted."

"Oh, man. Still, that's pretty vague. She didn't confide that she was terminally ill?"

"No. I could see she was deeply depressed, and I did wonder if she might be ill. But she never let on. Sally wasn't one for self-pity. She didn't want anybody thinking she was mortal. A hard road, but that was her generation, you know? Like my mom."

"When did she tell you about Max being Kevin's father?"

"Third meeting. Two nights before she died."

"Where were you?"

"My house. That time, she didn't seem upset at all. In fact, she was eerily calm. Looking back, everything seems as clear as day, of course.

She'd made her peace with death. I was the one who was upset that night."

"Did you suspect she was considering suicide?"

"I don't know. All three times we met, I begged her to see someone. A professional. I really tried. But Sally said she was past that kind of help. She said she was in the kind of situation where nobody could help you but yourself."

"Shit. So how did she tell you about Kevin's paternity?"

"I'll get to that. First she told me her plan. What I should do if anything happened to her. This made me think she was afraid of being killed, rather than thinking of suicide. And her plan was so detailed and masterful that I realized she must have been working on it for some time."

"Ever since she figured out Max was Kevin's father. But I've assumed that was only a few months ago, at most."

Nadine nods. "She got suspicious about three months ago. Which is pretty strange, really. Because Tallulah, their maid, had suspected it from the time Kevin was an infant."

"What do you think accounts for that?"

"Knowing what I know now? I think Sally had willfully blinded herself to something she didn't want to see. Something that would have destroyed her family. But when a doctor told her she was going to die, her denial crumbled. Her protective instinct for her grandchild burned through it. She saw things as they really were. And it terrified her."

I ask the question that has haunted me since last night. "Did Sally talk to Jet about the paternity issue?"

"What did Jet tell you about that?"

"She said they never talked about it. She thinks Sally died not knowing."

Nadine looks incredulous. "Jet really believes that?"

"She did until last night. I think I probably cracked her faith in that notion. She's out on the edge now, just like Paul."

"And you're in the middle." Nadine shakes her head in the dashboard light. "Sally told me she never confronted Jet about the paternity issue. She worried that might trigger Jet to do something desperate, like leave town with Kevin."

"Why did you say 'confronted' her? Jet was the victim in this."

Nadine hesitates before answering. "You're right. I don't know why I said that."

"You must have had a reason."

She cuts her eyes at me. "This is dangerous ground, Marshall. You said Max tried to rape Jet tonight. So I'm probably full of shit."

"Full of shit for what?"

Two pairs of headlights round a curve ahead and move toward us.

Apropos of nothing, Nadine says, "It's weird owning a bookstore like I do."

"What?"

"I'm there all day every day, alone a lot of the time. Men know where to find me. They have the right to come in and look at me, unless I bar them, which as a practical matter is tough. They can sit in my café for hours, even have me wait on them. It can make for uncomfortable situations."

I've never thought about it that way. I'm guilty of exactly that. "And . . . ?"

"I've learned a lot about men during that time. A lot of guys have hit on me in that shop. I've seen every type. Beau Holland is one of the worst. Vain, arrogant, pushy, no concern for anyone but himself. He can't imagine any woman saying no to him—or meaning no, rather."

"And Max? You told me he hit on you more than once."

"He has, absolutely. But not like Beau. Max has a sense of humor about it. He'll make a remark or whatever, some double entendre, but he knows when to back off. With me, anyway." Nadine turns to me as she drives, letting me see her eyes. "All my instinct tells me he's not the guy to try to take it when he's not wanted."

Something in her voice frightens me, but it also triggers anger. "You should have seen him trying to rip Jet's shirt off earlier tonight."

"You saw that happen?"

"I was across the Parnassus pool from them. He attacked her. That's when she hit him with the hammer."

"See? I'm an asshole. I've just been trying to make sense of why Jet never left that marriage."

"That bothered me, too," I admit. "I don't mean after Kevin was born, or even after she discovered she was pregnant. But right after the rape."

"Exactly. Jet wasn't a teenager. She was, what, thirty-three? And an attorney."

"I asked her about it. She couldn't give me an answer. Only that she wasn't as strong as she'd thought she was."

"I'm not criticizing her," Nadine says quickly. "And I'm not speaking lightly of this. I've been assaulted twice, almost raped both times. I managed to get out of those situations, but not unscathed."

"Did you report it?"

"The first time, no. Second time, yes. But we're not talking about me tonight."

"Jet has serious issues because of her father abandoning her. She was also worried that Paul would kill himself if she left. He was suicidally depressed. And remember what Sally told you: Max is a truly evil man. Jet discovered that fact thirteen years before Sally did. She told me he takes trips to Vietnam to have sex with young prostitutes. Who knows what really kept her in that family?"

"I'm sorry I brought it up," Nadine says, sounding genuinely upset.

"No, I understand. I've listened to a lot of stories in my life, and there's something that doesn't feel quite right about Jet's narrative. I hate saying that."

"Why did Sally give the cache to me?" Nadine asks. "That's the nub of it. Jet was the natural choice. She's a practicing attorney. She's Sally's daughter-in-law. She'd crusaded against the Poker Club. She seemed unafraid of Max. Why didn't Sally talk to Jet as soon as she suspected the truth? Unless . . ."

"She was afraid to," I finish. "That's what you're thinking. And not just because she might scare Jet into running with Kevin."

"Yes," Nadine says quietly. "I don't want to go any further than that. If you want to know more, you should go talk to Tallulah in the morning. She knows more than any of us."

"You spoke to her today, right? About your mom and Max?"

"I did. But let's leave it there. All this gets about as personal as anything can. And when you're dealing with human beings, everyone has their own agenda. You can't be sure you're getting pure truth from anybody. You know that. I'm not even sure I want to get to the bottom of this."

"Jesus," I whisper. "You're scaring me."

"I'm not suggesting anything weird, okay? Just . . . you need to go down that road on your own. I can't get between you and Jet. I don't want to."

Two semi trucks traveling in tandem blow past us, and the Acura shudders.

The implications of Nadine's reasoning have left me cold, almost disoriented. Maybe it's just sleep deprivation. For a few seconds I wonder if Jet is with Paul right now and, if so, if she's all right. After that scene at the hospital, there's no telling how he might treat her. For now, I have to trust that she'd text me if she were in trouble.

To distract myself from these thoughts, I say, "Did Sally ever consider killing Max? I mean, straight-up murder. Talk about having a good motive . . ."

"I know, right? She not only considered it, she *planned* it. But when the moment came, she couldn't bring herself to do it. Sally didn't go to church much, but she was deeply religious."

"That's too bad. Because the world would be a lot better for a lot of people right now if Max had died instead of Sally."

A darkened service station drifts past on the right.

"We're going to be at the barn soon," I tell her. "Tell me this: How did Sally compile such a damning data cache in only a few months? I mean, she was a housewife, not a private detective."

Nadine pops my chest with a stinging blow.

"Damn! That hurt."

"I should have smacked you in the face. Sally was sharp as a razor, and one of my best customers. Since 1865, the Poker Club has rotated meetings between the members' houses. The Mathesons' hacienda was better suited to a big group than most houses, so they hosted more than their share of meetings. As a first step, Sally started recording them. The last few months have been especially busy because of the paper mill. In no time she had enough damaging information to put most of the members behind bars. And that was before she cracked Max's password and started copying his emails. She even installed a keystroke recording program."

I laugh in amazement. "If Max had known that, he'd have died of a stroke weeks ago."

"Or murdered Sally," Nadine says in a cold voice.

"True. Look, I know you said Sally was sharp, but all this sounds pretty high-tech. Are you sure she didn't have the help of a tech-savvy young attorney?"

Nadine nods. "Positive. Sally had read mysteries and true crime for fifty years. She also watched a lot of TV. That may sound quaint to you, but while her friends were watching *Downton Abbey,* she was bingeing on *The Wire* and *The Americans.* It was actually *The Americans* that inspired her plan."

"How so?"

"Do you know the show? It's a Cold War setting. And one episode involved the so-called Dead Hand system. Are you familiar with that?"

"I did a paper on it when I was at UVA. It's a system that fires nuclear missiles even after your country has been destroyed. It's put in place to deter a first strike by the other side. Even if your whole population has been wiped out, the Dead Hand fires every missile you have left, destroying the 'victorious' opponent."

This earns me a smile from teacher. "Sally adapted that doctrine to marital warfare."

I think about this for a quarter mile. "Here's where I'm confused. How was the *cache itself* supposed to function? What were you supposed to do with it? Sally created this weapon, which she gave to you. Then she warned Claude Buckman that if Max ever revealed his secret, the Poker Club would be destroyed. But *they don't know what the secret is.* So how did Sally's Dead Hand system work? How does the cache keep Max quiet? Was it meant to be a threat only? Never used?"

"Oh, no. If it were only a threat, Sally wouldn't have needed to create it."

"Except to bolster the threat at the beginning."

"Uh-uh. That cache exists to destroy them all if Max ever tells Kevin or Paul the truth about Kevin's paternity. Sally was deadly serious about that."

"Well, that's a crappy plan. Once Max tells the secret, Kevin and Paul are screwed for life, whether Max and the Poker Club are ruined or not."

Nadine smiles with secret knowledge. "Unless there's an early-warning system. A trigger to alert me if it looked like Max was going to spill the beans."

"What could that be?"

Nadine raises her eyebrows. "You mean *who*. Tallulah, of course."

The elegance of Sally's system takes my breath away. "Tallulah practically lives with Max and Kevin," I think aloud. "She'd know if Max was coming apart, edging up to the line."

"Exactly."

"And she loved Sally. Tallulah probably saw Max becoming obsessed with Kevin long before Sally did. Max was lucky she kept quiet about it for so long."

"I think his luck is running out."

"I'm surprised the club didn't kill Max the day after Sally called Buckman. To remove all risk of the cache being used. Pine told me that some members wanted to do that."

"Give them time. They've only known about the cache for two days," Nadine reminds me. "You know they're shitting bricks right now. But most of those old bastards love Max. And from my analysis of the cache, Max seems to be the main liaison between the Poker Club and Azure Dragon. That probably makes him especially valuable to them."

"So . . . that night at the hotel, when Max and Sally fought in public. Was she planning to execute her plan? Or did the fight push her to it?"

"I think Sally knew what she was going to do that night. She started that fight to bolster her frame-up of Max."

I'm amazed by the cold precision of Sally's plan. "What if she hadn't been able to reach Buckman on the phone that night?"

"She'd have moved down the list to Blake Donnelly. If she couldn't get Blake, then down again until she reached a club member. But Sally knew all those men well, and their wives even better. She knew Charity Buckman would put her through to Claude—especially after seeing them fight at the Aurora."

"I can't get over how gracious Sally was to us that night, while *this* was in her head. But . . . you had to suspect something?"

"I didn't, really. Not that night. She looked so alive, even happy, right up until that argument."

I think back over the timeline of that night. "You stayed at my house that night. I'm the one who told you she'd been shot. You didn't show much emotion."

"I was shattered, Marshall. All I could see was Sally sitting at my kitchen counter, drinking wine and trying to pretend things weren't hopeless. That night, when I left you to get dressed for our digging expedition at the mill site, I stuck my finger down my throat and threw up."

"I'm sorry. You know, some of this would have been useful to know these past couple of days."

"I realize that. It's been hard watching you struggle to figure all this out, when I knew the answer all along. But I promised Sally I wouldn't tell a soul. And I took that promise seriously."

"I get it. She was your mother's best friend."

Nadine looks over at me, and I see her lower lip quivering. For the first time, I feel like she's about to lose her composure.

"There's the road," I tell her, and she looks grateful for the distraction.

We turn left, and kudzu-choked trees close around the car. Instead of voicing the next thing that comes into my head, I lay my hand on her arm, and she smiles sadly. Crunching over gravel in the dark, I feel the fatigue of an endless day burying me like sand. Then the trees open out to the clearing and the pond, which has a cold sheen in the moonlight. Three cars and a pickup truck sit outside the barn. Yellow light leaks from beneath the big sliding door, and as Nadine parks, I see a cigarette flare in the dark.

Opening the passenger door, I hear a deep voice say, "Yo. Who goes there?"

"Marshall McEwan. This is my dad's place."

"What's the password?"

"Purple Rain," Nadine says from behind me.

"Yes, ma'am. Welcome back."

A big black man holding a rifle materializes out of the darkness. He reaches out and slides the barn door to the side, spilling light into the night. The sentry who challenged me looks about fifty, and his rifle is an AR-15 with a forward pistol grip and military scope.

Once through the door, I smell chemicals, ink, and heated paper. Aaron and Gabriel Terrell stand over by the big German offset press,

while a group of teenagers sits in a circle of folding lawn chairs, all looking at their cell phones. Aaron waves and starts toward us. Before he
covers ten feet, the kids break into an a cappella gospel rendition of
Stevie Wonder's "Higher Ground."

"Looks like you recruited a youth army," I say, shaking Aaron's hand.

He grins through his white beard. "We gon' be all right on the foldin'
and delivery. Got some more drivers comin' soon."

Despite the excitement I felt about witnessing this spectacle—or
even taking part in it—I wobble on my feet. "I noticed you have some
security out there."

"My idea," Nadine says from beside me.

"That guy didn't look like any church security guard."

Aaron chuckles. "Hey, man, just 'cause I grew up in the church don't
mean I don't know some brothers from the other side of the street. We
got somebody riding shotgun with Ben, too."

Nadine says, "Is anybody using those army cots you found earlier?
Marshall's hit a wall."

"I see that. They're all free right now. Got three set up in the back
corner over there. Two more on the other side. We keep the boys separated from the girls when they lay down. On my watch, anyway."

"You going to be able to get that front page printed?" I ask.

Aaron smiles. "You're kidding, right?" He walks to the linotype,
reaches down to a stack of paper on the floor, then brings back an
eleven-by-seventeen sheet of paper. "We had some trouble with the Heidelberg. Had to use the old ABDick."

He hands me the page, which is topped by a beautifully printed version of the original *Watchman* masthead, with the eagle and the banner
in its beak. *Vincit Omnia Veritas.* Below the masthead runs a series of
large headlines with brief descriptions of the stories to be found within
what will be the most unusual edition of our paper ever printed. POKER
CLUB RIFE WITH CORRUPTION? blares the first. PHOTO PUTS HOLLAND AT
LIKELY MURDER SCENE WITH VICTIM, announces the second, in smaller
type. REAL ESTATE SCAM DEFRAUDS HOMEOWNERS, reads the third. Then
comes BONES DISCOVERED ON MILL SITE. Beneath that in smaller type are
the words: "New Artifacts Support Dr. Ferris's Theory. MDAH Must
Investigate."

"Truth conquers all," I say softly, looking at the eagle again. "Thanks for this, Aaron."

"Oh, yeah. I'm glad to give Duncan something to smile about."

"You're going to do more than that. The Poker Club's going to go to war. I'm glad you've got that security here."

"We'll be all right. Problem is our max size on the jobbing press was eleven by seventeen. It's a long way from perfect, but the kids are folding it around the main edition and then rubber-banding it. They takin' a break now, but they work fast. They been foldin' five hundred copies an hour per person."

"Wow. Well, we can live with the size difference. Wake me if you need me, or if Ben says get me up."

Gabriel Terrell laughs and walks up behind his brother. "Ben? That boy passed out an hour ago."

"Well, he did a good job."

"Look now," Aaron says, "ain't no blankets on them cots."

"We'll make do," Nadine tells him.

She leads me through the antique machines to a couple of Korean War–vintage army cots set up side by side against the wall. Three feet away stands a fifty-five-gallon drum with an Evinrude outboard motor bolted inside it. The prop has probably rusted to powder by now. Beyond the motor stands another cot with Ben Tate sprawled across it, snoring up at the rafters.

"Lie down," Nadine says, laughing softly. "I'll take the one on the outside."

The voices of the choir fade into empty silence. Then a soft tenor voice begins singing "Hey Ya!" by OutKast. Other singers mimic instruments beneath the vocal, filling the barn with sounds not quite like any I've ever heard.

"You're about to fall down," Nadine says, taking hold of my upper arms and easing me down onto a cot.

"What about tomorrow?" I ask, curling into the barn wall. "The meeting with the Poker Club?"

"We'll deal with that tomorrow. I've got a little treat you can take with you. A silver bullet."

"What's that?" I ask, my eyes already closed.

"A recording of Claude Buckman waxing poetic about committing treason with China. It was so damning that I made a recording to keep with me, separate from what's in the safe-deposit box. Fifteen seconds of it was enough to get you out of jail."

"Awesome," I mutter, not even sure what she's talking about.

A moment later I feel her drop something soft and heavy on top of me, and that sends me over the edge into oblivion.

CHAPTER 45

AT 7:55 A.M. I walk out of the elevator on the second floor of the Bienville Southern Bank. As thankful as I was for that army cot, I'm still shaky from sleep deprivation. I'm also a little nervous. Before going into the conference room, I duck into the men's room to take a leak. While I'm standing at the sink washing my hands, the door opens behind me. In the mirror I see Tommy Russo walk in, wearing one of his body-hugging suits. He doesn't go to a urinal or a stall, but stands by the door, looking at me. He's holding a folded newspaper in his hand.

"This a social call?" I ask, wiping my hands on a paper towel.

He takes two steps forward and slaps my back with the newspaper. Rubbing sleep from my eyes, I take the paper and hold it in front of me. It's this morning's edition of the *Watchman*.

"I thought we had a deal," he says, his eyes bright with anger.

"We did. Then Arthur Pine showed up and shut down my father's business. So, no, we don't have a deal anymore."

Russo takes back the paper and opens it to page two, where several photographs show the principals in the main Poker Club story. One pairs Tommy with a man who looks very much like him and is identified as "New Jersey syndicate figure Anthony Russo."

"That your brother?" I ask.

"Yeah. Tony. And he ain't happy today. My old man, either, who's still alive, the stubborn son of a bitch."

"Well, you're lucky, Tommy. Because my old man's in a coma. He's not going to be around long. And I wasted last night in the county jail."

"I feel for you, Marshall." Russo taps the photo. "But this ain't good for business. And there's worse ways to die than in a hospital."

I let his threat hang in the air.

"I thought we had a private understanding, you and me," he insists. "After we talked yesterday."

"We did. I listened to your speech about family and not messing with a man's living. And then you dropped a truck on my family."

"Look, that debt-purchase thing, that wasn't my call. With the paper, I mean. That was Buckman and Holland and that prick Pine. I thought they'd settled things with you. Next thing I hear, everything is off."

"That sums it up, Tommy. Business is business, right? But physics matters, too. You're a serious guy, I know that. But you're about to learn a lesson about leverage."

"You got some balls on you, McEwan. You know that?"

I look past him to the restroom door. "What are you really doing here, Tommy?"

He steps right to be sure he's blocking my exit. "You need to understand something. Those guys you're about to talk to in that conference room, those so-called Southern gentlemen . . . they're local, okay? My partners ain't local. They're from Jersey. So remember this: whatever gets said in that room in the next few minutes, those clowns don't speak for my partners."

"You got bigger problems than me, Tommy. That paper mill deal? Selling U.S. Senate votes? The FBI will bury you under a federal prison for that. Ask the governor of Illinois. Correction, the ex-governor. The thing is, you'd never get to prison, because the Chinese would kill you first. The Chinese intelligence services, Tommy. They make the mob look like Girl Scouts. So listen hard in that conference room and make sure I stay healthy. That's your best survival strategy. Now, let me out. I've got a meeting."

UNLIKE MY FIRST FORMAL encounter with the Poker Club, this time eight of twelve members are present. I feel like I'm facing an all-male Senate committee, not least because it's being chaired by an irascible octogenarian.

As before, Claude Buckman sits at the head of the long rosewood table, Donnelly to his right, Arthur Pine to his left. On Donnelly's side sit Senator Avery Sumner, Wyatt Cash, and Dr. Lacey. On Pine's side sit Beau Holland and Tommy Russo. I'm at the far end, opposite Buckman. Cell phones lie in front of each man, all switched off. This time, I was wanded and searched by a security man before entering the conference room, to be sure I'm carrying no recording devices. When he searched me, I suppressed a sigh of relief that I'd left Nadine's pistol in the Flex. As I prepared to leave the barn this morning, Nadine insisted that I bring her gun with me. I assented, but on the condition that she would remain behind while Aaron Terrell dropped me outside the sheriff's department to pick up the Flex.

Not one man has spoken since I entered the conference room. I suspect that's because of the Chinese man sitting in a plush chair against the wall to my right. Though no one has introduced him, he looks like the fiftyish man who made the speech at the groundbreaking ceremony three days ago. I believe the *Watchman* story referred to him as Jian Wu, a corporate officer of the Azure Dragon paper company.

"Mr. McEwan," Buckman finally begins in his gravelly growl. "This morning's newspaper articles have placed several members of this club in legal jeopardy. Azure Dragon has also informed us—privately—of their intent to pull out of Tenisaw County and relocate to Alabama. Mr. Wu is only here this morning as a courtesy to me. Needless to say, you have our full attention."

"Before I address the new developments," I reply, "I want to remind you that as of yesterday at twelve P.M. we had a deal that would have prevented those articles from running. You not only took that deal off the table, you chose to blackmail me instead. You also shut down my father's newspaper, which resulted in him having a massive heart attack. Last night, I was waterboarded in the city jail, and Beau Holland was present throughout. *That's* why we're all sitting here."

Blake Donnelly, the most likable member of the club—and also the second richest—gives me a wry smile and says, "Marshall, I heard you had a little trouble over at the sheriff's department. I want to apologize. Those guys get a little out of hand over there. They need to be kept on a tight leash. You know what power does to people."

"That I do." I look pointedly at Beau Holland. "I need to use my phone to play a recording. I'll switch it off as soon as I'm finished."

"Proceed," says Buckman.

From my pocket I remove a small Bluetooth speaker I borrowed from one of the choir kids this morning, then check to be sure it's paired with my iPhone. "I'll be as brief as possible, gentlemen. First, this is not a negotiation. To prove that, this recording represents a tiny fraction of the material Sally Matheson gathered to implicate this club in a broad spectrum of felonies."

The general feeling in the room seems to be a mix of repressed fury and extreme discomfort. I press PLAY, and a hiss of static fills the conference room. Then Claude Buckman's unmistakable voice says, "Gentlemen, before tonight's toast, let me say this."

Every face around the conference table goes pale.

"If, when you're away from the club, you start to ponder the *ethical* dimension of our undertaking, remember one thing. This is one of those times when sectionalism must trump nationalism. I don't say that lightly, but our ancestors lived through a similar period, one that led to the founding of this group. Every man here knows that in *our* time, the Yankees and Jews and California flakes won't put any more major factories in Mississippi until we give up the last of our traditions."

"Fuck 'em!" barks a voice that sounds like Donnelly's.

"And the Priuses they ride in on!" jokes someone else.

"After all," Buckman continues, "we long ago reached the point where national boundaries mean little. And if we must deal with a foreign country, I'd prefer the Chinese to a lot of others. My uncle flew the Hump in Burma, and he loved the Chinese. Hell, General Chennault himself married a Chinese woman."

Claire Lee Chennault, the commander of the Flying Tigers, was raised just down the river near Ferriday, Louisiana.

"The Chinese know their history," Max says on the tape. "Mr. Wu told me General Chennault had been a great friend to the Chinese people. That surprised me, given Chennault's anticommunist work, but the guys who run China these days are about as communist as Henry Ford."

"I'll take Chinks over Japs any day of the week," Blake Donnelly pipes up. "Nissan may have brought a lot of jobs to this state, but I'd never break bread with those bastards. I lost an uncle at Guadalcanal."

"All due respect," says the New Jersey accent of Tommy Russo, "I'd take a billion dollars from Hitler if he was offering. I could give a shit. Money's like pussy. You take it where you can get it."

Twenty seconds into my playback, Jian Wu blanched. Now he looks like he might slide from his chair onto the floor.

"My point," Buckman growls from the speaker, "is that helping China in the Senate isn't a one-time payoff deal. The mill is just the beginning. Once we're in bed together, they can't say no. It's going to pay off again and again for us. And if we can get Avery re-elected for a full six-year term, then the sky's the limit."

"The sky, my ass," says Wyatt Cash. "We're talking space. Satellites, rocket engines. The upside of this deal is *infinite*."

I press STOP on my iPhone app.

All nine men in my audience look like they might need paramedics.

"That recording is self-explanatory," I observe. "But I'll say this. If I use my D.C. contacts to break that story, the U.S. and China will effectively be on a war footing within hours, and Azure Dragon Paper will be the first casualty."

Jian Wu swallows audibly.

"That said," I continue, "as much as I'd like to win a second Pulitzer Prize and become the most famous journalist on planet Earth, I don't much like the idea of killing the goose that can guarantee my hometown's survival for the next thirty years."

The collective sigh of relief that follows this statement alters the humidity in the conference room. While they watch me with trepidation, I take out some notes made on a torn piece of newsprint I got from Aaron Terrell this morning.

"To keep me from breaking this story, you will do the following. There is no order of priority to these demands. If any single one is not met, you will find yourselves the subjects of an FBI investigation by day's end, and the story will start running on MSNBC and CNN by five P.M. Finally"—and here I look at Russo—"if you were to shoot me in the head while I sit in this chair, the story will still break around the world. Is that understood?"

Buckman nods with impatience. "Please state your demands."

"First, Azure Dragon will not be moving to Alabama. No matter what happens from this point forward, they must complete the planned paper mill and put it into operation within two years. However, the company must re-site the mill no less than fifteen hundred meters south of the present site, well clear of the Indian settlement discovered by Buck Ferris."

"Impossible," hisses Jian Wu.

"*Most important*," I go on, "all tax breaks granted to Azure Dragon to entice the mill to Bienville will be revoked. The company will pay the full ride to both the city and state throughout its years of operation."

Jian Wu stands white-faced—with anger or fear, I can't tell which.

"You wish to say something, sir?" I ask.

"None of this can be done! It's far too late."

"Is it? Think about you and your fellow corporate officers being charged for subversion, forfeiting all Azure Dragon property and holdings in the United States, and having the U.S. president demand that President Xi break up your company to prove that it's not a part of your country's intelligence services."

The Azure Dragon man's lips are quivering, but he takes his seat again.

"Please continue," says Claude Buckman, looking grateful to me for accomplishing what he could not with the Chinese.

"Second, within sixty days, Avery Sumner will resign his seat in the U.S. Senate for family or health reasons, whichever his preference."

Four chairs down to my left, Senator Sumner looks stricken, but he doesn't protest. Unlike Jian Wu, he's content to let Buckman fight his battles for him.

"Third, the Bienville *Watchman* will be returned to my father by noon today, for the sum of one hundred dollars. The newspaper will be unencumbered by debt. The building that houses the paper will be included in the sale. Further, the mortgage on my parents' house will be paid in full by this club and the house titled in my mother's name. The contracts completing these transfers should be delivered to my father's hospital room by Arthur Pine by eleven this morning."

"Consider that done," says Donnelly, glaring at Pine, who looks as though he's struggling with ulcer pain. "And I, for one, will be glad to see that happen. I didn't support that bullshit move yesterday, and I'm glad to see it rectified. The *Watchman* was founded the same year as the Poker Club, and it's only right that it should go into the future guided by the family that built it."

Beau Holland and Tommy Russo would love to strangle Donnelly right now.

"Fourth," I go on, "all real estate named in today's article—the homes and land Beau Holland scammed from homeowners along the interstate corridor, et cetera—will be sold back to the original owners for one-half of what they were paid for it. This will be done within ten days."

Holland has gone so red he looks like he fell asleep in the sun. He starts to argue, but from the corner of my eye I see Russo lay a restraining hand on his arm.

"Fifth," I push on, "in tomorrow's paper, I will run an interview with Claude Buckman in which he expresses the critical need for new public schools in Bienville and his intention to push forward a public referendum for a new high school. At a minimum that investment will be fifty million dollars."

Nobody comments on this point, and since it was offered yesterday, this must have already been factored into their expectations.

"Sixth, a community development fund totaling one million dollars per year will be funded by the Sun King Casino and the Bienville Poker Club. I will initially administer that fund, and I will determine who administers it after me."

Russo looks like a man with malignant hypertension.

"Finally, the local sheriff's department will request the assistance of the FBI in the murder of Buck Ferris, and whoever is responsible will either plead guilty or stand trial and accept whatever verdict and sentence result from said trial."

This demand turns out to be the bridge too far. Several mouths fall open. Then Beau Holland snaps.

"This is absurd!" he bellows. "Every damn word of it! It's extortion!"

"Beau," says Blake Donnelly. "Let's wait until he's finished."

"Why even pretend to humor this asshole? We're not giving in to this bullshit. You know McEwan won't keep his word. He's a goddamn reporter! He'll never be able to sit on this. Look at today's *Watchman* stories. He built his career blowing open scandals." Holland looks around the room. "You're not actually considering any of this?"

"*Beau*," croaks Buckman. "Wait until the man is finished."

Once Holland sits back in his chair, whispering angrily to Russo, I look down the table at Buckman. "In exchange for all of the above, I will withhold the contents of Sally's cache from publication for all time. It will be as though that cache does not exist. *Never* existed. Bienville will get its paper mill, the new bridge, and the interstate. The Indian site will become a huge tourist attraction. Many of you will still likely profit mightily from the various side deals you've made related to all the new development. And you can sleep well at night knowing you're not going to jail."

Buckman nods grudgingly. Donnelly, Cash, and Dr. Lacey are sighing with apparent relief. But the others look far from happy.

"*However*," I say, drilling Arthur Pine with the coldest stare I can muster. "If you fail to live up to any of these conditions, the FBI, the SEC, the IRS, and the Mississippi state tax authorities will be informed of every crime detailed in Sally's cache. The list is staggering. None, however, approaches the betrayal of the United States implicit in the auctioning of Avery Sumner's Senate votes."

The Azure Dragon man stands stiffly. "I must make a telephone call."

"Call whoever you want," says Buckman. "But you've got no choice, and you know it."

Without waiting for further comment, Jian Wu leaves the room.

"Mr. McEwan," says Buckman, "could you give us five minutes alone?"

I pick up my phone and walk to the door. Then I look back and say, "I don't want anybody coming out here to talk to me. Especially Russo. Make sure that whatever you decide, you're all on the same page. There won't be any second chances if I pull the trigger on this story. For this club, that's the end of the world."

I walk out into the anteroom, which is only a small alcove off the main second-floor hall. Even out here, the décor is old photographs of steamboats and cotton fields. I check my emails, then scan Twitter. Secretaries pass with brusque efficiency, and most look like they were chosen for their physical attributes.

Unless someone in that conference room has leverage I don't know about, they have no choice but to accede to my demands. What preys on my mind is the terrible awareness that I'm betraying the most basic tenets of my profession. After today, I'll be a traitor to every luminary of journalism whose book sits on my father's shelf of honor. Not one of them ever made a deal like this. Today I join the ranks of the second-raters and sellouts.

Today I become a whore.

Why? I wonder. *Is it because I live in a different time?* No. There were always robber barons trying to use their power to pervert and exploit the political system for gain. I'm part of the army that's supposed to stand in their way—

"We're ready, Marshall," announces Blake Donnelly, who has stuck his head out of the conference room door.

The oilman holds it open for me to go back inside.

Everyone is seated where he was before, including Jian Wu against the wall. Donnelly walks to his chair at Buckman's right, and I take my seat at the near end of the table. Of all the faces around the table, it's those of Pine, Holland, and Russo that look angriest.

"All right," rasps Buckman. "Azure Dragon will comply in full with your conditions, Mr. McEwan. They don't like it, but being proved guilty of espionage against the United States they like even less."

Buckman taps the table with his clawlike fingers. "Next, the Bienville *Watchman,* its associated real estate, and the mortgage on your parents' house will be returned to your father and mother forthwith by noon today, unencumbered by debt, as per your terms."

"Again," says Donnelly, "you have my apologies as to how that was done. No excuse for it, and I hope Duncan gets back on his feet soon."

Buckman grimaces at this mixture of sentimental courtesy with business. "The other real estate you mentioned," he goes on, "will be returned to the various sellers under the terms you described within ten days. Mr. Holland, give Mr. McEwan your word on that."

Beau Holland's jaw is set so tight he looks incapable of speech.

"Beau?" Buckman prompts him.

Through clenched teeth Holland says, "Agreed."

"For my part," says Buckman, "I will call for and support the public school referendum, as you requested, and I'll make sure those schools get funded. Same for the community development fund. Mr. Russo? Your word on that?"

Tommy nods once. He hasn't taken his eyes off me since the meeting began. It's like being watched by a tiger shark from the edge of a reef.

"As you've probably noticed," Buckman says, "I've left two of your demands to the end. Before we discuss them, I'll ask Beau to step outside."

"What the hell?" Holland demands, his tanned face going red again.

"Mr. Russo," says Buckman, "please take Mr. Holland outside for a drink or a cigarette. Keep him company."

Holland glares at me on his way out, but Russo gives me a pass, which only makes me worry that he intends to find me later.

"Two things," Buckman says, after they've gone. "Blake?"

"We'd like you to reconsider something, Marshall," says Donnelly. "Having a U.S. senator from Bienville is just too helpful for this town to give it up. This Chinese thing is just a sideshow. We can make sure Avery votes honest on those issues. But don't take that competitive advantage away from the town. My God, think what John Stennis and Big Jim Eastland did for this state. Trent Lott?"

"Good old pork," I mutter.

"Damn right!" says Donnelly. "We'd appreciate you giving that deal point another look, son. Seriously."

"What's the second issue?"

Wyatt Cash speaks for the first time. "This matter of Buck Ferris's murder. I'll say right up front, I'm no fan of Beau Holland. And let's say, hypothetically speaking, that he and Cowart turn out to be guilty. If they were arrested and charged—or, God forbid, indicted—they wouldn't hesitate to deal whatever cards they have to stay out of prison. And Beau knows more about the business of this club than Sally Matheson ever did."

Arthur Pine leans forward and says, "We can't risk that becoming part of a conversation with a district attorney. Even our own district attorney. And given Beau's temperament . . . well, you understand."

"So where does that leave us?" I ask.

"There's more than one way to skin a cat," Donnelly says in a tone I've never heard from him before. It suddenly strikes me that, despite his genial exterior, the oilman is just as ruthless as the rest of these guys.

"Exactly what are we talking about?"

Buckman says, "It's hard to justify putting the county to the expense of a trial if the guilty parties are known."

Donnelly nods with apparent regret. "A waste of taxpayer money."

"Especially considering the complexity of the case," adds Pine.

"There's precedent in the club," says Buckman. "Just after the war, there were instances of collaboration with the enemy that had to be handled this way."

He's talking about the Civil War. At least I hope he is. The coldness with which these men discuss the execution of one of their own—or two, including Cowart—chills my blood. Of course, they probably see Dave Cowart as a mere peasant, not one of them.

I shake my head and look from Buckman to Donnelly. "Gentlemen, I'm asking for justice, not murder."

"Justice is a tricky business," says Wyatt Cash. "What's the difference to you, so long as the guilty parties pay for what they did?"

"For one thing, the public needs to see justice done."

"The public doesn't give two shits about Buck Ferris," growls Buckman. "Maybe his wife does, but damn few others. Why don't you ask Quinn Ferris if she'd be satisfied with us burying her husband's killers in a gator hole south of town?"

I've got a feeling I won't win this argument. "That reminds me, the deal we made for Quinn Ferris yesterday stands. One million."

Buckman grunts with displeasure, but he nods assent.

I've pushed these men about as far as they're going to go, at least for now. "Why don't we revisit the two outstanding deal points later today?" I suggest.

Buckman looks around the room. With a warning edge to his voice, he asks, "Is our business concluded then? But for those two points?"

In the tense silence that follows, Arthur Pine says, "Claude, I'm worried that Beau might be right. Marshall said it himself: this is potentially the biggest story of his life. No matter how pure his intentions today, it's hard to believe that he'll sit on this forever. We could jump through all these hoops, and in the end he could still screw us."

Jian Wu is looking at me as he would at some dangerous criminal it would be better to execute immediately.

"That sounds like projection to me, Arthur," I observe.

"He'll keep his word," says Buckman.

"Why?" asks Pine. "He told me last night that he's going to take us down. Why believe him now?"

"Because he's a good son of Bienville," says Donnelly. "He's a home-town boy, just like his daddy. Duncan always treated us right, and Marshall's no different. Not when it counts."

If Donnelly had let Buckman answer, the old man would have said, *Because if he doesn't, his mother and everybody else he cares about will die.* But Donnelly kept everything smooth on the surface, in the Southern tradition. The subtext is always known, but never spoken.

I stand and look at each man in turn. "You guys need to understand something. Sally's material has been digitized. Even if you tortured me to get every copy, you could never be certain you got it all. It can live on any server in the world."

"Then what the hell are we getting for all our money?" Pine asks.

"Life outside jail. By the way, I've also set up what's known as a Dead Hand switch. If anything suspicious happens to me or mine, the media won't be your only problem. My contacts at the FBI, the CIA, and the NSA will receive full reports within thirty minutes, whether I'm dead or alive. Make sure Holland and Russo understand that. You may not like it, but this is the best deal you're going to get."

Blake Donnelly looks left at Buckman, who seems to wrestle with his decision, but finally gives the slightest of nods. Donnelly gets up and walks down the long table to me, switching on his iPhone as he comes.

"Tap your phone number in there for me, Marshall."

I do. "Oh, one more thing."

Buckman's pained smile tells me I'm stretching his goodwill. For a moment I think of something Nadine told me before we parted this morning: *They should put a fifty-foot-tall statue of Sally Matheson on the bluff. Because she's going to be the salvation of this town.* But what I say is "The cop who waterboarded me is named Farner. I want that son of a bitch fired by the end of next week. I want my arrest record from last night expunged. Also, Sheriff Iverson doesn't run for re-election."

"Getting awful greedy, aren't you?" Buckman mutters.

"Done, done, and done," says Donnelly. "Have a good day, Marshall."

The oilman extends his hand, and God forgive me, I take it. This is the way business is done in America in 2018.

"Walk me out, Blake," I tell him. "I don't want any bullshit from Beau or Tommy."

ON THE STREET OUTSIDE the bank, I check my text messages. One from Nadine informs me that my father is still unconscious, but his cardiologist plans to bring him out of the coma later this morning. Nadine is at her store, but she's staying in close touch with my mother. I text her back: *Deal terms agreed. Will pick you up on way to hospital, probably 1 hour from now. Have errand to run first.*

She texts me a thumbs-up emoji in reply. Then she adds: *Be safe.*

After a last look at the Greek Revival façade of the Bienville Southern Bank, I get into the Flex and head east out of town. I want to be back at the hospital to watch my father sign the papers that will return the *Watchman* to the McEwan family. But before I do, I need to speak to Tallulah Williams.

CHAPTER 46

THE BELLE ROSE neighborhood in late morning looks like the cover of a Frontgate catalog. Zero-turn mowers scuttle over perfect lawns like manta rays combing the floor of a green sea. A gleaming mail truck rolls slowly from oversize box to oversize box, looking like a prop from a Steven Spielberg movie. And set well back from the road on every lot stands a McMansion to shelter the white refugees of Jackson, Mississippi. A few prosperous Bienvillians live out here, though I'm told that more bought in Beau Chene, built just five years ago. Only the lowering sky ruins what would have been a perfectly saturated Technicolor morning in America.

When Paul and I were growing up, he lived in a subdivision about a mile away from mine. The houses in his neighborhood were newer than ours, and nicer, but the Mathesons at that time were fully integrated into the middle-class life of Bienville. Now Paul and his father own homes in this physical expression of Beau Holland's dream: an exclusive refuge from the black crime of both Bienville and the state capital, which is only twenty-two miles from the entrance to Belle Rose. Paul and Jet live in a conventional McMansion, which Jet claims to detest, but Max built a Spanish hacienda that looks remarkably authentic. Besides the house, the property boasts a lavish outdoor kitchen, an infinity pool, a pool house, and a seemingly endless terrace of clay tiles. Behind the pool house stands another outbuilding, styled like a stable. For the past few years it has housed the family maid, Tallulah Williams, and her husband, Terrence, who worked as the Mathesons' yard man until he got too old for outdoor labor.

I park at the side of the hacienda, trying to keep the Flex out of sight in case Paul happens to return from Jackson. Not wanting to give Tallulah a chance to brush me off by phone, I didn't call ahead. The maid is probably busy inside the main house, so I walk quickly around it on the terra-cotta pavers, cross the expansive patio, and step up to the glass doors at the rear of the house. I knock casually, hoping she'll assume I'm a pool boy or a neighbor.

I stand alone for half a minute, but as I raise my hand to knock again, I see a large black woman slowly making her way to the door. She's not wearing the white uniform I remember from childhood, but a pair of blue jeans and an enormous flower print blouse. When Tallulah reaches the door, she puts her palm over her eyes to shield them and peers at me. At first she looks suspicious, but then the light of recognition dawns, and she pushes down the handle.

"Sorry I took so long," she says, pulling open the door. "I was in the kitchen watchin' my story and sortin' socks."

Tallulah's face is old and heavy, with pendulous jowls, but her eyes radiate wisdom and perception that misses nothing. She's been a maid all her life, but as a boy I learned you had to get up damned early to pull anything over on her.

"What can I do for you?" she asks.

"I'm Marshall McEwan, Mrs. Williams. You might—"

"Oh, I 'member you, Marshall. You and Paul used to play together at the old house. You's just a little string bean back then. You filled out good."

"I remember you, too. You took good care of us."

"I tried, Lord knows. I liked that old house better than this one. Even when I was younger, this would have been too much. Who you lookin' for out here? Paul? He up in Jackson at University Hospital."

I consider telling her that I've come looking for Max, then decide against it. "Actually, Mrs. Williams, I came to see you."

She stands in the open door with hands on her hips, studying me with an expression I cannot read. She looks worried but also intrigued.

"You'd better just call me Tallulah. That's what you called me when you was seven. No use changin' now."

"Yes, ma'am. Tallulah, I believe a friend of mine came out to see you yesterday. Blond, cute, about five-foot-six—"

She smiles. "Name of *Nadine,* like that Chuck Berry song?"

"That's her."

"You're lucky to have her as a friend. That girl got a good soul. Treats people right."

"Yes, ma'am."

Tallulah glances behind her, then says, "I reckon I ought to let you in, but I got a feeling Mr. Max might not like you bein' here just now. Am I right to figure that?"

"You could be."

"Well, then. What you wantin' to know? Same thing Nadine ax me?"

"Did she ask whether you'd caught Max with her mother, Margaret Sullivan?"

Tallulah gives me a conspiratorial look. "Sho' did. But Mrs. Sullivan wasn't the first wife I seen in here with her clothes off. Or the last."

"Did you tell Sally about it? Catching Mrs. Sullivan?"

"No, indeed. I wouldn't have hurt Mrs. Sally for all the money in the world. Poor soul put up with more trouble than any two white ladies I ever knew. That Mrs. Sullivan was all right, too. Didn't have no business messin' with Mr. Max. But then . . . a lot of 'em was like that. Moths to the flame, I reckon."

"I think you're right." I hate to push her, but I need to know what she knows. "Tallulah, I don't want to get you in trouble with Max. I'm going to get right to the point."

The maid looks wary. She probably hasn't had many good experiences with white men who tell her they are coming to the point.

"I know Max is Kevin's father," I tell her.

The maid grunts down deep in her chest. "Who told you that? Nadine, I expect?"

"No. Kevin's mother."

Tallulah draws back her head and regards me with open suspicion. "You don't come around this neighborhood much, do you?"

"I haven't, no. I stay pretty busy."

There's a new light in the maid's eyes, cold and judgmental. "That the only reason?"

"Why do you ask?"

"'Cause I seem to 'member you and Miss Jet bein' an item back in the day. I wondered if maybe it's hard for you to be around her."

I try not to betray any emotion, but my odds of hiding anything from this woman are pathetically low. "I think it's probably best to leave the past in the past."

Tallulah nods slowly. "I think you're right about that. If only we could."

"Sometimes we can't. As much as we'd like to."

She looks like someone being coerced to speak against her will. "What is it you want to know, Marshall?"

"I'm not sure. Do you think Sally killed herself because she found out Max was the father of that boy?"

Tallulah looks at the ground for a while, but then she looks up and nods. "Two, three years back, I'd have told you Mrs. Sally couldn't do that. Take her own life."

"And now?"

The old maid shakes her head. "Those who don't cry don't see."

Something about her answer pulls my mind away from the present. "When did Sally find out the truth?"

"Two, three months back, maybe. She would have seen it before, but her heart blinded her mind to what her eyes took in." A wistful look comes into the old woman's eyes. "The thought first struck me about the tenth time I changed that boy's diaper. I pushed it away, or tried to, but it stuck. By the time he was walkin' and talkin', I knew for sure."

"How?"

"Same way his mama knew, I reckon. Just watchin'. I'd raised Paul since he was a baby, you know that. And something jus' told me li'l Kev hadn't come from him. Kevin's got Mr. Max's blood. Got his bones, muscles . . . his *way*."

"Kevin acts like Max?"

"Mm . . . I don't mean that, exactly. He don't have Mr. Max's cruel way. But he's more straight-ahead than Paul ever was. He don't hesitate with nothing. Paul did sometimes. Still does."

"I see." Tallulah still looks wary to me, which tells me she's holding something back. "I don't want to beat a dead horse, but what do you think finally made Sally see the truth?"

"Mr. Max. He loves that boy too much. It's natural for a grand-daddy to love a grandchild, even dote on him. And that helped Mr. Max hide the truth. He was hiding one light behind another, you see? But his feelings as a father just grew and grew, until nothing would hide 'em. You can't hide the sun behind a candle."

Her image leaves me shaken, and even more worried for Paul. "What kind of shape do you think Paul is in, Tallulah?"

"Oh, he's in a bad way. So sad. He never should've married that Jet. Or the other way 'round, maybe. She didn't love Paul—not really. She may have *wanted* to, but she never did."

To this I say nothing. Tallulah is validating the truth of Jet's life as she told it to me last night.

The maid tilts her head to one side and regards me with fresh suspicion. "I reckon you know who Mrs. Jet loves, don't you?"

"Tallulah . . . I'm going to ask you one more hard question. Maybe a stupid one. But I would really appreciate an answer."

"You done used up your time, Marshall. I need to get back to work."

"Wait—please. I was told that Max raped Jet. That that's how he fathered Kevin."

Tallulah's gaze settles on me with gentle but insistent pressure. "Who told you that?"

"Does it matter? I want to know if that's what you believe."

Tallulah looks down at a flower bed filled with Louisiana iris. "It's gon' rain this evening. These flowers need it." When I don't respond, she looks up and says, "I'll tell you this. Mr. Max been with a lot of women over the years, white and black. He's a hard-dick man. He broke a lot of hearts over the years . . . but I ain't ever known him to force nobody. He never had to."

How closely her words echo Nadine's. "Maybe this time he did," I suggest. "Maybe he had to. To get Jet to submit."

Tallulah nods slowly. "Mayhap that's how it was. But I 'member that time pretty good. Wasn't but thirteen years back. Hard times in this family. Paul was takin' pills, smokin' that reefer. Drinkin' every morning, passed out by dark. Mrs. Sally was having health issues. Female troubles, but worse things, too. Terrible diverticulitis. But Mr. Max? He was his same old self. Heck, he wasn't but fifty-three back then."

"What are you telling me, Tallulah?"

"Nothing. I don't speak ill of nobody. All I'm saying is things had a funny feeling 'round here for a month or so."

"What did you see?"

"Nothing! I'll swear that on the Bible. I never saw nothing untoward."

"But you felt something."

She shrugs her big shoulders. "Like I said . . . things just felt *funny* for a bit. Then they settled back down. And next thing I know, Jet had the big belly. Then she was bringin' li'l Kev into the world. After that, it was like a rainbow coming out after a storm. Everybody got better. Whole house had a glow in it, all coming from that boy."

The memory has lightened this woman's heart. "And now?" I ask.

Another heavy sigh, and her lips pooch out. "This house done gone dark again. Darker than before, even, 'cause Mrs. Sally gone. Now . . . you've kept me too long. I need to go." She puts her hand on the door-knob and starts to close the door.

"Did Paul ever sense anything?" I ask quickly. "This is important, Tallulah. I'm trying to avert bloodshed."

She stops, looks back. "Paul's smarter than people think. A lot smarter than his daddy ever give him credit for. He has a lot of Mrs. Sally in him."

"I know that. What about my question?"

"If Paul sensed anything, he shoved it way down deep, with all the other stuff been killin' him all these years."

That's the Paul Matheson I know. But what she's suggesting about Jet goes against everything I know about her. And I know her better than anyone alive. Yet what reason could Tallulah have to lie? As I stare at the anxious maid, an answer comes to me. It's not a pleasant one, but it's grounded in hard reality.

"Tallulah, Max's murder alibi rests on you. He told the police you told Sally you caught Max with Margaret Sullivan. You and I know that's not true. If the police ask you that question . . . what will you tell them?"

She sighs heavily, then looks at my feet. "I don't know. One thing's for sure, nothing I say gon' help Mrs. Sally now. She's with Jesus. Long past these earthly travails."

"But you're not. Do you feel you owe it to Max to protect him?"

She looks up, and I see harsh truths written in her lined face. "Owe him? Boy, that's like askin' me why I still work for Mr. Max, when he coulda killed Mrs. Sally."

I don't even blink as I stare at her. "Will you answer me?"

Tallulah closes her eyes, then shakes her head with a sadness that has a centuries-old provenance. "This be where I stay at, Marshall. Who else gonna give me my own house to sleep in? Bills paid, water paid, 'lectric paid. Health insurance, even. I got no choice, have I? Body my age? You know that."

There it is. Odds are, Tallulah wouldn't tell me Max raped Jet even if she'd seen it with her own eyes.

"I'll tell you somethin' else for free," the maid goes on. "You ain't helped Paul none. I always thought you were a good boy. Your mama and daddy were good folks. But this ain't right, what been goin' on these past months. If Jet don't know better, then you ought to. If you had sense, you'd marry that Nadine before somebody smarter does it first. Now, I gots to go."

As I stand openmouthed, she shuts the door in my face, then slowly makes her way back toward the kitchen and her story.

ON THE ROAD BACK to Bienville, the sting of Tallulah's last words takes a long time to fade. I remember staring after her through the glass, watching her waddle across the floor of a twenty-first-century hacienda owned by a man whom she would as soon let fade into darkness, if she didn't depend on him to support her into old age. As for myself, I don't much feel like going to Nadine's store just now. I need to think. Most of all, I need to talk to Jet. But not yet. Right now I need to see my father. If he comes out of his coma without brain damage, I will give him the only medicine that might yet bring him relief at this point in his life. If he doesn't, then I will still speak the words that, after my revelation in the jail, I know must be said. For who knows what sleeping minds might register, and how deeply? Perhaps even in darkness the soul can be healed before the last warm pulse of life fades.

CHAPTER 47

"MARSHALL?" SAYS MY father, blinking his yellow eyes in the ICU bed.

They brought him out of his coma thirty minutes ago. Often patients emerge from unconsciousness in a state of confusion that can persist for hours or days, but after about ten minutes, Dad oriented himself to both recent history and his present situation. I missed his awakening, but Mom told me that what brought him fully alert was the sight of this morning's guerrilla edition of the *Watchman*.

"Right here," I tell him, touching the thin cotton bedspread over his thigh.

A soft cacophony of beeps, whirs, and pumping sounds fills the room, and voices leak in from the nurses' station beyond the half-open sliding glass door. Dr. Kirby has come and gone, heading for the lab in search of some elusive test result, leaving my mother and me to perform the play I've authored with the Bienville Poker Club.

"Dad?" I say, moving closer. "I need to tell you something. It has to do with the future of the paper."

He closes his eyes. "I don't want to talk about that. All these years I clung to it . . . fought to keep it open . . . then I lost it right at the end, when you were making good use of it."

"Dad—"

"Blythe showed me your special edition," he whispers. "I haven't read it yet, but I saw the front-page headlines. Printed on the job press, I heard."

"Aaron and Gabriel tried hard, but they couldn't get the folder for the old Heidelberg up to speed in time."

Dad lifts a trembling hand and points at the paper lying across his lower legs. "That's all right. I'm damned proud of that. Proud you did it."

I haven't heard him say anything like that since I was a boy. The lump in my throat stops me from going on for several seconds. "Dad, listen to me for a second, please. I've got a present for you."

"Did your mother tell you Marty Denis came by this morning?" he asks in his reedy whisper. "To apologize for what he did? That took some guts. I was asleep. Seems Claude Buckman took over the debts of Marty's bank. Poor Marty had no choice in the matter—had to do whatever Buckman told him to."

I don't know whether that makes me feel better or worse about Marty Denis. But it makes me feel better about the next two minutes. "Dad, stop talking. You're about to get one of those moments that's very rare in life."

At last his bleary eyes find mine. "What are you talking about, son?"

I nod to Mom, and she goes to the glass door, beckons through the opening. A moment later, Arthur Pine walks into the room in a rumpled suit. In his left hand are some papers, which he begins to unfold.

"Arthur?" Dad says, obviously confused. "What are you doing here?"

"I've got some papers for you to sign, Duncan."

Dad squints at him, the malevolence in his eyes burning right through the drugs. "You get out of here. I already signed away my life's work. I've got nothing left for a vulture like you."

Pine steps closer to the bed. "I'm afraid you don't understand. This agreement formalizes the full return of the Bienville *Watchman* to you and your family. Also your home. Blythe owns it free and clear now."

Dad blinks in confusion, as if this is some cruel prank.

"Marshall, this is upsetting him," Mom says.

"Dad, it's true," I say quickly. "You're getting the paper back. And the house. Mom owns it now."

"But—" He blinks like someone coming out of anesthesia. "I don't understand."

"The *Watchman* is coming back to our family," I tell him. "Debt-free. I'm going to go downtown and open up the doors today. Bring the whole staff back on. And as soon as you can walk, I'm taking you down there to sit in your office."

He's shaking his head as though worried he's having another hallucination. "But . . . how?"

"Turns out your son here is a hell of a businessman," Pine says. He holds out the contract and a Montblanc pen.

"Don't worry about it now," I tell Dad. "Just sign your name, and the *Watchman's* yours again."

"Not if you bought us out of the hole," he says, shaking his head on the pillow. "I won't stand for that."

"Marshall hasn't paid a cent," Arthur says with ironic bonhomie. "I can assure you of that."

I grab an *Architectural Digest* that my mom was reading and slip it beneath the contracts so that Dad has something to press against when he signs. Still bewildered, he looks over at Mom, who nods and says, "Sign it, Duncan. Take your paper back. For old Angus McEwan."

"Well then . . . all right." He takes the pen with his trembling hand and, after some struggle, signs a semblance of his name.

Arthur flips some pages and has him go through this struggle twice more. "That's it," says the attorney, handing me a copy. "You're back in business, Duncan, and close to two million dollars better off than you were yesterday afternoon. I'd stay to help you celebrate, but considering the circumstances—"

"You'll get the hell out," I finish.

Before he leaves, Arthur gives me what I can only describe as a smile of grudging respect. He's screwed enough people to appreciate a good fucking when he's on the receiving end.

After he's gone, my father says, "What the hell just happened?"

"Poetic justice," Mom says with satisfaction.

His jaundiced eyes seek me out, then settle on my face. "How the hell did you do this, son?"

"The Charles Colson method. I got them by the balls, and their hearts and minds followed."

Dad closes his eyes and mumbles something I can't make out. Then in a stronger voice, he says, "You gave up something. You had to. They wouldn't have given it back to us. Not free and clear."

"I gave up nothing."

"Did you hurt your career?"

"No," I lie.

"Did you bury something for them?"

Jesus . . . "Do you remember your Greek proverbs, Dad? Don't look a gift horse in the mouth."

"We're not Greek. I *always* look gift horses in the mouth. That's what journalists do. If something sounds too good to be true, it is."

"Dad, you could ruin a—hell, I don't know."

"I know it. There's only one way this is worth it to me."

Oh, boy. Here it comes. "How's that?"

"You stay here and run the paper. I'm too old now. Too damn sick. You make it what it should be. If what your mother told me about this morning's issue is true, then you've already made a good start. You don't answer to me anymore. The *Watchman*'s yours. I'll sign it over right now."

My mother walks to the edge of the bed and lays her right hand on my father's arm. "Let's stop talking about the paper. There'll be plenty of time for that later on."

Will there? I wonder. Looking at Dad's waxy yellow skin, I feel like I'm seeing a preview of what he'll look like in death. We stand in silence for a few minutes, and his eyelids slowly fall closed. His breathing sounds shallow and irregular.

"I'm going to see if they'll let us bring two chairs in here," Mom says. "Jack said he'd speak to the nurses."

"Thanks, Mom."

"You stay with him. I don't want him to wake up alone."

"I'm not going anywhere."

After she tiptoes out, I stand at the foot of the bed and speak softly, voicing words I should have said years ago. Decades, even. The problem is, I didn't realize that until I'd been drowned on a bench in the Bienville jail.

"I've hated you most of my life," I tell him. "You made my last three years of high school hell. You acted as if I didn't exist. You blamed me for Adam's death. I blamed myself for it, okay? But I didn't kill him. I know he got in that river to look out for me, but that wasn't all of it. He had his own reasons. Anyway . . . I know what it means to lose a son. And you lost two children. I can't imagine that."

I pause, feeling short of breath, only half hoping he's heard me. He lies there with his mouth open, his arms jerking every few seconds as his brain misfires. Stepping closer to the bed, I lay my hand on his cold arm. He doesn't stir.

"I've always said you blamed me all my life," I go on. "But the truth is, you blamed me for three years. After that, I got the hell out of here and slammed the door behind me. You never reached out to me. But if you had, I wouldn't have listened. That's the truth of it. I blamed you for blaming me. And now . . . it all just seems stupid. A waste. I've spent years trying to prove I'm better than you were at this job, and you've drunk yourself to death. And for what? Nothing I can see."

The glass door slides open behind me, and Mom leads in a male nurse carrying two folding chairs, which he sets up on the opposite side of the bed.

"Y'all must rate pretty high around here," he says. "They don't usually let us do this for folks, but Dr. Kirby called somebody and laid down the law."

"He's a good man," Mom says. "Thank you for setting these up."

"Yes, ma'am."

After he goes out, Mom says, "Did I see you talking to your father?"

"Not really. I was just letting him know he's not alone."

She gives me a long look, but she asks no questions. "Well, I'm glad," she says finally. "I hope you had a good talk."

"Yes, ma'am."

We sit in companionable silence for about ten minutes. Then the nurse returns to tell me I have a visitor in the ICU waiting room.

"Male or female?" I ask.

"Male. Said his name is Mr. Russo."

Tommy Russo? *Shit.* Now I regret leaving Nadine's gun in the Flex.

"Is everything all right?" Mom asks, with her preternatural perception of danger.

"Yeah, it's fine. I'll just be a minute."

I FIND RUSSO CHATTING up a young nurse in the ICU waiting room. He's smiling at her, but when he sees me, he says something in a low voice and she scuttles down the hall.

"What can I do for you, Tommy?" I ask.

"I hear your father's not doing good."

"That why you're here?"

Russo looks around the waiting room. "What a dump. Can you believe this is the best they can do?"

"Tommy—"

"That deal you made this morning. With Buckman and the others."

"Yeah?"

"I can live with most of it. But you gotta tell 'em to forget that community development fund. That million-a-year bullshit."

"Why's that?"

"Buckman says I gotta fund that whole nut out of my new casino. I can't do it. My partners won't stand for it."

At this moment the concerns of Tommy Russo's partners don't interest me in the slightest. "That's your problem, Tommy, not mine."

He shakes his head once. "See, that's where you're wrong. What you gonna do with that money, anyway? Repave some streets for the moolies, do some drainage projects? Their cars are for shit anyway. I should know. They fill up my parking lot night and day, while the owners gamble away their Social Security."

"I don't have time for this, Tommy. What's a million to you? If that's the price of a new casino, it's cheap."

"It's a mil I don't need to pay, Doc. I ain't your only problem, either. Beau Holland ain't goin' to jail. I'm just telling you. He'll kill you before that happens."

My image of Russo as a snake with its fangs folded back returns, because now I sense the fangs being deployed. Tommy steps into my personal space, and I get a strong wave of his cologne mixed with sweat.

"Listen," he says. "I feel bad about your old man. But he just got his newspaper back, right? He's whole again. Your mother's happy, I know. Now, that article you ran this morning, that got me in some hot water. You run another story like that, you dig deeper, you're gonna set some things in motion."

So much for Russo's understated threats.

"It's like Newton's law, right?" he goes on. "Yeah, I went to school. Every action has an equal but opposite reaction. In other words, you fuck me this way, you get fucked right back."

I don't know what to say to this.

"I hope you don't lose your old man," he says. "But if you do, look at it this way: you still got your mother, right? God bless her." Russo grips my shoulder like we're old friends from the neighborhood, then walks to the open door, turns, and looks back with an altar boy's face. "Think about that, Doc. I'll be seein' you."

"I WANT OUT OF here, Marshall! Get me out!"

I blink awake beside my father's bed. I don't know how long I've been sitting here, but my left arm and leg are both asleep, and there's a painful crick in my neck. With Dad's limited vocal volume, there's no telling how long he's been trying to wake me.

"Marshall?" he rasps. "Wake up, son! I need to get out of here."

"Dad, you can't," I tell him, getting to my feet.

My mother touches my lower back, and I feel as though she materialized out of the ether. "You're in the ICU, Duncan," she says. "You have to stay here and rest."

"I'll rest when I'm dead," he says with a spark of his old gruffness. "Get me out of here. That's what I want. That's *all* I want. Get Jack Kirby in here! He'll understand."

Mom turns to me, imploring me to think of a way to calm him down, but we both sense that nothing short of a sedative will bring that result.

"Dad, Jack's going to tell you the same thing we are. You can't just walk out of the ICU."

"Jack will tell you to go jump in a lake," Mom says, trying to lighten the moment. "How about some ice cream? Marshall can run and get you some Blue Bell."

"I don't want any damned ice cream," he growls. "I'd give a thousand dollars to jump in a lake. Get Jack on the damned phone."

"Where is it you want to go, Dad? Home?"

"No." The immobile mask of his face seems somehow filled with emotion. "I want to go to the cemetery."

I feel Mom's gaze on my face. "The Bienville City Cemetery?" I ask.

"That's right. I want to see Adam's statue. And you're coming with me."

Mom clenches my hand below the line of the bed. She's worried that this fit of agitation might be the last burst of life before a final heart attack.

"How long has it been since you were out there?" I ask.

"Too long." He looks at Mom. "Isn't that right, Blythe?"

"Too long," she agrees, and I realize that she's crying.

"I know you have Jack's cell number," Dad says. "Call him."

Mom's iPhone appears in her hand. Holding it close to her face to see the numbers, she presses a few buttons on the screen, then passes it to me.

After three rings, Jack Kirby says, "Blythe? Is everything all right?"

I turn from the bed and walk into the corner, wanting to get some distance from Dad, but not wanting the nurses beyond the glass to see me using the phone. "It's Marshall, Jack."

"Has Duncan taken a turn for the worse?"

"I'm not sure. I've got an unusual question for you. He wants to leave the hospital."

"Oh. Hell. I can't say I'm surprised. It's a common request at this stage."

"I'm not sure it's a request."

The old doctor chuckles. "Where does he want to go? Home?"

"He wants me to drive him out to the cemetery, to sit with Adam's statue."

There's a long silence. Then Dr. Kirby says, "I see."

"What would that do to him, Jack?"

"Marshall, he's in failure now."

"Heart failure?"

"Yes. And his liver's close to failing, as I've told Blythe. I've just seen some new cardiac numbers. There's a lot of muscle damage from yesterday's infarction."

"Speak up!" Dad says from the bed. "Or let me talk to him."

I lower my voice still further. "Are you telling me that no matter what we do . . . ?"

"I think you know I am. I'm sorry."

I close my eyes, grimly absorbing his funereal tone. "So you don't have any problem with me taking him for a drive downtown?"

"Well, I can't recommend it. And I don't know if he'll survive it. But if you're asking me whether I think my old friend would rather look his last over the Mississippi River or at a blank wall in the ICU—I think you know the answer."

My last resistance gives way. "Okay. How do I get him out of here?"

"To take him anywhere but home, you'll have to check him out against medical advice. He'll have to sign something."

"No problem there. I'll talk it over with Mom, but I have a feeling she'll agree."

"I do, too. Let me call admissions and try to smooth the way for you."

"Thank you, Jack."

"By the way—I really enjoyed my newspaper this morning. That's the way to stick it to the bastards."

"It felt pretty good."

"You still carrying that pistol like I told you?"

"I am," I tell him, even though I left it in the Flex.

"Good. Head on a swivel, boy. Remember."

"Yes, sir."

After staring through the thin curtain at the nurses sitting before their monitors, I turn back to the bed.

"What did he say?" Dad asks.

"We're going to the cemetery."

My father's eyes shine with pleasure. "I told you. Jack's a good egg."

Mom looks from Dad to me, then back again.

"Are you coming, Blythe?" he asks. "Are you up for it?"

She gives him a smile that must have taken immeasurable strength to summon. "No, darling. I need to run back to the house and check on some things. To be ready for your homecoming. You two go ahead. You need this trip. It's been a long time since Marshall went out there."

Dad looks at her for a few seconds, then nods. "Just the men, then. Let's pull out these tubes and hit the road."

CHAPTER 48

IN THE END, it's Jack Kirby himself who helps me lift Dad out of the hospital wheelchair and fold his rigid body into my passenger seat. Thankfully, the Flex sits lower to the ground than any other SUV, but still my mother stands to one side, waiting to grab him if he starts to fall. After I close Dad into the vehicle, Jack takes Mom's arm and walks us to the rear bumper.

"Anything could happen at this point," he says, his eyes on my mother's. "We all know that, right?"

She nods silently.

He turns to me. "I'll be here a little longer, then over at my office. If something happens, just head back this way and give me a call. I'll meet you here."

Mom squeezes his hand. "We appreciate this, Jack."

The old doctor smiles and give her a hug, then walks back into the hospital.

"I think this is the right thing, Mom," I tell her.

"I do, too. Call me if you need me."

"Are you really going home?"

She shakes her head slightly, and I see the truth in her eyes. "I'll just wait here. I've got a book to read."

And with that we part.

THERE ARE BASICALLY TWO ways to get from the hospital to the Bienville Cemetery, and they take roughly the same amount of time.

Most people would take the bypass to the river, then drive along the bluff, through the Garden District, and up to the cemetery. But you can also skirt the town until you hit Cemetery Road, then drive in east to west, the way farmers and soldiers and slave traders came in during the heyday of the town. I choose that route, because it will take us past many of the landmarks of our lives, both nostalgic and sorrowful.

Dad doesn't speak as I take Highway 61 around the eastern edge of town. He shifts in his seat as I turn onto Cemetery Road, which grumbles under the tires, a dozen layers of too-thin asphalt and pothole patches, eroding under the weight of log trucks rumbling between the Matheson sawmill on the river and the north-south artery of Highway 61. In a few minutes we'll pass the turns for the barn and my parents' neighborhood. Then we'll enter the city proper, transect the northern quarter of town, and arrive at the rear of the cemetery, where the road sweeps in a great circle around the lush green hills of the graveyard. An unbroken wall of gray cloud stands to the west, towering over the river. I hope the rain will hold off until our pilgrimage is concluded.

Without turning to Dad, I say, "Sometimes I feel like Cemetery Road is the only road in this whole town. You know?"

He grunts but doesn't comment.

"No matter where you're going, you either cross it or end up taking it at least part of the way."

"Seems like," Dad whispers, and then he coughs hard, struggles to swallow.

I've become somewhat accustomed to his illness over the past months, but there's no denying that last night's coronary knocked him down hard. He doesn't seem to notice the turn for his neighborhood when we pass it.

"I have some really good memories of this road," I tell him. "On our end of town, anyway. The old Weldon barn, and Delphi Spring out at Parnassus Hill. But the other end you can have. The cemetery and the river. This is a road with life at one end and death at the other."

Dad grunts again, and before I realize where we are, we're bumping over the railroad tracks where his wife and daughter died, and where Jet disposed of Max's gun and bloody hammer.

"We're all on Cemetery Road," Dad rasps, turning his head enough to see the kudzu-choked ravine drift by under the gray sky. "All the time. Some of us are still near enough to that spring to pretend the road leads somewhere else, or maybe goes on forever. But we're all headed to the graveyard sooner or later. Or that river."

I turn and find him looking at me, his jaundiced eyes filled with the pain of all his years in a bottle. But beneath the glaze of exhaustion, I see a faint remnant of the dreams he once had, and memories of heroic things he accomplished before violence and death came into his life.

"They tried to change the name of this stretch once," he says, looking forward again. "Where the accident happened. Goddamn Chamber of Commerce. Called it *Azalea Boulevard*. What a crock. They even put up signs, but it never took. Everybody knew they were on Cemetery Road. Might as well call it what it is, right?"

Right.

"What do you want to do out here?" I ask as the green hills of the cemetery come into sight.

"Just sit," he says. "I don't think I can walk. Even with your help."

"We'll just park under the statue then, and stay in the car."

"Look at the river some."

Great, I think, feeling my stomach roll.

I pull through the rear entrance of the cemetery, a massive wrought-iron gate set on masonry pillars. The asphalt lane beyond the wall is smooth but narrow, maintained by the Bienville Cemetery Association. Under the steely sky, I drive slowly through cuts between gentle hills covered with marble stones, obelisks, crosses, and mausoleums that range in size from garden sheds to small houses.

Turning toward the river, we ascend the long road to Laurel Hill, the westernmost redoubt of the graveyard. Standing on one of the highest stretches of the Bienville bluff, it towers 250 feet above the Mississippi River. The McEwan family plot has occupied part of this ground since the 1840s.

"There it is," Dad says, pointing with his shaking hand.

The shoulders and head of Adam's statue have become visible above the stones on the back side of the hill. Strangely nervous, I drive the last hundred yards to the edge of the hill, then park on the grass before the brick-and-marble base that supports the monument. From the passenger seat, Dad can glance to his right for a full view of Adam, but in general he's facing Louisiana and the river.

From this spot, if you look upstream and down, you can see almost fifteen miles of the Mississippi. Looking westward over the delta fields, now planted with cotton and soybeans, you can see to where the land falls away with the curvature of the earth. To the south I see the great towers that carry the electrical cables across the river; the one on this bank is where Adam danced atop the pinnacle while I clung to the ladder in terror, four hundred feet below.

"Well, here we are," Dad says softly. "Good old Stavros."

This statement doesn't puzzle me as it would others. The origin of Adam's statue has been the grist for a dozen local legends. The truth is simple enough. During his work as a reporter for the army, Dad served as a correspondent in Italy for a year, and he took his chance to see all he could of the ruins of the classical world. He made friends everywhere he went, and one man he became close to was a sculptor. Half Greek and half Italian, Stavros Romano began his career as a promising artist, but by the time Dad met him he was sculpting memorial pieces for the private cemeteries of wealthy families. Several of his statues had been cast in bronze or concrete and were sold as copies around the world.

Shortly after Adam died, Stavros somehow heard of his passing. Five months after the memorial service, a large crate arrived on a freighter at the Port of New Orleans. There it was transferred to a barge headed upriver. Five days later, I drove my father and mother down to the Bienville port to see what Stavros Romano had sent them.

Inside the crate was a life-size marble angel of breathtaking beauty. The angel, a young male, sat on a stone with an air of weary melancholy, as though exhausted from dealing with the travails of the earthly realm. The statue had been hand-sculpted, and I was too young to grasp what that would have cost had my father commissioned it. My parents were so stunned, they weren't sure what to do with it. The magnitude of the gift seemed too great to accept. And yet, somehow the statue seemed to fit the hole that Adam's death had blown in our lives.

It was my mother who voiced our collective conviction: "It looks like Adam," she said with reverence. "Not exactly like him, but . . . the spirit of him. We'll put it in our plot, up on the hill." My father resisted at first. By that time, he had not merely abandoned the idea of God, but was enraged by it. If his friend's statue was going into the McEwan family plot, Dad wanted its wings removed, broken off, and the stumps sanded down to hide the fact that they'd ever been there. I could see his point. As beautiful as they might have been on an eagle, the folded wings gave the stone angel a supernatural aspect, whereas without them the figure would have appeared as a strong and handsome boy of about eighteen, the ideal of Greek beauty.

My mother refused to allow it. She said they hadn't the right to deface Stavros's sculpture, and besides, the town would probably rise up to prevent the desecration of a holy statue. Without his wings, she said quietly, the boy would possess an almost decadent, earthly beauty. In this he was like Adam, and in the end that may have been what swayed my father to permit this exotic object to become Adam's memorial, which now—thirty-one years after his death—is one of the most famous landmarks in the town. When I was in high school, I used to come up here alone sometimes, and I saw more than one tugboat captain shine his spotlight up on the high bluff to pick out the angel where it stood sentry duty at the edge of the cemetery.

"What do you think happened to him?" Dad asks. "Most people get found when they die in the river."

"I don't know," I answer warily. "I used to think about it a lot."

"I like to think he made it all the way down to the Gulf."

"Me, too," I confess.

"A river burial," he mutters. "I don't like that. They say Hernando de Soto's men buried him in the river so the Indians wouldn't realize he was mortal. That was about fifty miles south of here. I like the idea of burial at sea better."

"I do, too."

"I like the British navy burial service."

This conversation is surreal, but I suppose I should have expected something like it. "I think I remember some of that from Patrick O'Brian's books."

"*Master and Commander*," he says. "Think of it. Wrapped in your hammock and weighted with cannonballs. That's the way to go."

"Do you remember the words? I think they're from the Book of Common Prayer."

"Nothing's perfect," Dad grumbles. "I remember some—leaving out that nonsense about Christ."

"Say them," I tell him, feeling butterflies in my stomach. "This can be Adam's real funeral. For you, me, and him."

"The McEwan men, eh? Why not?"

He raises a trembling hand to his mouth and clears his throat. Then, in the strongest voice I've heard him use since I returned home, he recites, "*We therefore commit his body to the deep, to be turned into corruption . . . looking for the resurrection of the body, when the sea shall give up her dead.*"

In the silence that follows, I hear the cry of a far-off bird, the groan of a truck's engine down on Cemetery Road. "I like that," I tell him. "It's fitting."

Driving out here, I intended to repeat the explicit apology I made to Dad while he was sleeping in the ICU. But this doesn't seem the proper moment. He's staring fixedly at Adam's statue. "After I'm gone," he intones, "I want to be cremated. No worms for me. Blythe can keep some ashes. But the rest I want you to take out in a boat and cast over the river. I know you don't like going out there, but I'm asking you to do it. I'll follow Adam to wherever he went."

My God. He's still haunted by the loss of his eldest son. But then . . . am I not also?

"All right," I tell him. "I'll do it."

Dad raises his left hand a couple of inches in acknowledgment but says no more. Looking at the back of his head, the brittle white hair and frail shoulders, it strikes me how awful it must be to wither and die while your mind is clear. It's a terrible paradox, sufficient to kill religious faith in a thinking man. Of course, the reverse is also a paradox: to live for years with a ruined mind in a healthy body. Some might argue that's worse, but only from the outside. At least the victim suffering that fate remains unaware of the true horror of his plight.

Dad looks out over the river for a while, and I leave him be. At length he says, "I wish I had more time. To make up for some things. This body of mine's about used up. I haven't done it any favors with my drinking. But once I got Parkinson's . . . I just couldn't abide it. My vanity. I hate to confess that."

"You always had a lot of pride."

"It's vanity, not pride. And vanity's a low thing. That's one thing the Christians got right. Vanity's a weakness. That which is crooked cannot be made straight, and that which is wanting cannot be numbered. There's nothing wrong with being sick."

"No. But it's human to feel the way you do about it."

His eyes find mine, and I see despondency in them. "I don't recognize the world anymore, Marshall. Maybe when you stop feeling at home in the world, it's time to leave it."

Before he can go further down this road, an urge to confession takes hold of me. "Dad, back at the hospital, you asked if I'd agreed to bury anything in exchange for getting the paper back."

"Did I?" he asks, still looking toward the river.

"Yes. And I avoided the question. But I did agree to bury something. Probably the biggest story of my life. I sold out. And I'm not sure why."

"Something to do with the Poker Club? Burying their sins?"

"Yeah. Some big ones."

He takes a few shallow breaths. "I used to be a zealot about ethics. So damn self-righteous. But let me tell you something: I know of cases where guys buried stories—big stories—and I'm talking about legends. I'll carry that to my grave, but I *know*."

"You can't tell me more than that? Why they did it?"

He shrugs, still watching the Mississippi roll below us. "In one case, a president asked him to. Didn't think the country could handle it. In another, the story would have destroyed a friend. I also knew a couple of guys who took money not to print something. We're all human."

"These Poker Club guys. They basically sold a Senate seat. To a foreign country."

Dad cuts his eyes at me. "To get Avery Sumner in? Huh. Are they going to make it right?"

"Sumner's going to resign."

"What did you get in exchange for your silence? The newspaper? Our house back?"

"A lot more than that. A new public school, built by next year. Thirty years of full taxes for the city from the paper mill. Money for Buck's widow. A lot more besides."

Dad shifts in his seat, as though forced to by pain. Then he growls,

"Here's what I think. If that's the deal you made, you probably accomplished more good than you could in twenty years of reporting from your high horse. That may sound facile, but I believe it. If you can hold their feet to the fire and make them do what they promised . . . then sleep with a clear conscience."

I feel as though a killing weight has been lifted from my shoulders.

"It's a business of whores now anyway," he says. "Access whores. Everybody talks about the renaissance of journalism. Renaissance, hell. Reporters trade favorable coverage for access every day. I guess you can't blame them, since any day on the job could be their last. The bean counters are stripping our newsrooms bare. TV anchors recruited at beauty contests and modeling agencies chase ratings like hounds in heat . . . The politico-media complex is as bad as anything Eisenhower warned us about. At least you made a clean deal. In exchange for burying one story, a whole corner of this impoverished state gets a new lease on life. Thousands of kids get a better education? That's a fair trade, in my book."

Dad stops speaking, his chest heaving from the effort of speech. He coughs from deep in his lungs, a ragged sound that finally trails off into a worrisome wheeze. I mean to sit quietly with him, but another confession rises unbidden from my heart.

"I did that one other time in my career," I say softly. "I buried part of a story, betrayed my calling."

"When?"

"My Pulitzer book. That night Paul saved me in Iraq . . . he killed some civilians. While escaping the house, we got trapped in an alley with a car blocking us in. A Honda Accord. Paul riddled it with bullets, and we scrambled over the top. It turned out there was a family inside."

Dad looks out the window at Adam's statue. "War's full of horrors like that. You know that. What if Paul hadn't fired?"

"We might not have made it. There could have been insurgents in that car. But that's not my point. As we clambered over that Honda, I heard a child cry out from the backseat. A whimper, really. The parents were dead in the front, but this child had lived. I started to go back, but Paul jerked me to the ground. Seconds later, a heavy machine gun chewed the car to pieces."

Dad looks back at me but says nothing. He knows more is coming.

"Four years later, when my son drowned, I couldn't escape the feeling that his death was some kind of karmic payback for me not saving that Iraqi child. It may sound crazy, but I became certain of it. Obsessed with the idea. I'd let an innocent die, and my little boy had been taken as payment. A life for a life. The universe had balanced things out."

My father looks into my eyes without pity. "You think you've been tormented by that for ten years. But you haven't. You've been comforted by it."

Anger flares in me. "Did you understand what I said?"

He nods solemnly. "Better than most. But you're not looking hard enough at yourself. Believing your son's death was a price exacted by fate, or karma, or God, lets you believe there was reason to it—meaning behind it, however hard to bear. The *true* horror is that you're wrong. There's no universal tally of good and evil, balancing right and wrong. The Christians with their God-has-a-plan fantasy, the Hindus with their karmic balance . . . it's all wishful thinking. Primitive religious impulse. Linus's damned security blanket." My father's eyes burn with hard-earned conviction. "The truth is infinitely simpler and harder to bear. Your son died because your wife had four glasses of wine instead of three. Adam died because you and he tried to swim that damned river down there when you were drunk and exhausted. No other reason."

"Then why did you blame me for it?"

"Because it *was* your fault!" He shakes his head with what appears to be self-disgust. "But it was Adam's, too. His more than yours, because he was older. Old enough to know better. But Adam was dead. You were still alive. That was your bad luck. I should have borne all the pain myself. I should have let you be a boy. But I wasn't strong enough, Marshall. I'm so sorry for that."

I never thought I would hear these words from him.

"After my first wife and child died," he says, "I was lost. Searching for meaning, like you. But Adam's death taught me the terrible truth. There's no meaning to be found in tragedy. Only in our response to it. What we do matters, nothing else. That's what kept me at the bottom of a bottle for fifty years. I wasn't searching for an answer—I'd been *given* the answer. And I couldn't handle it. It's tough to look this life square in the face. The plight . . . the void. *For in much wisdom is much grief; and he that increaseth knowledge increaseth sorrow.* That's why your old man's a drunk."

"Ecclesiastes," I whisper. "From my atheist father. All this time, I've figured you blamed yourself for some sin I never knew about and transferred your guilt onto me."

Dad's face fills with loathing. "Freudian claptrap. If that were the answer, I'd have shot myself and been done with it thirty years ago." He squeezes my knee with surprising force. "You're alive now because Paul Matheson shot that family in Iraq. If you'd gone back for that child, you'd have died. Your own son would never have been born. You'll never penetrate the heart of that equation; the human brain isn't up to it. The randomness will drive you mad. Those Poker Club bastards could put a bullet in your head tonight. What's to stop them? Fate? Providence? Prayers? Hogwash. Maybe that deal you made today will save your life, or even your mother's. I sure hope so."

"That's a pretty grim vision of the world, Dad."

"Listen at your peril."

"I don't know what I'm going to do after all this. My personal life's a mess. And the country has drifted so far off course, nobody even cares about the truth anymore."

"You're right. We're witnessing the last gasp of white America, and it's a lulu. Our people think the land of liberty's their God-given country club and the caddies have forgotten their place. But revolution's coming . . . just not the one they think. I don't envy you, son."

"Things always come back into balance, though, right? Eventually."

Dad goes very still, eerily so considering his disease. "Eventually. Balance came back in 1918 after twenty million deaths. It came back in 1945 after seventy million. It's getting the pendulum back to the midpoint that's the killer. And right now it's being pushed *hard* right, all around the world. The last gasp of Ozymandias—once more, with feeling."

"Take it easy. We can't fix it from this hill."

"No . . . hell. You're right."

This may be the only time I've heard him speak that phrase to me.

"I can't fix it at all," he says, obviously exhausted. "It's your turn. But you can't do it from Mississippi."

"I thought you wanted me to stay here and run the paper. That's what you said at the hospital."

"Ah, hell. We're nothing but a backwater now. Back in the sixties, this was the front line. But the war moved on. There's still plenty of injustice here, but look at the rest of the country. I should have packed you boys and your mother up around 1973 and moved you to the new trenches."

"I was one year old in 1973."

"That's what I mean. Doesn't matter now. The Moving Finger has writ."

This Khayyam allusion is a flash of his old character. *"Nor all thy Piety nor Wit, Shall lure it back to cancel half a Line,"* I continue.

"Nor all thy Tears wash out a Word of it," he finishes.

In this moment, a blessed memory returns to me. I'm sitting on my bed with Adam, while Dad reads aloud poems from *The Oxford Book of English Verse.* I don't know how old I am, but even Adam is still a boy. Each week we must choose a poem to memorize. I usually pick some brief Byron or Shelley, but Adam has phenomenal recall. I've watched him recite all 109 stanzas of Oscar Wilde's *The Ballad of Reading Gaol* without a hitch. I do, however, remember choosing *The Charge of the Light Brigade* by Tennyson on one ambitious night.

How could I have forgotten poring over that text before I went to bed each night for a week? *Half a league, half a league, Half a league on-ward . . .* And then the evening I recited it, after Dad got home from work. I'd never been so nervous. I sweated, turned red, worried I'd pee in my pants. But somehow I started, working through the lines, word by rhythmic word. I remember Adam's glowing face, encouraging me all the way, just as he did by walking along the side of the pool when I practiced swimming. The rhythm helped me find the words: *Storm'd at with shot and shell, Boldly they rode and well, Into the jaws of Death, Into the mouth of hell, Rode the six hundred.* Behind Dad I could see my mother watching anxiously, worried I would stumble. But the words poured out with ever more certainty as I neared the end, like a horse running the last quarter mile to the barn. After I finished, Dad stared at me with a new emotion in his eyes: pride. He spoke not a word of criticism. Then he reached out and tousled my hair while Adam and my mother applauded.

How could I have forgotten this?

"Oh," Dad groans. "No, wait—"

As I turn, he twists in his seat. Then his arm flies up as though he's trying to reach around himself and grab his own shoulder blade.

"What is it?" I cry, my heart quickening. "What's the matter?"

"My back—oh, it's bad."

"We need to go." I reach for the key, but he grunts in a way that tells me not to start the engine. He's breathing hard and shaking his head. "It'll pass," he gasps. "Nothing to be done anyway."

"You don't know that. I want Jack Kirby to see you."

"Let's just sit here, son. I don't think it'll be long."

A wave of panic hits me, sending adrenaline crashing through my veins. "I'm taking you back," I tell him, cranking the motor.

"Damn it—"

"I'm taking you back and that's an end to it!"

He settles back in his seat. "All right. Hit the gas, then."

The Flex has a truck engine under the hood, giving it a surprising amount of power. Once we clear the cemetery gate, I switch on my hazard lights and use every cubic centimeter of horsepower as we roar down Cemetery Road, making for the intersection with Highway 61. I drive with my left hand only. My right rests on Dad's left forearm, gently squeezing at brief intervals to let him know I'm with him.

"Won't be long," I say every few seconds.

"Okay," he says once. A mile down the road he whispers, "Not bad . . . not as bad."

As I screech onto Highway 61, the vehicle swaying on its shocks, I realize there's something wrong with his breathing. The silences last too long, and when the breaths come, they're like gasps. Something like a snore follows these gasps, but it's not a snore. It's almost like he's trying to talk.

Lifting my hand from his forearm, I lay it across his forehead. The skin is cold. Unnaturally so. As this realization sinks in, somewhere out of the deep reservoirs of trivia in my brain—accumulated during the writing of thousands of news stories—two words rise: *agonal breaths*. That's what I'm hearing now. My father's in cardiac arrest. The gasps are his body's last-ditch effort to get oxygen to his starved organs. His brain has already winked out, like a guttering candle. *Oh, God*, I think, an image of my mother filling my mind. *Why did I take him out there?*

"Dad? Dad!"

Nothing.

He hasn't inhaled for thirty seconds. Maybe forty. Just when I think he's finally gone, he gasps again, a long inhalation like a breath—and yet not a breath. Then comes the long, rippling sound like a snore.

"I'm with you," I tell him, wondering if he knows I'm here. Maybe he can feel my hand, at least. "I'm with you, Dad," I tell him. "I'm with you . . ."

MY HAND IS STILL on my father's forehead when we reach the hospital, but his skin feels like the flesh of a mushroom. He didn't breathe or gasp as I drove the final mile. He never will again. Dr. Kirby and my mother stand outside the ER entrance. Jack has his arm around Mom, comforting her as best he can.

When I stop, Jack leads her to the passenger window. I press the window button with my left hand. As the glass sinks into the doorframe, Mom sees my hand resting on Dad's forehead. Thankfully, his eyes are closed.

"I shouldn't have taken him," I say helplessly.

"You did right," Dr. Kirby says. "He wanted to go."

"Did you talk about Adam?" Mom asks.

"We did. I learned a lot. I'm so stupid."

"No. You did the right thing." She looks up at me at last, and her eyes are clear. "I'm glad you were with him at the end."

"Me, too," I say, my voice breaking. "I talked to him all the way back, so he'd know he wasn't alone."

Dr. Kirby nods his approval. A single tear runs down my mother's cheek. "I know he heard you," she says softly. "It's over now. He's with Adam now."

CHAPTER 49

PAUL MATHESON TRUDGED up the fourth-floor hallway of the University of Mississippi Medical Center, watching his father's half-open door. He hadn't eaten in a while, so he'd gone down to the McDonald's on the first floor of the hospital for a cheeseburger. Paul was no health-food nut, but he wondered if Mississippi's medical center was the only one in the union shoveling Big Macs and fries into patients and their families during medical crises.

He was functioning on four hours' sleep. After the ER docs had evaluated and admitted his father last night, Paul had rented a room at the Cabot Lodge, just across Woodrow Wilson Drive, to have a place for Kevin and Jet to crash if they decided to stay over. They had stayed about six hours, but his father had been sleeping a lot, and Kevin had baseball practice, so they'd headed back to Bienville in her Volvo. Paul hated to miss the practice, especially since his father would also be absent, but the other dads would just have to handle it.

From what the doctors said, Max was lucky to be alive. If Warren Lacey hadn't managed to get him to a hospital when he did, his vital functions would have shut down on Parnassus Hill. Max had a depressed skull fracture, a subdural hematoma, and a bruised cerebral cortex. Surgeons had drilled a small hole in his skull to relieve the pressure on his brain, and now he was doing as well as could be expected. The neurosurgeon who'd informed Max about his close call during his post-op visit was surprised to hear his patient answer: "Doc, I walked out of an army hospital in Chu Lai and returned to my unit six hours after suffering worse than this." That was Max all over. Had to show the doc he was the toughest SOB he'd ever operated on.

But maybe Max was. For when Paul turned into room 437, he was shocked to find his father sitting up in bed—or at least he'd raised the bed to where he appeared to be sitting up. Max had his cell phone in his hand, and he appeared to be texting with somebody.

"What's going on, Pop?" Paul asked. "You trying to kill yourself already?"

Max looked up. "Duncan McEwan just died."

Paul felt a momentary dislocation in time.

"Seems Marshall drove him out to the cemetery, to Adam's statue. He had a heart attack out there."

"Mr. McEwan never got over losing Adam," Paul said. "Not even after, what, thirty years?"

"Thirty-one." Max was looking at his phone. "I remember it like yesterday. I put my boat in the river and spent two days searching for that boy. Damn shame. Adam was the best natural athlete to ever come out of this town. Best white one, anyway."

Paul nodded. "Them trying to swim the river that morning was the stupidest thing I ever saw."

"And it was Marshall's idea, you said. At least you were smart enough not to try it. Shows your sense. It's a miracle Trey and Dooley didn't drown, too. Idiots."

Paul went silent at the mention of his cousins. There was something about that morning he'd never shared with a soul.

"What's the matter?" asked his father. "You look like you saw a ghost."

"I'm just tired."

"Bullshit. Spill it, boy."

Paul wished he hadn't said anything about the river. "Two weeks after Adam drowned, I was over in Jackson with Dooley and Trey, staying at Uncle Richard's house. I heard them talking about that morning. They were high as hell, really out of it. Apparently while Marshall and Adam were separated out there, Dooley and Trey swam around and messed with Adam in the fog. Pulled him underwater eight or ten times. He eventually got away, but Trey was pretty sure they wore him out doing that."

Max stared at his son as though he'd rather not hear the rest, but

Paul couldn't stop himself. "Marshall said it was Adam cramping up that killed him. But Trey felt like him and Dooley had murdered him, pretty much."

Max's gaze drifted off Paul to the window blinds letting in shafts of late-afternoon light.

"Pop?"

"Things happen," Max said. "High school boys do stupid things. Best keep quiet about that from now on. Adam McEwan is still remembered as a saint in Bienville."

"I'm not stupid," Paul said angrily. "I was just telling you. And at least Duncan can never know about it now."

"That's right."

"How's your head feeling?" Paul asked, wanting to change the subject.

"Miniature jackhammer going off in my skull. Kevin gonna make it to practice in time?"

"Yeah. And I talked to Jack Bates. He'll practice the pitchers today."

"What Jack Bates knows about pitching would fit in my mother's thimble."

Paul gave his father an obligatory laugh.

"Sit down a minute, son. We need to talk about something."

"I can't hear standing up?"

Max sighed heavily. "You'll want to sit down for this."

Paul sat on the arm of a vinyl chair that folded out into a twin bed.

"I don't know if you know this," his father began, "but you're having marital problems."

"Yeah? I don't know a married couple that's not."

"This is different. This is a crisis."

Paul was too tired to get excited about his father butting into his marriage. "What are you talking about, Pop?"

Max lifted his left arm and pointed to the bandage on his head. "Your friend Marshall didn't do this."

Paul sat up straight. "Who did?"

"Your wife."

He blinked in disbelief. "What are you talking about?"

"I need to tell you a quick story. Wait till the end before you start asking questions."

Paul shifted on the arm of the chair, but he forced himself to remain silent.

"You know how I've been missing baseball practice lately?"

"Yeah. I thought you were working."

Max nodded. "It started that way. About six days ago I missed practice to ride out to the Zurhellen acreage and meet one of the heirs. You remember that?"

"Yeah."

"Well, I was going pretty fast, and I came up on Jet's Volvo out on Highway 36. From a couple hundred yards back I saw her turn on Blackbird Road, near Marshall's place, the old Mendenhall farm. For some reason I followed her. He's got a security gate out there on his private drive. Well, I saw Jet open that gate without fully stopping, like with a remote switch. I pulled up afterward to make sure the gate doesn't have some kind of automatic opener on it. It doesn't. That means she had a remote in her car."

Something fluttered in Paul's chest, like a skipped heartbeat.

"I left that day," his father went on. "But it bugged me. So the next day, before practice, I parked out near that gate. Sure enough, there came Jet, headed in the same direction and right back through the gate. Well, I locked my truck and walked through the woods to Marshall's house. I saw them together on his patio and filmed them with my phone."

"Are you the one who sent me that picture of them hugging?"

Max sighed with irritation. "I am. But let me finish. I went back the next day because I couldn't really believe what was going on. I had to be sure."

"Why didn't you just show me that damn picture? Why email it anonymously?"

"I wanted to warn you without making you too mad. Wake you up to what was going on, make you pay attention."

"Dad, you're stirring up shit over nothing. Jet and Marshall have been working on stories and cases ever since he got back. She recruited him into her crusading bullshit."

Max's face hardened. "Do you want to hear what I've got to say or not?"

"All right," Paul said, filled with irrational anger.

"I staked out that gate for three days. She's been going out there every day. Usually during Kevin's baseball practices, when you and I are a hundred percent distracted. Out of the way. Remember how many practices she came to last year? Most of them. This year?"

"Almost none."

"Busy working, right?"

Paul thought about it. Before he could get very far, his father said, "Open the email I just sent you."

"What?"

"Check your Gmail account."

Paul took out his phone and opened his email. A lot of messages had accumulated in his inbox, but the most recent was from his father, and it had a file attached. Paul clicked on the file and waited.

An image much like the one he'd received yesterday appeared, a long shot of Marshall's back patio, probably filmed from the tree line—only this image was video. At first Paul saw no one, but the whole image jiggled due to the shooter's unsteady hand. Then the frame zoomed a little, and he discerned a figure lying in a chaise on the patio. Just as Paul decided the figure must be Marshall, his wife walked into the frame naked. He recognized a once-familiar rocking of her hips, something he'd seen less and less over the years: the sexual arrogance and confidence Jet displayed when she was eagerly anticipating sex.

Paul felt like his father had handed him a venomous snake that he knew must bite him, but which possessed some hypnotic power that prevented him from dropping it. He was doomed to watch the writhing of the oily scales in his hands until the fangs sank home.

On the tiny screen Jet paused in front of the chaise, apparently talking to the man lying on it. Then she turned her back to him and reached around her hips, taking the cheeks of her behind in her hands. The camera zoomed to the limit of its power, and the image went grainy. Paul felt the fangs dig into his flesh as Jet pulled her cheeks apart. From his angle, he could see only her breasts and the dark tangle at her pubis, but he knew exactly what Marshall was seeing. Something moved at the level of the chaise. An article of clothing flew away.

Jet placed a foot on either side of the chaise and lowered herself onto Marshall's midsection. She went down smoothly, almost without hesitation, then began rising and falling above him, working with a powerful rhythm that Paul had once known like the rhythm of his own heart.

"What's it look like she's working on there?" Max asked. "A newspaper story?"

Paul barely registered the words. He was thinking that for Jet to go down so smoothly—without even a hint of foreplay—she must have already been wet. Purely from anticipation. Not just moist . . . but *wet*. He couldn't count how many years it had been since the prospect of sex with him had produced that response in her. In fact, the last woman he'd caused to get that way was a young waitress from the Twelve Bar, about three years back.

"You see how it is," Max said. "Can I talk, or do you need some time?"

It took Paul a few seconds to find his voice. "At least I have something concrete to take action on now. Evidence."

"That's where you're wrong," Max said. "This situation's far more complicated than you realize."

"How's that?"

"Because of *custody*. Who gives a shit about the marriage? Wives come and go. It's your son that matters. Kevin."

"What are you saying, Pop? Surely you have enough power to get me a clean divorce and guaranteed custody."

"There's a wrinkle in this situation."

Paul's bowels were churning down low. He tried not to let his father see how upset he'd become. "I'm listening."

"You know I like Jet," Max said. "I've protected her from the club's retaliation for years. When she got Dave Cowart sent to jail, then went after Dr. Lacey's license, I kept the club from hitting back at her. And they didn't appreciate that, I can tell you."

"Dad, for God's sake—"

"I talked to your mother about this before she passed."

Paul blanched. "You didn't."

"Had to, son. Sally saw a lot, and I wondered if she'd suspected anything. Turns out she did. She'd been worried about Jet leaving for a long time. She'd even talked to her about it, like women do. What she found out, I can hardly bear to tell you. But you have to know. Because who knows what they might be planning now? Look what they did to me.

They're desperate now. They've got to be worried I'm going to tell you everything."

"Are you telling me this has something to do with Mom killing herself?"

Max gave a somber nod. "No doubt about it. Your mother was already depressed about her illness. I didn't know she was sick, but I knew Sally. She dreaded any affliction like that. But this affair with Marshall . . . she worried it would drive you to suicide. She didn't know you like I do, Paul. I know you're going to do what's necessary, after we talk. This is why I had to tell the cops that bullshit story about Margaret Sullivan. I didn't dare tell them what really pushed your mother to the edge."

"Mama thought I'd kill myself over Jet having an affair?"

"No, no, hell no. Listen, son. You've got to steel yourself for this. It's the hardest thing you'll ever have to face in your life."

Paul had no idea what could push his father into this kind of mood. "I'm ready. What is it?"

"Kevin isn't your son. Not biologically."

A flash of heat crossed Paul's face.

"Did you hear me?" his father asked.

"That's bullshit."

"Not according to your wife."

"What are you saying?"

"Jet told Sally that she slept with Marshall back in 2005. When his Afghanistan book came out. He stopped in Jackson on his book tour. Marshall's wife had just had their kid. She wasn't on tour with him. Jet went to his hotel. Six weeks later she realized she was pregnant. Your mother told me you and Jet had been trying for a long time to have a kid, with no luck. Well, she popped Marshall during that stop in Jackson, and that was it. He planted one in her. That's Kevin, as much as I hate to admit it."

Paul got up off the chair, then fought to keep his balance. "I don't want to hear any more."

"I know you don't. But you have to. Because you have to be smart from now on."

Paul hated the way his father talked to him. *Smart from now on . . .* like he'd been stupid all his life up to now. Paul folded his arms across his chest to keep from punching something. "That lick to your head scrambled your brains, Pop. Kevin looks like me. Like us. Like our side of the family. Everybody says that."

Max nodded. "We see what we want to see. And other people tell us what they think we want to hear."

"Are you saying other people know about this? Or suspect it?"

"No. Just that seeing a resemblance is subjective. Next time you look at Kevin, you're going to see Marshall in his face. So get ready for it."

"Bullshit!"

Max sighed, then gingerly rubbed the bandage on his head. "I know this is tough. But you have to face it squarely. Can you swear to me you've never had a funny feeling about Kevin? A distance? A feeling that maybe he wasn't quite yours?"

Paul closed his eyes. He couldn't let those thoughts in. If he did, he wouldn't be able to hold himself upright.

"Listen to me, Paul, like you've never listened in your life. Jet's a lawyer, and she's been thinking about this for a long time. Marshall's no dummy, either. They've got a plan, I guarantee it. She wants to divorce you, go back to Washington with Marshall, and marry him. And she means to take Kevin with her."

"You're lying."

"She told me herself last night, right before she hit me with that goddamn hammer. What she didn't tell me, Marshall did."

"When? Last night?"

"Yes, but I went to see him the other night, too. I showed him the video. Tried to scare him away from her."

Paul could barely contain his fury, but at the root of it was shame. How could all this be happening without him even suspecting it? "Why didn't you tell me, Pop? Why did you waste all this time?"

His father looked at him with more empathy than Paul could ever remember seeing in his face. "I never wanted you to have to know this, son. I wanted to handle it for you. Protect you. You don't deserve what they've done to you. It would be tough for any man to handle. And you haven't had the easiest time these past years."

Paul felt his balance going. "So what the hell were you doing out on that hill last night?"

"I asked them both to meet me out there. I didn't want anybody seeing us together. I told them they were crazy and had to end it. I told them that if they kept on, things would end badly for them, but Kevin would go through hell, too. Marshall wouldn't listen. He and I got into it. I was getting the best of him, but Jet went to my truck and got my hammer. She would have killed me if Marshall hadn't stopped her. But they sure didn't mind leaving me out there to die of exposure."

"I'm going to take Kevin from her," Paul heard himself say. "She's never going to see him again."

"I know that's your first instinct—"

"First instinct! What else would I do?"

"Think, that's what. Kevin's very existence is proof that Jet committed adultery. But follow that string out a little. Say you get a DNA test proving Kevin was fathered by Marshall. The endpoint of that may be divorce, but not divorce with you getting custody. Because the god-awful truth is that *Kevin is Marshall's son.* You ain't gonna wind up with him. He'll be lost to us forever if you go that route."

"Surely not in Bienville," Paul argued. "What good is all the power your damn club has if it can't get a judge to give me custody of Kevin?"

"Ordinarily, I'd agree. But this paternity problem can't be got around. Blood outweighs everything else. Now, there's ways around it, of course. But they're not legal."

"Like?"

Paul saw a familiar light in his father's eyes. "Plant a pound of cocaine in Marshall's house. I've already broken in there once, just to take a look."

"Seriously?"

"Sure. But the thing is, that won't shut him up. He could still talk from prison. And Jet could still take Kevin away from you."

"Then what? I know you. I know this is leading to something."

Max ground his jaw as if in pain, then spoke in a voice devoid of all emotion. "There's only one answer to this, son. Something's got to happen that leaves only one parent alive. You. Then there's no doubt whatever. You'd have custody forever, and no one would ever ask for a DNA test. Why would they? Nobody alive would even suspect the truth."

"You're talking about murder."

His father shrugged. "I'm taking about justice. I'm talking about a woman taking another man into her bed and wrecking a marriage. A man whose life you saved in wartime, who then turned around and betrayed you when you were at your lowest point."

Paul could hardly make himself believe that Jet and Marshall were capable of that level of betrayal. "They *told* you they mean to leave and take Kevin?"

"Paul, you're nothing to them but an obstacle to be gotten around."

Paul leaned over and took hold of the bed frame with his left hand. He was afraid he might throw up.

"I told you I went in his house," Max said. "Look what I found."

Max reached into a slot in his cell phone case and brought out a folded piece of ruled notebook paper. Paul took it from his father with quivering hands and unfolded it. What he saw was the intricate pencil doodle of a talented junior high school girl, the kind of thing Jet would spend most of an hour on during history class. He knew Jet had drawn it, because of the Arabic flourishes around the letters, which made the whole thing look like some sultan's ceiling in an Ottoman palace. The shading variations alone looked like the work of a professional artist. All this Paul registered in the time it took to draw a breath. But what lasted longer, what burned itself into his brain and heart, were the letters at the center of the design: *Jordan McEwan*. Contained in those two words was the dream of young Jordan Elat Talal, who would years later become Jet Matheson. Scrawled across the bottom of the intricate design were more words, much smaller, yet even more painful, because they were obviously more recent. Written with a pen, they read: *Remember this?! Prophecy after all!*

"Son?" Max said.

A tear fell onto the paper, staining it gray. Paul had not cried in more years than he could remember, except on a couple of occasions when Kevin had made him so proud that he could not contain his emotion.

"It's gonna be all right," his father said. "I know it's bad now, but we're gonna make it right. We just have to work it out."

Paul slowly folded the paper, slipped it into his pocket, and walked out of the hospital room. As he boarded the big elevator with a legless black man in a wheelchair, he realized he had ascended to a plane where earthly concerns no longer mattered. That piece of paper, combined with his memory of the lovemaking video, had wounded him in a way that blades and bullets never could. But it was his father's revelation about Kevin's paternity—and the obscene ongoing deception that it implied—that triggered a dark epiphany unlike anything he'd ever experienced.

Max was right. All his life Paul had sensed some ineffable distance between himself and his son. He had never spoken of it to a soul. In fact, he'd hardly let himself dwell on the feeling long enough to analyze it. To do so would have been like walking out onto four inches of ice over a bottomless lake. But now . . . his father had dredged the unspeakable secret from that lake bottom and winched it to the surface. Paul's new awareness blotted out all else and could be expressed in a single sentence that played over and over in his mind: *I may be a fool, but you'll die before you take my son . . .*

CHAPTER 50

DEATH IS ABSOLUTE. It sweeps all before it. Death long expected arrives like the eye of a slow hurricane: days of wind, rain, and thunder—then silence. The rain will return as the storm moves through, but you won't feel it, being numb. Once the storm passes, you won't ever be the same. Feeling returns to a person changed.

When a parent dies, your center of gravity is altered. Even if you lived apart from them—even if you walled yourself off from all contact—you are irrevocably lessened by their passing. Death, like gravity, respects no barriers.

The hours since my father died have blurred into vignettes of my mother's old friends stopping by with foil-covered casserole dishes and Mom compulsively straightening up the house. Intermittent thunder has made the house shudder, but the rain never comes. I've checked my iPhone at least a dozen times, but as yet I've received no call or text from Blake Donnelly or Arthur Pine. Perhaps my father's death has made them reluctant to call, but I can't imagine sentimentality getting in the way of Poker Club business—especially with their reputations and even their liberty on the line. More than once I've worried that they might decide to kill Beau Holland rather than force him to stand trial for Buck's murder, then present me with a fait accompli. Claude Buckman and company are nothing if not practical.

I took it upon myself to remove the assistive apparatus of Dad's illness from the front room, though I could see it upset Mom to watch it packed away. She wanted it out of sight, but its removal was like an

erasure of his final months in this house. During the silent caesuras between neighbors' visits, she and I sit in the den, going through old photo
albums she dug from a cabinet in the guest room. Most date to before
Adam's death. Some of the best pictures are from those rare occasions—
once every year or two—that it snowed in Bienville, and we hauled pizza
pans out to the Indian Village to slide down the snow-covered ceremonial mounds. In one shot, Dad, wrapped like a Sherpa, carries me up a
steep mound while Adam, who looks about seven, trudges beside him
like Edmund Hillary summiting Everest. No one looking at these photos would guess that this happy triumvirate would be shattered only a
decade later.

"Duncan did his best," my mother says beside me. "He really did."

"I know," I tell her, granting her this fiction.

"I wish he could have lived to see you reopen the *Watchman*."

All I've done so far is pass the keys to Ben Tate, who has a skel-
eton staff downtown, setting up tomorrow's edition. Ben's more than
a little pissed that I've restrained him from going hard after the Poker
Club, and I can foresee problems in hewing to the deal I made with
Buckman. But right now Ben is content to focus on the murders of
Buck and Sally, as well as the imminent arrival of the Department of
Archives and History archaeologists who will assess the paper mill
site.

"We'll do it tomorrow in style," I tell her. "If you don't mind, I'd like
to take that portrait of Dad from your bedroom and hang it in the lobby
of the building."

This takes her by surprise, and moves her deeply. I have seen other
widows become faithful tenders of their husbands' legacies. "I think
that's a wonderful idea," she says. To hide her tears, Mom changes the
subject. "I've heard Buck Ferris's memorial is tomorrow afternoon, out
at the cemetery. Do you plan to go?"

"Sure, of course. I didn't know."

"I'd like to go with you. Buck did this family a great service."

That he did. "We'll go together."

As she turns the album's pages, I see the shining faces of people I
haven't spoken to in years. Bienville children who grew up and spread
across the country, though most remained in the South. In every photo-

graph, the kids seem oriented in relation to Adam, like bodies of lesser density finding their position in relation to a star.

"That boy was something," Mom says softly. "Wasn't he?"

"He was."

As she slowly turns the pages, moving through Christmas presents and Fourth of July firecrackers, I remember Tim Hayden talking to me in the little park up the street from Nadine's bookstore. "Mom, can I ask you something personal?"

"About your father?"

"No, Adam."

"Of course."

"Did you ever wonder if he might be gay?"

"Adam?"

I instantly regret the question.

Mom lays her hands flat on the plastic-covered album pages, draws back her head, and looks at me. "What makes you ask that?"

"I . . . never mind. I just wondered."

After a few moments, she smiles in a way I've never seen before, defenselessly, as though allowing her deepest self to become manifest on her face. "Of course he was," she says. "Your father never knew. I don't think Duncan could have handled it. Not back then. Although . . . for him, Adam could do no wrong. I suppose that would have tested his love."

"How long have you known?" I ask.

"Oh, I suspected when he was a little boy. Never mind why. Mothers know these things, if they pay attention. They don't always react well, of course. But they know. At least I did."

"Did you ever talk to anybody about it?"

Another smile touches her mouth and eyes, this one wistful. "Jenny Anderson," she says. "His girlfriend from junior and senior year. About ten years ago, she was in town for Christmas, and she stopped by to see me. Jenny knew. And she loved him like we did. For what he was. All he was."

"I must be blind," I murmur, feeling ashamed.

"We're all blind about some things. Different things for each of us. That's what makes life so hard."

I lean back on the sofa, and Mom lays her hand on my knee. "I'm not teasing you now, Marshall. You know who reminds me of Jenny Anderson? Nadine. That young lady has a pure heart and an old soul. I hope you're not blind to that."

Before I can answer, my burner phone pings in my pocket.

"Excuse me a sec, Mom. This is work." I get up and take the phone out of my pocket, feeling her gaze on me as I walk to the door. Looking down at the screen, I see a text from Jet: *Have to see you ASAP. I know it's worst possible time, but this is an emergency. Things falling apart. Leaving for your house now. I'll park in the woods till you let me know it's ok to approach house. So sorry about your dad!*

"Is everything all right?" Mom calls.

"Yes," I tell her, leaning back through the wide door. "It's just work. Would you be all right if I had to leave for about an hour?"

She nods without speaking, but in her eyes I see the knowledge granted by her phenomenal perception. "Be careful," she says. "That blindness we were talking about gets people hurt."

This is as close as she'll ever come to warning me away from Jet.

"I will, Mom. I'll be back before you know it."

FIVE MINUTES AGO I watched Jet walk from the tree line to my patio for the third time this week. As she did, I thought about all that's happened since she shed her clothes on the same walk three days ago. We live in a different world now—so different that had she stripped while making that walk today, I would have worried she'd lost her mind. As she walked, swiftly today, her gaze on the ground, I wasn't thinking about Max, or Paul, or even my father. I was thinking about my conversation with Tallulah Williams. Oddly, I also remembered how Jet left her earrings in my bathroom two days ago, as a test. She'd wanted to know whether Nadine would find them there. A human gesture, obviously. But it bothered me more than I'd realized at the time.

She sits before me now with a haunted face, her dark, long-fingered hands flat on the kitchen table. It's odd to have a table between us, but today it seems appropriate. Something about this visit seems formal, even forced. I have a feeling she's about to tell me why I feel that way.

"Max sent me here," Jet says simply.

"I thought he was in the hospital in Jackson."

"He is. He called me from his room at UMC."

"Max made you come here?"

She nods. "He told me that if I didn't, he would tell Paul and Kevin that he's Kevin's father."

My God. The man is lying half-dead in a critical care hospital, and he's still applying pressure to the object of his obsession.

"Why did he want you to come here?"

Jet closes her eyes, sighs heavily. "Do you know what it's like to carry a secret that can destroy your life? Your whole family? I've heard people describe it as dragging a weight, but it's not like that. It's more internal than that. I used to feel it like a tumor inside me, one that could turn malignant any time. Or an aneurysm that could burst. But that's not really it, either. Do you know what it's like?"

"No."

"An explosive vest. I strapped it on thirteen years ago, and Max has the detonator. I've been wearing this fucking thing for thirteen years, waiting for it to go off, and the man with the detonator has been slowly going mad."

I've never seen Jet in this much pain. How did she mask it for so long? I want to comfort her, but I have no idea how to go about it.

"I don't know if I can do this," she says. "I feel like I'm about to knife you in the heart. Or myself. I don't know if this feels more like homicide or suicide."

Jet reminds me of my wife in the pit of postpartum depression. There's a deadness to her voice that I couldn't have imagined until I heard it. And all the light has been sucked from her eyes.

"Let me try to make this easier for you," I say gently. "I think I know what you're about to tell me."

"How could you?"

"I spoke to Tallulah this morning."

"Tallulah?" Jet looks blank. "What about?"

"She's an observant woman."

Jet shrugs and shakes her head in puzzlement. "What did she 'observe'?"

"Well . . . nothing terrible, or even untoward. She just described to me a feeling that she had."

A sudden alertness in Jet's posture tells me she's made the connection. "Oh," she says softly. "Oh."

"Did you come here to tell me that Max never raped you?"

Her chin begins to quiver, and her eyes close. Even her hands are shivering.

"You don't have to tell me about it," I say, meaning it as a kindness. "I have no idea what you were going through then. It had to be a terrible time."

"I'd prefer to tell you," she replies, her voice braced with iron. "If you can listen. It's not what you think. Nothing like what you must think."

What can she mean? "Did he rape you?"

She looks stricken. "No."

"Then . . . what should I think?"

"Will you please listen to me? Five minutes. That's all I ask."

I nod slowly. "I'm listening."

Jet takes two deep breaths, then licks her lips like someone about to read aloud from a book. "The situation was pretty much as I described last night. Though Paul was, if anything, in worse shape than I let on. He had constant pain from his head wounds. He was addicted to Oxycontin. Warren Lacey wrote prescriptions for whatever he wanted, but Paul also bought street drugs from a worker at the sawmill. I think the multiple IED concussions had profoundly affected his brain. He would fly into rages, he was impotent nearly all the time, and he refused to seek help for any of it."

"And you?"

"I did what women always do. I blamed myself."

"Why?"

"For marrying him."

I feel like we're retracing old steps. "You said that last night. That you married a man you didn't love. But I don't think you're being honest with yourself. Or me. You feel that way now, but not when you walked down the aisle."

Frustration etches itself into her face. "You're so wrong, Marshall.

Did I not come to you in D.C. only weeks before Paul proposed to me?
Did I not ask if there was a chance for us?"

"Yes . . . sort of. But you waited until you were right at the edge of
the cliff."

Anger flashes in her eyes. "I still did it. That's more than you did.
But you shut me down. You slept with me, of course. But you let me
know you weren't ready to deal with it in a real way. With us."

"I wasn't ready. What was the hurry?"

"We were twenty-eight! Not eighteen."

I turn up my hands on the table. "To tell you the truth, I was still
hurt by you going back to Paul after college. I assumed you wouldn't
have done that if you didn't love him."

Jet's gaze flits over the surface of the table, as though she's looking
for crumbs that need sweeping up. "I've come to realize something,"
she says. "Marrying someone you don't love is a sin. Because it sends
both of you to hell. It destroys the other person first, but in the end it
gets you, too. The magnitude of what you've done, the damage you've
caused by forcing you both to live a lie."

Her words take me back to my own marriage. "I see the truth in
that. I've lived that. But that sounds like a lot of marriages, Jet. Wilde
said the one charm of marriage was that it made a life of deception absolutely necessary for both parties."

"Glib and depressing."

"Why don't we focus on you and Max?"

"There *is* no me and Max! There never was." Though Jet's outward
affect is melancholy, I sense fearsome anger beneath. "What happened
was simple, pragmatic, utilitarian. By 2005, Paul and I had been trying to have a baby for four years—since before he went to Afghanistan
after 9/11. All through his rotations home, even when he had that stupid contracting company in Iraq. After one year of failure, I got myself
thoroughly checked out. My plumbing was fine. But Paul refused to get
even the most basic fertility tests on himself."

"That I believe."

"He'd tried to kill himself twice that I know of in that time. He
pretended both episodes were accidental overdoses, but I knew. He was
about to become another VA statistic. I really believed a baby was the
only thing that might save him. He wouldn't consider adoption, and if

I'd mentioned a sperm donor, he'd have killed me. The thing is, even though I knew the situation wasn't my fault—the infertility, I mean—I felt like a failure."

Sitting here listening to Jet, I think of how people in the town see her—smart, tough, put together, in control—the mother of an athlete destined to become a star. No one could imagine the life she's describing to me now.

"So . . . what did you do?"

Something changes in her voice, an alteration in pitch that renders it more mechanical, less human. "It happened a lot like I told you last night. Sally was ill after surgery. I'd been taking care of her, but it was Tallulah in the bedroom with her that night. Max and I were in their living room, by a fire. We'd all been drinking. Paul was passed out twenty feet away."

"And?"

"Max asked me what was wrong with Paul. He could see his son dying before his eyes. Killing himself. He said he didn't blame me, but he wondered why we hadn't had any kids. He said Paul refused to talk to him about it."

"So you told Max the truth."

Jet nods. "He listened. He didn't say anything for a while. I just sat there, drunk, wondering what the endpoint of all this was. I was very near getting in my car and driving away from that family. I think Max knew that. Sally certainly did. She'd already begged me not to go."

At last, I realize, *I'm hearing the truth.*

"Max just threw it out there," she says suddenly. "I'll never forget it. He said, 'Hell, if the problem's that you can't get pregnant, we can solve that easily enough. No use anybody dying over that.' I just stared at him, trying to understand what he meant. I know it sounds sleazy, but . . . it wasn't like you think. Max wasn't creepy or lechy about it or anything. Not back then. It was a calculated solution. A transaction. Like, 'If this is what needs to happen to give Paul a chance, then let's make it happen.'"

I can't believe how reasonable it sounds. Maybe from the outside, someone would think she was crazy. But when I put myself in her place, I can almost understand it. "Go on," I say gently. "I'm not judging you. Seriously. Did you sleep with him that night?"

"No. I thought about it for twenty-four hours. The truth is, I'd considered desperate options before. I'd thought about going to New Orleans and picking up some stranger in a bar. Telling him a different name and having sex with him. But the risks of that just seemed insane."

Compared to sleeping with your father-in-law? I ask silently.

"I'd also considered asking a male friend to help me. But I didn't have any male friends I could ask that of. You, maybe. But you weren't exactly a friend."

"No. And there's the resemblance factor."

Her eyes flash. "Exactly. Any resemblance to you, Paul would have seen in a minute. I think that's what settled my decision. Because if the baby looked like *Max*, there'd be no problem. Everybody would simply say he looked like his grandfather, which is the most natural thing in the world. From a logistical point of view, the plan was perfect."

"But from a psychological one, a nightmare."

She sighs deeply. "I know that now. The thing is, Marshall . . . it *worked*. For the first nine or ten years. Max wasn't weird about it at all. He was a sperm donor, that's it. Once I was pregnant, he played his role perfectly. And as I told you last night, Kevin was Paul's salvation. The whole family's, really."

"Until Max started getting older?"

"Right. And Sally. We went through all this last night. Kevin started turning into the boy Paul never quite was, at least in Max's eyes—"

"And Max wants him. God, this is bad. If Paul *ever* learns the truth, it'll end in violence. No question."

Jet gives me a sickly smile. "Do you think anything else would have brought me here like this? The explosive vest, remember? Max has his hand on the detonator. And there are a lot of people standing close to me."

Me, for one. "He won't keep your secret forever, Jet. Max wants that boy. And he wants *you*."

"I know." Her eyes close again. "All I can do now is try to postpone that day."

"Or hope Max dies."

Her eyes open. There's a burning light in them that wasn't there before. "I did what I could in that direction last night. But the bastard lived."

I've got a much deeper appreciation than I did last night of why she wanted Max dead on Parnassus Hill. Very gently, I ask, "Did he really try to rape you last night?"

"He did."

"And six weeks ago? When you stabbed him?"

She looks away. "Not that time, no. That was the first time he threatened to tell Paul and Kevin the truth. He told me he loved me, that we were meant to be together, and Kevin was the proof. I lost my shit. I couldn't stand to listen anymore. I grabbed a knife off the counter and aimed for his stomach, but he jerked left and caught the blade in his side."

"Dr. Lacey must have patched him up that time, too."

"I guess. But last night was worse, Marshall. He told me if I didn't break it off with you and divorce Paul, he was going to ask Paul to step aside. He repeated that when he called me today, from the hospital."

The colloquial syntax sends a chill through me. "What does 'step aside' mean in that context?"

"Set Paul up in Dallas or Atlanta—in theory expanding their business. Once Paul was committed, Max would tell him the truth about Kevin. Threaten to cut him off completely if he resisted. No job, no inheritance, nothing. Then make sure my divorce went smoothly and I got custody."

"That's delusional," I whisper. "Paul wouldn't go for that, no matter how much money Max gave him. In fact, Paul would blow his brains out."

"Max's?" she asks. "Or his own?"

I think about this. "Max's first, then his own. That's my bet."

Jet slides her chair back and stands, then begins pacing between the table and the back window. "I think Max believes Paul would kill himself, leaving no obstacle between Max and a life with Kevin and me."

"Except me," I remind her. "And he sent you here to end that."

She nods but says nothing. Reflecting on Max's desire to remove me from his life makes me miss Nadine's pistol, which I slipped into the rag drawer by the refrigerator before Jet arrived. If Max were not bedridden in University Hospital in Jackson, I wouldn't risk being even that far from the gun. As I look into Jet's tired face, Tallulah Williams's description of the "funny time" in the Matheson home comes back to me.

"Jet, I get that you basically used Max as a sperm donor. But it's not like you used a turkey baster."

Her head turns sharply, and I see a warning in her eyes.

"I have to ask you something," I say in a low voice.

"Please don't," she says, reading my mind.

"How many times, Jet?"

She raises her hand to her face, covers her eyes.

"Jet . . . ?"

"Three, okay? I checked to be sure I was ovulating. Then I did it."

"Where?"

"Don't."

I wish I could save her the pain of this. But I can't. "I hate myself for asking, but I need to know."

She blows out a rush of air, trying to bleed off anger or guilt. "Once at their house. In the guest room, like I told you last night."

Only in a very different way than you described. "And the other two times?"

"At the spring."

This takes me aback. "Delphi Springs? On Parnassus Hill?"

She nods, looking at the curtained window.

"Where we used to go," I say softly. The awful symmetry of this makes me hate her for an instant. The thought of Max plunging into Jet's willing body beside that pool gives me vertigo—

"It was the most secluded place we could think of," she says, still refusing to look at me.

"Not Max. He manages thousands of acres of timber. Even you could have found some other place."

She turns back to me in desolation. "Does it matter what patch of grass my naked ass lay on? I did it, Marshall. I gave myself to him. Surely that's the only relevant fact."

She's right. We stare at one another without words. This is a new experience, to watch each other with something like loathing. Perhaps we don't loathe each other so much as ourselves. We say nothing, for there seems nothing to say. My mind makes a few silent forays into the twisted logic of the situation, but my instinct for self-preservation pulls it back. Jet giving herself to Max was like a snake eating its own tail. By consummating her relationship with him, she turned herself inside out, becoming a living negative of the person she was before, and subverting a fundamental family dynamic. She achieved the goal she sought, a son for her suicidal husband, but at what cost? It's hard not to believe that on the day Kevin Matheson was conceived, the seed of his family's destruction was planted. And three nights ago, Sally Matheson died.

Who will be next?

Given the true state of affairs in the Matheson family, it's easy to see how Jet might have viewed me as the only means of escape within her grasp. Knowing I'd never stopped loving her, she could have lured me here in the hope that I could somehow extricate her from the terrible web that bound her, without destroying everyone in it. But her hope was in vain. No one could accomplish that.

"So what now?" I ask, feeling exhausted and close to despair.

"I'm going to go," she says. "I know I've wounded you. I look in your eyes, and I see that you can't imagine touching me. Don't deny it. Maybe that will change, I don't know. I only want to be sure you know one thing. I loved you when we were kids, and I never stopped. I loved you when I came to you before I married Paul. I've loved you the whole time I was married. I know you don't trust me now. But when you think about all this later, consider one thing: to tell you the truth was to risk losing you. It meant that every time you looked at Kevin, you would think of Max. Every time you made love to me . . . the same. Which would have killed any hope for us. Telling you also meant confronting it myself—in the daylight world, outside of Max and me, who were the only two who knew for thirteen years."

"Tallulah knew."

"She never told me that."

"Do you believe now that Sally figured it out?"

Jet turns back toward the window. "I don't know," she says distractedly. "Did you hear something?"

"No. What?"

"A deer, maybe? A hoof on concrete?"

The sharp rap of metal on glass reverberates off the kitchen cabinets.

So loud and sudden that my heart begins hammering against my breast-bone. Jet whirls to me, paler than I've ever seen her.

Max? I mouth silently, remembering his earlier visit.

"He's in the hospital!" she hisses. "If that's Paul—"

"Open the goddamn door!" shouts a male voice.

Paul's voice.

CHAPTER 51

JET AND I stand frozen in my kitchen, staring at the back door. She's on the far side of the table. I'm nearer the island.

"Do we run?" she whispers. "Or open it?"

My mind goes to Nadine's pistol in the rag drawer, eight feet from my hand. But arming myself against Paul, who has Special Forces training in firearms, strikes me as a suicidal gesture. "We can't run from this. He'd hear the car start. He'd get there before we could back out of the driveway. Or he'd follow and catch us at the gate."

She nods in resignation, still watching the door. "He's supposed to be in Jackson. He's been with Max. He may know everything." She looks back at me. "He may have come to kill us."

Paul batters the door again with his fist.

"We've risked that from the beginning," I tell her. "There's no hiding the truth anymore. Whatever happens happens."

This time Paul hits the window with something hard, and it shatters.

Jet walks forward and lays her hand on the knob. Then she looks over her shoulder and whispers, "I love you. I never lied about that."

"I know. Open it."

She pulls the door inward and steps back as though she expects a hail of blows or bullets.

First I see only the empty doorway. Then Paul moves into it, fills it. If Jet looked haunted when she arrived, Paul looks possessed. Pale and unshaven, he's wearing the same clothes he had on last night at the hospital. But most unnerving are his eyes, which are so inflamed that the sclera appear bloodred. If he doesn't have an eye infection, then he's running on alcohol, adrenaline, and maybe something stronger.

"Well?" he says in a conversational tone. "Did I interrupt the foreplay or the afterglow?"

"Neither," Jet says. "We're just talking."

Paul steps over the threshold. The moment his body displaces air from my kitchen, I realize how wrong it is that I'm here alone with Jet. The fact that I loved her first means nothing. That she loved me first means nothing. They exchanged marital vows, and in this moment, in the eyes of the law and of the world, she belongs to him. As I ponder this, a black semiautomatic pistol swings into view, dangling from his right hand. He could kill me now with a reasonable expectation of being acquitted.

"Do not speak," he orders Jet. "Not unless I ask you a question. You've forfeited that right."

While she gapes at him, he turns his attention to me. "What should I do with you, Marshall? My good friend. Yesterday you denied you were fucking my wife. Today . . ." He waves his gun hand. "Today everybody's going to tell the truth. Is that understood?"

When no one answers, he looks at Jet. "I know it was you who hit Pop last night. Not Marshall. Correct?"

"Yes."

Paul takes a step toward the table, then digs a cell phone from his pocket. "To spare us any awkward denials, I want to play a little video short."

The floor shifts beneath my feet. He holds his phone out toward us.

"Paul, don't," Jet pleads.

"Why not? I've watched it all the way from Jackson. A forty-minute loop. I could have whacked off a couple of times if I hadn't had to drive. Noticed something new every time."

The sound of forest insects comes from the phone. Then the screen lights up with the green sweep of my backyard. Even from the kitchen counter, I can see Jet's naked body sitting astride mine on the patio steamer chair.

"That didn't come off Pornhub," Paul says. "That's the real deal."

Jet is looking at the floor.

"*Watch it, goddamn it!*" Paul roars, walking around the extended phone so that he can watch it with her. "At least have the guts to face up to what you did."

Jet looks at the screen. Both their backs are to me now, but I'm not stupid enough to think Paul isn't aware of every move I make.

The geometry of the kitchen suddenly seems important. There's ten feet of floor space between the table and the back wall. Jet and Paul occupy that rectangle. The table is six feet long and three feet wide and runs parallel to the back wall. There's eight feet of space between the table and the island, which is tucked into the U of cabinets and appliances. I'm standing between the table and the island. And Nadine's pistol—

"Here we go!" Paul says with false excitement. "First orgasm coming up!"

"Christ, please stop this," Jet pleads.

"Aaaaaand . . . *boom!*" Paul cries. "Good one!"

Jet gives him nothing.

"By my count," Paul says, "we'll have thirty-three seconds of rest, then the lady will start again, going for her second pop. Anybody want to wager on how long it takes her to get there? No?"

"Stop," Jet implores. "This is pathetic."

"*Then how could you do it?*" he shouts, so loudly that Jet draws back from him. "*Huh? I'm waiting!*"

Instead of yielding more ground, Jet stands straight and says, "You ask me that? Like you haven't screwed a dozen waitresses and assistants since you married me?"

I knew that Paul had cheated on her, but this revelation shocks me.

Paul doesn't blink. "Not like this! I never loved anybody else."

Jet shakes her head and looks at him with what must be painful frankness. "You've never loved anybody, Paul. Not really. Certainly not me."

This stops him for a few seconds. "That's a lie," he says finally. "I loved you."

"No. You wanted me to love you. There's a difference."

"You don't know what I feel!" he yells, trying to recapture his initial fury. In this moment Paul looks like a little boy trying to understand a painful world.

"But I do," Jet says. "Better than anyone alive. And you know it."

Paul waves his gun at her. "Here's what I know. You never loved *me*. You lied to me from the beginning."

"What tells you that?" She points at his cell phone. "That stupid video? What does that show? Sex. That's all."

A nasty grin stretches his lips. "You think I'm stupid?" He digs in his back pocket again, removes a folded piece of paper, then shakes it open and tosses it on the table. I lean far enough forward to see what it is. When I do, my stomach flips. Not only because of what it is, but because it means Paul has been in my house before today.

"Is that 'just sex'?" he asks.

He's pointing at an intricately embellished piece of calligraphy, one by someone with obvious skill. The letters at the center of the drawing read: *Jordan McEwan*. Jet gave me that drawing three months ago, shortly after we started sleeping together again. She stares at the scrap of paper without speaking, but then a choked sob escapes her throat.

"Well?" Paul says. "Nothing to say?"

She shakes her head.

"You've loved Marshall since middle school. He was always there between us, like a shadow in your heart. Your dream. Your secret life. I guess I hoped you'd outgrow it. But I didn't know how deep your betrayal went." Paul's eyes fix on me with alarming intensity. And yet I see a sort of pity in them, too. "You came home because she *summoned* you. Didn't you? Without even a word, I'll bet. Maybe only a look, right? During one of your visits home to see your dad?"

My God, how close he's come to the truth. I think back to the department store checkout line, Jet behind me with Kevin, her almost flirting manner. It wasn't flirting, really, merely a possibility revealed during conversation. An admission of unhappiness in her present state, openness to a different future. An unspoken invitation. That was all it took—

"That's her magic, man," Paul says. "It's effortless. She makes other women seem like girls."

He's right.

"I know your plan," he says to Jet. "Wait till old Duncan died, then let Marshall go back to D.C. You'd let a little time pass, then tell me you think we need some time apart. From there, it's on to divorce, and you try to get custody, never revealing that you were planning all along to take Kevin to Washington."

Right again.

"Well, now Duncan's dead," Paul declares. "So I guess it's time to pull the trigger. Pun intended."

"Paul," she pleads, "you don't understand—"

"Shut up! I *told* you. Don't speak!" He swallows like he has no saliva in his mouth. Then he yanks out a chair and sits at the table, laying his gun flat before him. I recognize the pistol: it's a Glock 19, a compact semiauto favored by Special Forces operators. Fifteen rounds in the magazine, enough to kill us seven times over.

"The thing I couldn't figure," Paul goes on, "is how you thought you'd get custody. I mean, come on. Pop and his buddies own this town. Judges included. But I wasn't taking into account what a *dumbass* I am. I should've known you had it worked out. You and your goddamned OCD brain."

I don't know what he's talking about, and from the look on her face, Jet doesn't, either. I feel like we've been locked into a cage with a gorilla armed with a pistol. At any moment he might pick it up and shoot us, without our ever knowing exactly why.

"You're not getting Kevin," he says flatly. "You know that, right? You're not taking him from me. *Ever.*"

"I know that," she says.

Paul nods forcefully. "So you'll leave him, then? You'll abandon Kevin? To be with Marshall?"

"No. I won't live without Kevin."

Paul jerks up his free hand and rakes it through his hair like a puzzled eighth grader trying to make sense of algebraic equations on a chalkboard. "The only way you get a life with Kevin is by staying with me."

"I understand that."

What is she doing? Trying to defuse the immediate threat by telling him she wants to stay married to him? I'm watching Jet closely for a clue as to what I should do, but she hasn't even glanced my way.

"That prospect makes you sick, doesn't it?" Paul says. "Living with me. Sleeping with me."

"Paul, stop it. Just stop!" Jet sounds like a mother disciplining her child. "You and I need to go home and talk."

"Home?" he echoes. "I figure you think of here as home now. Don't you? This is where you get your needs tended to."

"Paul—"

"*Isn't it?!*" he cries, slamming his hand down on the table.

Jet takes her time before answering. "I suppose it has been." She steps up to the table and lays her hands on the back of an empty chair. "Being with you doesn't make me sick. But we didn't get to this place by accident. And you sitting there with that gun doesn't say much for your confidence in your position."

"I've got my reason for this gun," he says, staring fixedly at the table. "You lying whore."

The venom in his voice sends a chill along my arms. *We're missing something,* I realize. *Whatever is driving this behavior, we don't know about it.* A faint buzzing starts in my brain, and a trickle of adrenaline into my veins. *He's working himself up to killing us.* I don't know why, but that's what he's doing. It isn't the sex on the patio. If Paul were going to shoot us for that, he'd have done it already. I need to warn Jet before he passes the point of no return—

"Take off your clothes," Paul says, his voice dead and cold.

I'm not sure who he's talking to until he raises his Glock and points the muzzle at my face. My stomach rolls over.

"You heard me. Strip." He waves his gun to hurry me along.

Jet is staring at him in confusion. This scene has taken on the dreadful banality of a true-crime show on late-night cable TV. "So you can shoot me and the cops find me naked?" I reply. "Crime of passion? Is that the script?"

"Take 'em off, Marshall."

"You'll have to do it after you shoot me. I might as well make you work for it."

"You too, slut," he says to Jet. "Get 'em off."

Her eyes go wide. "I will *not*. You plan to shoot me, too?"

"Not sure yet. Get 'em off, though. Let's see that coochie one last time. It's not like Goose and I haven't both seen it before."

Jet's glare would freeze motor oil. "You'll never see it again, unless I'm dead."

A strange smile touches Paul's mouth, and he nods as though confirming some secret suspicion. "How about you stop acting like the aggrieved party? I'm the victim here."

"*You!*" Pride makes her stand taller. "I think most people who know you would say you betrayed yourself—a long time ago. First yourself, then me. We could have had a child years before Kevin, if you'd been man enough to go to the doctor. But no, you'd rather sit in the house drunk, popping pills, whining about how the army screwed you in Iraq. Christ, even your mother knew that."

Paul recoils like he's been backhanded by a strong man. Actually, he looks more like he took a knife between the ribs. Shock first, then pain. But as I watch, his pain turns to rage.

"We're going to the bedroom," he says quietly. "I'm going to finish this. I'll have Kevin, and he'll be safe from you. It could have ended another way . . . but you picked this climax. Let's go."

Paul slides back his chair with a grinding screech, then stands and points the Glock at my chest, center mass.

"I'm not walking back there," I tell him. "You'll have to shoot me here."

"Yeah?" He racks the slide on his Glock. "Just remember, I'm not taking anything from you I didn't give you myself."

"*Paul, don't!*" Jet screams, sensing that he means to shoot.

"Get your clothes off," he says, "and I'll wait to fire."

With shaking fingers, Jet starts unbuttoning her blouse.

Yet again I sense death near, as I have so many times before. How many guises can it take? The barge in the foggy river with Adam . . . the hooded man with his water jug in the Bienville jail. There were other times, other faces, especially during the first years after my son died, when I took crazy risks on the job. But the memory that haunts me now is that night on the kitchen table in Ramadi, when Paul burst in and killed the men about to cut my throat. And now, defying logic, or perhaps fulfilling it . . . my rescuer has become my executioner.

"Paul, why are you doing this?" I hear myself ask. "You really want to kill me?"

He shakes his head slowly. Yet the words that come from his mouth are "I saved your life, didn't I, Goose?"

"You did."

"So all the years you've lived since then . . . you got from me. Right?"

"Absolutely."

"And this is how you repay me?" He points at Jet, whose blouse has slipped to the floor, revealing a flesh-colored bra against her dark skin. "By taking what's most precious to me?"

"That's a lie," she says. "If I were precious to you, our whole lives would have been different."

She's the one lying now. The truth is, Paul was never precious to her. Not really. And he knows it. He glances at her for a couple of seconds, then looks back at me. His right forefinger slips inside the trigger guard. Something goes out of his eyes, and my bladder turns to lead.

"Paul, *please*," Jet pleads with utter subservience. "I'll do anything. Let's go home right now, and I'll be your wife till the day you die. I swear to God. For Kevin. Come on. Just leave him standing here and let's go."

Nothing she could have said would have hurt him more. What more powerful proof of her love for me could she give than to offer to martyr herself by living with Paul for the rest of her life? I open my mouth to try to mitigate her words, but the scream that bursts from his throat knocks me back a foot.

Then he fires.

Jet's shriek barely registers against my eardrums. I stagger back, a delayed response to the eruption of flame from the pistol. No bullet hit me—none I've felt yet, anyway. At the last instant Paul pulled his aim left, putting a slug through a kitchen cabinet instead of my heart.

In the ringing aftermath of his shot, he screams once more, then sobs, but he doesn't lower his weapon. "You *liars*! If Kevin was his, why didn't you just *leave*? Why stay with me and live this goddamn lie? I thought you had more guts than that . . . both of you. Jesus, it's *sick*."

Jet and I stare at each other in stunned horror. Four words have burned themselves into our brains: *If Kevin was his . . .*

Max did this. If Paul just came from UMC, then it was Max who put this poisonous idea into his head. What agony must Paul have endured during his ride here? To believe, even for an hour, that I'm the father of the son he loves above all things?

"Paul, what did you say?" Jet asks. "About Kevin?"

"You gonna make me say it? All right. Kevin's Marshall's son! I know it now. And I know Mama knew it, too. Goddamn, you've been lying for twelve *years*. I just . . . I thought y'all were better than that. You've fucked us all up—Kevin most of all."

Jet stands shaking in disbelief. She clearly has no idea how to respond to this. But I do. There's only one path open to us now—one road to life.

"Paul, listen," I say firmly. "As God is my witness, *I am not Kevin's father*."

His eyes narrow, but Jet's widen in fear.

"Why keep lying?" he asks me.

"I'm not lying. I am not Kevin's father. But you're not either. Not his biological father."

Paul goes utterly still. "What the hell does that mean?"

"Try to ease back, man. Calm down. I'm not your enemy. The person who screwed up your family is your father. It's *Max*, bro. He's the cause of all this misery."

Paul is shaking his head now, almost violently. "What are you *talking* about?"

Jet silently begs me not to go on. But I have no choice now. "Paul . . . Max is Kevin's father."

"Oh, God," Jet gasps, backing away from the table.

"He raped her," I say quickly. "Max raped her in 2005. And she never told you about it."

Paul's initial response is one slow blink of the eyes, then another. But after a few seconds, I sense a tectonic shift within him. My words are leaching through years of accreted anger, pain, bewilderment, suspicion. When at last they sink into his mind, something vast and heavy slides into place.

"Thirteen years ago," I say as Paul's face undergoes a terrifying change. "You were passed out in the den. Max drugged her with Xanax and raped her."

I cut my eyes at Jet, who's paralyzed with fear. I can almost read her mind. *After so many years of lying, how can our salvation depend on another lie?* But it does.

"Is that true?" Paul asks, looking her square in the face.

She nods once, her chin quivering.

Paul closes his eyes, then wobbles on his feet. The Glock hangs loose in his hand, but death is in the room with us, hovering. While

Paul is blind, I glance at Jet, who sucks in her lips and nods quickly. Tears are streaming down her face. She gets it. Rape must be the story now. It's the only narrative that might allow her a life after this—a life with her son—and she knows it. For an insane moment I consider going for my gun, because there's no telling what Paul might do next. He could kill himself, or us—or us first, then himself. But I don't think he will. Somehow, he understands that what I just told him—at least Max's part in it—is the truth. And even if he means to kill himself at some point, Paul won't leave the son he loves under the power of the man who made his life a tragedy.

"Max told you I was Kevin's father, didn't he?" I say softly, trying to steer his anger away from Jet.

In the roaring silence of Paul's shock, the back door opens. Max Matheson walks through it, a pistol in his hand. The upper left quadrant of his face and skull is a Pollock painting of purple and blue, and his left eye is so swollen I can barely see it.

"What the hell happened?" he asks. "Paul? I heard a shot."

I back away from the door until the island stops me, and Jet follows. I have a feeling Max's life is now measured in seconds. Then again . . . I thought that last night, on Parnassus Hill. All I know is this: I need the gun from the drawer.

CHAPTER 52

PAUL TAKES A step toward his father, partially blocking my view. But as Paul speaks to Max, and Max meets his eyes, I move left and slide open the drawer that holds the .32 automatic that Nadine insisted I take this morning.

"What the hell are you doing here?" Paul demands. "How did you get out of the hospital?"

Max steps deeper into the kitchen and says, "The way you stormed out of my room, I was worried you might do something crazy. So I yanked out my IVs and got down here as fast as I could. I nearly passed out near the county line, but I made it."

Paul's back is to me, but I can see skepticism in his posture. "What did you drive? Your truck was here in Bienville."

Max doesn't miss a beat. "I went down to the employee lot and found a guy dropping off his wife for a shift. I waved two hundred-dollar bills in his face and asked if he could get me to Bienville in thirty minutes." Max touches the wrecked left side of his face. "I think this got me the ride. The guy felt bad taking my money. He drove eighty-five all the way to my house, and I got my truck there."

While Paul digests this, Max sweeps his eyes over the room, taking in the scene with military efficiency. He and Paul are on the far side of the table, Jet and I between the table and the island. Max looks surprised to find us alive.

"I thought for sure you'd shot this Jody bastard," he says, waving his gun at me. "Did you show them the video?"

Paul answers without looking at him. "Yeah."

"And?"

I slide the pistol a little farther behind my leg.

"And what?" Paul says.

"What did they say about it?"

Paul shrugs. "Doesn't matter."

Max's eyes narrow. "Doesn't *matter*? What are you talking about?"

"I been thinking, Pop. I think the best thing is to get a DNA test on Kevin. I won't tell him what it is. Just routine blood work for a sports physical."

Max's face betrays astonishment. "Why the hell would you do that? I told you where that'll lead. Them taking Kevin from us. From you. They're playing you, son. A DNA test is a bell you can't un-ring."

Paul nods as though he understands, but his voice remains firm. "Still . . . I think it's the best thing. Just to be sure."

I take a chance by speaking to bolster Paul's position. "A DNA test is the only thing that can settle this beyond doubt. And it will prove Jet and I are telling the truth."

"Of course he'd say that," Max argues. "He'll tell any lie he can think of to get out of this room. And remember, the DNA test tricks you into proving Kevin belongs to him. You've got to end this now. If you don't have the sand for it, I'll do it for you."

Paul faces his father with surprising grit. "Two minutes ago, I was an inch from killing Marshall. If it turns out he's been lying to me all this time—if he's Kevin's father—I'll kill him. But I want to be sure."

Anxiety bleeds into Max's face. He's shifting his weight from foot to foot, and his eyes flit from Paul to me and back.

"What about you, Pop?" Paul asks in an eerily calm voice. "You fine with a DNA test?"

Max stops shifting. "I've told you how I feel about that."

"I mean a DNA test on *you*. You and Kevin."

Max Matheson was always the coolest customer I ever knew. But in this moment, his legendary composure deserts him. The truth in his eyes is beyond concealment. He has wanted his illegitimate son for so long that he can't hide what he feels—and it's not the emotion of a grandfather. Tallulah's words come back to me in a rush: *You can't hide the sun behind a candle—*

"What the hell have these two been saying?" Max demands.

Paul shrugs again. "I'm just asking a question."

"You're wasting time is what you're doing! Marshall's got a gun right there behind his leg. He's just waiting for his chance."

In what may be the last risk I'll ever take, I toss Nadine's pistol onto the floor near the table. "I don't want to hurt anybody," I say evenly. "All I want is the truth to come out. And I don't think we should have a conversation about paternity while everybody's armed."

"What do you think about that, Pop?" Paul asks. "You gonna drop your gun, too?"

A nervous laugh from Max. "Hell, no. Marshall's probably got another pistol in one of these cabinets. You're not thinking straight, boy."

I take a step toward the table. "Why don't you own up to what you did, Max? For once in your life? Thirteen years ago you raped Jet in the guest room of your house, while Paul was passed out in the den."

Max blanches. "That's a goddamn lie! Is that what she said? It was rape?"

"You're damn right," Jet says with unalloyed hatred.

Max knows we're lying, and that knowledge has driven him to rage. But by responding instinctively, he's acknowledged that he had sex with Jet. I need to keep pushing him in that direction. On the other hand, if Paul's not ready to defend us, pushing Max could get us all killed.

Paul is staring at his father the way a bull once stared at me when I slipped through a fence and tried to sneak past him to a pond. I'm not sure Paul caught the full implication of what Max said, but he senses that his father has been lying to him.

"I hate to say it," Paul says, "but I can see that happening. I've seen you watch Jet's ass while she walked, concentrating so hard you don't even know where you are."

Max turns up his hands. "She's got a great ass. So what?"

Paul rocks back and forth like a man who wants to pace but has no room to do it. "Jet says you raped her," he intones, not taking his eyes from Max's face. "Marshall says the same thing."

Max shifts his gun to his left hand, then holds up his right as though taking an oath in court. "On your mother's name, Paul—it's a lie."

Truth has its own power, and Max spoke it with a prophet's conviction. But while our accusation of rape is technically a lie, the truth of Max's obsession with Jet is not. Max is consumed by a hunger—a sort of blood greed—to possess both Kevin and his mother. Paul may not know this at a conscious level, but the most primal region of his brain is pulsing with new awareness. He studies his father for a while longer, then looks back at Jet.

"That was either a damn good performance, or he's telling the truth."

Jet's face has regained some color, and her dark eyes move from man to man. When her gaze finally settles on Paul, she holds her hands out before her, almost like an enchantress casting a spell.

"Think about our life together," she says. "Think of everything you know about me. Then think about your father. Who's the liar, Paul?"

His bloodshot eyes betray deep conflict. "Until tonight, I'd have said Pop. But you've lied from the beginning about Marshall."

"Damn right she has!" Max exults. "She's been whoring for him ever since high school. Junior high, probably."

Paul's gaze remains on Jet. "You still say he raped you?"

"Think how Max treated your mother," she goes on. "There aren't many ladies like Sally left in this world. But Max screwed every woman who'd lie down for him, even her close friends. And think how he treated *you*. Always tearing you down, cutting your legs out from under you—"

"Don't listen to that!" Max roars, and his gun rises as he glares at Jet. "I won't apologize for being a man. But I loved your mother, goddamn it. You know that. Sally knew it!"

"He killed her, Paul," Jet says with pitiless conviction. "He either shot her or drove her to suicide. Whichever it was, he had the same motive—to silence her forever. Sally had figured out the truth about Kevin. I hate to admit that to myself. It *kills* me. But she knew Max had fathered Kevin. She saw that he wanted Kevin to raise as his own, and he wanted me for a wife. Sally would never let that happen. That's why she created that cache everybody's after. She couldn't bring herself to kill Max in cold blood, so she did the next best thing. She protected you and Kevin the only way she knew how. She gave her life to protect you, Paul."

My God, I think. *She's finishing what she started with that hammer—*

"Don't let her poison you like this!" Max pleads, and for the first time I hear fear in his voice. "This is what women do. They turn us against each other. She's *poison,* Paulie. Remember that video? She's humped your best friend a hundred times in this house. *Right in this kitchen.*"

"Paul?" Jet says in a voice as soft as a prayer. "If I've committed a sin, it's that I never told you he raped me. I was terrified of what would happen. I thought you might kill him and end up in prison. That would have killed Sally and destroyed the family. So I kept silent. But as horrible as what Max did was . . . I loved Kevin." Jet's face softens with undeniable love. "He's my precious baby, no matter how he came to be. So I can't look back and say I wish it never happened, no matter how bad it sounds. He's our son, Paul. Max was nothing." Her face hardens with implacable fury. "But he can't let go of me. He's obsessed. It's *Max* who poisoned this family—Max who's a threat to Kevin. I think that's what drove me to Marshall in the end. I can't live with your father's sickness anymore. Not another day."

Paul's face is terrible to see in this moment, but he believes her. Jet looks back at Max with perfect serenity, knowing she has won.

What will he do? Max stands at the threshold of violence. Could he shoot Jet before Paul reacts? No. He'd shoot Paul first. He'd have to.

His gaze moves from Jet to Paul, to me, then back to Paul once more. Survival instinct burns like phosphorus behind his blue-gray eyes.

"Come here, Paul," he says in a paternal tone. "I need to tell you something these two can't hear."

"Don't, Paul!" I say sharply, surprising myself. "He can say anything he wants from right there."

Max's eyes cut to me for a furious instant.

"Something's wrong," I think aloud. "Get your weapon up."

"Fucking drama queen," Max mutters, his eyes finding Paul's again. "I hoped I'd never have to tell you this. But they've left me no choice. You want the truth? All right, yes—Kevin's my son. Anybody with eyes can look at that boy and see it. I never told you because I knew it would break your heart."

Paul's mouth is hanging open. "How do you know he's yours?"

"I had a DNA test done when he was a baby. On a hair from that baseball cap I gave him. He's mine, Paul, same as you are. Kevin's your brother."

"Half brother," Jet corrects him. "You son of a bitch."

Paul's face has gone slack with horror.

"*But,*" Max goes on, "I never raped her. That part's a goddamn lie. I never stole pussy off a woman in my life, and Jet's no different."

Every atom of Paul's being resists this claim. "You're telling me Jet slept with you because she wanted to? She had an *affair* with you?"

Max shrugs. "That's not how it started. At first I was doing you a favor, strange as that may sound now. You and Jet, both."

"A *favor?*" Paul just looks at him. "Tell me about this favor you did me."

Max rakes his left hand over his stubbled chin. "It's not complicated. Jet told me how much trouble y'all were having conceiving a child. She was worried you might kill yourself. I was too, I won't lie. I know what war does to men. And your mother was a nervous wreck, worrying about you. Those were tough times in the Matheson house. Jet told me you wouldn't get your plumbing checked by the medics and you didn't want to adopt. Which I totally get, by the way. These days they wanna give you a Mexican baby or even a nigger. We figured the only way to pull you out of your tailspin was to give you a son. Your *own* son. A blood descendant. A reason to live. Best one there is. And we did."

Listening to Max now, it's tough to imagine Jet deciding to sleep with him to get pregnant. But that was thirteen years ago, and Max has probably changed a lot since then. A lot of friends I grew up with have begun to become their parents as they age: Gen X slackers morphing into racist xenophobes they would have hated in their twenties.

"It was that easy, huh?" Paul says, avoiding the third rail of this conversation. "One roll in the hay, and you did what I couldn't do in four years?"

Max struggles to portray an emotion he's never actually felt: compassion. "There's no *fault* to that kind of thing, Paulie. It's just medical. Like who gets cancer and who doesn't. There's no reason to it."

Paul knows as well as I that Max doesn't believe that. More than once I've heard him tell a father of only daughters: "Lemme know if you need some help getting a son over at your place." Usually on the sideline at football practice.

"You've all been lying to me," Paul says. "For *years*. I want out of this goddamn nightmare. I want straight answers." He turns to Jet. "Did he force you? Or did you give yourself to him?"

"He raped me," Jet says with conviction.

Paul turns to me. "You believe her?"

"I saw him try to rape her again last night, on Parnassus Hill." This, I realized earlier today, is not strictly true. I saw Max attack Jet, and I later saw her ripped blouse. But I can't be sure he was trying to rape her. He may have been trying to kill her. But the truth will not save us now.

As Paul turns back to his father, Max restates his basic argument. "I've been with a lot of women in my day, Paul. You know that. But I've never forced one yet. Not once. I *damn* sure never raped your wife. And I can prove it."

How the hell can he prove that?

"You shouldn't have lied about me," Max says to Jet, who suddenly looks afraid again.

"How can you prove it?" Paul demands.

Max lowers his head like a priest preparing to deliver last rites. Then he looks up, his eyes hard. "How do you think? I can tell you what she likes between the sheets."

The room temperature drops ten degrees.

"All right, I'll bite," Paul says. "Let's hear it."

Max looks directly at Jet while he answers. "When you go down on her . . . she likes to open the hood herself, so your fingers are free to work up her tailpipe."

A shudder of recognition goes through me, leaving nausea in its wake. As Paul and I stare at each other, white-faced, Max nods with triumph. "She comes harder that way. Right? Would I know that if I raped her?"

Jet's face has lost all color.

As crudely as Max spoke, he told the truth. In the first moment our eyes met, Paul and I shared the certainty that we've both serviced Jet in this way, and at her request. Apparently, Max has, too. What Paul feels I can only guess. But what's devouring me from the inside is the knowledge that less than an hour ago, Jet lied to me when she "confessed" how Kevin had been conceived. The "pragmatic" transaction she described as undertaken solely to produce an heir has turned out to be something else entirely—as Tallulah intimated to me this morning.

"My automotive analogy confuse you boys?" Max asks with a fraternal smile. "She likes to part the curtains herself so you can work on her backyard plumbing."

"*Shut up!*" Paul yells, but he's looking at Jet, who is crumbling before our eyes. Red blotches have appeared on her face and neck, and tears are pouring down her cheeks. It's a reaction to what she sees in our faces, I realize, a reflection of shame and revulsion.

"He's lying," she says in a tiny voice. "I mean . . . not about that. You've both been with me. But I've never done that with him. *Never.* How can he *know* that?"

"How indeed," Paul says in a dead voice.

"*Please*," she beseeches us. "Please believe me! He must have watched us with cameras or something. He's been stalking me. You *can't* believe him."

Paul looks back at her with something akin to pity. "I wouldn't have. But there's no other way he could know that."

"There has to be! This is *sick*. Please—"

"Boo-fucking-hoo," Max says in a mocking voice. "At least now we know where we stand. All that matters now is Kevin. And I know one thing: this whore is never getting custody of that boy again."

Jet looks wildly from Paul to me, like an accused witch in search of a champion.

"She's his mother," I say quietly.

"Lots of whores are mothers," Max observes. "What's your point?"

"Help me," Jet begs, looking from Paul to me.

Max steps toward the back door. "Time to put an end to this bullshit. Come out to the patio, Paul. I don't want these con artists to hear what I've got to say to you."

Alarm bells are clanging in my head. "Don't do it, Paul. Do whatever you want about Jet, but send Max home. Something's not right."

"*You* ain't right, Goose," Max says, raising his gun and aiming across the table at me. A trace of a smile tugs at the corners of his mouth. "The only person in here who follows *your* orders is Jet, and you were third in line, ace. I wonder who'll be next. You look like you might have soured on her a little bit."

He looks at Jet, contempt written on his face. "Can't say I blame you. She's been aging out of her prime for a while. She might perk back up after we relieve her of her motherly duties, though. Get a little nip and tuck where it counts."

"You won't get Kevin," she says with the last remnant of her defiance. "I'm the best lawyer in this town. I'll stop you."

Max grins. "I'd say that depends on the judge, darling. And I own the judges in this town. Not to mention, I'm the boy's father."

Fear morphs into panic on Jet's face. But something in Paul's posture changed during Max's last words.

"You're forgetting one other thing," Max says. "The only thing that really matters. In seven months, Kevin turns thirteen. Then *he* gets to decide who he lives with. And I took care of that a long time ago."

I can't bear to look at Jet while she realizes what this means for her future. Max's been coaching Kevin's teams since the boy's first season of T-ball, guiding him into what's now a perpetual spotlight of hero worship, even at twelve. Max owns and drives the luxury RV that ferries Kevin's traveling baseball team all over the Southeast. But what must Paul think of this picture Max is painting? Where does he fit into it?

"All right, outside," Paul says gruffly, walking toward his father.

Max reaches for the doorknob. "About damn time. I'll tell you how I see—"

"Max?" Jet calls.

He's still grinning when he turns, and his chest blooms scarlet before I hear the first gunshot. Staccato concussions send me reeling against the wall. Jet has snatched up my pistol from the floor. She fires four times, and at least three rounds plow through Max's upper body, spinning him wildly and dropping him on the floor by the back wall.

"*What the fuck!*" Paul shouts, whipping up his pistol and aiming at Jet. "You killed him!"

"*Yes!*" she shrieks, the gun shaking in her hands. "He's a liar! He can't do that to me!"

"Paul, don't shoot her," I beg, stepping in front of Jet and throwing up my hands. "We don't know what happened."

He shakes his head in stunned fury. "I *saw* what happened! She killed him to shut him up. She was scared he'd tell me more."

"I don't think so," I say quickly, staring at Max, who lies faceup at his son's feet. "He pushed her past her limit, man, saying he'd take Kevin away. But it's more than that . . ." The truth comes to me as I watch Max convulsing on the floor. "He was going to kill you. If you'd gone out on that patio, you'd be dead now."

Paul's face tightens in confusion, but he looks down at his father. "What are you saying?"

Max lurches up off the floor and gasps, then claws the air as though trying to pull himself to his feet. Watching him fight for life, I realize there's no other possible reason he could be here.

"He came here to get Kevin," I explain. "And for him to get Kevin, you and Jet had to die."

A grating rattle issues from Max's throat, then fades into a gurgle.

"He's trying to talk," Paul says. He drops to his knees and takes his father by the shoulders. "Can you hear me? Pop?"

A wet wheeze is Max's only answer, but his eyes are wide with urgency. I don't want Max Matheson voicing one more word. That bastard has the persuasive powers of Satan. But I can't very well finish him off while his son kneels over him with a pistol.

Max is shivering. Watching him bleed out, I remember how cocksure he was in this very room only two nights ago. Why couldn't I see then that he'd come not to protect his son's marriage, but to warn a rival away from the woman who held him in thrall?

"Did you kill Mom?" Paul asks, leaning low over his father's face.

Of all the things he could have asked . . . it's his mother that dominates Paul's thoughts now. Maybe he's already written Jet out of his life forever.

Max's head jerks up, falls back. "Shot . . . shot herself," he chokes out. "Cuh-couldn't believe it."

"What about Jet? Tell me the truth. Did you force her?"

Almost any father would lie at this point, even if the lie would damn him in the eyes of his son. Because a lie would give his son a second chance at life. But Max has always lived for himself alone. Glancing left, I see terror in Jet's face. She jumps as Paul slaps his father's face to bring him around.

"*Nuh,*" Max groans, a guttural monosyllable. "She gave it to me. We made that boy, her and me . . . that beautiful boy."

Paul swallows something sour, but he holds his place, unflinching, fighting to get the truth.

"I had to," Max croaks. "Had uh . . . do what you couldn't. Carry on the line. Don't blame me for that . . . or her. She loved me, you damn fool. Now you . . . gone and ruined it. You've took that boy's real daddy from him."

"Do you know what you're saying?" Paul asks in a cracked voice.

Max's eyes go wide, but instead of fear they hold inchoate fury. "God*damn*," he rages. "This isn't right. He's the son you never were to me. And now . . . *this*."

After looking down in silence for several seconds, Paul lifts his right hand from the floor and covers his father's mouth with it. Then he closes Max's nose between his thumb and forefinger. Max's shoulders jerk up off the floor again, but Paul keeps his head pinned against the wood. Paul's body appears relaxed, even as Max's legs kick wildly. Only in his arm do I see the force being applied. So tight is Paul's grip that Max can't even gasp. His eyes bulge in pain and terror, as if they'll burst from their sockets. His face darkens to purple, and his midsection bounces off the floor like he's copulating with an invisible woman—once, twice, and again. Then his back slams against the hardwood and stays there.

Still, Paul doesn't let go.

I look back at Jet, who's probably watching someone die for the first time. There's pain in her face, but behind that, a savage satisfaction, and perhaps also gratitude that her husband is finishing what she started. Maybe murder will bind them more deeply than love ever did.

After what seems an interminable delay, Paul releases his grip. No one moves. We don't even look at one another.

Max is dead.

CHAPTER 53

WHATEVER SHAPE PAUL was in before Max died, he's barely coherent now. He sits in a pool of his father's blood, hunched over, looking down at the bruised, motionless face. In the span of two days both his mother and father have perished, but that's not the worst of it. Today Paul lost his wife and son as well. And not in the way of a man who loses his family in a car crash. He's lost not only his future with them, but also the past. Every moment he ever spent with Jet and Kevin has been ripped away, tainted, invalidated by the knowledge that his wife loved his childhood friend and his son was sired by his father. Paul still has his gun in his hand. It hangs limp against the bloody hardwood floor, but I've seen Paul shoot in combat. He could put a bullet through both our heads in a second and a half.

"Paul?" I say, surprising myself.

He doesn't answer. Doesn't even lift his head. Jet looks as though she wants to comfort him, and in fact starts toward him, but something makes her pull up short. There's something brittle in the air, a sense that in this moment Paul is capable of anything, from murder to self-destruction. To touch him now would be like touching a wolf after a kill.

You just don't do it.

Jet turns, and her eyes find mine across eight feet of space. Where two days ago an arc of pleasure and anticipation would have passed between us, now there's only mutual awareness of all that's been lost. We're like hurricane survivors staring at each other through the ruins of our house.

Below my line of focus I see movement. Paul has lifted his pistol into his lap. He's staring at it more like a child than a military vet, an innocent who picked up a strange machine, unaware that death awaits in the steel tube. As I watch with increasing apprehension, Paul turns the gun until he's looking down its barrel. His finger isn't inside the trigger guard, but he seems hypnotized by the black hole. What does he see in it? A tunnel out of hell? An escape from unbearable pain? Is his suffering so all-consuming that oblivion offers the only peace?

As I watch him, half-hypnotized myself, Paul opens his mouth like a baby waiting to be fed. For a terrible fraction of time I consider simply standing here and witnessing what I know must be coming. His finger will enter the guard and compress the trigger, beginning the irrevocable pull—

I can't. No matter what the risk, I have to stop him.

But how? If I startle him, his training might trigger him to whirl and kill me out of reflex. Keenly aware that Jet has done nothing to intervene, I pad past her with my empty hands held out before me.

"Paul?" I almost whisper. "Hey, man . . . you with me?"

No response. How can I break through that death trance? As I ease forward, memories of our time in Iraq return, the weeks I spent with Sierra Bravo in Ramadi. *"Yo, brah,"* I call softly. "Rangers lead the way, right? Remember?"

Very slowly, like a man with a traumatic brain injury, Paul closes his mouth. Swallows. I crouch beside him, then sit, but I don't risk touching him.

"Paul? Can you hear me?"

He says nothing, only stares down at his father's motionless face.

"I want to talk to you, man. Kevin's still your son, okay? Nobody's taking him from you. *Ever.* You hear me?"

"Jet did this," he whispers. "Jet put us here."

A bubble of fear rises in my chest, and I sense Jet backing away behind me. "No, man, listen. Max did this. He told you I was Kevin's father. Remember? He lied. And he lied for a reason. He wanted you to kill me. Jet, too."

"Why?" Paul asks. "Makes no sense."

"Oh yes it does. He wanted to raise Kevin. He wanted custody of that boy."

Paul has yet to even look at me. But he says, "Killing you and Jet wouldn't get him Kevin."

"It would if you were dead, too."

"You're full of shit, Goose. It was her, man."

Jet's got to be petrified. I can't believe she hasn't fled the house. *"Think,* Paul. Max showed you that video of us. Then he told you I was Kevin's father. With all that rage, he was betting you'd come straight here and shoot us. And you almost did. He pointed you at us like a guided missile. He knew we'd be here, and he sent you to kill us."

At last Paul looks up with glassy eyes. "How could he know you'd be here?"

"Jet, what brought you here tonight?" I ask over my shoulder.

When she doesn't reply, I risk a look back. Her face is a finger-painting of tears and smeared mascara. But Nadine's gun now hangs by her leg.

"What was the first thing you told me when you came in?" I ask.

"Max sent me here," she says in a shaky voice. "He called from UMC and told me to end it with you. If I didn't, he'd tell Paul everything."

"There you go," I tell Paul. "He pointed you at us, and then he blitzed out of that hospital and followed you here."

"Why?"

"He was betting that once you killed Jet and me, you'd end up turning your gun on yourself. But if you didn't, he had to be here to finish the job. That's why he busted in when he heard your shot. A single shot didn't make sense to him."

Paul is shaking his head. "No, man. You're reaching."

"Shit. You think Max followed you here because he was worried about *you?* You know better."

"But *you* care about me?" Paul throws out his gun hand and knocks me off my heels. "You're lying, Goose. You've both been lying all along. She wants to take Kevin from me, and you're helping her."

"I don't want Kevin, man. He's yours. Use your head, damn it. Not your heart." As I scramble to my feet, a gleam of black at Max's ankle catches my attention. A flash of memory takes me back two nights, when Max's jeans rode up and I saw the pistol in his ankle holster. Only on that night the gun was nickel-plated.

"Check his ankle holster!" I tell Paul, pointing.

"What?" he asks dully.

"Max brought two guns. Why? Where'd he get them?"

While Paul stares at me in confusion, I reach across the hardwood with my shoe and slide Max's pant leg up over the nylon holster. Paul looks disinterested at first. Then his eyes narrow, and he pulls the gun from the holster.

"This is mine," he mumbles. "My compact Springfield."

"Did you lend it to him?"

Paul hesitates, then shakes his head. "It was in my desk at home. It was there last night. This morning, too. He . . . he must have stopped on his way into town and grabbed it."

"If the guy he paid drove him fast enough when he followed you from Jackson, he just had time."

"This is too crazy, man. This is wack."

"This is *Max*. Remember when he asked you to walk over to him so that he could whisper something to you? He tried it twice. *Twice*. The second time he asked you to go out on the patio. I knew something was wrong, but I didn't know what."

"No."

"You know I'm right. To fit his narrative, he needed a contact head shot. A contact wound with *your* gun. One that would look like suicide."

"But . . . why kill me first?"

"Seriously? You were the only real threat to him in here. He'd have shot us right after he shot you. But when he talked to the cops, he'd have told it in reverse. *I followed Paul out there, worried sick. I heard two shots and busted in. I saw Jet and Marshall dead, and Paul turned the gun on himself before I could stop him.*"

Paul blinks like a man struck with a club. "You really think he would have killed us all?"

"It's the only way he could get custody of Kevin. Last night he tried to talk Jet into leaving you. He had some crazy plan to move you to Atlanta or Dallas, offer you a lot of money. But Jet refused. No threat would make her screw you over like that." I turn back to her. "Tell him."

"It's true," she says in a ragged voice. "He'd lost his mind. He said he was going to cut you out of his will if you didn't get out of his way. He tried to rape me last night, I swear to God. That's why I hit him with the hammer."

"Don't talk to me," Paul says sharply. "Don't say one damn word."

Paul looks down at his father again.

What can he be feeling? I spent most of my life believing that my father wished I'd drowned instead of my brother. What can it feel like to know your father would disown you—even kill you—so that he could take your wife and child for his own?

Paul raises his head and turns until he can see Jet. His eyes are filled with what looks like Puritanical judgment. "Pop was right," he says. "This is your doing. All of it. You poisoned this family with your lies and betrayal. You seduced him. You wanted a kid by him. Then you brought Marshall here to take you away from the lie you made us all live."

"Paul, listen," she says in a quavering voice. "I'm not sure who fathered Kevin. Okay? You were with me three times that month. I never saw any DNA test report, and I don't want to see one. Our job is to make sure our son never questions who his father is. He's *ours*, okay? Yours and mine."

Paul gets slowly to his feet, and for a moment I think she's gotten through to him. Then he raises his gun and aims at her midsection.

"That's what you say now. But you'd say anything to get out of this room. You could always talk circles around me. But not tonight. Pop showed you for what you are. A liar. And a whore."

Jet recoils as though struck. Then she takes a step toward Paul and says, "A whore gets paid for what she gives up. What did you pay me with? I never had a husband. I've had two little boys."

With a long sliding step, I interpose myself between them, blocking Paul's aim. He's only ten feet from Jet, though, and he could still hit her almost anywhere with a snap shot. I hold out my arms, trying to make myself as wide a shield as possible.

Paul smiles strangely. "There you are, old *friend*—right where you've always been. Between us."

"I can't let you shoot her, man."

He takes a step closer. "I don't want to shoot you. You're just another sucker like me. But I will. She's not taking Kevin."

"You're not doing this for Kevin," Jet says from behind me. "Have the guts to be honest, at least. You're doing this because of what Max said. Your sense of ownership is offended. He got me pregnant when you couldn't. You're afraid he fucked me better than you. You think by shooting me you'll stop that pain? You won't."

Jesus, would you shut up? I think in desperation. *You're committing suicide—*

"You and Max were so blind," she goes on. "You think Kevin loves baseball more than his mother? For God's sake."

"I know he loves you," Paul says. "And I wish I didn't have to do this. But it's the only way I can stop you. As soon as the sun comes up tomorrow, you'll be charting out your legal strategy to steal him from me. And if I'm not his biological father . . ."

Nearly paralyzed by futility, I experience a thunderclap of revelation. "Paul, wait, man. You're missing the forest for the trees. Max is dead. You have his seat in the Poker Club now. *You* own the judges in this town. She can't get Kevin from you. Think, man! Come on."

For the first time since he got up, my words have struck home.

"But the DNA," he reminds me. "There's no way around that. Blood trumps all, like Max told me in the hospital. To get Kevin, I've got to be the only parent left. So nobody even raises the question."

"And me?" I ask, stating the obvious. "Are you gonna kill me, too?"

When he averts his eyes, I realize the answer is yes. To get custody of Kevin, he will kill me. Maybe I should have let him kill himself after all—

"Not if you don't make me," he says, an offer of clemency in his eyes. "Why would you defend her now, anyway? After what we heard tonight? Christ, you heard what Pop said. How disgusting was that? She fucked him, and she loved it. She fucked us all, betrayed us all. She's *poison*, man. End of story. Now step aside."

"You make me sick," Jet says from behind me. "Both of you. You say you love me? *Love* me. But tonight Max slandered me, and who did you believe? Him. A lying psycho, and you take his word over mine. If I didn't know how badly Kevin needs me, I'd just as soon you shoot me."

Paul is edging to his right, prepping for his shot. I move left with him, still using my body as a shield. My nerves are vibrating like I've taken hold of a live wire.

"Get out of my way, Goose," he says. "Let me do it clean. No pain."

Abject fear raises every hair on my body.

"Do it, Marshall," Jet says in surrender. "Move clear."

For a second I wonder if she means to shoot at Paul when I move. Surely she's not that deluded, to think she'd have any chance of killing him first. "Jet—"

"There's no use in you dying, too." Nadine's gun clatters to the floor. "He's past all sense, all caring. He doesn't see that by killing me, he's killing himself. But this is where we are. And maybe I did bring us here. I just wanted love. You know? I wanted to be loved."

As when Max spoke from the heart, truth has its own ineffable power. Paul's face goes from that of resigned executioner to a man tortured by the fires of hell. He stops moving toward me, and in this odd lacuna of time and intent, my eye is drawn to the white rectangle of notebook paper on my kitchen table.

My breath stops.

"Paul," I say, pointing at the note. "Where did you get that?"

"What?"

"That note was in my bedroom dresser for the last three months. Either you broke in here and stole it or Max did. Which is it?"

"Max gave it to me at UMC. Today."

Epiphany washes over me like blessed grace. "I think I understand! Max *was* lying about sex with Jet. Put your gun down for two minutes. That's all I ask. Come to my bedroom. I'm almost certain about this."

I can't risk moving out of the shooting lane between them. Instead, I reach back and catch hold of Jet's wrist, then spin and push her up the hall before me, as I've done so many times during these past weeks, anticipating hours of sex.

"Stop!" Paul warns, but I ignore him.

His heavy steps follow us up the hall.

Pushing Jet through the bedroom door, I hit the light switch and walk up behind her, to be sure I stay between them. Then I glance back and see Paul walk in, his eyes fixed on my chaotic, unmade bed.

"What the hell are you doing?" he asks.

"Max watched us," I explain, looking high into the corners for a wireless camera or even a small hole in the wall.

"What are you looking for?"

"We've all assumed that patio sex video was the first time Max watched us. But why?" I catch Jet's eye. "Didn't you tell me he'd been stalking you?"

She nods, and something in Paul's face tells me this makes sense to him, too. Even so, I see no sign of any surveillance gear. Keeping Jet in front of me, I move around the room, but nothing stands out as unusual.

Paul is still staring at my bed. His jaw works steadily, flexing and relaxing like he's chewing a piece of leather. I'm starting to wonder if coming back here was a mistake. In his mind, Jet and I are flailing naked on that bed, and she's screaming with an ecstasy she never experienced with him.

"I could shoot you both in this room," he says. "No jury in Mississippi would convict me."

He's right about that. Jet knows it, too. But even as I try to think of a graceful way out of here, she steps away from the protection of my body. She walks to the threadbare curtains covering the picture window that the old farmer who sold me this place cut into the wall after he became confined to his bed. Reaching out, she runs her right hand down the curtain, creating a wave in the thin fabric.

"Analog," she says. "Not cameras. The oldest recording device in the world: the human eye."

"We never thought about privacy out here," I realize. "Because of the acreage . . . and being behind the gate."

I walk to the door to the right of the window, turn the bolt, and yank it open. The scent of impending rain fills the room. I walk out into the dark. Jet follows, Paul on her heels.

The picture window is blocked by huge Elaeagnus shrubs, nine feet tall at least. But the light streaming through the bedroom curtains silhouettes the branches behind the thick leaves. Taking out my iPhone, I switch on the LED and push between two of the bushes.

Behind the outer layer of foliage, I see a sort of doorway consisting of broken branches. Somebody has created a comfortable "hide" outside my window, the way snipers do in the field. And from where I stand, I can see every detail of my bed through the thin curtain.

"Where are y'all?" I ask. "Come in here."

"What is this bullshit?" Paul asks in a warning tone.

"Just get in here, damn it. You'll see why."

He violently pulls aside the brush, then he and Jet push into the shrubbery. It only takes Paul one glance to pick up the broken branches.

Then Jet sees them. Switching on her LED, she drops to the ground, like a young Miss Marple searching for footprints.

"I don't see any shoe prints," Paul says. "The ground's pretty hard, but we ought to see something. And I don't."

"There is something here," Jet says. "It looks like dog poop. Or maybe . . . some other animal? A fox, maybe?"

"Get out of the way," Paul says, crouching in the darkness at the base of the brick wall.

He switches on his own light and illuminates what Jet was talking about: small brown clumps that look like animal scat. As I watch in disgust, Paul picks up a clump and crumbles it between his fingers. Then he lifts it to his nose and sniffs.

"Wintergreen," he says. "That's Skoal."

With one sweep of his gun arm, he pulls a mass of branches away from the wall. We all shine our lights on the exposed bricks, revealing a long brown line of dried splatter.

"He was here," Paul says. "Dipping. He spit behind these bushes to hide it."

"I told you!" Jet cries angrily. "I've watched Max suck that nasty stuff at the baseball field a thousand times, spitting in a cup or a Coke bottle." She shudders in revulsion. "I can see the outline of that little round can in the back of his Levi's, or on his truck dash. *Gross.*"

I almost feel Max standing with us, a chilling incarnation of lust and envy. "Well," I say softly. "Here goes nothing."

Inhaling deeply, I lean close to the window glass and exhale a rush of warm air against the pane. Out of the condensation appears the ghostly outline of a nose and forehead, leaving eerie spaces where the eyes should be. To the left and right of this ghostly face float the outlines of splayed hands.

A soft gasp escapes Jet's throat. "That sick fuck."

"Goddamn," Paul mutters.

Though Max Matheson lies dead in my house, his essence is alive here, staring back at us like a demon summoned by my breath. Radiating from the silhouette on that glass is pure obsession, the desire to possess Jet in whatever way he could. How many days and nights did Max stand here watching us make love in blissful ignorance, in the full glare of the bedroom lights?

"This is how he knew," Jet says. "My God. I told you. I told you both."

I'm shocked and shamed by the relief I feel.

She turns to Paul. "I told you, damn it. I'm not the poison in the family. *He* was."

"Great," says Paul, bulling his way out of the shrubbery. "*Such* a relief. I guess I'm supposed to be happy it was only Marshall's finger up your ass instead of Max's?"

Jet glares at him with fiery indignation, then pokes him hard in the chest. "*Yes.* And fuck you for believing otherwise."

Here we stand, three people stripped of illusions. Three people who have known one another since childhood and now face a future that seems unimaginable. Exhaustion gives Paul's face a haunted look, and surely mine must look the same. As I try to think of what to do or say next, the clouds open up, and the rain finally comes. Cold, heavy drops smack into my scalp and shoulders, making me want to run. But Paul stands oblivious, his gun in his hand, like a soldier assigned sentry duty. For him the rain doesn't exist. He probably does feel some relief, but the losses he endured tonight will never be made up. In his mind, he is utterly alone in the world.

"What now?" I ask. "A lot's happened, I know. But we've got an urgent situation in that kitchen."

"Nothing's changed," Paul says. "She still wants Kevin. And you."

"Oh, come on, man," I say in frustration. "If we just wanted Kevin, we could have stood there and watched you eat your gun. You were about to do it."

Paul shakes his head, but at some level he knows it's true.

"For God's sake!" Jet cries. "I meant what I said back there. The one thing I'm certain of is that Kevin will never—*never*—doubt who his father is. He's your son, Paul, and that's it. It's our job to make sure he never thinks different. No matter what happens."

She's finally broken his trance. "How do we do that?" he mumbles.

"I don't know yet. What I do know is that none of us is going to jail over this. Here's what's going to happen now. You two are going to get rid of Max and his truck. I don't know how or where. Just make it happen. I'm going to stay here and scrub that kitchen from floor to ceiling with Clorox."

"You think that'll keep us safe?" Paul asks.

Jet nods in the rain. "You're damn right. Max killed Sally, he lied about the assault last night, and today he jumped bail. For all we know, he's fled the country. I'll tell the FBI that he confided to me he was guilty. Max exits stage left, never to return. Now, let's get out of this damned rain."

I'm ready, but Paul doesn't move.

Jet claps her hands as though demanding the attention of toddlers. "Get it together! Come on!"

I look warily at Paul, who's staring at the bedroom window.

"Paul?" Jet presses, looking fearfully at me.

After fifteen or twenty seconds, Paul says, "I'll sink his truck in the river. Take backroads to the sandbar below the industrial park."

Jet's eyes flicker with hope.

"You call Tallulah," he goes on. "Tell her Kevin needs to sleep over with her. He's probably already asleep now. Tell her we'll pick him up in the morning."

Jet nods, somehow masking her immense relief.

"What about me?" I ask.

Paul spits on the wet ground, then looks over at me the way he has for most of our lives. "You and me are going down to the swamp."

CHAPTER 54

WHILE JET BEGAN scrubbing the blood and tissue from my kitchen floor and walls, Paul and I wrapped Max in a gray tarp and carried him out to Paul's F-250. I figured we needed at least a car with a sealed trunk, but after we laid Max in the truck bed, Paul pointed to an iron rack in my yard that held most of a cord of firewood from last winter. After ten minutes of steady work, we buried Max under the split logs. No cop without a canine escort would be likely to hassle us, even during a traffic stop.

After making a trip inside to hit the head, Paul went into the kitchen and spoke softly to Jet. I went inside long enough to change into dry clothes, but I avoided making eye contact with her as I passed the kitchen. They were still speaking with quiet intensity when I came back up the bedroom hall, so I exchanged the stink of Clorox for the wet leather smell of the F-250 and waited another five minutes for Paul to emerge from the house. Two minutes after that, we pulled out onto Highway 36, heading west toward the junction with Highway 61 near Bienville.

Instead of turning south and driving through Mississippi—which I'd expected—Paul remained on 36, then crossed the Bienville Bridge into Louisiana and turned south on Whitetail Road. Whitetail Road follows the big levee south toward St. Joseph, Waterproof, and Ferriday. In a few places the road ascends to the crest of the levee, but for most of its length it runs on the landward side. Just over that big wall of land lie the "borrow pits"—swampy, snaky sloughs filled with snakes and gar and alligators that live in the miles-long trench left by the excavators that built the levee. And beyond that trench runs the big river.

The rain has mostly stopped. Our headlights cut through the spring night, catching millions of bugs in the beams. Objects flash out of the night and vanish: a mailbox, an abandoned car, a snake crossing the road, the red eyes of a transfixed possum. The truck's air-conditioning makes me shiver, partly because my clothes are wet from the exertion of piling logs over Max's body. But sleep deprivation has also taken its toll. I have that flu-like feeling where any sudden noise makes me jump and curse. I suppose I could be in shock, but since the stress isn't likely to end any time soon, I have no choice but to gut it out.

Paul turns away from the levee and drives inland into Louisiana, but I don't question him. When we left Bienville, he tuned the radio to an album-oriented rock station and set the volume low, probably to spare us the awkwardness of sitting in silence that begs to be filled. To keep from confronting the obvious, I focus on the faint strains of Led Zeppelin, Traffic, the Allman Brothers, Pink Floyd. Though Paul and I are in our forties, both of us—me through Buck, him through Max—grew up listening to the music of the sixties and seventies. Not many of the later-era bands ever quite took.

At some point during this AOR parade, I must have drifted off, because when I wake up, we're driving along a levee again. Maybe it's exhaustion, but I feel like we've driven in a big circle.

I'm about to question Paul about this when he says, "How's your mama doing? Pop kind of freaked out after Mom died."

After Mom died? I'm not going to touch the question of whether Max murdered Sally. "She seems okay," I tell him. "Dr. Kirby told me to assume that's a front, though."

"Yeah. I imagine so."

Paul drives another mile in silence. At last I summon the nerve to ask him where we're headed.

"Boar Island," he tells me.

A chill runs up my damp back. "Isn't that the island Wyatt Cash owns?"

"Yeah."

I didn't know where we were headed, but I would never have guessed Boar Island. "Is Wyatt there?"

"Nah, it's off-season. Just the empty hunting camp."

"We're not dumping Max in the river, are we? He could float up anywhere tomorrow."

Paul glances at me in the blue-white dashboard light. "They never found your brother, did they?"

His casual mention of Adam's death disconcerts me. "That was an anomaly. Most bodies that go into the Mississippi get found."

Paul turns his attention back to the road. "Relax. There's plenty of old sloughs on Boar Island. We sink him in the right one, the gators and turtles will eat him in less than twenty-four hours. Bones and all."

Tactical considerations aside, this man is talking about his father. Paul's apparent detachment only adds to my disquiet. "I figured we were taking him to a swamp somewhere. When you turned inland a while back."

"I planned to," Paul says in a low voice. "But that's too far to go. Too risky."

I settle back into my seat, but I'm no longer anything like calm. Boar Island is less than fifteen miles from Bienville by road, and it's walked every year by dozens of hunters who pay thousands of dollars for the privilege. It's probably rooted up by hundreds of hogs and dogs as well. That makes it a damned unlikely place to dispose of a corpse—especially for a man who owns and manages thousands of acres of forest and swampland untrampled by human feet. Most worrisome of all, we've been on the road for an hour and we're not there yet.

"So, you made some kind of deal with Buckman today?" Paul says, not taking his eyes from the road. "To keep quiet?"

"How'd you know that?"

"Claude called me this afternoon to ask whether I thought you'd honor an agreement like that. I told him you would."

"Did he tell you the terms?"

"Not specifics. I didn't much care at the time. What did you ask for in exchange for keeping quiet?"

I don't see any way to avoid answering. "The moon."

"And the club agreed?"

"Except for two points, yeah."

"What two points?"

For a guy who just experienced one of the most harrowing traumas of his life, Paul seems damned curious all of a sudden. "Do you know about their China deal? The Senate thing?"

"I figured it out on my own. They had a little celebration one night, and I stopped in. Damn, they were proud of themselves. Sell out your country and pop the cork on the Veuve Clicquot. A half hour didn't pass before they were bragging about it."

"Except for the matter of treason, it's a hell of an accomplishment. I told them Avery Sumner has to resign. Give up his Senate seat."

"Huh. No wonder they had a problem with that. What was the other sticking point?"

"I said whoever killed Buck Ferris has to stand trial or plead guilty to murder. I assume that's Beau Holland. One way or another, I want him in Parchman."

Paul glances over at me again, his skepticism plain. "Beau's an ass-hole, but they'll never let him stand trial. Or plead out. He knows way too much to risk letting him talk."

"I gathered that. Buckman offered to have him killed instead."

Paul chuckles. "Claude's a hard old bastard. Why didn't you let him do that?"

"I want justice for Buck, not another murder."

Paul shakes his head like a sergeant dealing with a naïve recruit. "Eye for an eye's about as fair as it gets in this world, Goose."

"Yeah? Well. That's where you and I part ways."

"Maybe. Yet here we are with a corpse in the truck bed. You never stopped being a Boy Scout, did you?"

"A Boy Scout wouldn't have made the deal I made today."

He doesn't comment further. Soon our headlights are the only man-made illumination within our range of vision. The moon hangs on our left, slightly larger than it was when Jet hit Max with the hammer last night.

"*Do* you intend to hold up your end?" Paul asks. "Or are you just playing those guys for suckers?"

As I look over at him, anxiety crawls up my spine like a beetle under my shirt. "How would I play them? And why?"

"I figure you might want another Pulitzer to announce your re-entry to the D.C. media world."

I sigh heavily. "I don't even know that I'm going back to Washington."

"What would keep you here?" he asks, his voice tighter than before. "Jet?"

There it is. The unspoken question. "No," I say deliberately. "The newspaper. The *Watchman.*"

"Really?" Paul looks surprised at first, then skeptical. But after a few seconds he says, "A lot changes when our fathers die, I guess. I can see that."

"What about you? You gonna take Max's seat in the Poker Club?"

He shrugs. "Hard to say. I think it's going to get tougher for rich white guys to rule these towns in the world of Twitter and cell phone cameras. Even small towns."

"Maybe. I think their biggest problem may be the black community. They really got behind the coroner this week. They might decide to run a real candidate for mayor this year. Tell the Poker Club to keep their money and try to take over the Board of Aldermen."

Paul grunts. "That'd be a hell of a show."

In the silence that follows this exchange, I lean against my door and close my eyes. But Paul isn't through. Before ELP finishes "Lucky Man," he says, "So did you give it to them yet? The cache, I mean."

"No," I answer, still leaning against the door. "I can't really give it to them. It's mostly digital. They just have to accept that I'll keep it isolated."

Paul nods. "But there's a hard copy somewhere?"

Shit. "There's a couple of hard drives somewhere, I think." To push him away from this subject, I ask him something that's stumped me from the beginning. "I can't figure out who sent me those pictures of Dave Cowart and Beau Holland with Buck."

"Really."

"I wondered if it might be you. It had to be somebody in the club. Somebody with access to game cameras at the mill site."

Paul doesn't turn to me as he answers. "I'm no fan of Holland, but it wasn't me."

"Any ideas?"

"Wyatt Cash would be my guess."

"Why's that?"

"First, because the cameras were his. Second, he hates Holland. Beau screwed his ex-wife before she was his ex."

"Didn't you tell me there's a club rule against that?"

"Yeah, but that's not the kind of thing you want to bitch about to your friends. I think Wyatt waited for his chance, then hammered Beau hard."

"Wouldn't that be a huge risk for Cash? With the club, I mean?"

Paul lifts a hand off the wheel as if to say, *Not so bad that I wouldn't take it*. "Those cameras transmit data over the cellular network. In theory, they're hackable. Plus, some other people saw those shots. Nobody could pin the leak on Wyatt for sure."

I settle back against the door.

"But you've had them all along, right?" Paul asks. "The hard drives."

I sit up in my seat, the obvious question in my eyes. "I never had the cache, Paul. I only know who your mom gave it to—that's all. And it took me all week to figure that out."

His eyes glint in the dark. "Who was it?"

I don't answer.

He smiles strangely. "You're not gonna tell me who my mama trusted with our family secrets?"

"I made a promise, man."

"You haven't been big on honoring those lately. That must mean it was Jet. Does she have the cache?"

"Hell, no. The drives are in a safe-deposit box. That's all I can tell you. They can't be gotten to until Monday at the earliest."

After a few seconds, he nods and turns his attention back to the dark road. "Well, that's good."

And with that he falls silent.

My slow-building anxiety has shifted into fear. I don't think Paul was asking those questions for himself. And if he wasn't . . . then I may be mistaken about what we're doing on this lightless road. Am I here to help him bury his father? Or am I riding to the edge of my own grave? Does Paul plan to shoot me in the back and roll me in on top of Max before driving back to Jet and his son? If that's his plan, Boar Island suddenly makes a lot more sense. An island owned and protected by the Poker Club might be the safest place to commit one more murder and hide the evidence. Hell, they process deer carcasses out here all the time—

Okay, calm down, I tell myself. But my heart doesn't listen. It's hammering against my chest wall, and my blood pressure has skyrocketed. The pounding in my ears only allows "Free Bird" into my head in brief pulses.

If Paul is leading me to my death, I have only a couple of options. Maybe just one. I have a gun, but so does he, and his skill with firearms makes me like a child in comparison. My only chance would be to shoot him in the head while he's driving the truck. But we're still moving at sixty miles an hour. Would I survive the impact that would likely result? A head-on crash into a tree is usually fatal. If we tumble down the levee, same result. Besides, if Paul already means me harm, then he's prepared for anything I might try. If I even touch the gun in my pocket, he could have his out and held against my temple.

While I ponder these logistics, he turns onto a well-maintained gravel road, the kind that must be replenished every year after being washed out by backwater from the swollen river. He follows this for about a mile, and the trees close in tight as the land rolls by. Before long, we come to a hand-tooled wooden sign that reads:

PRIME SHOT PREMIUM HUNTING CLUB
Boar Island, Mississippi

Between these letters is a beautifully carved whitetail buck with a twelve-point rack.

"It's weird, isn't it?" Paul says. "This island's part of Mississippi, but it's on the Louisiana side of the river."

"I think that's pretty common," I reply, trying to keep the fear out of my voice. "At least on the lower Mississippi."

"The river goes its own way," he says. "Corps of Engineers might as well give up now."

I say nothing. It strikes me that the ever-changing river is like a woman caught between two men, snaking across the land from year to year, confusing boundaries and triggering conflicts that take the courts, and sometimes guns, to resolve.

The road runs a little smoother beyond the sign, and soon we come to a stretch paved with asphalt. As we roll through the dense hardwoods, it occurs to me that he and I have shared more than many brothers. We shared our childhoods, our adolescence. We've loved the same woman, and shared her as well, once long ago and now again. We shared the adrenaline rush and terror of combat and the after-action dilemmas that trail in the wake of modern war. He saved my life in Iraq, and back at my house tonight, I returned the favor. If I hadn't eased up behind him and begun talking, I believe he would have shot himself through the mouth. But will that save me now? Does he even remember it? And if he does, does he care? Or are Jet and Kevin the only things driving him? Jet's betrayal, and the desire for custody of his son?

White light blazes out of the forest after a sharp turn. Glancing left, I see that Paul is as surprised as I am. He brakes slightly, then lets the truck keep rolling. Up ahead stands the main complex of the Boar Island hunting camp. Like most of these facilities, there's a central lodge or bunkhouse, plus assorted outbuildings that serve various functions. As we near the bright bubble of light, I see that its source is a large pavilion in front of the main lodge, a tin-roofed structure set on huge wooden posts and beams, with a cement floor and what looks like an outdoor kitchen under the roof. Maybe a dozen vehicles are parked between the pavilion and the lodge.

"What the hell, Paul?" I ask. "Did you expect this?"

"No." He's counting the vehicles. "I expected Buckman and Donnelly, maybe Russo and Holland. But that's it."

"Russo and Holland?" Suddenly I understand. While Paul was alone in my house with Jet, he must have called Claude Buckman and told him to get some Poker Club members over to Wyatt's island. Then he drove around Louisiana long enough to let them beat us here. While I slept like a dumb steer headed to the slaughterhouse. "You called those guys?"

He parks twenty yards short of the pavilion, then turns to me, his face like that of a stranger. "Listen, Goose. You can't do what you've done these past few months and expect to walk away clean. You gotta know that. Some things have to be settled."

The fear in my belly almost unmans me. "What does that mean?"

He looks at the lighted pavilion. "Given what I see here, I'm not sure. But there's no running from it. For either of us. So let's find out."

"You could back your truck out of here and run for it."

"We'd never make it." He claps me on the thigh without looking at me. "Let's go."

He takes his keys when he climbs out of the truck, leaving me no choice but to follow. As I walk toward the pavilion, I see Beau Holland's Porsche 911 parked between two pickups. Fear makes my hands tingle. The drone of a big generator provides the basic soundtrack out here, punctuated by the sudden electrocutions of a bright violet bug zapper. The smell of whiskey and cigars rides the damp air, but there are undercurrents: rotting fish and vegetation, motor oil, mud, gasoline, horseflesh, leather, corn, wet dog fur, and spent gunpowder. This is like rolling up on an American military camp in the jungle, which I once did in the Philippines. Air-conditioned luxury in the primeval wilderness, powered by diesel generators.

Paul raises his hand in greeting.

Beyond him, I see a semicircle of teak chairs, each occupied by a member of the Poker Club. There are twelve chairs in all. Two stand empty. One must be Max Matheson's seat. I recognize most of the men in the chairs. Claude Buckman sits in the only seat outside the semicircle, and he faces the others, like an elderly general briefing his commanders. Nearest him sits Blake Donnelly. Then come the usual suspects: Senator Sumner, Arthur Pine, Beau Holland, Tommy Russo, Warren Lacey. Farthest from Buckman sit three older men I don't know. One might be a prominent insurance agent, the other a wealthy farmer. The third, I have no idea. Opposite the semicircle is a large bar and outdoor oven, including a fireplace big enough to warm a platoon. Above the mantel hangs a colossal flat-screen television. Beneath it sit several SEC football helmets, all autographed by Hall of Fame quarterbacks. Ole Miss, LSU, Alabama, Mississippi State, Tennessee, even Florida. Around the pavilion's perimeter I see at least three armed guards.

Nobody has football on his mind tonight.

As I come even with Paul, he walks out before the assembled Star Chamber and addresses Buckman. "This isn't exactly what I expected, Claude. Looks like a full meeting. Except I don't see Wyatt. This is his island. Where is he?"

"Mr. Cash will be along."

"So what's going on?"

The old man gives Paul a philosophical smile. "There's too much on the line to keep this small. We need to set everything to rest tonight. What did you learn from McEwan?"

"He means to keep the deal he made with you. As for Avery resigning, he's flexible. He still wants Beau to go to Parchman, though."

"Keep dreaming," Holland says from his seat.

Beau Holland is wearing his customary Izod shirt and chinos, the aquamarine shirt chosen to set off his tan. A sweating glass of whiskey sits in a hole in his chair arm, and his right hand holds a burning cigar. As I scan the circle, each man sees me marking his presence, but not one nods or raises his hand in greeting—not even Blake Donnelly. A result of today's newspaper stories, I'm sure. These men have come here solely out of self-preservation. They're treating me like I'm already dead.

"The situation has changed quite a bit this evening," Buckman explains. "We're going to have to make some big decisions. Final decisions. Beau, get the TV."

Holland lifts a remote control from his lap and presses a button.

The big screen above the mantel lights up, showing what looks like a scene from *The Texas Chain Saw Massacre*. In reality, it must be security cam footage of the interior of a deer-skinning shack. Hoists and hooks are bolted to the walls and ceiling joists, while knives, bone saws, and pliers hang from the wall. Tied to a six-by-six post at the center of the screen is Nadine Sullivan.

She's naked except for a pair of panties, and a rag has been tied around her mouth. Her eyes look glassy from fatigue, or fear, or perhaps narcotics. Behind her the wall is stained with blood. It looks like old blood, but with this video setup it's hard to be sure. The camera's wide-angle view shows me a big drain in the floor, surrounded by something wet. A small pile of clothes lies at Nadine's feet.

It's all I can do to hold down the contents of my stomach, which feel like nothing but acid and whatever casserole my mother's friends brought over after my father's death. I'm about to speak when Paul reaches out and grips my arm hard enough to stop me.

"Is that the bookstore girl?" he asks. "Nadine?"

"That's right," says Beau Holland. "She had the cache your mother made. The one designed to destroy your father. And us, if necessary."

Paul glances at me, then back at Holland. "How'd you find out she had it?"

"Your wife told us."

This throws Paul off-balance. "My wife?"

Tommy Russo answers the question. "We sent a couple of guys to talk to her this afternoon."

Holland can't bear to let Russo have the floor. "As soon as Jet realized her kid was in danger," he says, "*poof,* no more cache problem."

Paul takes a deep breath, sighs. I may be the only man under this roof who understands that he's already in the grip of homicidal rage.

"You sent men to interrogate my wife?" he asks softly.

"Had to, Paulie," says Russo. "And it's a good thing we did. 'Cause she gave up the Sullivan girl without hesitating. And Nadine talked just about as quick. She thought she was being smart. She hid the cache in a safe-deposit box in a bank in Monroe. Since the bank had just closed for the weekend, she figured we'd have to keep her alive at least till Monday so she could get it out for us."

"But . . . ?"

"But," Holland says with a grin, "she didn't realize that Claude knows every banker from Texas to Alabama. We had that cache in hand ninety minutes after Nadine told us about it."

Paul sniffs and looks over at Buckman. "Well, that's a relief."

"She also told us that Marshall never had anything more than what she fed him anonymously," Holland adds.

"What about some kind of fail-safe mechanism?" Paul asks. "She dies, and copies get sent out to the FBI and the media? There could be a dozen copies out there in the cloud."

"There aren't," Russo assures him.

"How do you know?"

Russo nods at the TV. "We made sure. Take my word for that."

My hands are shaking. It's all I can do not to jerk Nadine's gun from my pocket. Worst of all, I feel guilty for having the pistol at all. Maybe if she'd had it, Nadine could have defended herself against the men who abducted her.

"Okay," Paul says with what sounds like weariness. "So what's everybody doing here? Why the big confab?"

Buckman draws on his cigar, then answers in his gravelly voice. "You're going to have to earn your father's seat, son."

"How do I do that?"

"By killing McEwan."

Paul sniffs again and looks over at me. He doesn't look surprised by this order. "What about the Sullivan girl?"

"She's not your problem," says Holland. "Nadine and I have a little unfinished business."

Paul snorts. "Having a hard time getting laid, Beau?"

Holland grins with maddening arrogance. "Never."

Paul surveys the semicircle of faces, then settles his gaze on Buckman. "So the price of my father's seat is Marshall's life?"

Holland's grin widens. "That's right."

"Who'd you kill to get your seat, Beau?"

The real estate man's grin gets brittle.

"That's what I figured."

Buckman says, "The demands McEwan made this morning could cost us in the neighborhood of seventy million dollars, Paul. That's unacceptable."

"The club and the city together, you mean."

"Marshall was never going to honor that deal," Holland cuts in again. "He was going to write another book. Try for another Pulitzer."

"What if I don't kill him?" Paul asks.

The old banker leans forward. "Then we'll know your priority is not the club. But this is all academic. If you killed your father tonight, I can't see how killing Marshall could be any more difficult."

"Hell," says Holland, smirking, "I'd think you'd enjoy capping this asshole."

I hear muffled laughter from the semicircle, but Paul seems not to notice. There's a coldness in his eyes that I know is a prelude to violence.

"Let me be sure I'm clear on the terms," he says. "I kill Marshall, my family is free and clear. I ask because I know Pop protected my wife in certain circumstances. And he's gone now. If I kill Marshall, Jet is safe. Right?"

Buckman regards Paul through the smoke rising from his cigar. "It's a bit more complicated than that."

Paul rolls his shoulders, then cocks his head and looks down at the old man. "Why's that?"

"You'll find out in a minute," says Holland. He glances at his watch. "Less than a minute, actually."

"Have some Scotch," Russo suggests. "I'll pour you one. This is all gonna work out, bro."

"I don't know," Holland says. "Paul doesn't look too happy. I figured this would be a relief for him, but he looks a little constipated."

Paul gives Beau Holland his full attention. "That's because I'm not as confident as you seem to be about how safe we are." He turns to Buckman. "I told you Wednesday it was a mistake to kill Buck Ferris— which this asshole did, along with his sidekick."

Paul must be referring to Dave Cowart.

"Still, you made a deal to contain that damage, and Marshall means to keep his promise."

"That deal was too costly," Buckman declares. "Especially given that we don't need to honor it now."

"Are you sure about that? If Marshall and Nadine die, it'll draw a hell of a lot of attention to our little town. Especially after the newspaper that came out this morning. Marshall's a goddamn celebrity in D.C., which none of you seem to understand."

"That's as may be," Buckman concedes. "But we can't afford any more stories like the ones he published this morning. It's worth the risk to be sure we put an end to them."

Paul looks around the semicircle again. "I still don't know what you're all here for. To watch me put a bullet in him? I'd think you'd want to avoid that."

Before anyone can answer, I hear the sound of a helicopter over the trees. The distinctive *whup-whup-whup* I recognize from my early reporting days as a Bell 206B JetRanger. I know of only two locally owned JetRangers: Matheson Lumber has one; the other is owned by Prime Shot Premium Hunting Gear. Since Paul is the pilot for Matheson Lumber, I assume the pilot of the JetRanger overhead must be Wyatt Cash, the owner of the island beneath our feet.

Standing at the edge of the pavilion, I see a white nose-light boring in from the east. Red running lights appear behind it. Twenty seconds later, the JetRanger becomes discernible against the clouds, descending fast. Several men stand and turn away from the rotor blast while the chopper flares and lands in the space between the camp house and the pavilion, throwing up a hurricane of pinecones, pea gravel, and grit. If it hadn't rained earlier, the storm of debris would be worse.

Sure enough, the white JetRanger has the Prime Shot logo painted behind its door. As we stare, the aircraft's big side door pops open. A man wearing paramilitary gear gets out, then helps someone to the ground.

It's Jet.

While I stare in shock, the guy in body armor reaches back inside and helps a heavy black woman to the ground. Tallulah Williams. Last of all comes Kevin Matheson, who leaps easily to the ground, looking around like a kid stunned to find himself on a night adventure.

Turning to Paul, I see but one emotion in his face: fear.

CHAPTER 55

"WHAT THE FUCK is my son doing here?" Paul asks, standing rigid as a man waiting to be horsewhipped.

"You'll see," Beau Holland says over his shoulder.

Holland doesn't realize how close he is to death at this moment.

Two guards appear behind Paul. One takes the pistol from the small of his back. The other checks his ankles for a holster. Apparently they knew Max's carrying habits. Sure enough, they find a second gun. Paul must have put on Max's ankle holster before or after we loaded his corpse into the truck. While they set aside Paul's weapons, another guard wraps an iron-hard arm around me and snatches Nadine's .32 automatic from my pocket. Paul and I make momentary eye contact, but if he's sending me a message, I'm too thick to translate it. Paul didn't protest being stripped of his guns because he knows there's nothing he can do at this point but make a suicidal stand. And until he knows Buckman's intentions regarding his family, he won't do that.

His eyes go wide, however, when two armed guards take hold of Kevin and Tallulah and lead them into the main lodge. When Jet tries to follow, another guard restrains her and marches her toward the pavilion. There's a scuffle as Tallulah resists being led into the lodge, and Kevin tries to help her, but the guards quickly subdue both the maid and the boy. I can't help but feel that Paul is marking these transgressions on an internal ledger that he will square if it takes the rest of his life—however short that may be.

"Where are they taking my boy?" he asks softly.

"Kevin's fine," Buckman says. "He's safe."

"For now," adds Holland. "Let's see how this goes."

As the chopper's engine spools down, Wyatt Cash climbs out of the pilot's seat and trots across the ground, catching up to Jet as she's led into the pavilion. Cash seems surprised by the size of the gathering, and even more so by the mood of the men, which feels like the quiet before a crack of lightning.

In the threatening silence, Jet looks up and sees Nadine on the TV screen. "Oh, my God," she whispers. "What have you done to her?"

"What do you care?" Holland asks. "You gave her up to us."

"Sweet Jesus." She looks at me. "I'm so sorry, Marshall."

"We may do the same to you yet," Holland says, and I see Paul shift his weight.

Jet scowls at the real estate developer with contempt. "You sick bastard."

If Paul weren't here, I have no doubt that Holland would have struck her for that. Instead he walks to the fireplace and comes back with a roll of duct tape. While a guard holds Jet's head, Beau rips off a length and tapes her mouth shut. Wyatt Cash looks like he's about to protest, but Buckman waves a hand, silencing him.

"There's no call for this," Paul says to Buckman. "No reason for it."

"Here's the thing, Paul," croaks the old banker. "Nadine Sullivan poses no further threat to us. Neither does Marshall. The X factor is your wife."

"My wife? How do you figure that?"

"She was close to your mother. She's a lawyer. She's been trying to nail our asses for years. If Max hadn't been protecting her, she'd have had an accident a long time ago. She's the natural person for Sally to give another copy of this cache to."

"She doesn't have it, Claude."

"Well, Paulie," Russo chimes in, "you gotta forgive us if your word isn't quite enough. You're probably the last person who'd know what Jet's really up to. In fact, Marshall here's probably the only one who would."

"She doesn't have it, guys," I tell them. "Seriously."

Holland laughs, as do several other men—Warren Lacey the loudest.

Buckman signals Holland with a nod, and Beau picks up the TV remote again. The image changes from Nadine in the skinning room to security camera footage of a long balcony. It's the interior of the Aurora Hotel. The mezzanine. The view is from above, shooting along the balcony rail. The screen flickers as Holland presses a button to fast-forward. Two figures hurry along the rail at quadruple speed, and it's hard to make out what's going on. Then Holland removes his finger, bringing the playback to normal.

Panic hits me all at once, sending adrenaline shunting through my veins. Jet's eyes have gone wide above the duct tape, but I can't read her emotions. Fear, yes, but something else, too. The desperate drive for survival. She senses how close we are to being killed. Paul doesn't yet know what's coming, but he will any second.

On the screen, a woman who is unmistakably Jet leans against the rail in profile and hikes her dress over her hips. From the side she looks like a textbook illustration of lordosis, the behavior during which female mammals arch their backs and make themselves most receptive to being mounted by males. She glances back over her shoulder and speaks. I say something, then turn and walk away from her. The camera follows me.

"How about that tracking function?" Holland marvels. "Tommy's casino contractor set us up with pan-tilt-zoom rigs."

Paul stares wordlessly at this further evidence of his wife's infidelity—or desire for it. The view switches to a different camera, this one apparently near the service elevator. Now we're looking straight-on at Jet's behind, the dark tangle below the cleft in her derriere shockingly visible, even with the thong.

"I don't appreciate everybody looking at my wife's ass," Paul says quietly.

Holland chuckles. "If she didn't spread it around like she does, we wouldn't have to."

This guy is clueless, I think. *Or else he's betting that Paul won't make it through this meeting alive.*

"Can't believe she ever delivered a kid," says Dr. Lacey. "She's still high and tight. I'd like to give that a workout."

Paul cuts his eyes at Lacey, marking him down for future attention.

"Point is, Paulie," says Russo, "you don't know what the hell she's been up to, or how much of a threat she is to us."

"I think it's time we heard from the lady herself," says Buckman.

Holland rips off the duct tape. Jet yelps, then raises her hand to slap Holland, but he easily catches her arm.

She looks down at Buckman, her arm still locked in Holland's grasp. "You'd better tell him to let go, Claude. Because you are well and truly fucked already. And this is making it worse, I *promise* you."

Buckman assesses her with a practiced eye. "Let her go, Beau."

She focuses on the old banker, and in her eyes I see implacable fury. "You threaten my *child*? You kidnap me by force, when you could have just invited me here? What the hell were you thinking?"

"Business is business, dear."

"You're the one here to answer questions," says Holland. "Not us."

"*Why* is our son here?" Paul asks in a barely controlled voice.

"To ensure that your wife tells us the truth," Buckman replies, nodding to Holland once more.

Holland works the remote, and the video of Jet is replaced by an image of Kevin Matheson pacing a small bedroom, while Tallulah Williams sits at the end of a bed, looking frightened.

"You're saying you'd torture my son?" Paul asks, his eyes on Buckman, then Blake Donnelly, who looks away in shame.

"We didn't create this situation," says Buckman. "And I don't think it will come to that. But I'm very concerned about what your wife just said."

"You should be, you dried-up bag of bones," Jet says. "What I said is you're fucked. Screwed. Dead meat. Either you put us back in that chopper and fly us home, or the FBI will be kicking down your door by eight A.M. Every one of you. Federal prison. Bank on it."

"Bullshit," says Holland, clearly discomfited by her bravado. "She's bluffing."

Jet regards him with regal disdain. "Beau, you shouldn't think. You're not good at it. Selling time-share condos in Gulf Shores . . . that's your ceiling."

Holland laughs. "Big talk for an Ole Miss grad."

"You think? I figure my IQ surpassed yours when I was about ten." She looks around the semicircle. "Make no mistake, gentlemen. Each and every one of you has a sword hanging over your head. Sally Matheson put it there. You want to know if I have a copy of the cache? You bet your wrinkled old balls I do."

She's bluffing, I think. *She has to be—*

"She's lying," insists Holland. "She never had it. If Sally was going to give it to her, why bother giving it to Nadine, too?"

"That I can't tell you," Jet replies, still radiating supreme confidence. "But I can tell you this: Royal Bank of Seychelles, account number three-seven-six, six-eight-one-five, two-two-seven. That ring any bells for you boys?"

At least six men have gone bone white. Several sit up in their chairs as though a psychic has started reading their credit card numbers on television.

"Is that a yes?" Jet asks in a game-show host's voice. "Anybody need a Valium? Maybe a little nitro under the tongue? You will. Because here's the important thing: I don't just *know* that information. I've set up an automatic trigger to release it in the event that I go missing or die. That's my personal insurance policy. I set it up months ago, when I targeted Max. You put a bullet in my head tonight? You touch my child? You're paying a deposit on your prison cell."

She looks from face to face without a shred of fear. "And *you,*" she says, poking Holland in the chest, exactly the way she did Paul's an hour ago. "You will get down on your knees and *beg* me not to feed you to the FBI."

Holland gapes at her in astonishment.

"I said *kneel,* bitch," Jet repeats.

Holland looks from face to face, gauging his support. "You don't really believe her? Nobody would memorize account numbers."

Jet sighs as though bored with this game. "I don't have to memorize them, Beau. They just stick in my head. For example: CDB Offshore Bank of Seychelles. Account nine-three-six, seven-two-nine-nine, one-six-four-three."

Gasped obscenities burst from the semicircle of chairs.

Jet smiles with satisfaction. "Aaaand the Prince's Trust Bank, Seychelles. Account one-one-six, eight-five-one-seven, two-two-nine-six. Anyone . . . ? Bueller? No?"

One man comes up out of his chair.

"*There,*" Jet croons. "I believe Arthur Pine just wet his diaper."

I've never seen anyone turn the tables on a group of powerful men so fast. It's as though Jet took hold of the corner of a killing box and flipped it inside out with a single jerk. Suddenly she's protected, and everyone else is facing destruction.

She steps away from Holland as if to get some distance from a bad smell. "As you mentioned, Claude, I am an attorney. And I happen to know that the penalties for tax evasion and criminal fraud amount to a life sentence for most of the men under this pavilion. My little insurance policy also contains copies of emails between Max and officials of Azure Dragon Paper, which will prove conclusively the selling of U.S. Senate votes. I'm not sure what the Justice Department does to you for that. I'd call it treason. But that's only the beginning. I suspect the stock value of Wyatt Cash's company would drop ninety percent by market close Monday." She turns to Cash. "Say goodbye to this island, Wyatt. Also to your helicopter, which is nice, by the way."

"Okay, hold up," Cash says. "This is getting out of hand. It wasn't my idea to kidnap this lady's kid. Paul, you've got to take my word for that."

"You flew them here in your helicopter."

"Claude told me you wanted them here! Tell him, Claude."

"Your stock's going to take a hell of a beating, too, Claude," Jet goes on. "Selling out your country to the Chinese? You'll be off the board of your own bank in forty-eight hours."

"Goddamn it," Holland says. "Everybody's losing their nerve."

"Agreed," says Russo. "She may have some of this cache, or she may just have a set of balls. I know some tough women gamblers. I don't plan to spend the rest of my days living in fear of what this lady might do. I think she's bluffing. And I call. Let's tie her to a tree and spend fifteen minutes finding out exactly what we have to worry about."

"I second that motion," says Warren Lacey.

Somebody in the semicircle whoops in anticipation.

Buckman and Donnelly share a glance. They don't look happy with the turn things have taken. Buckman looks over at Pine. "Arthur?"

The old lawyer runs his hand through his silver hair and regards Jet critically. "Jet Matheson isn't my favorite person. But she's smarter than any two of us put together. On the other hand, if her life over the past year has proved anything, it's that she's a consummate liar. I think the only way to find out whether she's bluffing is to do what Tommy suggested—as much as I detest that kind of thing."

Paul shakes his head in disbelief. "My vouching for her isn't enough?"

"Regrettably, no," says Buckman. "Mr. Russo? If you would?"

Tommy signals some security guys at the periphery of the pavilion. "Take her to the skinning room, for the sake of our ears. You guys can watch on TV if you want."

"Wait!" I shout. "For God's sake, give me sixty seconds before you start this. You already tortured Nadine, and that was pointless."

Buckman is busy relighting his cigar. "On the contrary, Mr. Mc-Ewan. We learned that we don't have to honor the deal we made with you."

"But you do. Remember the audiotape I played you at the bank? Of you talking about the deal you made with the Chinese? I've made copies of that and placed them with friends, much as Jet did, I suspect."

"We'll find out soon enough," says Russo. "We'll take you to the shed, too."

The two thugs who took Paul's pistols move toward me.

"You can't win this thing, guys," I tell them, trying to hold my voice steady. "Not like this. But the real question is, why are you even trying to?"

"Because," says Buckman, "Mr. Holland and Mr. Russo have argued quite convincingly that you, as a journalist, cannot be relied upon to honor your end of the bargain. Sooner or later, you'll be tempted to publish the story. And we can't risk that."

"This is where you're wrong, Claude. We made one deal and you broke it. The result was the newspaper that hit you guys this morning. Then we made a second deal, and now you're trying to break that. But I fully intend to honor our deal. Nadine wanted that, too. She *never* wanted to blow up the paper mill and hurt the town. But you had to torture her. Stupid, man."

"You're lying," Holland says. "You've got too much ego to sit on this. It would kill you. This is your ticket back to the big leagues. You'd tell yourself you were breaking it to honor your father."

I shake my head at the Realtor. "Jet's right, Beau. You're not too smart. My father died earlier today, at my brother's grave. Before he did, I told him about the agreement I'd made with the club. I told him I'd betrayed every principle of our profession, and I thought he'd damn me for it. But you know what? He didn't. He said I'd probably done more good than I could have in twenty years of writing newspaper stories. Once he told me that, I knew I could live with it."

Blake Donnelly leans toward Buckman. "Duncan was a good ol' boy, Claude. I think the kid has a point."

"Think of the body count if you go this route," I point out. "You're gonna kill Nadine. Then me. Then torture Paul's son to be sure Jet's not lying. *Then* you torture Jet and kill her? That's insane. You'll have to kill Paul to stop him from killing you all in revenge. You think you can just write all that off like a tax loss? After Buck's death? And Sally's? You may control the local cops, but you're going to have the FBI setting up an office in Bienville after all that. That's *without* the fail-safes we've set up. That's crazy-level risk."

"I don't know," says Russo. "If we leave all the bodies at Paul's place, we can say he found you banging his wife and went crazy. White man on a rampage. Killed his whole family, then set the house on fire and shot himself."

"There you go!" cries Holland. "I read stories like that once a month."

Wyatt Cash is shaking his head. He steps closer to Buckman. "This is nuts. Paul and Max were as much a part of this club as any of us."

"There's a cleaner solution," I press on. "Hang everything on Max and Holland. Beau killed Buck Ferris, then fled the country because the photo we printed placed him at the scene. Max killed Sally, then jumped bail and disappeared. End of body count. Nobody else dies. Any legal problems resulting from today's story, you hang on Max and Holland. Wrap them up in a nice bow and kiss them goodbye. The paper mill still gets built; you guys stay free and rich. Richer every day."

I hear grunts of approval from the semicircle.

Buckman purses his lips, then visually takes the pulse of the men filling the half-moon of chairs. "Paul? You've been surprisingly quiet. What do you have to say?"

Even in stillness, Paul radiates considerable tension. "I told you guys that whoever killed Ferris was going to destroy the club. Well, here we are. And that's thanks to this asshole." He jerks his thumb at Holland. "Tommy's only standing with Beau because he's got so much money invested with him. Marshall's got the right idea. Hang it all on Max and Beau, then boogie on down the road. That's the surgical solution."

Buckman looks at Tommy. "Mr. Russo? What do you say?"

"He's right. I've got a lot of money tied up with Beau." Tommy looks at Paul. "Can you make me whole if I lean your way?"

Paul glances at Jet, then back at Tommy. "What kind of money we talking about?"

Russo thinks about it. "Ten million would get me most of the way there."

"Ten million."

"Right."

"Can't do it, Tommy. Not me alone."

Russo doesn't believe him. "You're about to inherit Max's fortune, right?"

"I didn't tell you to invest with Beau."

Feeling the mood shift against him, Beau Holland barks at the men in the semicircle. "What the hell are we talking about? They've got nothing! Tie this slut to a tree and go to work on her. Drag that kid out here. She'll cough up the truth in thirty seconds."

Paul looks calmly at Holland. "You're starting to piss me off."

Holland draws a derringer from his pocket and points it at Paul's belly. "How about now?"

Paul looks down at the gun with contempt, then surveys the ring of faces. "You guys act like I just got off a bus. Whatever happened to loyalty? Claude, you're a tough old bird, but you can't live forever. Tommy? You're a wop, and you're from out of state. They'll never let you run this club. If Max had lived, he'd have been next in line. Everybody knows it. But Max is dead. I killed him. What's the saying? 'The king is dead, long live the king'? Well, I'm not just taking Pop's seat—I'm taking his *place*."

Holland snorts at Paul's presumption, but I see a couple of men nodding. They're thinking that Max Matheson left big shoes to fill, but this kid might just be able to do it.

"Who else is going to run it?" Paul asks. He gestures at Beau with disdain. "You guys want to hitch your wagons to this soft-dick, spray-tan cocksucker with his pimp gun? Give me a break."

Claude Buckman shifts in his teak chair. Even the banker is considering Paul's argument.

"You got some balls on you, Paulie," Russo says, looking over at Holland. "You want to make your case, Beau?"

"You're not listening to this asshole, Tommy?"

"He makes sense."

Holland's face goes red beneath his tan. "He's a bullshit artist, like his old man! Look at him. You think he can run this club? He's got head wounds from two wars. He's been a drugged-out wreck for twenty years. He can't hold on to his own wife, because she's fucking his best friend. You want to chain yourselves to that?"

"Yeah, yeah, yeah," Paul mutters. His hard eyes focus on Russo. "You talk a lot about family, Tommy. I want every man out here to think about his son. Because you've got *my* son locked in that camp house, scared to death. He's worried about his mama. And for what? You sons of bitches ought to be ashamed. You know me. You knew my daddy. Some of you knew my *grand*daddy. You know the history. When it came to gunplay after the Civil War, which family did you count on to take care of business? The Mathesons, that's who. Well, what's changed? Nothing. And I hold every man here personally responsible for whatever happens next. I may not be a rocket scientist—that's my wife's department—but when the enemy's at the gates, I'm the guy you call. You don't believe me, ask Marshall here what he left *out* of that book about Iraq."

Rapt faces stare at Paul with something close to worship in their eyes. There's no respect among American men like that reserved for soldiers who have survived combat.

"One more thing," Paul says in a softer voice. "Marshall here screwed me over pretty good. But that's personal. I'm no angel myself. God knows I haven't treated my wife right over the years. And the thing is, me and him go back to kindergarten. Dixie Youth baseball. Jerking off to our first *Playboy*. Building forts in the woods. We fought together in Ramadi, and I can tell you this: when the insurgents overran us, he returned fire till his gun ran dry. Today we both lost our fathers. The same day. Now you got us out here for this bullshit inquisition?"

Paul looks at the ground and shakes his head. "I'm not killing him for you. I won't do it. He's gonna hold up his end of the deal. And if *you* kill him—and that bookstore lady, who hasn't done a damn thing to you, and whose coffee I like—then I put your names down in my book. And one night soon, you're gonna wake up just long enough to see the blood spurting from your carotids before you bleed out."

"I told you!" Holland cries with satisfaction, pushing his derringer closer to Paul. "We've got to kill him, too."

Holland seems to believe that Paul has condemned himself.

"He's right," Paul concludes. "You boys got a choice to make. Kill half a dozen people for no good reason, then pray the FBI doesn't kick down your door tomorrow morning. Or lay it all off on Max and this prick, and call it a day."

Holland swallows hard. He looks to Russo but finds no support there. Summoning all the conviction he can, he says, "None of this is up to Paul. Jet's the one with a copy of the cache. And remember that video. These two are about to wind up in divorce court. Guaranteed. How many of us have been divorced? Seven out of twelve? Think about it. No matter how you start, it ends up a war. No prisoners. Does anybody here think this bitch won't use everything in her arsenal to get custody of her kid? Be smart! Let's find out what she knows and put an end to the threat once and for all."

"You're thinking again, Beau," Jet says, stepping between Holland and the other men. "Who says I'm getting divorced? What did you see on that screen? Me having sex with Marshall? No. He doesn't want me. He's in love with Nadine. Sure, I strayed once. So what? It's nothing Paul hasn't done a dozen times. All you dinosaurs think if the woman strays, the marriage is over. Well, that's not how it is anymore. Paul and I have a son to raise—together. And that's what we're going to do." She looks at Russo. "As for your losses, that's your problem. If the club wants to make you whole, fine. There's no reason that should fall on Paul and me. Claude, assess every member of the club. Split eleven ways, that's $909,090.90 apiece."

I'm worried she's moving too fast for these old guys, some of whom appear to be trying to mentally check her math.

"Why eleven ways?" Holland asks.

Jet smiles at him. "Because you're going to be dead." She turns to Buckman. "You *could* get him to write you a check tonight. After all, you own the bank. You could still honor it Monday, even after he's deceased. Right?"

Her brazen confidence and mental acuity have stunned the assembled businessmen.

"Mr. McEwan," Buckman says. "What about Avery Sumner? I'd

very much like him to retain his Senate seat. Bienville needs him. He'll vote honestly on all China-related bills. You have my word. Can you live with that?"

I barely have enough spit in my mouth to form words. "I can."

Buckman looks over at Donnelly, who nods once. Then at Arthur Pine. Pine is slower to agree.

"This is crazy!" Holland yells. "You're willing to risk our security because of this bitch? Because you haven't got the nerve to do what needs to be done?"

"I'm about tired of this motherfucker," Paul says.

Holland's eyes blaze. "You don't get to—"

Like a rattlesnake, Paul's right hand strikes Holland's throat and clamps around his windpipe. Holland fires the derringer, but Paul's left hand has already parried it, and the bullet ricochets off the cement into the night. Holland tries to speak when Paul wrenches the little gun from his hand, but no sound emerges.

As Beau's tanned face darkens, Paul cracks his head against a vertical post, stunning him senseless. Tommy Russo whips out a pistol and aims at Paul, but Paul ignores him. Buckman looks at Russo and lifts a restraining hand.

"I'm a new member, Claude," Paul says. "Do I need a show of hands or what?"

The silence stretches while Buckman's mind races, calculating odds. In the end, he takes too long. In one violent motion Paul slams Holland down to the concrete, then rises and stomps his neck so hard that a shock runs up our legs.

Several men jump in their seats, and Jet turns away.

"Can I get a second?" Paul asks, straightening his shirt and looking around the circle.

"Second," says Wyatt Cash. "Goddamn."

"Well," croaks Buckman, staring at Holland's motionless corpse. "I guess that's that."

Paul looks around. "Somebody find a blanket and show Marshall where the skinning shed is. And lend him a truck to take Nadine home."

"What about my ten million?" Russo asks, staring at Holland's body.

Buckman's mouth works silently as he thinks about it. "The club will cover half your losses, Mr. Russo. What would that be, Mrs. Matheson?"

"Eleven ways?"

"Yes. I can assess a share from some of Mr. Holland's shadier deals."

Jet clucks her tongue. "$454,545.45 apiece."

Buckman smiles. "You have a job at my bank any time you want it."

"No thanks."

Paul looks at the semicircle. "Dr. Lacey, how about you step over here a second?"

Lacey looks left, then right, hoping someone will excuse him from this reckoning. No one meets his eye. The doctor rubs his knees, then gets up and walks slowly to where we stand.

"You like my wife's ass?" Paul asks.

Lacey's face goes red. "Paul, listen, I'm into the gin pretty good—"

Paul backhands the doctor with a blow that sends him reeling, then turns his attention to Wyatt Cash. "Wyatt, how 'bout you take Jet in there with Kevin and Tallulah? Once they've calmed down, put them in your chopper and fly them home. I'll stay here till Max is in the ground. Claude and I will work out the fine print going forward. Somebody needs to lose Beau's Porsche."

"Consider it done. All of it."

"What about Mr. Holland's remains?" asks Buckman.

Paul looks down at the corpse and snorts. "You can feed that motherfucker to the hogs for all I care."

Everyone present seems taken aback by the speed with which the situation has changed, yet no one looks displeased. It's as though Paul has so completely assumed Max's mantle that he seems a younger incarnation of his father.

"Paul?" Buckman says as Wyatt prepares to escort Jet inside. "There's still the matter of the cache. The Seychelles accounts, all the things your wife mentioned." The ruthless old banker looks Jet in the eye. "May we rely on your continued discretion, my dear?"

After several seconds, she nods. "Just don't cross me, Claude."

THE DEER-SKINNING SHED STINKS of blood and urine. Nadine whimpers when I open the door, but then she recognizes me. Her first response is a quick sucking in of breath. Then she says, "Are they going to kill us?"

"No." I go to her and cover her with a Pendleton blanket Wyatt Cash brought me.

She sobs and shudders against me. "I prayed you'd come."

"I'm so sorry I took so long." I squeeze her tight, trying to comfort her. "I'm sorry I had your gun. What did they do to you?"

"I don't want to talk about it." She draws back far enough for me to see revulsion in her face. "Except that Beau Holland. I never want to see him again."

"You won't. Paul killed him two minutes ago. You can look at his corpse if you want to."

A look of desolation crosses her face. "I almost do. But no."

"Paul and Jet got us out of here, believe it or not." I hear engines outside. The meeting must be breaking up.

"Can we go now, please?" she asks.

"They're getting us a truck. For me to drive you home."

"Thank God. I can't believe it."

"Unless you want to ride in a helicopter with Jet and Kevin?"

Her face hardens. "No. It was Jet who told them about me. Did you know that?"

"I just found out. I'm sorry." I feel I should try to defend Jet's action, even though I can't believe it myself. "They threatened her son."

Nadine nods, but it's plain that forgiveness will be a long time coming, if ever. "You said you're driving me home?"

"Yes."

"Could I stay at your house? Not to—you know. I just don't want to be alone tonight."

"Absolutely."

When I pick up her clothes, I realize they're tacky with blood. "Um . . . you've got blood on your things."

"I don't care. It's my blood. Just turn around for a minute."

I turn to the stained wall of the skinning shed, thinking how close we came to dying in here. Not just the two of us, but Jet and Kevin and Paul as well.

"I'm finished," Nadine says. "Can we go now?"

Hanging the blanket around her shoulders, I open the shed door and lead her out into the harsh light. An old GMC pickup stands waiting, keys in the ignition. I walk her around the truck and help her into the passenger seat, then climb behind the wheel and crank the engine. As I put the truck into gear, Wyatt Cash's chopper lifts into the night sky above the camp.

I gently press the gas pedal, and the truck rolls forward. Passing the Boar Island pavilion, I see a figure detach itself from the others and stand silhouetted in the light, one arm raised in farewell.

"Who's that?" asks Nadine.

"Paul."

She raises a hand and waves limply. "What the hell happened out there?"

"You'll never believe it."

"But you'll tell me everything?"

"Later. Once we're safe."

I gun the engine and blow past the vehicles and men of the Poker Club, back toward the mainland. Toward home. If Bienville is home. Before anything else, I need to do what I came back to Mississippi to do in the first place. Bury my father. Or in his case, scatter his ashes on the river.

Then we'll see.

CHAPTER 56

BUCK'S FUNERAL IS scheduled for three P.M. That worked out well, because Nadine and I slept twelve hours straight after getting home from the hunting camp. I wasn't sure Mom coming to the cemetery was a great idea, given that my father's funeral will be held in a couple of days, but she brushed away my concerns. She told me she's always been grateful for what Buck did for me as a boy and doesn't want his widow to have to bury her husband with only a handful of people to mourn him. That's the closest Mom has ever come to acknowledging Buck being my surrogate father.

Nadine, too, fears that the funeral will be a bleak affair, given that the town virtually disowned Buck after his work threatened the paper mill. I feel a little more hopeful since learning that most of the newspaper staff is going; every warm body will make Quinn feel a little better. Mom is riding beside me in the Flex, while Nadine sits in the middle of the backseat, wearing a dark navy dress that's quite a change from her usual jeans and T-shirts.

Two blocks from Cemetery Road, I recognize a couple of cars ahead of us. Hopefully they're headed to the service. One is Dr. Jack Kirby's, which lifts my heart. The other looks like it belongs to Byron Ellis, the coroner. Maybe we'll have a decent showing after all, enough to pay modest tribute to all the good work Buck did for the people of this town.

As we drive through the cemetery gate, something tells me I might have misjudged the occasion. A young Boy Scout stands beside the asphalt lane, staring ahead with military bearing, his green ball cap held flat against the red kerchief on his chest as a sign of respect. I remember exactly what that uniform feels like, though in my day we wore the iconic Stetson campaign hat or a military-style garrison cap. Thirty yards down the lane, another Scout stands in the same rigid posture.

"My goodness," says my mother, flattening her hand against her bosom. "What fine boys. What fine, thoughtful boys."

As we drive deeper into the cemetery, we pass Scouts every thirty yards, all the way to the burial site, where a tent has been set up. As I make the final turn, I see forty or fifty cars parked along the lane beside the gravesite.

"Thank God," I say softly.

"Look at the crowd down there," my mother says. "What do you notice?"

I gaze down the lane at the knots of people, mostly adults moving among uniformed boys. "I don't know. What?"

Nadine leans up between our seats. "It's nearly all male. I'll bet those men are Scouts, too. Men Buck mentored when they were boys."

"Must be," I say, feeling my throat tighten.

Mom squeezes my hand. "Good works never die. There's your proof. You think those men give a damn about some paper mill?"

"Come on," says Nadine, touching my shoulder. "Let's go pay our respects to Buck."

We walk down the asphalt lane and join the mourners. Through the bodies, I see Quinn Ferris moving from person to person, thanking each for coming. To my surprise, she's smiling a lot of the time. When Quinn gets to me, I worry that she'll ask me to say something over Buck's grave, but she doesn't. When I ask who is going to speak, she says no one. There will be no prayer, eulogy, or benediction, no Christian minister of any kind. But cryptically she adds that there will be a farewell ceremony of sorts.

"By the way," she says. "I got a call from Arthur Pine this morning."

"What did he want?"

"He said he had a check for me. An insurance policy I knew nothing about."

"Huh. That's weird."

"I thought so, too. Because it was a big one." She gives me a knowing look, then stands on tiptoe and kisses my cheek. "Thank you."

After Quinn moves on, we choose a vantage point on some elevated ground across the lane, where we can see the faces of the mourners nearest the grave. Through the crowd I pick out an old-school campaign hat resting on Buck's coffin lid. A fitting tribute to his lifelong avocation. A loud hum rises from the crowd, as people who haven't seen each other for years greet friends and reminisce. But as a bank of clouds obscures the sun, they slowly fall silent. Soon not a sound can be heard from the mourners. Each is reliving moments he shared with Buck Ferris. It's strange to hear no words spoken over the grave, no hymn or even pop tune sung with heartbreaking sincerity. As I wonder how this unusual gathering will end, a strange sound rolls over the ground, reverberating off the gravestones.

"What's that?" Mom asks, looking around in confusion.

"A drum, I think."

Half a minute later, a column of Indians wearing ceremonial shirts adorned with colorful ribbons marches over the hill behind the gravesite, a solemn file of men and women. It's been three decades since I attended one of the powwows Buck managed at the Indian Village, but I still recognize members of at least half a dozen tribes. Some wear their black hair long, others short. And while many have the pure blood of the first Americans to walk this ground beside the river, others have intermarried with whites and look like working-class people from any Southern town.

"I bet this is the first time this cemetery's seen a sendoff like this one," I say softly.

"It's not bagpipes playing 'Amazing Grace,'" Mom observes. "But it sure inspires respect and reflection."

As we watch in fascination, the Indians form a circle near the grave, the hide drum at the center, and eight of them begin striking it together. Then their voices rise in song.

Mom looks back at Nadine and me. "When Duncan and I first married, he came to the Episcopal church with me. We went to the adult Sunday school. The topic of discussion that day was whether or not Buddhists and Hindus could get into heaven. Can you imagine? That was the last time Duncan darkened the door of that church. I stopped going myself. Being with your father made me see the silliness of all that. The arrogance of it. Oh, Duncan would have loved this."

I remember Dad sitting with me in the car yesterday, beside Adam's statue, asking me to cast his ashes into the river. "I think you're right."

After the drum falls silent and the singing fades, a group of men lowers Buck's simple wooden coffin into the grave, and the Indians begin covering it with earth. As the shovels work steadily, I notice Jet making her way through the crowd. She's wearing a black dress and onyx earrings, and her height and dark skin make her easy to follow. I hadn't realized she was here. Once I'm sure she's moving toward me, I excuse myself and signal her to meet me at a tree that will give us some cover from the crowd, so as not to appear disrespectful.

"Are you by yourself?" I ask as she reaches the tree.

"Kevin's home with Paul. Sally's service is tomorrow. I think one funeral is enough for Kevin right now."

"Sure."

She hesitates, then gives me an unguarded look. "A lot happened last night. Some things need explaining. Could you meet me at the barn today? Four thirty?"

"The Weldon barn?"

She nods. "Too soon?"

"No, I can make that."

Jet smiles with gratitude, but then her face darkens. "How's Nadine doing?"

I'm not sure how honest to be about this. "She's all right."

She nods but says nothing further. "Four thirty, then."

"Four thirty."

We part without touching.

DESPITE THE FLEX'S LOW ground clearance and the path being thickly overgrown by weeds, I make it all the way to the clearing around the Weldon barn. Jet is already there, waiting in front of her Volvo. She's wearing the black dress from the funeral, and staring at the remains of the old cypress structure. The barn where she and I discovered each other has mostly collapsed. It's being slowly consumed by kudzu and poison ivy. The second story sits only four feet off the ground and looks like rattlesnake heaven. I wouldn't climb up into it unless I was running for my life.

While the barn itself has fallen in, the clearing looks exactly the same. The sun filters down through the canopy in thick yellow shafts, the only straight lines and angles the first people in this region would have seen. Lone wildflowers blossom in the shadows of the woods. I don't know their names, but they're more beautiful than any you'd find in the florist's shop on Rembert Street. I see fewer and fewer butterflies in the world, but they still thrive here, fluttering among the vines at the edge of the clearing.

I park beside Jet's Volvo, then walk over and hug her. After the cemetery, I worried that this might feel awkward, but here it seems natural. We hold each other for a full minute without speaking. We do not kiss. I feel myself responding to her body, and she must feel it, too, but we draw apart without going further. Then she leads me to the edge of the sunlight and sits in a patch of clover, tucking her legs demurely beneath her. I sit facing her with my arms around my knees.

"Do you remember the old black man who saved us from the druggies that day?" she asks.

"Hell, yes. It was night, really."

"What was his name?"

"Willis."

She laughs. "That's right! He said my twelve dollars would feed him for a week. I hope it did. If I could find him now, I'd give him twelve hundred."

She picks a white flower from the clover, then another. With delicate, assured fingers she ties one green stem around another with a tiny knot, beginning a necklace.

"What did you guys tell Kevin about Max?" I ask, stepping right into the unspoken issues between us.

Jet doesn't look up. "We told him Beau Holland got his grandfather tangled up in some serious financial crimes. We said that Max thought Beau had been murdered by some crooked partners, and he felt his only choice was to flee the country. I tried to give him the impression that Max is living on a beach somewhere, drinking tequila under another name. Costa Rica, maybe. I did tell him that I doubted we'd ever see his grandfather again."

"Did Kevin ever believe that Max hurt Sally?"

"I don't think so. Once news of her illness got out, he latched on to that as a legitimate motive for suicide."

I nod, thinking that's probably best.

"Last night was pretty crazy," she says, picking another flower and going to work on its stem with deft finger movements.

"That barely begins to describe it. I'd say the credit for saving us goes to you. You were ferocious. You scared those old guys to death."

She shrugs. "We all did our part."

"You made it sound like you and Paul are staying together."

She looks up at last, her eyes noncommittal. "I said what I had to. I read the moment."

"You read it well. I'm the only one who knew you were bluffing about the cache."

She laughs softly. "I wasn't bluffing."

"What?"

"One hour before they threw me in that helicopter, all I had was the number of the account I'd set up in the Seychelles."

"Then how—"

"Max's phone. Before you and Paul left to dump his body, I took the cell phone he had on him. I punched in the first password from Sally's necklace, and it opened like a charm."

"My God. What was the second password to?"

"A password vault application on his phone. That's what 'MaiLoc1971' opened. Once I got into that app, it was like Aladdin's cave. I could have emptied those accounts if I'd had time. I was still going through the stuff when Wyatt's guys showed up to grab me. I slid it under the credenza in your den two seconds before they kicked in the door."

"But you remembered some account numbers?"

Jet taps her temple and gives me an ironic smile. "'The Brain,' remember? I've never been so thankful for being a number freak. If I hadn't been able to quote those account numbers, we'd be dead now."

"Yes, we would." Given that we survived the ordeal under the pavilion, my mind has wandered back before those crisis moments, to the ones in my kitchen. "I've thought a lot about Max," I tell her.

Jet's mouth tightens. "He was going to kill us. All of us. You said that yourself. That was the only way he could get custody of Kevin."

"I know. I'm sure of that. Max would have shot Paul on the patio."

"Then he deserved what happened to him, didn't he?"

I don't answer. I'm thinking about a conversation I had with Nadine when she and I woke up this morning. It was that discussion that caused me to put Jet's sapphire earrings in my pocket and bring them to this meeting, to give back to her.

"It's changed, hasn't it?" she asks. "Between us."

"Yes."

Her dark eyes deepen. "When did it change for you?"

I'm not sure how to answer this. "I don't know if you ever really know something like that. You just feel one way—you see a future— and then you don't."

She peers into the shadows under the trees. "I know exactly when it was for me."

"Really?"

"Last night. When Max said what he did about me—the sexual thing—and you believed him, not me."

I don't respond to this.

"I know what he said sounded credible," she goes on. "But I told you he was lying. And you still decided that I was the liar."

"You're right. After we proved he had lied, I felt like throwing up. I was ashamed."

Her lips compress like a child's as she works to thread one trouble-some stem into a tiny knot. "I'm probably being unrealistic," she says. "But I want somebody who'll believe me, even if what I swear to seems impossible."

I know how she feels. On the other hand, two nights ago she completely fabricated the story about Max raping her, and I'd believed that. I can't help but feel that's what made me vulnerable to Max's lie. I'd just as soon abandon this line of discussion, but I feel one point must be made.

"Paul didn't believe you, either," I remind her.

"No. He didn't. But Paul and I have a child. That's the difference."

She's right, even if Paul isn't Kevin's biological father. In every other way, Kevin is his son. But I wonder if a man who Jet lied to for so many years will ever be able to give her the trust she craves.

I held something back a moment ago: I know the exact instant that

I realized Jet and I have no future together. It was last night under the Boar Island pavilion, when Beau Holland revealed that she was the one who had given up Nadine as the holder of Sally's cache. I understand Jet giving a couple of thugs what they'd demanded from her. After all, they'd threatened her child. But afterward . . . she chose not to warn Nadine, or even me. She abandoned Nadine to her fate. I don't know why she did that, and I'm not sure I ever want to know. But it changed my feelings about her forever.

"It's all right," she says, watching my face. "I understand."

"What?"

"Nadine. The cache. I can't really explain what I did."

"How did you even know she had it?"

Jet's fingers stop moving, but she doesn't look up from the string of flowers. "I didn't know. I guessed. Once I realized it was out there, that Sally had made this thing and given it to someone, the possibilities were pretty limited. I didn't think she'd trust any man with it, honestly. Not even an attorney. Not in this town. The Poker Club is large enough that any man could be beholden to them, and not even Sally would know. Once I got that far, I figured it had to be Nadine. If her mother had been alive, Sally would have chosen her. But she wasn't. That's it, really."

I don't know what to say. This is actually worse than what I imagined. She gave up Nadine without even being sure she had the cache.

"I know it's terrible," Jet says softly. "It's probably the worst thing I've ever done. But they threatened Kevin. I was terrified for him. I wanted it all to go away. The danger. I didn't let myself believe they would really hurt Nadine. But I was lying to myself. I know that, because it was my fear of what they would do to Kevin that drove my actions."

I wish I could say something to ease her conscience, but nothing comes to me.

"Please tell Nadine I'm sorry, even though it probably won't mean anything."

I nod and leave it at that.

"Look," Jet says, pointing under the trees. "Turn very slowly."

I do. Something is watching us from the edge of the clearing. It's a doe. A spotted fawn stands just behind her in the overgrowth, nervously watching its mother. The doe stares at us for perhaps fifteen seconds, then, with supreme indifference, leaps over a patch of briars and vanishes. The fawn looks lost for a moment, then scrambles after her.

"A good omen?" Jet whispers, plucking another flower from the ground. She has seven tied together now. Soon she will close the circle.

"For what?" I ask. "The future?"

She gives a slow shrug as her fingers work. "I've been worried about you. We talked about having a child together." She looks up, her eyes filled with concern. "You need one. Deserve one. And neither of us are kids anymore."

"That's about the last thing I've been thinking about."

Sadness creeps into her face. "Are you going back to Washington? Or will you stay here and run the paper, like you told Paul?"

So the two of them have been talking. "I don't know. Does it matter to you?"

"Of course." A strange smile tugs at the corners of her mouth. "But I can think of somebody who'd love to make babies with you, if you're still here."

This is the most surreal conversation I've had in a long time, maybe ever. And that's saying something. "You're a matchmaker now? For me?"

"Nope. Jealous rival. Always. *Voilà.*" She dangles her completed necklace before me from one finger. "My anniversary present to you."

"Anniversary?"

She stands and slips the necklace over my head, then pulls me to my feet. "We started growing up here. Maybe we've finally completed the journey. Maybe we're grown-ups now."

"I don't know about that. But it's definitely time to put away childish things."

She studies me for several seconds. Then she nods. "I need to get home. One kiss? Goodbye?" She moves almost imperceptibly toward me. Her eyes seem bottomless, and her lips grow larger, fuller in my sight. Even now, she radiates some mysterious field that draws me to her—

"Something tells me this is not a good idea," I murmur.

Jet goes still, then smiles and squeezes my hand, letting hers trail off mine as she turns and walks to the door of her Volvo. Watching her climb in, I remember the earrings in my pocket but decide not to stop her. She starts the engine, makes a hard turn, then heads down the overgrown path toward the real world.

Turning back to the barn, I take out the sapphire studs she left in my bathroom as a test to see whether Nadine would find them there. With only the faintest pang of regret, I toss the earrings through the barn door, into the kudzu and poison ivy.

This barn was my refuge from the world, long after I left it physically behind. Jet, too, was a refuge of sorts, a sanctuary from reality, a bubble of childhood in which everything seemed pure and new and the future always bright. We all carry those bubbles within us. But they're too fragile to bring out into the sun. They're like my brother's laugh or my father's pride. They're memories.

And the real world awaits.

ACKNOWLEDGMENTS

AT WRITERS HOUSE: Dan Conaway and Simon Lipskar.

At William Morrow: David Highfill, Liate Stehlik, Tavia Kowalchuk, Danielle Bartlett, Chloe Moffett, and everybody in the sales department—especially the reps!

At HarperCollins U.K.: Julia Wisdom, Charlie Redmayne, and all the team.

My all-hours co-conspirators: Ed Stackler, Jamie Kornegay, and Laura Cherkas.

Writers tend to know a little about everything and a lot about nothing. A novel like this requires the knowledge of many experts. I thank them here, and all mistakes are mine!

James Barnett, for sharing his deep knowledge of Native Americans in the Mississippi Valley. Dr. Chuck Borum, for his knowledge of scouting and Native American customs.

Terry Burkley, for sharing painful details about living with a loved one with Parkinson's disease.

Richard Grant, an insightful writer, for an outsider's perspective on Mississippi.

Wade Heatherly, banker, actor, and former rescue swimmer, for great info (and for acting in my son's movie).

Friends with details: Kevin Cooper, the newspaper business; Scott Slover, attorney; Howard Jones, the lumber business; James Lee, coroner; Dr. Barry Bertolet and Dr. Kellen Jex, medical expertise; Dr. Randy Tillman, aviation; Glenn Green and Mimi Miller, miscellaneous. Terri Aldridge for the last-minute read!

Friends with insights: Courtney Aldridge, Rod Givens, James Schuchs, Kevin Dukes, Billy Ray Farmer.

The loved ones who keep me going: first and foremost my wife, Caroline Hungerford. Madeline Iles, Mark Iles, newcomer Elliot Iles, Geoff Iles, Betty Iles, Dr. Jerry W. Iles, and Nancy Hungerford and Betsy Iles for babysitting Elliot!